"Brabazon's achievement in this comprehensive and exceptionally fine biography is to show how Schweitzer, faithful to the peculiar characteristics of his Alsatian origins, was able to be many men at once without contradiction or neurosis—dreamer and man of action, traditionalist and innovator, egotist and 'saint.' . . . A rich book, and a fitting tribute to a great if controversial man."
—*Publishers Weekly*

Albert Schweitzer
A Biography
by James Brabazon

Albert Schweitzer was surely one of the most remarkable and controversial figures of the twentieth century. Before the age of thirty he had achieved international renown for theological writings that flew in the face of accepted interpretations of both Jesus and the Bible. Also before the age of thirty, he had received equal acclaim for his studies of the piano and organ, his skill as a concert performer and his works on Bach. Not content with kudos that only a handful of men garner in a lifetime, he suddenly and dramatically turned his back on his previous careers, obtained a degree in medicine, all but renounced civilization and went to Africa, where, in the tiny village of Lambarene, he opened a hospital for the Africans that was to make his name a household word throughout the world.

(Continued on back flap)

ALBERT SCHWEITZER: A Biography

ALBERT SCHWEITZER

A Biography

by JAMES BRABAZON

G. P. Putnam's Sons, New York

To the solidarity of life

SBN:399-11421-1

Library of Congress Catalog Card Number:74-30545

PRINTED IN THE UNITED STATES OF AMERICA

CONTENTS

Illustrations will be found
following pages 128 and 320.

ALBERT SCHWEITZER: A Biography

ACKNOWLEDGMENTS

I was well into the writing of this book before I fully appreciated what I should have realized from the start—how rash it is to try to get to know at secondhand a man of Schweitzer's magnitude, and how hard it is to hold in balance and to convey in proper perspective what one hopes one has discovered. To those who unstintingly helped me to understand, I owe a tremendous debt of gratitude—and apology where I have failed to pass on to the reader what they tried to tell me.

First among these must be Mrs. Clara Urquhart, who provided me with the initial impetus to embark on the project, as she has in the past provided the impetus to many others to get to know Schweitzer.

Next I must thank Schweitzer's daughter, Mrs. Rhena Schweitzer Miller, for the confidence she placed in the book, for the help and encouragement she has given me, and for the labor of reading and checking the manuscript for accuracy. To her too I owe the authorization for the many quotations from Schweitzer's books, speeches, sermons, and letters. Most of all, perhaps, I am grateful for her objectivity about her father, a man about whom objectivity was not always easy.

I would like also to thank Ali Silver, for twenty years Schweitzer's right hand at Lambarene, and now the devoted and delightful keeper of the Central Archives in Günsbach, Alsace; and Mrs. Erica Anderson, whose Albert Schweitzer Friendship House in Great Barrington, Massachusetts, is a treasure both of written material and of recollection.

My first impression of the quality of Schweitzer as a man came from the quality of the many relatives and friends of his that I met—a most attractive combination of friendly directness and warm vitality. From his sister-in-law, Mme Emma Schweitzer, who knew him in his teens, to his granddaughter, Christianne, following in his footsteps as a doctor and musician; from M. Léon Morel, who was already a missionary on the Ogowe River when Schweitzer first decided to go there, to Dr. Weissberg, who ran the government hospital near Schweitzer's during the last years of his life; from Schweitzer's nephews, Gustav Woytt and Albert Ehretsmann, who knew him at home in Alsace, to Dr. Mark Lauterburg, who worked in Africa with him in the 1920's, and Dr. James Witchalls, who did so forty years later; from all these and many others I gained not only the information I needed but also something else—an idea of the kind of man Schweitzer must have been if he could impress, and sometimes overwhelm, people as varied and yet as vigorous as these. To all of them my warmest thanks both for what they told me and for what they gave me of themselves.

Sources of quotations, where they are not fully identified in the text, are indicated in the Notes and in the Bibliography. Readers who do not care for notes are reassured that these contain no additional information, but are confined to source reference only.

And I would like to make more formal acknowledgment of my gratitude for permission to make use of quotations to the following:

Erica Anderson, *Albert Schweitzer's Gift of Friendship* and *The Schweitzer Album*. Reprinted by permission of the author.

James Cameron, *Point of Departure*. Reprinted by permission of Weidenfield and Nicholson/ Arthur Barker/ World University Library. Articles from the *News Chronicle* by permission of Associated Newspapers Group. Broadcast talk by permission of the BBC and Nicholas Thompson.

Pablo Casals and Albert E. Kahn, *Joys and Sorrows*. Copyright © 1970 by Simon & Schuster, Inc. Reprinted by permission of Simon and Schuster, Inc., and Hughes Massie Ltd.

The Christian Register and *The Register Leader*. Articles by Charles R. Joy and Melvin Arnold reprinted by permission of the Unitarian Universalist Association.

Winston Churchill, *My African Journey*. Reprinted by permission of Neville Spearman Ltd.

The Convocation Record of the Albert Schweitzer International Convocation 1966. Reprinted by permission of the Aspen Institute of Humanistic Studies and Mrs. Elizabeth Paepcke.

Norman Cousins, *Dr. Schweitzer of Lambarene.* Copyright © 1960 by Harper & Row, Inc. Reprinted by permission of Harper & Row, Inc.

The Daily Herald. Letter from Albert Schweitzer reprinted by permission of I.P.C. Newspapers Ltd.

Albert Einstein. Letter to Albert Schweitzer and statement about him by permission of the Estate of Albert Einstein.

Frederick Franck, *Days with Albert Schweitzer*. Copyright © 1959 by Holt, Rinehart and Winston, Inc. Reprinted by permission of Holt, Rinehart and Winston and Peter Davies Ltd.

John Gunther, *Inside Africa.* Reprinted by permission of Harper & Row, Inc., and Hamish Hamilton Ltd.

Hermann Hagedorn. Correspondence with Albert Schweitzer by permission of Mrs. Hermann Hagedorn and Mrs. Mary H. du Vall, the George Arents Research Library for Special Collections at Syracuse University, and the Collection of American Literature, Beinecke Rare Book and Manuscript Library, Yale University.

Dag Hammarskjöld. Letter to Albert Schweitzer by permission of the Trustees of Dag Hammarskjöld's papers.

Charles R. Joy, *Music in the Life of Albert Schweitzer.* Copyright © 1951 by Harper & Row, Inc. Reprinted by permission of Harper & Row, Inc., and A. & C. Black Ltd.

Charles R. Joy and Melvin Arnold. Articles in *The Christian Register* and *The Register Leader.* Reprinted by permission of the Unitarian Universalist Association.

Nikos Kazantzakis. Letter to Albert Schweitzer by permission of Mrs. Helen Kazantzakis.

Oskar Kraus, *Albert Schweitzer—His Work and His Philosophy.* Reprinted by permission of A & C. Black Ltd.

D.H. Lawrence, "Thought." From *The Complete Poems of D.H. Lawrence,* edited by Vivian de Sola Pinto and F. Warren Roberts. Reprinted by permission of Lawrence Pollinger Ltd. and the Estate of Mrs. Frieda Lawrence. Also Copyright © 1964, 1971 by Angelo Ravagli and C. M. Weekley, Executors of the Estate of Frieda Lawrence Ravagli. All rights reserved. Reprinted by permission of The Viking Press Ltd.

Gerald McKnight, *Verdict on Schweitzer.* Reprinted by permission of Frederick Muller Ltd. and John Day Ltd.

Charles Michel and Fritz Dinner. Report of the funeral of Albert Schweitzer reprinted by permission of the authors.

Dr. David Miller. Report of the death of Albert Schweitzer reprinted by permission of the author.

John Middleton Murry, *Love, Freedom and Society.* Reprinted by permission of the Society of Authors as Representative of the Estate of John Middleton Murry.

Conor Cruise O'Brien. Article in *The New York Review of Books,* August, 1964. Reprinted by permission of the author.

Suzanne Oswald, *Mein Onkel Bery.* Reprinted by permission of the author.

D. Packiarajan. Letter to Albert Schweitzer by permission of the author.

Panorama. Television program for Albert Schweitzer's ninetieth birthday quoted by permission of the BBC.

The Paris Mission Society. Correspondence with and about Albert

J.S. Bach, tr. by Ernest Newman. Reprinted by permission of A. & C. Black Ltd.

Kant's Philosophy of Religion, tr. by Kurt F. Leidecker. Reprinted by permission of The Citadel Press. ©

Memoirs of Childhood and Youth, tr. by C. T. Campion. Reprinted by permission of George Allen and Unwin Ltd. Also Copyright 1949 by Macmillan Publishing Co., Inc. Reprinted by permission of Macmillan Publishing Co., Inc.

More from the Primeval Forest, tr. by C. T. Campion. Reprinted by permission of A. & C. Black Ltd. Also Copyright © 1931 by Macmillan Publishing Co., Inc., renewed 1959 by Albert Schweitzer. Reprinted by permission of Macmillan Publishing Co., Inc.

My Life and Thought, tr. by C. T. Campion. Reprinted by permission of George Allen and Unwin Ltd. Also Copyright 1933, 1949, © 1961 by Holt, Rinehart and Winston, Inc. Reprinted by permission of Holt, Rinehart and Winston, Inc.

On the Edge of the Primeval Forest, tr. by C. T. Campion. Reprinted by permission of A. & C. Black Ltd. Also Copyright © 1931 by Macmillan Publishing Co., Inc., renewed 1959 by Albert Schweitzer. Reprinted by permission of Macmillan Publishing Co., Inc.

Peace or Atomic War. Reprinted by permission of A. & C. Black Ltd., and of Holt, Rinehart and Winston, Inc.

A *Psychiatric Study of Jesus*, tr. by Charles R. Joy. Copyright © 1948 by The Beacon Press. Reprinted by permission of The Beacon Press.

The Quest of the Historical Jesus, tr. by W. Montgomery. Reprinted by permission of A. & C. Black Ltd. and Macmillan Publishing Co., Inc.

Religion in Modern Civilization. Copyright © 1934 by the Christian Century Foundation. Reprinted by permission from the November 21 and 28, 1934, issues of *The Christian Century*.

George Seaver, *Albert Schweitzer—The Man and His Mind*. Reprinted by permission of the author.

Ali Silver. Extract from the British Bulletin of the Albert Schweitzer Hospital Fund, by permission of the author.

Adlai E. Stevenson. Correspondence with Albert Schweitzer and statement by permission of Adlai Stevenson III and Princeton University Library.

Marie Woytt-Secretan. Extract from the British Bulletin of the Albert Schweitzer Hospital Fund by permission of the author.

PREFACE

ALBERT SCHWEITZER died on September 4, 1965. A presence which had made itself felt throughout the world was now an absence. He was mourned by Japanese schoolchildren as by European intellectuals, by peasants as by politicians, by blacks and whites, communists and capitalists, employers and wage slaves. Magazine articles had already appeared with headlines that described him as a twentieth-century saint and the greatest man of our generation. At his death, the superlatives poured again from the presses of the world.

Many of those who actually met him felt that the force of his personality came at least within measureable distance of living up to the myth. The impact of his physical presence was certainly tremendous. He existed in the confident, indisputable way that animals and children exist, his concentration at every moment focused completely on whoever or whatever then occupied his mind.

When he was part of the company, whether the company consisted of colleagues, friends, or strangers, jungle Africans or Nobel Prize-winners, he was the center of interest. He commanded attention by his knowledge, by his training as a preacher, which had taught him how to make people listen to him, but mostly by sheer personal magnetism—a combination of physical power, charm, dominating will, and a quick responsiveness to everything around him.

A formidable man. A man hard to say no to. A man of whom a friend said that his enjoyment of his own dominance was as naïve and endearing as that of a little girl with a new frock. Others found it less charming. But for good or ill, the power was there. Schweitzer was a force to be reckoned with.

Response to life was the mark of his personality. Reverence for life was the key phrase of his philosophy. The things he stood for were the things for which the new generation stands—a return to the earth and a re-

15

spect for nature; peace; simplicity; spontaneity; the stripping away of the false values of a materialistic civilization to rediscover the true values of human relationship—relationship with other people and with the whole of creation.

When he died, the things he was doing were left unfinished. The hospital which he designed, built, and presided over for so many years was still growing. The books in which he had hoped to explore the wider implications of his philosophy remain a series of disconnected notes, which others may try to put together. But his life is ended. There is no continuation. In that sense it is complete; the argument has been stated.

The statement he made by his life was intended to be about all life. To investigate his life therefore—to see whether it has the universal relevance he claimed—is not only a matter of doing justice to him—it may be of crucial importance to us.

My own quest for the truth about Schweitzer was spurred on by a sense that much could be learned from a philosopher who was not content with philosophy, a theologian who went beyond theology. It also seemed important to look for the hidden flaws, the human failings in the man who has been beatified by the popular press; and to discover which were right, those who were "for" him or those who were "against" him; or whether perhaps those words had no meaning.

He has often been hailed as an exceptionally good man. But a close friend of his said, "He was not so much righteous, as right." The world has utmost need of people who are right. Was Schweitzer? If so, his life must have been right, since he made his life his argument.

With this in mind, I set about trying to understand Schweitzer's life.

1

CHILDHOOD
1875-1885

SCHWEITZER simply means Swiss. The family seems to have lived in Switzerland until the end of the seventeenth century; what they were called there nobody knows, but when they moved north to Alsace after the Thirty Years' War, they were called Swiss as a means of identification; and for a while the name came to signify the occupations they had at that time—carers for cows and makers of cheese.

The Thirty Years' War had been a dreadful and consuming struggle. Luther's great challenge to the Roman Church a hundred years before had been followed by mounting religious bitterness which culminated in a vicious conflict that tore Europe apart. In some towns, it was said at the time, there were only wolves for the wolves to feed on; and now in many places dead men's land was to be had for little more than the asking. In Alsace, softer and more fertile than the country they came from, the Schweitzers settled, spread, and flourished.

Alsace is a lovely homeland. The people are cheerful and energetic and the soil is beneficent. On the mountainsides the timber grows straight and dense, and in the valleys the vineyards produce some of the most delicious white wines in the world. There is a saying that the Alsatians, who have no unnecessary scruples about taking the best of both worlds, eat as much as the Germans and as well as the French.

In this pleasant place the family took root, and during the next two hundred years contributed to the community a variety of sound citizens, among them a rich sprinkling of schoolmasters and pastors; leaders of their communities, cultivated people, often with a bent for music—the kind of solid bourgeoisie that Alsace values. There was little to suggest, though, that suddenly, at the end of the nineteenth century, they were to produce two of the most influential Europeans of their age, Albert Schweitzer and Jean-Paul Sartre.

Despite all its virtues—partly indeed because of them—Alsace has one

great drawback. It is very vulnerable; and from the point of view of the
large powers on either side, very desirable. Its borders, the crest of the
Vosges Mountains on the west side and the Rhine on the east, are both
natural barriers whose control is militarily important. Alsace was a battle-
ground in Roman times, when the legions set up their outposts along the
Rhine to protect their empire against the Vandals. Ever since then it has
played the role of buffer between France and Germany, much more so
than Lorraine, its neighbor on the west, which has only been linked historically with Alsace because they share control of the important passes
over the mountains which divide them. Whenever France and Germany
have resumed their perennial conflict, Alsace has become first a battlefield, and then, when the struggle was over, part of the spoils of war.

So it is that an Alsatian might be born a Frenchman and die a German,
or vice-versa, according to the outcome of the latest bout. Had Albert
been born five years earlier, he would have started life as a Frenchman.
But the Franco-Prussian War had ended with victory for Prussia and the
founding of the German Empire, and so he was born a German citizen.
For this crime he was to be imprisoned by the French during the First
World War, before being transformed into a Frenchman in 1918.

The Alsatians have had enough of this kind of thing to make them humorously resigned to the follies of international politics—though it also
makes them understandably alert to any shift in the political wind. But
though their natural feeling about their two large and aggressive neighbors is to wish a plague on both their houses, they have also contrived to
win what they can from the situation by adopting as their own whatever
suits them best from each side. Their eating habits have already been
mentioned. In the same way they have developed their dialect, an unwritten language which is largely formed by taking from French or German
whichever offers the shorter and simpler way of saying things. Alsatian
speech tends to be pungent, practical, and economical, like the people
themselves.

All this is very relevant to Schweitzer, for he was completely a man of
Alsace. One can begin to understand him better if one begins by understanding this obstinate, friendly, self-reliant little region; a region which
can never afford to ignore the march of history but refuses to be impressed
by it; which lives close to the soil, because the soil is good and profitable
and is all that people have.

Especially relevant is the way they have handled their religious differences. After the Thirty Years' War they were faced with all the usual
problems of communities where Catholics and Protestants coexist; but
there was also a special complication introduced by Louis XIV.

Soon after the war, Louis quietly annexed Alsace for France. In many of the towns there were Catholic minorities who had no place of worship, and Louis undertook to remedy this lack by a simple and ruthless method. Lutheran pastors were forced to hand over the chancels of their churches for the permanent use of their Catholic neighbors, and to allocate certain times each Sunday when the Catholics could have the whole church for the celebration of mass.

Part of Louis' intention was to humiliate a defeated enemy; and the natural reaction would have been one of extreme bitterness. The war that had just ended had been over precisely this issue, and numbers of Alsatians had died in it. Louis was giving Alsace every opportunity to develop a festering unease that could sooner or later break out into a painful sickness like that of present-day Ulster. But the mischief-making failed. The Alsatians, making the uncommon decision to put commonsense and loyalty before dogma, used the occasion to develop a degree of friendly and cooperative understanding between priest and pastor. Inevitably there were hard feelings among individuals—there still are—and the Catholics took the opportunity to cling to the rich plainland while the defeated Protestants tended to retreat into the hills. But in village after village God was worshiped in different ways at different times in the same church, and the congregations did not suffer. The two men of God cared together for their joint flock.

The Schweitzers set a good example of this kind of tolerance. Most families leaned to one side or the other, and there were not many houses where you would find, as you would in Pastor Louis' study, French and German classics side by side on the bookshelves, Rousseau and Luther both having a say.

Kaysersberg, where Albert was born, is a typical enough little Alsatian town. Half destroyed in the Second World War, it has been so lovingly rebuilt that only by looking very carefully can you see which houses are new. Beautiful, compact, damaged by wars, but virtually untouched by the cruder forms of progress, it reflects history from every corner of its timbered courtyards and every cobble of its winding roads. The very name means "Caesar's Mountain"; and here, on the hill that dominates the town, the Romans built a fort which commanded the mouth of one of the main valley routes over the Vosges into Gaul.

The ruins of a castle still crown that hill, but this was built much later, against a threat from the opposite direction. The Emperor Frederick II had trouble in the thirteenth century controlling the depredations of the Dukes of Lorraine, who came raiding over the pass and down the valley, and the castle was there to send them packing back before they broke out into the open plain.

So the past hovers above the town. And beneath it, behind a wire grille in the crypt of the church, you may still see a great pile of bones removed from a medieval plague pit. Here is the very imminence of mortality, the very presence of history in the jumble of dead burghers.

Even today's livelihood is owed in some degree to the soldiers who set out in the sixteenth century to campaign in Hungary and brought back vines from Tokay. Wine is a very serious matter in Alsace—a means of combining business with pleasure, with pride into the bargain. And Albert Schweitzer as a boy was glad to boast that the year of his birth, 1875, was an excellent vintage year.

He was born on January 14—a Capricornian subject. People born under Capricorn are supposed to combine the spiritual and the practical to an unusual degree, and though he would have laughed at the idea, Schweitzer might have been born to endorse that particular theory. It is tempting also to find symbolism in the place of his birth, standing as it does midway between France and Germany, between Catholicism and Protestantism, between mountain and plain. But the fact that Schweitzer turned out to combine in himself many opposing elements—the dreamer and the man of action, the traditionalist and the innovator, the servant of mankind and the hardy egotist—has nothing to do with symbolic connections. It is a simple matter of cause and effect. He was what he was because he was faithful to the place of his origins and its trick of absorbing multiple influences.

His father, Louis, was pastor to the Lutherans of Kaysersberg—a gentle, kindly man in his late twenties, with an inclination to ill-health that was far from typical of the Schweitzers. There was already a daughter, Louisa, a year or so older than Albert. But the pastor must have been eager for a son, for at Albert's birth this placid, bookish man jumped right over the crib in his excitement.

The vicarage where the family lived is a beautiful, sturdy old house with a spacious courtyard. It is at the upper end of the town where the street begins to widen as it leads out toward the hills. The room where his mother gave birth to Albert looks out over the street, muffled then with the January snow, past the big clock on the adjoining wall toward the inn, the tree-lined square, and the castle on the hill.

Schweitzer's mother was herself a pastor's daughter, from one of the villages in the next valley southward. Here Louis had wooed and won her, when he was assistant pastor to her father. The family moved back to this valley a few months after Schweitzer's birth, when his father was transferred to the smaller parish of Günsbach, only a few miles from his mother's childhood home in Mühlbach. Her father was dead now, but he was far from forgotten. His name was still a byword in the neighborhood for eccentricity, wide learning, a passion for organs, and a fierce temper. For her at least, the move was a homecoming.

Kaysersberg was predominately Catholic. Günsbach, farther from the plain, had a majority of Protestants. And in Pastor Schweitzer's new parish the ancient edict of Louis XIV was still effective, entitling the Catholic minority to a share of the time and space of his church. Dominating the little chancel was a gilded altar, with tall candlesticks; and above that two gilt statues stood and gazed down the aisle at Catholic and Protestant worshipers alike.

The house at Günsbach was an unhappy change from the one they had left at Kaysersberg. It was hemmed in by other houses, dark, and what was more serious, damp. About the time of the move Albert had developed a severe fever, and the new house did him no good. In August, when his father was inducted to the parish, and the visiting pastors' wives peered into the crib at the infant Albert, he lay so yellow and wizened amidst the splendor of his frills and ribbons that the good ladies could find nothing pretty to say about him, even to the daughter of the notable Pastor Schillinger of Mühlbach; and Mrs. Schweitzer, unable to stand the embarrassment, carried off her puny offspring and cried over him in the privacy of her bedroom. The story was told to Schweitzer—frequently—by his mother, but in the account as we have it in his *Memoirs of Childhood and Youth* the exact illness is not specified. Jaundice perhaps—the yellow skin suggests it—and so severe that the child's life was despaired of and ninety years of remarkable living were nearly canceled before they began.

Another boy, Paul, and two girls, Adèle and Margrete, were added to the family, and the pastor's stipend began to feel the strain a little. Though they were better off than the peasants who were their neighbors, they had a position to maintain and their hospitality was unstinting. Nevertheless they managed well enough. And Europe remained at peace while the children grew.

We know very little about this childhood except what Schweitzer himself has told us in his books. His was not a family of diarists or letter writers; nor were they communicative about their feelings and experiences. True, Pastor Louis had some literary skill. He used to collect stories from the valley villages and published a little book of them, the names of participants tactfully altered. The stories are simple, but shrewdly and vigorously told, and quite without ecclesiastical taint. He seems to have written little else, however, until the First World War, when he began to keep a diary, largely for the benefit of Albert, cut off in Africa, about the progress of parish affairs and the impact of a war that brought terror and death to the family's very doorstep.

But even had there been an ardent diarist in the family, he would have found only the most ordinary events to record. The peace that prevailed between nations was matched by the harmony within the family. The cycle of seasons and the normal incidents of growing up provided all the excitement that came Albert's way. The hard-packed snow in winter, the sunny vineyard in summer; picnics; the harvest; lessons at the village school; visits to friends and relatives in Colmar, the nearest big town, out on the plain beyond the mouth of the valley; and the occasional expedition as far as Strasbourg, Alsace's capital city, fifty miles to the north— these were the framework of Schweitzer's first ten years. And but for a chance meeting which resulted in his writing his *Memoirs of Childhood and Youth* when he was in his forties, almost nothing would remain to tell us of his intense interior response to these gentle events.

The book is one of the small classics about childhood—truthful, observant, and wise; quietly mocking (of himself as well as others) and full of amused understanding. But it leaves huge gaps in our knowledge. It was intended as a group of tales for use in a young people's magazine, and a great many things that we should like to know are not recorded in it. And so we see the boy Schweitzer in a series of disconnected images, as though caught by the intermittent flashes of a great strobe light. The images are vivid and important. But between them lies darkness.

Maddeningly lacking is any clear picture of Albert's relationship with the rest of the family. We hear for example almost nothing of the brother and sisters. We are told only that the family was happy, loving, and yet reticent about personal feelings. And if this seems improbable to a generation taught to believe that all genius stems from the repression of early family trauma, it seems nevertheless to be perfectly true. Though no one still living remembers those early years, there are several who visited the Günsbach vicarage regularly at the beginning of the new century and knew the Schweitzers well. And an account of the teen-age Albert by his sister Adèle, brief as it is, brings the family to life in all its unspectacular normality.

The family reticence, of which Schweitzer had his full share, is quite enough to explain the gaps in his narrative—together with the fact that the family was not the subject of the book. Schweitzer was writing about his own early experiences, and these were mostly solitary.

Struggles and agonies there certainly were—indeed, they were the mainspring of his life. But they were never repressed. They were fully conscious from the beginning, and jealously guarded for their importance. And they had nothing to do with the family.

Instead, the family was the stable basis for his inner security, the strength which enabled him to make his struggles fertile. Out of those first placid ten years in Günsbach flow all the different streams of Schweitzer's life. In his memoirs we can see, clearly marked because they spring from unforgettable experiences, the sources of each stream as it arose. And if his mature achievements are remarkable in scope and scale, they are the more astonishing for having sprung not from the compression of energies which had been thwarted in some way, but simply from a natural, free development of what was born and bred in a normal small Alsatian boy.

The *Memoirs of Childhood and Youth* are thrown together, as Schweitzer admits, just as they occurred to him. Their chronology is not always obvious; and here and there remarks occur whose significance is concealed by their apparent casualness. Only when one begins to fit the fragments together in their context and in the context of the rest of his life does the importance of some of the small pieces become clear.

We first see Schweitzer, through the eyes of his forty-year-old self, when he is very small—still in petticoats. He is sitting in a corner of the manse courtyard watching his father collect honey from their beehives. A bee settles on his hand and begins to crawl over the skin. He watches it with interest and approval—until it stings him and he howls.

Great excitement. The servant girl is trying to kiss it better, while his mother is scolding his father for not putting the child in a safer place. The hubbub is highly enjoyable—so much so that when Albert suddenly realizes that the pain has gone he goes on crying in order to prolong the satisfaction of being the center of all this fuss. But later, when everyone has calmed down, he grows so ashamed of having exploited the situation that he remains miserable for the rest of the day. So he records.

For the rest of the day? That argues impressive emotional stamina at a very early age. But something made that day stick in the memory—something more than the hurt and the crying, for those must have been frequent. The unforgettable thing was the little boy's vivid awareness of himself, the enjoyment with which he dominated the situation, commanding the limelight with tears; and then the uncomfortable realization that he was cheating—getting a larger share of sympathy than he deserved, and outraging that just and proper balance between behavior and consequence which children instinctively recognize and value.

About the same time that he was learning this lesson in honesty, his churchgoing began. When he was three or four he was, he says, "allowed" to go to church. Unlike many clerical parents, Albert's father managed to give him the feeling that coming to church was a privilege, not an imposition. Louis probably achieved this by the simple means of believing it himself, for children are dangerously sensitive to hypocrisy in such matters.

Church had its excitements for the small boy, and its terrors. He had the satisfaction of seeing his father presiding over the congregation, the respected focus of the village's attention. And years later he still remem-

bered the feel of the servant girl's cotton glove on his mouth, when she
tried to stop him from yawning or singing too loudly. He remembered too
the lady who sometimes came and told tales of strange heathen folk overseas, and who collected sous for the conversion of these poor creatures.
Nearer home and more alarming was the vision of the devil, who frequently peered down the aisle at the congregation but vanished whenever
the pastor was actually praying—a clear proof of the power of prayer,
which, wrote Schweitzer, "gave quite a distinctive tone to my childish
piety."[1]

The vision turned out to be nothing more diabolical than the reflection
of Daddy Iltis, the organist, looking in his mirror for his cue to play.
Much worse than the devil, who after all was safely caged in the House of
God and controllable by prayer, was the village gravedigger, sacristan,
and humorist, a veteran of the Crimean War, Jägle by name. Jägle's sense
of humor led him to divert himself by persuading the pastor's son that he
had horns growing. Albert's forehead had distinctive bumps, which lent
credibility to the story. So Jägle would trap the terrified boy and feel the
bumps for signs of growth, while Albert stood hypnotized, longing to run
away but powerless to move. Months passed before he could bring himself to speak to his father, even indirectly, about horns on human fore-
heads, and so exorcise his fear. Then Jägle had other jokes up his sleeve.
He told Albert that the Prussians were going to put all boys into armor,
and that the blacksmith would need him for a fitting. Schweitzer calls this
humor dry, but sour would be a better word. There are Jägles in most
communities and though their cruelty may be unintentional it can be
harmful. In the long run, however, they sometimes provide their victims
with an early innoculation against alarmist fantasies and teach them a useful skepticism about the statements of their elders. Later on, Jägle tried to
teach Albert to follow in his footsteps as a humorist, but Schweitzer comments, "I found his school a little too hard for me."[2]

On the whole though, these were years of contentment, before school
placed its dreaded restrictions between Albert and his liberty. He used to
go out tending the pigs and cows of the local farmers, and it became his
one ambition be a swineherd forever, roaming the countryside all day
long for the rest of his life. Günsbach is surrounded by an almost endless
variety of hill and field, forest and vineyard. Behind the village rise the
slopes of the Rebberg, the little mountain among whose folds lie secret
valleys quite cut off from the world. Follow the stream up, past the clus-
tering houses and you can soon be high above the villages; or you can
lose yourself in thick woodland; or stay in the valley and go fishing in the
little river Fecht or walking by the lake in the little park; or keep an eye on
the progress of the vines, some of them planted by Pastor Louis himself.

Albert knew when he was well off. He had no wish to grow up, no envy of the big boys who went to school

When the time for school finally came, he had to be led there and he cried all the way. His fears were well founded; the academic life did not improve on acquaintance. School and Schweitzer simply did not agree. He was dreamy and vague, and found even reading and writing too much for him. Soon his father was reduced to begging him at least to learn enough to become the local postman; the Schweitzers were not the sort of people to produce swineherds. Albert's maternal grandfather, that famous Pastor Schillinger of Mühlbach, had been a great student of current events in the political and scientific world, and would wait in the street after the Sunday service to pass on to his parishioners news of the latest invention or discovery. When the skies showed something of interest, he would set up a telescope in front of his home for public use. Could his daughter have produced this dunce?

Schweitzer, looking back, remembered his mother's eyes as frequently red with weeping over her son's school reports. But nobody seemed able to do anything about him. He continued to sit at his desk, staring out the window and chewing his pencil, considering the immense advantages of a swineherd's life over any other and quite unprepared to accept opinion of parent or teacher that he might be wrong. Book learning he regarded as waste of time, and he found it "terribly unnatural" that his father should be forever reading and writing in the musty study, where he could barely breathe for the smell of books.

But the country and its creatures were not the sum total of his interests. Both sides of the family had produced musicians—particularly organists—with grandfather Schillinger eminent among them. He had been a great improviser, both on the organ and on his square piano; and on his death the piano had come to his daughter and son-in-law at Günsbach. Louis too had a talent for improvisation and Albert would spend hours listening when his father played, and then learning how to do the same himself. Before he went to school he was already able to devise his own harmonies to the tunes of the songs and hymns he knew.

The singing teacher could only pick out tunes with one finger, and she and the backward Albert discovered with mutual astonishment that he could do at least one thing better than she could. But as with the story of the bee sting, the satisfaction of mastery was more than outweighed by his sense of shame and embarrassment. He was afraid he might seem to be showing off and trying to set himself up against the teacher.

A complex, introspective child. One would have expected, since he had so little success at school, that where he did find himself doing well he would have made the most of it. But things were not as simple as that.

The few early photographs we have of him, aged five onward, all show a dark, intense little face, watchful, almost wary, the deep eyes considering us from beneath lowered brows. No doubt some of his hostility is due to the circumstances. The unfortunate child has obviously been dressed up in the most uncomfortable garment for the occasion—stiff collar, huge bow, and what appears to be a velvet suit; and his hair has been plastered down, which he hated. After all that, after the posing and waiting and the standing still for the exposure, an angelic smile is not to be expected. But in pictures taken in groups, with the family or with his class, the same observant look singles him out; as though the blinds of his own spirit were down, and from behind them he were gravely absorbing the evidence of his senses, reserving judgment.

Although he refused to read or write, there were always stories. Despite philosophies and techniques of psychology the story is still as good a device as any that man has hit upon for understanding himself. A good story sticks in the subconscious and breeds all kinds of reflections and responses. And Günsbach was full of stories.

Albert's father was collecting tales of the valley people for his book; and his mother would tell him stories about her family, particularly grandfather Schillinger and her much loved half-brother Albert, after whom Schweitzer was named. In a settled pastoral community the past remains very close, and these dead were as present, as potent an influence as the living.

The spirit of Pastor Schillinger was unavoidable. He lived in the stories about him; he lived in the square piano on which the family played; but he also made himself felt through his daughter, who had inherited, along with some of his sternness and lack of humor, his alert, inquiring mind. While Albert's father concerned himself with the local interest of the valley, Mrs. Schweitzer was the one who followed world events, and hated it when a public holiday deprived her of her morning paper.

Schweitzer's recollections of his mother as being frequently in tears—about his school reports, about his father's chronic ill-health, about the family finances—might suggest weakness in her character. Wrongly, if so. She was the elder of the two parents by four years, and had the more powerful personality. Her tears were the result not of inadequacy, but of depressions as deep as her temper was violent. Both temper and depressions were inherited from her father. Both were passed on to her son. Her daughter-in-law, Paul's wife, speaks of her as "very hard, very severe." And one may guess from her photographs that she was a formidable woman in a rage. The features are strong, masculine, and far from beautiful. But the eyes are warm, and the lines bespeak firmness and justice rather than harshness. She seems to have avoided, perhaps because of her husband's softening influence, the extreme rigidity of old Schillinger, who insisted on parishioners dressing in frock coat when visiting him and who draped all mirrors in black when young women stayed in his house. The virtue Mrs. Schweitzer seems to have prized above all was kindness. And she had a deep romantic love of nature, especially of the countryside of her valley; a love bordering on sentimentality. Schweitzer quotes her as saying of a lake where they often walked, "Here, children, I am completely at home. Here among the rocks, among the woods. I came here as a child. Let me breathe the fragrance of the fir trees and enjoy the quiet of this refuge from the world. Do not speak. After I am no longer on earth, come here and think of me."[3]

When Schweitzer recalled those days, he himself was an old man, and the sentiment may have been affected by his own knowledge of approaching death. But the sensual richness of the Schweitzers' identification with nature is unmistakable—a depth of emotion that in some of the family may have substituted for sexual warmth and freedom of expression in personal relationships, but which in Albert himself was to prove the ground bass to the whole theme of his life.

Writing in 1944 to the American poet and biographer Hermann Hagedorn, who had asked him for details of his early years, he recalled:

> Even when I was a child I was like a person in an ecstasy in the presence of Nature, without anyone suspecting it. I consider Nature as the great consoler. In her I always found calm and serenity again when I was disturbed. And this has only become accentuated during the course of my life. . . . Unforgettable pictures of the country are engraved on my memory. I roam among these memories as in a gallery in which are hung the most beautiful landscapes painted by the greatest masters. . . . It is said I am a man of action. But at bottom I am a dreamer, and it is in reveries, reviving the living contact with Nature, that I gather the powers that make me an active being.[4]

Like his mother, Albert had difficulty in talking about deep feelings for people but none in expressing his love for nature. This shared delight seems to have been one of the strongest links, unspoken but acknowledged, between them. As a young man he spent some very hard-earned pocket money on sending her and his sister Adèle for a walking holiday in Switzerland, for whose mountains she had a passion. And she always hoped that one day, when he was rich and successful, he would take her to Scotland. The hope was never fulfilled. He had the wrong kind of success.

The relationship between these parents and their children was not an unusual one in Europe at that period; the dominant mother and gentle retiring father; the lack of any show of sexual feeling between parents, extending to an emotional reticence between parent and child. The only account of this family, apart from Schweitzer's own, is from Jean-Paul Sartre. It was written almost a century later, and dependent on impressions gathered much later during visits to the vicarage as a child—Sartre was nearly thirty years younger than Schweitzer—and on his recollection of the recollections of his grandmother.

Sartre was brought up in unhappy circumstances in Paris, in the house of his grandfather, Charles Schweitzer, Albert's uncle. His mother, who had been widowed soon after his birth, had been forced to return with her child, penniless, to the parental home she had only just left. Here, so Sartre suggests, she had been resented and humiliated, though she struck up a lifelong friendship with Albert, who used to walk Jean-Paul out in the pram when staying in Paris as a young man. At all events Sartre grew up feeling unwanted and out of place—a sensitive Parisian among robust Alsatians. His view of the Schweitzer family is accordingly jaundiced. His grandmother, so he believed, had not enjoyed her marriage to Charles Schweitzer; his mother was even more embittered; and his own sympathies lay with the female side of the family. But his acid little sketch of the family is worth quoting nevertheless. His evidence, though that of a hostile witness, is revealing in a way which he may not have intended.

Here then is his version of a visit made to Alsace made by his grandmother and grandfather, Charles and Louise, in the early years of their marriage. (The brothers mentioned are of course Albert's father, Louis, and his uncles, Charles and Auguste, both of whom had settled in Paris.)

"They spent a fortnight in Alsace without leaving the table; the brothers told each other scatological stories in dialect; now and then the pastor would turn to Louise and translate them out of Christian charity. It was not long before she produced good enough reason to exempt her from all conjugal intercourse and to give her a right to a bedroom of her own; she would speak of her migraine, take to her bed, and began to hate noise, passion and enthusiasm, all the shabby vulgarity and theatricality of life with the Schweitzers."[5]

So the Schweitzer household was noisy, passionate, and enthusiastic. Nobody would guess it from Schweitzer's own temperate account. But they are not bad qualities among which to grow up. There may be some literary license in the portrait of the genteel Louise, unaccustomed to country language and the presence of a vigorous man in her bed, marching off to have her lonely migraine. Other children were there during those holidays—Schweitzer's nephew and niece among them—who remember the little sharp-eyed Jean-Paul sitting with his ironic smile, absorbing but taking no part; and who remember the ladies tut-tutting at some of the language being used in front of the women and children, as ladies tut-tut the world over. It was no more serious, they say, than that.

Jean-Paul's own grandfather, Charles, with whom he had an intense love-hate relationship, was the most ebullient of the family, and used to annoy Albert's humorless mother with his jokes. The Schweitzers, for example, took their hospitality seriously enough to keep a visitors' book, whose flyleaf carried the inscription from Hebrews: "Be not forgetful to entertain strangers; for thereby some have entertained angels unawares." Charles added, "Others have found the devil slipping in"; which Mrs. Schweitzer did her utmost to erase.

Sartre adds this about their language: "Creatures of nature and puritans—a combination of virtues less rare than people think—the Schweitzers loved coarse words which, while they minimized the body in true Christian fashion, manifested their willing acceptance of the natural functions." [6]

Did they minimize the body? Charles used to jog Jean-Paul on his knee and sing, "I ride upon my bidet, and when it trots it leaves a fart."[7] Jean-Paul giggled and blushed, knowing that this was rude. The subject matter for the family's vulgarity was excretion rather than sex. But as an adult Albert exhibited a perfectly normal countryman's interest in the processes of procreation, animal and human, and though he had a strong dislike of immodesty appears to have been quite without prudishness. "He had no quarrel with the way God made men and women," said a friend. It is possible that he achieved this attitude in the teeth of his upbringing, but there is no evidence of any struggle of this kind in his youth. And looking at the life-styles of the two men, one can hardly feel that it is Sartre to whom one would go for a free and balanced attitude to human physiology.

The Schweitzers lived life with gusto and good humor and there was none of the pious hypocrisy suffered by the families of many Protestant clerics. But from Sartre we can safely accept that this bustling, energetic household lacked that physical intimacy, that easy tender relationship between husbands and wives that leads to easy tender relationships between parents and children. In families of this kind the mother often places more emphasis on action and achievement than on contentment and fulfillment—or perhaps such mothers equate the two. Certainly that period produced large numbers of men of achievement, explorers and adventurers—men who welcomed hardship. And many of them had mothers who, like the Spartan women, expressed their love by spurring their sons to endeavor and discouraging weakness.

But despite Mrs. Schweitzer's vehement temperament, her varied interests, and her passion for information, the man she taught her son to admire most was not her learned and imperious father but her gentle half-brother Albert.

The older Albert had been pastor at St. Nicholas' Church in Strasbourg. When Strasbourg was threatened with siege during the Franco-

Prussian War, he went in a hurry to Paris to fetch drugs and supplies for his parishioners. Getting what he needed was not easy, and by the time he finally returned, Strasbourg was already surrounded. The Germans allowed the supplies to be sent through, but Albert Schillinger was held, suffering agonies of guilt for fear his parish would think he had deliberately chosen to avoid their hardships. So when the war was over and there were food shortages, his guilt reinforced his natural benevolence, and he suffered considerable deprivations to help others who were in need. Since he had a weak heart this was not simply kind but dangerously sacrificial; two years later he was rewarded for his selflessness by a sudden heart attack which killed him as he stood talking with friends. The young Albert became haunted by the idea that he ought to provide some sort of continuation of the man whose name he had been given.

Such were the ever-present dead. From the living there were other lessons to be learned, and unlike school lessons, once learned they were never forgotten. Coming home from school one day he had a friendly wrestling match with a bigger boy, George Nitschelm. Albert won the fight and pinned the boy down. A triumph. But what happened next turned the tables on Albert forever. Lying there defeated, George said, "Yes, if I got broth to eat twice a week, as you do, I'd be as strong as you are."[8] And Albert, so he says, staggered home, overcome by this end of the game.

The excuse is not a particularly good one. It is hardly likely that George starved in that rich countryside. Albert might reasonably have dismissed the remark and forgotten the incident; or he might have been secretly pleased to have his superiority recognized. So what overcame him? The real accusation behind George Nitschelm's words was that Albert belonged to a different class, one of the alien bourgeoisie.

Albert certainly knew something about Socialism. A relation of the family was Eugene Debs, whose father had emigrated from Colmar to the United States, and who was himself to become a leading trades union organizer there, even running for the Presidency. The Schweitzers of Günsbach had maintained contact with Debs—Mrs. Schweitzer had a family photograph taken specially for him. So she would certainly have talked to the children about the poverty in the United States at the time, and the appalling conditions that Debs and other Socialists were fighting to improve.

Albert, his instincts always siding with the weak and disregarded, could not endure to be thought of as one of "them," the better off, the exploiters. More than anything he wanted to be exactly the same as the other boys, so that they would forget that he was a sprig of the gentry, bred from a line of pastors and, worse, schoolmasters. But he was caught in a cleft stick—nothing he could do could alter the facts, and in a way his very determination set him farther apart. The harder he struggled to escape his bourgeois background, the more he was proving himself an exceptional child.

He refused to wear an overcoat that had been made for him out of an old coat of his father's—not a particularly high-class garment, but the other boys had none at all. He refused to let his mother buy him a sailor cap, and made such a commotion in a Strasbourg shop that the customers came running to see what the trouble was. Before he could be pacified the shop assistant had to delve into the unsalable stock for a brown cap that could be pulled down over the ears; "like what the village boys wear,"[9] said this uncouth boy in the big Strasbourg store. To the added embarrassment of his mother, he dragged it on there and then, such was his need to establish his difference from the middle-class shoppers who were staring and whispering.

A school photograph adds point and poignancy to the story. There sits Albert among his classmates, the only one with a wide collar and a fancy suit, the young master to the life. The respectability of the Schweitzers shouts from the picture.

It became a running battle, poisoning, he says, their lives. Coat and cap were not the only issues. Gloves entered into it—he insisted on fingerless mittens; and boots—he would wear only clogs, except on Sundays. He endured beatings as well as entreaties, and against both he stood firm.

Oddly enough, his father was more perturbed about his deviation from propriety than his mother. Perhaps the dignity of the ministry was at issue. The gentle pastor was not too gentle to administer beatings to his "*sacré imbécile*" of a son. But Mrs. Schweitzer seemed to understand that there was more involved than willfulness. Albert was unable to explain to either of them. Against all beatings, reasoning, and entreaty he stood firm, and won by sheer obstinacy.

It was to no avail. The boys were not to be fooled by his disguise. In brown cap and clogs, fingerless gloves and no coat, he was still not one of them. They went on calling him a sprig of the gentry, and he went on suffering.

The difference must have been fairly evident, and concerned more than parentage or clothes. At its simplest, a boy who can teach the teacher how to harmonize is unlikely to find it easy to merge with the herd. But there were other, deeper differences.

In a neighboring village lived a Jew—a dealer in land and cattle, and reputedly a usurer, named Mausche. Jew-baiting was an accepted way of enjoying oneself in Günsbach as elsewhere, and the village had no Jew of its own; so when Mausche appeared with his donkey cart and drove through the village and out over the bridge across the Fecht, he was pursued by a horde of jeering boys. Schweitzer, when he reached an age to join in this sport, ran jeering with them—thus announcing, as he says, that he was beginning to feel grown-up. But he was also announcing his identity with the rest of the boys. He did it for no reason but because the others did. And he admired the daring boys who folded a corner of a shirt into the shape of a pig's ear and waved it in Mausche's face.

Mausche drove on, apparently unmoved. But once or twice he turned and smiled. That smile, like George Nitschelm's excuse about the broth, was never forgotten. "Embarrassed but good-natured"[10] Schweitzer called it—the smile of the perennial outcast. It taught him, he says, what it means to keep silent under persecution.

One need not be persecuted to know what persecution is. Children's imaginations leap ahead of their experience. But when this happened the boy was already beginning himself to know what it meant to be singled out for scorn. His sympathy went out to Mausche. He never again ran with the pack when the Jew and his donkey drove through; instead he greeted him politely. Coat or no coat, clogs or no clogs, this was not the way to win acceptance and approval from his classmates. He would have done better to join the boys who turned their shirttails into pigs' ears if he had really wanted more than anything else to be one of them.

Out in the fields and on the hillsides he had already become deeply affected by the sufferings of animals, both in the course of nature and at the hands of human beings. Not that the Alsatians are particularly cruel to animals. Jägle, the gravedigger, had a pet calf which he wept over when it ceased to recognize him after a season's hill pasturing. And today there is a clogmaker living opposite the house that Schweitzer built in Günsbach whose dream it is to stand still on a hillside until the birds come and settle on his outstretched arms. But country people are unsentimental about animals—sometimes indifferent. In Colmar Albert once saw an ancient bony horse being dragged and beaten to the knacker's yard. And there are the marks of nature's harshness in every dried-out shell of a bird caught by a cat, in every pile of rabbit's bones in the fields, every small scream in the night, every maggot that infests the dead or living flesh. For Albert these were enough to make him add privately to the prayers which his mother said with him each night a special prayer for "all things that have breath"; for he saw no reason why human beings should have the exclusive right to compassion.

In a much-quoted passage he writes, "Youth's unqualified *joie de vivre* I never really knew";[11] adding that he doubts that he was alone in this. It is highly unlikely that youth's unqualified *joie de vivre* exists at all outside the sentimental memories of adults. But the statement is worth setting against his claim to have had a very happy childhood—for these small clouds of distress were the beginning of a darkness that had immense results.

The thing that differentiates Schweitzer is not that he suffered, both in himself and on behalf of other people and creatures, but that the feeling remained fresh and active in him, where in others it becomes overlaid or dismissed. And experience with him was remembered and its lesson learned. This was due partly to the violence of his experiences, partly to the obstinacy with which he clung to them as something which he knew to be fundamental and true. Though he learned gradually to be more patient and tactful than he had been over the issue of the overcoat and the sailor cap, the pattern of events was constantly the same as when George Nit-schelm gasped out the fatal words and set Albert on a collision course with his parents. Experiences came to him with a vividness that forced him to a decision, from which subsequent events and the argument of the others had no power to deflect him.

Not that he was an unnaturally good child, in the sense of being squeamish or inhibited. His understanding of pain included the inflicting of it, as well as the suffering of it. People who hate cruelty only because they have been at the receiving end are in danger of becoming tyrants themselves if their chance comes to turn the tables. A safer basis for compassion is to have found the roots of aggression in oneself at an early age.

The Schweitzers had a dog, somewhat learnedly named Phylax, Greek for "Guard." Phylax's technique for guarding the family was to bite anybody who came to the door in uniform. He had once been rash enough to bite a policeman, but it was the postman who was regularly in danger and needed protection. Albert, the eldest son, was given the responsibility of holding off Phylax, and he liked to pretend to be a wild-beast tamer and pen him into a corner of the courtyard with a switch, striking him whenever he tried to break out. "When later in the day, we sat side by side as friends, I blamed myself for having struck him; I knew that I could keep him back from the postman if I held him by his collar and stroked him. But when the fatal hour came round again I yielded once more to the pleasurable intoxication of being a wild-beast tamer!"[12]

A neighbor's asthmatic old horse also learned to be wary of the young Albert Schweitzer, who was inclined to whip him into a trot although he was too old for trotting. Afterward Albert would "look into his tired eyes and silently ask forgiveness"; but next time he was allowed to drive, the same thing happened. The excitement of mastery over other creatures was too much to resist.

There were other experiences, less painful, that went as deep and had as lasting an effect. They are mostly to be found in the memoirs, but they need mentioning here, not for curiosity value but because they show us the child who is, if any child ever was, the father of the man.

Standing outside the classroom, waiting for a lesson, he heard inside the older boys at their singing lesson. They were singing Alsatian folk songs in two-part harmony. For some reason Albert had never heard this particular style of singing before—or more probably he had simply never heard it done properly. He was, once again, "overwhelmed"; he had to clutch the wall to prevent himself from falling, such was the ecstasy. And when in Colmar he first heard a brass band in procession, he nearly fainted away again.

One thing is evident from all these experiences. Albert's dreaminess was not due to any vagueness or lack of interest in life. His mind may have been absent from where the teacher wanted it, but it was vividly present somewhere else. Herding swine lost its appeal, and his imagination reached after other, more distant occupations. For a long while he wanted to be a sailor, and he covered his schoolbooks with pictures of ships. The world was full of romantic possibilities, and some obstinacy refused to let him pretend to be fascinated in the schoolroom when the schoolroom threatened to distract him from what he was really learning. "No-one," he wrote, "can do anything in defiance of his inner nature."[13] The remark is worth bearing in mind, coming from one who is commonly supposed to have been a model of self-sacrifice.

The early backwardness of brilliant men is not uncommon. Perhaps it is simply this, that most of us allow our natural turn of mind, to which we might apply all the energy of a growing creature, to be diverted into the common course of primary schooling—out of respect for our elders and fear of getting into trouble. We are slowed by preformed ideas, our wheels stuck in the ruts. But the interior direction of some men is so demanding that it will not be deflected; and so in the long run they travel faster.

Still hankering after his freedom to enjoy the open air, Albert used to take his homework to a rock seat halfway up the hill above the village commanding a view of the length and breadth of the valley. There he thrust his pencils into a crack in the rock and let his mind wander. A large pink statue now stands, or rather sits, on this rock—a piece of sculpture of which one of the few noteworthy features is the accuracy with which the sculptor has observed the odd way in which Schweitzer held his pen or pencil; not between his finger and thumb, but between first and second fingers. There is nobody left to tell us whether he already had this trait when he sat there as a boy. He is sometimes said to have developed it later as a result of writer's cramp. But his daughter has it, and says it was not learned from him. Could such a characteristic be instinctive—and hereditary?

Still his work did not improve. His mother's tears at his bad school reports distressed him but were unable to reform him. In the years of his fame he never forgot how much cleverer the boys of the village had been than he was—boys who remained farm workers and shopkeepers. The village school had made it impossible for him to be an intellectual snob, and he was grateful.

Not even the annual agony of writing, or failing to write, Christmas thank-you letters could spur him to work harder. These dreaded sessions took place in the pastor's study between Christmas and New Year's Day, and the anticipation was sometimes enough to reduce Albert to tears on Christmas day itself. As he sat despairing in front of his piece of paper, while his clever sister Louise rattled off letter after letter, each one different and yet each obeying the specified formula, and his friends "whizzed down the road behind the church on their sledges," the iron ate into his soul. Instead of emerging from the ordeal with a strengthened ambition to do better next year he merely found himself confirmed in his "horror of studies and letter writing"—a horror which took years to shake off.

Others however benefited in due course, for he determined that when he grew up the recipients of his presents should never salt their soup with their tears as he had done. And as he determined, so he did. Gifts to nephews, nieces, and godchildren were accompanied by notes forbidding them to write their thanks.

Colmar, for Albert, was "the big world." Bicycles had not yet reached Günsbach—the first penny-farthing arrived there while he was still at the village school and half the village turned out, adults as well as children, to see this strange object leaning against the wall of the inn, and to watch its rider emerge from the inn and pedal away—a sight even stranger than the bicycle, for who had ever seen an adult in knickerbockers?

So there was no getting away from Günsbach except for the regular holiday visits to his godmother's house in Colmar. But Colmar was sufficient. Here were parks, processions, brass bands, a museum, and real boats on a real river—of which more later. In addition Colmar presented Albert with moral issues more complex than any he had yet had to face.

One afternoon his godmother sent him out for a walk, escorted by the two maids—at that time even the petite bourgeoisie boasted two maids. The maids took him instead to the local fair, where they spent the time dancing. They danced, all three of them, hand in hand, Albert between the girls in the long row of dancers, and on the other side of each girl "a cavalier who interested her much more than I did!" So he learned the contredanse, a dance which he reports regretfully "you don't see anymore."

On the way home the girls made it clear that there was no need to mention to his godmother that they had been to the fair. "I came face to face," he says, "with the problem of Guilt. . . . On the one hand I was on fire with chivalry. On the other, I should have to tell a lie if I was to keep faith with these sterling girls." We learn a lot about Schweitzer from the capital *G* that he gives to Guilt, the mock pomposity saving the story from any hint of pretentiousness. And there is no moral. "Luckily, as it happens at times to all of us, I was spared the ordeal."[14] His godmother asked only whether they had a nice time. Yes, they said. Nobody mentioned where they had been.

There was another brush with Evil in Colmar which left its mark. Albert's godmother sent him out with a friend to play. The friend was a Colmar boy, a little older than Albert and a good deal more sophisticated, and Albert was put in his care with the strict injunction not to go near the river and above all not to go boating.the boy led Albert through narrow unfamiliar streets till eventually they reached the edge of the town—and the river. Albert was thrilled, for he had never before seen a real river with real boats on it "that floated on the water, with great loads of vegetables on board and a man in the stern to steer them." Besides, he had recently abandoned plans to become a coachman or a pastrycook in favor of going to sea as a sailor.

"Let's find one that's not properly tied up," said the boy; and promptly did so, jumping aboard and telling Albert to follow. Albert was shocked. He begged the boy to remember what they had been told. "We mustn't do it," he said. Then came the revelation. "He didn't deign to reply, but looked at me as if I had fallen out of the moon and was speaking some unknown language. He didn't even try to find excuses for not obeying. He merely implied by his attitude that obedience, in his eyes, was a prejudice to be abandoned: a notion so far beneath him that there was no point in acknowledging it. It was an attitude of mind that I had not imagined possible. When later, towards 1893, as an undergraduate, I read what Nietzsche had written a few years before—it was beginning to make something of a stir—I found nothing surprising in his intention to go 'beyond good and evil.' There was nothing in Nietzsche that had not been revealed to me, without a word spoken, in that scene on the banks of the Lauch. And for an instant, as I boarded the boat under the imperious gaze of my companion, I had been one with Nietzsche."[15]

Here, in the quiet deflation of the overblown elements in Nietzsche's philosophy, is the essential Schweitzer—the man who was not to be frightened by big words and pretentious notions but would always check them against simply human experience. Europe would have been saved a great deal if the German nation had had a greater share of his Alsatian commonsense and humor.

His Nietzschean escapade, like Germany's, ended badly. The boys were seen, reported, and punished. "Still," concludes Schweitzer, "guilty or not, I'd been out in a boat!"

The museum at Colmar was the object of regular expeditions, and here Albert found a great deal to interest him. This museum is remarkable for so small a town, and the attendance there is said to be second only to the Louvre in all France. The most notable exhibits are the paintings of two fifteenth-century Alsatian masters, Grünewald and Schongauer. Both painted religious subjects with a great deal of realism, placing the life of Christ in Alsatian surroundings with much naturalistic detail. The Grünewalds, which today are proudly and centrally displayed, were then badly placed and badly lit; but Albert singled them out for special attention. Life in Alsace had changed so little since the fifteenth century that the wooden bathtub that Grünewald had given to Jesus was just like the ones in Günsbach. And as at Günsbach a chamber pot lay handy.

The color, too, pleased Albert—"brilliant and unexpected"—but the naturalism impressed him most. Jesus was no mystery, for here he was, surrounded by people and things that Albert knew. Most gratifying of all, it seemed that St. John had a mop of unruly hair—like his own.

Albert's hair was totally uncontrollable, and the maid whose hopeless job it was to try to flatten it with fearsome brushings and a stick of brilliantine used to make disquieting remarks about the way in which hair could indicate character. "Unruly without, unruly within," she would pronounce, and Albert was beginning to wonder if his hair really did presage something like a criminal career. Grünewald's St. John reassured him. Schweitzer's disposition to let this kind of thing prey on his mind was characteristic. Jägle had poisoned his life with the threat of horns. The maid was able to "darken the skies" with her old wives' tales of character reading by hair. These things fed a deep anxiety—about existence, about nature, and about his own character—which he was unable to shake off and which was growing toward a climax.

Another of Colmar's sights, too, pointed to that climax—the big statue in the Champ de Mars of a reclining black man. The statue was made by Bartholdi, a native of Colmar, who also designed New York's Statue of Liberty. It was destroyed during the Second World War, but the head is preserved—dignified, leonine, pensive, a highly idealized conception of the noble savage. It touched the strong romantic chords in the boy's nature. He visited the statue again and again.

Why did this particular image appeal to Albert? It was only one of four that surrounded the main statue, which celebrated an admiral of local fame. The other three statues all represented races from other distant countries. We can only guess what was special about this one; but something in the pose of the head, lowered and brooding, is not unlike those early photographs of Schweitzer himself. St. John had hair like Albert's. Perhaps the Bartholdi black man seemed to the boy to share his sense of sadness.

So the long quiet years of childhood stretched out, undramatic but full of incident. One exciting day Mrs. Schweitzer returned from Strasbourg looking years younger because of her new set of teeth. Friends and relations constantly visited, for the country walks and the mountain air. In summer there were frequent family picnics led by father—bread and cheese and homegrown wine—and when young Paul was likely to be left behind, because they were going farther than he could walk, Albert knocked together a cart and towed him rather than see him deserted. In the winter evening the pastor would settle down with his piano or his books, the girls with their embroidery, Mrs. Schweitzer with her cooking or her mending, and Albert, unless some demand roused him to unwilling effort, with his dreams.

Spring would come and the storks would fly in from the south, to build their nests and to bring good luck to the houses where they settled. When the time came for spring cleaning, Mrs. Schweitzer would shut the dog out of the house so that his muddy pawmarks would not undo her labors. Ordinary events, but in every ordinary event Albert found significance. From images as simple as that of the exiled dog he would build the foundations of his philosophy.

His father was still far from robust in health. His digestion was unreliable, and Mrs. Schweitzer wondered guiltily if the cause was the cheaper food which the growing family made it necessary to buy. He suffered occasionally from rheumatism as well, to which the dampness of the house contributed.

In such circumstances as these an elder son takes on any tasks and responsibilities that his size and strength allow. The boy was certainly not driven hard, for he was to look back longingly to this period when he came up against a stricter disciplinarian in his great aunt a few years later. "My parents," he says, "trained us for freedom."[16] But during these growing years, when the father was often either ill or in his musty study, the mother and the strong son, working together, learned to understand and respect each other, and though their mutual reserve meant that they almost never spoke freely of their deeper feelings, she passed on to him a full share of her interest in world affairs as well as her love of kindness and her passion for nature. He understood only too well her shyness, her flaring temper, and those acute depressions. The constant troubled references in his memoirs to her reddened eyes show how aware he was of her mental state; aware and probably more than a little guilty.

In his ninth year important things happened. The first was simply that his legs finally grew long enough to reach the organ pedals. This was a great event, for the organ was in his blood, and as we have seen he was never inclined to fight his heritage. Daddy Iltis encouraged him to practice whenever he could; perhaps from sheer goodheartedness, perhaps partly because he had an eye to the moment when he could take some time off and leave the accompaniment of the occasional service to an enthusiastic deputy. If he had anything of this sort in mind he was not disappointed. Within a year Albert's face began occasionally to appear framed in the organ mirror as Satan's stand-in.

Besides being the organist, Daddy Iltis was also teacher to the senior section of the school, to which Albert had now graduated. And at last, under his friendly guidance, Albert began to show a little interest in learning. The ability to read and write, laboriously acquired and unwillingly exercised, were suddenly seen to have some purpose; and once that happened there was no stopping him. One of the first books he asked for was a Bible; when his father gave him one, he plunged into it with enthusiasm.

This was not simply a pious exercise. He had never yet had a satisfactory answer to his question, If Jesus' parents were given frankincense, myrrh, and especially gold by the Three Wise Men from the East, how was it that they remained poor? Other things puzzled him too. Forty days and nights of rain were said to have drowned even the mountaintops when Noah was afloat in his ark. In Alsace it rained nearly as long as that one summer, and the water never even reached the houses. Albert's father had explained this by the theory that in those days it had rained bucketsful, not mere drops, but unfortunately this was not confirmed by the Scripture teacher. Clearly, the Bible held clues to these and other mysteries; and Albert had an urgent need to know more about those important days when Jesus lived—about the springs of the religion to which his father and so many relatives had given their lives.

His ninth year then saw the beginning of Schweitzer the organist and Schweitzer the Biblical scholar. But more important still—more central—was a third development; an event, a moment, which hardened his childish tendencies and inclinations into a crucial conviction.

It happened a little before Easter. The soft snow had melted from the surrounding fields, and now lay only on the high slopes distantly visible at the head of the valley. Where it had lain hard packed in the streets, it had been chipped up to bare the buried cobbles. The naked branches were beginning to mist a little with leaf buds. What better time, thought Albert's friend Henry, to take one's new catapult up the warm hillside and kill a few birds? Henry proposed the expedition to Albert, who found himself in his familiar dilemma. He prayed for the safety of birds—why should he shoot them? On the other hand refusal might mean further mockery from his fellows.

The story has often been told, and justly. A vital thread of his life runs unbroken through this experience, the greatest of his childhood, through the greatest experience of his manhood thirty-two years later, and straight on to the end of his life. For a moment as important as this there are no better words than his own.

We got close to a tree which was still without any leaves, and on which the birds were singing beautifully to greet the morning, without showing the least fear of us. Then stooping like a Red Indian hunter, my companion put a bullet in the leather of his catapult and took aim. In obedience to his nod of command, I did the same, though with terrible twinges of conscience, vowing to myself that I would shoot directly he did. At that very moment the church bells began to ring, mingling their music with the songs of the birds and the sunshine. It was the Warning-bell which began half an hour before the regular peal-ringing, and for me it was a voice from heaven. I shooed the birds away, so that they flew where they were safe from my companion's catapult, and then I fled home. And ever since then, when the Passiontide bells ring out to the leafless trees and the sunshine, I reflect with a rush of grateful emotion, how on that day their music drove deep into my heart the commandment: Thou shalt not kill.

From that day onward I took courage to emancipate myself from the fear of men, and whenever my inner convictions were at stake I let other people's opinions weigh less with me than they had done previously. I tried also to unlearn my former dread of being laughed at by my school-fellows.[17]

The dilemma was resolved. The life of "things that have breath" was more important than the fear of being laughed at. The terror of being different from the others was at last overcome; not in a moment, naturally, for the conflict continued, never entirely to be resolved, between the need to stand out alone and the need to be one of the company. But the priorities were now clear and were never again to be in doubt. When at the age of nine and a half he went on to the Realschule in Münster, roughly two miles away, he would walk by himself over the hills, which is not the direct route, rather than go with the other boys along the road.

One other incident is undated, but should be reported. It must have happened about this period. One of the guests at a wedding which his father conducted was a crippled girl. Albert in his innocence asked whether this was the bride. They laughed at him; who would want to marry a girl with deformities? Albert privately determined that if that was the way the world went, he would be different. He would marry a cripple. It was one of those silly quixotic resolutions which children do make, and then when they learn better, forget about. But in Albert's case such resolutions often stayed with him and he lived to make them seem normal and reasonable. About this decision it is less easy to decide how important it was, and what, if anything, it meant to him later in life.

In the year in which he tramped across hills to the Realschule, he saw the Münster valley in every seasonal mood and fell more and more deeply in love with it. He tried to express his feelings in poetry and in sketches; both were complete failures. Only in musical improvisation did he ever feel he had creative ability. In fact, though, there are the marks of a major artist in the use he makes of imagery in his books and sermons. It is nearly always nature imagery. The countryside through which he tramped became the natural landscape of his thought.

Imagery of this kind can bring an argument down to earth, and at the same time bring it to life. He would have said that bringing to life and bringing down to earth were one and the same thing. Everything that happened to him was teaching him the same lesson. Truth lies in the concrete. Dogma and theory must check with common human experience. Eternity starts from here and now, or nowhere. Grünewald reinforced it with the chamber pot near Jesus' crib; and at the Realschule, Pastor Schaffler, the teacher of religion, had the gift of dramatizing Bible stories to such effect that when he wept over the story of Joseph making himself known to his brothers, rows of boys would sit sobbing on their benches in sympathy.

At this period Albert was nicknamed Isaac, "the Laugher," because he could so easily be made to giggle in class, and his schoolfellows made the most of this weakness. But this laughter was not the sign of cheerfulness. "I was by no means," he says, "a merry character."[18] Introspection still pursued him, and he had not yet learned to neutralize it by putting it to work. His giggles were of that uncomfortable kind that come from tension and self-consciousness.

The tension is made clear by one tiny incident, casually mentioned in the memoirs, but full of consequence. He was playing a game with Adèle, one of his younger sisters. Even in games he found it impossible to relax and enjoy himself. He played "with terrible earnestness, and got angry if anyone else did not play with all his might."[19] Not an entirely attractive boy, it must be admitted—little wonder that the other boys enjoyed making him laugh in class.

Adèle took this particular game less seriously than Albert thought she should, which infuriated him so much that he hit her. His mother had told him that he must never hit a girl, but most mothers say something of the sort to most sons at some time or other. More than a mother's reprimand is needed to account for the consequence, which was simply that Albert stopped playing games.

All he writes is this: "From that time onwards I began to feel anxious about my passion for play, and gradually gave up all games. I have never ventured to touch a playing card."[20]

The key word is "passion." Sartre wrote of the noise, passion, and enthusiasm of the Schweitzers. "Noise" and "enthusiasm" fit Albert badly at this age. He was the dreamy one. But "passion" is absolutely right. The passion for play, and that passion for dominance which he felt in taming the snarling dog, came head-on into conflict with the passion for kindness and justice. The struggle was cruel, because the feeling was so intense. That same intensity which peers out at us from the early photographs, which "overcame" him after his fight with George Nitschelm, which almost stunned him when he heard two-part harmony sung well, which drove him to those long and bitter fights with his parents over what he was to wear, now turned inward. He recognized a force in himself over which he was in danger of losing control. He had to tame it, for his own peace of mind. His own violence now had to be penned into a corner and stopped from biting. His desire for mastery had to be turned onto himself.

Jesus said, "If your eye offends you, pluck it out." Here was a child who set about plucking out his love for games because it offended him. He might easily at this point have swung fiercely toward puritanical self-repression, but some instinct saved him from this. The search for a right way of living continued, forced on him by the ease with which he felt he might go wrong. From now on he was to seek for a course by which his vehement nature could express itself positively, not destructively.

Instead of the subconscious wound which the psychoanalysts seek, the thing that troubled him was his awareness of the division and conflict in existence itself. In nature there was creation and there was cruelty. In himself there was love and violence. Something was fundamentally at odds and out of balance in the very stuff of which life and the universe were made. Once again, the exceptional thing about this particular boy was not that he felt this, for multitudes of people feel it, at all ages; what singles him out was the depth of feeling, the insistence with which it pursued him, and his refusal to evade it. The wound was not a personal one of his own. It was in everything, and it had to be faced.

In all these developing tensions of his mind, there was one sure place of peace and reconciliation, and ironically the thing that gave it its special quality was the ill-intentioned edict of Louis XIV. The Catholic chancel of the Günsbach church, with its gilded altar and the two golden statues flanking the east window, was a vision of mystical wonder to the Lutheran boy. Beyond the vision, through the window, he could see the real world of roofs and mountains, trees and sky. This world, he recollects, "continued the chancel of the church into an infinity of distance, and was, in turn, flooded with a kind of transfiguring glory imparted to it by the chancel. Thus my gaze wandered from the finite to the infinite, and my soul was wrapped in peace and quiet."[21]

Günsbach had given him everything he could need—quiet and disquiet, deep roots in the country and the community, and yet enough freedom to question and break away into his own world. As long as he lived it was part of him.

But now the time had come for him to leave it. His elderly great-uncle in Mulhouse, who was also his godfather, made it possible for him to go to the Gymnasium there for his secondary education by offering to board him free of charge. In addition he would have a small scholarship as a pastor's son. For such an opportunity one should be truly grateful.

He was not grateful. Secretly he wept for hours at the prospect; "I felt as if I were being torn away from Nature."[22] The ten years to which he was saying good-bye were his whole lifetime to date—years in which the most startling events in the physical world had been the arrival of the first bicycle in the village, and the first appearance of that alien and suspicious vegetable, the tomato; but in which he had laid down irrevocably the pattern of his life.

2

THE DARK YEARS
1885–1893

Mulhouse is an industrial town, as dreary as Colmar is enchanting. In this uninspiring spot Albert's uncle Louis occupied a gloomy residence that was actually part of the Central School; for after a lifetime of schoolteaching Louis had now become a school inspector. So Albert lived in a permanent atmosphere of education. The boy who hated school was now at school for twenty-four hours a day.

As though this were not enough, the discipline too was strict and pedagogical. Louis and his wife Sophie were of the old school. Childless themselves, they did not believe, as Albert's parents did, in bringing up children for freedom. The day was carefully regulated, to each task its proper time, to each hour its task. Aunt Sophie would encourage the lethargic boy with worthy considerations: "Think how lucky you are to be strong enough to make your bed!"

Looking back later in life he was to discover that he had learned something from Aunt Sophie, but at the time he was not impressed. Even piano practice (between lunchtime and afternoon school, and again if he finished his homework early) became a chore to which he had to be dragged. He was not allowed out walking alone, and visiting was confined to one or two carefully selected and approved friends. When he was finally old enough to be permitted to go for walks by himself, the lanky boy would make a pilgrimage to the top of a nearby hill, from which on a clear day he could see the distant outline of the mountains, a shadowy reminder of home.

What sort of correspondence passed between the two Louis Schweitzers, father and uncle, about the ill-disciplined boy and the need for a firm hand? It has all vanished. Sophie did her best to instill in him a proper respect for literature. Reading was a good and proper activity, but only within prescribed periods—in her case for one hour before supper and two after. Albert's homework restricted his time far more severely, and his method of

44

leaping on a book when he had the chance and devouring it at one sitting, skipping the dull bits, was entirely deplorable and needed correction. How could one appreciate the style if one read like that?

Albert privately disagreed. He believed that if there were bits one wanted to skip, the book was badly written. If it were good enough, the style commanded attention automatically. But he kept his opinion to himself because argument might endanger what little reading time the schedule allowed.

Things came to a head over newspapers, which he read as avidly as he did anything else. The only time he had for this was during the quarter of an hour while supper was being laid, but his aunt was convinced that he only looked at the murder cases and the fiction in the Literary Supplement, and she tried to persuade her husband not to allow him the paper. Albert claimed an interest in politics. His uncle, wise to the deceits of eleven-year-olds, instantly tested him on his knowledge of recent political events. When he had reeled off the names of princes and premiers in the Balkans, the three previous French cabinets, and the substance of a recent speech in the Reichstag, the grown-ups submitted. From then on Albert would solemnly discuss politics with his great-uncle over meals; but much more important, he was allowed additional time for reading the papers.

"Naturally," he wrote, "I used this time to refresh my soul with stories from the Literary Supplement."[1] For stories remained his passion. And even in his fifties, when he was traveling about Europe, he would get someone to keep any installments of a serial that he might have missed so that he could finish it when he got back home.

The battle of the newspapers was one triumph in a period which otherwise was largely disaster. Aunt Sophie's stern regime failed to work. The donkey in Albert's character, the beast that would never be driven in any but the direction that suited him, dug his heels in. One teacher after another found him totally unresponsive, and the day came when the headmaster had to speak to his father about the waste of time and money involved in keeping him on at the Gymnasium. He was the dunce again. Of all the lessons he gratefully remembered having learned from Aunt Sophie, one of the most vivid and valuable was how not to educate the young.

The ax did not fall. He was allowed to stay at Mulhouse, working at lessons he did not understand or want to understand, living in the house of rules, regulations, etiquette, and discipline, musty with the odor of those who, however kind and well-intentioned, were old not only physically but at heart. His feelings when he heard he was not to be expelled back into the Eden of Günsbach must have been mixed indeed.

Nor did Mulhouse do anything to help Albert with his shyness. Rather he sank deeper into himself. His struggles had always been solitary, even in the heart of his family. Here he was more isolated than ever. The never-ending schedule of activities at school and at his uncle's house kept his body occupied, but gave him no escape from his loneliness or his private thoughts. So deeply did his problems enwrap him that he barely noticed the distress his lethargy was causing. When his father came to see the headmaster about his possible removal from the school, the only reaction Albert could summon up was amazement that he was not scolded. It never occurred to him that his parents' worry had gone too deep for anger.

In practical ways, though, he was a dutiful and considerate son, prepared, when the family finances were at a low ebb, to freeze all winter in a summer suit rather than admit to his mother that his winter one was too small and he needed a new one. His aunt characteristically encouraged this Spartan gesture. His schoolmates laughed at him for his impoverishment, which was unpleasant, but at least the reason was no longer his superiority. Perhaps he found some satisfaction in reflecting that he was now among the underprivileged.

In Günsbach he had determined that he would never allow himself to become insensitive to the pain of the world. He would fight his way through the problem rather than take Peer Gynt's way, round about. "Even while I was a boy at school," he wrote in his autobiography, "it was clear to me that no explanation of the evil in the world could ever satisfy me; all explanations, I felt, ended in sophistries, and at bottom had no other object than to make it possible for men to share in the misery around them with less keen feelings."

He would not evade the issue or forget the experiences that had forced it on him. "It seemed to me a matter of course that we should all take our share of the burden of pain which lies upon the world."[2] Somewhere beneath the lethargic exterior the determination smoldered on, but it was now so damped by the rigidity of his godparents, by homesickness, and the longing for the lost world of the countryside that he himself was barely aware of it.

Aunt Sophie however had another lesson to teach him by reverse example. Withdrawn by nature, he found in her someone who was withdrawn on principle. Etiquette and decorum were her watchwords. Going to see friends was known as "knocking about outside."[3] Spontaneity was discouraged and humanity in general kept at arm's length.

This was a change from the vigorous, hospitable life of Günsbach, and Albert, seeking a way out of his distress, had to decide which was better. Aunt Sophie lost. Formal rules of society, Albert concluded, were not the key to relationships with the outer world. In Sophie he saw his own reserve writ large and sealed with adult approval; and he saw that it ran counter to his convictions about the unity of all life. Spontaneous warmth, the thing he was no good at, was the proper approach to fellow creatures. So he set out to achieve it.

A deliberate decision to be spontaneous sounds like a contradiction in terms; but the contradiction is more apparent than real. He was not really aiming to change himself—simply to release his true nature. Some native insight told him that the search for love and warmth is not a journey to a far country but the uncovering of a hidden spring. The difficulty of finding it is not that it is remote or alien but that it has been half obliterated by the superstructures of social taboo and the rubble of one's own attempts at self-preservation. It takes an act of faith to start excavating, for if the pessimists are right and the heart of man is desperately wicked, the well, once disclosed, will turn out to be foul smelling and poisonous, not fresh and life-giving. Albert, fortunately, had not been brought up in that negative stream of Christian thought, and he believed that man, once liberated, was inherently good. So he made his act of faith. But such a decision is only a beginning. Hard work follows. Habit and social sanction set like concrete over the spring water, and the man swinging the pick has his work cut out to get through.

Not that Albert was completely friendless. He had at least two good schoolfriends (awarded his godparents' seal of respectability), one of whom came regularly to Günsbach for the Whitsun holidays. But an odd feature is that in both cases he seems to have valued one of the parents as much as the son. One was a pastor—yet another pastor!—"an extraordinarily learned man." In the other case it was the mother whom Albert singled out. He describes her as "a woman much above average," and makes the rather curious comment that because of her "it was a great advantage to me to go so often to the house of Ostier." Not pleasure; advantage. Similarly he says of Anna Schäffer, a schoolteacher—yet another school-teacher!—who also stayed with Louis and Sophie, that "with her wise and kindly personality she contributed much more to my education than she ever suspected."[4] All the time the search is for understanding rather than delight. Surrounded by pedagogues and ecclesiastics, Albert stood a good chance of maturing into a sanctimonious prig.

Ann Schäffer however appears to have provided some relief from the strictness of the household, and what she taught him had more to do with how to treat people than how to analyze a sentence or a specimen. She and Mrs. Ostier were the first of a long line of women whose help and approval he was to enjoy and rely upon throughout his life—a humanizing, counterdogmatic influence that mattered a great deal to him. Not that he was sexually precocious—far from it. At puberty he began to worship an occasional schoolgirl from afar, like most middle-class boys. But it was older women whose company he sought. He could learn from them and he found them easy to get on with.

And there were still occasional moments when something happened vivid enough to penetrate the miasma and stir the impressionable mind to its old, excited response. Such a moment was his first view of the astonishing Marie-Joseph Erb, a virtuoso pianist from Paris, who came to give a concert at Mulhouse. Sixty years later Schweitzer still remembered the gowned women eating candy while they awaited the maestro, and the inadequacy of his own outgrown suit; he remembered the whirling fingers and his own thunderstruck attempts to work out how those incredible runs and "cascades of arpeggios" had been achieved. Afterward he could not understand how the audience could go back to exchanging sweets as though nothing special had happened. The concert was a revelation of the possibilities of the piano, and at practice that evening he even worked hard at the studies that were "starred with sharps and double sharps, which I had so detested before."[5]

He devised a system for mitigating the tedium of these scale exercises, at least when at home during the holidays, by propping a novel or a magazine serial on the music stand and reading while his fingers ran up and down the keyboard. The rest of the family, going about their business, had no such alleviation of the interminable din, and felt more than a little sore. He alone sat happily insulated from boredom, refreshing his soul with fiction. It is unlikely though that he tried this trick at Mulhouse. One can imagine the comments of Aunt Sophie had she caught him at it.

His music teacher at Mulhouse was Eugène Münch, an organist of considerable distinction, whose nephew Charles was to become the conductor of the Boston Symphony Orchestra. Eugène was an enthusiastic teacher and a tireless seeker after perfection, but he could do no more with this tedious boy than anyone else, and called him "the thorn in my flesh." The problem was that Aunt Sophie could lead Albert to the piano, but she could not make him practice properly. Münch gave him various pieces to learn, but Albert preferred to sight-read something that caught his fancy, or to improvise as he had learned to do on the old square piano at Günsbach. Perhaps from time to time he became in fantasy Mr. Erb of the flying fingers. So he came to his lessons ill-prepared and got into trouble. His surprise at not being scolded by his father about his bad report is only one indication that at that time trouble was more or less his native element.

The determination to break out of his shell was at work within him, but these decisions take time to become effective. With Albert it was a new teacher who made the first crack—not, needless to say, by any new form of stick or carrot for the donkey Albert. Those had all been tried and abandoned as hopeless. What forced itself through the fog of Albert's inattention was the single fact that Dr. Wehmann did his job properly. Exercise books were handed out, collected, and corrected at the proper time. The boys were not expected to be the only ones who were in the right place at the right time, with all their work done. Dr. Wehmann too had his obligations, and met them. The implication, unstated in Schweitzer's account but clearly enough implied, is that the rest of the staff were not like Dr. Wehmann. The same sense of justice which told Albert that animals had as much right to compassion as human beings also said that boys and masters had an equal obligation to work at lessons. Dr. Wehmann became his hero.

In one of his letters to Hermann Hagedorn about his early life, he wrote: "I could never tell you how indebted I am to him. I and many of my schoolmates feel that we owe our sense of duty to the mere example of his life. . . . He had a rare gift for encouraging his students."[6] And in his autobiography he writes: "Thanks to Dr. Wehmann I became firmly convinced that a deep sense of duty . . . is the great educative influence, and that it accomplishes what no exhortations and no punishments can."[7] But the word "duty" here must not be confused with that thin-lipped attitude which often serves as a substitute for love. Schweitzer never preached or practiced that rigid, external type of duty, which is in fact the enemy of the spontaneity he was seeking. What Schweitzer is writing of is example, the willingness to be the first to do what you are asking others to do, and an orderliness which enables good intentions to become effective.

The response to Wehmann's example was immediate, and the result startling. Between Christmas and Easter Albert moved from the bottom of the form to somewhere near the top. Any teacher who had written on Albert's school report "Could do better" would have been absolutely accurate. It was not that he had been unable to work—simply unwilling. He hadn't seen the point of it. Now he did. The spirit of enlightenment, as he put it, awoke in him in his fourteenth year.

In music too the time for the opening of the floodgates had arrived. Münch one day gave his unrewarding pupil a "Song Without Words" by Mendelssohn, saying, "I suppose you'll spoil this like everything else. If a boy has no feeling, I certainly can't give him any." Albert was hurt. His problem was that he had if anything too much feeling, but did not care to exhibit it. Münch's remark meant that now he could put his whole heart into playing the Mendelssohn and yet not feel he was endangering his carefully guarded emotional underbelly. He was simply answering a challenge. He practiced for once with great care, and at the next lesson gave Münch a considerable surprise. Münch's response was to sit at the piano himself and play another of the "Songs Without Words." Albert was accepted. They were musicians together.

The breakthrough was happening on all fronts. In music as in lessons the pent-up talent, once released, soared immediately to undreamed-of heights. At fifteen, after his confirmation, he began to have lessons on the big organ at St. Stephen's. At sixteen he was deputizing there for Münch at church services. And not long after that he was playing the organ accompaniment at a concert performance of Brahms' *Requiem*. A puff of wind from the right direction, and the smoldering fire burst out and leaped heavenward with a ferocity redoubled by its long suppression.

There came a new broadening of his musical horizon—a new experience to stun him and send him walking about the streets in a dream for days afterward—Wagner's *Tannhäuser*. It was his first visit to a theater—often exciting enough in itself to a susceptible boy. Wagner overwhelmed him. Where Bach fed the religious instinct in him, and the need for reason and order, Wagner nourished the wild romantic, the ecstatic side of his nature.

The release was longest delayed in religion—perhaps because in religion it mattered most. His teacher was Pastor Wennagel, an old man who, if he had ever had it, had by now lost the fire to which Albert's fire could answer. What he taught, he taught well. But in Albert there raged questions which Wennagel's kind of instruction never even knew existed, let alone how to answer. And in particular there was one fundamental difference between the ideas of the teacher and the pupil. Albert, fighting his way through to a command of his impulses and an understanding of life, had adopted Grandfather Schillinger's devotion to reason as his guiding light. Christianity was not exempt from its rule. Dogma, revelation, the tradition of the Church—all were subject to questioning, all had to be seen to stand up to rational examination. For Pastor Wennagel faith was a matter of submission to authority; Albert's probing into the mysteries of received truth seemed to him not only meaningless but bordering on blasphemy. The boy, approaching his confirmation with reverence and exaltation, knew instinctively that to bring his questions to Wennagel would be to expose both of them to fruitless hurt; so he hugged to himself both his questions and his joyous conviction of the universal power of reason to embrace the highest religious experience. To Wennagel's gentle questions about his feelings he could only give evasive answers, and the old man concluded with disappointment that Albert didn't care. Had he persevered with sympathy he might well have discovered the passionate emotion that seethed beneath the demand for reason. Albert was in fact "so moved by the holiness of the time that I felt almost ill."[8] Wennagel's disappointment awaits all adults who have the "correct" answer in mind when they question children, and it is their own fault, for the question is not sincere. They seek their own image in another person, and are hurt when they find that the other is truly other. Clergy and schoolmasters, upholders of tradition, are peculiarly prone to this mistake; and it is remarkable that Albert, with the blood of both professions thick in his veins, surrounded by both for most of his early life, managed to resist their pressures and retain his independence of mind. Even more astonishing perhaps that he was able to do this without any violent or rebellious reaction, without ever kicking over the traces like the traditional daughter of the parsonage who flees from the restriction of her upbringing to the arms of a multiplicity of lovers. Albert managed the difficult feat of remaining a lone sheep without ever leaving the fold. The worst that happened was that when he finally broke through the crust of his reserve he began to exhibit one or two alarmingly wolfish characteristics.

In the perspective of history, that period of his life simply looks like an abnormally late spring. Delayed by the frosts of shyness, of the struggle with his own passion, of uncomprehending adults, he finally blossomed into a sudden simultaneous flowering. For him, the release was almost a second birth. But for the bystanders it was an explosion, and it was wise to stand clear of the blast. The tall quiet lad was suddenly a prickly streak of aggressive argument. No unexamined statement was allowed to pass unchallenged. Casual remarks were subjected to scrutiny which they were never intended to stand up to. The passion for reason reached an unreasonable pitch as the search for truth switched from the inward landscape to the world outside. He became an intolerable nuisance, not to be taken anywhere with any degree of comfort. His aunt said he was insolent, and his father had to implore him, when they were visiting friends, to keep his mouth shut and not spoil yet another day.

Insolence was not the intention. All he wanted was to find out the truth. Other people seemed not to care about it and it had to be pointed out to them that this would not do. How could you go through life cheerfully making inaccurate statements based on false assumptions? No wonder the world was in a mess. Like Socrates, Albert demanded only that people should use the brains they were given to ask questions, to pull apart accepted notions, to think for themselves.

History began to fascinate him. Here was one vital key to human life and behavior. And the natural sciences were important, for they dealt with objective fact. The only trouble with science lessons was that there were not enough of them. Also there was something wrong with the textbooks, for they pretended to know too much.

Today the thought that science has its limitations is a familiar one. We have seen too much of the consequences of trusting our lives to purely technical criteria. But in the closing years of the last century science appeared to those who believed in it at all as a shining light, and the probable guarantee of a bright and constantly improving future. The mysteries of nature were capable of being dissected, analyzed, described, and eventually controlled. It was to conventionally religious minds that it mostly appeared a threat, likely to replace hallowed belief with some mechanical

explanation of the world's development such as evolution and natural selection. Worthy archdeacons contemplated suicide at the very thought.

This was not what worried Albert. He had no quarrel with the truth,
from whatever direction it came. If his grandfather could set up his telescope for the village to peer through at the night sky, Albert was not going to be an obscurantist about the universe. His problem was simply that
science was not scientific enough. If one stated that a thunderstorm was
caused by electrical discharges, this did nothing to explain it—it merely
provided a rather more accurate way of describing it. But the new description then needed further explanation. What was electricity? Where
did it come from? The confidence of the textbooks (which in any case
were out of date almost as soon as they appeared) was laughable and piti-
ful. "It hurt me to think that we never acknowledge the absolutely mysterious character of nature, but always speak so confidently of explaining
her."[9] Behind each new contribution of science is always further mystery. However deeply our knowledge penetrates, the only proper attitude
to the basis of nature is mysticism—wonder. And this conclusion is
reached not through a rejection of science but through the use of reason to
assess the proper place and function of science. "Thus I fell gradually
into a new habit of dreaming about the thousand and one miracles that
surround us, though fortunately the new habit did not, like my earlier
thoughtless day-dreams, prevent me from working properly. The habit,
however, is with me still, and gets stronger. If during a meal I catch sight
of the light broken up in a glass jug of water into the colours of the spec-
trum, I can at once become oblivious of everything around me, and unable to withdraw my gaze from the spectacle." History, too, came under
the same judgment. "I gradually recognised that the historical process too
is full of riddles, and that we must abandon for ever the hope of really understanding the past. In this department also, all that our faculties allow
us to do is to produce more or less thorough descriptions."[10]

In religion, truth began with personal experience. Since history was so
suspect, so capable of distortion, the historical side of religion must always be treated with suspicion; finally one could only trust one's own
heart and mind. This was one reason why he so much respected his father, whose sermons were as often as not a way of sharing his own
thoughts and problems with his congregation. This was not particularly
clever, but it was true. And who needed cleverness, if not to discover
truth?

Albert was a strong boy now, tall and thin, with a physical strength capable of matching the mental energy that had been released by the explosion of his spirit. The world was his oyster now, and he set about opening
it. And if there were subjects which he found particularly difficult, he be-

gan to look on them as challenges, not as tiresome irrelevances. Languages, for example, never came easily. Nor did mathematics.

Such was his determination that when he wanted to earn some pocket money by giving private tuition, it was mathematics that he taught—because mathematics was in demand. The reason he needed money was a compelling one. He wanted a bicycle. Bicycles had come a long way, in every sense, during the previous ten years, and were no longer the oddities they had been. To Albert his bicycle was the magic steed that opened to him the gates of the countryside. Mulhouse at last was no longer a prison, mentally or physically.

He saved up more money and gave a bicycle to his young brother Paul. He sent his mother and sister on holiday to Switzerland. He found himself able to talk to anyone about anything. Everything was delight and exhilaration, whether exploring the countryside with his brother during the holidays, conversing with pig farmers or professors, making a nuisance of himself in the cause of truth, or flooding a church with the sound of a big organ. And yet his very delight carried with it a penalty. The greater his happiness, the stronger grew his feeling that he owed something to somebody in return for it. Where this sense of debt came from is hard to say, but it was strong in him. It may be that those first few stifling years at Mulhouse taught him the value of his parents, his home valley, and his childhood freedom as nothing else could have done, and this too was a backhanded lesson from Aunt Sophie. Whether this was the cause or not, the little cloud now hovered intermittently on the horizon of his newfound happiness. It was not yet a very large cloud, but it was there, and it would not go away.

Finals were passed, if not in a blaze of glory, at least respectably. They were marred by only two things, his obstinacy and his trousers. The latter, which he had borrowed for the occasion (examinees were required to attend in black frock coat and trousers), were far too short. With singular lack of foresight he had failed to try them on until the day they were needed. He could eliminate the gap at his ankles by adding bits of string to his braces, but then the gap reappeared at his waist. Apart from the embarrassment, they must have been very uncomfortable. But Albert, who had once so hated being laughed at, was now prepared to turn like a mannequin to let his fellow candidates appreciate the full effect, which was best of all from behind. When the students entered the examination hall, the school staff enjoyed the vision, but the visiting commissioner was not amused and leaned heavily on the buffoon in the funny trousers.

The obstinacy lay in the fact that as usual Albert had not troubled to learn things that he considered irrelevant, and he could see no reason whatever to suppose that it mattered how Homer described the beaching of the Greek ships at Troy. The commissioner took the view that as part of the examination syllabus it did matter, and Albert was only saved at the last moment by his interest in history, which turned out to be the commissioner's subject. Albert finished with a special mention, and his days at Mulhouse were over.

Liberated from his shyness and looking back at the days of his enslavement, what he regretted most was failure to express his gratitude. He was genuinely grateful to many people—Uncle Louis and Aunt Sophie not excluded. Sometimes he was grateful for what they had given unwittingly, the chance remark finding the exact spot at the right moment; sometimes for what they intended, for the goodwill offered even if not accepted. He could hardly be said to have been easily influenced. The Rock of Gibraltar was more yielding than Albert Schweitzer when his mind was made up. But when he was searching, as he so often was, for a clue, a direction, then his response to the right stimulus was instant and uncompromising. These deep, barely acknowledged moments of communication he felt were the most important and precious gifts that human beings could give each other. They could happen by a word, an action, perhaps simply a smile; and their effect was unforeseen and secret. So education for him consisted as much as anything in being constantly ready and available with the healing and necessary presence. He assumed, generously perhaps but probably rightly, that other people were as anxious as he was to find their proper path, and needed, as he did, moments of guidance. Their search was their own affair, not to be dictated from outside; but they could be helped at any and every moment by the responsiveness of people they met. One must be ready therefore to give oneself freely wherever one was needed; but one must never demand results, for these might be long delayed or very different from what was anticipated. All that was necessary was the readiness to give, and the humility to know that the choice of gift was not for the giver. Only the receiver knew what he needed, and even he might not be able to find words for it.

Albert was conscious of debts of gratitude which it was now much too late to repay. He had been too shy at the time, or had taken things too much for granted, or had not recognized what it was he had been given. But if the debts could not be paid where they were owed, they could go back into the common pool of humanity. Benefit could be acknowledged by being passed on to others. And this became the plan of his life.

The cloud then was a cloud of obligation. The debts were piling up, and something in him was saying that sooner or later they would have to be reckoned with. But not yet. For the moment there were new avenues opening up in all directions. Life had become full of possibilities.

3

STRASBOURG
1893–1896

AT home things had greatly changed for the better. The son of a former pastor of Günsbach had died and left his house to the parish as a vicarage in place of the old one. The house was well built and dry, with a substantial cellar and a good garden, and the move had a rapid effect on Louis' health. Shortly after this a small legacy solved the worst of the family's financial problems.

The children had grown up with their mother's keen interest in all manner of things, and there was never a dull moment at the vicarage. With the easing of the financial stringency, the Schillinger passion to be up to date showed itself in Mrs. Schweitzer as a love for trying out new foods, new gadgets, whatever was the latest thing.

The family's pleasure at having Albert home was not entirely unalloyed, though by this time the worst of his argumentative phase was over and they could at least look forward to having a meal in peace. But he was still inclined to moodiness, and as always after he returned from Mulhouse it was some time before he was able to relax. He went about the house withdrawn and stiff, still dogged by the starchy image of Aunt Sophie, and from time to time, when he was not thinking, would call his mother "Aunt."

Even after the family atmosphere had reasserted itself and he had begun to thaw out, the visible manifestations of his inward struggles continued to plague those around him. One never knew when he would turn up late for meals (a considerable crime) or fly into a sudden rage. He would hurt his father by refusing to take part in the traditional stroll after church on Sundays, or by making it very evident that he only did so under protest. He preferred to loiter and dream. He would do his best to avoid any task requiring practical effort. He would practice his scales and arpeggios incessantly, despite all protest, or make abrupt and imperious demands of his poor sisters that they leave everything and pump the bellows of the organ while he practiced, and keep them there till they nearly dropped.

But these things were endured not only because he was a beloved son, not only because he was a big brother, but because it was becoming increasingly apparent that the *sacré imbécile,* the dunce of the village school and the near-despair of the Gymnasium, was developing into someone to reckon with.

Not that the family, even at the height of his fame, ever allowed themselves to show more than a surprised amusement that Bery, as they called him, should have attracted so much attention. And they did their best, as he did, to avoid meretricious publicity. But forty years later Adèle was prevailed upon to write about her memories of those adolescent years, and she makes it clear that even as early as this, and even to those who suffered most from his uncertain temper, something marked him out. They all felt the increasing dominance of his personality, and realized that what drove him was a passion for truth and a hungry quest for perfection. They understood what he called "the conviction that human progress is only possible if reasoned thought replaces mere opinion";[1] and they realized that anyone who held such a conviction was unlikely to live a very contented life.

Young Paul was different—all charm, thoughtfulness and good humor, never any trouble, and without any of his brother's prickliness, but also without the inner fire that gave meaning to his brother's flaws. They were different enough, both in age and temperament, these two, to be without jealousy or rivalry. Each admired, but had no wish to emulate, the other.

Schweitzer's pursuit of truth, it must be reported, did not preclude the odd social evasion. He was searching, he said, for what was "true and serviceable"; and sometimes a lie appeared a good deal more serviceable than the strict truth. One day he and a cousin, feeling the need of beer, explained to their grandfather (this was on a visit to Pfaffenhofen) that they were going to see an uncle. No sooner were they settled in the inn than grandfather appeared and sat down at their table. "An old man isn't as blind as you might think," he said. "And he's often just as thirsty as the young ones. Now pour me a drink." It was the sort of lesson that Schweitzer regarded as eminently serviceable, and he continued to tell the story till he was an old man himself.

With a month or two to spare between finals and the start of the university term, the student traditionally travels. No longer a schoolboy, no longer a slave of the timetable, he stretches toward manhood, he comes into his own as a free member of the human race and wishes to survey his inheritance.

Arrangements had been made for Schweitzer to visit his uncles in Paris. Here, one might think, was truly the big world, outclassing Colmar, Mulhouse, even Strasbourg; *fin-de-siècle* Paris, at that time widely regarded as the center and height of Western Civilization. But this Paris, the Mecca of sensitive Americans, where Left Bank artists experimented with new forms, where poets had sought significance through every degree of perverse experience; the Paris of Baudelaire and Rimbaud, Cézanne and Gauguin, where death came early from alcoholism, drug addiction, or syphilis; this was not the Paris Schweitzer came to know. His Paris was largely a kind of colony of Alsace, populated by those who had fled there when their country came under German rule at the end of the Franco-Prussian War.

These Alsatians were mostly professional people. The very fact that they had been able to make the move to Paris meant that they had a certain amount of enterprise and at least moderate means—sufficient to provide themselves with a fresh start and somewhere to live. They had none of the language problems that most expatriates suffer from, so they had no need to herd together physically. But they naturally kept in touch with one another and helped each other through the first difficult years. As expatriates often do, they throve, needing to work harder than the natives to achieve security in a strange land. Alsatian shrewdness and energy gave them a great advantage; but there was another reason for their success. Unlike the Bohemian colony of artists on the Left Bank, Parisian bourgeois society at that time was restricted by the most rigid conventions. "Paradoxical as it is," Schweitzer wrote, "no other citizenry in the world is for good or bad as conservative as that of the modern French Republic."[2] The more flexible Alsatians could maneuver with much greater freedom than the formal Parisians; when they wanted things done, they did not allow convention to impede them.

Uncle Auguste and Uncle Charles had both in their different ways achieved distinction and prosperity, and both were able to introduce Albert to a prosperous circle of friends and acquaintances. He was less of a country cousin in the big town than he might have been, being much among his own countrymen, who to some degree at least retained their native outlook and native accent. But when he ventured among the true Parisians he discovered, for example, that a visit to a friend necessitated a formal call rather than a casual arrival, and that certain afternoons were set aside each week for receiving. Besides, the trams never seemed to go where one wanted them to go. Any spontaneous impulse to strike up friendships was nipped in the bud.

Inevitably therefore such friends as he did make tended to come from within the Alsatian community. Auguste, with whom he stayed, was able to put him in touch with the business world. Charles had put his bilingual upbringing to good use by becoming a teacher of German at the Collège

Janson de Saylly, where he used a new and advanced method about which he had also written a textbook. His circle was accordingly more academic and, since he was something of an amateur both of poetry and music, artistic. A poem of his which has survived shows more enthusiasm and sentiment than talent, and suggests that there may have been something in Sartre's portrait of him as a histrionic figure, a striker of attitudes. But looked at another way, he was an impressive and memorable man, larger than life, flamboyant and highly entertaining.

Among the Alsatians the social life to which Schweitzer was introduced was not unrewarding, to judge by the one event we know of. This was the wedding of a M. Herrenschmidt, whom Schweitzer must have known passably well, for he was chosen as best man. One of the children of that marriage, Marcelle Herrenschmidt, grew up a friend of Schweitzer's and it was remembered in the family that he danced all through that night; the first record we have of Schweitzer as the enthusiastic dancer, the man who in his eighties, when invited to condemn jive, said, "Any young person who does not dance is an idiot."

Also at the wedding was a Mlle Adèle Herrenschmidt, the bridegroom's sister—a woman of forty, a teacher, who later became principal of a girl's finishing school. Between these two, says Marcelle, a great mutual attraction grew up.

Paris is renowned for its tales of the sexual initiation of young men by older and more experienced women, and the few pieces of evidence we have make it tempting, if rash, to embark upon conjectures on these lines. Certainly such a development is unlikely to have occurred during this first fairly brief visit to Paris; but Schweitzer was in Paris again three years later, and regularly thereafter, and his close friendship with Adèle lasted until her death in the early 1920's.

The details, as for all Schweitzer's personal life, are very scanty. We know that though younger women were much attracted to him, he seems always to have been impressed by older ones—perhaps because his mother had a personality and intelligence that few young women could match. We know that in the years before the First World War, when Schweitzer took his annual holiday, he would summon Adèle and some of the family (young Marcelle included) and they would all obediently journey to a remote inn in the depths of a little-known Swiss valley near Interlaken, where they spent ten days with the world shut out by the surrounding mountains. And we find in the section of the autobiography that deals with the period about 1905 one passing mention of Adèle—as brief and unemotional as the sentence with which he relates his mother's death: "While in Paris I also saw a good deal of Mademoiselle Adèle Herrenschmidt, an Alsatian lady occupied in teaching."[3] By the standards of Schweitzer's reticence that might well be a declaration of passionate involvement.

On the other hand it might not, and certainly Marcelle Herrenschmidt believes it was no such thing—though Marcelle was only ten when they began going for their holidays to the Grimmialp valley, and discreet grown-ups have ways of hiding such things from ten-year-olds.

About Schweitzer's private life we are forced by his reserve into speculation, and perhaps into folly—or else into the pretence that it did not exist at all. What is sure is that this friendship was an exceedingly important one to Schweitzer, and that this intelligent and sophisticated lady taught him things about the world of women that he could not have come by in the Alsatian valleys or the school buildings of Mulhouse.

Schweitzer and his generation were right to this extent, that private life—friendships and affairs and marriages and divorces—is common to all humanity, and therefore may if you wish be taken for granted. What singles an individual out is his public career. And we have no need to speculate about the importance of the fact that among Uncle Charles' circle of acquaintances was the organist of St. Sulpice, and organ teacher at the Conservatoire, Charles-Marie Widor.

Twenty years earlier Widor, then only twenty-five, had succeeded César Franck at the Conservatoire. Now he was the most famous organist in France; and as a composer he was respected even in Germany where French music on the whole was regarded with some disdain. For Widor, as for Schweitzer, the organ was more than a mere musical instrument. It was a means of reaching out to the infinite and the eternal. "Organ playing," he told Schweitzer, "is the manifestation of a will filled with a vision of eternity."[4]

Such an attitude inevitably led him toward Bach; and through a variety of historical accidents Bach's original style of organ playing had been passed down with much less distortion through the French school than through his native German tradition. Widor therefore was an acknowledged king among the interpreters of Bach, and the pupils whom he handpicked exclusively from the students at the Conservatoire were the élite of their calling. Besides this, the organ at St. Sulpice, recently rebuilt and enlarged by the great organ builder, Cavaillé-Coll, was recognized as one of the most magnificent in the world.

So an introduction to Widor was something of an awe-inspiring occasion for any budding organist. Schweitzer confessed to a continuing shyness in company which must have added to his nervousness, however confident he may have been in his abilities when he presented himself at St. Sulpice one October day, with his aunt's letter of introduction in his pocket.

Thus they came face to face, the small elegant Parisian with his punctilious courtesy and his secure international reputation, and the tall, abrupt country lad with the thick accent and the big hands, whom he was obliged, for politeness' sake, to hear play the organ. He enquired what

Schweitzer would like to play. "Bach, of course," said Schweitzer.[5] The answer was not as obvious as it might now appear. In the first place, one of Widor's own compositions might have seemed the more diplomatic choice. But apart from considerations of tact, Bach was not the acknowledged emperor of the organ that he is today. His rediscovery, after years of neglect, was comparatively recent, and not yet by any means complete. Schweitzer's "of course" might not everywhere have won agreement. But here, as it turned out, it was the right answer.

The playing was even better. So far had he come since, five years before, he had hated the sharps and double sharps and made himself the thorn in Münch's flesh, so well had he made use of the panting efforts of his sisters at the bellows of the Günsbach organ, that Widor instantly broke his rule of taking on pupils from the Academy; though, "I still don't understand why he did it,"[6] wrote Schweitzer at the age of seventy.

For both men the meeting was important—for Schweitzer vital. No encouragement could have given him greater confidence. Though there was little time during this stay to take advantage of Widor's offer, those few first lessons meant that he could embark on a fundamental improvement in his technique. "Plasticity" was the key word—a word which denotes the careful molding of a phrase, so that each note contributes its proper value to the entire musical structure. Smoothness is essential, but it must be achieved without loss of definition. Every note must be distinct, yet integrally linked with its neighbors. Structure was an aspect of music of which Schweitzer had hitherto been too little aware.

So he was able to go to college with a great deal to think about, a great deal to work on. Behind him he had the approval of the great man and the knowledge that he could return to Paris at any time to take up instruction where he had left off.

No longer the reluctant scholar, Schweitzer seems to have settled instantly into college life. It was an exciting time to be an undergraduate, and Strasbourg was as good a place as any to appreciate it. In every way the university was young. Founded only twenty years before, after the Franco-Prussian War had left Strasbourg in German hands, it had been provided by an astute government with some of the brightest young professors in Germany. The rising intellectuals of Alsace were to be wooed into the liveliest streams of German thought. As a result, the university offered ideas that were largely free from the trammeling influences of tradition and the prejudices of aging professors. "A fresh breeze of youthfulness," wrote Schweitzer, "penetrated everywhere."[7] The prevailing mood among thinking people was set by the cheerful view of Hegel that, however the pendulum of events might swing to and fro, the hour hand of history was advancing steadily toward the perfecting of civilization. It followed that nothing but good could come of the rather startling thoughts being put forward by Nietzsche and by those who were opening up a new approach to the study of man, known as psychology. One might happily and without qualms explore any new road, however dark or devious, for the truth was great and would prevail, regardless of individual error. Indeed it was only through individual error that it could prevail, for it was precisely the clash and conflict of views that would lead to further light.

The insights of psychology were being pounced on with glee and with varying degrees of appropriateness. All was grist to the mill of this new investigative technique. Some scholars, not content with demonstrating that the belief in Christianity, along with other religious faiths, was neurotic in origin, went on to claim that Jesus himself could be shown to have suffered from paranoia, schizophrenia, or at the very least hallucinations.

The excitement about Nietzsche went less deep, for the students found it hard to take his excitable mental antics seriously. But as his major books became known they began to read him for the brilliance of his style and the entertainment value of his epigrams. (Schweitzer thought his *Beyond Good and Evil* one of the two most perfectly written books in the German language. The other was Luther's translation of the Bible.) The young people enjoyed Nietzsche's shrill attacks on every shibboleth, his witty, catty disrespect for every moral and intellectual cliché, his demolition of the idea that pomposity was the same as profundity, his mistrust of any philosophy that tried to cram all of life into a system, his intoxicating combination of commonsense and hysteria. It never occurred to them that his demand for nobility would become an excuse for self-aggrandizement, or that his accusation that the Christian Church encourages weakness could be used to justify the abandonment of pity. He appeared to them a stimulating court jester, little more.

He was, of course, much more. His books opened the door to the abuses that the Nazis committed in his name, but he himself really cannot be held responsible for them. His own ideas were truly noble—but unbalanced. He proclaimed the need for self-transcendence, and he was right. He demanded that life should be affirmed, not denied, and he was right. He was even right when he pointed out that meekness and humility are encouragements to political and religious oppression. But he was wrong in saying that humanity should therefore discard meekness and humility. A virtue that can be abused is not therefore a vice. The vice is the abuse. Nietzsche, reacting against one abuse, opened the door to another.

Schweitzer understood this. He responded powerfully to Nietzsche's demand for heroism and the vision of the Superman, who could rise above his own weakness to his own full potential stature. It was of a piece with his own belief that reason was a better guide to behavior than convention. And it had echoes in the noble spiritual aim behind the grandiose romanticism of Wagner's operas, which moved Schweitzer so deeply. But he was not at all happy with the implication that ordinary simple qualities were to be despised in the process of self-improvement. He was only puzzled that none of the theologians and religious philosophers seemed able to answer Nietzsche, to take his ideas apart and show where they were inadequate.

These thoughts were no more yet than whiffs of apprehension. For the most part he went along with the general feeling among the young that any of the old beliefs that failed to survive the shovel of the psychologists and the gadfly attacks of Nietzsche were not worth keeping anyway. They embarked cheerfully on their voyages of discovery, and nobody at that time could be expected to foresee how many of those expeditions of the mind would end in wasteland or swamp, or whether some of the things being jettisoned to make the journey possible would later turn out to have been valuable and perhaps irreplaceable. One difference between Schweitzer and Sartre was simply that Schweitzer's intellectual life was given its direction at a time of hope, Sartre's at a time of disillusion.

Schweitzer's lodgings were at the St. Thomas' College, overlooking the river on the edge of the old town. Old Strasbourg, laced with little waterways, threaded with narrow streets, and revealing a rich variety of timbered houses at every turn, was exactly calculated to feed the romantic heart of the young student, particularly since it resembled the town of his holidays—Colmar.

Not far from St. Thomas' College is St. William's Church, where Ernest Münch, brother of Eugène, who had taught Schweitzer at Mulhouse, was energetically building up an audience for concerts of Bach's music. A great revival of interest in Bach had been going on for the past forty years, some of which had taken the misguided form of trying to "modernize" the music, by performing it as though it had been composed in that century. But Ernest Münch was of the other party—those who were beginning to seek out the composer's original manuscripts in search for clues to his precise intentions.

Schweitzer lost no time in introducing himself, and before long he and Münch were up half the night discussing points of interpretation, pacing to and fro, banging chairs on on the floor to emphasize an argument, and falling asleep over the pages. Münch's three children woke sometimes in the night to hear the commotion—Fritz, who himself was studying the organ; Charles, who was to become the conductor of the Boston Symphony Orchestra; and Emma, to whom Albert's arrival was most fateful of all. She was to marry Albert's young brother, Paul. She still lives in Günsbach, and it is to her that we owe much of what we know of Schweitzer's student life in Strasbourg.

The academic subjects he had elected to study were theology and philosophy. He was still eagerly interested in Biblical history, though his approach was now somewhat more sophisticated than in the days when he puzzled over the poverty of the Holy Family. Again he was lucky. For anyone with such interests, to be in Strasbourg in the last decade of the nineteenth century was to be in exactly the right plact at exactly the right time.

About a hundred years earlier a professor of Oriental languages named Hermann Samuel Reimarus had first dared to suggest that it was possible, even desirable, to apply historical judgments to the life of Jesus. Before that all had been a fog of piety, and nobody had thought fit to peer through the haze of omissions and contradictions in the gospels and try to distinguish a recognizable story of a recognizable man. The fact that the creeds, devised fifteen centuries before, had stated that Jesus was "true god and true man" had not encouraged the priests to take his manhood seriously and ask, What really happened to him? The life of a man who was also a god could evidently be a meaningless series of jumbled incidents instead of a consecutive history. Besides, it gave so much more scope for that enjoyable form of self-expression known as interpretation.

Luther's attack on the mystifications of the Roman Catholic Church and his insistence that the New Testament be published and read in a language that ordinary people could understand had gradually borne fruit. It was in his country and his language, though not till two hundred and fifty years after his death, that Reimarus made the breakthrough with a series of witty, scathing, and impassioned attacks on the priestly nonsense that surrounded the stories in the Bible. It was a bold venture, so bold that his work was not published at all during his lifetime, and after his death only in fragments, and anonymously. But once published by a courageous admirer, it could be seen for what it was—the first approach of rationalism to the New Testament; and then there was no stopping the avalanche of violently polemical works that it set in motion. Theory followed theory, each demolishing the last, each fatally weak at some point or other which became the target for the next attack. The orthodox continued to abide, as they always had done, by the principle laid down by Osiander in the sixteenth century, that if an event is recorded more than once in the Gospels, in different connections, it happened more than once and in different connections. So Jesus twice cleansed the Temple, and raised the daughter of Jaims from the dead several times over. But in the German theological schools the battle for the definitive historical life of Jesus raged on, sometimes going around in circles, sometimes making a little progress, but forever revealing fresh abysses of incomprehensibility in those four odd little books which the Christian Church regards as containing the ultimate revelation of God to man.

The battle was still in full swing when Schweitzer arrived at Strasbourg. In fact, his own lecturer, Heinrich Julius Holtzmann, had recently published a scholarly salvo on the origin of the Synoptic Gospels; the book had been very well received, and the views he put forward naturally formed the basis of his lectures on the subject.

On one or two points there was general agreement—that none of the Gospels had been written until at least forty years after Jesus' death—and that of St. John was the least historically reliable, having more of the character of a personal commentary on the significance of Jesus' sayings than of an accurate account of events. But the precise relationships connecting the other three Gospels, the so-called Synoptics, which at least presented a recognizable similarity of outline, was still heatedly discussed.

Holtzmann had made a powerful case for what was known as the Marcan hypothesis. He believed that Mark's Gospel, being the simplest and least elaborated, was therefore likely to be the earliest and most reliable. He was far from being alone in this belief; but the narrative in Mark has so many gaps that even when the decision has been taken to follow Mark in preference to the other Gospels, the scope for interpretation is practically limitless. The method chosen for filling in the gaps naturally affected the kind of Jesus that emerged; his personality and his purposes could be read a dozen different ways according to the way in which the interpreter laid together the elements left by Mark. The temptation was to read the story according to one's own predispositions and to impose one's own outlook on that conveniently shadowy Jesus.

Holtzmann was a kindly and right-thinking European liberal. The Jesus he saw in Mark was an idealist, like himself, who set out to found an ideal Kingdom of God, succeeded for a while in carrying his hearers with him, but encountering increasing opposition began to see himself as a suffering Messiah and finally put his fate to the test when he went up to Jerusalem to his death. The skillful way he told the story, the effective use he made of detail from Mark's Gospel, was so much to the taste of the time that it carried enormous conviction. When Schweitzer sat to hear his lectures he was the acknowledged and loved master of his subject, the man who had cracked the riddle of the Gospels and had given to that eager, optimistic generation a Jesus they could understand and identify with. In its general lines, of course, the picture is still recognizable as the Jesus of innumerable European and North American pulpits today.

Schweitzer, eager to please such a distinguished tutor, studied hard. His first term, disrupted by the usual problems of settling down, was also bedeviled by the difficulty of learning Hebrew, not an easy language at the best of times and particularly hard going for him, with his problem about languages. But once he had mastered its elements and passed the initial examination at the beginning of his second term, he was able to concentrate better on the Gospel problems.

In April he began his year's national service; but this did not seriously interfere with his studies. It was administered with a sane flexibility very unlike the strictness we have since learned to think of as the mark of German militarism. His captain arranged matters so that he could get away to attend the most important lectures, and he continued to grapple with both the Synoptic Gospels and the history of philosophy.

He enjoyed his military service. Physical activity was a pleasure to him, and he had grown into an exceedingly robust young man. His frame was filling out and he was able to make do with very little sleep. So the extra work was no hardship; indeed he now took delight in pitting himself against a challenge.

The discipline too was something he appreciated. Dr. Wehmann had taught him its value, but self-discipline still did not come easily and he relied more on enthusiasm and impulse. External discipline was a help. So for a while the military and the academic existences continued side by side.

In the autumn however the national servicemen had to go on maneuvers, and there was no more college life. Meanwhile Schweitzer had applied for a scholarship, and to qualify for this he was due to take an examination at the beginning of the winter term. Though students doing their national service were required to take only one subject in this examination instead of three, Schweitzer was anxious to shine in that one— which was the Synoptic Gospels. So in his haversack, when he set off on maneuvers, was a copy of the Greek New Testament, from which he wanted to study the text at firsthand to see how much he could remember of Holtzmann's commentaries. While his fellow recruits dozed around him, he was deep in the Greek original of the Gospels.

And so it was that in St. Matthew he came upon a problem. At first it merely puzzled him; then startled him, when he discovered that nobody else had taken much note of it; and finally proved the key to his whole interpretation which, so far as I can ascertain, has never been successfully challenged. Nor has it been openly acknowledged, since acknowledgment would be most uncomfortable for orthodox Christianity; it has simply been quietly absorbed as the unspoken basis for a great deal of modern thinking about Jesus.

What he noticed was as simple as his observation that forty days of rain is not enough to cover a mountain. His achievement in each case was simply to take quite practically something that hitherto had always been regarded as having only a "spiritual" meaning—and "spiritual" in this sense was all too often used to describe something that should not be brought into focus or looked at too closely, for it contradicted reason. In such circumstances it was thought best to allow the spiritual and the rational to pursue their separate courses. The invaluable word "mystery" was invoked a great deal more than it should have been; for though it may legitimately be used to describe a phenomenon which can be observed but not fully understood or expressed, it has all too often been used to mean "something which *you* cannot understand, but which is an open book to me, thanks to my superior connections with the Godhead."

Schweitzer, as we have seen, expected reason to be able to embrace every side of human experience, the spiritual included. There might be occasions on which it was not enough; there might even be times when reason itself said that reason here could go no farther. But it must never be abandoned while it had anything to contribute. And—one more important point—reason to him was not a dry logic. The German word "*denken*" has a much wider, deeper meaning than the English "think." It covers all the faculties of the concentrating, absorbed mind, which include intuition and experience as well as logic.

By now of course Schweitzer had long known that much of the Bible had been written by storytellers whose purposes were more complex than the mere description of facts and historical events, and who embellished their tales accordingly. Such embellishments were clearly at work in the stories of the Ark and the Flood. And passages in the Gospels themselves appeared to have received similar treatment. But he could see no reason why this should be true of the first half of chapter 10 of St. Matthew.

The chapter begins thus thus:

> And he called to him his twelve disciples and gave them authority over unclean spirits, to cast them out, and to heal every disease and every infirmity.
>
> [After naming the twelve it continues]: These twelve Jesus sent out, charging them, "Go nowhere among the Gentiles, and enter no town of the Samaritans, but go rather to the lost sheep of the house of Israel. And preach as you go, saying, 'The kingdom of heaven is at hand.' Heal the sick, raise the dead, cleanse lepers, cast out demons. You received without paying, give without pay. Take no gold, nor silver, nor copper in your belts, no bag for your journey, nor two tunics, nor sandals, nor a staff; for the labourer deserves his food. And whatever town or village you enter, find out who is worthy in it, and stay with him until you depart. As you enter the house, salute it. And if the house is worthy, let your peace come upon it; but if it is not worthy, let your peace return to you. And if anyone will not receive you or listen to your words, shake off the dust from your feet as you leave that house or town. Truly, I say to you, it shall be more tolerable on the day of judgment for the land of Sodom and Gomorrah than for that town.
>
> "Behold, I send you out as sheep in the midst of wolves; so be wise as serpents and innocent as doves. Beware of men, for they will deliver

you up to councils, and flog you in their synagogues, and you will be
dragged before governors and kings for my sake . . . and you will be
hated by all for my name's sake. But he who endures to the end will be
saved. When they persecute you in one town, flee to the next; for truly,
I say to you, you will not have gone through all the towns of Israel, before the Son of Man comes.''[8]

According to the Marcan theory, so stoutly defended by Holtzmann,
there was nothing in Matthew of any significance which was not to be
found, at least in simple form, in Mark. But the counterpart in Mark 6,[9]
though it mentions a mission, says nothing at all about the nearness of the
Kingdom of God. Was it therefore unimportant? A later fabrication? Certainly there was one very good reason for preferring to dismiss Matthew's
addition, and that was that it seems to lead nowhere at all. The incident is
incomplete. The twelve are sent off on an urgent missionary journey to
warn the faithful of the imminence of the Kingdom of God, and are themselves warned of all the dire experiences that they are to expect—hatred,
persecution, beating—before the kingdom arrives. Most solemn of all—
they are promised that even before their task is finished, the kingdom will
be upon them.

The episode is never mentioned again. There is no record of the disciples actually setting out on their journey, nor of any persecutions or disasters. Nor is there any explanation as to why these predictions were not
fulfilled. Admittedly the chronology is so sketchy that the order of events
is far from obvious, but within a few verses the disciples are around Jesus
as before, and there is no mention of the great mission and the nonappearance of the kingdom. The incident comes from nowhere and goes nowhere. It is untidy and pointless. Clearly it would be easier to ignore it or
explain it away. But this fails to answer the real question: If it is so incon-
clusive, if it shows Jesus making plans that get nowhere and prophecies
that are never fulfilled, why on earth would anyone want to invent it?
Why should the faithful, two generations later, preserve this evidence of
the fallibility of their master if it were false? Its very improbability
proved, to Schweitzer at least, that it was not a valueless addition to Mark
but a genuine record from some other source.

One thing the passage does then is to cast doubt on the sufficiency of
the Marcan hypothesis. But this is not its only or even its main importance. The really fundamental question concerned this Kingdom of God
which Jesus foresaw, for which he was forever urging preparedness.

We are accustomed to think of the Kingdom of God in a spiritual sense,
as a condition of peace which the individual can by grace or by endeavor
achieve in this life; and which may one day, if enough people achieve it,
come to reign over the whole world. Schweitzer's knowledge of and instinct for history told him that this was not the Jewish view. For the Jews

the Kingdom of God had a very specific, very material meaning, handed down by the prophets. It meant deliverance from their oppressors and the appearance of the Messiah, the Son of Man; a chosen human being to whom God would give command over the nations. He would bring the old order of violence and evil to an end and inaugurate a totally new age, without tears or sickness or death, a world remade. But it would not be a separate world, in the sense of an afterlife or a spiritual realm distant from earth. It would be the same world, renewed and perfected. And all that was necessary for its coming was that enough of the Chosen People should believe in it and prepare themselves for it by a change of heart.

This, said Schweitzer, was what every Jew of that period understood by the Kingdom of God. And where, in all the Gospels, was there any indication that Jesus meant anything different? When was there any suggestion that he wanted to "spiritualize" the phrase? If he had told the disciples that they were expecting the wrong kind of kingdom, that all Jewry had been misled by the prophets, and that they were going to have to find their own kingdom within the same old suffering world—in that case would there not have been great emphasis in the Gospels on this startling new interpretation?

If, then, Jesus believed in the same physical kingdom as his contemporaries and urgently predicted its arrival at a time when quite evidently it failed to arrive, what did this imply about the ministry of Jesus? Clearly it meant for one thing that he was fallible, as other men are fallible. This would be no great shock to Schweitzer, brought up on the down-to-earth paintings of Grünewald and the whole Lutheran tradition of a human and comprehensible Christ. But, asked Schweitzer, what must it have meant to Jesus himself, to expect the cataclysmic coming of the kingdom and to find himself wrong? What did that do to his own beliefs, and how did it affect his subsequent behavior? In short, Schweitzer saw that this passage, if authentic, must be a vital key to the progress of Jesus' thought and career; and one that nobody before had noticed.

This is a bald, brief, and unsubtle outline of the argument—which indeed was not yet an argument when he first began to wonder about Matthew Chapter 10 in the Alsatian hills. It was simply an uneasiness, a subject for private study. And it was complicated by a further problem in Chapter 11.

This was a more abstruse and scholarly question, concerning the meaning of the Greek phrase ' " 'ο ἐρχομενος.' ' It is translated into English as "he who is to come." John the Baptist sent a message to Jesus asking if he was "he who is to come." Jesus in reply said neither yes or no. His messengers are simply to tell John that Jesus is performing miracles of healing and preaching the good news to the poor.[10]

We are so accustomed, said Schweitzer, to the notion that John the

Baptist was the forerunner of the Messiah that we take it for granted that he himself was aware of it. But in those confused days, with fanatical religious and religiopolitical sects abounding, united only by their hatred of the occupying Romans, who was sure of what? John anointed Jesus in the Jordan, but never named him the Messiah. Jesus on the other hand describes John to his disciples in the same chapter as ' " 'ο ἐρχομενος." '

Moreover, in the Jewish tradition it was not the Messiah but his forerunner who was expected to come performing miracles, signs, and wonders. The Messiah himself was expected to come in glory, not before but *with* the new Kingdom. Could it be, wondered Schweitzer, that John, thinking of himself as simply a prophet, was not in fact asking Jesus "Are you the Messiah?" but "Are you the Messiah's forerunner?" For Jesus had given no word or sign at this stage that he regarded himself as the Messiah. Indeed, had he done so, the people would have been uncontrollable, and the authorities would quite certainly have been forced to act.

Further, Jesus' reply suggests, by its emphasis on the miracles, that he is sending a cryptic indication that he is indeed that forerunner; though later he is speaking of John as ' " 'ο ἐρχομενος." ' The puzzles multiply.

The point about these puzzles, whose pursuit took Schweitzer years of work, and which are far too complex to be gone into in detail here, is that they both centered on the same question—the question of the Messiahship of Jesus. The Christian Church has worshiped him for two millenia as the Messiah, adapting the meanings of that word and the phrase "Son of God" to suit its own beliefs and requirements. But Jesus was not a Christian; he was a Jew. Did *he* know he was the Messiah? And when did the disciples know? And what did they expect? And what did *he* expect, when he went to the Cross? Had he really, without a word, renounced the ancient Jewish hope of the age of peace—he who said he had come to fulfil the prophets?

Many of these questions had been the subject of attention from the writers who since Reimarus had been looking into the history of Jesus. Schweitzer was not exploring uncharted territory. Only he had a new starting point from which to set out and make his own map—the unfulfilled mission on which Jesus sent the twelve disciples, as remarked in Matthew Chapter 10.

It was evident that if his investigations were to lead in the direction he suspected, he would come into head-on collision with his respected tutor, Holtzmann, on Holtzmann's pet subject. He was not ready for this, nor did he want to hurt the kindly professor who examined him so gently on his summer's work when the scholarship time came. So in his replies he said nothing of his doubts about Holtzmann's theories.

Schweitzer was to get so enwrapped in his project that he did less work than he should have done on his set subjects. "No-one can do anything in defiance of his inner nature''; and his inner nature had not changed since the days when he rejected his schoolbooks for dreams of being a swineherd or a sailor. He still dreamed his own dreams, he still chose his own path; though now his deviations were less noticeable, since at least the path now led through the same countryside that he was officially supposed to be treading. And besides, he had grown craftier, or more tactful, at concealing what he was about. The impetuous quest for truth bequeathed him by Grandfather Schillinger was no less headlong. But he had learned that it was sometimes better pursued in quietness and solitude if it was to reach its goal.

He lived very simply. He could afford nothing else. Beer was cheaper than wine, so beer he drank, and very little of that. His room was without comforts—a workshop, not a place for relaxing or entertaining. He found relaxation in music, entertainment in the conversation of friends, and the occasional visit to the theater, generally to hear Wagner. Wagner had "overwhelmed" him. Like everything else that overwhelmed him, Wagner was to receive passionate and lifelong attention. Schweitzer not only listened to the music; he studied the scores, analyzed the productions, and generally made himself acquainted with every aspect of Wagner's work. His first emotional reaction was confirmed. "His music is so great, so elemental," he wrote to Hermann Hagedorn in later years, "that it makes of Wagner the equal of Beethoven or Bach. Such assurance in composition, such grandiose musical architecture, such richness in his themes, such consummate knowledge of the natural resources of each instrument, such poetry, dramatic life, power of suggestion: it is unique, unfathomable in its greatness, a miracle of creative power! Forgive me, my enthusiasm is running away with me."[11]

The same thoroughness that he gave to Wagner meant that in his study of the organ he was not content with learning to play it; he discovered how organs were built, compared their virtues, and studied how effects were achieved. His work with Ernest Münch on Bach's manuscripts led to further research on organ construction; understanding the music was helped by knowing the kind of instrument it was written for.

He had plenty of opportunity for playing, sometimes in concert conditions. When Münch conducted his Bach concerts his brother Eugène would come from Mulhouse to play the organ for him. Schweitzer would stand in for Eugène at rehearsals, and in due course took over at the actual performance if for any reason Eugène was unable to come. Since the concerts at St. William's were acknowledged as among the leading expositions of the new, authentic style of playing Bach, Schweitzer found himself in the forefront of musical advance. The Strasbourg orchestra with which he played was noted for its excellence, and there are few spurs to achievement like the challenge of playing in the company of first-class players.

St. William's had not of course been designed for this kind of enterprise. The organ, a magnificent creation by the eighteenth-century organ builder Silbermann, was so positioned that it was impossible to accommodate anything but a small choir and orchestra near it. When a full choir and orchestra were needed they had to be positioned behind the congregation, under the bell tower, where they could only be accompanied by a small organ with a single manual. When Münch gave a performance of the *St. Matthew Passion,* with its two orchestras and two choirs, the audience had a very early and rather surprising experience of stereophonic sound, since they had one choir, one orchestra, and one organ behind them, and another small choir and orchestra in front, under the great organ. Schweitzer played the latter, although he had only been at Strasbourg a year. "In spite of the distance," he wrote, "we obtained a perfect ensemble. But the audience was still a bit disconcerted by listening to music coming from two opposite sides. For us the experience was very interesting."[12]

The only solution to the problem was to move the organ farther back, to make room for the choir and orchestra in front of it. This distressed Schweitzer, for the organ's tone was matchless and even visitors who knew the Cavaillé-Coll organs at St. Sulpice and Notre Dame were astonished at it. But the move had to be made. The problem was how to pay for it.

The finances at St. William's were already under some strain because of the concerts. Münch wanted his music to be available to all comers, and he made no charge for entry. A collection taken as the audiences left was never enough to cover expenses. This led to fierce disagreements with the church treasurer, Herr Frick, who shared the view of the church council that the upkeep of a choir for church services was all very well but that concerts were quite a different matter. Both Münch and Frick had violent tempers and disagreements grew heated. The choir's continued existence was threatened.

Surprisingly enough it was to young Schweitzer that Münch turned as his mediator. Schweitzer's own temper was none too even; he never did master it entirely. But he was already learning to keep it in check when it was clear that a polite approach would pay dividends. He handled Mr. Frick with kid gloves; allowed him to let off a little steam, and then played on his pride in the fact that St. William's choir was regularly mentioned in the newspapers. The obdurate Mr. Frick softened under the Schweitzer treatment.

After a while it was decided that certain seats would have to be reserved at a mark each, to ease the strain. But even after that, and even with donations from wealthy supporters, the cost of moving and renovating the organ was much too great, and long-drawn-out negotiations for assistance from the city authorities themselves were necessary before the plan could finally be put into effect. The reviews for the first concert after the moving of the organ were unexpectedly poor, and Schweitzer now learned something about publicity. "As we thought it over we came to the conclusion that this might have been because the musical critics were all seated together, so that if one shook his head or puckered his eyebrows at some passage, none of his colleagues would risk giving a completely favourable report for fear of compromising himself. From that time on we saw to it that the critics did not sit together, and thus had their impartiality safeguarded; and this had a good result in their articles. The principle was once more proved that nothing must be left to chance."[13]

The significance of all this is that Schweitzer did not only concern himself with music at St. William's. He immediately plunged into the center of the whole enterprise, involving himself in all its aspects. He was part of an idealistic pioneering venture that constantly faced the quicksands of financial disaster and the thorns of other people's uncomprehending opposition. He learned that the idealist must be more practical than the realist, because he stands alone—that successful idealism cannot live on pure enthusiasm, but demands a willingness to muddy one's boots in incessant tedious detail and a certain cynical cunning in dealing with those who are in a position to be helpful or otherwise. It was a valuable foretaste of the difficulties of his own great adventure to come. It impressed on him unforgettably "that nothing must be left to chance."

The Münch family and their circle seem to have been his closest friends. If there were others, their names have been lost. If there were girlfriends, he kept them quiet, in accordance with his principle that a person is entitled to the privacy of his private life. We know from photographs that he was developing into a very attractive young man. And Emma Schweitzer, née Münch, remembers that there were plenty of girls who were fully aware of the fact. Who they were at this time she is not prepared to say, even if she remembers. But it is clear that she herself was not immune to his charm; she remembers that he was very fond of dancing and flirting, and says that he was not merely romantic but sentimental. Add the comment that he himself made to a friend toward the end of his life, that he regretted the introduction of lipstick for one reason only— that it added unnecessary hazards to a stolen kiss—and we probably know all we shall ever know about Schweitzer's love life as a student.

But whether there was any romance or none, one or several, much of his leisure time was spent in groups. Cycling parties jaunted into the country at weekends, along the flat empty roads that led out of the city, a couple of villages, and up into the hills. It is pleasant to think of early romances budding under cover of these groups of energetic students pedaling forth with the young ladies of Strasbourg. In the evenings they would dance deep into the night in the country inns among the folds of the mountains; and Schweitzer achieved such a reputation as a dancer that he was regularly invited to private dances—though his dancing was energetic rather than elegant, for he was not a physically graceful man; and he himself swore he was only invited when they needed someone who was prepared to play the piano all night long.

The occasional visit to a Wagner opera would provide a welcome romantic evening, ardent souls carried away on a flood of music. But we are fairly safe in assuming that whatever encounters there were went little further than gentle kisses and romantic hand-holding. Schweitzer's upbringing, though not strict, had been entirely conventional in sexual matters, and he showed no signs of rebelling against it. Besides, his many other interests would hardly have given him the time for the prolonged assault necessary to overcome the scruples of the average young lady from the respectable middle classes of the day.

He joined a student association attached to St. Thomas', which ran a kind of Robin Hood service, begging twice a year from the rich and distributing weekly to the poor. The conditions of the poor were nothing new to him. But he really dreaded the begging expeditions, which aggravated his natural shyness and sometimes made him extremely clumsy. He learned that "begging with tact and restraint is better appreciated than any sort of stand-and-deliver approach."[14] One can can imagine the sort of reactions he must have aroused before this lesson sank in, when he stood large and embarrassed on the doorstep of the big house, aggressively explaining the moral obligation of some wealthy merchant to hand over a part of his ill-gotten gains.

The battle with shyness continued, and he was making progress. But it required constant effort. He would take trouble to speak to any and everybody, in the street in Günsbach, on the train, in cafés and shops, wherever life took him. There were four classes on the trains and he would always travel fourth class. It was an economy, true, but it was also where he met people he wanted to meet—"the real people," he called them—swineherds and sailors, for example; no longer to argue with them or persuade then to pursue the truth; simply to get to know and understand them. He made it his business to make everybody's business his own—to share their interests and concerns, their work, their jokes and stories. From bakers he learned the secret of making dough, from carpenters, the tricks of cabinetmaking. He grew in his understanding of life, this theologian, this academic, from the point of view of those who lived it; from the underside, where things look very different from the perspective of the theorist; more varied, more interesting and funnier, as well as truer.

He still enjoyed stories above all—including those rude and ribald stories that delighted the heart of Uncle Charles. The semiliterate passengers of the fourth class were full of them. Schweitzer would sit quietly in his corner, scribbling notes and ideas on his cuff and listening to the conversation, until the opportunity came to join in. Since he quickly built up a repertoire of stories of his own, he was not an unwelcome companion. The faultless memory which was to win the respect of Biblical scholars was at work storing up excellent little *"blagues"*—partly for sheer entertainment, partly for what they said about human nature.

These things made Schweitzer much loved by those who came to know him, the villagers of Günsbach, the shopkeepers near St. Thomas' in Strasbourg. The few who still remember him speak of his cheerfulness and the way he would stop for a chat and a joke with everyone. Nor was it only talk. One day in the street he met an old lady who turned out to have no mattress. Schweitzer went to his room, fetched the mattress off his own bed, and carried it on his back to her house.

He was nineteen and a half when he first stumbled upon the mystery of Matthew 10, and decided to treat it as a mystery in the detective rather than the supernatural sense. In the eighteen months that followed he was busier than he had ever been, as he pursued all the different interests that absorbed him. He would work late into the night, his head wreathed in clouds of smoke—for he smoked anything and everything that came his way—scribbling illegibly in his haste. His room was strewn with books, musical scores, and sheaves of notes, more or less neatly arranged from a practical point of view, so that he could lay his hand quickly on what he wanted, but the despair of anybody who tried to sweep or dust. Both here and at home, Adèle complained, he was untidy, impractical in day-to-day affairs, and impatient of anyone who tried to alter him. Work was all-important, all-absorbing, both in term-time and vacations. He hated to be dragged away. Adèle and the youngest sister, Margrete, were at school at the Lutheran convent of the Good Shepherd in old Strasbourg, not far from St. Thomas', and Adèle recalled how reluctantly her brother came to take them out on Sundays—how ill at ease he sat in the parlor waiting for them, shy at the presence of so many girls and impatient to get his duty over with.

Chronically behind schedule, he would pelt from appointment to appointment on his bicycle, his energy responding to the unending pressure, his interest kept at high pitch by the constant change of subject. At the same time he was learning that to do all these different things he had to concentrate totally and exclusively on each in its turn.

He was happy. This was the life that his ancestry and his childhood had prepared him for, now raised to a level his forebears had never approached. All things came together for his good, and he knew it and reveled in it. But that was not the whole story. In this complex young man were many strands of character, each counterpointing the other. As an embryo exhibits at different times the different characteristics of its species' history, so the boy Albert Schweitzer had been through phases in which first one side of his nature took control, then another—the dreamer, the romantic introvert, with flashes of passion and insight, who was followed by the determined rationalist, forced by his own temperament to learn control; the shy boy nervous of others' laughter, who became the bold conversationalist and raconteur; the inattentive scholar who developed immense powers of concentration. But the earlier Schweitzer was never replaced by the later. The two existed side by side, thread behind thread. And now in his twentieth and twenty-first year, all the threads finally wove themselves into the complex but complete personality, in which each aspect settled into a harmonious whole. The whole was not without tension; that would not have been possible with so many extremes balanced at the center point. But the tension was always controlled, and guided toward creation; never released to destruction.

So in the most active and happy eighteen months of his life so far there were other forces at work below the busy surface. The energy and pace of his daily life is easy to envisage. But there was another side. A night's study is a long lonely affair. Two o'clock in the morning is an awesome time, especially for a romantic youth. And a long organ practice alone in a darkened church with an instrument that speaks of sublimity and power is another experience fraught with profound feeling. These two kinds of vigil were a regular element of this outwardly hectic life; and both were centered on one image—the figure of Jesus.

Bach's sonatas address Jesus intimately, confidently, as friend as well as master. They speak of a whole life interwoven with Jesus. Studying Bach, Schweitzer could not avoid being aware of the deep personal religion that gave meaning to the music. Alongside that, his own intense search through the Gospels was a search for the same man, the man with whom Bach shared his happiness and his agony, his hopes and fears. Schweitzer was saturating himself with Jesus—not as a scholar analyzing a remote historical personage, but as a man searching for the mind and motives of a man. All his capacity for emotional intuition, his ability to feel with other creatures, as well as his intellectual and historical skill, were bent on understanding Jesus.

The two quests—the quest for a knowledge of his fellow man and the quest for a knowledge of Jesus—were not wholly separate, though they occurred at different levels. The love of God and the love of one's own neighbor—the two great commandments—are not so alien to one another. In humanity Schweitzer found the raw material of Jesus; in Jesus the completion of humanity. And along with these studies—linked with them—there grew that sense of debt that had begun to make itself felt earlier; the happier he grew, the more the feeling oppressed him that he owed something to somebody in return. Other children's homes were so much less happy than his had been. Other students lacked his health and energy, or simply a godfather who would board them free of charge.

The German word for debt is the same as the word for guilt. Protestantism talks all too much about guilt, and has been responsible for unjustifiable guilt-complexes and Puritanical self-abasement of a most unhealthy kind. But translated into "debt" the word loses a lot of its venom, since debt is repayable. What in some men might have become a load of intolerable, irrational guilt became in Schweitzer simply a need to repay.

In a peasant society, never very far from hardship, debt is important. What is borrowed is not easily afforded; simple justice demands its return at the first moment possible. And Schweitzer's family had had to count the pennies. At his paternal grandfather's house in Pfaffenhofen he had been taught, when he ate an apple, to keep the core for the pigs and the stalk for the fire. Schweitzer understood debt. These first years at the university, the years when he was learning to master all the elements of his nature and harness them to his purpose; when he first began to feel the full potentiality of his mind and spirit; when through the Gospels and through Bach he spent so many hours face to face with the figure of Jesus—these were the years when that little cloud, the size of a man's hand, grew to cover the whole sky. The greater his satisfaction, the greater his debt. The cloud was becoming more than he could bear.

One stiflingly hot summer month, a certain Professor Lucius held a course of lectures on the history of missions. The heat and the unpopularity of the subject reduced his audience to half a dozen or so. One of these was Schweitzer, who as a boy had enjoyed his father's afternoon mission services and the letters that missionaries of the Paris Mission Society had sent from distant lands.

Lucius' theme was to do with debt. He spoke of the damage that white colonists had done in black countries and the way in which missionaries could do a little to make up for these depredations.

Ten years later Schweitzer recalled:

> It was there that I was struck for the first time by this idea of expiation. It had an extraordinary effect on me. Till then, in Dogmatics and New Testament commentaries, this word "expiation" had seemed heavy to handle—it had to struggle to explain why Jesus died for the world's sins. Everything we had hitherto been told was lifeless and petrified, and we noticed in the way the lecturers spoke of it that they seemed ill at ease and were none too clear about it themselves. But

now, launched as an appeal to work under the banner of Jesus, this
word took on life, it was a cry, a shock, something which sank into you
and took hold of you,—and as that day ended I understood Christianity
better, and I knew why missionary work was needed.[15]

The word worked within him, reinforcing all that he already felt. And
in the Whitsun holidays of 1896, a few months after his twenty-first birthday, he woke one morning of brilliant sunshine with the conviction that
the debt must be repaid, the cloud must be lifted—or persuaded to fall in
fertile rain. What was to be done?

In his childhood we have seen how experience was followed by decision, decision by action. He had not changed. "Proceeding to think the
matter out at once with calm deliberation, while the birds were singing
outside, I settled with myself before I got up, that I would consider myself justified in living till I was thirty for science and art, in order to devote myself from that time forward to the direct service of humanity.
Many a time already had I tried to settle what meaning lay hidden for me
in the saying of Jesus 'Whosoever would save his life shall lose it, and
whosoever shall lose his life for My sake and the Gospels shall save it!'
Now the answer was found. In addition to the outward, I now had inward
happiness."[16]

What the direct service was to be he had yet no idea. He had nine years
to look into that. But the decision had been taken—a decision which was
in no way startling, for it had been prepared for by everything he was and
had been. When he finally put it into effect it was to appear to observers as
though a whole lifetime had been wrenched violently off-course in unnecessary self-denial. From within it seemed no more than a natural development—one that was so much part of the man that the real self-denial
would have been to refuse it; because that would have deprived him of inward happiness.

4

PARIS
1896-1899

Outwardly, everything went on as before. The time bomb which Schweitzer had set for 1905 ticked imperceptibly. Not one of his family or his friends was consulted. Not one was even informed. Nothing could better illustrate how the separate layers of this complex character lay one beneath another than the way he kept this vital secret all the time that he was studying to be easy and outgoing in company. This was no longer compulsive shyness, but a matter of controlled reason and the will.

Not that he ceased to be regularly "overwhelmed" by one experience or another. The molten lava of emotion still seethed beneath the hardening crags of character. Knowing of his passion for Wagner, kind Parisian friends gave him tickets for a production of Wagner's entire *Ring of the Nibelungs* at Bayreuth—the first time the whole cycle had been performed since Wagner had first presented it there himself twenty years before, at the opening of his dream opera-house. Now, after his death, that enormous operatic event was being faithfully repeated under the direction of his widow Cosima; not with a new production, for who could ever improve on the Master himself? So far as was possible everything was identical with the original performance.

The occasion was not to be missed. The Tetralogy was the biggest theatrical event of the century. The opera-house-cum-temple in which it was performed was equally unique, born of an unlikely union between an opinionated genius of a composer and an enthusiastic young emperor, Ludwig II. Wagner, turning upside down every accepted canon of operatic presentation, aimed at a total experience, musical, theatrical, practical, religious, to which nothing less than a complete new building would do justice. In fact, Wagner went some way toward personifying for young Europeans the Superman that Nietzsche had demanded. Rising above bourgeois considerations of financial solvency and marital morality— Cosima was another man's wife when she became his mistress—he inhabited a high sphere, he achieved things that others barely dreamed of. To see his masterpiece at Bayreuth was to share in the consummation of the century. Schweitzer had his share of admiration for the Nietzschean ideal, and he responded to the event. "The very simplicity of it made it so marvellously effective," he wrote, and contrasted this production with others which he saw later, which had "all sorts of stage effects claiming attention alongside the music, as though it were a film show."[1]

Wagner had only himself to blame if recent producers have overelaborated the settings; for his stage directions are far from simple, demanding for example an underwater scene with a mermaid swimming gently in the middle distance. But it would appear that for such a scene he himself was content with a huge dominating painted backdrop and a few papier-maché boulders—a setting which casts an awe-inspiring mood over the whole action—and eschewed the mechanical tricks which, as Schweitzer noted, are admired for themselves rather than for their contribution to the performance.

To pay for his train ticket Schweitzer had to make do with only one meal a day; but turned this to advantage by taking lunch each day with members of the orchestra and listening to their views on the imposing Cosima—views which were respectful but by no means unanimous about the advantage of having "a woman of such an imperious will as Madame Cosima directing the performances."[2]

In fact, the disadvantage, as he came to see himself later, lay not in the will but in the fact that it was directed toward a sterile repetition rather than a re-creation, an act of personal homage rather than of artistic understanding. At the time however he was vastly impressed by the dominating spirit of Wagner, which brooded over the production. Schweitzer's character showed a marked degree of hero worship; but the heroes he chose were of the highest caliber.

On his way back to Strasbourg he broke his journey to sample the quality of a new organ in the Liederhalle at Stuttgart. It had been much publicized for the technical innovations that had been built into it, as into many new organs in Germany about that time—devices in the main made possible by the application of electricity to the bellows, and to the linkages between key and pipe and between different sections of the organ. This sudden access of new power opened up possibilities of swift fingering that before had been limited by the relatively cumbersome series of wooden push rods and pivots that connected the finger to the pipe valve—the principal one of which was known as a "tracker." In these new German organs the tracker was on the way out. At the same time the output of the organ could be increased, and the control of volume could be much simplified by bringing into action a revolving drum which, at one touch of hand or foot, activated an overall crescendo or diminuendo. Previously a complicated series of movements had been necessary to build up the volume by bringing in the different voices one by one. Finally, having liberated the organist from these chores, the designer felt able to add a multiplicity of new hand stops for the variation of tone. Each new organ had a different layout, according to the designer's perception of how to exploit these innovations.

Schweitzer was already, so he claimed, suspicious that in seeking new technical efficiency the designer had lost sight of more important factors. But his suspicions had not prepared him for the revelation which Stuttgart afforded him. He was to call it his "Damascus," after the Damascus road, on which St. Paul in a blinding flash saw the error of his ways.

The parallel is not very good, for it was the error of others' ways, not his own, that was revealed to Schweitzer at Stuttgart. His work with Widor at St. Sulpice had given him an excellent point of comparison, and his studies with Marie Jaëll and Carl Stumpf had sharpened his sensitivity to tonal quality. And when a good local organist played him a Bach fugue on the Stuttgart organ, he found it quite impossible to follow the separate lines of the music, on which the whole effect of contrapuntal music depends. It was "a chaos of sounds."[3] Not only this, but the tone too was harsh and dry.

His suspicions more than confirmed, he made it his business during the following years to seek out and play all kinds of organs wherever he went, in substantiation of his case. The quest did nothing for his popularity in the German musical world, for organists there were intoxicated with the novelty of their toys and were not at all pleased to be told that the despised and old-fashioned French were still doing these things better. But steadily, over the next nine years, Schweitzer went on building up his evidence.

In Strasbourg his life continued as the sort of peaceful rush that many students know. Too many things to do, not enough time, but never any real pressure, never any anxiety. The vacations at Günsbach were an unfailing refreshment. Nothing much changed there, except that Louise had married a Mr. Ehretsmann and gone to live in Colmar. However, she and her husband, and the children as they arrived, came regularly to the vicarage at weekends and holidays. And in the new, dry vicarage with its big flower-filled garden, and its cellar filled with chalk-marked casks of homegrown wine, the old pastor's health held up and constantly improved. The few small blemishes there had been on the family's happiness, poverty and ill-health, seemed to have been permanently removed.

When the academic year began in the autumn of 1897, a fresh impetus was given to Schweitzer's New Testament studies when the subject was set for the government test, a preliminary examination due to be held the following May. Students were to write a thesis on "The Last Supper— Schleiermacher's view compared with the New Testament conception and the Confessions of Faith of the Reformers." Schweitzer studied Schleiermacher on the Last Supper and in due course passed the examination. But a thought which Schleiermacher dealt with in passing and then never pursued to a conclusion gave a fresh impetus to his investigations into Jesus' sayings about the Kingdom of God.

Certain words reported as spoken by Jesus over the broken bread and the wine at that Last Supper form the very heart of the eucharist, mass or communion service, which is in turn the heart of Christian worship. But not all the words that the priest says in that solemn consecration are recorded in Mark and Matthew, the early Gospels. According to those Gospels Jesus did say, of the bread, "Take, eat; this is my body." He did not say, " . . . which is given for you. Do this in remembrance of me." Of the wine he said, "Drink of it, all of you. For this is my blood of the covenant, which is poured out for many for the forgiveness of sins." He did not say, "Do this, as often as you shall drink it, in remembrance of me."[4]

According to the most authentic documents, then, Jesus never gave his disciples any instruction to repeat the supper. Yet had he done so, how could any account have omitted anything so awesomely memorable— especially since the early Christians did in fact repeat the meal? No. If Mark and Matthew (and even some versions of Luke) say nothing of such instructions, it is more than reasonable to assume that Jesus never gave them. They were inserted by the early Christians to account for and justify their continuance of the sacred meal.

There are other words, however, which are recorded in all three Gospels, but which the Christian ritual omits. They are similar in all the Synoptic Gospels. In Mark they read: "Truly, I say to you, I shall not drink again of the fruit of the vine until that day when I drink it new in the Kingdom of God."[5] Here again, at this moment of ultimate solemnity, is the insistence on the coming kingdom—which, Schweitzer believed, had one meaning for Jesus' Jewish hearers and one only.

What then was the true significance of the meal? If Schweitzer was right in thinking that Jesus genuinely believed in a kingdom whose arrival was only days away, would this not account for Jesus' words as the Gospels report them? No repetition would be necessary, because this would be not merely Jesus' last supper, but the last supper of any of them in the old order; a preparation, in Jesus' eyes, for the First Supper of the New Kingdom. Was it as such that the early Christians celebrated it freshly each week, as they still waited for their master's reappearance and arrival of the Apocalypse? And was it because the kingdom never came that they were forced to change the meal's significance to one of remembrance, and to insert the words that explained this?

Schweitzer was not ready to make his conclusions public; as with the scholarship examination three and a half years earlier, he confined himself at the government test to what he was asked, and kept his own investigations to himself. He still needed to do a great deal of work, for example, on the Old Testament prophecies, and the influence and meaning they had for the Jews of Jesus' time, the people who heard him speak.

Schweitzer did well enough in the test for Holtzmann to propose him for another scholarship worth 1,200 marks a year for six years; not a princely sum—barely enough to live on—but it obliged the holder to take the degree of licentiate in theology within those six years. Applying for this, Schweitzer was committing himself to academic life.

He won the scholarship. Already he was evidently a prize student, the protégé and pet of poor Holtzmann, who still knew nothing of the theological rebellion hatching in the young man's bosom. Ironically enough that very licentiate in theology for which Holtzmann was grooming him was to be the occasion for Schweitzer's declaration of independence.

Meantime however Schweitzer switched for the moment to philosophy. He had two excellent tutors in the subject, one of whom specialized in ancient Greek philosophy, the other, Theobald Ziegler, being an ex-theologian and an expert in ethics and the philosophy of religion. The philosophers who interested Schweitzer most at that time were the speculative school of the seventeenth and eighteenth centuries on the one hand, and on the other the "modern" school, who had finally declared the speculatives bankrupt and had begun to look for the secret of life in their own responses to it, in emotion and will rather than abstract thought. Of these Schopenhauer and Nietzsche were the outstanding examples. But the eighteenth century was where he really felt intellectually at home. He liked the eagerness for truth and justice that he found in the philosophers of that period, and he wanted to know why it had now dwindled into disillusion and skepticism.

One great man of the eighteenth century, however, he found hard to understand. His tutors seemed enthusiastic about Goethe, but their enthusiasm puzzled Schweitzer. At a time when thinker after thinker was striving to grasp the secrets of the whole of Creation and weld them into a gigantic pattern of thought, Goethe was humbly studying natural science. Instead of speculating, he was observing. Instead of trying to master nature, he made himself its servant. He appeared totally unmoved by the whole exhilarating impulse of his age, and Schweitzer, deeply admiring that age, dismissed Goethe as a man out of step. One of the remarkable things about Schweitzer was how swiftly his intuition normally seized upon what was important to him, and how very rarely he changed his

mind. Further experience nearly always confirmed rather than contradicted his first impressions. Goethe was to be the exception that proved this
rule.

In the brilliant young man who was combining theology and philosophy Ziegler saw a student after his own heart, and before long suggested a
subject for study that suited them both well. Huddled together against the
rain one day under Ziegler's umbrella they decided that Schweitzer
should work at a dissertation on the religious philosophy of Kant, for his
philosophy degree.

Of all the great logic-chopping philosophers of the German speculative
school, Kant was the one most calculated to appeal to Schweitzer—precisely because he had views on ethics which transcended logic.

This kind of philosophy means little to anyone but an expert in the
field. It needs a special vocabulary for its own purposes; and it deals in
abstractions, using them as counters for an elaborate game whose rules
and results are obscure and, to the uninitiated, quite lacking in practical
outcome.

For our purpose it is enough to note how Schweitzer fared in this field,
so artificial compared with his other interests; and what effect it had on
him. For out of every new mental encounter he took something that he
needed, leaving the rest behind. He picked out the kernel and threw away
the husk—never making the mistake of assuming that there was no kernel, just because the husk was dry.

In the autumn of that year—his twenty-third—he went to Paris to work
at the Sorbonne. The library there was more comprehensive, and the instruction should have been better than at Strasbourg. Besides, it was an
opportunity to see more of Widor.

For this period of intensive study he decided not to stay with Uncle Auguste. The select and spacious northern suburb where Auguste lived in
the Boulevard Malesherbes was three or four miles from the university
and St. Sulpice, which lie within half a mile of each other in the center of
the city, near the Luxembourg Gardens. The tram service was of little
use, and for Schweitzer, accustomed to working any or all hours of the
twenty-four, the restrictions imposed by the obligations of hospitality and
the consideration owed to a family home would have made his kind of
concentration impossible. So he took a small room in the rue de Sorbonne
and set to work.

It quickly became apparent that however superior Paris might be in the
matter of organs, the planning of its university left much to be desired.
The lectures at the Sorbonne were excellent, but the organization of the
syllabus made it impossible for students to get full value from them. At
Strasbourg, Schweitzer had been used to courses of several lectures

which comprehensively explored their subject from many angles. Here the lectures were confined to special subjects, unrelated to their background. Schweitzer did not attend many lectures.

The National Library was equally disappointing. The system of obtaining books for the Reading Room was so cumbersome that the impatient Schweitzer decided that he had no time for it—he would ignore all that had been written *about* Kant and concentrate instead on what had been written *by* Kant. The instinct was typical—disregard the rubble, go for the foundations.

One thing that must be said about his *Sketch of a Philosophy of Religion in Kant's "Critique of Pure Reason"* is that he seems when it suited him to have been able to adopt the abstract philosophical style and to match the subject of his study in obscurity. It never happened in any of his other writings, which are limpidly clear and unpretentious. But here he was capable of whole pages of this kind of thing: "Thus, in the interrelationship of transcendental hypotheses with the assumptions of reason for practical purposes, there lies, at the same time, the relation of critical idealism to the philosophy of religion which is based on it." [6] To be fair we have to remember, apart from the difficulty of translation, that this, unlike his other writings, was intended for the eyes of professional philosophers only. When he wanted his philosophy to reach a wider public his style was very different.

There are several good reasons why Schweitzer was interested in Kant, and why we should be interested in his interest. Kant was the most outstanding thinker of the eighteenth century, a child of the Enlightenment— that period when reason began to dispel superstition, at least among thinking men; when philosophers began to attack the intolerance of the Christian Church and question its dogmas; when a whole series of thinkers set about reexamining the most basic presuppositions about human nature, the purpose of society, and man's place in the universe. They refused to accept the priests' assertion that God was this or that, even that God existed; they wanted proofs of their own, logical and unanswerable. They wanted to know what morality meant, whether good behavior was desirable as an end in itself, or as a means to happiness, or simply as a social necessity to keep the community stable. They even questioned the nature of knowledge itself—whether it came entirely from experience, or whether there were things that the mind could know or could discover by a process of pure logic quite independent of experience. In France, Germany, and England philosophers rang the changes on these themes; and their ideas began to have an effect outside their academic circles. Whole nations felt the impact, for these philosophers concerned themselves with the happiness of mankind in general, not merely of the chosen few; and happiness here and now, not only in the afterlife. They concerned themselves with the meaning of freedom, the search for justice, and the proper conduct of authority. Kings and ministers listened to them. Voltaire, who chastised the French government mercilessly at any sign of persecution or injustice, was for a few months the honored intimate of Frederick the Great; and had he lived two years longer he would have seen torture abolished in France as a result of the new humanitarian wave of thought. The effects were not enormous, perhaps, and in the perspective of the whole century it could be argued that harm resulted as well as good. The violence as well as the splendors of the French Revolution can be laid at the door of a belief in the rights of the common man. But for Schweitzer, as for grandfather Schillinger, the eighteenth century was a time when philosophers had both hearts and heads in the right place, when reason was both humane and effective, and when Europe at least took a few hopeful steps toward universal justice.

Among the philosophers of the Enlightenment, Kant had a special place. As a young man he followed his teachers in believing that the existence of God and the basic principles of ethical behavior could be known and proved without either divine revelation or the experience of the senses. He himself was not a man of much more experience of the world; his whole life was dominated by academic study; and at the age of thirty-eight he was still engaged in the rarefied pastime of proving the existence of God by purely intellectual propositions.

But he was coming under the influence of English and Scottish philosophers who, as Britons are apt to do, had a more practical, empirical approach; that is, they insisted that knowledge and understanding can come only from experience, and that metaphysics, which claims that it is possible to know through intellectual reasoning alone, is (in Hume's phrase) "nothing but sophistry and illusion."

Hume's attack on metaphysics woke Kant, so he said, from his "dogmatic slumbers"; and he embarked on his first great work, A Critique of Pure Reason. "Our age," he wrote, "is essentially an age of criticism, to which everything has to submit." Now he decided to turn reason on to reason itself, to discover its scope and limitations.

It would be irrelevant to this book to attempt a full account of Kant's "critical idealism"—to delve into the definitions and redefinitions, the qualifications, and distinctions that go to make up the argument. Suffice to say that, once convinced of the inadequacy of pure reason, but concluding that sense experience was also insufficient to account for all human knowledge and behavior, he introduced a new idea that fell between the two, and shared, so he felt, the advantages of both. This was Practical Reason. The Critique of Pure Reason was supplemented by the Critique of Practical Reason, in which Kant concluded that certain propositions, which could never be proved by pure reason, must nevertheless be assumed for practical purposes by ordinary men if they were to give their lives any meaning at all. These he reduced to three ultimate "postulates"—God, Freedom and Immortality; belief in which he showed to be necessary to human beings as guarantees of the value of ethical conduct. There was no point in people trying to behave well unless they could depend on these three postulates to support their efforts; God, as the ultimate giver of the moral law; freedom, without which one could not choose whether or not to obey it; and immortality, as the end toward which the individual, obviously unable to achieve complete goodness in this life, could look for an opportunity to complete his self-perfection.

So one point at which Kant's thought suited Schweitzer was in his desire, without losing the guidance of reason, to find value in the ordinary man's experience and way of thinking. An even stronger link lay in the conviction which for Kant was more fundamental than anything else—the conviction that an understanding of the moral law, a respect for right conduct, was the basic, unalterable fact of human consciousness. This moral sense, he believed, was not the product of teaching or experience. It was inborn. Nor was it conditioned on circumstances. It was categorical. He sought by long analysis to define this law, rejecting all definitions that were partial or provisional or questionable.

In the end he defined this universal obligation thus: "Act only on a basis which you can will to become universal law." This was his "categorical imperative"; the one unquestionable starting point for all ethics, and all religion. Even God was only to be understood as the founder and guarantor of this law.

This emphasis on a basic principle of ethics impressed Schweitzer more than anything else about Kant. In fact the main part of Schweitzer's thesis is devoted to showing that Kant's conception of the moral law grew deeper and deeper, and in the end destroyed the arguments put forward in the *Critique of Practical Reason;* that his search for a rational design in the universe came into conflict with the search for ultimate morality; and it was reason that, almost unnoticed, got left behind as he was driven back, against his own logic, to a conviction that somewhere in man is a need for righteousness and right action that has nothing to do with the hope of immortality or any other reward or guarantee. This, said Schweitzer, was the real greatness of Kant, that despite his dry academic approach, his moral intuition was so powerful that it shattered his elaborate intellectual structure.

Schweitzer claimed that he was the first to have noticed these destructive contradictions and inconsistencies. In the summary that concludes his thesis he boldly states "every type of reflection has been investigated by itself, and only after it was thoroughly understood compared with the reflections in other writings and brought into relationship with them." As a result he claims to have demonstrated that "a philosophy of religion tailored and oriented to the pre-suppositions of critical idealism is a product which is disintegrating."[7]

Kant, like other speculative philosophers, attempted to erect a huge and indestructible edifice of thought on basic presuppositions that simply could not stand the weight of the structure. It is the classic blindness of academics; they become so involved in their mental gymnastics as the scaffolding grows higher and higher, that they never notice how the whole thing is tilting where the joints are weak; so that a few taps from a critical hammer at the right point can bring it all crashing to the ground. The ruin can be interesting and instructive, but is not for living in. As Winston Churchill is reported to have said, "The only trouble with great thinkers is that they generally think wrong." It would take a professional philosopher to say whether Schweitzer's long and detailed thesis really justified his claim to have found the flaws in Kant. But his tutor Ziegler said afterward, "A new philosophical genius is arising in our midst."

One other point about the Kant thesis is of great importance in showing the development of Schweitzer's mind at this time. One of Kant's works which he deals with is *The Critique of Aesthetic Judgement* in which Kant considers the relationship between nature and art; "although," as Schweitzer dryly observes, "he was without native artistic ability or any close contact with the performing arts."[8] Schweitzer's analysis of the argument is of no general interest, until the moment when he unexpectedly takes off at a tangent, more or less deserting Kant, and develops his own account of artistic theory. This then extends into a statement about genius—first about artistic genius, and then, by further development about religious and moral genius. Since there are those who claim that Schweitzer himself was certainly a moral genius, probably a religious one, and perhaps a musical one, his own views on the subject at the age of twenty-four are worth some attention.

He begins by stating that any object is dependent on certain ideas in the viewer before it can become art. "Thus a heap or rubble on a mountain becomes art because around it hovers the romantic spell of the Middle Ages. If we were to discover that it was contemporary, we would fail to find in it any aesthetic unity; it would remain . . . a picture of loathsome disorder. A couple of broken columns and a bit of blue sky, and the landscape becomes art if the viewer's memory, and his insight into the splendour of ancient Greece, should awaken; failing this, the infertile imagination cannot complete the vision."[9]

Genius, he goes on to say, is the ability to extend the range of appearances which can be seen as art; "to accomplish an aesthetic unity at a point where it had not been accomplished before."[10] And for this reason genius is often misunderstood. Genius has perceived a unity which is not perceived by others; to them it is still loathsome disorder. "Thus when Bach breathed into counterpoint, which in itself is an empty pattern, the idea of a unified development, by virtue of which all his works possess such a surprising perfection and unity, his music was felt, particularly by capable contemporary musicians, to be noise."[11]

Then he turns to religious genius:

> If it is the religious or ethical nature of the person which seizes the world of appearances and its events in a corresponding unique unity, one calls it moral or religious genius. Therefore, the nature of every religious genius is shown in that he constructs a unity by working over the wreckage of a religion destroyed either deliberately or unconsciously as the exigencies of his religious personality dictate it without concern as to whether, for the average person, the broken pieces do fit together into a structure or not. The genius seizes only what he needs for his new, unified image, lit by his own light—and the rest becomes blurred in the shade. Thus, for Jesus of Nazareth, only that exists in the Old Testament which proves to be in harmony with his religious talent. It is from here that light is shed; "On these two hang all the law and the prophets. . . ." Thus Luther, being the religious genius that he was, fits together the most contradictory portions of medieval dogma because he brings a unified principle to bear on it; he voices contradictions, but he never felt them.[12]

Thus Schweitzer also? We shall see.

There are many echoes of Kant's ideas in Schweitzer, despite the arrogant young man's confident dismissal of his philosophical system as "self-disintegrating." Both of them hold the conviction that the moral principle in man is a starting point, and both search for the fundamental moral law. Both maintain that reason can be practical, can take account of common experience, without ceasing to be reason. And both believe that in thinking of God, we have to start with what we know of man. Less important, but noted by Schweitzer as significant, is Kant's abandonment of the idea of immortality as prerequisite for morality. Schweitzer too was to express doubts about immortality.

Which came first? Was Schweitzer interested in Kant because he already held similar views? Or did he develop these views through his study of Kant? Evidently some of each. Schweitzer was initially attracted because Kant tried to hold together religion, philosophy, and ethics—Schweitzer's preoccupations—in one grand design. But Kant in turn reinforced Schweitzer's convictions that all things could and should come under the sway of reason, and that a fundamental principle of life should be sought and could be found. Though Kant had failed, Schweitzer felt, he had failed nobly. Those who had followed him had done worse, and had gradually abandoned reason altogether as a guiding principle, in favor of instinct, or nature, or the State. Kant pointed in the right direction, and gave his pupil courage.

This was the last time that Schweitzer ever concerned himself with purely speculative philosophy, except to dismiss it as too abstract. But it would be a mistake to suppose that even this encounter was purely cerebral. Nothing was ever purely cerebral for Schweitzer. Other philosophers could, and often did, lead lives that appeared to be totally unaffected by their theories and speculations. Not so with Schweitzer. We are watching a young man who was to make his life his argument. At this stage in his career he was still developing the argument. After that he made his argument his life. Only in the final process did he make his life his argument. But at every stage there was the closest possible connection between the two. That is the significance of Kant for our present purpose—that every mind that Schweitzer encountered added something vital to the pattern of his living; and that this kind of critical analysis provided him with much more rigorous intellectual exercise than many theologians are called upon to face.

The tussle with Kant was not the only reason, nor in the long run the most important, for this trip to Paris. Kant he could have studied anywhere. But Paris meant Widor, it meant music.

Since he first met Widor five years before, the promising lad fresh from school had become a confident young man with the beginnings of a reputation of his own. His studies on Bach in Strasbourg had taught him things that he could teach his teacher; and according to Widor himself it was during this period that a conversation took place that was to lead to two heavy volumes and the founding of Schweitzer's reputation as one of the world's foremost authorities on Bach.

Widor was puzzled. He understood the musical logic of the fugues, indeed of all the instrumental works, except some of the choral preludes. These troubled him, because they "passed abruptly from one order of ideas to another, from the chromatic to the diatonic scale, from slow movements to rapid ones, without any apparent reason."[13] Schweitzer, as a German-speaking Lutheran, might know what literary idea Bach was trying to express by these odd and unexpected progressions.

Schweitzer knew exactly. The words of the chorales on which the music was based were quite familiar to him—he had them by heart. As he recited them, the meaning of the music's changing moods became clear to Widor. "Music and poetry were tightly clasped together, every musical design corresponding to a literary idea. In this way the works which I had admired up to that time as models of pure counterpoint became for me a series of poems with a matchless eloquence and emotional intensity."[14]

This was a revolutionary insight. The current school of Bach interpretation emphasized that he was above all a mathematical composer, in contrast to the romantics, the Berliozes, the Wagners, who expressed rich personal emotion in their music. There was war in the musical world between the adherents of the romantic and the classical, and the latter required that the music of their hero, Bach, should be austerely remote from the changes and chances of life, obeying only the laws of its own changelessly beautiful world.

So it needed the many-sided Schweitzer to open Widor's eyes to a whole new dimension of Bach's arts. And though still instructor and pupil, the relationship was approaching that of colleagues and friends. Widor now taught Schweitzer free of charge and proudly introduced his young lion of a protégé to a much wider circle of artists and intellectuals in Paris than Uncle Charles could command. This did not of course include the socially questionable avant-garde of art on the Left Bank, for that was not the world of the fastidious little professor from the Conservatoire; it was mainly the musical establishment, sharing the rigid social code of middle-class Paris, that opened its doors to Schweitzer. He enjoyed the social life, but found it far from irresistible, and dragged himself away without difficulty to the little room with the oil lamp where he and Kant were trying conclusions.

Widor taught only the organ. For the piano Schweitzer needed somebody else—and in fact went to two teachers, widely differing in approach. The more interesting of these, Marie Jaëll-Trautmann, was very advanced indeed. As we have seen, Schweitzer found the native Parisians a pretty conventional lot, and it is not surprising to find that Marie Jaëll was Alsatian by birth. This formidable lady, a friend of Liszt, married to a piano virtuoso and herself a notable concert pianist, had abandoned performance to develop her theories about touch and fingering in piano playing. Like all the best teachers, whether of art or of life, she aimed as it were to liberate the natural talent, to release the performer from the tensions which inhibit his own instinctive control. In piano playing this meant that the student had to discover and isolate all the muscles from the shoulder down, so that none of them should be affected by involuntary tensing, conscious or unconscious.

Other teachers might recommend exercises that aimed at strength or flexibility of the fingers, a purely mechanical virtuosity. Marie Jaëll believed that that would all follow once the finger was put into uninterrupted touch with the mind. Once the muscles have been brought out of the bondage of unwanted tension, they can convey the player's intuition to the fingertips without obstruction, so that it seems as though each finger is thinking for itself. The finger must be aware not only of the movement required but of the actual sound it wants to produce. And it must be aware that the sound is affected by the way the key comes up as well as by the way it goes down. Phrasing depends on the right sequence of movements, either joining the notes in an organic unity or separating them by the subtlest rolling of the fingers in different directions as the notes are pressed.

So the fingers grow increasingly sensitive to the relationship between touch and tone, and the player becomes acutely conscious of tone color.

To make sure that her theories were physically sound Marie Jaëll called in a physiologist, a M. Féré, to advise her. And the voluntary guinea pig at their experiment (as though he had not already enough to do) was Albert Schweitzer. It was all worth it. He learned an immense amount in a comparatively short time; proving once again that the "liberating" technique of teaching is not only surer but swifter than the "hammer-it-into-them" technique. It sharpened his musical ear and "completely altered" his hand. "I became more and more completely master of my finger, with great benefit to my organ playing."[15]

But he went only so far with Marie Jaëll. She was afflicted by that terrible need of pioneers to find in their discoveries some kind of universal key to the whole of nature, and this led her into strange extravagancies in the books she wrote, which for many people concealed the practical value of her teaching. Schweitzer, maintaining his almost infuriating common-sense even in the midst of the most progressive experiments, hedged his bets by going at the same time, and unknown to Marie Jaëll, to another piano teacher; a conventional, traditional pedagogue, J. Philipp. "This protected me from what was one-sided in the Jaëll method."[16] He got the best out of both by never telling either that he was studying with the other, for they each mistrusted the other's teaching and would have regarded him as a disloyal and less-than-serious student had they known.

That tangled web that we weave when we first practice to deceive involved him in having to lie even with his fingers, which had to play "with Marie Jaëll in the morning à la Jaëll and with Philipp in the afternoon à la Philipp"—in itself something of a feat of concentration and technique. But Schweitzer's ethics never dealt in any commandment as simple as "thou shalt not lie." As we have seen, he agreed with Kant that morality had its origin not in the needs of society but in those of the individual. Nietzsche was emphasizing this at the time with his appeal for moral heroism and the dismissal of bourgeois scruples in the interest of a higher standard. Like others in the intellectual swim, Schweitzer believed in making his own moral rules, not in having them made for him. If a lie was necessary to maintain good relations with two people both of whom he valued, the trouble the lie caused him was a fair price to pay.

So the winter wore on. There were nights without sleep and days with too little to eat; though Widor often decided that the large young man needed nourishment and took him to the Restaurant Foyot, his regular eating place near the Luxembourg; and sometimes he would dine with one of his increasing circle of friends in the university and musical worlds before going back to the midnight oil.

To keep himself awake as he worked he sat with his feet in a bowl of cold water. And he smoked—ceaselessly. Cigarettes, pipe, cigars—any method of burning tobacco was equally welcome. He worked with his head wreathed in clouds of smoke, and even reached that grim condition in which a cigarette is necessary before it is possible to get up in the morning.

But on December 31 he made a New Year's resolution. On January 1, 1899, he gave up the habit and never smoked again for the remaining sixty-six years of his life. He thought he had detected a weakening of his memory—that extraordinary memory over which people marveled till the end of his life, and which nourished him not only with the facts he needed for his intellectual work but also with the recollections of people, places, and events which fed his spirit.

Nine days before this, on the Friday before Christmas, he stopped work for a while to write a letter to a little girl, his niece and goddaughter Suzanne, Louise's eldest child, not yet two years old. It is an odd letter, full of a homesickness that perhaps he could not quite express directly to adults; it confirms Emma's remark that he was sentimental. And it is a long letter, and worth quoting at length, for it is the first personal utterance we have from these ill-documented years.

> My Suzi cherie!!!—Now stay still and don't make faces,—you are in front of me, leaning against a book by Kant. Ordinarily you are on the mantelpiece, because on the table you distract me too much. I have kissed you and placed you in front of me on the table. You are the only photograph in my room. . . .
>
> I have just been dreaming a little and thinking about you. Do you remember when you didn't want to be alone when you went to bed, and I had to hold your hand? You cried—I opened the door; "Pa'ain, pa'ain" [her word for *parrain*—godfather]. I couldn't resist such tender trust—I came to your side, you took my hand; and you were calm and peaceful. It was dark in the room and I talked in a low voice—I told you things you didn't understand. Sometimes I passed my hand over your forehead as my mother does over mine, loving me. I said "Suzi" very softly—I thought you were asleep—but no—I started to get up—"Pa'ain, pa'ain"—I tried to creep out on all fours—"pa'ain, pa'ain"!—oh, I believe I can hear you say the word now.

He goes on to talk of Christmas:

Daddy has written that he has chosen a pine from the forest for the
Christmas tree and it was snowing. . . . O Suzi, Suzi! Last year I
carried you in my arms! You had a lovely long dress, you couldn't yet
say "Pa'ain" and I loved you all the same. Do you know, will you
ever know what you are to me? What place you hold in my heart? And
on Sunday I shan't be with you! . . .
Grandmama from Günsbach and your mama will cry a little—you
know, they love me a great deal. . . .

A little later, a didactic note creeps in:

You are right, you know, to be gay at Christmas as long as you can;
plenty of sad Christmasses will come later—my first sad Christmas was
when I brought back a bad report, grandmama cried, and I couldn't
bear to see her cry, I took her head in my hands and kissed her and
promised to work. It was then that I realised I loved her more than I
could tell her. I've kept my promise. . . .
When you're big, you'll re-read this letter . . . what shall I be
then? Perhaps they'll tell you that I'm hard and cruel, that I'm heartless. And you will know that I'm not heartless—I have almost too
much heart; when one loves deeply, one is not happy.
And now as I look at your photograph, I have to smile. Do you know
what they'll say? Pa'ain is writing to his Suzi, but Suzi doesn't know
how to read! . . . But it isn't true. You will understand better than all
the rest; they will say: it is a sad letter—and you will smile. Pa'ain has
written me a letter, he has told me a lot of things and the others think
it's sad, because they don't understand. . . . It's funny, people
imagine one must know how to read before one can understand a letter—no, it's only necessary to love pa'ain to decipher it.[17]

So few personal letters from the young Schweitzer have survived that
one is tempted to read all kinds of things into them, as archaeologists will
try to reconstruct whole civilizations from a few cooking pots and a hiero-
glyphic shopping list. But at least we clearly have on display here that
vulnerable heart, which was so frequently overwhelmed by this experience or that. Schweitzer said himself, in his later years, "I have the heart
of a dove inside the hide of a hippopotamus."
Also apparent is the distance Schweitzer has progressed in that quest
for spontaneity that began sixteen years earlier, that day in Lent when he
spoiled Henry Bräsch's bird-shooting expedition. About that incident he
wrote: "From that day onward I took courage to free myself from the fear
of men. . . . I tried also to unlearn my former dread of being laughed at
by my schoolfellows. . . . "[18] And in the *Memoirs of Childhood and
Youth*, about the struggle he had with his shyness and reserve: "The law
of reserve must be broken down by the claims of the heart, and thus we all

reach a moment when we should step outside our aloofness, and to some fellow man become ourselves a man. . . . . I gained courage to try to make my actions as natural and hearty as my feelings were. . . ."[19]

Here in this letter is the result. He was attempting in everyday life exactly what Marie Jaëll taught him about piano touch—the liberation of all his faculties from involuntary blocks and tensions, so that word and action would be completely at the service of his intention and would seem to flow directly from the heart. The unguarded sentiment of the letter comes from the same impulse that made him unhesitatingly take the mattress from his bed and carry it cheerfully through the street to a needy old woman.

Plato has an image of the life of man as a chariot drawn by two horses, the emotional impulses, which if not controlled constantly by the charioteer, reason, will pull in different directions and overturn the chariot. Schweitzer's horses were magnificent, powerful creatures, and his reason fought to keep them both at full stretch and yet in complete harmony. Such a fight never ends. Some who knew him said he was a man of will, a hard man. Others were conscious only of a glowing warmth. Once, when somebody's insecurity was mentioned in conversation, he asked, "Who is secure?" And in this letter the most revealing and moving thing of all is the sudden outburst of doubt: "What shall I be then? Perhaps they'll tell you that I'm hard and cruel, that I'm heartless. . . ." What made him think that? Had anything been said to him? And if so why? We do not know. Later he was called hard because he ignored all advice and pleas when he went to Africa; could he already have been anticipating such a development, and the reaction to it? Or was it simply that his family had begged him to be home for Christmas and he had refused, feeling that his work was more important, his concentration must not be broken? Certainly he must have known that this letter would be passed around the family at their Christmas festivities, and they would all read his plea for understanding, the admission of a chink in his armor, and the hint of the change to come.

To understand Schweitzer we have not only to be aware of the balance he achieved between the different sides of his nature—we have also to know how precariously it was maintained, the effort it continually cost. I have found a tendency, not only in others but in myself, to feel about Schweitzer that he had it too easy to be a good guide. We feel somehow that because he mastered himself he lived too high above the struggle to be able to help those who are embroiled in it. Those thinkers and writers like Sartre who not only suffered the full sickness of the century but explored its fever chart with gusto seem more sympathetic. "They understand," we say; "therefore they can heal."

But unfortunately the blind cannot lead the blind. All they can do is commiserate more easily with each other's infirmities as they totter together into the ditch. They can also condemn as patronizing any seeing person who suggests that they might be better off on the path and offers to lead them there. But it is true that the sick can get little comfort from the hearty encouragement of a healthy optimist who has never known what sickness is. The nervousness of the twentieth century is a valid reaction against the false optimism of the nineteenth; and it is very easy to see in Schweitzer a figure of robust, uncomplicated health, and to feel that he has nothing to offer us.

It is not true. He stood exactly between the two centuries. Though he used the phraseology of the nineteenth he spoke of the despair of the twentieth. He felt, sooner than most, the abyss that lay under the crust of progress, and before existentialism was a word he was an existentialist— with this one difference from the others, that where they seemed interested in sickness for its own sake, his only interest in disease was how to cure it. In a sick time, Schweitzer was for health.

He himself experienced its sickness—less dangerously than others, because of the solidity of his upbringing, but acutely enough to make him devote his life first to doctoring himself and then to finding medicines for civilization. Until his stay in Paris the points where he had been conscious of something wrong were in his own personal life and in the common agonies of the world at large—pain, poverty, sickness, and cruelty. But now he began to be increasingly aware of a special sickness—the stink of a decaying civilization which in Paris was more noticeable than elsewhere. With that political sensitivity which he had shown at his uncle's dinner table at the age of eleven, he found himself contrasting the high concerns and noble intentions of Kant and the Enlightenment with the general attitude of society to the events of his own time. "My impression was," he wrote, "that the fire of man's ideals was burning low without anyone noticing it or troubling about it. On a number of occasions I had to acknowledge that public opinion did not reject with indignation inhumane ideas which were publicly disseminated, but accepted them, and that it approved of, as opportune, inhumane courses of action taken by governments and nations."[20]

In fact, though Schweitzer barely mentions it, Paris in 1898 was buzzing with a political scandal so poisonous that three quarters of a century later it is still an international household word—the Dreyfus case.

In 1894 Alfred Dreyfus, a young Jewish army officer, had been found guilty of selling military secrets to the Germans and sentenced to life imprisonment. His brother Mathieu, convinced of his innocence, had spent the intervening years gathering evidence of a miscarriage of justice and collecting allies—one of whom, incidentally, was an Alsatian, M. Scheurer-Kestner, who had risen to be vice-president of the Senate.

On November 15, 1898, a month before Schweitzer wrote to Suzi, Mathieu Dreyfus had shocked Paris by claiming that the documents in question bore the handwriting not of Alfred Dreyfus but of a dissolute and aristocratic officer, Major Count Esterhazy. Esterhazy demanded an opportunity to clear his name, and on January 9 was acquitted by court-martial. Clemenceau, at this time forwarding his career by a deep involvement in journalism, took an interest and four days after the court-martial published Emile Zola's famous letter, *"J'accuse,"* alleging miscarriage of justice and corruption in high places.

France was split in two. The Royalist/Catholic faction felt that the honor of France, her army, and her nobility was at stake; it was expedient that one unimportant officer (Jewish at that) should be sacrificed for its preservation. The other party, tending to be Lutheran and Republican in its sympathies, supported Dreyfus and Zola in their attempt to get justice done. The pro-Dreyfusards formed themselves into an organization with a title calculated to please Schweitzer: The League of the Rights of Man. The anti-Dreyfusards countered with The League of the French Motherland.

The case rolled on for eight months, its ripples widening; in the distant Alsatian hills, Schweitzer's mother was moved to write a passionate letter to the papers about it. Little by little the lies and forgeries that had convicted Dreyfus were uncovered, and in September he was finally pardoned and released. As the anti-Dreyfusards had feared, the honor and self-confidence of France was shaken for years to come—and by their own conduct.

For Schweitzer the case was no more than the boil where a deep-seated poison had come to a head. Indifference to justice, he felt, was far too widespread. Too many people were abandoning true patriotism for "a short-sighted nationalism." The banner that they carried bore the word *"Realpolitik,"* and all the nations of Europe were infected. "From a number of signs," he wrote, "I had to infer the growth of a peculiar intellectual and spiritual fatigue in this generation which is so proud of what it has accomplished. It seemed as if I heard its members arguing to each other that their previous hopes for the future of mankind had been pitched too high, and that it was becoming necessary to limit oneself to striving for what was attainable."[21]

With the ending of the century, people were looking around them and summing up the achievements of the past hundred years. Material progress had been enormous, and was clearly only beginning. This gave a sense of confidence which to many spelled advance, unalterable and unending. To these people, man had now reached his highest point so far, and was poised to go higher. But Schweitzer's own impression was that "in our mental and spiritual life we were not only below the level of past

generations, but were in many respects only living on their achievements . . . and that not a little of this heritage was beginning to melt
away in our hands."[22] Reason was giving way to superstition and astrolo-
gy was growing popular, with its implication that human effort could not
affect events predestined by the stars. It made Schweitzer very uneasy
that people suffering from this sort of moral exhaustion should imagine
that they had really advanced since the eighteenth century. The little pool
of light where he and Kant met night after night seemed a haven of sanity
and security, surrounded by advancing shadows.

5

BERLIN
1899

IN March he took his completed thesis back to Strasbourg and read it to
Ziegler. And Ziegler made his pronouncement about the advent of a
philosophical genius.

If there was genius in the thesis, it was due to a combination of three
qualities. First, that characteristic instinct to bypass the commentators
and get to grips with the original writings of the man himself. Second, the
intuition that searched beneath the words and the arguments for the character of the thinker, and valued him for his aspirations more than for his
logic. And third, that infinite capacity for taking pains that led Schweitzer
to track various key words through the different writings, to count their
frequency, and to analyze the way their meaning varied as the thought of
Kant developed. Genius or no, the sum of these qualities is impressive.
Ziegler looked hopefully forward to the second part of the examination,
the viva-voce interview, which was set for July. Schweitzer had four
months to prepare.

He decided that this time he would try Berlin, which boasted excellent
lecturers in philosophy. Theology too was well represented, and although
that was not the subject on the agenda at the moment, Schweitzer would
not have been the man he was if he had resisted the temptation to drink at
all the springs at once.

Three years had already passed since his decision to abandon the academic life at the age of thirty. Only six of his nine years were left; into
them he needed to cram as much as possible of the life he loved and ex-
celled in. Meanwhile he was searching for the path that his service was to
take when the time was up. He had no idea as yet what it was to be.

He took a room on the third floor of a courtyard house in the Koch-
strasse. In his reading in Berlin he intended to get a good working knowledge of all the major philosophers, ancient and modern, as well as rounding out his study of Kant. But Berlin proved much more seductive than

Paris in distracting him from his syllabus. In the first place there was none of that rigid social etiquette that made it so hard to penetrate French family life. Here the hospitality was easy and swift, and social life so much the more enjoyable. Similarly the intellectual life was informal and vigorous; one did not encounter professors only at lectures, but might find oneself invited to their homes, there to meet others and carry on the debate among friends.

Intellectual leaders thronged to the house of Frau Curtius, widow of a great scholar of ancient Greece, whose stepson, Frederick, was district superintendent of Colmar and an excellent administrator in the Lutheran Church. Schweitzer knew Frederick a little, and through him was made welcome in the Curtius household. Every fortnight Frau Curtius would hold open house, and everyone who was anyone in the academic world would drop in for beer, sandwiches, fruit, and conversation about the day's work. Schweitzer would retire shyly into a corner, and for the most part was content to listen as the discussions of his elders and betters raged furiously, but without rancor, around him. Looking back from fifty years later he remembered particularly Wilhelm Dilthey, H. Diels, and above all Hermann Grimm, a theologian who backed the highly unfashionable view that St. John's Gospel was historically consistent with the other three, and who was forever trying unsuccessfully to enlist Schweitzer's support for this view.

All around were lectures to be sampled, interesting theories to be followed up, organs to be tried out. He found the organs, on the whole, displeasing; also the style of the organists. The same openness to new ideas that made Berliners more attractive to him than Parisians also made them more vulnerable to the blandishments of technical progress, and many of the organs had been renovated on the same lines as the new instrument at Stuttgart. He found their sound "dull and dry," and their organists more concerned with speed and virtuosity than with Widor's "plasticity of style" or Marie Jaëll's sensitivity to tone. However, he played regularly, deputizing for the organist at Kaiser Wilhelm Memorial Church; and at the organist's house he met musicians, painters, and sculptors, and so was able to keep one foot in the academic camp, one in the artistic.

Among the lectures that meant a great deal to him, though they were no part of his present studies, were those of the great Adolf Harnack, a highly fashionable preacher and theologian, a man of immense charm and erudition. His learning was so overwhelming that it actually reduced Schweitzer to a total inability even to answer his questions; so Schweitzer records.

There might, however, have been another reason for his paralysis. Harnack's view of Jesus was diametrically opposite to the one burgeoning in Schweitzer's mind. Schweitzer was convinced that the clue to Jesus' thought lay in taking seriously the fact that he was a Jew. Harnack on the other hand believed that the Jewish background was quite irrelevant; Jesus had come to preach the brotherhood of man under the fatherhood of God, and the fact that he happened to have been born in Roman-occupied Palestine was quite without significance. The proper way to study the Gospels then was to eliminate all the historical circumstances and to lift the essential, universal Jesus, freed from his "Jewish old clothes." Harnack's famous series of lectures on this theme, "The Nature of Christianity," was delivered the following winter to enormous acclaim. Before such a compelling opponent, the speechless Schweitzer had plenty of opportunity to check the validity of his theories.

Among the philosophers was Georg Simmel, to whose lectures Schweitzer, sipping here and there, was drawn back time and again. Simmel was concerned with the work of Nietzsche and the philosophy of self-transcendence, which, as we have seen, intrigued and troubled Schweitzer. Nietzsche, gradually going mad from syphilis, had in a lucid moment pumped out a final burst of frantic works including *The Twilight of the Idols, Antichrist,* and *Ecce Homo.* In these, with increasing hysteria but enough uncomfortable insight to make them impressive, he flayed the hypocrisy of Europe's Christian bourgeois standards and appealed to everyone to do what he himself in his weakness impotently yearned to do—to stand alone, to think alone, to act alone, heroically, without reference to others and responsible to no one. As we have seen, the doctrine of standing alone easily became a doctrine of stamping on anyone whose mediocrity impeded one's self-perfecting. Already in Nietzsche's own books there were signs of this ruthless arrogance.

Simmel's lectures were an attempt to disentangle the good from the bad in Nietzsche, placing the emphasis on self-transcendence that involved no conflict with others. The actual self had to be overcome in order to release the higher self which was potentially already in existence. The notion is far from unfamiliar, being simply a philosophical restatement of a basic religious idea, the idea of self-denial, of losing one's life in order to save it. But for Schweitzer, with his dual interest in philosophy and religion, it was of great importance that religious thought should be expressible in nonreligious terms. Not only Nietzsche but the whole current of feeling was swaying against established Christianity, and the old religious language was suspect. But if religious ideas could be proved in philosophic terms, it was a guarantee that they were still valid outside the context of the Church. For Schweitzer, philosophy and theology were not so much separate subjects as different approaches to the same truth. And since every instinct told him that the greatest truths were the simplest, it followed that anything that mattered could be said without using ecclesiastical jargon.

And still, in the list of things which occupied him in these astonishingly crowded four months, we have not reached the principal distraction from his work on Kant—the intriguing investigations of Carl Stumpf.

Stumpf was an experimental psychologist who was also something of a philosopher, and his view of the eighteenth century was quite different from Schweitzer's. He regarded it as the Dark Ages, when foolhardy thinkers speculated on matters about which they had no real knowledge at all. Stumpf had no interest in conclusions or systems. All he wished to do was observe facts. Until sufficient facts had been observed with sufficient thoroughness, he believed it was impossible even to start to construct a philosophy. A man in his way far ahead of his time, and probably a considerable influence in the weaning of Schweitzer from the speculative philosophers to that great observer of nature, Goethe.

Stumpf concentrated particularly on the psychology of sensation. Too many philosophers had discoursed freely about sense experience without knowing what it really was. So he investigated the actual effects on human beings of heat, light, and especially sound.

Once again Schweitzer stepped forward as the willing guinea pig. His ear, trained by Marie Jaëll, was cocked to analyze the effects of simple tones, of variations of pitch and intensity. What happened when you added echo? Or tried to eliminate it? And how did you isolate a note from its overtones? And what did that do to its psychological coloring?

Stumpf and Schweitzer spent hours at this fascinating game, in churches, halls, and rooms of different sizes. Kant took a back seat. At the very end of the nineteenth century Schweitzer was plunging into the experimental techniques of the twentieth. Though he may have mistrusted the aberrations of technical progress, he never believed that the remedy was to retreat into a prescientific past. His argument was not with physical discovery, but with the unthinking use that people made of it. The way forward was through more knowledge, not less; but knowledge itself must be exercised in the service of a true ideal, such as the ideals of the eighteenth century. Nor was any of this inconsistent with Christianity, since Schweitzer was convinced that "truthfulness in all things belongs to the spirit of Jesus."

In this conviction he stretched his mind in all directions. He worked hard and long, but without rush and without strain. His sister Adèle says that however hard he worked, he never appeared to lose his inward serenity. And this is borne out by a second letter we have to his goddaughter Suzi, dated simply "Berlin, June '99, one Thursday evening." Like the first, it reads like a love letter, long and warm and leisurely. And it makes it quite clear that a close correspondence of letters and gifts flowed between him and the rest of the family. "Grandma tells me in her letter that the strawberries sent from Colmar did something unpleasant to your digestion; this is the kind of thing that often happens in this world. . . ." He describes the house where he lives: "As you come in you have to take care not to step on the porter's feet as he sits smoking his pipe; remembering the days when these delights weren't forbidden me, I slow up to catch a noseful of it." He describes his young friend, Hänschen Müller, who "is very well brought up, better than you (but that need go no further)"; and who tends to get beaten for other children's crimes. "The latest thing was that the others shouted 'old Schachtel' after a lady who was climbing the stairs; his father was listening at the window and Hänschen caught it; it was only later that the lady came along and said that he was innocent. I couldn't help thinking of the number of times my father beat my bottom when I wasn't guilty; it didn't happen often, but the memory is comforting. . . . Kiss Grandmama for me and tell her that her letter delighted me all evening. Help grandpapa when he bottles the wine to send me. . . . Give my regards to Turk [the family's latest dog] when you take him for a walk and tell him a bit about what I'm doing, he'll find it interesting. . . ."[1]

Before Schweitzer returned to Strasbourg, yet another seed was sown, almost by chance, in the highly fertile pasture of his mind. A group who had attended a session at the Prussian Academy of Sciences had gathered for afternoon coffee at Frau Curtius' house to discuss it further. Through the hubbub of conversation a phrase reached Schweitzer in his corner: "Why, we are all of us nothing but *epigoni.*" He never knew who said it, but "It struck home with me," he wrote, "like a flash of lightning."[2]

"Epigoni" is a Greek word without an exact English meaning. It is something like "followers on"—"successors"—"latecomers"—"heirs of something past." The idea was not particularly novel or striking. But it summed up all that he had been feeling about European civilization. A chance incident as slight as this often sets the seal on a whole semiconscious complex of ideas in the mind of a writer. It is the spermatozoon that fertilizes the egg. And now Schweitzer was pregnant with a book.

It was to be called *We Epigoni.* Fired by the thought, he discussed its theme with his friends, but they were not particularly impressed. They thought the idea was a good example of paradox and *fin-de-siècle* pessimism, but none of them actually found it true or significant. How could they, when Germany, so recently unified, was growing steadily more powerful and influential, and an infectious national euphoria bathed each new day in a hopeful halo? Schweitzer, the alien Alsatian who knew too much about history, gave up talking about his book.

So he returned to Strasbourg, full of his experiences, full of his book, but somewhat empty of research on his proper subjects. In his written thesis he had been able to conceal the fact that he had skipped the commentaries and read only Kant himself. But it became painfully apparent under questioning. His examiners, full of expectation, had to admit to being disappointed and somewhat let down. The bud of genius appeared a little blighted. Stumpf and his experiments had eaten away more time than they should have.

But a favored student has to be allowed to stray a little. There was no question of his failing. And in August, 1899, Schweitzer had his first degree.

6

TWO EXAMINATIONS
1899–1900

FOR the new academic year Ziegler, undeterred by his disappointment, urged Schweitzer to go on to the next step in philosophy by qualifying as *Privat-Dozent*, or lecturer/tutor. Meantime a warm recommendation from the generous Holtzmann ensured publication of the thesis, despite its length and the obscurity of the author.

Unfortunately for his plans Ziegler happened to mention that if Schweitzer were to continue on the philosophy side he would have to give up any thoughts of preaching. It was time now to decide between the two fields of study, and sermons from a professor of philosophy might be regarded as out of place. That settled it for Schweitzer. He had already had experience of preaching, both in his father's church at minor services and in village churches to which he was sent as part of his theological training. Generations of pastors and schoolmasters had left their mark on his character, and "preaching," he wrote, "was a necessity of my being. I felt it was a wonderful thing to be allowed to address a congregation every Sunday about the deepest questions of life."[1]

So he decided instead to study for his licentiate in theology, which in any case he was bound to take by the terms of his Goll scholarship. He had plenty of time—nearly five years remained before the scholarship expired and its 1,200 marks a year would keep him in the modest style to which he was accustomed until he was within a few months of his thirtieth birthday and the end of his academic career. The moment seemed ripe to travel farther afield.

He had sampled university life in Paris and Berlin, the two capitals whose languages he spoke already. Now he looked forward to seeing new countries, learning new languages, taking at least a small step toward those faroff lands which had fascinated his childish imagination and which, once he had embarked on his life of service, were likely to be lost to him forever. At least part of his study for the licentiate he hoped to do in England.

104

While he was planning this he learned of the plight of another student, Jäger by name, whose brilliant career in Oriental languages was threatened by lack of funds to continue his studies. Jäger needed scholarship money. He needed, specifically, the Goll scholarship. But the Goll money was Schweitzer's until the end of his six-year term—unless he released it by taking the licentiate. For Jäger's sake Schweitzer gave up all plans to go abroad and decided to attempt the licentiate as soon as possible. The earliest opportunity to take the examination was the following July—a very tight schedule, for a licentiate was more than an ordinary degree, and qualified its holder for a full professorship.

Since he was staying in Strasbourg, he had to find somewhere to live, for having graduated, he was no longer entitled to his beloved rooms in St. Thomas'. But by a special dispensation he was allowed to stay there as a paying guest, at a rate which, if he was careful, he could just afford. "It seemed to me the fittest place for the work which now lay before me."[2]

What lay before him was no less than the upheaval of all established views of the life and mind of the founder of Christianity. For the subject of his thesis was a foregone conclusion. Now was the time to put together all his thoughts and studies on the meaning of the Gospels, focusing them on the Last Supper—the moment when, Schweitzer believed, Jesus felt the old order passing over into the new. The twenty-five-year-old son of the village pastor, the ex-dunce of Mulhouse Gymnasium, was setting himself, apparently without a qualm, a task which had baffled theologians and historians alike, and which was found to bring him into conflict not only with the academics but with the whole bulk of the Christian Church, of every persuasion. All this he knew. But the ideas had been maturing in the dark of his mind long enough. Now it was time to set them in order and put them on display. It was not the mind of Kant that he sought now in the pool of light on his desk, but the mysterious figure of Jesus, on whom half the world laid its hopes, calling him Saviour, Lord, and Son of God. Schweitzer was proposing to tell them in the name of Jesus that through the centuries they had never known who Jesus was, but that he, Schweitzer, could set them right.

This was the task of the quiet hours. Meanwhile, organ playing still took up as much time as ever. Eugène Münch had died unexpectedly of typhoid fever the previous September, when he was only forty-one years old; and Schweitzer, in the midst of his other activities, had written a touching tribute to him, for his family and friends. Now Schweitzer was St. Williams' official and permanent organist. He also had to think of providing himself with an income of sorts. The scholarship was barely enough to cover his expenses, and that would cease as soon as he received the licentiate. He applied for the post of deacon, a sort of noncommissioned officer of the church, licensed to preach but not to hold services, at the church of St. Nicholas, across the river from St. Thomas' college. St. Nicholas is an unpretentious church, but an obvious choice for Schweitzer, for he was already bound to it by many links. His uncle, Albert Schillinger, had been incumbent here thirty years before; and Herr Gerold, one of the two elderly ministers who now staffed it, had been Uncle Albert's closest friend. The other minister, Herr Knittel, had been pastor at Günsbach before Schweitzer's father.

He was accepted as deacon on the first of December. The same month, the last month of the century, saw the publication of his thesis on Kant— his first published work apart from his memoir of Eugène Münch.

Life now was more restricted than ever before. It revolved around a few fixed points—the growing book in his room at St. Thomas', music at St. Williams', the preaching and work of a junior assistant at St. Nicholas. A time of steady and serene concentration set in. His inaugural sermon took as its text St. Paul's advice: "Be joyful always."

The originals of most of Schweitzer's sermons were destroyed by fire in the Second World War. We shall never know what else went up in smoke during one or other of the wars, but we know that he was a tireless correspondent, and that later in life he liked to preserve the letters he received; so the loss probably was considerable.

Fortunately, typed copies of about a hundred and fifty of the sermons were made by a friend during World War II, and these survive. Fortunately, because, like his father, Schweitzer used sermons not to huff and puff with inflated rhetoric, not to expound subtle points of doctrine, not to distribute condemnation or praise, but simply to share with a congregation his feelings "about the deepest questions of life." He himself was reluctant to allow publication of his sermons, particularly those he preached in Africa. But the very grounds he gave for refusal—that they were designed as explorations of a subject with friends rather than a full and final statement—is the reason why they are so valuable to us. The sermons are more personal than anything else that has come down to us except the letters. In them we hear his own true voice speaking about his deepest convictions.

In May he preached a series of sermons on the Beatitudes, that great series of statements of blessedness which many, Schweitzer among them, would say are the heart of Jesus' teaching. On the twenty-fourth he was struggling with "Blessed are those who weep, for they shall be comforted"; the eternal problem of unhappiness, the great mystery which had overwhelmed him as a boy and driven him to set his life from the age of thirty in the balance against it. Now the apprentice preacher was trying to find the words to reconcile his congregation to the harshness of the world. The sermon, it must be said, is comparatively conventional. The young deacon (not yet even a curate) has not yet achieved the experience and the ruthless honesty that mark his later sermons. But already we find notable features.

First the simplicity. The scholar who could not only unravel the knots of Kant's verbiage but also create a few entanglements on his own account now studies to be understood by every member of the congregation. "I do not preach as a theologian," he said, "but as a layman." Clear, vigorous and confident, this style is unmistakably the man.

Then the warmth. One gets the sense of a strong and practical hand stretched out to help and reassure—above all to reassure. And behind the reassurance, a secure confidence in Jesus as the source of reassurance and compassion: "This is exactly what is marvelous about Jesus: he does not address himself only to our spiritual being, but he puts himself also on our level, he understands us man to man. . . . Christianity has been accused of consoling believers for the evils of the world by making them gaze at the mirage of the promise of heavenly bliss. This is wrong, Jesus was never touched by such thoughts, for he did not say 'Happy *shall be* those who weep today,' but 'Happy *today* are those who *today* weep.' "
And against those who through the ages have seen suffering as a punishment from God, he quotes the story of the man blind from birth, of whom Jesus was asked, "Who has sinned, he or his parents, to bring this evil on him?" And Jesus said, "No one."

"Now we have reached the heart of the meaning. It is this: 'Do not despair. Do not believe that God wants to chastise you, to punish or reprove you, but know that in suffering also you are in his kingdom, you are still his children and he sustains you in his fatherly arms.' "

But Schweitzer had not yet eliminated all traces of pious cliché. The sermon ends by asking "What teacher was the first to show you that we do not live for ourselves alone? Suffering. . . . What bred in you the desire for a more noble life? Suffering. . . ."[3] And so on, and so on. Schweitzer has still not really suffered himself—or not recently, not since he was a child. The reconciliation is too easy.

But it is hard not to warm to the humanity of the preacher, and what Georges Marchal calls "his smiling and virile confidence." There is confidence in the way in which he invokes the friendly Jesus who "understands us as man to man"—the human Jesus whose portrait, as we know though his hearers did not, was nearing completion on his desk.

Along with the licentiate thesis, however, he was also required to prepare for another examination, which would qualify him for ordination as a curate. The situation was somewhat absurd, as though a racing driver, in training for a Grand Prix, should find himself compelled to pass an elementary driving test. And in fact Schweitzer nearly failed his driving test.

The two examinations were held within six days of each other, that for the curacy first. A curate's qualifications do not include controversial views on higher theology, and the examiners were mostly elderly clerics of a fairly orthodox and prosaic turn of mind. It is not surprising that Schweitzer, with the licentiate giving him more than enough to think about, and with an unconquered disposition to neglect what did not interest him, failed to observe his own precept of leaving nothing to chance. He left a great deal to chance here, and trusted to spur-of-the-moment improvisation to see him through. It was a close thing. One question, about the authorship of a certain hymn, he tried nonchalantly to turn aside by saying that the hymn was too insignificant for him to trouble himself over. Regrettably the hymn had been written by the father of one of the examiners. Aging clerics do not love to be made mock of by clever young fellows with a superior air, especially if the young fellow is suspected of advanced ideas.

But as in his final examination for the Gymnasium, a common interest with an influential examiner tipped the scales at the last moment. Old Pfarrer Will was an expert on the history of dogma, and Schweitzer's knowledge of the subject saved him from humiliating failure. With anything but unanimous acclaim, he became a curate, a minister of the Lutheran Church.

The examiners for the licentiate were of a different breed. Scholars themselves, they could recognize the scholarship and enthusiasm that had gone into the thesis on the Last Supper. Whether or not they were convinced, they were definitely impressed. Within a week of his curate's examination Schweitzer had won his second degree and lost the Goll scholarship. It so happened that his curate's stipend exactly equaled the scholarship money, so he was no worse off; but had he not scraped through to the curacy he would have gone very hungry. No doubt this fact added to the annoyance to which he confessed when Jäger, after all that, failed to make use of the scholarship.

Four and a half years ahead loomed the watershed of Schweitzer's thirtieth birthday. Four of those years he might have spent, without financial worries, traveling and meeting new minds. Instead, he was a pastor, committed to a job, and so far as he knew he would never again have the chance to see the world. "I never ceased to regret," he wrote, "this misplaced consideration for others." Those who suspect Schweitzer of being too "good" may be reassured by this evidence that his goodness had nothing to do with masochistic self-denial but was concerned with very practical ends.

However, what was done could not be undone. And the Last Supper thesis had not exhausted what he had to say about the life of Jesus. There was plenty of work ahead.

7

THE SCHOLAR-CURATE
1900–1901

HAD there not been enough to do, Schweitzer would have invented something. He was becoming a driven man, the sort of man who had forgotten how to stop. Everyone who knew him in Strasbourg at this time says the same thing. Social life? Where would he find the time? Girlfriends? Where would he find the time? Dancing? Where would he find the time?

But social life is for those whose daily life is not social. A good pastor's life is constantly social—Schweitzer's more than most, urged on by his determination to become what his convictions had told him he should be—the man for all men, the universal neighbor. Whether in his everyday affairs or in his great intellectual interests Schweitzer could only understand life by understanding people. Reading his books we find that his thirst for understanding always emerges as a need to enter into the mind of a human being. His theological books were quests for the minds of Jesus and St. Paul; his book about Bach sought for the man behind the music; and even the great books about civilization were in the last analysis a search for himself. In them he mined for what in himself was absolutely fundamental and universally human. He sought therefore for humanity.

To this understanding everything was relevant. To know a man you needed to know his interests. Schweitzer wanted to hear about a man's trade or his craft, his problems and victories, the way business was going and what he thought of the political situation. When it came to a person's private life, though for Schweitzer it was indeed private, and no more to be discussed in public than the secrets of the confessional, he knew well enough what went on and he was not a man to be shocked. When family problems were brought to him, as they are to any pastor, he was gentle and understanding, never censorious.

It is true however that he could never, all his life, accustom himself to the new freedom of discussion of sex in public, and in old age was upset by a photograph of the birth of a baby—an event which he had witnessed times without number and always rejoiced in. He even tore from a magazine an article on prostitution. Such matters were only to be spoken of between friends, not to be paraded in print.

Outside sex, though, family life was as interesting as public life, and he saw no conflict between the two. In his book on Bach he confesses to a frustrated curiosity about "Bach's intimate life"; and as to Jesus' rejection of his family, Schweitzer always found that sad. He could only suppose that it happened "because his relatives wished to take him home and obstruct his public ministry." But he could never quite fathom why universal love should come into conflict with family ties; though it was a conflict from which he was himself to suffer before the end.

Every moment then was filled with the need to know more about people and the things people did and suffered. In conversation, in his study, in the pulpit, this was what exercised him. The philosophies he studied he judged not by their interior logic but by their truth to life. What was the value of a magnificently coherent system of thought which never touched ground? To interest Schweitzer, truth must be serviceable, and its service must be to all men.

He came back constantly to the ideas behind his Epigoni book. What was happening to civilization? Somehow or other, his intuition told him, civilized man had lost sight of civilization's purpose. He searched the philosophers to find out if any of them dealt with anything as fundamental, basic, or "elemental" as this. No. They all took civilization for granted, along with the ethics that make civilization possible. The tree had grown so large, and the branches so complicated, that the roots had been forgotten. Worse—the stem had been attacked and the sap was ceasing to flow. Among thinkers, only Tolstoi seemed to be writing about the elemental factors, love and compassion, and he was an artist, a man of imagination rather than logic.

What was it that civilization had lost? Nobody seemed to have a compelling ideal to set against Nietzsche's vision of proud and dominating individualism, which was everywhere gaining ground.

One quality that soldiers and politicians are said to need is the instinct for the jugular—the knowledge when and how to go for the kill. In philosophers, Schweitzer looked for something else and rarely found it—the instinct for the tap root, the root that draws nourishment from the soil. He himself had it. He believed that civilization, like everything else, needs constant nourishment if it is not to wither and die. What is that forgotten nourishment? It must be some quality deep in the nature of man; indeed of life itself.

Schweitzer found himself dissatisfied with any philosophy that confined its attention to human life. Kant had tried to capture the whole universe in a web of thought. That had proved a failure; the universe was too vast for that kind of thinking. But at least Kant had known that man does not live in isolation from the rest of Creation. Schweitzer scanned the philosophers for any sign that they acknowledged other life than human. In childhood he had included in his prayers "everything that had breath." Now, seeking for the root principle of the way we live together on earth, he again felt an emptiness if animal life were not included. None of the philosophers included it. Even in the Bible, the only words he could find of compassion toward animals were in Proverbs, Chapter 12: "A righteous man regards the life of his beast." The taproot instinct told Schweitzer that in this respect philosophy and the Bible were less rich and less real than everyday life, where animals were man's constant, valued companions and assistants, with as much right as any human creature to the world they were born into. Philosophy and religion should be man's servants, not his masters. They existed for man, not man for them. Schweitzer measured the great thinkers against the man in the street, and the thinkers were found wanting.

Had Schweitzer been Anglo-Saxon he might well have stopped worrying about the thinkers and got on with living. But being what he was, deeply imbued with the German need for a pattern in life, he found it impossible to let go. Instinct and thought must be brought into his harness. His own passionate nature still needed the guidance of a ruling principle, an ideal. His misfortune was that the principles that satisfied others left him cold; wherever he looked he found ideas that had lost touch with life. "I have often thought," he said in later life, "how lucky I was not to be brilliant. It forced me to be profound."

Such a man could never dwindle into the average kind of curate. Nor was it so. Within a month of the examinations we find him preparing a lecture, the first of a series, for the Foreign Language Society of Paris. The subject was his old bugbear, Nietzsche. While he was working on it, he heard that Nietzsche had finally, after his years of madness, died. The lecture became a kind of obituary, a valediction. Schweitzer saluted Nietzsche's courage, originality, and honesty; but was sad about his limitations, warned against his conclusions, and wished that Superhumanity could have been achieved without sacrificing humanity.

A few weeks later he had managed to get to Bayreuth for more of his beloved Wagner. And meeting there with his Aunt Mathilde, he accompanied her to Oberammergau for the Passion Play. "She wanted someone to look after the baggage," he said.

He liked the scenery—the mountains behind the open-air stage—better than the play. He admired the devotion of the performers and the way in which they struggled to preserve the simplicity of the original design in face of the flood of foreign visitors. But the structure of the play he found wanting, the display excessively theatrical, the text imperfect, and the music banal. It has to be admitted that a Biblical scholar with a specialist interest in Bach might be as hard to please as anyone in the Oberammergau audience that year, but his criticisms are not unjust.

Back in Strasbourg life settled to a steady rhythm that was to last without serious disruption for the next six years. The restrictions were less severe than he might have feared, since Gerold and Knittel, proud of the attainments of their new curate, were thoughtful and helpful about arranging free time. He was generally required to take the afternoon service and the children's service on Sundays, and an hour's confirmation class for boys three times a week. Occasionally he would deputize for one of the old gentlemen at the morning service as well, but he enjoyed the more intimate afternoon services better. Person to person he was at ease. In front of a crowd less so.

His comments on his confirmation class are worth quoting, not least because of the contrast between his teaching methods and those of Aunt Sophie of Mulhouse:

> I tried hard to give them as little homework to do as possible, that the lessons might be a time of pure refreshment for heart and spirit. I therefore used the last ten minutes for making them repeat after me, and so get to know by heart, Bible sayings and verses of hymns which they might take away with them from these classes to guide them throughout their lives. The aim of my teaching was to bring home to their hearts and thoughts the great truths of later life so they might be able to resist the temptations to irreligion which would assail them. I tried also to awake in them a love for the Church, and a feeling of need for a solemn hour for their souls in the Sunday services. I taught them to respect traditional doctrines, but at the same time to hold fast to the saying of St. Paul that where the spirit of Christ is, there is liberty. . . . In these lessons I first became conscious of how much schoolmaster blood I have in me from my ancestors.[1]

Mrs. Clara Urquhart, his long-standing friend in later years, has said that if one element in him predominated over others, it was the teacher.

For the younger children, who went to L'Ecole de Dragon, St. Nicholas' Sunday School, Schweitzer adopted the bribery technique. Each week he came to class primed with a story, which he saved up to tell in the final few minutes if the children had been good. Fritz Schnepp, who went to Sunday School at L'Ecole de Dragon seventy years ago, remembers the joy of the stories to this day; stories mainly of animals, of adventure, and hunting in distant lands. The big energetic friendly young man was more than capable of inspiring hero worship in the boys, with his ready laugh, his swift understanding, and his spurts of amiable fury. "His temper was quick," says M.Schnepp, "but never frightening." And Dr. André Wetzel, who also knew him from the early days, says, "There was so little humbug about him that people were often amazed to hear he was a pastor."

As to his afternoon sermons, Schweitzer regarded these, he says, "as simple devotional exercises rather than sermons"; so much so that they often lasted less than a quarter of an hour, and a complaint was lodged with Pastor Knittel about their inadequacy. "He was much embarrassed as I was. When he asked what he was to reply to the aggrieved member of the congregation, I replied that he might say that I was only a poor Curate who stopped speaking when he found he had nothing more to say about the text. Thereupon he dismissed me with a mild reprimand, and an admonition not to preach for less than twenty minutes."[2]

Confirmation classes were Schweitzer's only obligatory task—and since they only occurred during the school terms, he was free during the holidays to find a replacement preacher and to go where he would. This gave him a month at Easter, which he generally spent in Paris, and two in the late summer, which he took at home in Günsbach. But besides these he frequently had to make hurried journeys to Paris to play the organ at some concert with the Jean Sebastian Bach Society, whose official organist he now became. Sermons were written on the train or while waiting at stations. Cuffs were covered with thoughts that occurred en route. The trouble about these dates was that they sometimes clashed with his organ duties at St. William's, and now the wheel was coming full circle there— just as he had deputized eight years before for Eugène Münch, so now some of the young organ pupils whom he and Ernest Münch had trained were called upon to stand in for him.

When he made these forty-eight-hour dashes to Paris for a quick rehearsal, a concert, and back the next day, there was no time to reach his uncle's house in the suburbs, no money for a hotel. At any hour of the day or night he would hammer unceremoniously on the door of any handy friend who was used to his informal ways. Pfarrer Christian Brandt, who lives now in Strasbourg, remembers being awakened at five in the morning by an apparently tireless young man who wanted a bed for a few hours and, in the manner of the perennial student, was prepared to cadge one without shame or apology.

During the longer spells in Paris Schweitzer stayed with his uncle. Happy hours were spent with Widor at the organ of St. Sulpice, hours which, he wrote in 1962, "count among the most beautiful of my life."[3]

This was also his opportunity to extend his knowledge of French-built organs, which he was still busy comparing and contrasting with the new German organs. The two kinds of organ demanded different methods of playing, and Schweitzer studied the French style not only with Widor but also with Fr. Alexandre Guilmant, organist of the Church of the Trinity, and Eugène Gigout of Saint Augustine, both of whom were composers as well as performers. Guilmant, like Widor, had studied under the great Belgian organist Nicholas Jacques Lemmens, who himself had been a pupil of Adolf Hesse, the brilliant and faithful interpreter of Bach who had made his church in Breslau a place of pilgrimage for Bach lovers at the beginning of the nineteenth century, when Bach's name was almost forgotten. With the aid of these two French organists, heirs of the true Bach style, Schweitzer was building up a crushing case against German organ building. The attack was on three main fronts—ease of manipulation, touch control, and tone.

On manipulation the issue was one of hands versus feet. Schweitzer states it graphically:

> The basic principle of the French system is the arrangement of all the resources of the instrument in the pedals. The French organs have no pistons under the keyboards. What system shall we decide upon?
>
> I do not sit for five minutes beside Father Guilmant on the bench of his beautiful house organ at Meudon without his asking me, as if he had just remembered where we left off last time: "And in Germany do they still build pistons? That I can't understand. See how simple it is when one has everything under one's feet. . . ." And the short agile feet press couplers and combination pedals silently then in a trice let them up again.
>
> On another day Widor, for the twenty-fifth time, begins on the same subject. "Tell my friend Professor Münch at Strasbourg that he must point out for me a single place in a Bach prelude or fugue when he has a hand free for a moment to reach for a piston. Let him name anyone who can play on the manual and at the same time press the piston on the key strip with his thumb."
>
> I keep my silence, for the first German organist into whose hands I fall a few weeks later, and to whom I put this controversial question, answers me invariably, "The French are very backward. Formerly we too had all this in the feet; now, however, we have our beautiful pistons."[4]

Schweitzer summed up in favor of the French system. An organist often has a free foot, seldom a free hand; he had heard the jarring hesitations and dislocations of rhythm on German organs when the hand had to leave the keyboard to reach for the piston. And if helpers were introduced to pull the stops something always went wrong.

The question of touch control was the issue between pneumatic action and tracker action. When the electric bellows made unlimited power available to organ builders, they made use of it to eliminate the pushrod system that connected the key to the valve which opened the pipe.

Now the lightest possible touch instantly produced the note; no pressure was required, the finger had no "knowledge" of the moment the valve opened and closed, no sensitivity was needed. The difference was something like that between a manual and an electric typewriter, except that a dead precision is a desirable quality in a typewriter, not necessarily so in a musical instrument.

> The player must exert himself to overcome this dead precision. . . . It lacks the vital and elastic quality of the lever. . . . With the tracker the finger feels a certain tension exactly when the tone comes; it feels the contact point. And the depressed key pushes up under the finger, in order that, when the finger shows the slightest impulse to leave it, it may immediately rise with its own strength and lift the finger up with it. The strength of the keys co-operates with the will! With the tracker even the mediocre organist cannot smear. With pneumatics there is no such co-operation on the part of the keys. It makes the playing worse instead of better, and brings to light the slightest fault.
>
> Only with the tracker does one come into really intimate relationship with one's organ. In pneumatics one communicates with one's instrument by telegraph.[5]

The effect of Marie Jaëll's lessons on touch is apparent here. He went so far as to say that the average pneumatic organ was an instrument "which one leaves in a high state of nervous despair."[6]

For judging tonal quality Schweitzer devised a technique of his own.

> In order to judge the tone of an organ, one first pulls out all the eight-foot stops and plays a polyphonic movement. in the midst of the web of tone the alto and the tenor must come through well; and the tone, even when the stops are played in the upper register, should never be unpleasant. Thereupon one lets the four-foot and two-foot stops enter, and repeats the test. Finally, one plays Bach fugues for a half-hour without interruption on the full organ. If the hearer is able to follow the voices clearly, and if he finds the sustained fullness of tone is not exhausting, then the organ is good.[7]

German organs often failed this test because of their makers' tendency to build in too much power. The high pressure of an electric bellows could increase the volume, but at the expense of tone. "A fat person," commented Schweitzer disparagingly, "is neither beautiful nor strong. To be artistically beautiful and strong is only to have a figure with a perfect play of muscles."[8]

Schweitzer himself was both beautiful and strong. A glance at the photographs taken about this time shows that he had grown strikingly handsome by any standards. But almost more impressive than the good looks is the powerful masculinity of the face—the piercing eyes, dark springy hair, and strong square jaw and cheekbones would turn heads in any company. It is not a face to suggest deep devotional piety, or profound scholarship and long, late hours of study. A scholarly reputation combined with vigorous physical authority is a very attractive combination.

He also possessed a quality which his friend Werner Picht described as "total presence." To illustrate this quality Picht described an occasion which he witnessed some years after the time we are now concerned with, when Schweitzer's work on organ building had borne fruit in the form of commissions to design new organs. But since we are talking of the impression that Schweitzer could make I shall quote it here. At twenty-five he may have had it to a lesser degree than at thirty-five, but it was assuredly already well developed.

> Total presence in every situation is the infallible sign of the significant human being. Schweitzer has this sign in the highest degree. Napoleon needed an actor's training. But with Schweitzer the effect is unconscious and obtained without any gesture. During his years in Strasbourg a new organ was built in the Sängerhaus according to his instructions. The organists of Strasbourg came together at the inaugural celebration, and each sought to demonstrate the capacities of the new instrument and his own mastery of it. When everyone else had played his piece, the man who had created the organ walked slowly up to it in his usual fashion, his arms hanging loosely by his side, sat down at the organ, and played the Chorale—it was Advent—*"Wie soll ich dich empfangen"*—and then walked away again. And yet the one figure that moved with the least fuss is the one which remains in the memory after the passage of half a century.[9]

This "presence" arose from a total and unselfconscious concentration on the business at hand. Because he was unaware of it, it did not detract from his gaiety and good humor, and in addition he possessed that swift apprehension and sympathy which appeals to women. Besides all this, he was becoming something of a dandy—so he himself related in old age to Mrs. Erica Anderson, the documentary filmmaker whose film about him won an Oscar in 1958 and who became a close friend. Fortunately we have a photograph that shows what he meant. There he sits in all his glory—straw hat, cane, and all—the very model of a maiden's prayer, posed with conscious elegance on a rock in the middle of a field. His brother took the photograph, so it may have been intended for the family album. But the impression it makes is less that of the pious and devoted son of the vicarage, more that of the debonair young man about town.

An odd little story he told to Mrs. Anderson adds to the picture of the dandy. He was out for a walk with relations one day when a fashionable hat came flying over a clump of bushes and landed at his feet. "It was a nice hat, so I tried it on. It fitted well enough and I was very much tempted to accept this unexpected gift. But in the end I tossed it back where it came from."

Those of course were the days when the appearance of a camera was the cue to strike a pose—a habit he never entirely grew out of. The informal Schweitzer cannot be found in early photographs or in his published works, in both of which he appears as it were in his Sunday best.

In life, however, he had achieved a naturalness, a way of making himself instantly at home, which was one of his greatest attractions. He was the kind of man who would follow a housewife into her kitchen to steal a bun fresh from the oven (for his was a very sweet tooth), and do so with such charm and appreciation that it was a compliment, not an impertinence.

Those who tell us that he never had any time for social life or women friends say that this was also true of the holidays in Paris. But there seems no reason why life should have been quite so hectic there; there was no imminent examination to worry about, no pastoral duty to attend to. And his own autobiography tells us that he "made many valuable acquaintances"[10] at that time.

We do know that at dances, both in Paris and at Strasbourg, he would go out of his way to dance with the wallflowers. True to the spirit which as a boy had made him vow to marry a cripple, his sympathy went out to the girls who, for whatever reason, sat around the dance floor partnerless. With the boldness of conquered shyness he put his sympathy into practice, and enjoyed the happiness he gave. Not for him the priggish self-satisfaction of an unpleasant duty done. He gave pleasure and he took pleasure, physical and mental. "He was," say his friends, "a man for touching"—the light touch on the elbow or shoulder. Gaiety, activity, and contact with other human beings were the gifts of God. Delight itself was a duty—unhappiness was the enemy. The unhappiness of others diminished one's own happiness, so kindness was the practical thing, for one's own good as well as that of others.

Fifty years later, when he was visiting Europe in the intervals of his spells at Lambarene, Erica Anderson used to act as his chauffeur, to save him the trouble of long and tiring train journeys. Modern life offers few better opportunities for intimate conversation than a long car journey. Enclosed, uninterrupted, unable to do anything but talk, on these occasions Schweitzer could relax with a trusted friend more completely than anywhere else. On one long drive from Günsbach to Paris, she remembers, he talked nearly all the way about the women in his life. She has not said who they were, nor what exactly is meant by "the women in his life";

nor perhaps should she, since Schweitzer himself took such care to protect not only his own private life but that of everybody he knew. But she
has said that several appear to have lived in Paris; and that, oddly enough,
he seemed to have had a partiality for Jewish women.

In view of the lack of any firm information as to the identity and number of Schweitzer's lady friends—quite apart from the precise role they
played in his life—it might seem wiser not to go into the subject any farther. By passing it over, however, I run the risk of giving an impression
that may well, I believe, be false—namely that Schweitzer never knew
the physical love of a woman until his marriage at the age of thirty-seven.

It is impossible of course to prove that he did *not* have love affairs. And
if anyone still living is in a position to prove that he did, they have never
come forward yet and for good and sufficient reasons are unlikely to do so
now. Schweitzer was not the sort of man whose confidence one would
breach any more than he breached that of others.

So if we are not to abandon the subject altogether we are left with the
assessment of probabilities. To this end I can only put together the impressions I have gathered, state my tentative conclusions, and leave others to agree or disagree as they wish.

First, it is quite certain that Schweitzer was very attractive to women
and that he in turn enjoyed their company—if anything rather more than
he did that of men, which may have been partly, though I think not wholly, because they gave greater scope to his autocratic streak.

For a working colleague he chose—or allowed himself to be chosen
by—Hélène Bresslau. And when on holiday he needed to get away from
the world with a friend in whose company he could relax in complete trust
and serenity he sent for Adèle Herrenschmidt.

He certainly had an eye for female beauty and took an interest in fashion, but the women who appealed to him most at that time were those of a
strong and independent character. His partiality for older women would
seem to have been due less to any sexual predilection than to the fact that
they had more to offer in the way of wisdom, authority, and experience of
life.

But it would be wrong to suppose that he did not appreciate women as
women. Along with his new social poise he was developing a great and
gallant charm, and fortunately something of this charm is captured in letters he wrote to women friends and continued to write almost till the day
he died.

Whether any of these will ever be published I do not know, but for the
moment none are being made public. Those that I have seen come mostly
from his later years, but their style is so like that of those early letters to
his goddaughter Suzi that we are safe in assuming that this was a lifelong
style—tender, playful, intimate, and quite free from the formality that

dogged most of his other correspondence. Though they carry no implication of physical liaison, these can really only be described as love letters and could only have been written by a masculine man to a woman whose femininity he valued.

His dandyism too suggests an awareness of sex, a courting instinct, and a self-confidence which must have come from a knowledge that he was found handsome. Mrs. Clara Urquhart, his translator, confidante, and close friend in later years, is certain that as a young man he fell deeply in love. Erica Anderson, whose excellent and characteristic remark, "He had no quarrel with the way God made men and women," has already been quoted, also says, "Schweitzer believed in experience. He wished to experience everything, for he believed it was the only way to learn. There was no rigidity about him. The only rule was that one must never treat experience lightly or irresponsibly; and one must try never to hurt other people." "Schweitzer," she says, "was a complete man." And Schweitzer's daughter, Mrs. Rhena Schweitzer-Miller, says, "There is only one phrase to describe what he had, and that is sex appeal."

That such a man should reach his thirty-seventh year without experiencing sexual love I find incredible. To others it may not seem so. If love affairs did occur I am certain that he would have felt them deeply and taken them seriously; though I think he would have been wary of any involvement that threatened to overmaster him and his work. And if in fact he never did make love with a woman it was surely because he knew he could never give the relationship the time and consideration it demanded and deserved.

But if, as I think probable, his eagerness for life embraced this experience as it embraced others, then Paris in the early years of the century seems the most likely place and time for it to have happened. His life in the college at Strasbourg was too much of an open book for romances to have passed unnoticed, and it is those who knew him in Strasbourg who all swear that he had no time for such things. In Paris he was on holiday— free from the constraints of his position as professor and pastor, and with a little leisure. Here as in Strasbourg he was in touch with people from many different walks of life—business people, teachers, artists, musicians, students—as well as the shopkeepers and artisans with whom he was everywhere on good terms. There was no shortage of possible partners. As to his partiality for Jewish women, Mrs. Anderson has suggested that an association with someone from a different religion would be less likely to burden him with any sense of spiritual responsibility.

Should it be asked whether even this amount of discussion of Schweitzer's private life is legitimate, I can only answer yes, and for two reasons. The first is the same that he himself gave for publishing what he believed about Jesus, even though it would be unpalatable for many, and to some destructive of their faith: "Truth is in all circumstances more valuable than untruth, and this must apply to truth in the realm of history as to other kinds of truth."[11] And, quoting St. Paul, "We can do nothing against the truth, but for the truth."

The second is that Schweitzer has far too long been a plaster idol, removed from the sphere of ordinary feeling. His name is a byword for inhuman perfection, which is grossly unfair to a most human man. The care with which he protected his relations with women has led the world to believe that he was spotlessly chaste, and made it possible for the puritans to quote him as their hero. But though the myth elevates him as a shining example for aseptic preachers to point at, it also removed him from the common run of humanity, who were his true friends. The ordinary sensual, life-loving human being finds the Schweitzer figure too pure for understanding or sympathy.

As the twentieth century wears on we grow steadily less inclined to believe that physical abstinence is necessarily good and that holiness involves a denial of the body. We are more likely to feel that if a man knows nothing of the love of a woman until he is thirty-seven, it is a defect rather than a mark of perfection. We are beginning to understand holiness in its proper sense, as wholeness.

If it could truly be shown that Schweitzer had no relations with women before his marriage, then of course that should be clearly said. But I believe that the evidence points the other way. I believe he was a whole man.

During the summer breaks at Günsbach, he was capable of relapsing into the moody lad whom elsewhere he had outgrown. Here he could for a while relax from the effort of will that went into the rest of his life and forget the self-imposed struggle for ever-increasing self-mastery. The family routine was unchanged. Meals were on the table at the stroke of the clock, and woe betide anyone who was not in his seat. Traditional food was taken to traditional picnic places. Year after year fruit was bottled, jam was made, and sometimes, after a family expedition, the whole house would smell of the wild strawberries that they had picked.

But Schweitzer never forgot his work for long. The very peacefulness of the vicarage and its ordered ways would aggravate his restlessness and make him irritable and abstracted. When the bell sounded for lunch all the family would appear except Albert. Albert would be sent for. Albert would explain that he would be down when he had finished this paragraph. But the paragraph would spread into a page, or two or three, before Albert appeared and took his place with a somewhat querulous expression on his face. He would gaze out the window through the rest of the meal, saying nothing; and make it clear, if any remark was made about his lateness, that he had better things to worry about than punctuality.

On the whole the family bore it well. They were increasingly proud of him and convinced of his rightness. Perhaps the old pastor was the least impressed, being something of a disciplinarian, and seeing no reason why Albert should spend so much time over theological notions which he was convinced nobody would take seriously. But he recognized—he could hardly help recognizing—that his son now dominated the house when he was home. And mother was as proud as could be; only a little grieved that Albert rested so little and could spare so little time for the family.

Louise would often be there with her husband, Jules, and the family, little Suzi and her baby brother. Jules shared Albert's apprehensions about the increasing size and power of the great industrial empires witn their insistence on a slavish loyalty to predigested schemes rather than initiative and free thought. And this insistence on conformity and crushing of individuality was infecting churches as well as nations, political parties, and industrial concerns. Realpolitik, the worship of expediency and self-interest, was rife everywhere. The forebodings Schweitzer had felt in Paris and in Berlin about the way Western Civilization was going grew steadily more gloomy. Increasingly he felt himself "out of step with his age"; and the more Europe seemed to be dispensing with individual thought and succumbing to the cozy dogmas of nationalism and material progress, the more convinced he became that civilization began with the individual. Individual reason alone could find the way through the fashionable parrot-cries to the "elemental" in man; individual will could carry out the decisions of reason. Enslavement to causes, however worthy, was the end of truth and liberty.

All this was very like Nietzsche. The difference lay in what Nietzsche and Schweitzer regarded as elemental. For Nietzsche it was man's power to dominate. The individual he had in mind would rise above humanity to a splendid pagan nobility, freed from normal human concerns. For Schweitzer, the free man was Jesus, the figure he traced in his study and his prayer and his preaching. Jesus was no idealistic vision, but a man who actually had delved into himself for the essence of humanity, and in pursuit of his conviction had forced the authorities to kill him. What Nietzsche had said about the need for heroism, which was becoming increasingly relevant in an unheroic world, added fuel to the fire of Schweitzer's admiration of Jesus—an irony which might not have pleased the author of *Anti-Christ.*

In Schweitzer's room the new Jesus was almost ready to make his appearance.

8

THE HISTORICAL JESUS
1901

IN May, 1901, an extraordinary thing happened. The principal of Strasbourg's Theological College had died, and a certain Gustav Anrich was
appointed to the post. Anrich needed some time to wind up his affairs in
his parish, and an interim deputy was required. Schweitzer was twenty-
six, had earned his degree nine months before, and was not even a fully
fledged pastor. And yet by general agreement of the theological faculty he
was the only serious contender for the position; such was the esteem in
which he was held. And evidently he made a success of it, for two years
later, when Anrich went on to another post, Schweitzer was an automatic
choice as his successor.

He held the deputy principalship from the beginning of May to the end
of September, when the new term began. And now, during this term of
office, the book at last came out: *The Problem of the Last Supper,* together with *The Secret of the Messiahship and Passion. A Sketch of the Life
of Jesus.* Only the latter part was translated into English (and that not until
1914) under the title *The Mystery of the Kingdom of God.*

If you ask English-speaking scholars the name of the book about Christ
for which Schweitzer is famous, the chances are that they will say *The
Quest of the Historical Jesus.* They may well add that it was a highly important work for its time, impressively researched, unconvincing, over-
emphatic, and unfortunately they have never read it.

Still less have they read *The Mystery of the Kingdom of God.* The reason is partly that though it is the earlier book it was translated later, and
the furor that was caused in England by the *Quest* had blown over by the
time *The Mystery* arrived on the scene. It therefore seemed somewhat
déjà vu, since the arguments it puts forward are summarized in the *Quest.*

But the arguments are far more closely knit and compelling in the earlier book. The *Quest* had quite another purpose—it was designed as a survey of all the previous attempts to make historical sense of the Gospels;

and Schweitzer, having already put forward his own solution in *The Mystery of the Kingdom of God,* saw no reason to repeat his ideas in full. He sketches them in as a conclusion to the *Quest,* and inevitably they are not wholly watertight or convincing in this form.

The Mystery of the Kingdom of God then is the important book. Schweitzer never found cause to alter the views there expounded and though you will find scholars who claim that he was only able to hold to his theories by totally ignoring subsequent developments in theology, his introduction to the third edition of the *Quest,* written when he was seventy-five, shows that in fact he had remained closely in touch with these developments but found nothing in them to make him change his mind.

Indeed his views had not changed in any material respect since he first hit upon the problem while on maneuvers at the age of nineteen. The intuition that then struck him had now broadened and deepened into considered conviction, and he had confirmed it by wide-ranging studies of other possible theories, of the historical background of Jesus' life, and of the texts themselves in Hebrew and in Greek. The theory no longer depended on the passage in Matthew about the sending out of the disciples and the prophecy that the kingdom would be on them before they returned. This was not only one of many passages, all of which combined to prove to Schweitzer's mind that Jesus lived in constant expectation that the world was about to be remade and that he would reappear as its Lord, the chosen one of God.

In comparing Schweitzer's books with those of other theologians one is struck by one great difference that permeates all his writing. He does not *read* like a theologian. There is a sort of transparency about his presentation, the thoughts come clear and unmuddied. No preconception comes between Schweitzer and the subject under discussion, no dogmatic discoloration tinges his observation. With every other writer one is aware that some undeclared bias is tilting the argument to port or starboard. Centuries of Church teaching about Jesus have so impregnated the imagination of Christians that fact and dogma have become indistinguishable. For example, a scholar may know very well that the phrase "Son of God" could be applied by a Jew to every male Jew—to be human was to be a child of God. Yet when the phrase is applied to Jesus he finds it virtually impossible to forget that for 1,700 years the Christian Church has used the phrase to mean something quite different—the divine second person of the Holy Trinity, a unique creature, part of the Deity Himself. The two images become confused. And since our scholar is writing as a Christian for Christians, he may also be afraid of seeming to betray his own faith if he really manages to drive all Christian reactions from his imagination. It takes great courage to divest the mind of the doctrines which support and comfort it—great courage, and also a rare imaginative power, the power to enter an alien thought-world without feeling challenged, frightened, and defensive. We shall find that many of the reactions to Schweitzer's books show symptoms of this anxiety.

Schweitzer shows no such fear. There is a fine defiance, almost a ruthlessness about the way in which he claims the right to make up his own mind; "the judgement of the early Church," he writes, "is not binding upon us."[1] Such a claim is of course easier for a Lutheran than for a Catholic, for the latter is committed to the view that the Church is itself divine, that it possesses Christ's spirit and is indeed in some mystical way the continuation of Christ's own body. But Protestants too have a sense of the holiness of the Church, and to set oneself up against its judgments, though absolutely necessary for Schweitzer's purpose, can feel something like blasphemy.

Schweitzer's unique quality then was his ability to look at the subject afresh, undeterred by the claims of loyalty or the fear of what disastrous consequences his discoveries might provoke. On the crucial question of Jesus' Messiahship, for example, he writes, "One should not forget that if Jesus did not take himself to be the Messiah, this means the death blow of the Christian faith."[2] No mystical doctrine, he believed, could possibly justify a church which posthumously promoted its founder to a status he never claimed in his lifetime.

In this century we have seen how the Che Guevaras of this world can be transformed after their death into demigods to satisfy the need of their followers for someone to worship. Schweitzer was right. If this is how the Church was founded, it is proof only that man can set up a dead hero higher than he stood when he lived—and that Jesus was less than the image they made of him. This was the danger Schweitzer faced—and he knew it. And perhaps he exulted in it a little. His book glows with a sense of enjoyable challenge. And he did, after all, believe in heroes—the one man pitted against the many.

As we have seen, Schweitzer's instinct, whether dealing with philosophy, music, or religion, was to drive straight through to the mind that gave it birth. Instead of treating the texts as a series of abstract propositions, he paid Jesus the unusual compliment of acknowledging that he was both a comprehensible human being and a Jew of his time. The most pious Christian is committed to believing that Jesus was Man as well as God. Schweitzer took this seriously, knowing that the side of him which was God is not approachable by the historical method but the side which is Man can be understood in the way we understand other men—by sympathy and imagination, combined with an understanding of the surrounding circumstances.

Most professional theologians are less noted for their imaginative insight into human behavior than for their skill in literary analysis of dog-

matic manipulation. Their skill in chopping logic and devising phrases
sometimes has a fairly tenuous link with human reality. Schweitzer, entering the battle as a human being trying imaginatively as well as intellectually to understand the story of another human being, gave himself a
very excellent chance of discovering things which others had failed to notice. But at the same time he put himself outside the club. He was not
working entirely within the rules. And this may be one reason why the
theological fraternity, while respectfully acknowledging his industry, his
versatility, and his admirable humanitarian work in the jungle, has failed
to take his arguments as seriously as they deserve.

To understand these arguments at all we must make a brief plunge into
the history of the period. The little Jewish nation in Jesus' day was already well acquainted with suppression, and the resentful acceptance of
domination by a foreign power which did not understand or care about
their God. Since the great captivity in Egypt and their long flight to the
Promised Land their history had been a succession of enslavements by aggressive neighbors. Their holy books were almost all concerned not with
the mysteries of internal prayer or personal salvation but with the promises made by God that he would deliver the nation from this captivity or
that. They dealt also with the behavior required by God as a condition of
deliverance. But the hope to which they looked was not that of individual
bliss or a vision of God in another life, but of the Jewish society living in
peace and perfection, harmoniously obeying its own laws and worshiping
its God. Different prophets offered different pictures of the coming society and different prescriptions as to what kind of offering would be acceptable to the Lord before he ushered in the kingdom to come; some spoke of
sacrifices of beasts, some of repentance of heart, and one, the second
writer of Isaiah, foretold the sacrifice of one just man for many.

But in all of them the future glory would be found in a specific human
community, altered certainly almost beyond recognition, but on earth and
in time. In this sense the religious instincts of the Jews were social and
political rather than spiritual in the common modern sense of "other-
worldly."

For some of the prophets, the kingdom would be ruled over by God in
person. But for Daniel, God was too great, too transcendent for such a restricted task—he would send instead his chosen one, the Son of Man, to
rule on his behalf. The Son of Man would be human, but his origin would
be heavenly. Other prophets had spoken of the Messiah, a king descended
from David, who would rule in heaven on God's behalf. By the time of
Jesus' birth, these various conceptions had become an amalgam of ideas
and hopes. But at all events it was widely agreed that the kingdom was
coming—that the prophet Elijah would reappear as the forerunner of the
kingdom, announcing himself by doing signs and miracles—and that the

Messiah, now identified with the Son of Man, would then appear in glory to usher in the kingdom. When this happened, he would select the faithful and rule over them in peace and justice forever—the faithless having been consumed in the disasters that attended the inauguration of the new order.

These beliefs and hopes are now summed up in the word "eschatology"—the study of the ultimate things.

When Jesus was born, a great many Jews had cause to believe that the kingdom might be due. Apart from sayings in the prophecies which upon calculation put the date at about this time, many contemporary events suggested that deliverance was necessary. Half a century before, the Romans had occupied Israel, and a Roman general had walked boldly into the Temple's Holy of Holies, into which nobody but the high priest was allowed. Since then the occupation had become increasingly harsh and repressive, in answer partly to the resistance movements which had sprung up among the Jews. Herod the Great had imposed what was virtually a police state, impious and detested. On top of this there had been earthquakes, droughts, and pestilence—quite enough to convince the pious that the end, and the beginning, were near.

Many groups had left the cities and awaited the cataclysm in the desert, and communities of believers flourished. Others, though they might pursue their normal lives, could not fail to be aware either of the all-pervading presence of the occupying forces or of the hope of divine intervention and deliverance. On or below the surface, Palestine at that time was emotionally turbulent, sometimes hysterical, electric with apprehension and revolutionary fervor. And the fervor was both religious and political, since the two things for the Jews were the same.

Into this society, desperately alert to every possible hint of the arrival of salvation, came Jesus, born of the family of David, with a personality and style of preaching which drew crowds to him in his lifetime and which have echoed unceasingly, if confusingly, down the whole of subsequent history.

The only records of Jesus' life that have come down to us, the four Gospels, are absurdly confusing and incomplete. Why? To this question all scholars of any note are in agreement in answering that, whatever Jesus himself may have thought, his followers after his death were convinced that his return as the Messiah was to be expected at any moment. This is why nobody troubled to write his history—his life story was not needed. And in any case his life so far was of little significance—it was merely the overture to the perfected life to come. It was only when the kingdom failed, day after day, month after month, year after year, to break upon the world—when some of the disciples had died and new recruits had to be instructed in the expectations of the group—that people began to collect the stories told of Jesus and to write them down. But they were still not interested in Jesus' life history—only in what he had said that was of significance and value in fostering and refreshing the disciples' faith in the return of the Messiah and the birth of the kingdom. The task of picking the history of Jesus out of the Gospels is not so very different as that of tracing the story of Chinese Communism from the thoughts of Chairman Mao.

As time passed and the kingdom was still delayed, it became obvious that someone had made a mistake. That it should be Jesus was unthinkable. By definition the Messiah does not make mistakes. So it must have been the disciples. They must have misunderstood him. And so the great game of reinterpretation began, open to anyone with a theory that could remotely be made to fit those ambiguous brief records in the Gospels. The game has gone on ever since, with efforts being made from time to time by the various churches, notably the Roman Catholics, to check the confusion by laying down a party line and reinforcing it by the claim that it had been dictated by the Spirit of Jesus which had entered the disciples at Pentecost and dwelt in the Church ever since. After a time it began to be seen, in retrospect, that since the Spirit of Jesus dwelt still in the Church, the kingdom had in fact come after all. It had been in the world all the time, ushered in by Jesus and held in trust by the Church.

Thus it could be shown to everyone's satisfaction that nobody had made a mistake after all. God had moved in a mysterious way, the kingdom had arrived, and *this* was what Jesus had been talking about all the time.

But was it? The Church's claim to the exclusive representation of Jesus in the world has had good results and bad. Often it has imposed order, the order of conformity, on conflicting sects. Great and holy men have sprung from its soil (though also from other soils). It has also been responsible for some of the most disgusting horrors in human history. Who can say whether the scales tip toward good or ill in the long run? The parable of the Grand Inquisitor, in Dostoievski's *The Brothers Karamazov,* is probably the world's greatest statement of the pros and cons. But one thing the Church has not done. It has not been able to make its image look even remotely like the image that rises from the pages of the Gospels. The Church cannot do without Jesus. And so we are back to the question—who was he? What was he? What *did* he mean?

We have seen that Schweitzer's tutor, Holtzmann, believed that all the really essential historical material about Jesus could be found in Mark—and that the additions in Matthew, having been inserted by the writer for some purpose of his own, could therefore be disregarded as historical information. The story which Holtzmann picked out from Mark was essentially the one still told today in a great many pulpits.

Jesus came to tell the Jews—indeed to tell the world—that God's king-

dom was not after all to be the crudely materialistic world in which the
rivers were eternally full of fish, the trees of fruit, and the fields of corn,
where love and peace reigned and there were no more tears. (The fact that
churchmen dismissed this vision as being "too sensual" shows what extraordinary people churchmen can be, but many of them did.) Instead Jesus offered them a new conception—a new way of living in the world as it
is today. Love and peace not through a change in the world but through a
change of heart. He came as an example, to show how it could be done,
as well as proclaiming that it should.

At first his mission met with great success and popularity. But later he
encountered opposition and increasing misunderstanding. And concluding that he must now make the ultimate gesture of love and self-giving by
incurring a humiliating and agonizing death, in which he would take on
himself the pain and guilt of all the world and by his own suffering reconcile God to the wickedness of humanity, he went to Jerusalem and
allowed the authorities to crucify him.

The fourfold arguments by which Schweitzer demolishes this picture
involves a close knowledge of the text and need not concern us here.
Suffice it to say that he found no evidence (1) that Jesus ever spoke of a
new conception of the kingdom. The few passages that are regularly
brought forward to prove that he did so, such as "the Kingdom of God is
within you,"[3] have other possible meanings. This particular sentence can
also be translated "the Kingdom of God is within your grasp" or "suddenly the Kindgom of God will be among you." The new Revised Standard Version of the Bible, accepted by all major denominations, translates
it as "the Kingdom of God is in the midst of you"; (2) that there was any
"unsuccessful" period in his mission. Crowds continued to surround him
from beginning to end; (3) that Jesus ever gave the disciples the idea that
he was offering himself for the world's sins. St. Paul put forward this idea
as an explanation of the crucifixion *after* it had happened.

What was Schweitzer's alternative? What *did* Jesus mean when he
spoke of the Kingdom of God—and how much did he speak of it? This
crucial problem gave Schweitzer's book its title. *The Mystery of the
Kingdom of God* does not mean, as it would in the hands of most theologians, "the Mysterious, Mystical Fact of the Kingdom of God." It means
"The Puzzle of the Kingdom of God." Schweitzer was not writing a metaphysical tract but a detective story.

Although in Mark we find a number of instances where Jesus speaks of
the Kingdom of God, they are much more frequent in Matthew. Holtzmann and the Marcan school put this down to the fact that Matthew himself was a convinced eschatologist, and "end-of-the-world" man, and
has therefore put his own views into Jesus' mouth. But Matthew's Gospel, like the other three, was approved by followers of Jesus as a true and

1. Kaysersberg, Schweitzer's birthplace.

2. Pastor Louis Schweitzer's
   vicarage in Kaysersberg.

3. Schweitzer's maternal grandfather, the
eccentric Pastor Schillinger.

4. Schweitzer's parents.

Marie Woytt-Secretan, Strasbourg

5. Schweitzer's collar singles him out among his classmates.

6. Schweitzer, age seven.

Marie Woytt-Secretan, Strasbourg

7. The Schweitzer family. Albert stands in the middle.

8. The Schweitzer family at the Günsbach vicarage. Albert stands at far left.

9. The statue of a black man that
fascinated young Schweitzer.

10. Schweitzer as a student in 1900.

11. Schweitzer as a dandy, age thirty-one.

12. Young Schweitzer and friends on a night out.

13. Hélène Bresslau.

Marie Woytt-Secretan, Strasbourg

14. Schweitzer in prison
in France, 1918.

Marie Woytt-Secretan, Strasbourg

15. Friends help pack for the second expedition in 1924.

16. The first house in Africa, at the Andende mission.

17. Building the first hospital at Andende. Schweitzer's first African assistant, Joseph, stands at the foot of the ladder.

proper record. Were they all blind to the fact that Matthew had overdone it to the extent of making Jesus, the beloved Lord, utter false prophecies—he who had in other passages been so scathing about false prophets?

The standard procedure for theologians, when faced with awkward questions of this kind, is to reject the passage as "unauthentic." They decide what they want Jesus to say, select the passages that support it, and reject the rest. Christians thus let themselves off the hook of disagreeing with their Lord.

Schweitzer's clinching point was that if we accept that Jesus *was* a man of his time, and did in fact believe what Jews of his time believed, nothing has to be rejected. Everything fits. Everything makes sense. To the question, for example, whether or not Jesus regarded himself as the Messiah, Schweitzer's account points out that the Messiah was not expected until the kingdom came. By definition he was the ruler of the new kingdom. So Jesus knew that he was called to Messiahship, but *not yet*. Not until the kingdom came. For the present he was only the man whom God had chosen for future glorification. The secret was imparted to him when John the Baptist baptized him in the Jordan. There was no need to tell anyone, because all would be revealed when the world ended. Meantime it was a secret between Jesus and God, shared later in strict confidence with the disciples. The first and only time he openly claims to be the Messiah, he is on trial before the high priest—and the claim means certain death. He brought his death upon himself, because he believed the moment of the kingdom had come. By the manner of his death he hoped to save his followers—all the believers who had gathered to hear him in the previous months—from the woes and calamities that were supposed to precede the kingdom and thereby purge Israel of its sins; because it was also said in Isaiah, "Surely he has borne our griefs and carried our sorrows . . . he was wounded for our transgressions, he was bruised for our iniquities . . . and with his stripes we are healed."[4] Jesus, steeped in the prophets, took the salvation of the Jews on himself, fulfilled the prophecies deliberately, and deliberately died, having warned the disciples in parables what to expect. The fact that they did not fully understand was of no importance. All would be made clear at the day of rejoicing.

Throughout his preaching period Jesus allows the crowds to think that he may be, at best, the expected forerunner of the Messiah—or else simply one of the prophets. But when he realizes that the kingdom is not coming as soon as he expects, and concludes that the Chosen People are not yet faithful enough, he decides to sacrifice himself before God to atone for their shortcomings. From then on he plans his own death. He reveals to the disciples the secret of his Messiahship, knowing that if this is discovered by the authorities it will mean his arrest—something he has hitherto carefully avoided. And he knows there is a traitor in the group—Judas. When Judas excuses himself and leaves the Last Supper, Jesus knows where he is going—and encourages him. The message that Judas takes to the authorities is not, as commonly supposed, where Jesus is. Jesus' whereabouts are no secret; he has been constantly in and around the temple. The message is that Jesus claims to be the Messiah. At last the authorities have evidence against him.

Even so, false witnesses have to be bribed, because Jesus is too popular with the people. But in the event they are not necessary. Here, where it is most fatal to make the direct statement, he makes it. "Are you the Christ, the Son of the Blessed One?" "I am." And then comes the great defiance: "And you will see the Son of Man seated at the right hand of Power and coming with the clouds of heaven."[5] He has condemned himself to death.

The story here summarized is, of course, supported in Schweitzer's book by chapter and verse. And it is interesting that the only other "life of Jesus" that I have been able to find that proposes a similar outline is one written by a Jew, Dr. Hugh J. Schonfield. Dr. Schonfield's book, *The Passover Plot*, shows, with great scholarship and a deep admiration of Jesus, how that extraordinary career can look to someone not brought up in the Christian tradition. It was published in 1965, and there is no reason to suppose that the author had ever read Schweitzer's book, from which it differs in some respects, bearing more heavily on the political circumstances. But the similarity is a remarkable tribute to Schweitzer's insight and his ability to enter into the Jewish thought-world of the period.

There is no question that at this level Schweitzer is extremely convincing. It is true, as he claims, that to read the Gospels afresh after studying his arguments is to bring a great deal that was obscure and "mysterious" into clear light and sharp focus. But what remains then of the Christian Jesus? What does Schweitzer think of the Resurrection? Of the miracles? Of the Transfiguration of Jesus on the mountain? And how can he go on claiming to be a Christian if his Christ is so fallible, so limited by his own time and place?

This last is of course the most crucial question of all, and is the challenge that has been thrown at Schweitzer's theology from that day to this. He did answer it, in his own way, though it was a way which his critics consistently failed to understand. We shall look at that in a moment.

First, the Resurrection and the other supernatural events in the Gospels. What place have they in Schweitzer's story?

Schweitzer was a skeptic—a doubting Thomas. He would certainly have wanted to thrust his hand into the wounded side of the risen Jesus, to test if it was really he. To this extent he was a true child of the Age of Reason that he admired, and of the Age of Doubt that bred him. He was a scientific-thinking man, in the sense that he only trusted what he could personally observe and test. This does not mean he was a materialist, for he found it perfectly possible to observe and test consciousness, emotional reaction, and thought itself. But the metaphysical, the supernatural, were no part of his world. A visitor to Lambarene in 1954, Richard Kik, quoted him as saying, "I never could understand anything overspiritualized . . . and as for the transcendental, I've never been able to understand it at all."[6] The theologian in him was always under the strict eye of the rationalistic philosopher.

Immortality and the afterlife therefore he regarded as not proven. And he knew enough about psychology to be very wary of claims to visions and so forth. His reading of the miracles was that some of them were cases of faith healing—the effect of Jesus' personality on sufferers from psychosomatic complaints. Others he regarded as the experiences of highly excited minds, which had become amplified in the process of word-of-mouth retelling down the years before they were put on paper.

Into this category he put such reports as the turning of the water into wine, walking on the lake, etc. The feeding of the 5,000, he suspects, was actually a symbolic meal of the same kind as the Last Supper—a ritual sharing of bread among those who had gathered to Jesus, who were, simply by being there, believers in the kingdom. The transfiguration of Jesus, observed by three disciples only, on top of a high mountain, occurred very shortly after an event of the most intensely emotional nature. Jesus had declared himself to be the Messiah; had enjoined strict secrecy; had demanded their total dedication to his cause; and finally had promised "there are some standing here who will not taste death before they see that the Kingdom of God has come with power."[7] The emotional effect on a group of Galilean fishermen, says Schweitzer, would put them into the ideal condition for the experiencing of hallucinations.

And similarly, he suspects, the distraught disciples after Jesus' death found themselves "seeing" him; as widows and widowers "see" the loved one whom they cannot believe dead. Such was the Resurrection. Armed with these visions, and the memory of Jesus' promises, the disciples set about preaching the doctrine of Christ, the risen Messiah. But Christ was not risen in the flesh. He was dead. He had been wrong.

"You are probably right about it," Schweitzer's father said, "but no one will believe you." And so it proved. None of the theologians was convinced. Indeed little attention appears to have been paid to the book at all, except by Holtzmann (to whom incidentally Schweitzer had dedicated it, "with sincere respect and devotion," calling himself "his grateful pupil").

Holtzmann's reaction was inevitably motivated by a degree of personal pain. "You have ruined everything I taught," he told Schweitzer. And in his own next book, *Das Messianische Bewusstsein Jesu,* he referred to Schweitzer as "this crushing critic" with his "merciless edifice of theory."[8] The book did nothing to refute Schweitzer's arguments, simply granting him a few points in his eschatological claims, but asserting, without evidence, that he had taken it much too far and reiterating that there was a spiritual side to Jesus' teaching which Schweitzer had not allowed for. Christian Brandt, who was a young student at the time, and used to read Schweitzer's proofs for him, remembers meeting Holtzmann at Baden and asking him what he really thought of Schweitzer's ideas. Holtzmann seemed very agitated. "He is right," he said, "but only partly right."

Unfortunately Schweitzer had not left room for the "partly right" verdict. His own phrase for his contribution to the study of Jesus was "*Konsequente Eschatologie.*" It is generally translated "thoroughgoing eschatology," but this hardly does justice to the phrase. "*Konsequente*" means coherent, logical, consistent. And Schweitzer made it clear that in his view the attempt to have it both ways was a lost cause.

A theologian called Weiss had written a book shortly before Schweitzer's, asserting the importance of Jesus' sayings about the Kingdom of God. Where Schweitzer had pushed matters farther was by saying, in effect, "If a man is forever saying that the Kingdom of God is around the corner, he will inevitably behave accordingly." And finding that word and action matched, and that on this simple basis the whole Gospel made sense, he declared a position of no compromise. A man who speaks and acts in the belief that the world is coming to an end in a couple of weeks does not hedge his bets. Either he believes it or he does not. The suggestion that he believes it part of the time, but part of the time is thinking in terms of normal history stretching out ahead, simply is psychological nonsense. "If *any* of Jesus' sayings about the kingdom are true," says Schweitzer, in effect, "then the whole of my theory inevitably follows. If on the other hand you believe that Jesus was spiritualizing the message for generations to come, you must reject *all* the eschatological sayings as later interpolations. *Tertium Non Datur*—there is no third alternative. Jesus was not a man to blow hot and cold, nor to say one thing and mean another."

With his uncompromising *Tertium Non Datur,* Schweitzer left no room for equivocation. It was impossible to slide out of the alternative he posed with a "but" or an "if" or an "on the other hand." And being still, as he said himself, the same "intolerable young man" who had made everybody's life hell as a schoolboy with his demands for truth, he had not written too tactfully about the theories he was now attacking. Here, for example, is what he says at one point about the way in which "the modern-historical school" (that is to say, Holtzmann and all the leading "liberal" theologians) account for the crucifixion of Jesus: "It is after all a lifeless thought! The feeble modernity of it is visible in the fact that it does not get beyond a sort of representative significance of Jesus' death."[9] Feeble! Lifeless! One begins to see perhaps why scholars found it preferable to ignore a book which attacked so vigorously but to which they appeared to have no convincing answer.

One can see too why people found it hard to assess Schweitzer's situation in the university. A much-respected young acting principal of a theological college, a working curate, comes out with a book that appears to demolish large parts of the faith he is working for. Is he right? Then where is Christianity? Is he wrong? Then should he go on holding office?

Though he did not know it till later, two members of the faculty protested against his acceptance as a lecturer, fearing that he would "confuse" the students with his unorthodox approach. It was Holtzmann, whom he had hurt most, who with characteristic generosity and integrity threw his authority into the balance and swung the vote in Schweitzer's favor.

It hurt Schweitzer that Holtzmann was hurt. He found it painful that his conclusions must inevitably wound a lot of Christians. "The satisfaction which I could not help feeling at having solved so many riddles about the existence of Jesus was accompanied by a painful consciousness that this new knowledge in the realm of history would mean unrest and difficulty for Christian piety. . . . I find it no light task to follow my vocation, to put pressure on the Christian Faith to reconcile itself in all sincerity with historical truth. But I have devoted myself to it with joy, because I am certain that truthfulness in all things belongs to the Spirit of Jesus."[10]

We must postpone for a moment looking at the paradoxical claim that the spirit of Jesus led Schweitzer to announce that Jesus was fallible and dead. It lies at the heart of that difficult question—what kind of Christian could he call himself now? But for the moment we are considering only the reactions to his historical theories.

It was Schweitzer's ruthless logic, the dominating clarity of his argument, and his refusal of compromise that most perplexed the readers of *The Mystery of the Kingdom of God*. The silence that greeted its publication was almost audible. The two professors who opposed Schweitzer's lectureship did so in secret. Dr. Walter Lowrie, in the excellent introduction which he wrote to the English translation in 1914, says:

> Obviously it was not the weakness of the book, but rather its strong originality and in particular the trenchant way in which it demolished the "liberal life of Jesus" which accounts for the passive hostility with which it was greeted. In fact it contained more than could be readily di-

gested at once either by a liberal or a conservative mind. Most of the
New Testament students in Germany had collaborated in the fabrication of the "liberal life of Jesus" and they could not patiently endure to
see their work destroyed. Those among us who fancy that German
professors are bloodless beings who live in an atmosphere purified of
passion and prejudice, need to be informed that on the contrary they
are human, all too human. The animosities of party and school and the
jealousies of the cathedral have been proverbial for generations. The
reception accorded to Schweitzer's work does not seem creditable. It
was met by something like a conspiracy of silence.[11]

Christian Brandt confirms that the silence by no means indicated as-
sent. "They all thought he was wrong," says Brandt. "But he only
tapped the side of his nose with his finger and said, 'I can wait.'"

Schweitzer is still waiting. Through all his theological writings he never changed his mind about Jesus, though he kept in touch with all the
subsequent developments in theology. We can only assess his achievement therefore if we look to see how later theologians reacted to his view-
point, after the first stunned silence; and whether any of them, from that
day to this, has found any convincing proof that he was wrong. For this
purpose we must consider the reactions to *The Quest of the Historical
Jesus,* which appeared in 1906, as well as to *The Mystery of the Kingdom
of God.*

The German attitude can perhaps be summed up at its most charitable
by Holtzmann with his "he is only partly right"; and at its most uncompromising by the Olympian Harnack, who wrote, "If anyone finds it impossible to accept the antinomy 'the Kingdom is future and yet present,'
argument with him is useless."[12]

In England Schweitzer fared better, at least for a time. Canon William
Sanday, a professor at Oxford, read *The Quest of the Historical Jesus* in
German and welcomed it in a series of lectures in 1907, endorsing almost
everything that Schweitzer had to say. Before long the students at both
Oxford and Cambridge were in a furor about the new ideas and Schweitzer looked set for the leadership of the new theology at least in England.
Two years later however Professor Ernst von Dobschutz came to Oxford
to give a series of lectures and brought with him the official line;
Schweitzer had gone too far, had pressed his alternatives too hard, had
not allowed for the ambiguity which clearly lay in Jesus' words and
which Jesus had evidently intended.

At this point it became clear that Canon Sanday, in his championship
of Schweitzer, was not wholly disinterested. He disapproved of the whole
tendency of the Protestants in Germany to "modernize" Jesus and what
he liked most about *The Quest* was Schweitzer's exposure of the weak-
nesses in the modernizers' case. He had not, however, read the earlier

book, *The Mystery of the Kingdom of God,* where Schweitzer's own case is most closely argued.

Von Dobschutz's lectures shook the shallow roots of Sanday's enthusiasm, and in 1910 Sanday published a recantation in the *Hibbert Journal,* Britain's foremost philosophical and theological magazine. In it he apologized for having been "attracted unduly by Dr. Schweitzer's freshness and force," and overimpressed by his "audacity and exaggeration." Sanday now found that he could not agree with Schweitzer's "tendency to push things to extremes at the dictates of logical consistency." "Such drastic logic" he claims, "was not to be looked for on the soil of Palestine."[13]

This last remark is a good example of the befogging of issues which was the order of the day. In the first place he seems to be saying that Jesus, along with all the other Jews, was unable to coordinate thought with action—a suggestion which is unsupported with reference to the race in general, but in the case of Jesus an attack more damaging to the founder of the Church than any mounted by Schweitzer.

More basic however is Sanday's failure to understand where the logic lay. Schweitzer does not claim that Jesus was logical in the intellectual sense (though there is no reason why he should not have been). Schweitzer claims that he himself is logical in saying that if a man is obsessed by the end of the world, that obsession will underlie all his words and actions—a part-time obsession is not possible. It is not logic that makes such a man connect his sayings with his belief. It is the necessity of his being. Either Jesus was obsessed or he was not. There is no third alternative.

Once again we see that other theologians trade in words, without understanding the reality behind the words, where Schweitzer trades in understanding of human beings. Once again we see how his very strength, his honesty and commonsense, make him an odd man out in the theologians' club.

So Sanday (who had still not read *The Mystery of the Kingdom of God*) retreated from Schweitzer's logic into ecclesiastical doublethink, and the waves of the establishment closed over him. In 1910 *The Quest of the Historical Jesus* was published in English, with a preface by Professor F. C. Burkitt of Cambridge. In recommending the book Burkitt suggests that the most important element is not Schweitzer's own solution, but his survey of all the other solutions. "It is not to be expected," he writes, "that English students will endorse the whole of his view of the Gospel History, any more than his German fellow-workers have done."[14] It is a typical scholar's approach. The game is the study of problems, not the discovery of answers. But Burkitt's coolness, which has been echoed down the years, is also partly the result of the accident that *The Quest* appeared in the English language before *The Mystery.* Having read it, people assumed they had Schweitzer's arguments in their entirety and could the more easily dismiss them.

The British reviews clung fairly closely to Burkitt's line. The Glasgow *Herald,* for example, praised *The Quest* as "the only book in which any attempt has been made to give a full and connected history of the whole course of that wonderful movement of the German mind . . . which has had for its single aim to reach the exact truth about the Christ of history. In this aspect the book is invaluable." But the reviewer is not much impressed by what he calls "Dr Schweitzer's 'stand-and-deliver' style of calling upon the Christian world to declare itself either eschatological or non-eschatological."[15] The same phrase which Schweitzer himself used of his less successful attempts at begging for charity, "stand and deliver," suggests one reason why his book failed to endear itself to its readers.

The Manchester *Guardian* too spoke admiringly of "fullness of detail and brilliant perception" in Schweitzer's summary of previous books, but "some readers will feel that his own solution has become an obsession, and they will possibly resent the extreme dogmatism of his tone. . . ."[16]

The Nation rated the book "by far the ablest work which has hitherto appeared in this difficult and tantalising field,"[17] and summarized its conclusions with fairness, but was quite convinced that eschatology was foisted on Jesus posthumously by ecstatic disciples.

Several reviewers were so confused by the fact that Schweitzer's Jesus does not believe in a "spiritual" kingdom that they told their readers that the teaching, too, of this Jesus was without spiritual or even ethical content—the exact opposite of the truth. Others, more perceptive, were glad to be able to agree with Schweitzer's final conclusion that the Jesus of the heart is independent of historical discoveries—so their historical disagreements hardly matter.

What is quite evident, through the various degrees of nonacceptance and dismissal, is that the book had caused a considerable flutter in British theological dovecotes. And we are not surprised to find the *Times* reporting that the shadow of Schweitzer had fallen across the Church Congress held that year.

It had also made enough impression to be accorded considerable space in an *Encyclopaedia of Religion and Ethics* published in 1912. Professor J. A. MacCulloch, contributing the section on eschatology, has this to say: "The Eschatological theory, that Christ thought that the Kingdom would be inaugurated immediately after a short period of messianic woes . . . cannot be proved . . . nor can it be certain that Christ looked forward to an immediate coming of the [future] Kingdom."[18]

Having dismissed the whole theory on this bare assertion, he goes on to counter it with a series of unsupported guesses ("if he is correctly reported his purpose may have been to show that. . . ."); and upholds the view that St. John is more accurate than the other Gospels simply because its interpretation is more spiritual.

In his anxiety to give no quarter to the dreaded eschatologists, MacCulloch translates and interprets Biblical phrases in a manner that gives no indication that there are other possible meanings, proving the opposite to what he desires; he starts an argument with an "if" or a "perhaps," and then proceeds to a conclusion as though his "perhaps" were an established certainty; and he never genuinely queries the assumption that Christ thought what the later Church required him to think, or seeks truthfully to start from the beginning. He exhibits all the characteristics of what we have learned in a different context to call brainwashing. Schweitzer, hopeful that "truth belongs to the spirit of Jesus," had reckoned without the conditioning that affected the outlook of so many members of Jesus' Church.

Such were the initial reactions of the theological world. *The Mystery of the Kingdom of God* was not translated into English until 1914—a bad year in Britain and the United States for books with German-sounding authors. It seems to have passed almost without notice in Britain, where it was not reviewed seriously until the second impression in 1925. In the United States the publishers grew so alarmed at having a "German" author on their hands when war broke out in Europe that they sold the whole edition to jobbers at ten cents per volume and the jobbers got rid of them at twenty-five cents apiece at the drugstores. By the time the war was over the whole eschatological issue was old hat. Theologians had moved on to other problems, and Schweitzer was accorded a respectful wave of the hand as someone who once made "a useful contribution" but could now be ignored. It was convenient that he had meanwhile disappeared into the jungle and everybody could then change the subject by talking about his saintly self-sacrifice.

The fact is of course that when Schweitzer posed his stark alternatives he committed the grievous error of leaving no room for discussion. This was not playing the game. Theologians in their disputes are far from gentle creatures, as Dr. Lowrie points out. Their works are liberally scattered with warlike images—the opposition routed in hopeless disorder and so forth. Schweitzer played this game as well as any of them. But in most cases the routed opposition could, and did, rally and reform and fight a return battle. That was part of the fun.

Schweitzer's challenge was different—that third choice which he denied his readers was vitally necessary to their comfort. They could not deny the force of the eschatological argument, but if they accepted it with the unshrinking honesty of Schweitzer, they found that the beliefs on which they had pinned their faith and hope vanished like sand through their fingers. So the third choice *had* to be true. The spiritual Jesus, operating through the ages, had to coexist with the eschatological Jesus who lived for his own time. How? A mystery! Schweitzer's book, rejecting that mystery as impossible, was like one of those remarks dropped by a stranger into the middle of a pleasant party discussion, which all of a sudden demolishes the basis of the whole conversation and leaves an embarrassed hush behind.

As on those occasions, the first thing that everybody did was to change the subject and pretend the remark had never been made. Suddenly it became the mode to dismiss the whole search for the historical Jesus as useless. The Gospels are so difficult to interpret, it was decided, that we must abandon any attempt to read them for information about Jesus—we must now read them for what they can tell us about the people who wrote them and for whom they were written; that is to say the early Church. Behind the early Church we know there lies a misty figure, almost certainly an actual person but possibly not even that, called Jesus. We are not concerned with what that figure really said and did—only with what the Church said he said and did; and why they said it.

This new approach is called "form criticism," and it studies the Gospels as a series of totally unconnected episodes that have been thrown together in a manner so arbitrary that we have no hope now of disentangling them. In studying these episodes we first decide in each case what purpose the writer hoped to serve by telling this particular story. For the stories fall into several groups, each with its particular form (hence the name of the method), and the form suggests how the story was used. For example, miracle stories would be needed to convince doubters of the Messiahship of Jesus, pronouncement stories might be required to give the young Church guidance on conduct or doctrine, and so forth. So only those parts of Jesus' life and teaching which were useful for the daily survival of the early Church would have been preserved and these would have been so adulterated and altered in the process of being used as propaganda that their historical value is nil. Schweitzer's whole labor, as well as that of all his predecessors, was therefore a waste of time.

Schweitzer was not unaware of these developments. Introducing the third edition (1950) of *The Quest* he says, "My book deals with practically all conceivable arguments against the historicity of Jesus. Here . . . the old is always appearing in a new form."[19] And it is true that something very like form criticism had appeared in the middle of the nineteenth century in the work of Bruno Bauer; Schweitzer spends twenty-three close-packed pages on it in *The Quest,* and concludes that the figure behind the Gospel stories must be more solid and comprehensible than this theory allows.

Farther on in the Introduction he writes, "Later works on the life of Jesus cannot be included here. The introduction of new chapters, owing to the size of the book, would necessitate considerable abbreviation of what I have already written. But I cannot bring myself to spoil the thoroughness with which I have treated the earlier period. I therefore bequeath to another the task of introducing order into the chaos of modern lives of Jesus, which I performed for the earlier period."[20] Nobody has yet come forward to take on this task, but Schweitzer evidently had no qualms about his ability to demolish twentieth-century theories of the life of Jesus as effectively as he did those of the nineteenth.

For the moment let me say simply that form criticism itself unwittingly provides the most convincing proof possible of Schweitzer's eschatological theories.

Let us assume that none of the Gospels incidents can be proved to have originated with Jesus—they are derived from his sayings and acts, yes; but their selection and their final form are dictated by the needs of the young Church.

This Church is waiting for the second coming of the Messiah—all the records agree at least about that. They expect it daily. They feel some embarrassment that it delays so long. The very fact that the Gospels have to be written means that some fairly desperate measures have become necessary to preserve the faith—measures undreamed of in the first twenty or thirty years after Jesus' death.

At this juncture, any remark that Jesus might have made about a new, spiritual meaning of the kingdom, would have been, literally, a Godsend. It would have explained the whole delay if someone—anyone—had remembered Jesus telling them that the kingdom was not of the kind they expected, that history was to go on, and that they must find the kingdom in themselves. According to the rules of form criticism, such a hint would have been exploited to the full, both to comfort the Church and to turn aside the jeers of outsiders.

The fact that the Gospels contain no accounts of this kind is conclusive proof that Jesus never spoke to his disciples in these terms. If he was concerned to spiritualize the kingdom, he died with his secret unspoken. It was not the early Church, but a much later one, forced by history to spiritualize the idea of the kingdom, that put that thought by hindsight into his mind.

Form criticism has been the more sophisticated branch of recent New Testament study. Along with it has gone a new version of the old way of thinking, adorned with a new label, "realized eschatology." Schweitzer's influence is acknowledged by the word eschatology, but his meaning is obliterated by the whole phrase, which refers to the notion that Jesus did in fact usher in the kingdom simply by appearing on earth. The end of an era did arrive, though for some reason nobody noticed the fact for some while afterward. The disciples, awaiting the arrival of the kingdom, had already begun to live in it, by virtue of the new vision of life bequeathed them by Jesus. Similarly for all Christians thereafter, the kingdom is here and now, in love and faith.

Professor C. H. Dodd, doyen of British theologians today, is a leading exponent of this theory, which is widely accepted as a satisfactory solution of the eschatological question. It is of course nothing of the kind. It may adequately represent what has perforce happened to the Church over the years, but it evades all the historical difficulties about Jesus' own expectations which were thrown up in those hundred years of searching German criticism, as though they had never been.

So we are left hanging between those who, for all practical purposes, accept most of the Gospels as "Gospel" and continue with the game of "interpreting" them to their own convenience, and those who reject them totally. Schweitzer is not merely forgotten, but actually suppressed by the religious establishment. The BBC's attitude, for example, when challenged in the early 1940's by a keen Schweitzerian, Colonel E. M. Mozley, was that Schweitzer's theories must not be discussed on the radio, on the grounds that they were "not in the stream of the Christian tradition."[21] This ban was lifted only in 1947.

Apart from the way in which theological schools have avoided the issue of eschatology, what have recent individual theologians had to say about Schweitzer himself?

In Switzerland a small group headed by Martin Werner continued to work on his lines, applying his insights to the later history of the Church. In Britain, however, you may look in vain for any serious consideration of his work.

Such attention as there is still concentrates on *The Quest of the Historical Jesus*, rather than *The Mystery of the Kingdom of God*. The latter appears to be totally unknown, or ignored. The former is treated with a sort of distant respect accorded to the great statues of Easter Island. "A seminal work," says Professor Evans of Kings College, London, "since which nothing can be the same again; but flawed unfortunately by faulty methodology." He quotes that passage in Matthew which gave Schweitzer his starting point as being of doubtful authenticity anyway. He seems not to have realized that the full structure of Schweitzer's theory has no longer any need of this passage; the full-grown tree dispenses with the seed it sprang from.

Professors Davidson and Leaney, joint authors of *The Pelican Guide to Modern Theology*, call it "one of the most brilliant and interesting books of the century''; and then proceed to misunderstand it so radically that they can write, ''Such a reconstruction rendered a view of Jesus which saw him at his end a deeply disillusioned man, uttering a cry of despair from the cross as he died.''[22] On the contrary—Schweitzer's Jesus died in the full hope of immediate reawakening into a world made new.

Professor A. M. Hunter, of Aberdeen University in Scotland, says that Schweitzer, ''having destroyed the liberal portrait of Jesus, set about painting a new one in terms of his own eschatology—a portrait which satisfied no one but himself and reminds us, as Streeter says, 'of the Superman of Nietzsche wearing Galilean robes.' ''[23]

The only way in which Schweitzer's Jesus resembles the Superman is in his heroic stature. In every other way, as we have seen, he is totally unlike. Apart from that enormous error, the striking thing is Hunter's happy assumption that Jesus existed to satisfy modern Christians. This comforting belief finds echoes in many writers. W. J. Wolf says that The Quest ''brought an end to the 'Liberal lives,' but presented a Jesus totally foreign to our day.''[24] The fact that the figure is foreign apparently makes it unnecessary to decide whether it is true. Jesus is not allowed to be foreign (which he obviously was) because thereby he becomes less useful to the modern Church. It is a curious criterion of truth.

Several present-day New Testament authorities whom I have approached have simply admitted that they know too little about Schweitzer to be able to make any useful comment. Their knowledge is secondhand. We have seen enough of the travesties committed by firsthand commentators to realize that those present-day theologians who have relied on them have gained a quite inaccurate impression of Schweitzer's work.

This might account, for example, for an extraordinary paragraph about Schweitzer in D. M. Baillie's book, God Was in Christ. Elsewhere Professor Baillie admits that since the ''Jesus of History'' movement there is an almost universal recognition that Jesus' knowledge was limited by human conditions, and that likewise his healing activities and his moral and religious life were fully human. But of Schweitzer's Jesus he writes: ''The effect of Schweitzer's own interpretation, as he saw plainly, was to produce a portrait of the historic Jesus so grotesquely 'eschatological' in outlook as to make Him a complete stranger to our time, so remote, mysterious, and even unintelligible to us that it seemed to bring to an impasse the whole attempt to make the historic Jesus real as a basis for the Christianity of the modern world.''[25] The picture Baillie draws of Schweitzer's Jesus is so entirely different from Schweitzer's own that he must surely be supposed to be making it up from hearsay. On top of this he claims that Schweitzer ''saw plainly'' what Baillie sees. In fact what Schweitzer says of this ''grotesquely eschatological stranger, remote, mysterious, and unintelligible,'' is this: ''Even if the historical Jesus had something strange about him, yet his personality, as it really is, influences us much more strongly and immediately than when he approached us in dogma and in the results attainted hitherto by research."[26]

In fact even Schweitzer overstated the strangeness involved. Among theologians it may not be customary to exercise the imagination; but among writers it is well known that a figure placed firmly in its true historical context will always have a more universal significance than one which is set in some sort of limbo. We can identify much more easily with a genuine person whose circumstances, climate, and mental background are different from our own than we can with some kind of faceless creature with no definable place or time. We do not find it difficult for example to understand the predicament of King Oedipus, though his thought-world was not remotely like ours. We can detach his problem with ease from its circumstances and apply it to our own. Only the Church's self-imposed blinkers make it hard to do the same with Jesus.

All too often the spokesmen of the Church impose on Jesus the humiliating discourtesy of employing him as a helpless prop for their own preconceptions. He is required to be like themselves and judged according to that likeness. C. H. Dodd writes, "We no longer accept a saying as authoritative because it lies before us as a word of Jesus, but because we are rationally convinced that it is a word of His, and that will mostly mean in the last resort, because we are convinced that it is worthy of Him, that is, true and important."[27]

We are it seems to be the judges of truth and importance. It leaves Jesus at our mercy, the all-purpose symbol of any nation that goes to war, of authority and of rebellion, of Black Power and white racism, of Protestant and Catholic at each other's throats.

Small wonder that Schweitzer wrote, "How strong would Christian truth now stand in the world of today, if its relation to the truth of history were in every respect what it should be! But instead of allowing this truth its rights, Christianity has mistreated it in various ways, conscious or unconscious, whenever it became embarrassing, but always by either evading, or twisting, or suppressing it."[28] Things have not changed.

Schweitzer spoke of his own work on the Gospels as "scientific" and "historical." By adopting these standards, he put himself out of the game. In a race where most runners have their feet tied in a sack of dogmatic preconceptions or emotional dependency, he cut loose and ran on two good legs. He reached the post first, but found himself disqualified. As he mildly remarks in the Introduction to the third edition of *The Quest,* "The fact remains, however, that the eschatological solution has not succeeded in dominating the latest writing on the life of Jesus, and is not within sight of doing so. . . . It is an axiom for tradition that Jesus preached truth utterly beyond and above the time-process. But this is contradicted by the eschatological picture of Jesus, which shows him sharing the expectations of his contemporaries. Faith is asked to give up something which it has always held and cannot contemplate abandoning.''[29]

My own feelings are better summed up in a passage he wrote about the earliest of Biblical critics, Reimarus, which could be applied word for word to himself and the fate of his books:

> The fact is there are some who are historians by the grace of God, who from their mother's womb have an instinctive feeling for the real. They follow through all the intricacy and confusion of reported fact the pathway of reality, like a stream which, despite the rocks that encumber its course and the windings of its valley, finds its way inevitably to the sea. No erudition can supply the place of this historical instinct, but erudition sometimes serves a useful purpose, inasmuch as it produces in its possessors the pleasing belief that they are historians, and thus secures their services for the cause of history. In truth, they are at best merely doing the preliminary spade-work of history, collecting for a future historian the dry bones of fact, from which, with the aid of his natural gift, he can recall the past to life. More often, however, the way in which erudition seeks to serve history is by suppressing historical discoveries as long as possible, and leading an army of possibilities out into the field to oppose the one true view. By arraying these in support of one another it finally imagines that it has created out of possibilities a living reality.
>
> This obstructive erudition is the special prerogative of theology, in which, even at the present day, a truly marvellous scholarship often serves only to blind the eyes to elementary truths, and to cause the artificial to be preferred to the natural.[30]

Schweitzer's historical instinct, like a water diviner's rod, led him unerringly past the dry places of fruitless academic bickering to the spot where the important truths lay hidden. There he began to dig. He himself was hardly aware what a large part instinct played in his research. He attributed all his results to reason. But in every field of discovery it is instinct, a kind of esthetic sixth sense, that tells the great investigators what questions to ask. To answer needs only application and skill. Many people have those qualities. The real secret is in the asking.

Truth belongs to the spirit of Jesus. Yet truth declares that Jesus died a terrible death in pursuit of a mirage. This is the apparent contradiction in Schweitzer's argument. There is no connection, say the critics, between Schweitzer's historical theories and his Christian devotion. What kind of Christian can he be if the Christ he follows is no more than a deluded rabbi? The question has rankled down the years with Schweitzer's admirers and detractors. Books and articles have been written showing that he was, or was not, a Christian, and in what sense.

In many cases these assessments have started from a definition of Christianity which Schweitzer would not have accepted. And their authors frequently appear not to have read what he himself said on the subject—or to have read it with very little attempt at imaginative understanding.

Schweitzer made a first step toward clarifying his attitude at the end of *The Mystery of the Kingdom of God,* and though later he refined and amplified the statement he then made, his answer always remained essentially the same.

Jesus' death, says Schweitzer, changed everything, but not in the way Jesus intended. Jesus and the disciples expected the Kingdom of God in the eschatological sense. The spiritual understanding of the kingdom was forced on the Church by the failure of the eschatological Kingdom to arrive. The Church had to interpret—and misinterpret—the belated records of Jesus' sayings, so as to make them fit in with a future which Jesus never envisaged. *But*—such was the immense ethical and religious power of Jesus' personality that it did now become possible for those who followed him to live in a totally new way—to live, in fact, in a "kingdom within-the-world" which Jesus himself never envisaged. "The Christian view of the world which he founded by his death carries mankind forever beyond eschatology."[31] But we must not, says Schweitzer, impose these later ideas on to the historical Jesus. That is where untruth starts, because we all begin to saddle Jesus with the outlook and ideas of our own place and time. If we allow Jesus to remain in every way a man of his time, conditioned by the beliefs prevalent in his place in history, we can then see how superhuman his personality really was. His spirit was such that he attempted to bring history to an end—the most heroic act that anyone of this time could conceive of. Schweitzer uses a marvelous image in *The Quest of the Historical Jesus:* " . . . in the knowledge that he is the coming Son of Man [Jesus] lays hold of the wheel of the world to set it moving on that last revolution which is to bring all ordinary history to a close. It refuses to turn, and he throws himself upon it. Then it does turn. And crushes him. Instead of bringing in the eschatological conditions, he has destroyed them. The wheel rolls onward, and the mangled body of the one immeasurably great man, who was strong enough to think of himself as the spiritual ruler of mankind and to bend history to his purpose, is hanging upon it still. That is his victory and his reign."[32]

We can see the influence of Nietzsche in Schweitzer's vision of Jesus as the hero. Nietzsche had looked in the wrong direction for his Superman, sickened as he was by the hypocrisy of the very people who profess to follow the hero of Galilee. Jesus, dying in the greatest cause the world could offer, a cause foredoomed to failure, shattered the eschatological dream. But the spiritual power that led him to that adventure is untouched by the fact that he was mistaken about results. With his limitations as a man he had no choice but to follow the highest that he saw. It was a mirage. With its disappearance his spirit is freed, to be applied anew to all other situations and civilizations. The liberated spirit can pervade all history as it once "quickened and transfigured Jewish eschatology. . . . Theology is not bound to graze in a paddock. It is free, for its task is to found our Christian view of the world solely upon the personality of Jesus Christ, irrespective of the form in which it expressed itself in his time."[33]

Schweitzer intended in due course to trace the process whereby the Church was forced to adapt its thinking little by little until it finally formulated the Creeds several hundred years after Jesus' death. The outlines of the process were already clear in his mind—particularly the first great steps taken by St. Paul, whose brilliant and deeply religious mind was confronted by the agonizing problems caused by the nonappearance of Jesus and the Kingdom.

The book on St. Paul was not to be completed for many years yet, and the later one, about the subsequent development of the Church's beliefs and the formulation of the Creeds was so whittled away by the lack of time that it finally appeared only as a short essay. But following the trail through the years, one finds that he accounts as convincingly for the errors of the Church as he did for the errors of Jesus. Not only is he convincing—he is deeply sympathetic. He sees the necessity of what the Church did and he believes moreover that in one sense those early churchmen were right. They did the only thing possible. A spiritual understanding of the kingdom was the only course left open to them: They had to learn to see the existing world afresh, in the spirit of Jesus. This is precisely how Schweitzer himself lived.

But however right they were spiritually, they were absolutely wrong historically. The error of Jesus echoed down the ages, forcing fresh errors on generation after generation, as they attempted to reconcile the first great mistake with the facts. The complicated dogmatic formulas of the Creeds were efforts to fit all the conflicting and paradoxical pieces together. Thus Jesus became more and more strange, because Greek ideas of what a God should be became mixed with the original Jewish expectations, and the resulting God-man of the Christian Church was born, flanked by the other two persons of the Trinity. Christians now find the Jesus of Schweitzer strange only because they have been accustomed from childhood to believe in the far stranger Jesus of the catechism.

So Schweitzer's Christianity was nothing more nor less than a total devotion to the spirit of the original Jesus—a man who was limited by the knowledge of his time, but whose spirit was so great that he attempted to crack open time and reveal the kernel—the hidden realm of God. Success or failure was not the issue. The grandeur of the attempt made Jesus superhuman, even divine, supremely worthy of devotion.

But what kind of devotion can this be, to the spirit of a mortal man? And in what sense can it be called religious?

Though he did not understand the transcendental or the supernatural, Schweitzer understood mysticism—because he experienced it. Indeed he found it a universal human characteristic, in one form or another. The highest form of mysticism, he believed, "takes place through an act of thinking. Whenever thought makes the ultimate effort to conceive the relation of the personality to the universal, this mysticism comes into existence. . . . It attains the power to distinguish between appearance and reality, and is able to conceive the material as a mode of manifestation of the spiritual. It has sight of the eternal in the transient."[34]

We have already noted that the German "*denken*" has a much wider and deeper meaning than the English "think," and embraces overtones of awareness and contemplation as well as cogitation. "Thinking" mysticism, in this sense, was Schweitzer's manner of understanding Jesus—not because Jesus was a resurrected God, but because his spirit had manifested the eternal truth of heroic humanity as nobody before or since. Schweitzer found communion with Jesus deep in himself, in the depths of contemplation.

In a sense therefore it might seem that the whole quest of the historical Jesus was a scholarly irrelevance. Schweitzer's allegiance was to the Jesus within, not to the Jesus of history. But things are not so simple as that. In Jesus the eternal was manifested in a real man—not a figment. His reality was essential—a guarantee that the greatness of his spirit was not an invention. The kingdom might have been a mirage but Jesus was not. The connection between the inner Jesus and the historical Jesus is a close one after all. "Whoever preaches the Gospel of Jesus must settle for himself what the original meaning of his sayings was, and work his way through the historical truth to the eternal. During this process he will again and again have opportunity to notice that it is with this new beginning that he first truly realises all that Jesus has to say to us."[35]

At the end of *The Mystery of the Kingdom of God* Schweitzer wrote [author's italics]: "The judgments passed upon this realistic account of the life of Jesus may be very diverse, according to the dogmatic, historical, or literary point of view of the critics. Only with the *aim* of the book may they not find fault: *to depict the figure of Jesus in its overwhelming heroic greatness and to impress it upon the modern age and upon the modern theology.*"[36] At the end of *The Quest of the Historical Jesus* he wrote a passage that has been quoted again and again, often for the wrong reasons: "He comes to us as One unknown, without a name, as of old, by the lake-side, He came to those men who knew Him not. He speaks to us the same word: 'Follow thou me!' and sets us to the tasks which He has to fulfil for our time. He commands. And to those who obey Him, whether they be wise or simple, He will reveal Himself in the toils, the conflicts, the sufferings which they shall pass through in His fellowship, and as an ineffable mystery, they shall learn in their own experience who He is."[37] It sounds magnificent. "Unknown"—"Without a name"—no wonder it pleased those readers who were dismayed by the clarity of the rest of the book. It seemed that Schweitzer had at last relented and would allow his reader a Jesus who is vague, unfocused, faceless, drifting like a wraith by the water.

But it means nothing of the kind. Schweitzer has simply pulled out the stops of his pulpit oratory for the last few chords of the book. What he is really saying is clear if you add the sentence preceding the quotation: "The names in which men expressed their recognition of Him as such, Messiah, Son of Man, Son of God, have become for us historical parables. We can find no designation which expresses what He is for us."[38] All Schweitzer is saying is that "Messiah" and "Son of God" are now meaningless phrases; our Jesus must do without these titles. The compelling power of his spirit is what remains, dominating the lives of his followers. What then is this power? What exactly was it about the spirit of Jesus that made him so unique, yet so universal? Simply this, that without altering his vision of what the kingdom would be, Jesus totally altered men's vision of what was required to enter it—"the mighty thought underlying the Beatitudes of the Sermon on the Mount, that we come to know God and belong to him through Love."[39] He did not speak of the kingdom because he took that for granted. "The subject of all his preaching is love, and, more generally, the preparation of the heart for the Kingdom."[40]

The unique ethical insight with which Jesus spoke of the preparations needful to bring in God's kingdom—*that* was universal—*that* was divine—Jesus' total understanding of the human heart, of what man must become before the world can be renewed. That, for Schweitzer, was what mattered about Jesus; because regardless of the changing views of the universe or the meaning of God the deepest needs of man and his society remain unaltered. We still yearn for the kingdom of love and peace which has not yet dawned. If it is ever to come, it will always require the same change in men's hearts that Jesus demanded. Therefore we must follow Jesus. So still for us today, "The one important thing is that we be as thoroughly dominated by the idea of the Kingdom as Jesus required his followers to be."[41] . . . "The true understanding of Jesus is the understanding of will acting on will. The true relation to him is to be taken possession of by him. Christian piety of any and every sort is valuable only so far as it means the surrender of our will to his."[42] So Schweitzer wrote in *My Life and Thought* at the age of fifty-six.

His critics want to know how he could write this about a fallible, dead human being. Is it logical to submit one's will to the will of a man two thousand years dead? Perhaps not. One can only say that for Schweitzer truth was a matter of experience and observation, not of logic. It was clear from the evidence that the historical Jesus was dead. It was clear from the evidence that the the spirit of Jesus was alive. Does that seem unreasonable? Schweitzer claimed always that his thought was based on reason (which is not the same as logic). And reason told him that to believe the facts of one's experience, even if they seemed contradictory, was more reasonable than to deny experience because it seemed at first sight unreasonable. Must history and the spirit obey the same laws? If they clearly did not do so, reason must accept that: "Spiritual truth is concerned with the knowledge of what we must become spiritually in order to be in a right relationship to God. It is complete in itself. It is intuitive knowledge of what ought to be in the realm of the spirit. All other knowledge is of a different kind, having to do, not with what happens in us, but with what goes on in the world—a field in which understanding can only be limited and liable to change."[43]

Werner Picht, who knew Schweitzer from the Strasbourg days, and who married into the Curtius family, wrote in his fine book about him, "He is present *in person* in his scholarly writings to an extent which is regarded as quite improper in the scholarly world."[44] In something of the same sense, Nietzsche wrote of his love for what was written with the author's blood; those who wrote with blood, he said, would learn that blood was spirit.

There were overtones to Nietzsche's remark which Schweitzer would have totally rejected—yet he too wrote with his blood. He wrote what his blood told him. He entered by intuition into his subject and then applied reason to what he found. Thus he was saved from both extremes—mindless emotional indulgence and sterile logic. Between the two he held a precarious balance; trusting, Picht says, to a sleepwalker's instinct that skirts precipices. I would prefer to say that he trusted something much more wideawake—a sort of inspired normality. Professors find it hard to understand what Schweitzer means. It is easier for peasants. He was a peasant—born where many opposites meet. However long he took to prove it, what he had to say was always in the end very simple. He returned to the center, where things are real. He was the scholar of the obvious. He is to be trusted because he kept his eyes fixed on the facts, both internal and external, and refused the seductive satisfactions of intellectual consistency.

In a letter to Oskar Kraus, dated February 5, 1926, he wrote,

> In spite of external differences in form, I feel that Jesus' outlook on the world [*Weltanschauung*] is identical with mine in what I would call

the simplicity, the infinity, the heroism of his ethics. Through the outlook on the world and view of life which gradually developed in my
mind, I was able to understand the eschatological views of Jesus and
was thus enabled to do justice to the historical Jesus. What attracts me
so tremendously in him is the simplicity of the rationalism inherent in
his fantastic outlook on the world.

Jesus, in short, reasoned out the implications of his beliefs, however
strange they may be to us, and followed them to the uttermost in simple
faithfulness. And—here the final piece of Schweitzer's theory clicks into
place—it was precisely *because* the end of the world was so near, because
God was so near, that his ethics were the purest ever preached. There was
no need to compromise anymore. In those last few months, love and
goodness could be absolute, with no glance over the shoulder at the
consequences. What though you went hungry or cold, or were beaten or
imprisoned? The reward was in sight, a hundredfold. At the end of the
race you may push the car to its limit. It was precisely because Jesus believed in a mirage that he could be the greatest hero and teacher in history, totally without reservation, therefore totally right. No subsequent doctrine, alloyed by the continuation of history, could match that blazing purity. Thus Jesus was the Lord.

When he was older, Schweitzer would generally evade the question,
"Do you call yourself a Christian?" But once he said, "There are two
sorts of Christians—the dogmatic and the undogmatic. The latter follows
Jesus and accepts none of the doctrines laid down by the early Church or
any other church. That's the sort of Christian I am."

The Churches naturally find it hard to acknowledge such a person as a
Christian at all. But outside the Church's ranks are millions of people.
disillusioned with organized religion, who feel much the same way about
Jesus as Schweitzer did, yet have little intellectual foundation for their
feeling. They may look to Schweitzer for their authority.

Schweitzer's view of Jesus offers us as it were a filter with which we
may separate the temporary from the eternal in Jesus' thoughts. We are
not obliged to accept or reject the package as a whole or to swallow obvious untruths along with deep spiritual understanding. Schweitzer makes it
possible to be a skeptical rationalist and at the same time a disciple of Jesus, without dishonesty.

To found a church would have been the last thing Schweitzer wished to
do. But to reassure millions of individuals that they had as good a right to
their respect and love for Jesus as anyone else—indeed that to meet Jesus
face to face, as individuals, was the only true way—that would have been
his wish.

9

THE DECISION
1902–1904

In the previous chapter we have surveyed most of what Schweitzer wrote and said about Jesus at various periods of his life. It seemed right to do so, because even the ideas which for lack of time were not written down for nearly half a century were already clear in his mind by 1902. And so consistent was he that once we have grasped what he said at twenty-seven, we know fairly accurately what he would have said at any moment in the following sixty-three years.

But a certain change of emphasis occurred as time went on. In the early books, *The Mystery of the Kingdom of God* and *The Quest of the Historical Jesus,* comparatively little stress is laid on Jesus' doctrine of love. What most seems to impress Schweitzer is his heroic stature, the will which measured itself against the end of history. Schweitzer's need for hero worship is expressed in romantic statements such as, "Before that mysterious person . . . we must be forced to lay our faces in the dust, without daring to wish to understand his nature."[1] This is pulpit rhetoric, deeply felt no doubt but carrying still a slightly hollow ring, a touch of Germanic self-abasement; it has little in common with the confident investigations of the rest of the books and the easy assurance of that sermon where Schweitzer speaks of Jesus understanding us "as man to man."

The emphasis on love comes later, in letters, in Schweitzer's autobiography, in the essay on the history of the Church, all written after he had abandoned the academic life and learned in his own person something about the suffering that he recommended as so beneficial.

For now, when *The Mystery of the Kingdom of God* was published, he was still a good and obedient Lutheran pastor and in his sermons we find a much more conventional approach than in the book. Orthodox doctrine is still struggling to work in harness with unorthodox research, and when in February he preached "On the meaning of the death of Jesus," though he says nothing that contradicts his theological findings, the tone is quite different: "He [Jesus] declared that his blood would be shed for many, for the remission of sins. But why and how? He kept silence on this point, that it might remain a mystery, the source of adoration. . . . He indicated what kind of death he was to die, not only to allude to the cross on which his blood was to be shed, but to make us understand the deep and hidden meaning which this holds for us as well." [2]

And about suffering: "To suffer and to endure, this is to feel the clasp of the Lord's hand, the hand who seizes us and encourages us: 'Higher! Always higher!' "[3]

He spoke rather differently of pain when he knew more about it.

In March he was finally inaugurated as *Privat-Dozent* in spite of those two dissenting professors. His inaugural lecture was on St. John, and the new Greek doctrines which John and others were grafting on to the ideas of the young Church in an effort to account for the phenomenon of the Messiah who had never returned. "In the beginning was the Word," declares St. John. No Jew knew of a Messiah who was the Word of God. The very word "logos" is Greek. Jesus was well on his way to becoming a mystical, more-than-human figure.

A sermon Schweitzer preached that May shows vividly how his ideas were moving away from the academic and toward the active. The sermon was about the seventy men whom Jesus sent out to preach the kingdom, and about whom, when they returned exulting in their success, Jesus thanked God who had "hidden these things from the wise and understanding, and revealed them to babes."[4] Schweitzer comments: "Thought and analysis are powerless to pierce the great mystery that hovers over the world and over our existence, but knowledge of the great truths only appears in action and labour."[5] He had always known this. Speculative philosophy had seduced him for a while. Now he was shaking himself free. As he did so his style began to expand from the cramped diction of academic argument into the great natural images that became a hallmark of his mature thought. "Knowledge of life is like a man, sitting at his window, who looks at the flight of the billowing black clouds, chased by the March wind, and says: 'How sad and desolate it is!' And that's as far as he goes. At the same time the farmer, working in the fields, also watches the columns of cloud chased by the wind. But he goes further. He feels the passing of the breath of life, everywhere at work in the universe, the triumphant force of renewal which nothing can hold back. He alone understands the purpose of the March wind."[6]

And then, the deathblow of the intellectuals:

> You all know the name of the philosopher Schopenhauer who tried
> to convince men in his writings that the greatest wisdom was to see in

life nothing but suffering and struggle and distress. I can never open one of his books without asking myself this question: What would have become of him if, instead of retreating with distinction into his ivory tower, far from professional and human contact, he had been forced to take the post of schoolmaster in a poor mountain village, where he would have had the task of turning a haphazard mob of children, with slack habits, into self-respecting men? He would never have written the books that made him famous, never have been surrounded by clouds of incense, nor had the crown of laurels placed on his white locks; but he would have had more understanding; he would have acquired the deep conviction that life is not only a battlefield, but that it is at one and the same time a struggle and a victory.[7]

Here too was a text for Schweitzer the fighter. "'These undying words [of Jesus], 'Rejoice, for your names are enrolled in heaven,' are not spoken to the fortunate nor to those who rest from their labours, but to the combatants, to those whom Jesus Christ has chosen to announce the victory.'"[8]

Schweitzer was turning now to his new hero, Goethe, the odd man out in eighteenth-century philosophy, the man who let speculative thought pass him by and involved himself in every kind of activity, town planning, bridge building, economics, playwriting, poetry, and natural science. Goethe was to have a greater influence on Schweitzer than anyone except Jesus and perhaps St. Paul.

This interest in action was inevitably connected with the abiding problem—what was to be the manner of Schweitzer's service when he reached the age of thirty? He had decided initially to leave it to circumstances to guide him. Circumstance now pointed toward some kind of social service for the poor, an area of need which he constantly encountered.

As in intellectual life, so in social awareness, Strasbourg was very advanced. The central government at Berlin had recently confirmed the appointment of a young and enterprising mayor named Schwander, who had risen from the ranks of local government. He had devised a half-professional, half-amateur organization for the relief of poverty and distress. Simple tasks such as the distribution of food and fuel and the delousing of uncared-for children were entrusted to a corps of volunteers. Where problems were more complicated the paid social workers took over.

Among the volunteers was a group of young people attached to the university. Members of this group also formed the nucleus of the cycle club with which Schweitzer rode out on free days into the country—to explore a castle, to picnic by the river, to gather flowers—though Schweitzer himself preferred to leave the flowers growing where they were. The group included Paul and Adèle, who were living in Strasbourg at the time and with whom Schweitzer lived for a while after his deputy principalship was over. Others were the Münch children, among them Charles, Fritz, and Emma; the Curtius girls, and their literary brother, Ernst Robert; Elly Knapp, daughter of the rector of the university, whose husband, Theodor Heuss, was to became Chancellor of Germany immediately after World War II; and an energetic gray-eyed German-Jewish girl, daughter of a distinguished professor of history—Hélène Bresslau.

Though Hélène's parents were Jewish by blood, her father had severed all connections with the Jewish community and had had his children baptized as Christians. He might even have become a Christian himself, his granddaughter believes, but that his pride and integrity would never let him take a step which might seem to have been motivated by expediency. Like many of the older generation at that time, like Schweitzer's godfather and to some extent like his father, Professor Bresslau could be strict and disapproved of laxity, and to some of the young of Strasbourg he appeared uncomfortably stern. But his granddaughter remembers him as a gentle and kind man.

Hélène's social conscience was almost as highly developed as Schweitzer's and in addition she had enthusiasm, efficiency, and a fine disregard of social convention. She worked among verminous children at a state orphanage. She helped to found and run a home for unmarried mothers, which was not at all a proper thing for nice young ladies to do. She was one of the first women skiers. She played the organ. At a time when young women were taking eagerly to emancipation all over northern Europe, she was as liberated a woman as Strasbourg could offer. And she had decided, like Schweitzer, that she must one day devote herself entirely to social service—only her deadline was the age of twenty-five not thirty. She was four years younger than Schweitzer, almost exactly; so her moment of decision was due a year ahead of his.

All the girls adored Schweitzer, we are told. But Hélène Bresslau, with her practicality and zeal, had more to offer him than most. She offered him criticism instead of flattery and at the dinner party at which it seems they met she asked, "What gives you the courage to go into the pulpit every Sunday and preach in that awful Alsatian dialect? The accent's ugly and the grammar's dreadful." Schweitzer was sufficiently impressed to ask for her help, and before long she was reading his proofs for him, correcting his German and purifying it of some of his cruder Alsatian usages; though some readers, it must be said, prefer those books of his which retain the vigor of the country dialect.

She helped him in other ways too. Her knowledge of the organ—she accompanied the children's services at St. Nicholas'—meant that she knew when and how to pull the stops when he played. In general she made it her business to keep an eye on him, to organize him, and to further his career in the way it should go. Romance was nowhere in the picture however. This was simply the collaboration of two like-minded people—for Schweitzer a great convenience, for Hélène a happy way of furthering her dedication to work; or so it seemed to observers.

By the end of 1902 there was another book on the way. The germ of this one was that conversation between Widor and Schweitzer four years earlier, when Schweitzer explained that the curious progressions and key changes in Bach's cantatas were reflections of the words. Since that time Widor had been troubled that the French had no book about Bach's music, only about his life; and had asked Schweitzer to fill the gap by writing an essay for his pupils at the Conservatoire.

Schweitzer had set about this in the autumn holiday. But in his usual thorough way (and this reflects his German training) he had found himself writing much more than he had intended. It became clear that the essay "would expand into a book about Bach. With good courage I resigned myself to my fate."[9]

He was lucky enough to pick up, very cheap, a set of the complete edition of Bach's music which the Bach Society had been publishing, bit by bit, for the past fifty years—a landmark in the new appreciation of the composer. Armed with this, he set to work.

For once he felt slightly alarmed at his own temerity. He felt himself to be an amateur in musical history and theory. His sole ambition, he explained, was that "as a musician I wanted to talk to other musicians about Bach's music."[10]

But he had something new to say, and knowing what a fighter he was, we are not surprised to find that the book took shape as a challenge. Even the title throws down the gauntlet. *J. S. Bach. The Musician-Poet;* this about a man who was regarded as the most mathematical, least poetical composer ever to dot a crochet.

The musical world was fiercely divided at this time into two main schools, classic and romantic. The romantics loved the sweeping emotionalism of Wagner, Mahler, and Tchaikowski. The classicists defended the formality of Bach, which was supposed to be emotionless, rarefied, and cerebral. Wagner in particular had stirred up violent enthusiasm and equally violent reactions among the writers of the time. Men as different as Baudelaire, Thomas Mann, and Tolstoi found music both fascinating and frightening. Like the sea, it could carry you into deep waters and drown you.

Schweitzer understood and loved the emotional flood. The sound of a great organ at full volume is as overwhelming as any in the world, comparable to the superamplified din of modern pop, which young people use to reach states of cataleptic ecstasy. But he had no fear of it. Nor was he afraid to step between the two warring factions with his assertion that Bach, the idol of the antiromantics, was himself a painter of emotional colors.

Schweitzer, we are beginning to see, was never happier than when taking a lone stand against the consensus of the world. Once he had picked his cause, he always did it the fullest justice. To his own consternation, the book grew and grew, and was not to be ready for nearly two years.

An incidental effect of this book, the first he had to write in French, was to clarify his style. Although the family normally corresponded in French, it was not their native tongue. Alsatian is closer to German, and under German rule the main language taught in the schools was German. Schweitzer found French difficult, its rhythms more exacting.

He came to the conclusion that nobody is truly bilingual. "My own experience makes me think it only self-deception if any believes that he has two mother-tongues. He may think that he is equally master of each, yet it is invariably the case that he actually thinks in only one, and is only in that one really free and creative. If anyone assures me that he has two languages, each as thoroughly familiar to him as the other, I immediately ask him in which of them he counts and reckons, in which he can best give me the names of kitchen utensils and tools used by carpenter or smith, and in which of them he dreams. I have not yet come across anyone who, when thus tested, had not to admit that one of the languages occupied only a second place."

As to the difference between the two languages, "I can best describe it by saying that in French I seem to be strolling along the well-kept paths in a fine park, but in German to be wandering at will in a magnificent forest.

"Always accustomed in French to be careful about the rhythmical arrangement of the sentence, and to strive for simplicty of expression, these things have become equally a necessity to me in German. And now through my work on the French Bach it became clear to me what literary style corresponded to my nature."[11] His criterion once again is a personal one—not the strict correctness wished upon him by Hélène Bresslau.

Hélène's name appears for the first time in the Günsbach visitor's book in the Easter holiday of 1903. The new generation of children there christened her *Tante Anstand*—"Aunt Prim and Proper." With her it was always "Sit up straight," "Wash your hands." They were not entirely at ease, these country Alsatians, with the wellborn German-Jewish lady, however much they admired her classical features and respected her courage in involving herself with Strasbourg's flea-ridden orphans. But they were accustomed by now to entertaining all kinds of notable people, professors and musicians and politicians, as well as students and local folk. No ceremony was observed. Visitors had to take the Schweitzers as they found them. Hélène, at all events, became a regular visitor.

Gustav Anrich, the principal of St. Thomas' college, for whom Schweitzer had briefly deputized in 1901, now moved, only two years later, to a different post. Without opposition, it seems, Schweitzer was elected to take his place. The students, once having had a taste of Schweitzer, were only too delighted to have him back so soon.

"Principal" is perhaps a slightly misleading word. A *Stiftsdirektor* has no administrative functions; he is charged with the direction of students' studies and generally with oversight of their spiritual and mental welfare—a high responsibility for a man of twenty-eight; and one which, had he wished, he could have held for the rest of his life.

On October 1, the start of the new academic year, he moved his belongings into the "roomy and sunny official quarters on the second floor [in Britain, it would be called the first] of the college of St. Thomas"[12]— though even now he still kept his book-littered study for his literary work.

The beautiful new quarters were no match for Schweitzer. Despite a stipend of 2,000 marks a year to add to his curate's pay he had no inclination to change his way of life. The new rooms soon acquired a topsoil of books. All his belongings were kept in a quantity of linen baskets, which served in place of cupboards and chests. There was a grand piano, littered with scores of his favorite composers—Bach, Wagner, Mendelssohn, Widor, César Franck—on which at a moment's notice he would expound, with illustrations, the inner significance of anything from a Bach cantata to the whole of Wagner's *Tristan*.

As principal he seemed almost like one of the students. He ate in the students' dining hall, and he was at their disposal at any time. A standard nickname for principals—slightly disrespectful—was "Popel." Nobody ever called Schweitzer *Popel. Popel* was for "them"—the superiors—and Schweitzer was not like that.

He taught Greek and Hebrew, and twice a week directed a course on the Old and New Testaments. With these, and his curate's duties, and the book on Bach, he was again working late into the night—sometimes till 7:30 in the morning. Then he would tell the maid to keep the students quiet and take two or three hours' sleep while she kept watch.

He never needed to be roused. He could wake himself at any time. Like many of those who work exceptionally hard, he knew how to take catnaps. Sometimes in the middle of a discussion he would say, "I'm tired. Come back in twenty minutes." He would sleep for twenty minutes and wake of his own accord, fresh for hours more.

This was enough to earn the students' respect. What earned their love was that in the midst of it all, if any of them was sick or in trouble, he would come to their room at any hour of the day or night and ask what he could do.

Only two years were left in which to decide what he was to do with the rest of his life. The teacher in him directed his attention to children first. One plan, which would seem likely to have involved the collaboration of Hélène Bresslau, was for adopting a number of orphaned or abandoned children and educating them himself. Thus he would have virgin soil in which to implant his ideas about life; and along with them he would implant his own sense of indebtedness, so that the children would grow up to care for other derelict children in their turn; a self-perpetuating form of kindness.

Whether in fact he would have succeeded in imbuing others with the gratitude that came naturally to him is a matter for doubt. Human beings do not seem notably grateful for charity. But if anything could have done it, it would have been his faith and optimism, his trust in man's hidden goodness.

His feelings about gratitude come out clearly in a sermon he preached some fifteen years later, when he spoke of the Biblical story of the ten lepers whom Jesus healed, only one of whom returned to thank him. For Schweitzer this did not prove that the other nine were ungrateful—he was sure that they never forgot what they owed to Jesus. But they were forgetful, too taken up with their delight and the excitement of their families to express their thankfulness. The trouble with neglecting to express one's gratitude was that it made men believe that kindness was pointless. It "paralyses moral action in the world."[13]

Even those of us who feel, with Schweitzer, that people are basically good are often afraid to say so openly or to put the belief into action. It leaves us vulnerable, we feel, exposed to exploitation. So we in turn cover up the good that we feel, and the vicious circle continues. One of Schweitzer's great gifts was his readiness to stand unprotected by cynicism. And in the end he gained from it far more than he lost.

However, in this particular instance it was never put to the test, for he could find no organization that was prepared to accept his assistance. We sometimes suppose that stuffy bureaucracy is a recent development; but stuffy bureaucracy and nothing else crushed Schweitzer's first sorties into the world of charitable action. "For example, when the Strasbourg orphanage was burnt down I offered to take in a few boys, for the time being, but the Superintendent did not even allow me to finish what I had to say."[14] Knowing something of his temper, we can guess at the feelings which made him remember that incident so clearly when, twenty-seven years later, he wrote of it in his autobiography.

But though he made strenuous efforts to find other channels for his service, such as the welfare of tramps and ex-convicts, Schweitzer was constantly aware that something independent in him was restless for a task that was his alone. He realized that the welfare work he engaged in needed the resources of an organization—and he was a loner, a soloist, anything but an organization man, however worthy the organization. He needed the space to stretch his wings, freedom to work at his own pace and in his own way. Call it arrogance, which it was in a sense; or romanticism, hungering for something grander than the benevolent societies of Strasbourg could offer; or heroism, which some have called it—in the end it was simply an instinct that guided him unerringly past the blind alleys where his talents would have been smothered and kept him waiting until the right road opened ahead.

> One morning in the autumn of 1904 I found on my writing-table in the College one of the green-covered magazines in which the Paris Missionary Society reported every month on its activities. A certain Miss Scherdlin used to put them there knowing that I was specially interested in this Society on account of the impression made on me by the letters of one of its earliest missionaries, Casalis by name, when my father read them aloud at his missionary services during my childhood. That evening in the very act of putting it aside that I might go on with my work, I mechanically opened this magazine, which had been laid on my table during my absence. As I did so, my eye caught the title of an article: "The needs of the Congo Mission."
>
> It was by Alfred Boegner, the President of the Paris Missionary Society, an Alsatian, and contained a complaint that the Mission had not enough workers to carry on its work in the Gabon, the northern province of the Congo Colony. The writer expressed his hope that his appeal would bring some of those "on whom the Master's eyes already rested" to a decision to offer themselves for this urgent work. The conclusion ran: "Men and women who can rely simply to the Master's call, 'Lord, I am coming,' those are the people whom the Church needs." The article finished, I quietly began my work. My search was over.[15]

With the deadline only three months ahead, the quiet mechanism of instinct had finally found the road.

10

BACH

1904–1905

STILL he said nothing about his imminent change of course. He went about his work as though nothing had happened or was going to happen. There must have been times, when plans for the future were being discussed in the college or the church, that caused him some embarrassment. But he was not going to make his decision public until the details were clear in his mind. His instinctive fear of the opposition of his friends (justified, as it turned out) was reinforced by the example of St. Paul, who after his conversion to Jesus "did not confer with flesh and blood," and waited three years before getting in touch with the disciples. But his main reason was simply that "I am by nature very uncommunicative as to everything that concerns my personal life. I have to make an effort to be articulate to others."[1]

Only one person—"one trustworthy friend"[2]—knew what he was planning. He never named this friend, and indeed when Hermann Hagedorn included in his inquiries the specific question, "Who was the trustworthy friend?" Schweitzer replied, "This is unimportant. Permit me not to answer it."[3]

Yet the friend was important enough for Schweitzer to mention his—or her—existence in his autobiography; important enough also for the identity to need keeping secret. We might guess it was Hélène Bresslau; but would he not have said so, since she was to become his wife? Or Adèle Herrenschmidt, with whom he spent those quiet holidays in Grimmialp?

In fact the clue seems to lie in the introduction to Werner Picht's book, *The Life and Thought of Albert Schweitzer*. There, in an oblique and modest passage, Picht describes himself as "The man who, as a youth, sat at the feet of the preacher of St. Nicholas' Church at Strasbourg, who sat at his side at the desk in Günsbach when *Bach* was written, who drew the stops for him at the ancient Silbermann organ of St. Thomas's in Strasbourg, who was with him when his decision to go into the wilderness was first conceived, and who accepted it at once as a matter of course. . . . ''⁴

Though this cannot be called absolutely conclusive it seems hard to avoid the implication that the trustworthy friend was indeed Picht. And it is not hard to guess why Schweitzer wanted his name kept secret when we read in the autobiography, ''Almost more than with my contemplated new start itself [my friends] reproached me with not having shown them so much confidence as to discuss it with them first. With this side issue they tormented me beyond measure during those difficult weeks.''⁵ Schweitzer, in short, was protecting his trustworthy friend against the jealousy of all the others.

Two Sundays before his birthday was the Feast of Epiphany, the day devoted to the celebration of missionary work. None of those who heard Schweitzer's sermon on this occasion—except perhaps one—knew that what they were listening to was an announcement of his intentions and a discussion of his reasons. From the pulpit he could speak openly of his secret plan, and even those who knew him well had no means of knowing what he was telling them. Afterward, looking back, we can understand.

The sermon is a long one. I have picked out, as it were, the themes. For at this crucial moment all the major themes of his life come together, as at the climax of a great fugue—the theme of human compassion; the theme of devotion to Jesus; the theme of the degeneracy of civilization; the theme of fascination with faraway lands; the theme of action; the theme of simplicity.

He was to make his life his argument. But now the argument is still in words. And here it is, the *apologia pro vita sua;* in this magnificent sermon he gives an account of his life not after he has lived it, but before. And nobody knew what he was doing.

Jesus said to them; ''I will make you fishers of men''—this was the text. Other festivals, says Schweitzer, look backward to past events. But this festival is one ''when we look straight ahead of us, when it is not the past that we summon, but the present hour and the future, and when we prepare ourselves to face the tasks of tomorrow.'' He goes on to look at missions as they are, with an undeceived eye.

> Missions are not popular; you have no more illusions on that subject than I have. . . . Recently in Paris a generous donor said in my presence to a lady who was collecting: ''You can always call on me. My door and my purse are always wide open. But never in any circumstances ask me for anything for Missions—not a farthing. It's money thrown out of the window.'' As for me, I have argued so much, I have broken so many lances on behalf of Missions, by sea and by land, in coach and train, mountain and plain, with friends and strangers, that I

know pretty well all the objections that people bring against them. . . .

The first objection, endlessly repeated, is this: we must leave those races their religions, we must not go to them and take away the beliefs which have kept them happy hitherto, for that does nothing but disturb their spirit. To that I reply: "For me, a mission does not concern itself primarily or exclusively with religion. Far from it! It is above all a task of humanity, which neither our governments nor our peoples have understood. . . ."

What is it our governments and our peoples think of when they look beyond the seas? They think of the lands which they will take, as they say, under their sovereign protection, which they can attach to themselves in one way or another; they think of what they can seize from them for their own greater profit. . . . Our States, these States so confident of their high civilisation, come to grief there. They are nothing more than predators. Where in these highly civilised nations are the workmen, the craftsmen, the teachers, the wise men, the doctors, who will go to those distant lands and do the work of civilisation? Where can one see our society undertake some effort in this direction? Nowhere, absolutely nowhere!

The only true civilisation consists in living as a disciple of Jesus, for whom every human being is a person who has a right to our help and our sacrifice. . . .

Ah, fine civilisation, which can talk in such edifying terms of human dignity and the rights of man, and which at the same time mocks and tramples on human dignity and the rights of man among the millions of beings whose only crime is living overseas, having skin of another colour, and being unable to manage their affairs singlehanded. . . .

If anyone were to ask me why I think Christianity is the unique religion, dominating all the others, I will happily throw in the dustbin everything we have been taught about the relationship between religions, about the hierarchical structure, about the criterion of excellence, and I will only hold on to one thing: that in the first command the Lord gave on earth, a single word stands out: the word "man." He does not speak of religion, faith, the soul or anything else, only about "men." "Come, I will make you fishers of men."

In short, Missions are nothing but an expiation for the violence committed far away by nations that call themselves Christian.[6]

By today's standard what he says could be called paternalistic. He sees the black races as poor, distressed, needing help; and the true Christian as the benefactor who from his abundance can offer health, education, an improvement of life. But the word "paternalistic " begs too many questions to be useful. The question to ask is whether Schweitzer's words were true; they were. Were his motives sincere? They were. Did he place the responsibility and the blame where they belonged? He did. There is nothing patronizing about his attitude. To say what he said about white imperialism, when he said it, from a pulpit, was as enlightened, courageous, and far-sighted as it was possible to be at that time. Seventy years later the great mass of Europeans have still not caught up with him.

In these same days, leading up to his birthday, he was sitting for a portrait. He had handed over a room in his official residence on St. Thomas' Quay to a painter friend who needed a studio—Ada von Erlach, sister-in-law of that Frederick Curtius whose mother kept open house for the academics of Berlin. Ada had recently had a serious operation, halting though not curing a fatal disease, presumably a cancer. Her aged mother, the Countess von Erlach, lived with Frederick in Strasbourg—a wise old lady who had been the governess of a grand duchess. Schweitzer was treated as a member of the family, and to solace the old lady for not being able to get out any longer to concerts, played the piano to her for an hour every evening. In return she took him in hand and helped him, so he says, "to round off many a hard angle in my personality."[7]

It was the old countess who persuaded Schweitzer to sit for his portrait to Ada, hoping that by getting back to her painting she would gain a fresh interest in life which would help her back to health.

The last of these sittings happened to fall on January 14, 1905—Schweitzer's thirtieth birthday. Sitting there motionless—not his favorite occupation—he had plenty of time to face the implications of his decision. He was "like the man in the parable who 'desiring to build a tower first counts the cost whether he have wherewith to complete it.' "[8]

What was the cost? First and most obviously the loss of his job, his respected place in the university, his friends, the whole happy life he had built up, for which he had worked so hard; above all the loss of his music—the concerts in Strasbourg, the happy spells in Paris, the daily practice, the Sunday services, the freedom of the organs of Europe. What he was going to do could be seen as a continuation, in a way, of his pastoral and even his theological work. But music must be lost. And music, to a man who rested so little, *was* his rest—his balm, his solace, his relaxation. That would really be hard to leave.

There were more practical considerations. For several reasons it seemed better not to think of going to Africa as an ordinary missionary. The steady veering of his thoughts toward practical action, his disenchantment with theory, with words, urged him toward something different. Besides, he had enough experience of what the average Christian divine thought of his theology to doubt whether missionaries would find him particularly suitable as a preacher to the heathen. The Paris Mission Society had always been his father's favorite, because it was less inclined than most to talk in "the sugary language of Canaan";[9] there was an exceptional liberality about their attitude. But even so Schweitzer thought them likely to balk at his ideas.

On the other hand the society desperately needed medical help. The missionaries on the spot were constantly reporting their distress at the physical condition of the Africans who came to them. As a medical missionary surely he would be acceptable. Active, practical, merciful—everything pointed to this as Schweitzer's field of work, except that he knew no medicine.

He was thirty years old. How long would it take to learn? Could he learn it, starting so late in life? Could he face the effort of starting from the beginning in a totally new field? Such were the costs he had to count.

By the end of his birthday the decision was made. He would step down from professor to student at the start of the next university year, when the medical course began; and in due course offer his services as a doctor to the Paris Mission Society. The prospect was daunting. But the will which he had already trained to ignore the laughter of schoolfellows, exhaustion, the disapproval of theological colleagues, was equal to the new challenge. Still, however, he would tell no one what he intended. He must cross the river and set the boats on fire first. Then there would be no going back.

For another nine months he worked secretly at his plans, going about his many occupations as before.

The Bach book was finished. He had been sending the chapters one by one to Widor as he wrote them and in October the previous year, with the end in sight, he had asked Widor to supply the introduction he had promised. Widor, holidaying in Venice, promptly obliged. Schweitzer could hardly have asked for a more enthusiastic recommendation:

"Better than all the speeches in the world, the pages you are about to read will show the power of Bach's extraordinary brain, for they will give you examples and proofs. . . .

"As we read Monsieur Schweitzer's book, it seems to us that we are present at the inauguration of a monument; the last scaffolds, the last veils have fallen; we walk around the statue to study its details, then we withdraw a little to a point from which our eyes can survey the whole; and then we pass our judgement upon it."[10]

Although the book disagreed with most current opinion about Bach and trod on a few toes in so doing, the musicians were more generous than the theologians had been. Schweitzer had only intended to fill a gap in the musical education of French students—he had not felt qualified to do more. But the combination of scholarship and insight in the book attracted attention in Germany as well, and he was soon asked for a translation. What with one thing and another it was a year or more before he found time to attend to this commission, and when he did, he found that the difference between the two languages made a simple translation impossible. He would have to begin afresh.

Let us break the chronology of the story and consider the German version now. For although it turned out to be nearly twice as long, everything in it was already in his head when he wrote the French version. The scale of the project was all that had changed. And perhaps one can detect a slightly less reverent note in the later book (on which the English translation is based) as though the company of medical students had rubbed away a faint trace of pastoral respectability in Schweitzer's outlook and left him freer to look without alarm at his hero's foibles and failings.

When the time came to begin the new version he found it hard to get down to it. This was cold meat reheated, and he still had trouble concentrating on what did not catch his interest. The impulse to start finally came at Bayreuth, in the summer of 1906. He returned exhilarated to his hotel room after a particularly exciting performance of *Tristan* and found that at last the words were beginning to come. Once started, that evening in the Black Horse Inn at Bayreuth, "while the babel of voices surged up from the Bierhalle below, into my stuffy room,"[11] he wrote all night and on past sunrise.

The English translation (beautifully done by Ernest Newman in 1911) runs to two volumes and 926 pages; and Bach is not even born until page 99. In his usual thorough way Schweitzer has led up to his subject by going into the history of German music that produced his hero, and an account of the extraordinary musical family into which he was born. In the French version this is much more sketchily dealt with, but in the long run the long-winded German method pays great dividends in understanding; partly because Schweitzer by now was writing so well that length is not matched by tedium.

The next 125 pages are devoted to Bach's life—another forty to the cause of his reputation since his death—and the rest of volume one to a detailed survey of the instrumental works and the proper manner of playing them.

The first part of volume two goes into Bach's approach to writing for the voice. Here we come to the controversial part of the book—the argument that Bach is essentially a painter of pictures in his music, different motifs in the music representing specific images; dragging footsteps, placid water, storms, steep ascent or headlong downfall; that he deliberately and brilliantly illustrates the main theme of the words he is setting to music; and that he was happiest and most successful with words whose image was strong and clear. The argument is chiefly directed at Philipp Spitta, who had recently published the first full biography of Bach. Spitta's historical work was admirable, particularly in view of the scarcity of information about Bach, and Schweitzer made good use of it. But Spitta was a leader of the fashionable view that Bach's work was at the opposite pole to the descriptive composers, Berlioz, Schubert, Wagner, and obeyed only the pure laws of music; in short that Bach was, as the phrase has it, "the celestial sewing-machine." Spitta believed that the occasion when the music of a cantata seemed pictorial were subconscious accidents, to be ignored by the listener. Though how anyone could ignore for example, the desperate, heartbroken wail in the *St. Matthew Passion* that tells of Peter's remorse at betraying Jesus, when he "wept bitterly," is hard to understand.

Schweitzer believed that these descriptive elements were of the essence of the music; and moreover that proper performance was impossible until the performer had understood the pictorial purpose of the writing. With enormous care Schweitzer goes into the precise function of tied phrases, staccato notes, and so forth, showing how these build up the detailed rhythmical pattern that sets the scene. The whole vitality of this sort of music depends on this wealth of delicate and precise detail, rather than on the emotive masses of sound, swelling crescendos, dramatic climaxes, and tapering diminuendos of composers from Beethoven onward.

In one fascinating chapter on art in general, Schweitzer suggests that whatever medium they may work in, all artists experience the same artistic impulse. Their particular talent dictates how this impulse is expressed, whether in music, poetry, or the pictorial arts. This being so, he says, we often find a painter whose vision is poetic—even perhaps narrative; another whose painting is closer to music. A poet may be half musician or half painter. And a musician may paint pictures in his music, or may on the other hand evoke the emotional overtones of poetry. For Schweitzer, Bach was the painter, dealing in tableaux; Wagner was the poet, creating in the mind not visual images but flooding sensations.

Perhaps these classifications of the different types of artist and musician are too precise. Perhaps we can accept here the charge that was brought against Schweitzer's views on Jesus—that he pushes the argument too far. For, as he says himself, all writing about art is imprecise and subjective, incapable of either proof or disproof. Statements about art are oblique; they have the nature of parables. But even if we find it impossible to go along with Schweitzer all the way, this section of the book is full of stimulating ideas and insights, and well worth reading on its own. (I find myself using here almost exactly the same terms as critics who wrote about *The Quest of the Historical Jesus.* This suggests that they thought of the Gospels as some sort of art form, about which one could be stimulating, imprecise and above all subjective; whereas Schweitzer, as a historian, was trying to be objective and asking others to make the same effort.)

The 400 pages which conclude the second volume, in which Schweitzer deals exhaustively with all Bach's vocal works, are not for the general
readers, though they form a marvelous work of reference and the writers of
the blurbs on record jackets still regularly quote what he had to say about
this cantata or that motet. It is not hard to see why. No one before or since
has combined such extensive technical knowledge with such esthetic insight, enthusiasm, and power to express himself.
One typical example must suffice:

> The other alto cantata, Widerstehe doch der Sünde (No. 54) begins
> with an alarming chord of the seventh—

> The trembling of the basses and violas, and the sighs of the violins, be-
> tween them give the movement a somewhat disturbing effect. It is
> meant to depict the horror of the curse upon sin that is threatened in the
> text. Of a similar character is the aria "Wer Sünde tut, der ist vom
> Teufel" (The sinner is of the devil). It is strict trio between the voice,
> the violas and the violins. The theme runs thus—

> Harmonically the movement is of unparalleled harshness.
> The opening aria of the solo cantata for tenor, "Ich armer Mensch,
> ich Sündenknecht" (No. 55) is, as a rule, phrased so inanimately that
> the whole sense of the despairing wail is lost. The characteristic accent
> should fall on the second beat. The orchestra must phrase thus—

> This passage—

should be played with a strong crescendo, the last quaver being always heavily accented in contradiction to the beat, thus obstructing the rhythm, as it were. This motive belongs to the words "Ich geh' vor Gottes Angesicht mit Furcht und Zittern zum Gerichte" (I go in fear and trembling into the presence of God). It suggests painful striving, as in the theme of the introduction to the cantata "Herr, gehe nicht ins Gericht" (No. 105), of which it strongly reminds us.[12]

Perhaps what is most impressive in this book is the extraordinary memory and the concentration which seems able to seize on so many facets of a subject—historical, esthetic, technical, and human—all at once. Bach is seen simultaneously as a man, gentle and friendly, but capable of meanness and bad temper and chronically unable to control his pupils; as a historical climax to a whole musical movement; as a virtuoso keyboard player (his chief, almost his only fame in his own day); as a supreme artist, who paid so little heed to his own talent that his manuscripts were never properly preserved, and their classification is still in a state of chaos; and as a mystic, whose passionate, almost morbid attachment to Jesus and to the death which would unite him to his Lord was in a totally separate compartment from the contented family life of a man who liked the good things of the world and knew the value of money.

The historical element is vital, for it was not only Schweitzer's musical insight that led him to the pictorial function in Bach. Reaching back into the eighteenth century, he was simply disinterring a musical language, commonplace then, which the nineteenth century had buried. Bach was one of a school of composers which "took for itself by preference the title of 'expressive' (*affektvoll*) in distinction from all others, meaning to indicate thereby that its purpose was graphic characterisation and realism. Although our musical aestheticians must have known this—for the histories of music testify sufficiently to it—they made no attempt to examine the music of that epoch thoroughly and to enquire what light it might throw on the nature of the art, but took the line of sweeping aside these phenomena as merely transitory pathological perversion of pure music."[13]

At the very beginning of the nineteenth century one man, Johann Nicolaus Forkel, a musical historian, wrote of Bach as "the greatest musical poet and greatest musical rhetorician that has ever existed, and probably that ever will exist."[14] But his voice was barely heard in the surrounding silence, the mood of reaction which found Bach simply old-fashioned.

Another twenty years were to pass before the great rediscovery began and thirty more before it was really under way. But even then the words of Forkel were not taken seriously. Schweitzer's steady perseverance, his relentless amassing of detailed evidence, were necessary before people could again see Bach as he saw himself—an "expressive" man.

As we have noted, though Schweitzer was so unforthcoming about his own private affairs, he had no qualms about investigating Bach's daily life. In the French version he laments: "Unfortunately we possess very few details about Bach's intimate life, about the husband and the father of a family."[15] And in the German version he writes of "the shameless curiosity that characterises our boasted historical sense."[16] That he condoned this curiosity in himself may make us easier about our curiosity toward him.

Amusing to note other parallels between Bach and himself: "The other deliverances upon him [Bach] run on general lines of admiration and amazement and rhetorical analogies from ancient mythology. . . . We would gladly exchange all these for a single sentence of someone who, at the first performance of the St. Matthew Passion, had an intuition of the real spirit of Bach's music."[17] We suffer in the same way from the unthinking adulation of Schweitzer. How accurately, too, Schweitzer describes himself in these words about Bach: "He is one of those rare personalities that do not become, but always are."[18] We see the practical Schweitzer emerging from the academic when he writes:

> Bach was self taught, and as such had an aversion to all learned theories. Clavier-playing, organ-playing, harmony, composition,—he had learnt them all by himself; his sole teachers had been untiring work and incessant experiment.
>
> To a man who had made the fundamental rules of art his own in this manner, many theories that were interesting or new for others were a matter of indifference, for he had been to the roots of things. Now Bach lived in the epoch when it was thought that the perfect art could be discovered by aesthetic reasoning, while others, again, thought that salvation for music lay in mathematical speculations upon the numbers that underlie intervals. To all these endeavours Bach opposed a robust indifference."[19]

And we can see the sort of humor that pleased Schweitzer in his obvious enjoyment of the anecdotes he relates. Bach's tightfistedness amused him so much that he mentions three times the letter in which Bach wrote: "My position here is worth about 700 thalers, and when there are rather more funerals than usual the perquisites increase proportionately; but if the air is healthy the fees decrease, last year, for example, being more than 100 thalers below the average from funerals."[20] "He cannot help showing," says Schweitzer, "his indignation over the healthy year 1729, when the Leipzigers took so little pleasure in dying that the burial fees brought the cantor a hundred thalers less than usual."[21]

A close link between author and subject was Bach's dislike of working under the imposition of a governing body. At St. Thomas', Leipzig, Bach was answerable to both the church council and the consistory. But arguments broke out between the two bodies about his responsibilities. "We cannot say," says Schweitzer, "that Bach suffered from this tension. It ministered admirably to his own need for independence, for he played the consistory off against the council and the council against the consistory, and the meanwhile did what he liked."[22]

These personal notes enliven the long learnedness of the book. Schweitzer never forgot the man behind the masterpieces. But above everything else what attracted Schweitzer about Bach was his religion. All Bach's technical skill, like all Schweitzer's, went to serve an overriding mystical purpose. Things must be done beautifully because that was the clearest, most unencumbered path to the vision of eternity. It is worth noting in this connection that however much Schweitzer loved and admired Mozart and Beethoven (and we know that he did), the Protestant composers delighted him most; Bach, Mendelssohn, Wagner—as unlikely a trio as you could assemble, in style and talent. They are united only by a specifically religious mystical fervor which was not in the nature of Mozart or Beethoven, greater though they were than Wagner and immeasurably superior to Mendelssohn. Indeed, if it were not for Bach we would have to say that Schweitzer's musical taste was almost deplorably romantic. The truth is that whatever his esthetic insight he ultimately valued the intention, the mystical frame of mind, quite as much as the achievement.

Though most of the technical sections of the Bach book are to be skipped by any but practicing musicians, one of the side issues is of great general interest—both in itself and because it shows that Schweitzer had already reached conclusions which he only published in full a good deal later. It concerns the type of bow which Bach had in mind for the soloists in his violin works.

It was not until 1932 that he returned to this subject, in an article entitled "The Round Bow" in the *Schweitzerische Musikzeitung*. But here in the Bach book we find him already hot on the trail.

Compositions for stringed instruments often include chords as well as single notes. The only way to play a chord of more than two notes on a modern violin with a modern bow is by playing the notes in quick succession, altering the angle of the bow to touch one string after another. The chord thus becomes a sort of arpeggio. But the word "bow" now means exactly that—a bow; a curved piece of wood with a string stretched between the ends, held taut by the spring in the wood. This was the early musical bow, as can be seen in paintings of the time. By Bach's day the straighter bow, with a screw for tightening the strings, was coming into use. But the old bow was still in evidence, and Schweitzer was convinced that Bach had the old bow in mind when he wrote chords. For the strings of a bow of this kind, pressed firmly down across the strings of a violin, will give a little, so that they are touching all the strings of the instrument at once, and can play a simultaneous chord.

The straight bow, its strings screwed tighter than the old bow could ever be, has a brighter, more piercing tone, and can fill a larger hall. By comparison the old bow produced a softer, mellower sound. You can reproduce the tone of an old bow, said Schweitzer, by unstringing a modern one, turning it upside down, and restringing it with the strings above the violin strings and the wood under the neck of the violin. Draw this across the strings and you get an ideal of Bach's violin tone.

A Norwegian named Ole Bull, who had died as recently as 1880, had played with a round bow. But Schweitzer never heard a bow of this kind being used properly until 1929. Nobody was prepared to sacrifice the strength of tone produced by a modern bow—or to learn the complicated technique of using the thumb to tighten and relax the tension of the bowstrings.

Schweitzer's constant insistence on old organs and old bows was accompanied by a dislike of modern pianos, at any rate for Bach's music. To his ears all the later developments had added power at the expense of beauty. The accusation often leveled at him that he lived in the past and was not interested in the present or future is only true to this extent, that his historical sense enabled him to feel the pulse of a bygone culture, to live imaginatively within it, more completely than most of us, who observe it only from outside.

The pulse of the eighteenth century was very different from our own. But it is reasonable to suppose that a mind tuned to that pulse would be in a better position than most of us to compare old sounds and new. Schweitzer's experiments with Marie Jaëll and Carl Stumpf showed that he was far from reactionary. He had listened more widely and carefully than most men of his day. He never advocated a return to the imperfect techniques and instruments of a past age. All he asked was that modern ingenuity should seek ways of preserving and increasing beauty, not destroying it.

What would he have thought of the way in which Bach has recently become the darling of pop groups and been synthezised on an electronic organ? Bach's vitality fortunately lifts him clear of the clutch of his less discriminating admirers, but it must be said that some of them leave him temporarily a little bruised.

The campaign which Schweitzer launched a little later for his kind of organ has very largely been won. The harpsichord and other keyboard instruments which pluck rather than strike the strings have found a new popularity since Schweitzer's time. But the round bow is still as dead as the dodo and shows no signs of resurrection.

The accusation against all three of them was of softness, gentleness, a lack of volume that made them unable to be heard properly in a large concert hall. Perhaps another technical innovation can solve this problem. Electronic amplification need not always be crude and unmusical. Sensitively amplified, the sound of a clavichord can fill any hall, or can be heard on records in the intimacy of one's own home. Perhaps with this help the round bow too will come back into its own.

While he was working on the book, Cosima Wagner came to stay in Strasbourg with her daughter Eva. She had heard about Schweitzer's new views on Bach and wanted to learn more of them; so Schweitzer accompanied her as she walked about Strasbourg, and played for her on the organ of the Temple Neuf.

Hitherto he had only met the great lady at Heidelberg, when she was imperiously receiving visitors after a concert. Now they got to know each other better, and Schweitzer was bowled over by her as by none of the young women of Strasbourg. Christian Brandt remembers the casual pride with which Schweitzer introduced her when they met accidentally on the college stairs. And she in her turn must have been impressed by the intense and knowledgeable young man, for when he went to visit her in her declining years after the war the news of his arrival put her into such a flutter that she was unable to see him.

Schweitzer's theories about music were born of practical experience. And in turn the theories bore practical results. A new organ was required for his church, St. Nicholas', and as we may imagine the design incorporated many of his ideas. The stops and the couplings were planned as a compromise between the French and the German systems, aiming at the fullest flexibility combined with simplicity of operation. The result seems to have been most successful, and it must have delighted him enormously to see his notions taking physical shape. The new design cost only marginally more than a conventional one would have done; a point he stresses in writing about it, for many churches were being seduced by the cheapness of the "factory" organs which were beginning to dominate the organ-building world, in which smart complicated consoles were featured at the cost of inferior metal in the pipes and corner-cutting in quality all around. The treasurer of St. Nicholas' was no doubt breathing down Schweitzer's neck, and it must have been a relief to both of them that the custom-built instrument performed as anticipated and still only added 200 marks to the bill.

Meantime, in Paris Schweitzer had banded together with several of his musical friends and associates to found a new society—the Paris Bach Society. The leading light was the conductor Gustave Bret, but he was supported by Widor, Guilmant, Gabriel Fauré, Vincent d'Indy, Paul Dukas, and Schweitzer himself, a cross section of French music that excluded only the two greatest names of all—Debussy and Ravel.

They met in Widor's rooms at the Conservatoire and Schweitzer's function, apart from contributing to the interpretation of the music, was to play the organ accompaniment at the society's concerts and to write their program notes, a few of which survive.

It is interesting sometimes to note the things Schweitzer did *not* write about, the people he apparently did not find important. Debussy, though a very different composer from Wagner, feminine and sensitive in his music where Wagner is aggressively masculine, followed closely in Wagner's footsteps as a composer of the music of "sensations"; and his friendships with Mallarmé and Gide, and the direct influence he had on Impressionist painters, helped him to fulfill in his own way Wagner's demand for a linking and unity of all the arts. Yet Schweitzer never mentions him. The reason, I feel sure, is temperamental. The "softness" of Debussy (and of the Impressionists) was not for him.

The planning of the Paris Bach Society's concerts naturally involved a good deal of correspondence. Schweitzer was already a good and reliable letter writer, but his previous activities had never stimulated such a volume of correspondence as began now. The society was one cause, the book another. Congratulations, questions, and challenges began to pour in. It was as well he had no idea how this correspondence would increase, how nearly it would overwhelm him as his name became known in other, wider spheres.

In the summer of this year Schweitzer discovered that his students, studying the life of Jesus, had been given no idea what previous work had been done on the subject. It so happened that the university library was uniquely well equipped with relevant books and other material, and Schweitzer, after consulting his old mentor Holtzmann, decided to lecture on the subject. "I attacked the work with zeal, but the material took such a hold of me that when I had finished the course of lectures I became absolutely absorbed in it."[23] So began *The Quest of the Historical Jesus.*

At the same time something else needed winding up—his conclusions about organ building must be made public before he vanished into his new life. With so little time left, he went at the two things like a whirlwind—the booklet which was, in the long run, to change the face of organ construction; and the huge tome, with its wealth of learning, which was to land rather like a dud shell in the battlefields of theology.

Within six months he had virtually completed both—and this despite preaching, despite lecturing, despite concerts in Paris, despite duties at the church and in the college—and despite an explosive fistful of letters which he slipped into a Paris letterbox one October day of 1905 announcing to his unsuspecting family and friends that "at the beginning of the winter term I should enter myself as a medical student, in order to go later on to Equatorial Africa as a doctor."[24] Another letter resigned his post as principal of St. Thomas' college. There could no longer be time for those responsibilities. He makes a point of the date in his autobiography. Knowing how he disliked superstition, it is tempting to wonder if this was some kind of defiant gesture—except that even this could seem to give superstition more than its due. But, for the record it was Friday the thirteenth.

11

MEDICAL STUDIES
1905–1908

HIS mother seems to have been the hardest hit. She had defended him in his dreamy days and encouraged his ambitions. She had watched the seeds she planted in him burst into an unheard-of flowering. Her passion for knowledge and novelty had become in him an unremitting search for truth, saluted by great men. How she must have basked in the praise and admiration he constantly provoked! There seemed to be nothing to prevent him going higher and higher, conquering one territory after another. And now this! All of it was wasted on a quixotic, self-destructive impulse. She made efforts to understand and to hide her disappointment and disapproval, but she was never reconciled.

Whatever support he may have hoped for or expected from friends and relatives was not forthcoming. As is the manner of friends, they resented not having been taken into his confidence. No doubt they felt betrayed that this frank and cheerful companion could have chatted and joked with them and yet kept so great a project, the best of himself perhaps, hidden from them. It was bad enough that he was going, throwing away God's gifts, but could he not at least have consulted them first? Most of us have found to our cost that our friends think they know better than we do what is good for us. Schweitzer was no exception, and it was a very shrewd instinct indeed that told him to leave his great plan gestating, nine years and nine months, before he revealed it, fully formed, to his startled friends. He was dismayed to find that the theological friends were the least understanding of all. He quoted the precedent of St. Paul, and the three silent years he had spent before declaring his conversion. But they seemed not to be able to see things as simply as Schweitzer himself. St. Paul had not had to throw away such gifts, such achievementts.

Widor told Schweitzer he was "like a general who wanted to go into the firing line with a rifle."[1] A lady, of whom Schweitzer says only that she was "filled with the modern spirit," demonstrated that he could do more for the Africans by lecturing than by action. She told him that "that saying from Goethe's Faust 'In the beginning was the deed' was now out of date—today propaganda was the mother of happenings."[2] The modern spirit has evidently altered very little in the last sixty-five years.

And Elly Knapp, the enterprising young lady who with Hélène Bresslau was to startle respectable citizens by running a home for unmarried mothers, was surprised, looking back, that they all had been so little aware of Schweitzer's qualities. "We students," she wrote, "were unmercifully critical of one another."[3]

So this was a traumatic time for Schweitzer. The simple confidence that friends who knew the Gospels must understand what he was doing was constantly shaken. He was reluctant to expose his feelings and speak of "the act of obedience which Jesus' command of love may under special circumstances call for";[4] and when in desperation he did so he found himself accused of conceit. Or if in defiance of his habitual reserve he allowed people "to have a glimpse of the thoughts which had given birth to my resolution,"[5] they did not believe him. They were convinced that something else lay behind it, disheartenment about his career, or an unhappy love affair. So for the most part he did not trouble to explain. Werner Picht remembered his saying, "My friends have no more patience with my paradoxes. It's time for me to go."[6] He said, "*J'irai!*" (I'm going!), and that was that.

Many people can still be found who will explain with a shrewd and knowing air some theory that they have either read or invented for themselves about Schweitzer's decision to go to Africa. I have met clergymen who believe that he went to atone for the dreadful things he had done to Jesus in his books. Others, of course, bring his mother into it somewhere, believing that Freud has the answer to all things. It may encourage such people to know that they are in the good company of Schweitzer's own friends, who could not possibly believe it was as simple as he said it was.

In a way he had himself to blame, having kept his thoughts hidden so long. But he certainly found himself confirmed in the wisdom of his silence. "How much I suffered through so many people assuming a right to tear open all the doors and shutters of my inner self! . . . I felt as a real kindness the action of persons who made no attempt to dig their fists into my heart, but regarded me as a precocious young man, not quite right in the head, and treated me correspondingly with affectionate mockery."[7] Schweitzer had always known, and now had engraved on his heart, that simple truth, so rarely observed, that the greatest kindness we can do to anyone is to let him be himself.

In Schweitzer's case he knew himself pretty well—far better than his well-wishers did. His own estimate of himself is worth quoting: "I held the venture to be justified, because I had considered it for a long time and from every point of view, and credited myself with the possession of health, sound nerves, energy, practical commonsense, toughness, prudence, very few wants, and everything else that might be found necessary by anyone wandering along the path of the idea. I believed myself, further, to wear the protective armour of a temperament quite capable of enduring an eventual failure of my plan.''[8] This is not the estimate of a neurotic seeking escape from some childhood trauma or theological guilt.

To his congregation he would say what he could not say to his friends. On November 19 he preached a sermon. He took as his text the story of the disciples on the dark lake, beating against the wind to the far shore, who saw Jesus coming across the water toward them in the night and thought he was a ghost; when Peter, always requiring practical proofs, said, "Lord if it is you, bid me come to you on the water"; and Jesus said "come"; and Peter stepped out of the boat but then grew frightened and began to sink, and Jesus stretched out his hand and saved him.

For Schweitzer this was not a miracle, but a parable which had been transformed into a miracle in retrospect; and the parable spoke directly to him. To an age battered by winds of doubt Jesus appeared like a phantom, and nobody knew whether he was real or not. There was only one way to find out—to go toward him and see. If one became frightened and seemed to be sinking, then his hand would be there to protect and save.

This sermon, like others, could appear unremarkable enough (apart from Schweitzer's usual sturdy style) if we did not know what was going on in his life at the time. But this was no pious exhortation from a book of published orations—it was like his father's sermons, a sharing of his own struggles. Listen then to Schweitzer, beleaguered by his friends, misunderstood, and attacked on all sides, stating his case:

> It is hardly an uplifting task to be a pastor in these days of doubt and indifference. One wishes to give the people of our time some spiritual encouragement, to bring them the message of Jesus, and that is not possible. The age wants its doubts dissolved without trouble or effort. But if the proclamation of the gospel were simply the dissolution of doubts and the defence of a doctrine, the preacher's would be the most taxing and thankless of tasks; that would be as though one were trying to enrich people's lives by straightening out their sums on a piece of paper. Fortunately it is not that at all—it is much, much finer. It is saying to people: "Do not stay where you are, but move ahead, move towards Jesus!" . . . Do not ask yourself whether the road is firm or practicable, fit for the man who follows his inclinations, but look only to see that it is really the road that leads straight to Jesus. Peter is able to walk towards him, the moment he dismisses all human considerations. . . .

How is Jesus alive for us? Do not attempt to prove his presence by formulations, even if they are sanctified by the ages. Of late I have very nearly lost my temper when some pious soul has come to me saying that no-one can believe in the living presence of Jesus if they do not believe in his physical resurrection and the eternal existence of his glorified body. Jesus lives for everyone whom he directs, in matters great and small, as if he were here among us. He tells them "Do this or that." And they answer, quite simply, "Yes!" and go about their job, humble and busy. . . . The fact that the Lord still, in our days, gives his orders, proves to me—and for me it is the only proof—that he is neither a ghost nor dead, but that he lives. . . .

If you will let me explain in my way this living presence, I will say to you: "The eternal body of Jesus is simply his words; for it was about them that he said 'Heaven and earth shall pass away, but my words shall not pass away!' "[9]

To the music critic Gustav von Lüpke he wrote more simply, but the message was the same:

I hope you will give me the pleasure of showing a deeper insight than most people . . . and that you will find the course I am taking as natural and right as I do myself. For me the whole essence of religion is at stake. For me religion means to be human, plainly human in the sense in which Jesus was. In the colonies things are pretty hopeless and comfortless. We—the Christian nations—send out there the mere dregs of our people; we think only of what we can get out of the natives . . . in short what is happening there is a mockery of humanity and Christianity. If this wrong is in some measure to be atoned for, we must send out there men who will do good in the name of Jesus, not simply proselytising missionaries, but men who will help the distressed as they must be helped if the Sermon on the Mount and the words of Jesus are valid and right.

Now we sit here and study theology, and then compete for the best ecclesiastical posts, write thick learned books in order to become professors of theology . . . and what is going on out there where the honour and the name of Jesus are at stake, does not concern us at all. And I am supposed to devote my life to making ever fresh critical discoveries, that I might become famous as a theologian, and go on training pastors who will also sit at home, and will not have the right to send them out to this vital work. I cannot do so. For years I have turned these matters over in my mind, this way and that. At last it became clear to me that this isn't my life. I want to be a simple human being, doing something small in the spirit of Jesus. . . . "What you have done to the least of these my brethren you have done to me." Just as the wind is driven to spend its force in the big empty spaces so must the men who know the laws of the spirit go where men are most needed.[10]

After that there can be no mistaking what kind of Christian Schweitzer was—at least at that time, and probably for the rest of his life. Nor can there be much doubt why he went to Africa.

In fact Schweitzer had been rather more circumspect than he admitted in the pulpit, and had done a good deal of looking to left and right before setting out. Writing his autobiography twenty-five years later he acknowledged that he had been lucky in his time. In those days "anyone who gave up remunerative work could still hope to get through life somehow or other, while anyone who thought of doing the same in the difficult economic conditions of today would run the risk of coming to grief not only materially but spiritually as well. I am compelled therefore, not only by what I have observed, but by experience also, to admit that worthy and capable persons have had to renounce a course of independent action which would have been of great value to the world, because circumstances rendered such a course impossible."[11]

The claim to be a hero, which others often make for Schweitzer, was one he never made for himself—indeed he specifically renounced it. "There are no heroes of action," he wrote, "only heroes of renunciation and suffering. Of such there are plenty. But few of them are known, and even these not to the crowd—but to the few."[12] In his letters to Hermann Hagedorn, too, he steadily reiterated that there was nothing exceptional or unique about him.

When, later on, others came to him for advice about their wish to make the same sort of break that he had made, he would discourage any who seemed to be suffering from restlessness or frustration in their own jobs. "Only a person who can find a value in every sort of activity, and can devote himself to each one with full consciousness of duty, has the inward right to undertake some out-of-the-ordinary activity instead of that which falls naturally to his lot."[13] Extremely practical and clear-sighted! But despite this plenty of people have accused Schweitzer of the very thing he warned against, running away from something that he could not face to lose himself in the anonymity of the jungle. It is hard to see what he could have been running away from. As he points out himself, "I had received, as a young man, such recognition as others usually get only after a whole life of toil and struggle."[14]

No, there is no doubt that for years he had been loved, admired, successful, and happy. He was simply running true to form, to that obstinate necessity of his being which since his childhood days had linked action inevitably with experience and thought. He felt—he considered—he acted. In the Gospels he had found the guidance he needed, not in a set of rules to obey but in a man to follow. He was complete—his course was set. In a sense everything that happened afterward, exciting though it was, though it brought him worldwide fame and esteem, was now programed. He had set the countdown in motion. It was only a matter of awaiting the lift-off and the actual adventure.

The situation was quite irregular as far as the University was concerned. Professors in one subject could not enroll as students in another. And unfortunately only duly enrolled students were allowed to take examinations at the end of courses. Schweitzer seemed to have no alternative but to resign as a professor; but this he was not inclined to do. He enjoyed both teaching and preaching far too much to give up either until he was compelled to. Apart from all else there was a financial problem. He had sent in his resignation as principal, and when this took effect in the following spring he would lose both his official residence and his comfortable salary.

The university, once over their astonishment, proved admirably cooperative and flexible. The professors agreed to let him attend lectures free, not as a student but as a colleague, so his resignation was not required. And he was to be allowed to sit for the examinations on the strength of certificates from the professors stating that he had attended.

So he gave his name in to the dean of medical faculty (whose first reaction was to hand him over to the psychiatric department) and one day of thick fog toward the end of October he set out for his first lecture on anatomy.

Though it was hard to begin again, at thirty, learning a totally new subject, he rejoiced in the practicality of it. He had had enough of words. He had always loved natural science, but had largely deserted it for subjects where speculation and argument were interminable and proof was impossible. Now he was dealing with solid facts, capable of demonstration and conclusion, and it was a great relief.

When the time came to leave the principal's quarters, his friend, Frederick Curtius, came to the rescue. Curtius' official residence as president of the Lutheran Church of Alsace was inside the same big building which housed the principal's rooms, and he offered Schweitzer four small attics in his residence, one of them equipped as a kitchen. So, "on the rainy Shrove Tuesday of 1906 the students carried my belongings out through one door of the house on the St. Thomas' Embankment and in through another."[15]

Here Schweitzer installed himself and his books, now augmented by fat medical tomes. *The Quest of the Historical Jesus* and the long essay on organ building had been finished in the winter, before he moved. Now, for the moment, there was no literary work going on—only his pastoral work, his theological lectures, his organ playing, and his medical studies! The German version of the Bach book had been commissioned but he was—understandably—finding it hard to settle to it.

The organ playing was in fact increasing. He was in constant demand for the Bach Society's concerts in Paris, and he could not afford to turn any down, for he needed the fees to help out his diminished income. And indeed he was going ever farther afield, for he had caught the eye of Luis Millet, conductor of the Orfeo Catala of Barcelona, who invited him to play in the Bach concerts there. One of these concerts was to be held before the King and Queen of Spain, and Schweitzer felt that the occasion demanded something better than the clothes he normally wore. Many, many years later he told the story of the frock coat to Frederick Franck, a dentist working in his hospital in central Africa:

> I had my frock coat when I had to play the organ for the King of Spain in Barcelona. It was in 1905, yes, 1905. Or was it 1906? No, no, it was 1905. I remember it very well, for I said to my friend the tailor in Günsbach, "You have to make me a frock coat for I have to play for the King of Spain." He got very embarrassed. "You mean to say, Albert, I have to make the frock coat you are going to play in for a king?" With a worried expression on his face he then said, "All I can do is my best." It really became a beautiful frock coat, very strongly built, and I have always worn it on all great occasions. Of course I haven't got it here, so I can't show it to you, for in Africa it's no use. I keep it in Günsbach. But I wore it when I performed the marriage of Theodor Heuss, the present President of Western Germany, in the church of St. Nicholas in Strasbourg in 1907, when I was minister there. Of course I wore it, too, when I gave the lectures in Edinburgh, when I got the Goethe Prize, when I received the Nobel Prize, and when the Queen of England decorated me. And the last time Theodor Heuss saw it he said, "My, my, Albert, don't you look elegant! You must have a very good tailor in Günsbach."[16]

After the concert the King asked Schweitzer, "Is it difficult to play the organ?" "Almost as difficult as to rule Spain," replied Schweitzer. "Then," said the King, "you must be a brave man."[17]

In 1906 Schweitzer was already beginning to make overtures to the Paris Mission Society—La Société des Missions Evangéliques chez les Peuples non Chrétiens—of which his father approved as having a more liberal outlook than most. There were unfortunately no missions specifically belonging to the liberal sections of Protestantism. The dogmatic elements in the churches had been the quickest to send representatives to preach to the heathen at the beginning of the nineteenth century, their purpose being simply "to save souls"—meaning thereby to baptize as many black people as possible. By contrast, the liberal Christians wanted, as Schweitzer put it, "to set the Gospel working primarily as a force for the restoration of mankind and the conditions of human society in the heathen world."[18] But this kind of Christianity had no spokesman in the mission world

—which is why missions gained the bad name which still clings to them. Liberal Christians therefore tended to support the dogmatic missions for lack of anything better; and naturally they gave the most support where they discerned the most liberal spirit. But Schweitzer rapidly discovered that the simple and humane reports that come from the missionaries themselves were no reflection of the policies of the society's head office. The director himself, an Alsatian named Boegner, was the author of the article that had made up Schweitzer's mind for him; and he was moved and delighted at Schweitzer's application. But he still had to confess that he was somewhat oversimplifying when he wrote, at the conclusion of his article, "Men and women who can reply simply to the Master's call 'Lord, I am coming,' those are the people whom the Church needs." Schweitzer had indeed said, "Lord, I am coming." But he had not also said, "I believe in X and Y and Z," and therefore members of the committee were likely to raise objections. Boegner was reassured when Schweitzer explained that he wanted to come only as a doctor. But some of the good committee members were not to be so easily appeased, evidently feeling that the souls of their converts might be infected by the healing touch of a less-than-true believer. The two Alsatians, Boegner and Schweitzer, decided to wait and see whether the intervening years would bring these frightened people to what Schweitzer called "a truly Christian reasonableness."[19]

In fact, as it turned out a more liberal mission organization did exist, the General Union of Evangelical Missions, based in Switzerland, under whose auspices Schweitzer could have gone, he reckoned, as either doctor or missionary, and on his own terms. But he made no attempt to do things this easy way, for two odd and very Schweitzerian reasons. First, that "my call to Equatorial Africa had come to me through the article in the Paris Mission Magazine"[20]—and therefore a sort of emotional loyalty tied him to that society. And second, sheer obstinacy—"I was tempted to persist in getting a decision on the question whether, face to face with the Gospel of Jesus, a missionary society could justifiably arrogate to itself the right to refuse to the suffering natives in their district the services of a doctor, because in their opinion he was not sufficiently orthodox."[21] Behind that persistence one senses the same anger that crept up on him when pious souls told him he must believe in the Resurrection before he could believe in the living Jesus. His notorious temper must have had a trying time these months, when he felt himself surrounded by people who not only did not understand him but did not understand the Christianity they all professed. One cannot help suspecting that he learned the hard way the lessons he speaks of in his autobiography: "These favoured persons [that is, those like himself who are lucky enough to be able to strike out on an independent line] must also be modest, so as not to fly into a passion at the opposition they encounter; they have to meet it in the temper which says: 'Ah well, it had to be!' Anyone who proposes to do good must not expect people to roll stones out of his way, but must accept his lot calmly even if they roll a few more upon it. A strength which becomes clearer and stronger through its experience of such obstacles is the only strength that can conquer them. Resistance is only a waste of strength.''[22]

Under these stresses, Schweitzer's already powerful will was being tempered into a flexible but truly formidable weapon.

That summer, at Bayreuth, his literary inactivity came to an end when, inspired by *Tristan,* he began the German version of the Bach book. He was busy also with thoughts about St. Paul. If eschatology provided such dramatic clues to the puzzles in the Gospels, might it not be fruitfully applied also to the parts of Paul's Epistles which still baffled scholars?

While preparing a series of lectures on the subject, he became convinced that he was on to something. It was generally thought at that time that the difference between Paul's notions and those of other early Christians was due to the fact that he had been brought up in Asia Minor, where the Greek Mystery religions were dominant; and that this accounted for his opposition to the Jewish law and his mystical image of dying and being reborn ''in Christ.'' The Greek Mysteries centered around a God who died and was reborn. Mithraism too had a similar central myth. What more natural than that Paul should introduce these ideas into the Christ story?

Schweitzer, however, claimed that these religions did not reach a state that would make sense of this theory until a hundred years after Paul. So either the Epistles of Paul were written much later, and foisted on Paul to give them authority, or there must be another explanation of Paul's novel ideas. Working on this, Schweitzer was once again seized by the old need to begin his research with a survey of all that had hitherto been written on the subject. So he started collecting material for a brief historical introduction to his own discoveries; but like the Bach book, the thing stretched and grew under his hand, and he realized that he was going to have to write a whole separate book, leading up to the book he really wanted to write.

And so the overcrowded months passed, in what he described as ''a continuous struggle with fatigue.''[23] Günsbach provided a relaxation, and when really overtired he recharged his energies by getting out into the country and drawing strength from nature. Sometimes his goddaughter, Suzanne, would climb with him up the hill behind the village and sit happily while he made notes in his notebook—or if the notebook ran out, on his cuffs.

She remembers how even then, long before his philosophy of Reverence for Life was formulated, he would take the greatest care of every living creature, and teach her to do the same. Above all he would teach her to be grateful. Nobody could know, he would say, where we came from or where we are going. The only sure thing was existence, and the only way to affirm life was to take responsibility for our existence. Thankfulness strengthened the good in the world. For him it was a matter of the greatest thankfulness that he could call this beautiful valley home.

His young cousin, Jean-Paul Sartre, who had been born in Paris a year or so earlier, was to pick up the theme that all we could be sure of was existence itself, never its purpose. But for Sartre this meant futility and distress, not thankfulness. The word "Existentialist" could be applied to both; but it was Sartre's version, not Schweitzer's, that gained currency in the philosophical world. And Schweitzer, the champion of existence, never laid claim to the title of Existentialist; indeed he rejected it outright, for the associations it came to have were entirely alien to him.

When he was late for lunch at the manse it was often Suzanne who was sent to fetch him. She knocked first, and if there was no reply put her head around the door—cautiously, because as often as not it would be greeted by a flying book. Schweitzer was still unpunctual and disinclined for domestic chores. It was his job to draw the wine for the meal from the cask in the cellar; one day he dropped the jug on the stairs and his father said, "That is the last time the *sacré imbécile* draws my wine!" The job thereafter was Suzanne's; and she had the impression that uncle Albert had achieved what he intended.

In 1907 Widor came to stay at Günsbach en route for Germany, and Schweitzer met him off the express at Colmar. Widor had been traveling first class, as befitted his age and distinction. But for the last eight miles up the valley on the local train he traveled fourth class with Schweitzer.

Widor was quite a surprise to the family at the manse. They had met a variety of people, but never had they entertained anyone who kissed his hostess' hand at breakfast every day; and they were astonished at the courtly way he would reply to a hospitable offer: "I am quite overwhelmed, madame." It gives us some idea of the force of Schweitzer's character that he could prevail on such an elegant old gentleman to travel fourth class among the peasants.

That force could still erupt in anger. Suzanne's younger brother, Albert, remembers a day when Schweitzer was helping him with his Latin translation. He made no mistakes at all, and Schweitzer sent Albert to his grandfather to tell him how well he had done. When Albert returned, Widor was with Schweitzer and Schweitzer made him do it again for Widor. This time he made a mistake, and Schweitzer slapped him so hard it made his nose bleed. Thereafter Schweitzer swore he would never help him again. Not till years later did he apologize, and asked if Albert had minded very much.

Schweitzer's energy was volcanic. As when a child he had struck his sister over a game and then determined to give up games, so still he had to fight to fetter and guide that impatient energy. The wisdom that we find in his books is not the wisdom of a man to whom it was easy to be right, but that of a man who knew that if wisdom failed the abyss was waiting.

There is no mention of Hélène Bresslau in his autobiography before the brief statement that in 1912 he married her. So we have no notion what she had felt when she heard of his proposed African venture—unless of course she was the trusted companion he wrote of as the only sharer of his secret. But the similarity of their self-dedication probably helped her to understand him better than most. Her moment of decision had arrived a year before his, and she appears to have done nothing about it at the time—so perhaps she was privy to the plan. At all events, while Schweitzer trained to be a doctor, she enrolled as a student nurse. There seems to be no question that this was a direct result of his plan, and that her intention was to go to Africa with him. "We met," she wrote in 1945 to one of Schweitzer's biographers, George Seaver, "with a mutual feeling of responsibility for all the good that we had received in our lives, and a sense of duty to pay for it by helping others. It has been the joy and pride of my life to follow and assist him in all his activities. . . ."[24] So we may assume, and this is confirmed by those who knew them then, that she was his constant companion and assistant in his writing, his studies, and his music. There was no inkling of romance, however: indeed Christian Brandt at one time had an idea that Schweitzer might be going to marry Olympia Curtius.

In September, 1907, he finished the massive German Bach book, and on the thirtieth he wrote to Gustave Bret, conductor of the Paris Bach Society: "I take the first morning of the first week of liberty—the ms of the Bach book was finished on Wednesday 25th September 1907 at 6.45 P.M.—to study the question of cuts." The cuts refer to a projected performance of the *St. John Passion,* and Schweitzer lists a number of points: "The general principle is to keep the action intact, and as many chorales as possible." . . . "Fifty years of Purgatory if you suppress the first Kreuzige." Of the *Air avec Choeur* he comments: "To tell the truth nobody knows how it should be sung. One is only aware of the contest between the bass and the orchestra." He suggests replacing the *oboe di caccia* by the *cor anglais*—"identical instruments"—but, "on the other hand we have a marvellous *oboe d'amore* if you want one." And he proposes adding a piccolo, to bring out the flute parts. "Above all, use plenty of oboes, and put them right in the forefront, *in front of the violins.* The effect is superb!''[25]

From this letter, and from an article which Schweitzer wrote for the Berlin magazine *Die Musik* about the difficulty of organizing a choir in Paris, we get an idea of the considerable part he was playing in the running of the Paris Bach Society. This article has so much in it of social as well as musical interest that it demands some attention. It gives us some idea of the meticulous thoroughness with which he approached every one of his enterprises.

> When my friend and I a few years ago started to organise a Bach Society in Paris to produce the Passions and cantatas, people everywhere expressed the opinion that sooner or later our enterprise would certainly go on the rocks, since it was impossible to keep a good choir together very long in Paris. When we said that what succeeded elsewhere should certainly be possible there as well, we received only sympathetic shrugs of the shoulders.
>
> The fact is that none of the choirs composed of society volunteers has enjoyed a very long existence in Paris. Usually they died with their founders, if not before. For the most part they were not purely Parisian organisations, but were undertaken by the Alsatian community resident in the capital city. This is the reason that Paris had the best mixed choirs in the middle of the eighties, when the Alsatian community and its adherents from the departments of the east, by virtue of the exodus from Germany after the year 1870, had achieved the greatest importance and had taken a leading place in politics and intellectual culture.

He goes on to complain of the high cost of running a choir with professional singers; the result being too few rehearsals, and "under these circumstances a profound analysis of the works is impossible. . . ."

> The discipline is not very rigorous. It has always impressed me how little the conductor is heeded even in the choirs of the Conservatory concerts. More than three-quarters of the singers watch their notes from beginning to end for lack of discipline and skill. The director must make all possible concessions to them. The rehearsals are usually conducted with the singers seated. Men and women often keep their hats on. Intermittent pauses are numerous. And under no circumstances may the time agreed on be lengthened.[26]

The lack of enthusiasm and morale Schweitzer attributes to a complex of social causes. The inadequacy of the tram was a contributory factor, making it necessary for a woman going out at night always to take a carriage unless she lived close to a main street. But the main difficulties lay in the Parisian attitude to family life. The fact that young unmarried women were never allowed out unchaperoned made for a permanent shortage of sopranos. And the Parisians' devotion to their families to the exclusion of any larger social unit meant that the conductor of a choir was forever fighting the prior claims of family visiting days. Once at rehearsal, French individualism came into conflict with choir discipline. The French singer "does not become a member of the choir, a stop that the director pulls, but remains Mr. So-and-So or Mrs. So-and-So, who wants to be recognised as such. The modern Frenchman has an instinctive anxiety about anything that is called discipline; he sees in it nothing but a submission that is unworthy of a free being."[27]

Schweitzer contrasts this approach with the musical tradition in Germany and Switzerland, which had originated with the choirs and orchestras maintained by the small separate states and their courts in the eighteenth century. In France the monarchy had sucked the life out of the provincial cities:

> Most of all, however, the general musical education suffers from the lack of choirs. Only by rehearsing together and singing together can we arouse an interest in polyphony. Anyone who has never experienced a work of art which he has helped to create, in the midst of which he stands as it passes by, which he hears from within out, never emerges from the position of mere musical feeling to that of genuine artistic perception. The educational value of choral singing, which we may assume as a matter of course in the German people—at least for much the greater part of them—is lacking in the French. The feelings of the French are probably just as elemental and vital as those of the Germans, but the power of judgement that can be gained only through artistic activity is wanting.[28]

As to Schweitzer's musical contribution, a rare glimpse is given us by a Dr. A. T. Davison, who sang in the choir at that time, when he was studying the organ with Widor, and who went on to become a professor of music at Harvard University. In an article in the *Albert Schweitzer Jubilee Book of 1945,* he describes how Schweitzer's playing stood out against what he calls "the mechanical and heartless perfection of the choir and the orchestra." Bret's conducting he thought "more competent than inspired," and the somewhat underrehearsed choir lacked fire. "Schweitzer's contribution," he felt, was "easily the most distinguished of all."

> I was struck first of all [he says] by Schweitzer's indifference to any "effectiveness" in registration or manner of playing, the entire process being concentrated in the presentation of the music in its proper setting without the slightest effort to make it "telling" of itself. And it must be

remembered that the question was not of the great organ compositions; it was solely of the organ background to, let us say, one of the cantatas. My early studies had centred about the instrument as a vehicle of display, and from Widor I was discovering that the organ and the organist were the servants; the music—especially that of Bach—the master. The unpretentious accompanimental parts must always be a pretty routine affair to the organist who loves his playing better than the music he plays. Schweitzer however, never once obtruding himself, lavished upon them all the scrupulous attention they deserve but all too seldom receive. I realise now that my feeling about his skillful and appropriate support was primarily a technical one, albeit an as yet undiscovered clue to the impulse that converted these stylistic marvels into an almost biographical record of Bach himself.[29] [Widor himself had described Schweitzer as "One of the most skillful and experienced players that any conductor could desire to have at the organ during the performance of a Bach cantata or Passion."][30]

As far as I can remember [Davidson continues] Schweitzer, in spite of his authoritative knowledge, was never consulted—publicly, at least—regarding any of the questions involved in the performance of Bach's music. In fact the only occasion upon which I remember his forsaking the near-anonymity of the organ bench was at a rehearsal when the conductor, wishing to judge an effect from the rear of the hall, put his baton in Schweitzer's hand and asked him to direct the choir and orchestra. At that time, at least, Albert Schweitzer was in no sense a conductor, and it is significant that he made no pretense of being one. Turning his back squarely upon both orchestra and choir, one hand thrust in his trouser's pocket, his head back, staring up into the dark of the Salle Gaveau, his arm moving in awkward sweeps and unorthodox directions, it was quite obvious that if he gave himself a thought—which I doubt—it was only to consider himself the agent who should bring the music to life. Beyond that he had no responsibility. It was for the conductor to judge whether the balance of tone or the seating of the participants was satisfactory. Above all, there was complete detachment; entire absorption in the sound of the music. To this day I can remember the intense admiration I felt for Schweitzer's indifference to externals. How I swelled with indignation at the pitying smirks of the orchestral players as they condescendingly shrugged their shoulders and ostentatiously disregarded the vague gestures of the conductor pro tem. It was then, I feel sure, that I first sensed the stature of the man.[31]

Schweitzer was not yet a solo concert organist. It was circumstance, the need to collect money, that resulted in that development. At present he was still only—and happily—an accompanist, a member of the ensemble.

With a short while to go before the first medical examination, it became clear that he had indulged once too often in his passion for trying to learn everything about a subject, rather than confining himself to the issues in hand. He enjoyed working on the physical sciences so much that he tried to cover the whole field, and neglected the syllabus. He was not helped by the fact that he could not, at thirty, rely on a memory as perfect as he had enjoyed when he was twenty. In the last few weeks his young fellow students finally persuaded him to join a cramming club, which studied previous examination papers and the sort of answers required.

When, four weeks before the examination, he officiated at the wedding of his friend Elly Knapp with Theodor Heuss, a delayed birth at the gynecological unit barely gave him time to exchange his white gown for his frock coat, and some of the guests were surprised to note that the handsome young pastor smelled so strongly of iodoform.

The examination began on May 13. The subjects were anatomy, physiology, and the natural sciences. When he entered, his fatigue was greater than at any other time of his life; so at any rate he wrote in 1931—when of course he did not know what was to come. But he passed, and passed well; better than he had ever expected. Now, the worst over, the back of the new subject broken at last, he could drive on with fresh confidence to clinical study and his finals.

12

THE DEPARTURE
1908–1913

So the odd student toiled on, ten years older than the rest of the class, a professor one minute, a pupil the next, and the next again an organist of rising international reputation. His greatest difficulty was staying awake hour after hour at medical lectures.

Traveling to Paris or to Barcelona on the hard wooden seats of the fourth-class compartment, he dug deep into the resources of his extraordinary stamina, all the time strengthening it still further, making of himself what he wanted to be, the man without needs who was always at the disposal of the needs of others. Food he did like—that was an essential fuel; but he was able to go for long periods even without food when the occasion demanded.

When he took a holiday, the routine was the same year after year: First, a summons to Adèle Herrenschmidt, now a woman of fifty-three and head of a finishing school at Neuilly, to gather herself and her niece, Marcelle, together and meet him in Switzerland—a summons that was never disobeyed. Once among the Alps at Oey they took a horse-drawn carriage up the small side valley for two hours or more till the mountains were all around them and they reached the lonely Kurhaus Grimmialp, where year after year they had the same table, and year after year Schweitzer would say: *"Hier ist wo die Welt zu ist"*—"This is where we leave the world outside."

English has no equivalent for the word *"Kurhaus,"* which is somewhere between a sanatorium and a hotel—a place where the air is good and treatment is available. The only treatment Schweitzer needed was the remoteness and the quiet; the only person it seems that he trusted to share it, Adèle Herrenschmidt—which prompts the speculation that she was perhaps the one person in whom he confided his plan to become a doctor before announcing it to the world.

Here they stayed ten days or so. And even here Schweitzer spent most

189

of the day working. Then they drove back down the valley, back to trains and bustle and civilization; Schweitzer refreshed for his breakneck life by his perennial nurse and consoler, nature.

His booklet on organ building began to show results. The eighteenth-century Silbermann organ in St. Thomas' needed attention, and Schweitzer managed to persuade the church council not to scrap it and replace it, as all the other churches were doing, but to restore and renovate it. The man they commissioned to supervise the restoration, on Schweitzer's recommendation, was none other than that virtuoso pianist Marie-Joseph Erb, whose dazzling fingerwork had stunned the young Schweitzer in his schooldays at Mulhouse, and driven him back, reinspired, to his sharps and flats.

Erb now lived in Strasbourg and Schweitzer had got to know him a little. He was not only a pianist, but also an organist and a composer; not only a virtuoso, but also a mature musician. Schweitzer, Erb, and the organ builder, Härpfer, spent a great deal of time planning how best to replace the worn-out parts and to introduce new diapason pipes into the old organ without sacrificing any of its quality.

When it was done, Schweitzer was well satisfied. Thirteen years later, the same Archibald Davison who had admired Schweitzer's playing in Paris had the chance to hear him play the renovated St. Thomas' organ, and for the first time was able to see and hear for himself the kind of organ for which Bach wrote. "There it was, very much as it was in Bach's day, devoid of all the labor-saving devices of the modern instrument, cumbersome, and, from the point of view of one who had been used to the mechanically effortless instruments of America, calculated to set up for the player almost every conceivable impediment to easy and comfortable manipulation."

When Schweitzer began to play, he noted that "The 'machinery' of the old organ was plainly audible"; and that when the assistants had to pull out a number of stops in the middle of the G Minor Fantasia and Fugue, it caused a "terrific clatter." But Schweitzer appeared not to be aware of the noise; and he himself barely noticed it—"so overpowering was the effect of the music and its registration."[1]

This picture gives us a good idea of what Schweitzer did and did not think important about organ building. He would have been totally uninterested in the technical fussiness that goes into today's recordings, the obsession with exploiting electronic effects and so forth. If the spirit was right, it obliterated other imperfections. If not, what possible profit could there be in polishing something that was hollow at heart?

Not long after the restoration of the St. Thomas' organ, Schweitzer was invited to prepare an address on organ construction for the Third Congress of the International Music Society, which was to be held in Vienna from May 25 to 29, 1909. The organizer, Guido Adler, had decided that organ building was a question of sufficient importance to warrant the creation of a special study group in the congress, and presumably expected some sort of recapitulation of his booklet. But having cause to suspect that support for his views was thin on the ground, Schweitzer, despite all his other preoccupations, decided first to conduct an opinion survey. He sent a questionnaire, financed by the society—to organists and organ builders all over Europe. The questions were grouped under twelve headings, and covered everything from the desirability of different sorts of wind chest to the prices of the organ installations. Paragraph 5, for example, runs: "5. What dimensions do you consider the best for manuals and pedals? Are you for little or big keys, for keyboards near one another or rather far apart? Do you prefer the straight or the curved pedals? How should the pedal lie under the console? What range of notes should it have?"[2]

Schweitzer wrote later:

> This effort revealed how little sympathy there was for raising the question of organ construction at all. Instead of answering to the point, many of those addressed came out with threats against those who would encroach upon the freedom of the organ builder, and, as one man wrote, "would like to make all organs on one last." Worst of all were the answers of many organ builders and many organ inspectors. There were organ builders who did not understand what it would mean to them to have minimum prices set which would permit them to do artistic work. They saw only that a movement was on foot that would make it impossible for them to drive their new rivals from the field by underbidding or by means of the newest inventions.[3]

These responses were counterbalanced however by a great many positive replies, which Schweitzer analyzed and incorporated into his lecture. When the congress began, the members of the organ-building study group immediately put their heads together and decided that this opportunity should not be missed; and ignoring the social side of the congress they set about drawing up a list of regulations for the guidance of future organ builders. The Alsatian, Härpfer, who had rebuilt the St. Thomas' organ, was there. And Schweitzer's own initiative is clear from the fact that he was co-chairman of the group's sessions; the other chairman also coming from Strasbourg, Dr. Xavier Matthias of the Catholic theological faculty. Barely taking time to eat or sleep, the group completed the fifty pages of regulations in the four days of the congress, laying down a detailed set of standards which were subsequently accepted by the society and circulated to the same list who had originally received the questionnaire.

The results took time to emerge; but even within the next year or two it was evident that the tide was turning, that people were everywhere beginning to rethink their assumptions about organ building and to experiment with ways of using technology to maintain quality, not simply to cut down price or to devise complicated and unnecessary additions. By 1927 Schweitzer was able to write, "Today the fight is won";[4] not that the destruction of fine old organs had been halted (it still goes on even now) but when it happens now, it is generally through the ignorance of parish councils rather than the recommendation of the profession itself.

Next it was St. Paul's turn for the Schweitzer treatment. He was determined if possible to finish the work that had begun with *The Mystery of the Kingdom of God,* and show through the book on St. Paul how the process that started with Jesus' expectation of the new order had shifted gradually but inevitably toward the Church's quite different interpretation.

Something of the strain he suffered at this time is shown by the number of letters to him which mention that he had been ill. Ernest Newman, who was busy translating the German version of the Bach book into English, writes on November 5, 1910, thanking him for the French version and the correction of a mistake in it; "I am grieved to hear of your ill health," he writes; "you work too hard, I am afraid." What the illness was we do not know; nothing serious evidently, but certainly during this period Schweitzer's massive constitution was showing cracks.

He did in fact get the introductory book on St. Paul ready—the one that covered other people's research leading up to his own; this was called *Paul and His Interpreters,* and was duly published in 1911. And he was, he says, within weeks of completing the major work, *The Mysticism of Paul the Apostle,* when he realized that he would never be able to pass his finals if he did not put it aside.

Meantime another distraction had entered Schweitzer's life. Schirmer's, the New York music publishers, had asked Widor to edit Bach's organ works, with advice about the best way to play them. Widor agreed only on condition that Schweitzer collaborated with him, and Schirmer's accepted the stipulation. In fact Schweitzer did all the donkey work—he prepared the first draft, which he then worked over with Widor. Anyone who has done work of this kind will know how much easier it is to amend and refine something that has already been put on paper than it is to arrange those first thoughts and find those first words. And all this of course necessitated numerous extra visits to Paris—though twice Widor came to Günsbach for a few days to get on with the work without disturbance.

Schirmer's commission was a recognition that Widor's style of playing Bach was the nearest possible to an authentic reproduction of Bach's own. And this edition still holds an honored place on organists' bookshelves.

Widor and Schweitzer had firm ideas about everything to do with the performance of Bach's organ music—proper phrasing, proper fingering, bearing in mind that Bach crossed one finger over another rather than turning the thumb under; proper registration, which corresponded to what was possible on Bach's own organs; and moderation of volume, so that the individual lines of melody remained clear and were never swamped by an indiscriminate fortissimo such as Bach could not have achieved even had he wished to.

But these suggestions were never incorporated in the actual score. That was left as Bach left it—or as nearly so as could be discovered. The comments were separate, to be used or ignored as the player wished. Schweitzer had had enough of those editions which offer the player, even while he is playing, "the fingering, the phrasing, the fortes and pianos, the crescendos and decrescendos, and not infrequently even the pedantic analyses of some editor or other, even when I entirely disagree with them."[5]

The recommendations in this edition, incidentally, do not hark back to Bach's ways with total rigidity. After explaining what the limitations of Bach's days imposed on the composer himself, they go on to suggest "experiments to discover how far beyond that use could be made, without spoiling the style, of the variations in the volume of sound and its tone-colours which are desirable and possible on the modern organ."[6]

In September, a month before his finals began, Schweitzer went for a week to Munich for the Festival of French Music, where Widor was to conduct a new work of his, the *Symphonia Sacra* for organ and orchestra. Schweitzer was to play the difficult organ part; he needed the fee to pay for his examination charges. At the beginning of the week's rehearsals he was eating in small restaurants for economy's sake; but a wealthy count who bottled champagne and had to eat at the hotels to which he sold came to Widor and asked if he knew of any students who would care to keep him company at lunch and dinner. Widor suggested Schweitzer, who thus suddenly found himself living off the fat of the land, champagne being naturally a regular feature-of the menu. At the count's table incidentally Schweitzer met Saint-Saëns for the first time, but what they thought of each other remains a fascinating mystery.

The evening of the concert Schweitzer and Widor were both invited to dinner. Schweitzer thought it prudent to decline, but Widor went. The rest of the story is best told in the words of C. R. Joy in his excellent collection of stories and writings, *Music in the Life of Albert Schweitzer:*

At eight o'clock, when they were to begin, Widor was not there. At five minutes past he had not arrived. At ten minutes past he appeared, rushed to the rostrum, and began at once to conduct the orchestra with one hand while he searched for his glasses with the other. He was unable to conduct the symphony without the score, and neither he nor the orchestra was thoroughly familiar with it. With his baton first in his right hand and then in his left he searched in his pockets, one after the other. They were a quarter of the way through before he found them. Had not Schweitzer been so sure of himself and supported so well with the organ, the whole thing would have been disastrous. Said Schweitzer afterwards, "You see, I was right in not accepting the invitation."[7]

The state medical examination, the climax to six years' work, began in October and ended on December 17. When it was finished, "I could not," he wrote, "grasp the fact that the terrible strain of the medical course was now behind me. Again and again I had to assure myself that I was really awake and not dreaming."[8] The surgeon who conducted his last examination was telling him that but for his excellent health he would never have got through those last months and years; but he hardly heard him, the voice seemed to be coming from far away.

What the surgeon said of that time was true of Schweitzer's whole life. His achievements were only possible for a man of great physical strength. "Energy," said Blake, "is eternal delight." Lack of energy can bring to nothing all kinds of brilliance, insight, and good intention. Even love can fall a victim to weariness; to express it can become too much effort. This is not to decry the passion and determination that made Schweitzer what he was; and it may well be that by remaining true to himself and to his vision of excellence he saved himself from those interior complications and conflicts which can lead to neurotic illness. His goodness, in short, may well have contributed to his health; but his health certainly helped him to make the most of his goodness.

When Schweitzer walked unbelievingly out into the night he still had a thesis to write for his medical degree, and he still had to take a specialist course on tropical medicine before he could go to Africa. Moreover, the final arrangements had not yet been made with the Paris Mission Society.

For the thesis he decided to combine two of his fields of study and put into practice something he was increasingly preaching—the harnessing of religion with science. He would write a psychiatric study of Jesus. At least the subject was unlikely to encounter much competition from other medical finalists!

In fact he had something of a personal reason for choosing the subject. With the recent upsurge of interest in psychopathology, a vogue had arisen for applying psychological tests to Jesus. Three writers had published theories that Jesus suffered from one kind of mental abnormality or another; he had a tendency to delusions and hallucinations which amounted, they claimed, to paranoia, the definition of which was a good deal more chaotic than it is now.

Among those who were supposed to have contributed to the notion of a mentally disordered Jesus was Schweitzer. Holtzmann and others, so he tells us in the preface to his thesis, were constantly reminding him that he "had portrayed a Jesus whose object-world looked like a structure of fantasies."[9] A Jesus, they felt, who believed in the coming of a practical Kingdom of God was obviously out of his mind; and Schweitzer had done as much as any man to establish how central this was to Jesus' thought.

Schweitzer's existing knowledge was already more than enough to make mincemeat of the books that made Jesus out a madman, on two main scores. First, that the three authors had been entirely uncritical about their historical sources—the bulk of the passages they used to make their points came from St. John, whom no reputable scholar regarded as historically reliable. And second that they had ignored a very basic and very obvious principle in the analysis of ideas that look like delusions— namely that these ideas should be investigated in relation to the ideas current in the society of the time. As Dr. Winifred Overholser pointed out in her introduction to a new translation of Schweitzer's booklet in 1948: "To the Haitian native a belief that necromancy may be employed against him is a part of the folkways, is 'normal'—for the educated resident of Park Avenue such a belief would properly be classified as delusion."[10] It was as normal for Jesus to believe what he did as for the men before Copernicus to believe that the sun moved around the earth.

Equipped though he was with these potent arguments Schweitzer, in accordance with his principle of getting to the bottom of any subject he touched, read deeply about paranoia and other forms of psychosis, so far as they had then been studied, and took a year over writing his thesis. So his mistrust of psychoanalysis cannot be blamed, as it often is, on ignorance. Indeed the opening paragraph of his thesis is actually a defense of the method, and puts the blame where it belongs, on imperfect practitioners:

> The psychopathological method, which conceives its task to be the investigation of the mental aberrations of significant personalities in relation to their works, has recently fallen into disrepute. This is not because of the method, which with proper limitations and in the hands of professional investigators can produce and has produced valuable results, but because it has been faultily pursued by amateurs. The prerequisites which are essential for successful work in this field—exact source knowledge, adequate medical, and particularly psychiatric experience, both under the discipline of critical talents—are very seldom found together.[11]

So deeply did he believe in truth, including psychiatric truth, that he embarked on his analysis of his beloved Jesus with his eyes open to the possibility that he might in fact find genuine signs of mental disorder there.

> Should it really turn out that Jesus' object world must be considered by the doctor as in some degree the world of a sick man, still this conclusion, regardless of the consequences that follow from it and the shock to many that would result from it must not remain unuttered, since reverence for truth must be exalted above everything else. With this conviction I began the work, suppressing the unpleasant feeling of having to subject a great personality to psychiatric examination, and pondering the truth that what is great and profound in the ethical teachings of Jesus would retain its significance even if the conceptions in his world outlook and some of his actions had to be called more or less diseased.[12]

In fact however he found no cause to alter his belief that Jesus was perfectly sane, no reason to suppose that the ethical genius sprang from an unbalanced vision; always assuming that he was, as Schweitzer insisted, a man sharing the life and thought of his fellow men.

While this booklet was in the making a great many other things were happening. To study tropical medicine he had to go to Paris—Strasbourg could not teach him all he needed to know. So now at last he was forced to give up his teaching at the university, his preaching at St. Nicholas'. The last series of lectures he gave, in the winter of 1911–12, insisted on the belief behind his thesis, went deeply into the reconciliation between religion and science, a subject that concerned him more and more. With his combination of mystical apprehension and vigorously disciplined research he was qualified to speak for both as few others have been. What was science? What was religion? Both were life, both were truth. The names were unimportant.

On the religious side there is one subject on which we have not yet heard his views—sin. Sin would seem to be an important part of a preacher's concerns, but Schweitzer was not particularly interested in it. He touched on the subject in a sermon he preached in January, 1912.

> I cannot speak to you about sin like those terrifying preachers of penitence who have arisen through the ages. And I would not wish to. They always remind me of those fearful storms which beat on the earth but give it none of the refreshment that a fine rain gives when the water, instead of falling in torrents and carrying all before it, gently penetrates the soil. John the Baptist was a powerful orator. But Jesus, speaking to the people gently, certainly touched them much more

deeply and convinced them more deeply of their sin. Whoever speaks to others of guilt and sin should preach as a sinner; everything he says that is true is an episode from his own experience.[13]

The thought is echoed in his autobiography when he writes: "It is not where sinfulness is most talked about that its seriousness is most forcibly taught. There is not much about it in the Sermon on the Mount. But thanks to the longing for freedom from sin and for purity of heart which Jesus has enshrined in the Beatitudes, these form the great call to repentance which is increasingly working on man."[14]

On February 25 Schweitzer preached his last afternoon sermon to the congregation that had shared so many of his thoughts.

His text this time was "Be faithful unto death and I will give you the crown of life." "No doubt," he told them, "you have often noticed that during these last years I have been tired out, and have only been able to do my work by drawing on the last of my strength; and I have had the impression, as I came down from the pulpit, that you have had to be very indulgent with me. . . .

"And now that our ways are going to part, we must find a vantage point from which we can encompass a huge horizon. . . . You will understand that this saying—'be faithful'—offers us just the wide view that will rule our meditation."[15]

Faithfulness, he said, is the interior force of life, through which we direct our lives into strong-flowing channels, and save ourselves from spreading into shallow streams like a river with weak banks. There is faithfulness to oneself, without which our soul is wounded and slowly loses its blood. There is faithfulness toward men, which means nothing less than responsibility for everything we do to every man and woman alive. There is responsibility to the spirit of Jesus, which lies in placing ourselves at his service.

And the crown of life is not some prize to be awarded after it is all over.

"The crown of life is simply the joy and peace which fill the heart of the man who is faithful, which never desert him, but which grow more and more brilliant like the sinking sun, that at the very moment of its setting floods the whole world with light."[16]

So he said good-bye to St. Nicholas' and the university—and going around Strasbourg afterward, he could hardly bear to look at the places where he had taught and preached throughout those ten crowded years.

In Paris he got in touch with M. Boegner's successor at the Mission Society, M. Jean Bianquis. An agreement with the committee had gradually been reached over the years, and all seemed well; the basis of the agreement was that Schweitzer would come without involving the society in any expense whatever—"I know what heavy expenses the overseas missions represent for you. . . . I am counting on devoted friends who have given me to understand that they will help me within the limits of their capacities."

Schweitzer in fact had been going around Paris and Strasbourg ringing the doorbells of the wealthy and influential Protestant families he had come to know. And though he found that the tone of welcome changed noticeably when he mentioned the subject of his visit—particularly when it became clear that he was asking for money for a project that did not even exist yet—his personal involvement finally got him the help he needed. His experience of begging for the poor as a student in Strasbourg stood him in good stead. One family would suggest another, and so he begged his way around the cities.

In April he found a new way of raising money. He had never, it seems, given a solo organ recital in public before, but now he did—as part of a concert given by the Paris Bach Society "For the benefit of the Ogowe Mission." Gustave Bret said later that this was the first time that Schweitzer was recognized as a virtuoso soloist. The concert was a great success.

Meanwhile collections were being made in parishes in Alsace, whose pastors had been at college with him. Strasbourg professors contributed, even though they were German and the enterprise was for a French colony. There was another concert at Le Havre, and a lecture to go with it. And of course royalties from the Bach book were still coming in.

And so, when he had enough money for all the necessary equipment, for the voyage, and for the first year's running expenses, he told the Mission Society, in a letter dated May 11, that he was fully equipped and ready to go, asking only for a piece of ground and if possible some sort of building. On May 13 M. Bianquis, with an almost audible sigh of relief, agreed.

But in the meantime, a new pastor had joined the committee, a M. Edouard Sautter, and naturally the situation now had to be explained to him. M. Bianquis spoke to him, and found him somewhat disapproving. He then wrote to him, a long, closely reasoned and fervent letter, pointing out how much the mission would benefit from the presence of a doctor, particularly one who came full of love of Jesus, having trained for just this task. He summarized the history of the case, mentioning how the other committee members had had their doubts but now had been persuaded of Schweitzer's fitness to be associated with their work. He was confident that M. Sautter would also come to see it in this light.

M. Sautter quite failed to see it in this light. M. Sautter knew clearly what a Christian was, and Schweitzer was not one of them. He was obdurate. And he swung one or two other members of the committee to his way of thinking. M. Bianquis sent Schweitzer copies of his correspondence with Sautter, and his letters grew increasingly desperate. Schweitzer, already at the end of his tether, already beginning to make lists of equipment, already in communication with a M. Ottman in Africa about what to bring (tough crockery—the Africans break it—and envelopes *without glue*), suddenly found himself requested to appear before the committee and satisfy them as to his religious orthodoxy. Schweitzer was very wary. He knew of a minister whom the society had refused to accept simply because he was not prepared categorically to say that the fourth Gospel was written by the apostle John. The minister was right; the evidence is not conclusive. But his historical integrity branded him as undesirable.

Schweitzer accordingly sent a message to the committee which the more rigid among them must have seen as the confirmation of their worst fears. He refused to be examined by the committee, and "based my refusal on the fact that Jesus, when He called his disciples, required from them nothing beyond the will to follow Him. I also sent a message to the Committee that, if we are to follow the saying of Jesus: 'He that is not against us is on our part', a missionary society would be in the wrong if it rejected even a Mahommedan who offered his services for the treatment of their suffering natives."[17]

Instead, he offered to meet all the twenty or so committee members individually, to give them a chance to make a personal assessment, and this was agreed. As he went the rounds it became clear that some at least of the committee were afraid that with his great learning he might "confuse" the missionaries; and also that the temptation to preach might become too much for him even though he went as a doctor. Only when he solemnly promised that if he went he would be "as dumb as a carp" on the subject of religion did they relax and give him their blessing; as well they might, since they were sending out a fully qualified doctor, dedicated, humane, and hardworking; tamed, muzzled, and obedient, at no cost whatever to themselves. Even so, at some moment during this struggle it seems that the Swiss-based Union of Evangelical Missions actually wrote to Schweitzer, offering him a post on his own terms—the easy way out of his difficulties. When exactly this happened is hard to determine, since we only have a reference to this offer in another letter written in 1921. But Schweitzer's obstinacy, his desire to prove his point in his own way, had clearly not softened with the years and he turned the offer down.

The strain of this time, mental as well as physical, must have been tremendous. Almost all the letters that survive speak of some illness or other. Schweitzer was in a state of permanent exhaustion. But there was, in addition to the other complications of life, a more personal one. Hélène

Bresslau, who had for long been his constant assistant, helping not only with his books and his organ practice but with lists and prices and correspondence, was determined to go to Africa with Schweitzer. She was not, many say, the only one; but she was the one whom he chose. Whether they really intended to get married is a moot point. Opinions of those who were there agree that Hélène's father very understandably put his foot down and declared that his daughter was not going to disappear into the jungle with this beefy Alsatian unless a wedding conferred respectability on the situation.

If that is the case, the question arises whether in Schweitzer's mind the association was even now a sexual one or whether it was not still a union of goodwill. These two had known each other, after all, for almost nine years. A sudden development of passion after so long seems highly unlikely, and there had surely been no deep attachment earlier or why did Hélène never go with him on those holidays to Grimmialp? The union, whatever it may have been, was signaled on January, 1912, when Hélène's name appears for the first time side by side with Schweitzer's in the Günsbach guest book. The friendship became, as it were, official. But either before or shortly after this something happened which was to have a fateful and permanent consequence.

One day of thaw, Hélène went out to ski with Schweitzer's brother, Paul. She was, as we know, a skillful and intrepid skier. Schweitzer, feeling the thaw, was worried that the snow might be treacherous and warned them not to go. They went nevertheless, and Hélène fell badly. When Schweitzer saw her after the fall he knew that the injury would affect her permanently for the rest of her life. The damage was to her back. Accounts vary between a slipped disk and a broken spine, but it was certainly serious. It seems possible also that even at this time Hélène already suffered from other disabilities. Her daughter believes that she had already had a slight attack of tuberculosis due to overwork, though it is hard to be sure of this—central Africa was not a good place for a tubercular subject and Schweitzer would never have allowed her to go there had the attack been serious and had she not fully recovered. There was also said to be some heart weakness, though when this made its first appearance is doubtful.

She was soon active again after the skiing accident, her vitality and courage undiminished. But physically she was affected, and Schweitzer knew it.

It was pure coincidence that in his childhood he had determined to marry a cripple—Hélène's qualities were the very opposite, energy and enthusiasm. Yet one cannot help feeling that when her father—and she too—wanted the marriage, the prospect may in some degree have satisfied Schweitzer's instinct for compassion.

The engagement took at least the younger members of the family by surprise. They knew that the two families did not entirely get on. His was too Alsatian, hers too German—and Jewish into the bargain. Hélène's mother was a sweet woman, but her father was not much liked by some of the Schweitzers. Besides—the old cry—they really didn't think he had time for that kind of thing.

However, it happened. The engagement party was held at Strasbourg. Champagne was drunk, Mrs Schweitzer wiped her eyes, the men smiled indulgently, and Suzi had a loving pinch on the arm from her Uncle Bery.

The wedding was arranged for June 18. Earlier that month a stranger arrived at the Günsbach manse to pay his respects to Schweitzer, but Schweitzer was upstairs in bed worn out, and the stranger had to be content with talking to his mother. "You have an important son," said the man. "If he was less important I might see more of him," she replied; and then the unhappiness came out: "When he has something new in his mind he gets it all ready secretly, and when it's too late for anyone to do anything about it he lets people know. Now he's off with his wife to Africa as a mission doctor."

"What?" asked the man. "He's got a wife?"

"He will have, if he finds the time to marry her."

He did find the time, and "Aunt-Prim-and-Proper" became a real aunt. So far as one can tell, there was no honeymoon worth the name—for that there really was no time. Preparations for Africa went on apace. And as the day of departure drew nearer, the unhappiness of Schweitzer's mother grew deeper.

Part of Schweitzer's preparations consisted of an assiduous picking of useful brains. He had always gone out of his way to understand and share the problems of butcher, baker, and candlestick maker. Now his interest was more personal, for in Africa he would have to combine all those functions and many more in himself. He had to discipline himself to the chore of making orderly and accurate lists, of estimating budgets and keeping accounts. He learned a good deal about handling money from a Mrs. Fischer, whose husband had been a professor of surgery at Strasbourg but had died young. Having undertaken to go to Africa independently, Schweitzer could not count on any support from anywhere once he was out there. There could be no cables to headquarters for more funds or a couple of extra nurses. There could be no replacements for himself unless he himself found them. If a house needed repair, he would have to repair it. And all this in an environment totally strange to him, full of problems he had never encountered.

Everything must be foreseen now, or it would be too late. One particular apprehension was nagging at him. The Russian representatives in Paris were openly saying that war was not far away. And in both France and

Germany civil servants were increasingly being paid in paper money, not in gold. Gold was being held back. It seemed ominous. For Schweitzer in the Gabon would be an alien—a German citizen on French territory. His political antennae twitched, and he made provision for taking 2,000 marks in gold, which would keep its value regardless of developments.

On the literary and artistic side three projects were still unfinished— the thesis on the psychology of Jesus, the Bach organ-works, and a new edition of *The Quest of the Historical Jesus.* The last was made necessary by a number of British writers who had been attracting attention with the theory that Jesus never existed at all; he was a mythological figure, they said, invented like the Greek gods as a symbol of a new faith.

In answer to this entertaining theory, which still enjoys periodic resurrections, Schweitzer demonstrated at some length that though it may be hard to prove that Jesus existed, it is quite impossible to prove that he did not. Like those writers who had tried to prove Jesus mad, these Britishers—notably Robertson, Smith, Frazer, and Drews—seemed to have no knowledge of the critical work that had been done on the differences between the Gospels, and used all four indiscriminately to make their points. But more important, they never tackled the real issue, which was that if the early Christians had wanted to invent a mythological founder, it was inconceivable that they would have invented the Jesus who appears in the New Testament—a Jesus full of inconsistencies and hard sayings, quite unfitted to be the mythical hero of a folk cult. This section of the book unfortunately never found its way into English translation.

The Bach organ edition would never be finished in time—that was obvious. Despite all he could do, three volumes, dealing with the Choral Preludes, still remained to be dealt with when he left for Africa. But while he was in Europe work went on ceaselessly on the first five.

The Psychiatric Study of Jesus was finally completed early in 1913. Now Schweitzer was three times a doctor—of philosophy, of theology, and of medicine. Whether the triple doctorate is indeed unique, as some claim, I do not know. But certain it is that there have not been many of them. And we may be fairly sure that no one else has ever taken a third doctorate with the precise intention of escaping the academic world of the first two.

One further administrative problem faced Schweitzer. His doctor's diploma was a German one, and he wanted to practice in a French colony. Here the "old-boy network" came into action. Influential friends in Paris went to work, and special permission was granted. All the formalities were over. All that remained was the packing and the going.

The Paris Bach Society, which Schweitzer had helped to found seven years before and for which he had played so faithfully presented him with a magnificent parting gift—a piano specially equipped with a pedal attachment, and on which he could simulate playing an organ. From Samkita on the upper reaches of the Ogowe, where the missionaries waited with eager excitement for the doctor they needed so badly, he received instructions from M. Ottman how to preserve the precious piano, lining it with zinc against the ravages of the ubiquitous insects.

In deciding on the best site to commence operations, Schweitzer had consulted a M. Morel, another missionary from the Ogowe River, who was also an Alsatian. The Ogowe was navigable for several hundred miles inland from Cape Lopez, and in the days when the jungle had not yet been pierced by road or rail such a river was the main, almost the only, highway. A hospital at a strategic point on the river would be accessible to villagers for many miles up and down stream.

The Ogowe had already been opened up by traders in the nineteenth century, and settlements of both Catholics and Protestants were scattered along its shores. (The book which appeared in the 1920's purporting to be the memoirs of Trader Horn was based, whether fictionally or not, on the experiences of one of the Ogowe traders. After the traders came the missionaries.)[18] About 150 miles from the coast lies the village of Lambarene, and a few miles beyond that the mission station of Andende. Here Schweitzer, on M. Morel's advice, had requested and been granted a house for himself and his wife, and a site for some sort of hospital building. Thirty or forty miles farther upriver lay Samkita, where M. Morel and M. Ottman worked.

So the last of the equipment and provisions were bought, the crates were packed and labeled (one of the cellars of St. Thomas' Church having been pressed into service as a storeroom and packing place, somewhat to the verger's displeasure); and finally in February the packing cases—seventy of them—were sent off in advance to Bordeaux. It only remained to conclude the arrangements by which fresh supplies could be ordered and sent on to Africa, and then to say good-bye.

Apart from the personal leave-takings there was a last good-bye to be said from the pulpit, and Schweitzer returned to St. Nicholas' for a sort of farewell guest appearance on March 9. The text he chose for this occasion was that passage from St. Paul's letter to the Philippians which is so often used as a blessing at the end of a service: "And the peace of God which surpasses all understanding keep your hearts and your minds in Jesus Christ." Schweitzer had always used this parting benediction, and now used it for a greater parting. But what he wanted to say about it was slightly different from what the congregation might have expected. He wanted to emphasize that St. Paul was talking about minds as well as hearts. He wanted to strike another blow against an age which was increasingly separating thought (*i.e.*, science and technology) from faith (*i.e.*, religion). His last lecture series was about the reconciliation of the two, but those lectures are lost to us. In this sermon we have a glimpse of the way he was thinking, and it is important for what was to come later.

Schweitzer had now spent over six years working among medical men, studying the hard facts of natural science and biology. He had a right to speak for science. And he believed, more and more deeply, that thought led to religion. If it did not, that was because it did not go deep enough but gave up too soon. If the mind did not lead toward God, of what use was the mind? Was God irrational? If so the very heart of things must be irrational, and reason was of no use at all. But reason was one of men's noblest functions. Therefore God must be at the heart of reason as well as at the heart of love. All the true and excellent capacities of man must meet at the same point; and that point must be in some way divine:

"The more I felt I grasped the personality of Jesus, the stronger grew my conviction that in him there was an interpenetration of faith and simple natural thought. The further I went in my study of the history of Christianity, the clearer it seemed to me that so many errors and conflicts amount to this—that from the first generations to our own day people have constantly renewed the opposition of faith and piety against reason, and so dug a ditch in the hearts of men where God placed a harmony."

Then he defines what he means by reason—or what it is not. "You realise that reason is quite frankly not just the ability to think about superficial everyday affairs; it is the light which illuminates the spirit from within, which helps us to unravel the meaning of things, of the world, of the enigma of existence, the value and the purpose of our own being, and which allows us to discover the guiding thread of our own life. And this can only be what leads to the peace of God, the harmonisation between ourselves and the outside world. . . ."

And how does this peace surpass all understanding? "Just as the distant snow-covered peaks, shining in the sun, seem to rise in a solitary jet above a horizon of mist—but in reality stand behind the mountainous fortifications over which they tower, and which no-one can reach without first crossing all the intervening country—so does the peace of God seem to tower in the distance beyond reason, but in truth stands upon it."

So for Schweitzer reason was always driving farther, because "true happiness only breathes from the depths of inward peace." Reason "increases our thirst for peace. It drives us to climb the steep flanks of the mountains, and when we reach the shining barriers of the glaciers it encourages us—'Higher! Higher! Always higher! On to the shining light of the peaks, to the peace and the silent grandeur of the summits.' "[19]

So Schweitzer spoke, like one of those doomed heroes of Ibsen who are drunk with the romantic intoxication of the far-off peaks of the spirit. But Schweitzer, as we have seen, was the man who contrived to balance the extremes at the center point; and while he kept one eye on the distant snow, the other scanned every step of the way. As he spoke, his seventy cases were on the way to Bordeaux, and his 2,000 marks in gold were ready for packing in his hand baggage.

One final gesture: He took a ninety-nine-year lease on the Rocks of Kanzenrain—those rocks on the hill above Günsbach where he had sat and looked out over the valley since he was a child. A piece of the land that had bred him now waited for his return, and nobody could touch it without his knowledge. And so the last few days passed and the morning of March 23 dawned, Good Friday, 1913.

Suzanne was there and remembered how it was. How his mother got up early and went about the house with her face set; how Schweitzer came down and asked for his favorite breakfast, and Mrs. Schweitzer left the room tight-lipped. The uneasy morning passed, and lunchtime, and it was time to leave the village and cross the stream by the bridge where the children used to chase and mock Mausche the Jew on his donkey cart, and wait in the station for the single-track train that would come down the valley and take them to Colmar for the Strasbourg connection and the Paris express. The church bells rang for afternoon service—the same bells, at much the same time of year, as had rung thirty years before and cued the boy Albert to drive away the birds from the threatening catapults. If it seems sentimental to mention this, we must remember that he *was* sentimental—particularly about his homeland, his village, and his father's church. Throughout his life this had been home; there had been no break, no reaction to interrupt the flow of his feelings toward it.

The train arrived as the bell ceased, and Schweitzer and Hélène climbed onto the platform of the last coach, from which they could wave good-bye and look for the last time at the valley. The train started and they all waved—except Mrs. Schweitzer. The hard Schillinger spirit would not melt. The will that drove the son to Africa held back the blessing of the mother. He was not to see her again.

Schweitzer and Hélène spent the night in Strasbourg. On Saturday they took the Paris train and on Sunday went to the Easter celebrations at St. Sulpice and heard Widor at his organ. At two o'clock they were off again, to Bordeaux.

That Easter day was brilliant with sunshine, warm with spring, and the people were out in their holiday clothes. Finally to be on the move after seven grinding years of preparation, and on such a glorious day, seemed like a dream.

What was ahead was totally unknown. Everything that foresight and imagination could do had been done, but the break with past experience was complete. Schweitzer was going to Africa to work, to serve, to heal, to try to pay back something of what the white races owed the black. But behind that dedication was also the romantic child, unable to attend his lessons for dreaming of foreign lands and drawn constantly back to the great sad figure of the noble black man on Colmar's Champ de Mars. His whole life had been a preparation for this moment. Poised between one life and the next, he looked out at the sunshine and knew that whatever sacrifices he might have made, whatever happiness he might have left behind, he had made the right choice. It would have been harder to stay.

13

AFRICA
1913

W HEN you think you have thought of everything there is always something you have not thought of; for example, that the customs offices at Bordeaux will be closed on Easter Monday. The ship waited at Pauillac, thirty miles farther downriver. The boat train from Bordeaux was due to leave for the docks before long, and the big packing case which had been sent in advance sat inaccessible in the customs. The situation was fraught with disaster, for customs officials are not noted for their willingness to bend the rules in the interests of distracted travelers. Somehow or other however Schweitzer found an official who was prepared to do just that, and with minutes to spare the baggage was hurried by motorcar from customs to train, by train from Bordeaux to Pauillac, and so on board the steamship *Europe*.

After the jostling and shoving and finding the cabin (comfortably forward, away from the engines) and cleaning up and settling in, lunch was served. The Schweitzers felt ''poor untraveled home birds'' among the old Africa hands at their table—a couple of doctors, some officers, two wives returning to their husbands in the colonial service. Schweitzer ''could not help thinking of the fowls my mother used to buy every summer from Italian poultry dealers to add to her stock, which for several days used to walk about among the old ones very shyly and humbly.''[1] And he noticed ''a certain expression of energy and determination''[2] in his fellow passengers.

The Bay of Biscay provided further unforeseen hazards. The traditional foul weather set in, and the storm lasted three days. The Congo steamers were particularly shallow of draught, to enable them to go far up the Congo, and they rolled correspondingly. Schweitzer, unprepared, had not made the baggage fast, and in the night the cabin trunks ''began to chase each other about. The two hat cases also, which contained our sun helmets, took part in the game without reflecting how badly off they might come in it, and when I tried to catch the trunks, I nearly got one leg crushed between them and the wall of the cabin. So I left them to their fate and contented myself with lying quietly in my berth and counting how many seconds elapsed between each plunge made by the ship and the corresponding rush of our boxes. Soon there could be heard similar noises from other cabins and added to them the sound of crockery, etc., moving wildly about in the galley and the dining saloon.''[3]

That passage comes from Schweitzer's first book about Africa, *On the Edge of the Primeval Forest.* The style is new. Neither the formal style of the scholarly books nor the near-rhetorical style of the early sermons, here is the style which is the man himself. Disasters and dangers are treated with humor and even rampaging baggage elicits a sort of affectionate sympathy, as though it had a right to its "game."

This, I feel sure, was the Schweitzer his friends loved, the Schweitzer by whom every living creature, and by a comic extension every inanimate object as well, was appreciated and enjoyed simply for existing, for doing what it was its nature to do.

And what did the man of God do as the ship was flung to and fro? Did he pray? No. With a more scientific spirit he counted the seconds between the lurch of the ship and the suicidal rush of the baggage. Perhaps he prayed as well, but that is not what he remembered and reported.

Eventually the storm ended and the ship plowed on to calmer, sunnier waters. Schweitzer occupied himself in picking up tips from more experienced passengers. A lieutenant expounded his views on the evil ways Mohammedanism brought in its wake—not because the religion was false but because, so he said, it made the Africans anti-European, opposed to material improvements, and therefore idle. A military doctor gave Schweitzer two hours' discourse every day about his experiences of tropical medicine.

Once past the Canary Islands the troops on board were ordered to wear sun helmets when on deck. Schweitzer was surprised, since the weather was not particularly hot. But he was warned by an old Africa hand that in tropical latitudes the sun was man's worst enemy, to be dreaded even more in the cool of sunrise and sunset than at midday. He took the hint to heart, for he was to become notorious for his insistence that all the people at his hospital should wear something on their heads; often clashing with travelers who had gone bareheaded in tropical climates for years before meeting him. But before he became so rigid he was to have some practical experience of sunstroke himself—not personally, but in colleagues.

More curious—indeed extraordinary—is the fact that he also wore a hat after sunset! This seems to have had no practical reason at all, nothing but the fulfillment of an apparently pointless promise. The promise was made to the old Countess of Erlach, Frederick Curtius' mother-in-law, in the days when Schweitzer used to play the piano for her in the evenings, in the chapter house of St. Thomas'. An uncle of the countess who had worked for years in the tropics had told her that the reason he never contracted malaria was because he never went bareheaded out of doors after sunset. The old lady, who had greatly taken to Schweitzer and had decided to exercise a civilizing influence on him, made him promise to do the same. Schweitzer kept his promise. And never, as a matter of fact, caught malaria. Though, as he says himself, "of course the disease does not result from going with uncovered head in the tropics after sundown."[4]

What can we make of this blind obedience to an irrational promise? Schweitzer did not normally feel himself tied by bonds of sentiment when they turned out to be contrary to sense or to his own convictions. Truth normally reigned over all other considerations, and the truth was that the opinions of the countess' uncle carried no medical weight at all. So this obligation to which Schweitzer bound himself was no more than a gesture. I can only think it was a combination of two threads in Schweitzer's character, both of which were so deeply part of him that he had no alternative but to do as the countess said.

The first was his sense of debt. He owed the countess a great deal, and he could repay it only by doing as she wished. The other was his almost romantic sense of fidelity. When in old age he said, "*Je suis fidèle*," he was speaking of fidelity to the influences which made him what he was. All his life he was faithful to the deep experiences of his early years, because in them dwelt a richness of feeling which he never wished to lose. Without them "the soul lost its blood." I think that this habit of wearing a hat after sundown was a ritual of remembrance, by which he not only acknowledged gratitude but remained in touch with one of the sources of his strength. For despite his Protestantism, despite his scientific turn of mind and his hatred of humbug and his incomprehension of the transcendental, he had a strong sense of the value of ritual. As a boy he had loved the Catholic chancel of the Günsbach church. He remembered and honored anniversaries and birthdays. His wife said of him, "He really does know how to give presents." His rituals were the rituals of his own life and experience, not the imposed rituals of an organization. But they were no less important to him for that.

At Dakar came the first symbolic landing on African soil, and the first taste of African cruelty to animals. When he saw two Africans sitting on a loaded cart that was stuck in the mud and beating their horse to make it pull harder, Schweizer rapidly had the two astonished blacks off their cart and pushing. "If you can't bear to see animals ill treated," said the lieutenant, "don't go to Africa."[5]

Schweitzer was well prepared for the horrors that the white man had brought to Africa. Whether he was ready for the Africans' own defects is harder to say. The statue in Colmar was romanticized. Was he, at least subconsciously, expecting to find the noble savage sadly but with dignity enduring the rule of the white man? Mrs. Urquhart thinks he was. She thinks that the real Africa was a deep shock to him. Even on the Ivory Coast, where he saw finely built blacks who might have been models for the Colmar statue, he noted in the seaport Africans' eyes a "haunting vision of sullen and unwilling subjection, mixed with insolence."[6]

As the ship sailed, close inshore, past the Pepper Coast, the Ivory Coast, the Gold Coast, and the Slave Coast, Schweitzer's imagination was dwelling on the suffering those lands had seen. The sympathetic insight which had taken him into the minds of Bach, Paul, and Jesus was focused now upon the slaves who had been dragged in their thousands from these shores to the plantations of the New World. The schoolboy dreamer, the lover of travelers' tales, the follower of Jesus—all the layers of his personality were touched. And as he sat at table he tried similarly to guess at the thoughts—the responsibilities, the experiences and the ideals of his fellow passengers. "If everything could be written down that is done during these years by all of us who are now here on this ship, what a book it would be! Would there be no pages that we should be glad to turn over as quickly as possible?"[7]

The heat grew more intense. It was worse when the sky was overcast than on the clear days, and the intermittent storms did nothing to cool the air. After nearly three weeks they finally reached the equator and the capital city of the Gabon, Libreville—so called because freed slaves were landed here in the days when France and Britain had finally abandoned slavery and with the enthusiasm of reformed sinners had suddenly turned from capturing slaves to capturing their captors.

In Libreville the Schweitzers were welcomed by an American missionary, Mr. Ford, and since it was a Sunday were introduced to some of his black congregation. Schweitzer noticed that they showed none of the sullen looks of the seaport blacks, but looked "free and yet modest."[8] Mr. Ford was to prove a useful friend when war came. The last few miles, from Libreville to Cape Lopez, at the mouth of the Ogowe, were spent in worrying how much duty they would be charged on their equipment. The other passengers had told frightening tales of the ferocity of customs charges. But again they were lucky, and in due course transferred to the paddle steamer *Alémbé* which was to take them upriver. The equipment however had to be left behind. There was no room in this boat; and the next was not for another fortnight.

And up the river, into Africa, they went. Any first visit to the tropics is not merely a new experience—it is a new kind of experience. The feelings it arouses are unlike anything you have felt before. You do not recognize them. You do not recognize yourself. You are a new creature, with new perceptions. And so Schweitzer found, for all the care with which he had prepared his imagination.

> River and forest . . . ! Who can really describe the first impression they make? We seemed to be dreaming! Pictures of antediluvian scenery which elsewhere had seemed to be merely the creation of fancy, are now seen in real life. It is impossible to say where the river ends and the land begins, for a mighty network of roots, clothed with bright-flowering creepers, projects right into the water. Clumps of palms and palm trees, ordinary trees spreading out widely with green bough and huge leaves, single trees of the pine family shooting up to a towering height in between them, wide fields of papyrus clumps as tall as a man, with big fan-like leaves, and amid all this luxuriant greenery the rotting stems of dead giants shooting up to heaven. . . . In every gap in the forest a water mirror meets the eye; at every bend in the river a new tributary shows itself. A heron flies heavily up and then settles on a dead tree trunk; white birds and blue birds skim over the water, and high in the air a pair of ospreys circle. Then—yes, there can be no mistake about it!—from the branch of a palm there hang and swing—two monkey tails! Now the owners of the tails are visible. We are really in Africa!

The scale, too, overwhelms the mind:

> Each new corner, each new bend, is like the last. Always the same forest and the same yellow water. The impression which nature makes on us is immeasurably deepened by the constant monotonous repetition. You shut your eyes for an hour, and when you open them you see exactly what you saw before. The Ogowe is not a river but a river system, three or four branches, each as big as the Rhine, twisting themselves together, and in between are lakes big and little. How the black pilot finds his way through this maze of watercourses is a riddle to me.[9]

Let me quote the impression of two other writers about these African jungles—for it was among these jungles, and partly because of them, that Schweitzer found the key to all his thinking. Here then is Mary Kingsley, a magnificently humorous and intrepid English spinster who journeyed in the 1890's up this same river and wrote a book of unparalleled adventure, comedy, and scientific interest, *Travels in West Africa*:

> Not only does this forest depend on flowers for its illumination, for there are many kinds of trees having their young shoots, crimson, brown-pink, and creamy yellow: added to this there is also the relieving aspect of the prevailing fashion among West African trees, of

wearing the trunk white with here and there upon it splashes of pale pink lichen, and vermilion-red fungus, which alone is sufficient to prevent the great mass of vegetation from being a monotony in green.

All day long we steam past ever-varying scenes of loveliness whose component parts are ever the same, yet the effect ever different. Doubtless it is wrong to call it a symphony, yet I know no other word to describe the scenery of the Ogowe. It is as full of life and beauty and passion as any symphony Beethoven ever wrote: the parts changing, interweaving, and returning. There are "leit motifs" here in it, too. See the papyrus ahead; and you know when you get abreast of it you will find the great forest sweeping away in a bay-like curve behind it against the dull gray sky, the splendid columns of its cotton and red woods looking like a facade of some limitless inchoate temple. Then again there is that stretch of sword-grass, looking as if it grew firmly on to the bottom, so steady does it stand; but as the "Mové" goes by, her wash sets it undulating in waves across its broad acres of extent, showing it is only riding at anchor; and you know after a grass patch you will soon see a red dwarf clay cliff, with a village perched on its top, and the inhabitants thereof in their blue and red cloths standing by to shout and wave to the "Mové," or legging it like lamp-lighters from the back streets to do so, and through all these changing phases, there is always the strain of the vast wild forest, and the swift, deep, silent river.[10]

But it was Winston Churchill, writing in *My African Journey* of the Uganda forests, who expressed something else about them that entered Schweitzer's soul—a sense of awe at the unimaginable energy with which in these jungles life destroys life and then arises again from death:

One becomes, not without a secret sense of aversion, the spectator of an intense convulsion of life and death. Reproduction and decay are locked struggling in infinite embraces. In this glittering Equatorial slum huge trees jostle one another for room to live; slender growths stretch upwards—as it seems in agony—towards sunlight and life. The soil bursts with irrepressible vegetations. Every victor, trampling on the rotting mould of exterminated antagonists, soars aloft only to encounter another host of aerial rivals, to be burdened with masses of parasitic foliage, smothered in the glorious blossoms of creepers laced and bound and interwoven with interminable tangles of vines and trailers. Birds are as bright as butterflies; butterflies are as big as birds. . . .[11]

Scattered throughout this immensity are the people Schweitzer has come here to care for.

After a long run we stop at a small negro village, where, stacked on the river bank, are several hundred logs of wood, such as bakers often use, and we lie to in order to ship them, as wood is the fuel used for the engines. A plank is put out to the bank; the negroes form line and carry the logs on board. On the deck stands another negro with a paper, and as ten logs have passed, another on the plank calls to him in musical tones, "Put a one." When the hundredth log comes, the call, in the same pleasant tone, is, "Put a cross." The price is from four to five francs a hundred, which is rather high when one considers that the logs are all windfalls and only have to be collected.

The captain abuses the village elder for not having had logs enough ready. The latter excuses himself with pathetic words and gestures. At last they come to an agreement that he shall be paid in spirits instead of cash, because he thinks that the whites get their liquor cheaper than the blacks do, so that he will make a better bargain. . . .

Now the voyage continues. On the banks are the ruins of abandoned huts. "When I came here fifteen years ago," said a trader who stood near me, "these places were all flourishing villages." "And why are they so no longer?" I asked. He shrugged his shoulders and said in a low voice, "L'alcohol [sic]. . . ."

I feel more convinced than ever that this land needs to help it men who will never let themselves be discouraged.[12]

So long as the moon is high they can continue by night, while "a heat that is almost unendurable"[13] streams out from the forest wall. They move on till past midnight. This also is strange in the tropics, that because of the heat night has a different nature. In cooler climates you are glad to be indoors at night—the air grows chilly. But near the equator it is a good time to move, to go out, to be active—so long as you can see and so long as you are not in danger. You can sleep by day, when it grows too hot to stir.

So at first light, five o'clock, they are on the way again. And finally, well over a hundred miles from the coast, they see at last the village whose name the world has learned to link with Dr. Schweitzer's—Lambarene, which in the local dialect means "Let us try."

The mission station itself is not in the village but farther upriver still, an hour's journey by canoe. Mr. Christol and Mr. Ellenberger have come to meet the Schweitzers in two canoes rowed by boys from the mission school, singing and racing.

The dugout tree trunks seem very unstable—and are. The river is wide and full of dangerous beasts. The boys decide to race the paddle steamer—the Schweitzers grow very nervous. But after half an hour they manage to relax. The canoes swing into a side stream. In the distance a group of buildings gleam white on the side of a hill—the end of the journey— the terminus of a decision made seventeen years before, between waking and getting out of bed—the beginning of a life's work.

14

ANDENDE
The First Hospital
1913

THE wooden bungalow that the Schweitzers had been allotted stood on rows of iron piles, which lifted it above the threat of torrents that regularly flowed down the hill after the storms. A veranda ran all around, shaded by the wide roof. In every direction the view was of forest, though the river broke the middle distance on one side, and a range of hills stood blue on the horizon.

A little after six, before they were properly settled in, darkness fell suddenly and the hot moist night began. Twelve hours of darkness, twelve hours of light—the rhythm of days scarcely varies so near the equator. Schweitzer sat on a packing case and listened, entranced, as the children's evening hymn floated through the night air, competing with the din of the crickets.

An enormous spider crept down the wall. "An exciting hunt," he wrote, "and the creature is done for."[1] More slaughter followed. The house, left empty for a while, had become infested with spiders and flying cockroaches, and Schweitzer, lover of life in all its forms, began his sojourn in Africa with an evening of mass destruction before he and Hélène could get to bed. An unreasoning sentimentality was never part of his philosophy and the first priority here was to make their new home habitable.

At six A.M. the sun rose, the bell rang, the children sang their dawn hymn, the day began.

So did the stream of patients. Strict instructions had been issued that the doctor was to be given time to settle in, but they were ignored. There had been white men in Lambarene before with medical skill, and the villagers had learned to trust them. The news of the new doctor's coming had spread wide, and the sick were not going to wait.

Unfortunately there was nowhere to treat them—except in the open air.

The local timber traders had been enjoying a good season and had attract-ed all the available labor at rates the missionaries could not hope to com-pete with; so the corrugated iron "hospital" Schweitzer had been prom-ised had not materialized. Moreover, the bulk of the equipment and drugs was still a hundred and fifty miles away on the coast, and the black teach-er whose services Schweitzer had counted on as interpreter and assistant (he had been in correspondence with and about him for a year) had failed to turn up because he was engaged in a legal dispute in his village. Legal disputes, Schweitzer was to discover, were very popular with the Afri-cans and took automatic precedence over any other project or promise. This, said the missionaries, was the beginning of his education—you could never rely on an African.

So the job started, without accommodation, equipment, or assistance. All Schweitzer had was a small quantity of drugs in his trunk—and of course the patients.

From east and west they came—the cannibal Fangs from the interior (the French called them Pahouins)—from downstream the Galoas and others, survivors of the coastal tribes decimated by the slave trade and by intertribal warfare. Now Schweitzer could begin to study on the spot the results of the white man's interference and greed, the debt he had come to lighten.

There was little here of the noble savage of Colmar. For centuries the slavers had taken the strongest and best of the stock. The tribes nearest the coast had themselves turned slave traders and had raided up the river, draining the villages. Even when the English and French slavers saw the evil of their ways, other nations found it comparatively easy to evade their gunboats and the trade went on. When finally the United States abol-ished slavery, and the demand fell off to the point where the risks were no longer worth running, the tribes' troubles were not ended. White traders found their way at last through the devious channels of the estuary and up the river—a route which the coastal Africans had so far kept secret—and the porters they brought with them from the Congo carried smallpox and sleeping sickness to districts which had never known them before. Half the population around Lambarene died in the first smallpox epidemic. Into the lands of these weakened tribes came the warlike Fangs from the highlands farther up the river, and there was virtually no resistance to their slaughtering.

At last the white man did something toward undoing the harm he had caused. The killing was stopped, the Fangs held in check. The point where their dominance came to a halt was roughly at Lambarene. Peace of a sort prevailed, but there was no love lost between the tribes.

Then the missionaries came; and the Ogowe, unlucky in climate and in history, was at least lucky in its missionaries. The first who ventured up the river was an American, Dr. Nassau, who came with a group of American Presbyterians to the west coast of Africa and from there explored deep into the interior. Mary Kingsley believed he might have ranked with Livingstone and Burton as an explorer had he troubled to take notes of his expeditions.

Nassau established a mission station at Andende, and for a while the Americans ran it. Then the French authorities decided that all instructions to Africans in their colonies must be given in French and the Americans had to withdraw, handing the station over to the Paris Mission Society. Schweitzer's judgment in picking on this particular station is confirmed by Mary Kingsley, who had very little use indeed for missionaries in general but who wrote of the Andende group that their "influence upon the natives has been, and is, all for good; and the amount of work they have done, considering the small financial resources behind them, is to a person who has seen other missions most remarkable, and is not open to the criticism lavished upon missions in general. . . . I regard the Mission Evangélique, judging from the results I have seen, as the perfection of what one may call a purely spiritual mission."[2]

Such, briefly, was the history of the hill on which Schweitzer, hemmed in by the immeasurable forest, under the beating sun of what experienced travelers have called the worst climate in the world, set up his open-air clinic for the sad dregs of half a dozen lowland tribes and their cannibal foes.

He knew, of course, what diseases he might expect to encounter—but he had never imagined the sick would be so numerous, nor that so many patients would be suffering from so many diseases at the same time. A curious myth has arisen that Schweitzer's hospital dealt solely, or mainly, with leprosy. In fact practically every disease under the sun was represented—not only the specifically tropical diseases but European ones as well. Cancer and appendicitis seemed not to have reached Africa, but everything else cropped up sooner or later, from pleurisy and whooping cough to nicotine poisoning. Schweitzer listed the commonest as "skin diseases of various sorts, malaria, sleeping sickness, leprosy, elephantiasis, heart complaints, suppurating injuries to the bones (osteomyelitis) and tropical dysentery."[3] Hernias were also very frequent, often becoming strangulated and causing intense pain followed by death. And, unprintable in those days but widespread nonetheless, venereal diseases brought by Europeans. "Here among us," said one man, "everybody is ill." "Our country," said one old chief, "devours its own children."[4] Almost worse than the multiplicity of the diseases was their sheer extent. Africa does nothing by halves. An ulcerated leg would be simply one running, stinking open sore. All kinds of burrowing creatures beneath the skin set up irritations all over the body which were scratched till they too developed into open wounds. The swellings of elephantiasis can be so huge one can barely believe that people could still carry on something like normal existence with these burdens.

So of the walking wounded who came to Schweitzer's clinic many were in a state which, had they been Europeans, would have had them in hospital long since, or perhaps on a mortuary slab. The hardihood which kept them alive, active, and even cheerful was Schweitzer's only ally against the ubiquitous onslaught of death.

Among other things which contributed to the general ill-health of the area was the poverty of diet. Staple foods that other countries can rely on—corn, rice, and potatoes—produced no usable crops in the intense damp heat of the Ogowe climate. The people lived mainly on manioc (the ground-up root of the cassava tree), on yams, and on bananas. Even these were not indigenous but had been introduced from the West Indies by the Portuguese. In the districts where they had not been established the people lived permanently near famine level, and a great many would eat earth in their starvation. In defiance of the comforting belief that a man who knows the forest need never starve, these jungles produced no nourishment whatever; a man lost there would certainly and swiftly die.

Apart from the physical diseases there were mental and psychological complications to deal with. Taboos, curses, and the dread of witch doctors dominated the patients' minds; no amount of medicine would cure a man who was convinced he had broken a taboo and would die. Poisoning was common; the fear of it commoner still. Terror and superstition were as deadly as bacilli.

These things Schweitzer learned little by little. For this first fortnight he could do little more than ease pain and begin to build up trust. When work was over in the evenings he and Hélène would walk with the missionaries the length and breadth of the station—650 yards one way, less than 120 the other—cramped quarters of a man who for years had regarded half Europe as his workshop. Little wonder that he wrote: ''One seems to be living in a prison.'' But tiny and airless though the station was, it was better than the suffocating tracks that led through the tall dense forest to nearby villages. At least on the station there were fruit trees planted by earlier missionaries—mango and paw-paw, citrus fruits, coffee, cocoa, and oil nut palms.

After a fortnight the steamer came upriver again, and Schweitzer's cases arrived in Lambarene village. A fleet of canoes fetched them up to Andende, a monster dugout taking the crated piano. Dozens of African helpers hauled the equipment up the hill to Schweitzer's bungalow—but where was it to go?

There was one empty building on the station; one of the missionaries, a M. Morel, had used it to house his hens. The roof leaked, the main room had no window, and naturally it was filthy, but Schweitzer decided to promote it to the rank of hospital. ''I got some shelves fixed on the walls, installed an old camp bed and covered the worst of the dirt with whitewash, feeling myself more than fortunate."[5] Here the work went on, and at least did not have to be interrupted by a rush to the veranda when the rainy season's regular evening storm began. Even so most of the medicines still had to be kept in the bungalow, for lack of space, and Schweitzer had to cross the yard to prepare each prescription—wasting time and energy when both were in short supply.

Hélène, suffering like her husband from the first impact of the stifling heat, put all her vitality into the work to which she had given her heart and for which she, like him, had prepared so long. The housekeeping alone in these circumstances took a great deal of thought and effort; more particularly since a demarcation of function worthy of the toughest trade union operated among the black servants; each when his job was finished went and lay down, and any task that none of them catered for was left to Hélène. On top of this she sterilized the instruments, prepared patients for surgery, assisted at operations, and kept the bandages and linen washed.

One day an unusual patient arrived. He spoke French well and seemed particularly intelligent. His name was Joseph Azowani, and had the Schweitzer story been fiction he would have figured among the notable lieutenants of literature. He had trained as a cook, and when Schweitzer, impressed with his ability, asked him to act as interpreter and general medical assistant he was inclined to refer to the various sections of the patients' anatomy as though they were joints of meat on a butcher's slab. "This woman has a pain in her upper left cutlet, and her loin."[6] A human leg would be a "*gigot*," French for a leg of lamb. Or a man would have a wounded fillet.

He was no fool however. Schweitzer came to rely on him more and more, and as Joseph learned from Schweitzer so he also taught him, steering him through the tricky thickets of African prejudice and superstition. Unusually for an African of that place and time he had no fear of blood and pus, which normally they would never touch. With a few lapses he was to remain faithful to the hospital, an unmistakable figure with his strutting walk, until the distant end, more than fifty years ahead.

With Hélène and Joseph, Schweitzer now had something of a team, and the work ritual was laid down. At 8:30 the patients were waiting in the shade by the fowl house, and the doctor's standing orders were read out in both dialects.

1. Spitting near the doctor's house is strictly forbidden.
2. Those who are waiting must not talk to each other loudly.
3. Patients and their friends must bring with them food enough for one day, as they cannot all be treated early in the day.
4. Any one who spends the night on the station without the doctor's

permission will be sent away without any medicine. [It happened not infrequently that patients from a distance crowded into the schoolboys' dormitory, turned them out, and took their places.]

5. All bottles and tin boxes which medicines are given in must be returned.

6. In the middle of the month, when the steamer has gone up the river, none but urgent cases can be seen till the steamer has gone down again, as the doctor is then writing to Europe to get more of his valuable medicines.[7]

The arrangement Schweitzer had made with the Paris Mission was evidently conditioned on a trial period, for on June 18, about six weeks after his arrival, we find him writing to Paris to say that he now wants to make the agreement permanent, and to stay "as long as God gives me strength and as long as the Mission can accommodate me."[8] He had by this time decided that the place originally suggested by the missionaries for the hospital building was not the most suitable—too small, and too far from his bungalow—and he now asked for permission to start building on the lower part of the hill between the bungalow and the river. This request had to be considered by the conference of missionaries which was to be held at the end of July, thirty odd miles upriver at Samkita. At four o'clock one morning Schweitzer and two of the missionaries embarked with twelve rowers in their canoe for the long day's paddling against the swift current.

The conference confirmed Schweitzer's guess that the missionaries themselves, unlike the Parisian head office, had better things to worry about than doctrinal niceties. "Necessity," he wrote, "compelled them to put forward Christianity as before all else an ethical religion" (necessity being the simple need to be understood by the Africans).[9] The sermons of the missionaries centered around the great but simple statements of the Sermon on the Mount—which Schweitzer regarded as the heart of the Gospels.

M. Morel, the only survivor of those distant days, can hardly remember what all the fuss was about and obviously regarded the head office ban as absurd. "He was a pastor, wasn't he? So he should preach." But Schweitzer adhered strictly to his vows to remain "as dumb as a carp" on theological matters and simply enjoyed "the refreshing atmosphere of love and goodwill."[10]

The missionaries in their turn warmed to Schweitzer, and before long came to trust him so far that they released him from his vow of dumbness and invited him to share in the preaching. So one of the happinesses which he had sacrificed to come to Africa was restored to him—and in good measure, for he found a special delight in speaking of his own simple devotion to Jesus among people whose reactions were not straitjacketed by centuries of dogma.

The conference fully approved Schweitzer's building plans and voted 4,000 francs toward the cost. But if the thought even crossed his mind that his troubles were now over he was rapidly disabused. It was almost impossible, with the timber trade in full swing, to find laborers even to level the site of the first building. And once they were found, it proved quite impossible to make them work. This put the fiery Schillinger temper under heavy strain; and Schweitzer, knowing he would never be able to contain himself at the sight of such frustrating idleness, took precautions against his own wrath. He selected from the jungle sticks of a wood that snapped on the slightest impact, so that when his own breaking point was reached he could lash out with one of these and relieve his feelings without doing any harm. In the end the laborers had to be dismissed, eight porters were borrowed from a nearby timber merchant, and Schweitzer himself took a spade and led the work—"while the black foreman lay in the shade of a tree and occasionally threw us an encouraging word."[11]

The building itself was to Schweitzer's own specification, based on suggestions from missionaries. Already as early as this he had worked out the basic elements of the design he was to use for all his hospital buildings, from now till the day he died; a design which owed little to tradition, something to experience, but most of all to applied commonsense; but which is still more comfortable than the air-conditioned concrete of a luxury hotel, and which was to draw groups of architects to Lambarene from all over the world.

The main principles were two: first, that the buildings should run east and west, along the line of the equator, so that the unvarying route of the sun traveled along the length of the roof and never penetrated under the wide overhanging eaves; and second, that the long sides of the buildings, instead of having walls and windows, were made entirely of tough mosquito netting, The ends were corrugated iron or, later, hardwood, and ran right to the tops of the rooms. Thus the sun never entered, but every breath of air circulated in the house almost as freely as outside. And the warm rising air was never trapped in the ceiling but flowed out and added to the circulation. The ceiling itself was made of stretched calico, against mosquitoes. The floor was of beaten earth, wood, or concrete, and the roof was of stitched palm leaves, which were cool but not very durable and constantly needed to be renewed. In later buildings Schweitzer made the roof of corrugated iron, which normally makes for great heat, but which was the only available material of sufficient strength and durability. He also added a wooden ceiling, forming an insulating cavity under the iron roof to absorb the heat. Wooden shutters were provided for the open sides as a protection against storms. Apart from its coolness, this design had an additional advantage, that the whole building was mosquito-free—unlike the average European house in the tropics, in which mosquito netting only covers the bed, involving complicated struggles on retiring and a permanent hazard if one has to get up in the night.

Thus, from the start Schweitzer's hospital was in a special sense his own, paid for by money he earned or begged, and built to his own requirements—requirements which not only reflected his personality, homespun yet original, but fitted exactly both the needs and the facilities of the upper Ogowe.

The largest rooms in this first "hospital" building were only thirteen feet square—the casualty room and the surgery. The dispensary and the sterilizing room were smaller still. With the aid of the mission's two practical workers, Schweitzer himself lending a hand, it was finished in November, early in Lambarene's "summer," which is the rainy season. After that, work began on a hut for Joseph and a dormitory for the patients, the first of whom constructed their own beds—dried grass hammocks lashed to upright poles driven into the earth floor. About forty patients a day soon needed housing, and along with them the friends and relatives who had brought them,

When the dormitory was finished another hut was started, on the opposite bank, for sleeping-sickness patients. Isolation was a perennial problem, as was sanitation. Increasingly Schweitzer found his time divided between medical work and building. Without his presence as supervisor and exemplar, no progress was made. The tension of deciding how to divide his time between the two was worse than the actual work. In Strasbourg he had credited himself with sound nerves and a tough temperament. Now he was to find that

> I belong unfortunately to the number of those medical men who have not the robust temperament which is desirable in that calling, and so are consumed with unceasing anxiety about the condition of their severe cases and of those on whom they have operated. In vain I have tried to train myself to the equanimity which makes it possible for a doctor, in spite of all his sympathy with the sufferings of his patients to husband, as is desirable, his spiritual and nervous energy.[12] With this continual drive, and the impatience of the waiting sick, I often get so worried and nervous that I hardly know where I am or what I am doing.[13]

As an indication of what this "continual drive" amounted to, Schweitzer and Hélène treated nearly 2,000 patients in the first nine months—this in addition to the building work.

Perhaps Schweitzer's anxiety was connected with another discovery, about suffering. In his sermons in Strasbourg he had proclaimed the value of suffering as a searcher of souls, a strengthener of faith. Now he was less sure. "Pain," he wrote "is a more terrible lord of mankind than even death himself."

The remark comes in a passage which he wrote in June, 1914—a passage which has often been quoted, but generally without the medical detail. Without that detail the passage is all sweetness and light, the guts are gone—which is less than fair to Schweitzer. The full passage reads thus:

> [The blacks] also suffer much oftener than white people from strangulated hernia, in which the intestine becomes constricted and blocked, so that it can no longer empty itself. It then becomes enormously inflated by the gases which form, and this causes terrible pain. Then after several days of torture, death takes place, unless the intestine can be got back through the rupture into the abdomen. Our ancestors were well acquainted with this terrible method of dying, but we no longer see it in Europe because every case is operated upon as soon as ever it is recognised. "Let not the sun go down upon your—strangulated hernia," is the maxim continually impressed upon medical students. But in Africa this terrible death is quite common. There are few negroes who have not as boys seen some man rolling in the sand of his hut and howling with agony till death came to release him. So now, the moment a man feels that his rupture is a strangulated one—rupture is far rarer among women—he begs his friends to put him in a canoe and bring him to me.
>
> How can I describe my feelings when a poor fellow is brought to me in this condition? I am the only person within hundreds of miles who can help him. Because I am here and am supplied by my friends with the necessary means, he can be saved, like those who came before him in the same condition and those who will come after him in the same condition, while otherwise he would have fallen a victim to the torture. This does not mean merely that I can save his life. We must all die. But that I can save him from days of torture, that is what I feel as my great and ever new privilege. Pain is a more terrible lord of mankind than even death himself.
>
> So, when the poor, moaning creature comes, I lay my hand on his forehead and say to him: "Don't be afraid! In an hour's time you shall be put to sleep, and when you wake you won't feel any more pain." Very soon he is given an injection of omnipon; the doctor's wife is called to the hospital, and with Joseph's help, makes everything ready for the operation. When that is to begin she administers the anaesthetic and Joseph, in a long pair of rubber gloves, acts as assistant.
>
> The operation is finished, and in the hardly lighted dormitory, I watch for the sick man's awakening. Scarcely has he recovered consciousness when he stares about him and ejaculates again and again: "I've no more pain! I've no more pain!" His hand feels for mine and will not let it go. Then I begin to tell him and the others who are in the

room that it is the Lord Jesus who has told the doctor and his wife to
come to the Ogowe, and that white people in Europe give them the
money to live here and cure the sick negroes. Then I have to answer
questions as to who these white people are, where they live, and how
they know that the natives suffer so much from sickness. The African
sun is shining through the coffee bushes into the dark shed, but we,
black and white, sit side by side and feel that we know by experience
the meaning of the words: "And all ye are brethren" (Matt. xxiii.8).
Would that my generous friends in Europe could come out here and
live through one such hour![14]

Emotion apart, how good a doctor was he? Good intentions are one
thing, results another. In fact eight months after arriving he was able to
record with some pride, but even greater relief, a success rate for his operations of 100 percent. For a man with no previous experience, limited
equipment, minimal assistance, and nobody to turn to for advice or a second opinion this speaks for itself—particularly since Schweitzer never
adopted the practice, common in all medical communities and strongly
urged by the practical Joseph, of refusing to operate on the more difficult
cases for fear the patient should die under the knife and injure the surgeon's reputation.

As trying as anything else was his isolation. He notes briefly how he
envies doctors in Europe, who can always ask a colleague for a second
opinion. Dr. Weissberg, who thirty years later was to go through much
the same experience in the government hospital on the island of Lambarene (one borrowed lantern between him and his wife, so that if he
needed it for an emergency operation, she had to sit in the dark), puts in
more strongly. "I always think," he says, "of Charlie Chaplin. The
bomb lands, the General hands it to the Colonel, the Colonel to the Adjutant, the Adjutant to the Corporal, the Corporal to Charlie Chaplin. Charlie looks round for somebody else but there's nobody. Out there, you are
always Charlie Chaplin. With one hand you hold the patient, with one
hand you hold the lantern, with one hand you hold the knife, and you trust
to luck." Weissberg became a friend and ally of Schweitzer in the later
years and had no doubt that he was a good doctor.

From the first Schweitzer established the principle that those who could
do so should offer some token payment for their treatment. The payment
might be an egg, a bunch of bananas, or money. It helped the hospital to
survive, but also it served as a reminder that there were benefactors in Europe who by some effort and sacrifice had made the treatment possible.
Schweitzer's sense of debt, of mutual help and mutual obligation, never
let him take any benefits for granted, and he would not let others do so
either. As we shall see, this constant awareness of the value of what he
was given, particularly the small gifts that cost the giver a good deal, is

the clue to some decisions in later years which have puzzled a number of observers.

All the while Schweitzer was learning more about the life around him. Slavery, he discovered, still existed, though not in any organized way. Sometimes it survived because it still suited the slaves themselves, who preferred the total dependence and the lack of responsibility that went with it. Cannibalism was much feared and probably did go on, but so secretly it could never be confirmed. The domination of witch doctors and taboos was all-prevailing; and much of Schweitzer's trouble came from fighting the psychological influence of superstition, particularly when the witch doctors began to resent his influence and to put pressure on his patients. His own name among the Africans was Oganga—Fetishman—the only name they had for a man with the power of curing (and also causing) disease. The fact that Schweitzer, with his anesthetics, could kill a man and then bring him to life again cured, made him a very great fetishman indeed.

The Africa that Schweitzer came to know was of course one of the most primitive, undevelopable areas in the whole continent; indeed in the world. To find an equivalent today you would have to search among the tribes of the upper Amazon. The people were wretched—undernourished and without hope of improvement. Much of the slavery was due to the starvation of the tribes of the interior; they would rather sell a child into servitude downriver, where it had a chance of survival, than watch it starve among the earth eaters.

Schweitzer was especially interested in the relationship between black and white, the effects of the confrontation of the two ways of life. He discovered rapidly that for all their subservience to superstition the Africans had a keen interest in the meaning of life and questions of right and wrong; and that for all their indifference to his building program, they were far from completely idle.

Faced for example with the need to build a new village (which frequently happened, either because the banana plantation had exhausted the soil and they had to clear a fresh part of the forest, or because a feud within a village led to a split), they would work virtually without stopping for days on end. Or they would row tirelessly for hours and days to bring a sick friend, black or white, to the hospital. But for anyone with whom they had neither personal nor tribal connections they would not lift a finger. Humanity at large was no concern of theirs, and the notion of universal love was so novel to them as to be more or less meaningless.

For any white man trying to get work done on the Ogowe this presented problems. Schweitzer's own difficulties were echoed by all the traders up and down the river—particularly the timber merchants.

Coming from the timber country of Alsace to the timber country of the

Gabon, Schweitzer took a great and knowledgeable interest in the problems of the Ogowe's main export—the huge trees of mahogany, okoume, rosewood, coralwood, and ironwood. Profitable though this trade was, it was attended by every kind of complication and hazard. Trees had to be found close to the river, for it was impossible to shift the gigantic trunks more than a few yards from their felling point. Once safely in the water and floated down the estuary they might be caught by an offshore wind and driven irretrievably out to sea. And the problems created by nature were compounded by the attitude of the Africans, who would work just so long as they needed money for a specific purpose, such as buying a wife or a pair of shoes, and no longer; and if a fiesta called they would let pass the few precious days in the year when the river was high enough to float trunks lying some distance from the river bank, and leave timber worth hundreds and thousands of pounds to rot into uselessness before the next year's floods.

In July, 1914, Schweitzer himself fell ill with an abscess which needed attention. He went with Hélène to Cape Lopez to see the military doctor there, and while convalescing he wrote an essay on the timber trade, and also began to set out his thoughts on what he called "Social Problems in the Forest." The seventeen pages in which he wrote these thoughts down, while a slow trading-steamer took the couple back to Lambarene, still stand up as a concise and acute analysis of the colonial situation. Schweitzer saw the problem, he foresaw the future, he faced the tragedy. The roots of all the subsequent conflicts between black and white are here laid bare.

First he inquired why it was that the African would not work when he was required by the white men to work; and answered that it was not because he was lazy but because he was a free man. Within his village he could find all that he actually required for existence. He did not need money. He only went out to earn it when he or his wife wanted some luxury such as sugar, tobacco, rum, dress material, or a pair of boots. Once he had what he wanted, why go on working? He was still the master, not the servant, of his economy.

Such casual, unpredictable labor was useless to the white man, enslaved by the demands of productivity. Trade and State therefore combined to create need in the African, so as to force him into permanent work. The State imposed taxes (for the building of schools, hospitals, and roads, which indeed were often very needful); and trade seduced him with desirable objects such as sewing machines, safety razors, collars and ties, corsets, openwork stockings, concertinas, and music boxes.

Still, however, the African would not work steadily. His freedom was too deeply ingrained. And here the real tragedy began. "The child of nature becomes a steady worker only so far as he ceases to be free and be-

comes unfree'';[15] so the white man learns never to let him work near his
village, for there he is his own man—and never to pay him the whole of
his wages, for then he would be content and stop working. Half his
money is put by till the end of the year.
What happens?

> Many get homesick. Others cannot put up with the strange diet, for
> as no fresh provisions are to be had, they must as a rule live chiefly on
> rice. Most of them fall victims to the taste for rum, and ulcers and dis-
> eases spread rapidly among them, living, as they do, a kind of barrack
> life in overcrowded huts. In spite of all precautions they mostly get
> through their pay as soon as the contract time is up, and return home as
> poor as they went away.
> The negro is worth something only so long as he is in his village and
> under the moral control of intercourse with his family and other rela-
> tives; away from these surroundings he easily goes to the bad, both
> morally and physically. Colonies of negro labourers away from their
> families are, in fact, centres of demoralisation, and yet such colonies
> are required for trade and for the cultivation of the soil, both of which
> would be impossible without them.
> The tragic element in this question is that the interests of civilisation
> and of colonisation do not coincide, but are largely antagonistic to each
> other. The former would be promoted best by the natives being left in
> their villages and there trained to various industries, to lay out planta-
> tions, to grow a little coffee or cocoa for themselves or even for sale, to
> build themselves houses of timber or brick instead of huts of bamboo,
> and so to live a steady and worthy life. Colonisation, however, de-
> mands that as much of the population as possible shall be made avail-
> able in every possible way for utilising to the utmost the natural wealth
> of the country. Its watchword is ''Production,'' so that the capital in-
> vested in the colonies may pay its interest, and that the motherland may
> get her needs supplied through her connection with them. For the un-
> suspected incompatibilities which show themselves here, no individual
> is responsible; they arise out of the circumstances themselves.[16]

Some colonial states enforced compulsory labor. This too tended to
drag men away from their village roots. In some districts large commercial companies with concessions wielded more power than the state itself,
making all the local Africans dependent on them. The power might be
used with wisdom and discretion; but there was no guarantee of this, and
in any case the principle was wrong.
Since the white man's influence falls heaviest on villages near the white
man's towns those villages vanish, only to reappear far away in the jungle. A no-man's-land grows up between white and black. Enforcement

becomes more difficult, and more severe. The breaking up of villages goes on in an increasing spiral.

Schweitzer goes on to look at the problem of "the educated native":

> Both Government and trade require natives with extensive knowledge whom they can employ in administration and in the stores. The schools, therefore, must set their aims higher than is natural, and produce people who understand complicated figures and can write the white man's language perfectly. Many a native has such ability that the results of this attempt are, so far as intellectual knowledge goes, astounding. . . .
>
> But what becomes of these people? They have been uprooted from their villages, just like those who go off to work for strangers. They live at the store, continually exposed to the dangers which haunt every native so closely, the temptations to defraud and to drink. They earn good wages, indeed, but as they have to buy all their necessities at high prices, and are a prey to the black man's innate love of spending, they often find themselves in financial difficulties and even in want. They do not now belong to the ordinary negroes, nor do they belong to the whites either; they are a tertium quid between the two.[17]

Civilization for the African, says Schweitzer, should not start with book learning, but with industry and agriculture, "through which alone can be secured the economic conditions of higher civilization."[18] This is a prophetic comment, belatedly being put into practice in a number of African countries today. The timber trade, sporadically attracting every able-bodied male, made any sort of regular employment impossible. And Schweitzer complains of the way in which cheap European goods are destroying the African's craft of making household utensils out of wood and bark fiber. He speaks of the dilemma of governments who, even if they wish to abolish the import of cheap liquor, never do so because they have no other equally profitable revenues to replace the tax on them.

On the issue of polygamy Schweitzer sees clearly that it suits the local conditions far better than monogamy. (He used to say that the emphasis on monogamy arose when a society became settled and the men began to value the permanence of their possessions—their land, their houses, their wives. A nomadic culture had different values.) Polygamy safeguards the children, in a society where the only milk available is mother's milk and the mother must suckle her child for a long time. While she does so, other wives can solace the father, leaving her to give her time to the child. Polygamy ensures that every woman can be married, in a society which has no place for the unmarried woman. Polygamy protects the widows and orphans, who can simply join another family. In short, to abolish it on doctrinaire grounds could only cause the greatest confusion and hardship. (My own aunt once met Schweitzer on a lecture tour in Switzerland. When asked what he would speak about he said that to such a respectable bourgeois community he would like to commend the benefits of polygamy.)

Wife purchase too seemed to work well enough, and Schweitzer concluded that "we should accept, but try to improve and refine, the rights and customs which we find in existence, and make no alterations which are not absolutely necessary."[19] He believed that changes would come of their own accord, if and when they were needed.

One should not pretend that Schweitzer's opinions on African marriage customs were particularly advanced or daring. Most observers who went there from Europe with an open mind came to the same conclusions, and Schweitzer himself wrote that his views have been reached "after conversation with all the best and most experienced of the white men in this district." The cry to change the ways of the villagers came only from the more rigid type of missionary and the more obtuse and unimaginative sort of visitor—the same sort who later was to be horrified at the way Schweitzer ran his hospital.

Most liberals of today would probably agree with Schweitzer's analysis of the situation so far. The white man, committed to productivity, encounters the unconcern of the black man, free from such commitment. Slavery is no longer permissible, so the free black man must be bound by other means. New needs must be created in him, which he can only satisfy by offering the white man his labor. And the white man ensures the fulfillment of the contract by separating him from the source of his freedom, his village. The dreadful labor camps of South Africa today are the logical conclusion of the process, the new slavery incarnate, as evil as the old with a touch of hypocrisy added.

The only point at which Schweitzer and the modern liberal might part company is that Schweitzer also understands and sympathizes with the white man, whose job depends on the willingness of black laborers to do what they have promised, and who finds that, for his purposes, they are totally unreliable.

Which brings us to the vexed question of paternalism—the word that has been thrown at Schweitzer a great many times—as at many other whites of his generation. Like all such emotive and generalizing words it is best abandoned as soon as mentioned—but it must be mentioned before it can be abandoned. What matters is not the word, with all the taking up of attitudes and judgments which it presupposes, but the truth. Was Schweitzer in some way patronizing and "superior"? The key passage is to be found in the essay on social problems in the forest, and it runs thus:

A word in conclusion about the relations between the whites and the

blacks. What must be the general character of the intercourse between
them? Am I to treat the black man as my equal or as my inferior? I
must show him that I can respect the dignity of human personality in
every one, and this attitude in me he must be able to see for himself;
but the essential thing is that there shall be a real feeling of brotherli-
ness. How far this is to find complete expression in the sayings and do-
ings of daily life must be settled by circumstances. The negro is a
child, and with children nothing can be done without the use of authority. We must, therefore, so arrange the circumstances of daily life
that my natural authority can find expression. With regard to the negroes, then, I have coined the formula: ''I am your brother, it is true,
but your elder brother.''[20]

So Schweitzer takes for granted what the modern African and the
modern liberal white man would at least question if he did not hotly dispute: that the African—that is the primitive Ogowe African whom he
knew sixty years ago—is a child, and that the white man must exercise
his natural authority over him.

He quotes two stories to illustrate what happens when this natural authority breaks down. One concerns a missionary who some years before
had left the mission staff ''to live among the negroes as their brother absolutely. From that day,'' says Schweitzer, ''his life became a misery. With
his abandonment of the social interval between white and black he lost all
his influence; his word was no longer taken as the 'white man's word,'
but he had to argue every point with them as if he were merely their
equal.''[21]

From this and from the other story, about a black cook who took
advantage of his employer's easy ways to grow overfamiliar, it is evident
that at this time Schweitzer, however enlightened about the causes of the
situation, could not envisage anything so revolutionary as a white man
genuinely abandoning his superior position and putting himself on a level
with the blacks as a partner.

The missionary was certainly unwise to want to live as the brother of
the blacks if he was unprepared for the implications. He wished to be
their brother yet not their equal, and Schweitzer seems not to have noticed
the inconsistency. The cook, too, was expected to understand that white
men draw the line on social freedom at a certain point—and to know
where the line is and not overstep it. The moral that Schweitzer seems to
have drawn from such tales, as did almost everyone else of his generation, was that social freedom must not be allowed to go too far, for it
opens the floodgates to total equality which is unthinkable.

In Schweitzer's particular situation, of course, total equality was indeed unthinkable. He was not a missionary with a spiritual task only—he
was the controller of a jungle clinic with lives at stake, and anywhere in

the world a man in such a position must have authority or his work is destroyed. He was undoubtedly right in thinking that on the Ogowe the only way to maintain such authority was by preserving a distance between himself and the tribesmen, for the Africans were simply not accustomed to thinking on the lines necessary for self-discipline and voluntary cooperation. Authority had to be imposed. And we shall see in a moment how for all that authority their lack of discipline regularly endangered the hospital. But there was another reason why Schweitzer needed authority in Africa, and that was because he needed it everywhere. It was in his schoolmasterish nature. His paternalism, if we must use the word, was not toward the blacks only but toward everyone. He had come to Africa to avoid theorizing argument and to put his feelings into action and he was not likely, once there, to suffer interminable palavers with his staff and his patients, whether black or white. Without authority he could neither have been what he was nor done what he came to do.

But he did not believe that authority was something automatically conferred by black upon white.

> A white man can only have real authority if the native respects him. No one must imagine that the child of nature looks up to us merely because we know more, or can do more than he can. This superiority is so obvious to him that it ceases to be taken into account. It is by no means the case that the white man is to the negro an imposing person because he possess railway and steamers, can fly in the air, or travel under water. "White people are clever and can do anything they want to," says Joseph. The negro is not in a position to estimate what these technical conquests of nature mean as proofs of mental and spiritual superiority, but on one point he has an unerring intuition, and that is on the question whether any particular white man is a real, moral personality or not. If the native feels that he is this, moral authority is possible; if not, it is simply impossible to create it. The child of nature, not having been artificialised and spoilt as we have been, has only elementary standards of judgement, and he measures us by the most elementary of them all, the moral standard. Where he finds goodness, justice and genuineness of character, real worth and dignity, that is, behind the external dignity given by social circumstances, he bows and acknowledges his master; where he does not find them he remains really defiant in spite of all appearance of submission, and says to himself: "This white is no more of a man than I am, for he is not a better one than I am."[22]

Schweitzer too measured men by the moral standard, the most elementary of them all. For all the differences in their social backgrounds Schweitzer found more spiritual affinity with the Ogowe African than with the industrial European. Authority then, for Schweitzer, must be fairly won. It is not a guaranteed attribute of Europeans, a side-effect of whiteness. And he himself was not in Africa looking for a respect he had failed to win in his own country. He had held authority—intellectual, spiritual, and physical—over students, musicians, theologians, philosophers, and women in the capitals of Europe. He was not born with it—he had achieved it. Schweitzer had the right to speak of authority in Lambarene as elsewhere.

Having put the case as fairly as he can for the Africans, Schweitzer now has something to add about the white colonists:

> I am not thinking merely of the fact that many unsuitable and not a few quite unworthy men go out into the colonies of all nations. I wish to emphasise a further fact that even the morally best and the idealists find it difficult out here to be what they wish to be. We all get exhausted in the terrible contest between the European worker who bears the responsibility and is always in a hurry, and the child of nature who does not know what responsibility is and is never in a hurry. The Government official has to record at the end of the year so much work done by the natives in building and road maintenance, in service as carrier or boatman, and so much money paid in taxes; the trader and the planter are expected by their companies to provide so much profit for the capital invested in the enterprise. But in all this they are for ever dependent on men who cannot share the responsibility that weighs on them, who only give just so much return of labour as the others can force out of them, and who, if there is the slightest failure in superintendence, do exactly as they like without any regard for the loss that may be caused to their employers. In this daily and hourly contest with the child of nature every white man is continually in danger of gradual moral ruin. . . .
>
> The greater the responsibility that rests on a white man, the greater the danger of his becoming hard towards the natives. We on a mission staff are too easily inclined to become self-righteous with regard to the other whites. We have not got to obtain such and such results from the natives by the end of the year, as officials and traders have, and therefore this exhausting contest is not so hard a one for us as for them. I no longer venture to judge my fellows after learning something of the soul of the white man who is in business from those who lay as patients under my roof, and whose talk has led me to suspect that those who now speak savagely about the natives may have come out to Africa full of idealism, but in the daily contest have become weary and hopeless, losing little by little what they once possessed of spirituality.
>
> That it is so hard to keep oneself really humane, and so to be a standard bearer of civilisation, that is the tragic element in the problem of the relations between white and coloured men in Equatorial Africa.[23]

So the blame he laid on the whites from his pulpit in Strasbourg is not so easy to apportion on the spot. Two ways of life come face to face, and there is a good chance that they will destroy one other. Again South Africa shows the consequences writ large. The struggle there has crushed the blacks physically. Morally it has rotted the whites. The blame is theirs, for they have been in control. But beyond the blame is the tragedy.

Remembering that Schweitzer had deliberately chosen to work among some of the most primitive, remote, and socially ruined tribes in the world, it is important to hold a clear picture in our minds of what exactly the difficulties were that the traders faced, that made Schweitzer call the Ogowe Africans "children," and that drove him to an unceasing use of his rational authoritarianism. For he was indeed driven to it. He had not expected or wished to have to waste time imposing his will. "When, before coming to Africa, I heard missionaries and traders say again and again that one must be very careful out here to maintain this authoritative position of the white man, it seemed to me to be a hard and unnatural position to take up, as it does to every one in Europe who reads or hears the same."[24]

But in fact he found he had to tell the Africans the same things over and over again—not because he was white and they were black, not for the pleasure of dominating them, but simply, for example, to make sure that they came at the right time for their injections and remembered to take their medicine. He found he had to lock everything up, to become a "walking bunch of keys,"[25] not for the preservation of private property, for he never locked up his own belongings, and certainly not to save time and effort; simply because everything left unlocked was liable to "take a walk," and once gone could not be replaced for months, if at all. Drugs, instruments, equipment were not his to take risks with. They had been bought from the gifts of dozens of benefactors, many of them far from wealthy, and he owed it to them (and to the patients) not to lose them.

He found that nothing could safely be left to Africans to do by themselves—all had to be supervised and checked:

Not long ago the termites, or white ants, got into a box which stood on our verandah. I emptied the box and broke it up, and gave the pieces to the negro who had been helping me. "Look," I said to him, "the ants have got into it; you mustn't put the wood with the rest of the fire-wood or the ants will get into the framework of the hospital building. Go down to the river and throw it into the water. Do you understand?" "Yes, yes, you need not worry." It was late in the day and, being too tired to go down the hill again, I was inclined to break my general rule and trust a black—one who was in fact on the whole intelligent and handy. But about ten o'clock I felt so uneasy that I took the lantern and went down to the hospital. There was the wood with the ants in it lying with the rest of the firewood. To save himself the trouble of going the twenty yards down to the river, the negro had endangered all my buildings![26]

It is fair to ask the critic, "What would *you* have done—what would you have thought—given the remoteness, the responsibility, the lack of assistance, the climate, the weariness, the many better things one might wish to do?" In a European the action would have amounted to criminal negligence or sheer idiocy. By a kind of perversity it is now often suggested that it would have been kinder always to judge Africans by European standards, that not to do so was deplorably patronizing, was "paternalistic." In Schweitzer's context simply to state that view is to show how nonsensical it would have been, how fatal would have been the results.

Finally we must remember that "child" in Schweitzer's vocabulary was by no means a derogatory word. Schweitzer's hero had told his listeners: "Except ye become as little children ye shall in no wise enter the Kingdom of Heaven." It was not simply a question of being fond of children. Most people are fond of children. For Schweitzer, as for Jesus, the child had understandings which the adult had lost. Likewise the African.

They both had the gift of simple, direct response to life, an appreciation of what really matters. Martha, in the Gospels, was irritated with her sister Mary for much the same reason as the whites were irritated with the blacks. Mary sat about talking and listening instead of helping with the housework. Jesus sided with Mary. Schweitzer in his childhood had been a Mary, dreaming when they wanted him to do something useful. Now perforce he was a Martha, and was to remain one for the rest of his life. But at least part of him remained the dreamer, and he had every sympathy, even while he tongue-lashed them into activity, with those who would rather have sat and let life flow around and into them.

For his own relaxation and refreshment he had always in the past relied upon nature and music. Here nature was all around him, to an oppressive degree. As for music, though he had gone to great trouble to bring his organ-pedaled piano all the way to the equator, he made little use of it at first. It reminded him too vividly of the delights he had given up and would never, he believed, taste again. "The renunciation," he thought, "would be easier if I allowed fingers and feet to get rusty with disuse."[27]

But there were three volumes left uncompleted of the Bach edition he had undertaken with Widor. In his spare time he put in some work on these; and one evening, playing a fugue "in melancholy mood" he was struck by the thought that here in Africa, with no concerts to perform for, he could work gradually, at his own speed, on deepening his understanding of music. He could perfect his technique and study individual works in the greatest detail, eventually learning them by heart. So once again, as when he was a student, he began to use music as a retreat from stress; and found new depths in Bach, as he played into the hush of the jungle night.

15

WAR
1914–1915

TWO years was generally regarded as the longest a white man should stay in that climate before coming back to Europe to regain energy. According to Dr. Weissberg the white mortality in the Gabon in 1913 was 20 percent per year. According to Mary Kingsley the strong, robust, full-blooded type was the most likely to succumb. After a year and a quarter Schweitzer was exceedingly tired. We have to remember that he was already suffering from periods of total exhaustion before he went out to Africa and in one of his long and very conscientious reports to the committee he writes of the extra fatigue of a night journey upriver on the steamer to treat a patient at another station.

By this time he was already adding to the plantation of fruit trees and had started a garden. During the dry season every growing thing had to be watered daily. He used the families of the patients for this chore, giving each one a cup of rice if they would carry a jar of water to the garden. Tomatoes, radishes, and beans were on the way, and trees were already bearing oranges and mandarins. At least, in that climate nature helps those who help themselves, and crops, once planted and watered, are swift and heavy. Pineapples were a weed.

The Schweitzers began to plan their first trip home. After one more rainy season they would take a break—in the spring of 1915. It was not to be. Europe went to war. On August 5, in the evening, the Schweitzers were informed that, as German citizens, they were to regard themselves as prisoners of war.

He had seen it coming, of course. And its consequences. He had the gold, which he had brought instead of paper money. But it was of little use since he was now placed under house arrest and forbidden to practice as a doctor. A black officer and four men were posted outside the bungalow to see that he and Hélène spoke to nobody, white or black.

The guards' task was a thankless one. The local Africans, who had no

235

idea what the war was about, were only aware that suddenly they could get no treatment and that some of their fellow blacks were ordering the doctor about. The guards became very unpopular.

For Schweitzer life had suddenly come to an abrupt halt. For the first time for perhaps thirty years, instead of too much he had nothing whatever to do, except think. And the thoughts were not happy. His own family and friends, and Hélène's, were in the direct line of fire between the two main combatants, as Alsatians always were. They themselves were unlikely to hear from their families, since communications now ceased between German-occupied Alsace and French-occupied Gabon.

Had Schweitzer's temperament been other than it was, he might well have sunk into a despairing lethargy. Instead he instantly made the best of the situation and almost with relief went back to his writing. The book on St. Paul was so nearly finished that it was the obvious first task.

When he started to think about it, however, Schweitzer found something else in the forefront of his mind. Long ago in Berlin he had sat in the corner of the room, a shy student, while the great brains of the university exchanged ideas—and had heard someone say: "We are nothing but epigoni." He had planned a book then, but no one had been interested in his thoughts on the decay of civilization, and the whole idea had been overwhelmed by all that had happened since. Now it was clear that he had been right in his pessimism about the way Europe was going, and the teacher in him was eager to analyze the reasons why. By the second morning of his internment he was at work on his philosophy of civilization.

At first the writing was only for his own satisfaction. It was his way of combating the stress of the news. Whether it would even reach publication he doubted, for the authorities might not allow him to keep the manuscript. He was not even sure that he would ever see Europe again. He worked with a sense of detachment born of complete isolation, cut off, as he was, not only from his home, his work, and his friends but also from his future.

Little by little the isolation eased. The idiocy of having a doctor idle while sick people went untended aroused such protests that the local district commandant began, before long, to send sufferers to Schweitzer with special notes to the guards to let them pass—isolated cases at first, then in increasing numbers. Meanwhile his friends in Paris—Widor in particular, but also the influential friends of Uncle Auguste—had been active on his behalf, and at the end of November the internment order was lifted and he was free to go on practicing medicine as before. What he could not do, however, was return home. So the two-year stretch in the tropics was extended indefinitely.

Now he made time in his schedule to go on with the philosophy of civilization. In his imagination he was with the soldiers in the trenches and with his family at home. This imagination was the stimulus for the book. Such a horror must be traced to its root causes.

Schweitzer knew as much as or more than most people about the immediate political events leading up to the war. He had always been politically aware, as his godfather had discovered when he was only eleven. His uncle's friends in Paris had kept him in touch with political movements more recently—hence his insistence on bringing gold to Africa; and he is reported to have said sharply to Hélène, when she complained one day about the postal services in Alsace, "What do you expect? You [*i.e.* the Germans] are so busy building warships you have no time to organize the mail."

But the book was not about this kind of cause of war at all. The specific incidents were irrelevant for him. The search was not a survey or conglomeration of facts. (Spengler, who was also trying to account for the breakdown of European civilization, approached it that way, and his two massive, incredibly knowledgeable, totally unreadable volumes were for a while very popular among the intelligentsia after the war.)

Schweitzer was interested in the attitudes behind the incidents—the spirit which allowed the incidents to happen and which, if these incidents had not happened, would have allowed others, with the same result. The precise tracing of events was not "elemental" enough for him. He believed, after all, that he had, at the start of the century, discerned the trend long before the events occurred.

So the book was to be about what people expected of civilization, and what they were prepared to give to it. When it finally achieved publication, the opening chapter was entitled How Philosophy Is Responsible for the Collapse of Civilisation, and the opening words announced the theme: "We are living today under the sign of the collapse of civilisation. The situation has not been produced by the war: the latter is only a manifestation of it. The spiritual atmosphere has solidified into actual facts, which again react on it with disastrous results in every respect."[1]

After several months of isolation an occasional letter began to arrive via neutral Switzerland. Hélène's father, wealthier and with better contacts than Schweitzer's parents, was more successful in getting messages and letters through, and wrote asking if the couple would like pressure exerted to get their internment transferred to somewhere in Europe. It would seem that they replied in the negative; at least where they were they could go on working.

Schweitzer was a less dutiful correspondent than his wife. Hélène wrote conscientiously to her parents, and the Bresslaus passed on messages to the Schweitzers and transmitted their replies.

Pastor Schweitzer meanwhile had begun keeping a diary of these wartime days, to show his son when he should return. It is one of the most valuable and revealing documents we have of this relationship, and of the whole gentle, unremarkable atmosphere of the Schweitzers' family life.

By the summer of 1915 Günsbach was really in the front line. The Germans had dug themselves defensive positions on the hills on either side, dominating the valley. The French were challenging the heights. The villages were all taken over by the military, and not only the vicarage but even the church was occupied; Louis Schweitzer could no longer hold services, and his house was no longer his own. All he could do was to minister to his parishioners and, when it was necessary, bury the dead— of both sides—and write to the next of kin. In his diary he wrote of parish news and of the war almost in the same sentence. He had one consolation; the local commandant was billeted in his house, which meant he could usually arrange some sort of military transport for his visitors. This was just as well, for the passenger trains no longer ran up the valley from Colmar, and even army trains stopped at Hammerschmeide (now La Forge), three or four miles down the valley. After that it was horsedrawn transport or a long walk.

Stray bullets and shells made it dangerous to move about in the valley by day, and the villagers grew accustomed to doing much of their work by night. The cellars of the vicarage proved invaluable as protection. Mrs. Schweitzer tended to be very nervous—understandably, since one day in August a mortar shell came through the roof and landed on the dining-room table. After this she went to Colmar for a while to stay with Louise and her family, but after a month or two she rejoined her husband in Günsbach.

In Lambarene Schweitzer was suffering from nothing worse than tiredness and a heavy cold, caught after a sudden drop in temperature. All day he treated the physical ailments of his patients; by night he went on with the diagnosis of Europe's disease.

Europe, he believed, had gone to war because Europeans had lost touch with their own ideals. He blamed Nietzsche as much as anyone. Philosophy might seem remote from international politics, but he had himself experienced the way in which Nietzsche's influence had seeped down from the academic heights, and had permeated politics, business, and everyday life; not in its pure form but distorted and oversimplified. Europe had taken happily to the idea that the victory of the strong man over the weak led toward the perfection of the species.

From Hegel people had acquired a general feeling that progress inevitably developed out of conflict and that mankind automatically advanced by the sheer processes of history. Scientific and material improvements seemed to confirm this. So if history itself provided the world with a sort of automatic pilot, who needed compasses? The search of the eighteenth-century philosophers for some kind of rational pattern in nature by which men should set their sights had been abandoned as both hopeless and unnecessary.

So the war into which Europe had stumbled was marked by two new and hideous features—the absence of ideals and the presence of machine guns. Schweitzer was going to tell the world why it had happened.

The book as we have it, *The Decay and Restoration of Civilisation,* is the result of two separate drafts, one written after the war. But the lines on which he was thinking, out there in the jungle, are clear enough; and they are startlingly modern. Today we are still complaining that we are drilled and dominated by large impersonal organizations. We are aware that great cities cut us off from the natural life of the country. We know that long hours of meaningless factory work cannot be dignified by the name of honest labor, and that after a day in an office or on a production line the mind is in need of vacuous entertainment rather than meaningful recreation. We know that we are stunted by specialization, that few people have the satisfaction of mastering a complete job, that the word "creative" has become so debauched that it is now applied without a smile to advertising copywriters. And we know that we suffer from having too many acquaintances and associates, and too few friends. All these are concomitants of the highly organized industrial society, devoted mainly to production and the growth of the gross national product.

But we feel that the period before 1914 was part of the golden age before any of this had begun to happen. The postwar generation is generally held responsible for the beginning of the end of the old values. Not so, according to Schweitzer. He had felt it in the air years before and had seen or foreseen all these developments.

In the book he pinned them down with his usual accuracy and economy.

At this stage of the writing of the book Schweitzer was still only concerned with the causes and the symptoms of Europe's disease. He had reached the conclusion that a specific mental conflict had crippled the image which Europeans had traditionally held of the world they lived in. Briefly, the argument runs thus: Europeans in general believe that life is worth living. They have, that is to say, a positive approach to life (unlike, for example, Buddhists, who believe that the way to perfect oneself is to detach oneself as far as possible from life, since all worldly satisfaction is illusory). The endeavor of European philosophers has been to prove that this positive approach to life is justified by the fact that the universe itself is beneficent—that goodness, or love, is part of the nature of things. Many splendid theories have been evolved to demonstrate the excellence of the universe, and they all had two things in common: that their ideals were admirable; and that they had the practical advantage of confirming

people in general in their trust in divine providence (or whatever it might
be called).

Unfortunately, each theory in turn (Kant's included) proved vulnerable
to criticism. And when finally in the nineteenth century the study of natural science began to be taken seriously and people began to look for truth
not in academic theories but in physical observation and experiments, it
soon became clear that there is really nothing in nature at all that one can
truly call loving. Nature is an indifferent force, creating and destroying
impartially. For every sign of kindliness there is an opposing cruelty. The
idealistic pictures drawn by philosophers, clerics, and moralists were
simply wish-fulfilling figments of the imagination.

Since European morality had always depended on this supposed universal pattern (man's mind being seen in some way as the mirror of the
universal mind) the shattering of the pattern left morality without any basis. It was now felt that because nature moved blindly ("evolution" was
the new watchword) man could afford to do the same and evolution would
take care of the results. Civilization abandoned all the ideals which had
hitherto sustained it and believed it could do without them. Philosophy
ceased to be the study of ethics and human improvement and became a
matter of observation and description, without moral content. "Value
judgment" became a dirty phrase. In short, since man could find nothing
in nature on which to peg his ideals, he was free (this was never quite stated but was implied) to become as amoral as nature.

Such, put crudely, was Schweitzer's "apparently abstract, yet absolutely practical thinking about the connection between civilisation and
world-view." But for him to leave anything at a negative stage was quite
against his nature. "Everything," Erica Anderson remembers his saying,
"should end in a major key." Suddenly, one day in the summer of 1915,
it came to him that criticism was not enough. "I awoke," he wrote,
"from a sort of stupor."[2]

And the search began for the antidote to Europe's sickness. Somewhere, Schweitzer felt, some basic principle of civilization had been
missed, or mislaid—a principle which would underwrite the validity of
human ideals, proving that love was not simply a sentimental invention or
a convenient way of holding society together. He could never return to
the old-fashioned view that the universe itself was kindly—more particularly since he had been exposed to nature's blind and destructive force on
the Ogowe. But what other connection could there be between ethics and
the universe at large? This now became the great question, hammering at
him day in, day out, while he worked. It was now not only a matter of
rescuing civilization; in his own person he now faced the ultimate question—have we any sort of guarantee that it matters in the least whether we
behave well or badly? Was his devotion to other human beings no more

than a romantic whim? If so, not only was civilization doomed but so in a way was he.

Being Schweitzer, he was never in any danger of being content with any political or economic formula. The suggestion that a redistribution of wealth, however desirable, would guarantee civilized behavior was a non sequitur of absurd proportions. The question went much, much farther back. What did a human being really need? What indeed *was* a human being? What was the indestructible, rock-bottom fact about humanity, from which everything began?

What we want badly enough we generally find. It could be claimed that what happened next to Schweitzer was simply the result of his great need. It could also be said that intuition strikes truest where the need is greatest. This is for the reader to decide.

The actual event I shall leave to Schweitzer's own words. I hope the reader will not blame Schweitzer for the fact that some sentences sound so clumsy in English. Translation of this kind of passage, where some words have no English equivalent, is an impossible task. I only ask the reader to try to penetrate to the sense, noting merely that the phrase "world-and-life-affirmation" (*Welt- und Lebensbejahung*), so impossibly cumbersome in English, is Schweitzer's phrase for the European attitude we have noted—that life is valuable and the universe is beneficent and that the two things are connected.

> So it was necessary [he wrote] to undertake to grasp as a necessity of thought by fresh, simple and sincere thinking the truth which had hitherto been only suspected and believed in, although so often proclaimed as proved.
>
> In undertaking this I seemed to myself to be like a man who has to build a new and better boat to replace a rotten one in which he can no longer venture to trust himself to the sea, and yet does not know how to begin.
>
> For months on end I lived in a continual state of mental excitement. Without the least success I let my thoughts be concentrated, even all through my daily work at the hospital, on the real nature of the world-and-life-affirmation and of ethics, and on the question of what they have in common. I was wandering about in a thicket in which no path was to be found. I was leaning with all my might against an iron door which would not yield.
>
> All that I had learnt from philosophy about ethics left me in the lurch. The conceptions of the Good which it had offered were all so lifeless, so unelemental, so narrow, and so destitute of content that it was quite impossible to bring them into union with the world-and-life-affirmation. Moreover philosophy could be said never to have concerned itself with the problem of the connexion between civilisation and world-view. The modern world-and-life-affirmation had become to

it such a matter of course that it had felt no need for coming to clear ideas about it.

To my surprise I had also to establish the fact that the central province of philosophy, into which meditation about civilisation and world-view had led me, was practically unexplored land. Now from this point, now from that, I tried to penetrate to its interior, but again and again I had to give up the attempt. I was already exhausted and disheartened. I saw, indeed, the conception needed before me, but I could not grasp it and give it expression.

While in this mental condition I had to undertake a longish journey on the river. I was staying with my wife on the coast at Cape Lopez for the sake of her health—it was in September 1915—when I was summoned to visit Madame Pelot, the ailing wife of a missionary, at N'Gomo, about 160 miles upstream. The only means of conveyance I could find was a small steamer, towing an overladen barge, which was on the point of starting. Except myself, there were only natives on board, but among them was Emil Ogouma, my friend from Lambarene. Since I had been in too much of a hurry to provide myself with enough food for the journey, they let me share the contents of their cooking pot. Slowly we crept upstream, laboriously feeling—it was the dry season—for the channels between the sandbanks. Lost in thought I sat on the deck of the barge, struggling to find the elementary and universal conception of the ethical which I had not discovered in any philosophy. Sheet after sheet I covered with disconnected sentences, merely to keep myself concentrated on the problem. Late on the third day, at the very moment when, at sunset, we were making our way through a herd of hippopotamuses, there flashed upon my mind, unforeseen and unsought, the phrase, "Reverence for Life." The iron door had yielded: the path in the thicket had become visible. Now I had found my way to the idea in which world-and-life-affirmation and ethics are contained side by side! Now I knew that the world-view of ethical world-and-life-affirmation, together with its ideals of civilisation, is founded in thought.[3]

When the phrase came to him it was not of Christianity that he thought, not of Goethe, not even of Jesus. His mind went eastward, to Buddha. The antecedents of his great idea were worldwide.

That same month, September, 1915, half-trained French troops crept up the mountain slopes of the Lingen, above Münster, and tried to storm the entrenched German positions on the crest. By the end of the battle 30,000 men had died and the military situation remained unchanged.

16

"REVERENCE FOR LIFE"
1915

FROM this moment on, almost everything that Schweitzer did, almost everything that Schweitzer wrote, led back in some way or other to Reverence for Life. In a sense it had always been so, since the first apocalyptic moment when the church bells rang and he frightened the birds away rather than catapult them. The discovery of the phrase Reverence for Life was a turning point only in the sense that it was the recognition and naming of something that had always been there.

What, first of all, does it actually mean? And what does Schweitzer mean when he says it is "founded in thought"—or more positively, that it is "a necessity of thought"?

Reverence for Life is a translation of the German *Ehrfurcht vor dem Leben,* and the word "reverence" is really not quite adequate—though it comes closer in some ways than the French translation, *respect de la vie.* "Reverence" can perhaps carry the sense of mystical awe that is present in *"Ehrfurcht"* (though lacking in the rather matter-of-fact *"respect"*); but it is more specifically religious in tone than *"Ehrfurcht"* and it lacks the German word's overtones of "fear before an overwhelming force." *"Ehrfurcht"* is respect carried to ultimate lengths. It holds reverberations of the feelings we experience on the tops of high mountains, in a storm at sea, or in a tropical tornado. This was the element that the African jungle gave to Schweitzer's thinking—the acknowledgment of immensity and of overwhelming power. Like the farmer in his sermon, listening to the fierce winds, Schweitzer felt the force of continuing life in the vastness of nature.

This is a Wagnerian concept. Or perhaps in English we should look rather to Wordsworth, Blake, or Walt Whitman, the great mystic nature-poets, for a parallel. At all events it is a poetic concept. It came to him after much diligent thought, true, but it came out of the blue, an intuition, not a logical answer to an intellectual problem. So how can he call it a product of thought, or worse still, a necessity of thought?

Numbers of readers of Schweitzer have been troubled by this problem. John Middleton Murry, who was so impressed by Schweitzer that he wrote half a book about him in 1948, spent chapters berating him for failing to notice that Reverence for Life is *not* a necessity of thought, that no logical sequence of propositions compels any man to arrive at Reverence for Life. It is instead, said Murry (and many others), simply Schweitzer's own personal view of life summed up in a phrase, and thought has nothing to do with it.

This is a tempting conclusion to draw. Many thinkers tend to start with the presuppositions that their own natures require and then try to rationalize them. Schweitzer seems a blatant example.

"Schweitzer," says Murry, "does not see that he has, throughout his recorded career, been bent on imposing himself upon experience. He began with various elements in his character; a very pronounced will, a desire to relieve human misery, a determination not to subordinate himself to any organization, and a conviction that whatever was true in the Christian religion could be established by rational thinking. These were the main distinguishable elements. The will was the driving force behind the other three."[1]

There is certainly some truth in this. If it was the whole truth, we might take off our hats to a man whose nature is so generous, so universal, that it leads him to find Reverence for Life as his guiding star; but we would have no obligation to follow him, for he would have failed to establish it as a principle for all men.

It is of course, so patently obvious that Reverence for Life is *not* a necessity or a product of *logical,* step-by-step thinking that one is only amazed that anyone troubled to pursue that line of argument. Murry failed to ask the simple initial question: Is "thought" an adequate translation of what Schweitzer wrote? We have already seen that *"denken"* does in fact carry other connotations, of meditation, of brooding absorption in a subject, which the word "thought" does not encompass. Murry would have saved himself a great deal of irritation and effort if he had realized this. Curiously enough, in the other half of his book, which is a study of D. H. Lawrence, he quotes a poem of Lawrence's which is the precise answer to his problem:

Thought, I love thought.
But not the jaggling and twisting of already existent ideas,
I despise that self-important game.
Thought is the wellingup of unknown life into consciousness,

Thought is the testing of statements on the touchstone of the
conscience.
Thought is gazing on to the face of life, and reading what can be read,
Thought is pondering over experience, and coming to conclusion.
Thought is not a trick, or an exercise, or a set of dodges.
Thought is a man in his wholeness wholly attending.

That precisely, is *"denken."*

Murry himself was in fact trying hard to find in Schweitzer a confirmation of his own idealistic Socialist ideas and was not truly attending to
what Schweitzer wrote. Otherwise he would have noticed the similarity
between Lawrence's poem and Schweitzer's own definitions of thought at
various points in his writings. For example, in *The Decay and Restoration of Civilisation*: "[Thought] is no dry intellectualism, which would
suppress all the manifold movements of our inner life, but the totality of
all the functions of our spirit in their living action and interaction."[2] And
in his Hibbert Lectures in 1934: "Thinking is a harmony within us."[3]

Perhaps the clearest statement of his attitude and the way he reached it
comes from a statement he made in an interview on Radio Brazzaville in
1953:

I was always, even as a boy, engrossed in the philosophical problem
of the relation between emotion and reason. Certain truths originate in
feeling, others in the mind. Those truths that we derive from our emotions are of a moral kind—compassion, kindness, forgiveness, love for
our neighbour. Reason, on the other hand, teaches us the truths that
come from reflection.

But with the great spirits of our world—the Hebrew prophets,
Christ, Zoroaster, the Buddha, and others—feeling is always para-
mount. In them emotion holds its ground against reason, and all of us
have an inner assurance that the truth of emotion that these great spiritual figures reveal to us is the most profound and the most important
truth.

The problem presented itself to me in these terms: must we really be
condemned to live in this dualism of emotional and rational truths?
Since my particular preoccupation was with problems of morality, I
have always been struck by finding myself forced to recognize that the
morality elaborated by philosophy, both ancient and modern, has been
meager indeed when compared to the morality of the great religious
and ethical geniuses who have taught us that the supreme and only
truth capable of satisfying man's spirit is love.

I reached a point where I asked myself this question: does the mind,
in its striving for a morality that can guide us in life, lag so far behind
the morality that emotion reveals because it is not sufficiently profound

to be able to conceive what the great teachers, in obedience to feeling, have made known to us?

This led me to devote myself entirely to the search for a fundamental principle of morality. Others before me have done the same. Throughout history there have been philosophers who believed intuitively that reason must eventually succeed in discovering the true and profound nature of the good. I have tried to carry their work further. In so doing, I was brought to the point where I had to consider the question of what the fundamental idea of existence is. What is the mind's point of departure when it sets itself to the task of reflecting on humanity and on the world in which we live? This point of departure, I said to myself, is not any knowledge of the world that we have acquired. We do not have—and we will never have—true knowledge of the world; such knowledge will always remain a mystery to us.

The point of departure naturally offered for meditation between ourselves and the world is the simple evidence that we are life that wishes to live and are animated by a will in the midst of other lives animated by the same will. Simply by considering the act of thinking, our consciousness tells us this. True knowledge of the world consists in our being penetrated by a sense of the mystery of existence and of life.

If we proceed on the basis of this knowledge, it is no longer isolated reason that devotes itself to thought, but our whole being, that unity of emotion and reflection that constitutes the individual.[4]

In his preface to *Civilisation and Ethics,* the book in which he first unveiled the notion of Reverence for Life in all its glory, Schweitzer writes time and again of the way in which rational thought must give way in the end to the nonrational. Only "inexorably truth-loving and recklessly courageous thought is mature enough to learn by experience how the rational, when it thinks itself out to a conclusion, passes necessarily over into the nonrational."[5] In this passage the key phrase is "by experience." There is no *logic* by which the rational must arrive at the nonrational. We simply discover the fact, says Schweitzer, by experience:

If rational thought thinks itself out to a conclusion, it arrives at something non-rational which, nevertheless, is a necessity of thought. This is the paradox which dominates our spiritual life. If we try to get on without this non-rational element, there result views of the world and of life which have neither vitality nor value.

All valuable conviction is non-rational and has an emotional character, because it cannot be derived from knowledge of the world but arises out of the thinking experience of our will-to-live, in which we stride out beyond all knowledge of the world. This fact it is which the rational thought that thinks itself out to a conclusion comprehends as the truth by which we must live. The way to true mysticism leads up through rational thought to deep experience of the world and of our will-to-live. We must all venture once more to be "thinkers," so as to reach mysticism, which is the only direct and the only profound world-view. We must all wander in the field of knowledge to the point where knowledge passes over into experience of the world. We must all, through thought, become religious.[6]

Schweitzer's experience was that rational thinking led inevitably to "thinking experience," and so to mystical apprehension—and this whole process he called "thought." As a result he could speak of the "thinking man" when he meant not the academic but the man who is aware of the depths in himself and of his deep links with the rest of nature—the man who has not blocked off, in the interests of "growing up," the warm instincts of childhood.

This point is so important and so alien to our technological way of thinking that I make no apology for quoting two other passages. The first is from *Civilisation and Ethics,* Chapter 19. Schweitzer is describing the role which thought plays in the origin of ethics. "It seizes on something of which a preliminary form is seen in an instinct, in order to extend it and bring it to perfection. It apprehends the content of an instinct, and tries to give it practical application in new and consistent action."[7]

The other passage comes from the beginning of *The Mysticism of Paul the Apostle,* the book which he had had to leave unfinished when he went to Africa. Here he is distinguishing between different kinds of mysticism—the superstitious mysticism of primitive races, the magical mysticism which involves sacramental initiations, and the mature mysticism which is a personal comprehension of the universal:

> When the conception of the universal is reached and a man reflects upon his relation to the totality of being and to Being in itself, the resultant mysticism becomes widened, deepened, and purified. The entrance into the super-earthly and eternal then takes place through an act of thinking.
>
> In this act the conscious personality raises itself above that illusion of the senses which makes him regard himself as in bondage in the present life to the earthly and temporal. It attains the power to distinguish between appearance and reality and is able to conceive the material as a mode of manifestation of the Spiritual. It has sight of the Eternal in the Transient. Recognising the unity of all things in God, in Being as such, it passes beyond the unquiet flux of becoming and disintegration into the peace of timeless being, and is conscious of itself as being in God, and in every moment eternal.
>
> This intellectual mysticism is a common possession of humanity. Whenever thought makes the ultimate effort to conceive the relation of the personality to the universal, this mysticism comes into existence.[8]

In this process then of instinct, reason, and mystical intuition, what are the steps by which Schweitzer reaches his goal, the foundation of civilization, Reverence for Life?

First comes the clearing away of the rubble. "If a man wishes to reach clear notions about himself and his relation to the world, he must ever again and again be looking away from the manifold, which is the product of his thought and knowledge, and reflect upon the first, the most immediate, and the continually given fact of his own consciousness."[9] With a single sweep Schweitzer dismisses the doctrines and traditions of the churches, the theories of philosophers, the folklore of nations, all that man had thought or written or handed down. These are merely "the product of his thought and knowledge." They are partial and fallible. The only thing man really is certain of is his own existence, and his awareness of it. From there he can start. Descartes began, "I think; therefore I am"—*Cogito, ergo sum.* "With this beginning," says Schweitzer, "he finds himself irretrievably on the road to the abstract."[10] For "*cogito*" is the word for intellectual reflection, which is certainly not the first step. Existence and its awareness come long before we reach the point of cogitation. "The most immediate fact of man's consciousness is the assertion: 'I am life which wills to live, in the midst of life which wills to live.' "[11]

So Schweitzer lays down the basis of his thinking—the simplest, most fundamental or, as he would say, "elemental" starting point of consciousness. It is universal as well as elemental. I live. I want to go on living. So too do others live and want to go on living.

(As to those individuals and philosophies which claim that life is not worth living, Schweitzer observes that if they were consistent they would simply expire; so long as they go on living, there must be *some* will-to-live stronger than the will not to live. The true despair of the suicide is of course something totally different.)

From this simple beginning Schweitzer proceeds: "As in my will-to-live there is ardent desire for further life and for the mysterious exaltation of the will-to-live which we call pleasure, while there is fear of destruction and of that mysterious depreciation of the will-to-live which we call pain: so too are these in the will-to-live around me, whether it can express itself to me, or remains dumb."[12] With the next step we begin perhaps to enter the nonrational: "The man who has become a thinking being feels a compulsion to give to every will-to-live the same reverence for life that he gives to his own. He experiences that other life in his own. He accepts as being good: to preserve life, to promote life, to raise to its highest value life which is capable of development; and as being evil: to destroy life, to injure life, to repress life which is capable of development. This is the absolute, fundamental principle of the moral, and it is a necessity of thought."[13]

It could well be argued that the contrary is true. The world being what it is, my will-to-live is likely to find itself in conflict with other wills-to-live. It does so every time I eat a lamb chop. As Schweitzer himself writes, a few lines later: "The world, however, offers us the horrible drama of will-to-live divided against itself. One existence holds its own at the cost of another; one destroys another."[14] So finding my will-to-live in conflict with others my reaction is surely to strengthen myself against them, to prepare to destroy them before they can destroy me. This, the law of the jungle could certainly be described as logical, therefore rational. But this is not the thought of Schweitzer's "thinking man." "In him," says Schweitzer, "the will-to-live has become conscious of other will-to-live, and desirous of solidarity with it."[15] Schweitzer's type of thinking process leads to a precisely opposite conclusion to the logic of the law of the jungle.

At this point it becomes important to decide whether or not we accept Schweitzer's mode of thinking as a proper approach to philosophy. This semirational, semimystical technique may be all right for poets—it may even yield important insights which we apprehend more with our pulses than our brains. But can it be made the basis of a complete view of life? Can it convey something which is sufficiently accurate to be generally acceptable?

In the mystical stage of his thinking, is Schweitzer not really being subconsciously swayed by the Christian teaching of his childhood? Is he not generalizing from his own particular good fortune and subconsciously seeking for a philosophical justification for his own uncommon impulse to goodwill? Is he not alloying true thought with other mental functions in order to reach the goal he desires? Is thought not really much more calculating than he makes out, leading us to the behaviorists' belief that we are conditioned creatures who operate according to learned reflexes which enable us to survive; and that love itself is only another such reflex, a useful cement for securing the fabric of society?

These are questions which we must all answer for ourselves. Do we agree with Schweitzer in experiencing thought as something more than a logical thread of reason? Are we conscious of an impulse toward solidarity with other creatures? And if so, do we believe that impulse is something rooted in our nature, and in all nature? Or is it the result of some sort of social brainwashing?

Schweitzer's own childhood history seems to make the brainwashing theory less than convincing. His reactions at that time were often violently emotional, even uncontrollable and very much his own. They certainly do not seem to have been designed to please his parents. Yet these reactions were the start of his mystical identification with nature.

Indeed, he himself claimed that the brainwashing was the other way—

that life and adult society took pains to eliminate the spontaneous loving response of the child, so that growing up was a process of mental impoverishment. If he was right about this, then the kind of thought that is merely rational is artificially attenuated. The rich contents of the mind have been diminished to a colorless adding machine; and for some reason this adding machine has been regarded as much more scientific than the more complex mechanism it has replaced—as though science were concerned only with semihuman creatures.

This notion that science is only concerned with the physical, the practical, the technical, has arisen because the physical and the practical are so much easier to approach scientifically than the mental and spiritual—they are easier to measure and assess. We have even been assured that because mental and spiritual factors cannot be measured accurately, they do not exist—or at any rate have no significance.

The true difference, however, between the scientific way of looking at life and any other way is simply this—that the scientist is prepared to make the most careful observations possible before forming a theory, and then to check his theory by experiment. This is certainly difficult in studying mental processes, but not impossible. What is extremely unscientific is to ignore complicated mental phenomena simply because they are difficult. A truly scientific approach takes account of all phenomena, emotional impulses included.

In any case, Schweitzer is far from being alone in finding that "thought" is much more than emotionless intellectualization.

Einstein said that there was no logical path to a great scientific discovery—the mind had to make a leap, like that of a great painter or poet. And Arthur Koestler, in his monumental book, *The Act of Creation,* sets out to show how all discovery, scientific or artistic, occurs as a flash of vision, unexpected though not unsought-for, which instantly perceives a connection between things never before connected, making a new pattern never perceived before.

After the vision comes the hard work. The scientist begins his experimental checks. The artist begins the laborious business of transferring the vision to paper or canvas. Neither of them can trust the vision unless it works, in physical terms. If it does, the vision was a true one. If not, not.

So with Schweitzer, Reverence for Life came upon him as *Peer Gynt* came upon Ibsen or the theory of relativity came upon Einstein. Ibsen had to write the play and make it work. Einstein had to find the mathematical proofs. And Schweitzer had first to check his vision against the theories of other philosophers, and then, because he was talking about life, had to make his life his argument.

The word "thought" really is a red herring. Schweitzer, trained in the academic schools of philosophy, remained under their influence even when he had rejected their results. Goethe, with the same kind of vision, expressed it in poetry. Schweitzer could not. He wrote books of reasoned argument. He went back through all the types of philosophy he knew of— Chinese, Indian, and ancient Greek as well as European—checking the new vision against them and them against the vision. If there is something uneasy about the endeavor, it is because it often brings together two different kinds of thought, academic and visionary. But the purpose is clear—to check whether it can be shown that previous philosophies have all failed for lack of this one life-giving foundation.

The only way for the reader to satisfy himself about this is to read *Civilisation and Ethics*. The final chapters should be read in any case, for they are the fullest and most exhilarating exposition of Reverence for Life that he ever wrote, a paean of delight in the new possibilities of living. But the earlier chapters are optional, for the real experimental checks on the theory are to be found not in the writings but in the rest of his life.

Let us recapitulate a little. Schweitzer, concentrating his whole mind upon his whole mind, observed that deep within it was an ethical impulse. The impulse to solidarity with other creatures is so profound that it is almost a part of that first element of consciousness. "I am life, that wills to live, in the midst of life that wills to live." He believed that the impulse had been there since infancy. It was not implanted—it was inborn. It was not invented—it was discovered. It was undeniable. The fact that it was discovered at the heart of all consciousness by the brooding mind, and once discovered could not be denied, led Schweitzer to call it a necessity of thought.

Moreover, he had discovered it, and believed that everybody else could discover it, without any appeal to supernatural causes. To discover it one did not need any belief in God, or in Divine Providence, or Eternal Essence, or any transcendental pattern beyond earth. One simply sought in the depths of one's own being. The fact that this human impulse found no reflection in Nature, or the Universe, or History, or any other of those great abstractions, was puzzling, because human beings in general had always felt that there must be a Divine Pattern to which our nature corresponds and philosophers had always obliged by attempting to discern it. This attempt had finally collapsed, as we have seen, demolished by the study of natural history—the last blow perhaps delivered by Darwin when his *Origin of Species* showed that the only "pattern" needed to account for man's superiority to other animals was the pattern of natural selection and the survival of the fittest, a doctrine which gave plausibility to Nietzsche's plea that man should become dominant rather than good. The belief in goodness and gentleness had so long and so completely depended on a belief in the Divine Pattern that it was unthinkable that the two could be separated.

Schweitzer separated them. In his own eyes he seemed extremely daring. Long chapters are devoted to the novelty of the claim that one *could* be agnostic about the design of the universe and still find significance and the foundation of ethics in man—that world view could be dissociated from life view. "To understand the meaning of the whole—and that is what a World-view demands!—is for us an impossibility. . . . I believe I am the first among Western thinkers who has ventured to recognise this crushing result of knowledge. . . ."[16] So he writes in the Preface to *Civilisation and Ethics,* and many passages echo the same idea. A world view is inaccessible to knowledge. It remains a mystery. The only valid attitude to it is resignation—we can never know. We can only know ourselves. And from *that* knowledge we can build an affirmation of life, and in a sort of way an affirmation of the world as well—not because we *know* it but because we experience it.

Schweitzer never fully explores the possibility that man affirms the universe precisely because he affirms himself—that he projects his own secret knowledge of the solidarity of all life onto the universe and then seeks to find an intellectual justification for what he has subconsciously done by inventing Divine Patterns, reversing cause and effect. On this view there could be a connection, but a psychological one, not the philosophical one Schweitzer's training led him to argue against.

Be that as it may, he is much to be honored for what he did. It was a brave and truthful thing for any man at that time, particularly a pastor, to dispense with Divine Patterns without, at some time, succumbing to disillusionment and cynicism. The philosopher-scientist John Wren-Lewis makes this point strongly—and goes on to point out how subsequent scientific developments have confirmed Schweitzer's conclusions.

For ever since then our understanding of the physical universe has been changing. What we know now about the formation of matter, the origin of the stellar system, the operation of the brain, and so on are far from complete, but they are totally different from what Schweitzer knew at the time of the First World War. Any belief about man based on man's relationship with the physical universe has been irreparably shattered time and again in the intervening years—as Darwin and others shattered the beliefs of the nineteenth century. We have reached the point of being able to control and alter nature to an ever-increasing degree—even to alter man himself, his very brain structure. There is no settled relationship possible any longer. All we have is ourselves, in whom we may or may not find something we call divine. Where other prophets and philosophers have repeatedly become out of fashion, Schweitzer's elemental discoveries are still valid. The man whom many regard as old-fashioned is still up-to-date.

It would not be true to say that Schweitzer saw these implications when he divorced life view from world view. But events have shown that the human heart *could* come first. It *could* mold the world to its will, rather than be molded by the whim of the elements. To interfere with nature seems sacrilegious to those who feel that nature contains some divine order. To those who feel that this view is superstitious, an aftermath of the centuries when man was at nature's mercy, it may seem a responsibility to be seized with thankfulness, courage, and good hope. And whether it works out well or ill lies certainly not in the stars but in the human heart.

Schweitzer's bold stroke then, which still discredits him in the eyes of conventional philosophers, seems to point accurately to the future. He himself was not troubled about that. Enough for him that his intuition, which had led him to his own personal, profound understanding of Jesus, of Bach, and of St. Paul, now like an opening shutter printed indelibly on his mind a vision of life itself. The haunting passion for nature which he had felt since childhood fused with his desperate quest for the foundation of human ethics, and the vision was born. Everything led to life itself, everything stemmed from it. Good is what promotes and preserves life. Evil is what destroys and injures life. That is enough.

One of the difficulties about Reverence for Life is that it seems so extraordinarily naïve. Schweitzer believed in and trusted naïveté, but at first sight this is so oversimple as to be meaningless. Not until one begins to consider the consequences of living by such a simple belief does one realize its potency.

In the first place, Reverence for Life is so basic an idea that it is hard for anyone to refuse to acknowledge it. Unlike pacifism, vegetarianism, or any political or religious creed, it is an attitude of mind, not a code of rules or a set of propositions. It commands nothing. It forbids nothing. All it requires is that whatever is done should be done in full and deep awareness. Unlike creeds and codes, which provide human beings with preconstructed decisions and take away the need for choice, Reverence for Life lays on everyone the responsibility for every action. Imagine what the result would be if no human being could appeal any longer to country or party or creed to justify his actions but had to give a personal account for all he did.

Reverence for Life involves awareness—it begins with sinking deep into oneself, as in meditation—but it does not stop there. It proceeds to action. It must, because life is everywhere under attack and needs protection and enhancement. Its wounds cannot be ignored. In this way Reverence for Life bridges the chasm between the contemplative and the active. It avoids the kind of busy and unconsidered helpfulness that often stems from guilt feelings and generally does as much harm as good—and it avoids the self-centeredness of dedicated navel-gazing. Its very simplicity makes it a kind of zero point on a scale—the point where measurement begins. Because if you do not know where you begin, you have no idea what your measurements represent. Reverence for Life is not in itself an activity. It is a means of checking all activity.

Often, when writing of Reverence for Life, Schweitzer made the point that every previous attempt to find the basis for morality had confined itself to the human race. Ethics were always seen either as a technique for perfecting the individual human soul or for improving human society. Very rarely did anyone include other forms of life.

In fact, though Schweitzer never mentions it, Jeremy Bentham, writing in the eighteenth century of the need to treat all individuals with equal humanity, had this footnote to add about animals [author's italics]:

> The day *may* come when the rest of the animal creation may acquire those rights which never could have been withholden from them but by the hand of tyranny. The French have already discovered that the blackness of the skin is no reason why a human being should be abandoned without redress to the caprice of a tormentor. It may one day come to be recognized that the number of the legs, the villosity of the skin, or the termination of the os sacrum, are reasons equally insufficient for abandoning a sensitive being to the same fate. What else is it that should trace the insuperable line? Is it the faculty of reason, or perhaps the faculty of discourse? But a full-grown horse or dog is beyond comparison a more rational, as well as a more conversable animal, than an infant of a day, or a week, or even a month, old. But suppose they were otherwise, what would it avail? The question is not, "Can they *reason?*" nor "Can they *talk?*" but "Can they *suffer?*"[17]

The idea then had been mooted, but only as a footnote, not as an essential part of the argument. And even so, Bentham referred only to animal life, not to life as a whole, which included vegetable life. For Schweitzer even the cutting of a flower or the lopping of a tree were matters for responsible consideration. What Bentham tacked on in a footnote Schweitzer made a central point of his thought. The sense of solidarity with life to which his brooding had brought him made this inevitable. One could only, Schweitzer believed, understand civilization by understanding life. One could only understand life by sharing life. Unless one went as deep as this, one was always faced with conflicts and difficulties which arose from the principle being insufficiently inclusive. Even humanity was not embracing enough, for the one absolute value shared by all humanity was life itself, and that was shared also by all other creatures.

Journalistic distortion has presented Reverence for Life as a sort of perverted love for mosquitoes. And it is true that Schweitzer, with a thoroughgoing consistency that would almost seem absurd were it not the very reason for his achievements, would put a mosquito out of a room rather than kill it. "What?" cry the critics. "A doctor saving the life of a disease carrier?" The action is indeed a *reductio ad absurdum* of the argument, and for that reason valuable—for the responsibility of Reverence for Life meant in Schweitzer's instance that he was never prepared to kill if there were any other means of self-defense. In the hospital there were other means. As we have seen, his mosquito netting side-walls were a better protection for people indoors than any amount of swatting and slaughtering. And out-of-doors there were drugs for protection, on which Schweitzer was very insistent; besides which, what good would the death of one mosquito do among so many millions?

Few people would be so meticulous about the details of their belief. Schweitzer was in a special case, feeling that he had to be a living embodiment of his argument. But he was right in a sense. Halfheartedness would have been the death of the argument. The validity of a law is best seen in extreme cases. Blake, with the same kind of vision as Schweitzer's, wrote: "A robin redbreast in a cage/ Puts all Heaven in a rage." Many would accept that proposition, from love of robin redbreasts. The real issue arises when you ask whether a poisonous spider in a cage would put all heaven in a rage. I suspect Blake would have answered yes. Schweitzer certainly would have.

Unless of course it was caged for its own good or the safety of others. Schweitzer was quite prepared to restrain, or if necessary kill, creatures that were genuinely harmful—witness the spider hunt on his first night in Andende. Not to do so would itself be an offense against Reverence for Life, for where life is harmful to other life a choice must be made.

The choice, for Schweitzer, always involved qualms. The exercise of responsibility for death, even the death of harmful bacilli, visible only under a microscope, he found painful. He cultivated this sensitivity; for he had concluded that the loss of sensitivity was what had led the world astray. And the tough hide he had grown since childhood to protect his sensitivity against the jeers of his fellows was now quite capable of dealing with accusations of sentimentality. The formula he used to recommend, the soul of a dove in the hide of an elephant, was accurate enough of himself; he cultivated it and carefully maintained it, using determination to reinforce conviction, conviction to stiffen instinct.

That his sensitivity did not make him sentimental is evident from a number of stories. James Cameron, who visited the hospital in 1953, tells one in his book *Point of Departure:*

> One day luncheon began with a reprimand; the Doctor was concerned at my having walked alone up the forest track past the settlement: Did I not realize the danger from gorillas? This was a bad place for gorillas. I said, with rather fatuous lightness (since I did feel guilty), that it might be possible that by now the neighbouring gorillas had themselves developed the rudiments of Respect for Life.
>
> He replied with acerbity: "Doubtless if you communicated to the gorilla that you were a member of the British Press, he would stand aside; if by chance you had no time to do so he would first break your arms, then your legs, one by one: following that he would tear off your scalp. Gorillas I know."[18]

Clearer still is the story told by Dr. Frank Catchpool, who worked with Schweitzer for a number of years in the fifties, speaking at a convocation at Aspen, Colorado, after Schweitzer's death:

> As I was going down to the pharmacy one day, I saw Dr. Schweitzer's pelican struggling in for a landing. He made three attempts to land and I saw something was wrong with the undercarriage, because one hand was hanging down. I watched it carefully and it tried again, again and again . . . these birds with a five foot wing span, they fly so beautifully. Finally it made a clumsy crashlanding and came to a halt and I sent a message with Ali and said: "Tell Dr. Schweitzer that his pelican has a broken leg." An hour or so later Dr. Schweitzer came to the pharmacy and he said, "Do you have a moment? I would like you to come and consult with me about my pelican." I said, "*Sofort,* Doctor, I come. . . ." He said, "No . . . your patients first!"
>
> This was important to me and I was glad he said that. He had very clearly established the priorities of medical treatment: humans first, the worst cases first, and his own pelican, which he loved very much, was not to be put ahead of even the most minor human case. After lunch we went and looked at the pelican. Its leg did not seem to be broken but it was paralyzed in some peculiar manner, but we couldn't see anything else wrong with it. Then I noticed a couple of specks of blood on its feather and I said, "Well, could it possibly have been shot at? As it flies around it is such an easy target for someone with a shotgun." So, I said, "May I take an X-ray?" He said, "Well, X-rays are precious and hard to come by . . . if you like to. I'd like to know what's wrong with my pelican, too."
>
> This is another point I'd like to bring out. We had all things we needed in X-ray for making accurate diagnosis. On this picture you can see some of the pellets are flattened out against the bone, indicating the

shot had considerable velocity. Also, from the nature of the spots it was pretty certain that the intestines of the pelican had been perforated in numerous places. I said: "Dr. Schweitzer, this pelican is going to die. I can't do anything for it, unless you like me to open it up and we can sew up all these multiple lesions that he's got." He said, "Are you crazy?" He said, "No, leave this pelican alone. I don't want you to waste your time. I don't want you to waste the materials of the hospital on this. I'll look after my pelican." So, he put his pelican outside his window. After four or five days went past and the pelican wasn't eating . . . he tried forcing it to eat himself, he went to me one day at lunchtime and said, "Do you have another minute . . . will you come and look at my pelican?" I said, "Yes, it's dehydrating, it's not taking any fluids, it will surely die." Dr. Schweitzer said, "If he's not better tomorrow I'll chop his head off." This, again, to me is important to show that this man would not let his sentiment overrule his reason. He knew that this animal was doomed, he couldn't save it. He knew he was troubled by this animal's suffering. So, he brutally said, "I will knock its head off."[19]

The Alsatian countryman, bred of those Schweitzers whom Sartre found so crude of speech, is still there.

Attempts were made from time to time to persuade Schweitzer to tabulate Reverence for Life, laying down an order of priority among creatures. From Dr. Catchpool's story it is clear that human life came before animal life in Schweitzer's own personal tabulation—though several people noted that he was more able to demonstrate his tenderness to animals than to humans. But he refused to lay down a scale of values for others. To ask for a scale of values in fact implies a considerable misunderstanding of the whole idea of Reverence for Life. Reverence is an attitude of mind, not a set of rules. Schweitzer was asking that people should follow him in sinking into their own minds and hearts and finding there, as he was convinced they would, a place where separateness from other life ceased and solidarity began. Once there, they would not need rules. Each person would have to make decisions from time to time, about the relative importance to him or to her of different creatures. To keep alive a fallen nestling you must find worms. To keep a falcon you must sacrifice mice. Each decision must be personal, but must be taken under the overall guidance of Reverence for Life. Nothing must be arbitrary or irresponsible. The moment you publish a list of priorities you take away that personal responsibility, that fresh openness of heart and spontaneity of reaction that is of the essence of Schweitzer's thinking.

Responsibility is a hard thing. Most people prefer to accept some common code of behavior which takes from them the need to make choices and leaves them simply with the obligation to obey. No doubt Schweitzer's teaching would have been much more enthusiastically received had he issued clear instructions about the relative value of cats and birds, birds and caterpillars, caterpillars and leaves. It was not his way. Schweitzer was the ultimate revolutionary who will not take orders even from revolutionaries but only from his own conscience, and asks only that others do the same. "It is not by receiving instruction about agreement between ethical and necessary, that a man makes progress in ethics, but only by coming to hear more and more plainly the voice of the ethical, by becoming ruled more and more by the longing to preserve and promote life, and by becoming more and more obstinate in resistance to the necessity for destroying or injuring life.

"In ethical conflicts man can arrive only at subjective decisions. No one can decide for him at what point, on each occasion, lies the extreme limit of possibility for his persistence in the preservation and furtherance of life. He alone has to judge this issue, by letting himself be guided by a feeling of the highest possible responsibility towards other life."[20]

Responsibility being a hard thing, so is Reverence for Life. In his hospital Schweitzer lived face to face with decision all the time. When young pelicans were brought in by African boys who had shot the parent birds, fish had to be caught to feed them. Life demanded death. So, said Schweitzer, the responsibility for Reverence for Life demands constant guilt. There is no way of avoiding the awareness that in preserving we destroy, and we are responsible. If we are not aware of this, something is wrong with us.

"We must never let ourselves become blunted. We are living in truth, when we experience these conflicts more profoundly. The good conscience is an invention of the devil."[21]

This aspect of Schweitzer's thinking needs to be clarified. We are accustomed to the post-Freudian notion of guilt as purely destructive. For Schweitzer it simply meant an awareness of our involvement in the harsh necessities of life; it meant a refusal to pretend to be outside or above them. It meant too (the German word "Schuld" meaning debt as well as guilt) that something or someone is constantly having to pay for our decisions, however honestly and wisely we try to make them. To the creatures that have to pay—the fish for the pelicans for example—we owe a debt which we are not entitled to ignore.

Such awareness in fact should have a precisely opposite result to the deadening effect of a destructive guilt-complex. To be conscious of the price paid should sharpen the value of the life for which it was given. Schweitzer's own legendary alertness is the outward and visible sign of the state of mind he was talking about.

This alertness, this responsiveness, is perhaps the most obvious effect of Reverence for Life. Once reverence is established, everything that exists is important. Boredom is not possible. There can be no superiority, no isolation, no detachment. Everything is a subject for concern, nothing is beneath notice. The world is there to be appreciated and enjoyed. As Schweitzer once wrote of a girls' school which had adopted his principles: "The awareness of the meaning of my philosophy of kindness towards all creatures had made them at once serious and gay."[22]

The gaiety he spoke of arises from the freedom offered by Reverence for Life. To make up for the burden it imposes of responsibility for choice, Reverence for Life lifts many other burdens and demolishes many other problems. It overrides questions of nation and of party, and every kind of limited loyalty to race or creed. For though at first Reverence for Life may seem a vague ideal, the consequences if it is taken seriously are very practical. Cruelty, any kind of cruelty, for any purpose, becomes impossible. Racism and all prejudice become impossible. Censoriousness and self-righteousness become impossible (since one's regard for other beings depends only on their existence, not on any virtues they may possess). So also does that prevalent modern disease, self-hatred, become impossible. For oneself is also part of life, demanding reverence. As the second great commandment of Jesus was to love your neighbor *as yourself,* implying that you must love yourself before you can love your neighbor, so Reverence for Life can operate from a secure foundation only if the life of others is valued as a result of valuing one's own.

In *Civilisation and Ethics* Schweitzer makes this point clearly and with power:

> Why do I forgive anyone? Ordinary ethics say, because I feel sympathy with him. They allow men, when they pardon others, to seem to themselves wonderfully good, and allow them to practise a style of pardoning which is not free from humiliation of the other. They thus make forgiveness a sweetened triumph of self-devotion.
>
> The ethics of reverence for life do away with this crude point of view. All acts of forbearance and of pardon are for them acts forced from one by sincerity towards oneself. I must practise unlimited forgiveness because, if I did not, I should be wanting in sincerity to myself, for I would be acting as if I myself were not guilty in the same way as the other has been guilty towards me. Because my life is so liberally spotted with falsehood, I must forgive falsehood which has been practised upon me; because I myself have been in so many cases wanting in love, and guilty of hatred, slander, deceit, or arrogance, I must pardon any want of love and all hatred, slander, deceit or arrogance which have been directed against myself. I must forgive quietly and unostentatiously; in fact I do not really pardon at all, for I do not let things develop to any such act of judgement. Nor is this any eccentric proceeding; it is only a necessary widening and refining of ordinary ethics. . . . It is not from kindness to others that I am gentle, peace-

able, forbearing, and friendly, but because by such behaviour I prove
my own profoundest self-realisation to be true. Reverence for life
which I apply to my own existence, and reverence for life which keeps
me in a temper of devotion to other existence than my own, interpene-
trate each other.[23]

In this philosophy there is nothing negative, nothing repressive or divi-
sive, there is no conflict either between man and beast, man and man, or
man and himself.

The liberating effect of Reverence for Life makes it the enemy of every
form of establishment, every authoritarian code of ethics. One reason
why the appeal of Schweitzer's philosophy fell for the most part on deaf
ears was that the period just after he wrote his book saw the emergence
into history of the theories of another thinker, whose books had been written sixty years before—Karl Marx. Intelligent Europeans between the
wars found themselves faced with very practical issues, as Communism
began to emerge as the hope of the exploited classes, and Capitalism and
Fascism fought back. In this situation people of conscience had no serious
choice. Whatever the defects of Communism (and they only gradually appeared), it was for most thinking people the only viable opposition to social injustice, and he who was not with the Marxists was against them. A
generation of generous souls dedicated themselves to the Marxist future,
and found itself destitute when that ideal turned to ashes in Stalin's
Russia.

The great Socialist ideal is still with us, and great numbers of honest
men and women are still convinced that the class struggle is the key to
history. The more bitter that struggle, the more rigidly the partisans on
each side cling to the party ideology and feel it a virtue to sacrifice their
identity to the party good. To be committed to something or other is automatically a virtue—though commitment may mean signing away your
power of individual judgment and your conscience to a cause which can
and often does override humanity.

At such a time the voice of Schweitzer proclaiming that the individual
is supreme had as much chance of being heard as a solo flute in an artil-
lery barrage. "With the spirit of the age I am in complete disagreement,"
he wrote in his autobiography, "because it is filled with disdain for thinking. . . . The organised political, social and religious associations of
our time are at work to induce the individual man not to arrive at his convictions by his own thinking, but to make his own the convictions that
they keep ready-made for him. Any man who thinks for himself and at the
same time is spiritually free is to them something inconvenient and even
uncanny."[24]

Since so many people are still convinced that ethics consists in dedicating oneself unreservedly to a party or a cause, it is worthwhile quoting Schweitzer at some length on the subject—not only to make it clear how unlikely he was to get a hearing, but to show how early he saw the flaws that took years to become apparent to others:

It is impossible to succeed in developing the ethic of ethical personality into a serviceable ethics of society. It seems so obvious, that from right individual ethics right social ethics should result, the one system continuing itself into the other like a town into suburbs. In reality however, they cannot be so built that the streets of the one continue into those of the other. The plans of each are drawn on principles which take no account of that.

The ethics of ethical personality is personal, incapable of regulation, and absolute; the system established by society for its prosperous existence is supra-personal, regulated, and relative. Hence the ethical personality cannot surrender to it, but lives always in continuous conflict with it, obliged again and again to oppose it because it finds its focus too short.

In the last analysis, the antagonism between the two arises from their differing valuations of humaneness. Humaneness consists in never sacrificing a human being to a purpose. The ethic of ethical personality aims at preserving humaneness. The system established by society is impotent in that respect.

When the individual is faced with the alternative of having to sacrifice in some way or other the happiness or the existence of another, or else to bear the loss himself, he is in a position to obey the demands of ethics and to choose the latter. But society, thinking impersonally and pursuing its aims impersonally, does not allow the same weight to consideration for the happiness or existence of an individual. In principle humaneness is not an item in its ethics. But individuals come continually into the position of being in one way or another executive organs of society, and then the conflict between the two points of view become active. That this may always be decided in its own favour, society exerts itself as much as possible to limit the authority of the ethic of personality, although inwardly it has to acknowledge its superiority. It wants to have servants who will never oppose it.

Even a society whose ethical standard is relatively high is dangerous to the ethics of its members. If those things which form precisely the defects of a social code of ethics develop strongly, and if society exercises, further, an excessively strong spiritual influence on individuals, then the ethic of ethical personality is ruined. This happens in present-day society, whose ethical conscience is becoming fatally stunted by a biologico-sociological ethic, and this, moreover, finally corrupted by nationalism.

The great mistake of ethical thought down to the present time is that it fails to admit the essential difference between the morality of ethical personality and that which is established from the standpoint of society, and always thinks that it ought, and is able to cast them in one piece. The result is that the ethic of personality is sacrificed to the ethic of society. And an end must be put to this. What matters is to recognise that the two are engaged in a conflict which cannot be made less intense. Either the moral standard of personality raises the moral standard of society, so far as is possible, to its own level, or it is dragged down by it.[25]

We have seen, and still do see, plenty of examples of personal moral standards being dragged down by the moral standards of society—to such an extent that people in public life have come to be regarded with a sort of despairing disgust. Communist, Socialist, Capitalist—none is seen to be any better than the others. Corruption and dishonesty corrode every organization and every party.

But, in the ironical way in which history often works, Schweitzer's ideas, largely neglected in his own time despite all the personal admiration he received, are now being followed by a new generation that knows little or nothing about him. The course of history has forced them to acknowledge what he saw years before.

The young of today, or at least a large and articulate body of them all over the world, have like Schweitzer come out wholeheartedly for life as a whole. Born under the unifying dread of the mushroom cloud, they have seen, as he did, the lunacy of pretending that we can survive separately. The disastrous results of unfettered nationalism combined with unfettered industrialization and technological progress have been felt in this generation's bloodstream. They need no telling that polluted air, earth, and sea are bound up with the very existence of themselves and their children and that unless we reverence life we all die. Just as Schweitzer did, they have therefore rejected the traditional ethics that were limited to loyalties to one small community or another, one self-important creed or another. Life itself is precious, and the old divisions which made people kill each other for living in the wrong place or thinking different thoughts are seen as so ridiculous as to be almost incomprehensible.

In all too many cases, unfortunately, these young people have simply dropped out of society without knowing where to go next, and in the end the established order has got them back again. But their outcries have nevertheless become part of the world's consciousness, and even governments have had to take notice.

To determine the extent to which any of this was due to Schweitzer's influence would be quite impossible. What is sure is that the movement, now searching for its own foundations by turning inward to meditation and drug-induced mysticism, badly needs a prophet who combines mystical insight with common sense and practical knowledge as Schweitzer does. If this generation can hold on to and consolidate its instincts and convictions, and can find a secure foundation from which to go on challenging the nations and institutions that bred them, we have some hope of the radical change of outlook which alone can master the social and technological turmoil of our age.

Schweitzer's banner, which looked so irrelevant and old-fashioned in the 1920's and 1930's, could well now lead the field.

17

INTERNMENT
1915–1917

Now Schweitzer had a philosophy that satisfied both his instinct and his intellect, that provided a place where religion and philosophy met. Once he had hit upon Reverence for Life as the starting point (though all its implications were not yet worked out), it more or less took the place of Christianity in his mind. Jesus of course remained what he always had been—the supreme man. But Schweitzer was convinced that he had thought his way to a level deeper than the Churches dealt with; their language and ideas were no longer adequate for his purposes. So, for example, though he continued to use the word God when that would best convey his meaning to his hearers, or when not to use it would only upset or startle people, he used it less and less in general conversation and not at all in his writings. For he had declared himself agnostic about one of the manifestations of God, as creator and ruler of the universe; and the spirit he discovered within himself he preferred to define a good deal more closely, as "Will to Live, seeking communion with other Wills to Live." He felt that here he was in touch with some sort of universal Will, but the word God was so blurred by a hundred other connotations that it was useless as shorthand for what he was talking about, and he was only prepared to talk about what he himself had experienced.

Medical work continued as before; and now, to maintain supplies, Schweitzer began to run into debt. He could no longer get into touch with his sources of financial assistance in Strasbourg, and he had not budgeted for so long a stay. Joseph fell victim to the inevitable economy drive—Schweitzer had to ask him to accept a cut in pay, and Joseph felt that it was beneath his dignity to work for so little. So he went. And Schweitzer's work increased.

By December he and Hélène were both beginning to feel the effects of tropical anemia. The four-minute walk up the steep hill to the bungalow grew quite exhausting. "In the tropics a man can do at most half of what he can manage in a temperate climate. If he is dragged about from one task to another he gets used up so quickly that, though he is still on the spot, the working capacity he represents is nil."[1] Adding to all the other labor was the savage rate of depreciation in the tropics. Floods, termites, weevils, traveler ants—life was a perpetual battle against the depredations of any or all of these. While one foe was being thwarted, the others were creeping in. "Oh, the fight that has to be carried on in Africa with creeping insects! What time one loses over the thorough precautions that have to be taken! And with what helpless rage one has to confess again and again that one has been outwitted!"[2] Meantime reserves of European food were running short, and the Schweitzers trained themselves reluctantly to eat monkey flesh. At Christmas they burned the stubs of the candles they had saved from the previous year.

Letters to and from Europe were getting through fairly regularly now, and news arrived also by telegraph from Libreville or Cape Lopez. Newspapers which reached them seemed unbearable, not only because of the news they brought but because they appeared so grotesquely shrill and feverish. "All of us here live under the daily repeated experience that nature is everything and man is nothing. . . . It seems something almost abnormal that over a portion of the earth's surface nature should be nothing and man everything!"[3] At sermon time on Sundays Schweitzer was faced with the complicated task of explaining how it was that the whites, professed followers of Jesus, had turned on each other in a destructive fury quite incomprehensible to the Gabonese blacks. "About this time it became known that of the whites who had gone home to fulfil their military duties ten had already been killed, and it made a great impression on the natives, 'Ten men killed already in this war!' said an old Pahouin. 'Why, then, don't the tribes meet for a palaver? How can they pay for all these dead men?' For, with the natives it is a rule that all who fall in a war, whether on the victorious or on the defeated side, must be paid for by the other side."[4]

Time passed and weariness became a part of living. But Schweitzer went on working on his book, for he reckoned that the work he did on that was a recreation rather than an additional burden. "Mental work one must have, if one is to keep one's self in moral health in Africa; hence the man of culture, though it may seem a strange thing to say, can stand life in the forest better than the uneducated man, because he has a means of recreation of which the other knows nothing. When one reads a good book on a serious subject one is no longer the creature that has been exhausting itself the whole day in the contest with the unreliability of the natives and the tiresome worry of the insects; one becomes once more a man!''[5]

In the dry season, from May to October, the temperature dropped and the river shrank, leaving broad sandbanks exposed. One could walk there and enjoy the breeze blowing up the river. The work eased, too, in these cooler, drier, healthier months. In July, 1916, Schweitzer was writing about this relief, in one of the occasional essays which he still wrote in the hope that sooner or later they would reach his supporters. He did not know that early in the month his mother had died, her premonition fulfilled that she would never see him again.

In his autobiography Schweitzer says only this: "My mother was knocked down and killed in 1916 by cavalry horses on the road between Günsbach and Weier-im-Tal,"[6] a statement so bald that some writers have assumed from it that Schweitzer cared little for his mother. Others, their imaginations working in different directions, have dramatized the scene by describing her as having been "trampled to death."

The truth about the whole sad and pointless accident is told in Louis Schweitzer's diary. On Monday July 3, a sultry, wet day, he and Mrs. Schweitzer went to lunch with a friend, Frau Kiener, in Walbach, only a mile or two down the valley. After lunch the two women contentedly fed the ducks and hens, they all strolled for a while in the park, and the Schweitzers left about six P.M. Their friends came with them as far as the bridge, where they all stopped and looked at the scenery. Then the Schweitzers strolled on.

They took the footpath through the fields as far as Weier, where they sat and rested awhile on a bench. When they moved on it began to rain, so they put up their umbrellas and kept to the left of the road, under the trees. At a bend in the road two soldiers came galloping up behind them, one whipping his horse all the way, and rode past. When these were a hundred yards or so ahead, a third soldier, also riding hard, swung around the bend behind the Schweitzers. With the rain splashing on their umbrellas they only heard him when he was almost on them and then, "Mama turned to see what was coming—I couldn't pull her back." The horse struck her and she fell with a cry on the back of her head, her arms outstretched. There she lay, her eyes closed, foam on her mouth, her breathing deep and heavy.

The soldier came back, explaining that his horse had been out of control; and then went for help. Meanwhile a friend passed with a cart loaded with grass. They lifted Mrs. Schweitzer onto the bed of grass and set off for the village. A doctor from Strasbourg who came by diagnosed a fractured skull and returned with them to the manse. There the doctor bandaged Mrs. Schweitzer's head and tried to ease her breathing by massage and arm movements, meanwhile sending to Sulzbach for camphor. At eight thirty a doctor came from Sulzbach with the camphor, which was injected; and Mrs. Schweitzer's breathing improved briefly.

Before long both doctors had to leave. Mrs. Schweitzer's condition remained unchanged till two A.M. Then her pulse weakened. Then stopped.

Louis wrote to Louise, then slept uneasily for an hour or two. From eight A.M. onward the villagers came to offer their sympathy; and at eleven Louise and Jules arrived—Louise badly shaken.

At eight that evening shooting began in the valley and they had to go frequently to the cellar. The following day at eight in the morning Mrs. Schweitzer's face began to swell, because of the bandage.

It so happened that the village she came from, Mühlbach, where her father had been pastor and where Louis had first met her, was largely destroyed about the same time; the destruction included the church and the organ on which her father had lavished such enthusiasm and which Albert had helped to restore before he went to Africa. In Lambarene Schweitzer had already read of the damage to Mühlbach in a Swiss newspaper by the time the letters come through with the news of his mother's death.

It was August 15. On that day he wrote to Louis: "I write to tell you that I know that mother lies in the graveyard. The omens were remarkable. When the boat's siren sounded in the distance, I knew what news it brought. Through the room her picture greets me. Today we decorate it with palms and orange blossom. I am still too shattered to make sense of it, and I see in my mind's eye the corner of the graveyard in all its summer beauty; and I think how it will be when Hélène and I greet her on our return home."[7]

None of this found its way into Schweitzer's public writings. "At the end of the summer," he wrote, "we were able to join our missionary neighbours, Mr. and Mrs. Morel, of Samkita, in a visit of some weeks to Cape Lopez, where a trading company, several of whose employees had benefited by our treatment and hospitality during illness, placed three rooms in one of their stores at our disposal. The sea air worked wonders for our health."[8] That is all he says about that summer.

They had occasionally spent recuperative weeks at Cape Lopez before. They were there in December, 1915, and Schweitzer wrote that he felt so refreshed his philosophical work must be good. Now, with the rainy season approaching again and Hélène's health getting worse, they planned to stay there throughout the winter months. A timber merchant had offered them a house now lying vacant because of the war, and by the middle of October the baggage was packed and ready for the journey to the coast. It comes as something of a shock to discover that the baggage included not only chickens, but parrots and antelopes—fifty crates all told. The Schweitzers were traveling with a menagerie. As indeed they presumably had to, for who was to look after their animals if they left them behind?

Perhaps Hélène was not entirely delighted about it all. Aunt Hélène, so Schweitzer wrote to his niece, still had problems about respectability— her beloved pet dwarf antelope was inclined to wet all over the place and make little balls wherever it fancied.

A doctor is never entirely on holiday. Someone is always needing attention, everywhere. But the medical work at Cape Lopez was only occasional, and most of Schweitzer's time was divided between his book—at low tide—and at high tide helping to roll huge logs up the beach. This was to preserve the logs until they could again be shipped back to Europe—it was Schweitzer's way of paying the timber merchant for his lodging. They swam, too, and lived, Schweitzer wrote, the life of Robinson—presumably a reference to *The Swiss Family Robinson*, that classic adventure story about a family on a desert island. As to food, the bay was alive with fish. One day Schweitzer caught 400 herring. They grew tired of eating fish.

In January, 1917, Schweitzer formally rented the cottage, together with some land, for his use or the use of any of the society's members who were passing through. The contract stipulated that he might build accommodation for Africans visiting the coast; and also chicken houses. But one clause shows that Schweitzer was far from certain about the future. It provided that should the authorities compel him to return to France, the contract was nullified by *force majeure*.

They stayed a long while at Cape Lopez, while the war rolled on in Europe; and Louis Schweitzer recorded in his diary: "5th April, 1917. America declared war on Germany. I heard the first cuckoo in Altenbach."

Schweitzer and Hélène finally gathered their cases together and went back up the river to work some time in the early summer. There was much to do. In addition to the normal ailments of the local Africans, dysentery was rife among military carriers from the Cameroons who were passing through. They had not long settled to the task when the half-expected blow fell. The suspended sentence of internment that had hung over their heads for so long suddenly became a reality.

Clemenceau had decided that security in the French colonies was far too lax (and judging by Schweitzer's case he would seem to have had some justification for the view). He wanted the laxity stopped; and so the Schweitzers found themselves ordered immediately to Europe. Mercifully the ship that was to take them was a few days late, so they had time at least to make some dispositions of their effects.

The contract for the cottage at Cape Lopez had to be torn up—invoking the *force majeur* clause. And on October 9 Schweitzer wrote a letter to M. Félix Fauré, head of the mission station, that reads like a will. The whole pharmacy as it stands, surgical instruments and all, is left to the mission station—he estimates the value at about 6,000 francs. The micro-scope is a personal gift to M. Fauré. The piano is to be left where it is, if possible in its zinc-lined case; and the harmonium is to go to the American missionary, Mr. Ford, who happened to be in Lambarene on a visit from Cape Lopez at the time. To Mr. Ford also Schweitzer entrusted his precious drafts of *The Philosophy of Civilisation*, for safekeeping until the end of the war. It was written in German and was hardly likely to sur-vive French internment, besides which it would make a weighty item out of the 110 pounds which was all they were allowed to take with them. Mr. Ford undertook the task with some reservation, for he himself be-lieved philosophy to be a dangerous waste of time. If he ever brought himself to read the manuscript entrusted to him he must have felt better about his responsibility, for he would have discovered how closely Schweitzer agreed with him. For his own purposes Schweitzer made a brief summary of the book's ideas, in French, disguised as a harmless study of the Renaissance, wholly irrelevant to contemporary life.

In the previous year or two Schweitzer had occasionally met people on their way to prison camps and had always given them a supply of drugs from his own dwindling store, with careful instructions how to use them. Few things would be more useful in the conditions to which they were go-ing. Now he crammed as much as he could in the way of drugs and equip-ment into his own limited baggage.

Even while they packed, an African was brought in with a strangulated hernia. Among the packing cases, Schweitzer performed the last opera-tion of these four and a half years.

Two days later, an hour before they boarded the river steamer, he went to see an English timber-merchant friend and exchanged his carefully hoarded gold for French notes. Then they went aboard. Before they could push off, the father superior of the Catholic Mission thrust his way through the guard to shake hands with Schweitzer and thank him for all he had done for the country. Then they set off—all that they had built, all their friends, all the patients, all the animals, left behind.

On the way down the river they sewed the French money into their clothing, and thus clad they boarded the liner at Cape Lopez. Once again, as when they were first treated as dangerous prisoners of war three years earlier, they were isolated under guard. Last time Schweitzer began writ-ing. That was not possible this time, so instead he set about memorizing some Bach fugues and Widor's *Sixth Organ Symphony* . He had them by heart before they reached Bordeaux. And he practiced the organ—with a table as keyboard and the floor as pedals, as he had done when a child.

It was November when they disembarked in Europe. After four and a half years of tropical heat they found themselves in a chilly army barracks, without winter clothing, facing the sharp nip of late autumn weather. Even the normal barrack comforts were missing, since the place was designed for troops on the move through the port. On the seventeenth Hélène and Schweitzer wrote to their respective homes, both in much the same terms. Hélène's letter arrived first—so much so that Louis Schweitzer heard the news of his son's arrival in Europe on December 17 via the Bresslau family, two days before his own letter arrived from Albert. Louis' diary for the nineteenth records:

> At last a letter from Albert in Bordeaux, dated 17th November like Hélène's. He writes, "Dear Father: This note to say we have arrived in Bordeaux. You have doubtless heard the news—(where from?)—that an order came for us to leave Africa by the next passage, for internment in France. For the moment we are temporarily interned at Bordeaux, at 136 rue Belleville, where there are also some refugees. It is normally a barracks. At the moment it only houses civilians. Luckily the weather is dry, which allows us to get reacclimatised. Don't worry too much about us. If you can make any representations about us, such as you spoke about earlier, that would be good, for the mountains would be what's most beneficial for our health—Hélène and I send our love. Greetings and news to our friends. Yours, Albert Schweitzer."
>
> To start with [Louis continues] I was delighted at the news that they had come to Europe. But since Albert's letter, the more I think about it the more puzzling the affair becomes. Why have they got to leave Africa and be interned? Why just at the time of year when the passage from the tropics to Europe must be so injurious to the health? Have Albert and Hélène deserved no better consideration? Have written to Albert and the Bresslaus.

In Louis' suggestion that Clemenceau should have postponed his plans until the weather suited Albert and Hélène better, there sounds the authentic note of parental indignation. But he was right to worry. Hélène in her letter had been more explicit about the temperature: "Our only discomfort is the cold, which is natural after so sharp a change of temperature following a long spell on the equator. But we have been able to procure some warm clothes, which we were short of." Despite the warm clothes, Clemenceau and the Bordeaux barracks achieved what all the bacilli of the Ogowe had failed to do. Albert and Hélène were only there three weeks but during that time they caught dysentery, which the drugs they carried with them failed to arrest, presumably because they were so run down.

In addition, so Schweitzer later told his nephew, Gustav Woytt, Hélène also contracted tuberculosis in those barracks, from infection left behind by previous occupants. Whether or not her lungs already bore the scars of a previous slight infection, this one was not to be thrown off lightly. From the aftereffects of this brief incarceration Schweitzer was to suffer for at least two years, Hélène for the rest of her life. Those three weeks were a tragic turning point for both of them, for never again was Hélène fully fit to work beside her husband in Africa.

They had their wish for mountain air, however, for Garaison, where they were sent, lies close to the Pyrenees and the peaks shine in the near distance. The internment camp had in fact once been a monastery devoted to healing; the very name means healing, for "Garaison" is Provençal for "*guérison.*" Despite the cold, the couple began to feel better here.

During the previous year the inmates of the camp had done a great deal to put the abandoned monastery into good repair. The governor was a fair and tolerant man, and matters could have in many ways been worse. Heating was minimal, but the food was tolerable, the couple had a room to themselves, and provided one did not give in to apathy there was more to be learned from this haphazard collection of prisoners, gathered from every race, every class, and every profession, than one could normally gather in a lifetime.

Some of the bread which Schweitzer had earlier cast upon the waters returned deviously in the form of a table. In Lambarene one day he had given drugs to a man destined for a prisoner of war camp in Dahomey. This man, sent subsequently to a camp in France, had cured the wife of a mill engineer by means of Schweitzer's drugs. Now the mill engineer was at Garaison and wanted to repay the debt. The table he made for Schweitzer out of wood rifled from the loft meant that now Schweitzer could write again, as well as "practise the organ."

Further alleviation came when a group of gypsy musicians decided to enroll him as one of themselves because he figured in Romain Rolland's book, *Musicians of Today.* After a while the initial prohibition against his practicing medicine was sensibly lifted, as it had been in Africa, and he was busy as a doctor again.

Friends were active in Paris on the Schweitzers' behalf all this while, for it was indeed ridiculous that Schweitzer should be imprisoned by a country which was half his own, many of whose distinguished citizens were his relatives and friends, and in whose capital he had made his name as a musician.

Meantime the Bresslaus sent them 1,500 francs, and a local lady, Madame Dessacs, used to send in food. In later life Schweitzer never failed, when in that area, to visit her grave.

They wrote home that they were getting over their chills and holding their heads high, so far as it was possible with the tropical tiredness that still pursued them. Schweitzer was studying prison mentality and the killing effect of despair. The ones who had given up interest in life, he found, were hardest to treat. Drugs could not reach their disease.

After a while the activities of the Paris friends resulted in their being offered a choice of prison; they replied that they would stay where they were. The climate was not bad, they had made friends here, and there was work to be done among the sick. When Hélène was sent some warm material, tailors competed for the job of making it up, to have something to do.

Further revelations about human nature came early in 1918, when the French authorities decided to use some of the internees as pawns in an international blackmail game. The Germans had taken certain unpleasant measures against civilians in Belgium, and in return the French threatened to send the more distinguished inmates at Garaison to a special reprisal camp in North Africa. Schweitzer was obviously one of those in danger. Some of the notables however turned out in this crisis to be less notable than they had let it be supposed. "Head waiters, when delivered here, had given their profession as hotel directors so as to count for something in the camp; shop assistants had elevated themselves to the rank of merchants. Now they bewailed to everyone they met the danger which threatened them on account of the rank they had assumed."[9]

The Germans, fortunately, yielded, and the distinguished persons remained at Garaison, some of them less distinguished than before. The effect a reprisal camp might have had on Schweitzer, sick and exhausted as he was, is not hard to imagine. It might well have been the end of the Schweitzer story.

The winter was severe, but spring came at last and with it the order to move again to a camp at St. Remy, set aside for Alsatians only. The Schweitzers appealed against the move, but it seems their freedom to choose their place of incarceration had been withdrawn, and nobody took any notice. Even the camp governor put in an appeal. He wanted to keep them. But on March 27 they were moved regardless. Louis Schweitzer did not receive the news till June 1—the day he picked his first strawberries.

The camp at St. Remy had also been a monastery—but it had also been something else.

> The first time I entered the big room on the ground floor which was our day-room, it struck me as being, in its unadorned and bare ugliness, strangely familiar. Where, then, had I seen that iron stove, and the fluepipe crossing the room from end to end? The mystery was solved at last; I knew them from a drawing of Van Gogh's. The building in which we were housed, once a monastery in a walled-up garden, had till recently been occupied by sufferers from nervous or mental diseases. Among them at one time was Van Gogh, who immortalised with his pencil the desolate room in which today we in our turn were sitting about. Like us, he had suffered from the cold stone floor when the mistral

blew! Like us, he had walked round and round between the high garden walls![10]

Here too the governor was a reasonable, jovial man; and here the Schweitzers met many people they already knew. But the climate was very different from Garaison and did not suit Hélène at all. True to the pattern, Schweitzer was barred from practicing medicine at first, but once he had gained the governor's trust, and when the camp doctor was sent home in an exchange of prisoners, he graduated to camp doctor; and indeed was let out occasionally to attend the local sick. The bleak winds and the cold stone floors troubled Hélène greatly. And Schweitzer himself was suffering from the aftereffects of the dysentery attack at Bordeaux—a languor that he could not shake off and that made him unable to join the vigorous walks that were organized for the inmates' exercise. Hélène too was too weak for these walks, and "we were thankful that on those days the Governor used to take us and other weaklings out himself."[11]

It was here, chilly and tired and unwell, that Schweitzer begot his first and only child. Why now? That child herself, Rhena, thinks that her parents must have been practicing some form of contraception hitherto, which now, through mischance or carelessness, failed. Certainly it hardly seems the time or place to begin planning a family. And since they never had another child, and since neither of them proved to be a very good parent, we may guess for lack of other evidence that she was right. Hélène was approaching forty and in no state to bear the extra physical trials of pregnancy. And it must immediately have been clear to the Schweitzers that this pregnancy threw great doubt over future plans for Lambarene—for Hélène at least, probably for both of them.

Among the relics which Schweitzer kept from this time is a poem written by a fellow prisoner, Harry Wollman, about the eternal beauties of sky and earth outlasting pain and grief, and about the mothers of the world, with their soft hands, standing waiting at their doors for the return of their children. A poem of yearning, of homesickness.

And home was at last in sight. The efforts of friends had placed the Schweitzers' names on a list of prisoners to be exchanged (though by accident only Hélène was listed at first, and Schweitzer himself was added at the last moment); and on July 12 they were roused in the middle of the night with orders to get ready to go home.

As the sun rose we dragged our baggage into the courtyard for the examination. The sketches for the Philosophy of Civilisation which I had put on paper here and at Garaison, and had already laid before the Camp Censor, I was allowed to take with me when he had put his stamp upon a certain number of pages. As the convoy passed through the gate I ran back to see the Governor once more, and found him sitting, sorrowful, in his office. He felt the departure of his prisoners very much. We still write to each other, and he addresses me as "mon cher pensionnaire" ("My dear boarder").[12]

They were taken to the railway station at Tarascon to await their train. Neither Schweitzer nor Hélène was in any fit state by now to carry their baggage, and as they dragged themselves through the shingle between the tracks toward the freight shed where they were to embark, a cripple, whom Schweitzer had treated in the camp and who had no possessions of his own to carry, offered to help them. Much moved, Schweitzer accepted. "While we walked along side by side in the scorching sun, I vowed to myself that in memory of him I would in future always keep a look-out at stations for heavily laden people, and help them. And this vow I have kept."[13] Years later, companions were sometimes embarrassed by Schweitzer's irrepressible eagerness to carry the baggage of puzzled strangers.

At one stop on the way the party was entertained to an excellent meal by a welcoming committee who, it turned out, actually intended the feast for a group of French being repatriated from Germany rather than Alsatians returning from France. By the time the mistake was realized the food was gone, and the Alsatians journeyed on to Lyons full and contented without ever discovering what happened when the correct group steamed in from the other direction.

More and more coaches joined the train filled with internees from other camps, until they reached the Swiss frontier. Here they had to wait a long while for cabled confirmation that the trainload for which they were being exchanged had also reached the frontier. When they at last reached Zürich, early on July 15, Schweitzer found himself greeted, to his great amazement, by a group of friends who had known for weeks—longer than he had—that he was coming home.

Louis Schweitzer too had known for some time that the couple were soon to be released. This particular day, July 15, he chanced to meet a man who had had a telegram from a friend reporting that Schweitzer and Hélène had passed through Zürich that morning and were now in Constance, safe and well. He went to Strasbourg to wait for them, staying with his daughter Adèle at nearby Oberhausbergen.

Constance, lying on the border, separated prosperous, war-free Switzerland from a Germany nearing defeat. "Dreadful was the impression we received in Constance. Here we had before our eyes for the first time the starvation of which till then we had only known by hearsay. None but pale, emaciated people in the streets! How wearily they went about! It was surprising that they could still stand!"[14]

Here Schweitzer stayed till the formalities were completed, while

Hélène was allowed to go straight on to her parents in Strasbourg. According to his father, Schweitzer stayed on an extra day to help fellow internees with their papers. He did not reach Strasbourg till late on the seventeenth, long after dark. "Not a light was burning in the streets. Not a glimmer of light showed from any dwelling-house! On account of attacks from the air the city had to be completely dark. I could not hope to reach the distant garden suburb where my wife's parents lived, and I had much trouble in finding the way to Frau Fischer's house near St. Thomas's."[15]

His sister Louise was waiting for him at Mrs. Fischer's. So was his niece-godchild, Suzanne, now in her early twenties and too old to be called Suzi anymore, with whom he had kept up a steady correspondence. This was the first reunion. At eleven the next morning the three of them went to meet Louis off the train from Oberhausbergen. "We meet again," Louis wrote, "after five years and four months."

In the afternoon Louise went back home to her family in Colmar. Albert went with his father to stay with Adèle, and soon Louis was worrying about the unaccustomed unreliability of Albert's stomach.

There was no question of Schweitzer's going to Günsbach yet, to greet his mother's grave. A pass was needed to go up the valley into the battle zone and these passes were not easily come by. Louis had to go back to his parish alone, and two weeks passed before he received a letter from Louise to say that Albert and Hélène were coming to Colmar. Two days later, on August 7, a telegram arrived asking him to pick up Albert and Hélène in Colmar at nine A.M. The passes had finally, "after many visits and many entreaties,"[16] been granted.

Presumably the picking up in Colmar was arranged by courtesy of Louis' military friend, Captain Frick, the area commander, who lodged at the vicarage. Hélène and Schweitzer arrived at eleven thirty, after a night of gunfire.

> So this was the peaceful valley to which I had bidden farewell on Good Friday 1913! There were dull roars from guns on the mountains. On the roads one walked between lines of wire-netting packed with straw, as between high walls. These were intended to hide the traffic in the valley from the enemy batteries on the crest of the Vosges. Everywhere there were brick emplacements for machine-guns! Houses ruined by gun-fire! Hills which I remembered covered with woods now stood bare. The shell-fire had left only a few stumps here and there. In the villages one saw posted up the order that everyone must always carry a gas-mask with him.[17]

The inhabitants of Günsbach had grown so accustomed to having the fighting on their doorstep that bringing home the hay crop by night had become a matter of course, as had the periodic rush to the cellars and the constant possibility that a threatened attack might mean immediate evacuation of the village. Louis Schweitzer no longer even retreated to the vicarage's capacious cellars during a bombardment, but sat it out in his study.

Much more than by the war the villagers were worried by drought. The harvest was in serious danger that year. "The corn was drying up; the potatoes were being ruined; on many meadows the grass-crop was so thin that it was not worth while to mow it; from the byres resounded the bellowing of hungry cattle. Even if a storm-cloud rose above the horizon it brought not rain but wind, which robbed the soil of its remaining moisture, and clouds of dust in which there flew the spectre of starvation."[18]

They visited the grave after lunch. The same day, records Louis, the poppy harvest began.

Albert stayed for the next ten days, till the eighteenth, when the people of Günsbach held a festival, arranged without the pastor's knowing, to celebrate the forty-third anniversary of his installation in that parish—that installation when the yellow baby Albert had caused such embarrassment to the visiting pastors' wives and such distress to his mother. Now Albert, who was in on the secret, played the organ and preached for his father's festival, and the church was packed.

The following day he went to Strasbourg for a few days but was soon back, seeking the long-awaited rest and recuperation of his native climate and his native hills, trying to throw off his languor and the intermittent fever that had troubled him since the last weeks at St. Remy. He got worse instead of better. The fever became more acute and he was in increasing pain. The dysentery at Bordeaux had left a legacy in the form of an abscess of the rectum. By the end of the month he could not conceal the extent of his illness from his father, and on the thirty-first Louis records that when fetching Louise and "Bebby" (Suzanne's younger brother, Albert, the one who suffered Schweitzer's fury over the Latin lesson) from a military train at Türkheim, he also collected medicine for his son from the chemist.

When he returned two crises faced him. Albert's fever was acute and Captain Frick had had disturbing news. An attack seemed imminent and two fresh battalions were coming to Günsbach. Everyone who did not absolutely have to stay must unfortunately leave. Nor, he was sorry, could he offer them transport. Had he known it earlier, he would not have let Louise and Bebby come.

An empty munitions train was leaving Walbach for Colmar an hour before midnight. Louise and Bebby set off immediately to catch it. At nine thirty Schweitzer and the pregnant Hélène also set off down the road for the walk of three and a half miles to Walbach; with them went Suzanne, who had been staying at the vicarage. To distract himself from the pain Schweitzer sang chorales, interspersed with tirades against the idiocy of all the politicians who had failed to prevent the war and now were incapable of bringing it to an end; but he laughed when he asked Suzanne what she had in her basket and she replied, "Love letters, a prayer of yours and my washing things."[19]

He managed to reach Walbach, but could go no farther. While the others went on to Colmar in the munitions train, Schweitzer and Hélène stayed at the house of a friend, Frau Kiener. The next day Hélène went back to Günsbach for some belongings that had been left behind and then returned to Schweitzer. Frau Kiener found a carriage and on this Schweitzer was taken to Louise's house in Colmar. Suzanne was immediately sent for a doctor but it was seven P.M. before she found one. The doctor diagnosed the abscess and prescribed immediate surgery. At eight thirty Schweitzer, on a stretcher, was on a train to Strasbourg, accompanied by Hélène and Louise. The pain was now almost unbearable. They reached Strasbourg at eleven thirty and had to wait half an hour in the waiting room while an ambulance was fetched from the hospital. With the ambulance came an assistant, who gave Schweitzer opium.

At nine thirty the next morning Schweitzer was operated on—a fairly straightforward operation, lasting only a quarter of an hour. It appeared completely successful.

Hélène reported that while she stayed with him that day, he talked a great deal. About what we are not told. But that experience of pain gave him a new understanding of suffering. It added to his sense of debt that he had been delivered from the agony and danger of his illness by medical knowledge and skill. He conceived a new notion—"the Fellowship of those who bear the Mark of Pain."

> Who are the members of this Fellowship? Those who have learnt by experience what physical pain and bodily anguish mean, belong together all the world over; they are united by a secret bond. One and all, they know the horrors of suffering to which man can be exposed, and one and all they know the longing to be free from pain. He who has been delivered from pain must not think he is now free again, and at liberty to take up life just as it was before, entirely forgetful of the past. He is now a "man whose eyes are open" with regard to pain and anguish, and he must help to overcome those two enemies (so far as human power can control them) and to bring to others the deliverance which he has himself enjoyed.[20]

18

THE LOST COIN
1918–1924

WHILE Schweitzer recovered, the war ground at last to an end. On October 6 the Germans made peace overtures to President Wilson. Wilson replied on the tenth. And on the thirteenth, Schweitzer preached a sermon at St. Nicholas' Church, his first for five and a half years; years of shattering experience for his congregation, and for him years of remoteness, of an existence whose perspectives were quite unlike theirs. "I have looked forward Sunday by Sunday to this day when I should be permitted to speak to you again. . . . And now this dream so long awaited becomes fact, at a moment especially crucial and agonising, when our destiny is about to be decided and our future is darker than ever."

He spoke of the sufferings they had seen, every one of them; and recalled the words of benediction he had left with them in 1913—"the peace of God which passes all understanding. . . ." How to reconcile these things? How to arrive at resignation to the will of God? (For here he still spoke of God, though he also used the phrase "universal will").

The passage which follows is truly magnificent in its resolute refusal to pretend that things are other than they are or that horror is anything but horror.

> How to arrive at resignation to the will of God? Are we to confront this idea face to face, and gaze fixedly at it till we are enveloped and hypnotised by it? I would not dare to set you on that path, for I very much doubt whether it leads to the true peace of God. Forcing oneself to yield to the idea that everything comes from God seems to me the despairing act of those who have given up thinking: they shatter their own intelligence, they renounce the making of natural and reasonable judgements on things, they empty themselves of energy. They have peace, but only because their spring is broken.

Not a trace is left now of the pious cliché, of the comforting phrases about the nobility of suffering.

It often happens, certainly, that looking back we discover some sense in what at the time seemed obscure; so we decide that good has come out of evil, and reason has emerged from the absurd. . . . The tumultuous threat of the mountains that loomed round us as we travelled through the valleys is transformed to tranquil ranges when we see them from the distant plain. But there also exists . . . a multitude of occasions in which the absurd does not change into the reasonable, nor the evil into the good.

Anyone who tries to explain why a mother has to lose her only son, why friend betrays friend, why empty phrases carry greater weight than the truth, will only entangle himself in the undergrowth.

All we can know, says Schweitzer, is that the will of God tends toward

the blossoming of the spirit. . . . You who have passed through so many grievous experiences, you have certainly found the consolation of feeling inwardly free in face of the blows of fortune. You have amazed yourselves, at those moments when to human thinking you should be crushed by misfortune, by finding yourselves, on the contrary, uplifted by the triumph of spiritual forces over material catastrophe. . . . If we can lay hold of this passing experience as a permanent conviction, this is where the peace of God begins.

The peace of God is not rest—it is an active force . . . It is finding a progress within oneself that marches through life's events. Men and women of all nations can and must find this together—not through politics, not through "grand conferences about this League of Nations which they wish to found." What we must seek is the Kingdom of God, which arises naturally where men's thoughts are noble. . . .

. . . from the depths to which we have fallen let us proclaim our faith in the future of humanity and our desire to rescue it from destruction as the most precious ideals to bequeath to the coming time and the rising generation. The sun of hope does not shine on our path. Thick night still covers us, and the dawn of better days will not brighten for our generation. But if we have succeeded in preserving our faith in the sunrise which must come, the quivering light of the stars will be enough to illuminate our way.

May the peace of God fill our hearts and uphold our courage.[1]

*   *   *

Schweitzer had some need of courage at this time. His abscess did not properly clear up, and although his friend, Mayor Schwander, offered him work in the Municipal Hospital and St. Nicholas' took him back as curate, he had the debts of the war years at the hospital hanging over him and no means of repaying them.

Strasbourg had changed greatly. The war had bred antagonisms between pro-French and pro-German factions and the less scrupulous had used these to enhance themselves at the expense of their rivals. A new generation had sprung up who knew and cared nothing for Schweitzer's reputation. He felt, he said, like a coin that has rolled under a wardrobe and been forgotten. Nothing went right at this time. One day early in November he was driving back from Günsbach in a borrowed two-wheeler when one of the wheels caught in some tramlines, the horse slipped on the cobbles and fell, and Schweitzer and the driver were thrown out. The frightened horse, struggling to regain its footing, kicked Schweitzer's arm and caused a slight fracture. Not a serious accident, simply an additional nuisance, with Hélène now seven months pregnant.

Then came the revolution in Germany, the Kaiser's abdication, and the armistice. Günsbach was suddenly full of French troops instead of German, and French officers were quartered in the manse. The end of the shooting and the sleepless nights. And with the ceding of Alsace to France, Schweitzer was now a French citizen. For a while he found himself in sole charge at St. Nicholas'. Mr. Gerold had been openly anti-German and had been dismissed by the German authorities. When the armistice came and Strasbourg came under French rule, his colleague, Mr. Ernst, was removed because he was anti-French. It took a little while before the new authorities reappointed Mr. Gerold, and meanwhile Schweitzer, who had offended nobody, had to do all the work.

For once in his life Schweitzer had no objective—and no spirit to seek one. In these bad times he still remembered those worse off still and regularly sent what food he could to friends in Germany. He would cross the border at the Rhine bridge with a rucksack full of provisions and dispatch the parcels from Kehl. One of the friends he made a point of helping was the aging Cosima Wagner, now desolate among the neglected splendors of Bayreuth.

On January 14, 1919, his own forty-fourth birthday, Hélène bore him a daughter. Rhena Fanny Suzanne arrived at eleven P.M. in the clinic at Strasbourg hospital. Amid all the rejoicing it must have seemed as though Albert Schweitzer was a man with a great future behind him, settling down now to a belated domesticity.

The drafts of *The Philosophy of Civilisation* had not arrived from Africa, so Schweitzer, his mind still full of the importance of Reverence for Life, began the book all over again. As yet he had never spoken in public of his idea, apart from a brief use of the phrase in a sermon in December in memory of the dead. Here he had asked, as everyone at that time was asking, that the dead should not have died in vain; if life were reverenced, such deaths would never again be required of man.

The sermon is notable for its graphic insistence on the ghastly details of death, when so many sermons were inclined to surround such details in a comforting cocoon of rhetoric:

Piercing bullets have drained them of their blood; lying in the barbed
wire, they have groaned and suffered all day long and no help has been
able to reach them; stretched out on the frozen earth, they have died of
cold in the night; exploding mines have entombed them, or flung them
into the air, sliced to pieces; or else on the deep sea, the water has
come boiling into their ship; they have fought the waves till exhaustion
came; or imprisoned in the hull of the ship they have clung to the bulk-
heads, seized with helpless terror. And those who have not perished on
the battlefields or at sea have succumbed after weeks and months in
military hospitals, fighting to hold on to a life of mutilation.[2]

All this, he said, had happened because the world had not taken seriously "human life, that mysterious and irreplaceable value"—a world
"which plays the fool with Reverence for Life."

A month after Rhena's birth however he could contain himself no longer. He needed, as of old, to share with his congregation the thoughts that
mattered to him. This first public announcement of his great discovery,
taking place as it did in a religious context, is stated in religious terms.
And what terms! For if in his philosophical books he had to show the
inadequacy of every previous philosophy of ethics, so now he had to
prove the shortcomings of every previous religious statement—including
those of Jesus!

On February 16 he preached the first of two successive sermons on
Reverence for Life. He took his text from Mark 12; the passage in which
Jesus, questioned as to which is the first of the commandments, answers
that there are two—first, to love the Lord your God with all your heart,
with all your soul, with all your mind, and with all your strength—and
second, to love your neighbor as yourself. The sermon begins by asking,
as Schweitzer had asked himself in Africa, what is the fundamental basis
of all ethics. For Christian morality "has become bankrupt in the world.
It has not penetrated men's souls in depth, it has been accepted only su-
perficially, and always more readily in words than in deeds.

"This is why it is a waste of time ceaselessly to repeat and to comment
upon the commandments of Jesus, as if thus they must in the end wear a
path into men's consciousness." And moreover, "It is not easy to present
them in a form that makes them applicable in practice. Let us take, for example, the verses of the first and great commandment. What can it really
mean—to love God with all one's heart, and for the love of God never to
do anything but good? Pressing the idea to its depths, a host of questions
arise: have you ever done something good solely for the love of God, and
can you say that without this love you would have chosen to do ill?

"As to the second commandment, 'You shall love your neighbour as
yourself,' it is truly magnificent. I could expound it to you with the most
edifying examples. But is it truly applicable? Suppose that from tomor-

row you were to decide to abide by it to the letter, where would you find yourself at the end of a few days?''

Because these commandments are so impossible to act upon, he goes on to say, there is a great danger that people will content themselves with exalted lip-service. Another danger—it is an open door to pride. ''While we pardon our enemies, we glorify ourselves for our nobility of soul; when we render some service to someone who needs us, we admire our generosity . . . our sin of vanity brings us lower morally than those who act without pretending, as we do, to conform to the commandments of Jesus.''

Now he summons reason to help solve the problem—reason and the heart together—and defines reason thus: ''I understand by reason a force of comprehension which penetrates to the heart of things, which grasps the entirety of the world and which seizes the control-handle of the will.'' Reason is ''at one and the same time a thirst for knowledge and a thirst for happiness, mysteriously amalgamated within us.'' This thirst for knowledge tries to penetrate into the numberless forms with which life clothes itself; it seeks to comprehend the miracle of an ice crystal, it realizes that ''the beetle stretched out dead by the side of the road was a creature which lived, struggled for existence—like you; it experienced fear and suffering—like you; and now is no more than matter in decomposition—as you will be, sooner or later. . . .

''To respect the endless immensity of nature—no longer to be a stranger among men—to participate and share in the life of all. . . . Thus the final result of knowledge connects with the commandment of the love for one's neighbour. Heart and reason are at one. . . .''

To found a new world everyone must ''decipher, letter by letter, this single commandment, as great as it is simple; Reverence for Life—a commandment more charged with meaning than the Law and the Prophets. . . .''[3]

One could hardly make a greater claim. Those who believe that Schweitzer suffered from megalomania could find their text here, for the claim seems so much more startling in religious terms than it does in philosophical. Christian doctrine, unlike philosophy, claims to be revealed truth, once and for all absolute. Schweitzer is treating it like any other human attempt at understanding—magnificent but incomplete. There is no sign here of the doctrine of the Trinity. God is simply, ''the unfathomable principle of eternity and of life that we call God.'' So the claim to be able to criticize the great commandments of Jesus, and to improve on them, is not so extraordinary. Schweitzer is not, as some of his critics have claimed, setting himself up as God, or pretending to be a second Jesus. He is asserting his right as a man to his own discoveries about life—discoveries he could never have made without a lifetime's absorption in the insights of Jesus.

It would be unfair to assess this sermon without reading it all, and to set it all down here is out of the question. In any case a sermon is not a theological treatise; it is inevitably a simplified exposition, designed to convince by inspiration as much as by logic. There is no time for more. In this summary I have tried simply to show the way Schweitzer's mind was working in relation to the religion of his upbringing.

In the second sermon he amplified a number of points and dealt with some difficulties. "The great enemy of ethics is insensitivity." Several times he used a word about the processes of nature that now seems strikingly modern—he talks of their "absurdity." In recent years the notion that life has an element of absurdity has become fashionable, in contrast to the old conception that a hidden providence guided all things. Schweitzer was saying it in 1919. "Nature knows nothing of reverence for life. She creates life in a thousand ways with a prodigious ingenuity, and destroys it in a thousand ways with an equally prodigious absurdity. . . ."

"Her cruelty is so absurd! The most precious life is sacrificed to the benefit of the most ignoble. . . ." And he goes on to speak of a child's life destroyed by a tubercle bacillus, an African ravaged with pain and moaning all night because of a few minute organisms, ten to fourteen thousandths of a millimeter long, the carriers of sleeping sickness.

But why the notion of the Good and of Reverence for Life arise in man but not in nature, that is a question he leaves unresolved. The puzzlement and confusion which this arouses he regards as the first great hazard to be faced in devoting oneself to Reverence for Life, and we have no choice but to accept this puzzlement as one of "the contradictions which flow from the nature of the world like a devastating tide."

Two other hazards, or "temptations," threaten the follower of Reverence for Life. The first is the thought that "it will do no good! All that you do, all that you *can* do, to prevent or mitigate suffering and to maintain life, is insignificant in relation to what goes on in the world around you, of which you cannot change one iota. . . ."

Schweitzer's answer is interesting, for it shows how clearly he realized that his work in Africa fulfilled his own needs as well as benefiting others, and how strongly he believed that by yielding to their impulses toward good others could fulfill themselves in the same way. It is true, he says, that "compared with the size of the task the little you can do is no more than a drop of water in the midst of a torrent, but it gives your life its only true meaning and its value. Wherever you may be, and to whatever extent things depend on you, your presence should bring deliverance. . . ." For "compassion and mutual help are an inner necessity to you."

The final temptation is the thought that "to feel compassion for others means suffering. Anyone who is one day seized with the grief of the world can never again rediscover happiness, as mankind thinks of it. . . . In the middle of a group where gaiety reigns, suddenly his spirit is elsewhere.'' And the tempter comes, saying, " 'Come on, not so much sensitivity! Do as others do and stop thinking, if you want to live a reasonable life.' " To this temptation Schweitzer replies that "compassion also brings with it the ability to rejoice with others. If your compassion is blunted, you lose at the same time the possibility of responding to others' happiness."[4]

The "temptations" Schweitzer spoke of are so frequently brought forward in any discussion about the psychology of a life devoted to others that Schweitzer's own facing of them and answers to them are a necessary part of our understanding of the man. As to the effectiveness with which he applied them, there are plenty of people who will tell you that he did often, simply by his presence, bring deliverance and that he did enjoy the rejoicing of others as much as he grieved over their unhappiness. He himself was an illustration that his method of enriching life could actually work.

* * *

The year that followed held less interest and excitement than any in Schweitzer's life before or after. Neither he nor Hélène was fully recovered in health. Tropical exhaustion had eaten deep and their resilience was a long while returning. Schweitzer himself had to have a second operation in the summer, about which we know very little, except that it was a follow-up to the first. Either just before or just after the operation, in a sermon on his perennial theme, gratitude, he spoke of hospitals: "A sick man is in hospital at Strasbourg's surgical clinic, and he is due for an operation; to whom will he owe his recovery? Not only to the doctor who performs the operation, to the assistants who renew the dressings and the nurses who have cleaned him up; but also to many others, shadowy figures from the past."[5] The founders of the hospital, for example, and the discoverers of anesthetics and disinfectants.

Here is Schweitzer's morality at work. He is deliberately cultivating his sense of debt, as Baudelaire cultivated his hysteria. He is feeding his imagination with thoughts designed to nourish gratitude and solidarity. Thus he continually refreshed the springs of his personality.

In October, briefly and unexpectedly, the world opened out again for Schweitzer. His friends of the Orfeo Catala in Barcelona invited him to give a concert there. Permission to travel was hard to get—so was money; but the invitation meant a great deal and he went. He had been playing regularly, of course, in church; but whether because the disruptions of war had put a stop to all concertgoing or because those who were now arranging concerts did not know him, this was the first time since the war that he had played in front of an audience rather than a congregation.

He was hurt by the neglect of Strasbourg, where once he had ridden so high. "This first emergence in the world let me see that as an artist I was still of some value."[6] Equally if not more painful was the indifference of the academic world. "In learned circles I could have believed myself entirely forgotten, but for the affection and kindness shown me by the theological faculties at Zürich and Berne."

The neglect was not personal. Seven years is a long time in the life of any institution, and groupings change. For ten years and more he had been one of the darlings of his group of professors, and his circle of friends was like a family. All this was broken up; the more so because Strasbourg University, as we have seen, had enjoyed the special favor of the German government which now was no more. Political divisions existed in the university as elsewhere, and the new European situation was reflected in the staffing.

Failing other musical activities, Schweitzer tried to get on with the remaining volumes of the Bach edition for America. But the notes he had made for these were with the manuscript of *Civilisation*, which he had left in Africa; and the publisher was less enthusiastic than he had been; not surprisingly, for the arts suffer first when war comes, and recover slowly. Bach was as important as he had ever been to Schweitzer, but not to the rest of the world.

In this disheartenment Schweitzer turned to Eastern religions and philosophies. In his studies for *The Philosophy of Civilisation* and in the revelation of Reverence for Life he had already discovered in his thought strong affinities with Buddhism.

He began to explore the differences and the similarities between the two, using as a criterion his distinction between philosophies that were "world-and-life-affirming" and those that were "world-and-life-denying." The latter contained no impulse to ethical activity and to the betterment of human conditions, but were content to concentrate on personal spirituality in detachment from the world; despite his emphasis on mysticism Schweitzer had no use for these. But he did admire the emphasis in Buddhist mysticism on the thought that all life was one, a thought which he found nowhere in the West.

Hinduism and Christianity he saw as having in common an attempt to combine affirmation and denial of the world and of life. In Hinduism denial was the stronger element. In Christianity, as he saw it, denial had predominated throughout the Dark Ages, the centuries during which the Catholic Church reigned supreme in Europe and when the world was seen as a vale of tears to be endured in the expectation of bliss after death; affirmation of this life had only broken through with the Renaissance which is why Schweitzer loved the seventeenth and eighteenth centuries, when the Renaissance came to flower. No similar movement had occurred in India, where personal mysticism was still the be-all and end-all of religion. And in Europe, he felt, the negation which had been rejected in the eighteenth century had begun to creep back in the nineteenth; to that extent "Christianity ceases to be a force making for civilisation and begins to attract attention as a hindrance to it, as is amply shown by the history of our own time."[7]

Schweitzer was still suffering from the aftereffects of his abscess. The second operation had been no more successful than the first, and the wound would not heal. So discomfort, embarrassment, and world-weariness combined with the loss of his aim in life, the restrictions of movement, the poor food, and the all-pervading postwar shock to pull him down.

George Marshall in his recent study of Schweitzer goes so far as to say that at this time Schweitzer was suffering from a nervous breakdown. He brings to bear, I believe, some extremely dubious evidence, including a chance visit to a psychiatrist who happened to be a friend of his and the fact that Schweitzer on several occasions set about repairing and cleaning out old organs. This, says Marshall, was a special work-therapy for his condition.

In fact, of course, Schweitzer was forever plunging into work of this kind. He had come to enjoy and value manual labor, particularly when it was in the interest of one of his beloved old organs. It certainly proves nothing about his health.

All the same it was a period of profound depression. "Nervous breakdown" is misleading only in that it suggests a specific period of collapse, followed by treatment; there is no evidence of this whatever. As Marshall points out, however, there is a photograph of Schweitzer as an internee which, even allowing for the well-known lying characteristics of the camera, tells a story. Schweitzer sits hunched up like a morose Charlie Chaplin, almost unrecognizable as the vigorous character of most of his photographs.

Such was the outlook as Christmas approached—a Christmas which the Schweitzers "expected to celebrate in sorrow and distress as we had all the other holidays since the beginning of the war."[8] So he wrote thirteen years later, in a grateful memorial article to Archbishop Nathan Söderblom, the man who brought him back to life.

Before the war, Schweitzer had known of Söderblom as a scholar of historical religions with a particular interest in the relation of religion to science. In the meantime, unknown to Schweitzer, the scholar had become Archbishop of Sweden. Also unknown to him, Söderblom knew about Schweitzer—knew his work and knew that he had been interned. In fact the archbishop was actually under the impression that Schweitzer was still detained.

Söderblom was involved in the organizing of an annual series of lec-

tures sponsored by the Olaus-Petri Foundation at the University of Uppsala, and had a number of distinguished names on his list. He had somehow heard that Schweitzer was formulating a new theory of ethics and so
Schweitzer figured on the list, though not at the head of it. But it occurred
to Söderblom that an invitation to give the coming year's lecture might
help release Schweitzer from the imprisonment in which he believed him
to be languishing. Accordingly he asked the Archbishop of Canterbury
(presumably as representing the war's victors) to find out where
Schweitzer was and pass on the invitation. And so it came about that a letter arrived at Schweitzer's lodgings two days before Christmas, and sat
on the mantelpiece waiting when he came home from work. "I was not
after all so completely forgotten as I had thought."9

So run-down was he that he seriously thought of refusing the archbishop's invitation. But Söderblom dismissed these doubts. The change of air
would do Schweitzer good, and the food in Sweden was better than in the
defeated German dependency. Another difficulty, the travel restrictions
imposed on Alsatians, was overcome by admirers of Schweitzer's who
had authority to secure him a visa.

How long Schweitzer might have continued in his trough of depression
had he not been able to get out of the cramping circumstances of postwar
Strasbourg into the freedom and cheer of Sweden no one can say. But it is
important to realize that at this time he was a defeated man. Without
money, energy, or position he would have had to drag himself back by his
own bootstraps, and that would have been a long process.

Söderblom was right. The air and the cheerful and vigorous company
gave him a new lease on life. And perhaps even more important was the
opportunity to spread out his ideas in a place where they would be noticed, and the promise of publication after delivery of the lectures.

Schweitzer and Hélène reached Uppsala in April. The archbishop, they
found, was a remarkable man. When part of his rod of office was mislaid,
he cut a syringa twig and happily marched with that in procession. Even
more impressive, Schweitzer found, was the way he conducted local
church business. Schweitzer went into his room one evening to find him
sitting on a trunk settling the problems of the local priests, who were
strewn over the sofa and the archbishop's bed. He had a genius for combining authority with informality. This kind of episcopal relationship with
the priests struck Schweitzer as something the Alsatian church sadly
lacked.

A day or two after the last lecture, as Schweitzer was preparing to go
home, Söderblom took him out for a walk one rainy evening, the two of
them under one umbrella. Schweitzer spoke of his anxieties about the
debts he still owed to the Paris Mission Society and to friends in Paris—
debts he saw no means of repaying. Söderblom, practical and vigorous,

said that the obvious solution was to tap some of the money that had come Sweden's way during the war. Collecting money was out of the question in either France or Germany now, but the war had brought prosperity to the nearby neutral countries. Söderblom was convinced that a tour of organ recitals and lectures about his African experiences would pay Schweitzer handsomely. And he set about arranging it, planning the itinerary, writing letters of introduction, and arranging accommodation. He also got in touch with a publisher, Lindblad, about the subsequent publication of a book based on the lectures. Schweitzer, the dynamic organizer, was for once being organized. And to good effect.

Sweden responded to Schweitzer unforgettably, the country districts even more than the cities. He toured for six weeks, from mid-May to the end of June, and by the end of that time was well on the way to paying off the 17,000 francs he owed. His spirit, too, was so refreshed that now there was no doubt in his mind that he would go back to Africa. "If Archbishop Söderblom had not called me to Sweden and stimulated interest in my life work as a doctor in the primeval forest among his countrymen, I am not at all sure that it would have been possible for me to return to Lambarene."[10]

What did the decision cost Hélène? "For the fact that she so far sacrificed herself as to acquiesce under these circumstances, in my resumption of work at Lambarene, I have never ceased to be grateful."[11] The sacrifice was very real. She must have known that she had no real choice. With Rhena to look after, she could not go back; and every principle she believed in made it impossible to deny Schweitzer the work which he craved and which he had proved he could do. Whatever misgivings she may and must have felt, they were fully justified. She and Schweitzer were never again to be so close as they had been, and she was to see other women working at his side as she had planned so long and labored so hard to do. Mercifully, though, she could not have known at this time the extent of the sacrifice she was making, for she fully intended to rejoin her husband when she was stronger and Rhena was a little older. She could not have foreseen how long the years of illness stretched ahead nor how totally Schweitzer would become attached to Lambarene.

But Schweitzer, as he wrote to Suzanne, felt like a fir tree that shakes off the snow and straightens up after the winter. Back in Strasbourg he went full tilt at the book for Lindblad and had it finished by August. Since it was for the general public it had to be a good deal shorter than anything he had hitherto written: A salutary discipline, he felt—he was learning to condense his thought.

It appears that in the previous year Schweitzer had begun to make moves toward rebuilding an academic career, this time in Switzerland,

and in the summer of this year he was made an Honorary Doctor of Divinity at Zürich University. But all that became irrelevant now. Africa's call was insistent.

The manuscript which he had left with Mr. Ford in Lambarene at last reached Strasbourg, and he set to work with a fresh eagerness to collate his two drafts and get this book finished as well. Now once again life offered him the variety he throve on. After the deadening sameness of the past years he was again doing everything at once—writing, planning, lecturing, and playing the organ; often traveling miles to do so.

Apart from the book, there were the letters to write—letters, for example, on philosophical matters to Oskar Kraus, an admirer who wrote anxiously from Prague beseeching him to have the first chapters of his uncompleted book translated into English. In England, said Kraus, everyone is talking about Spengler and *The Decline of the West*; Schweitzer's book was needed as a corrective.

There were letters to his old friend, Morel, on leave in Rothau from Lambarene who reported how the antelopes and monkeys were faring out there and how much everyone was looking forward to having Schweitzer back.

And then there were letters to the Paris Mission Society, with whom negotiations had to begin all over again. Schweitzer's first spell on the Ogowe had evidently failed to convince the society's central committee that he was a totally acceptable type, however well he had got on with the missionaries on the spot. In spite of these complications he clung obstinately, as before, to his intention to begin again at Lambarene and nowhere else, though he received renewed offers from Zürich of posts whenever he wanted and on his own terms.

He went again to Barcelona, to play at the first performance ever given there of the *St. Matthew Passion*. In Strasbourg he saw a lot of his friend Mr. Erb, the organist and composer; and Widor called upon him as he passed across Europe. The old rhythm of life was reasserting itself.

In June, 1921, the book about Africa was published; first in Sweden, translated by one of Schweitzer's hostesses on his Sweden tour, Baroness Greta Lagerfeld; soon after that in Switzerland, Germany, and England; and finally in Holland, France, Denmark and Finland. *Zwischen Wasser und Urwald* was the German title—"Between Water and Jungle." In English we know it as *On the Edge of the Primeval Forest*.

With its combination of adventure, humor, and practical morality, all attractively served up in Schweitzer's sturdy style, the book was immediately successful—and with its success Schweitzer's fame spread out from the confines of the specialists into the broad reaches of the general public.

Success meant money too, and before long Schweitzer was able to resign his curacy and his medical post in Strasbourg and move with the family to the Günsbach vicarage, where his father still lived, a hale old gentleman. Here he was able to concentrate on his plans for the future, and from here he made frequent money-raising forages to parishes all around. A chance meeting with an Englishwoman and her son in Colmar was to prove fruitful. He kept in touch with young Noel Gillespie and was to take him out to Africa with him when he went two and a half years later. This was the first of many such meetings with enthusiasts for his work who were to provide the steady flow of volunteer help on which his hospital lived. From now on, wherever in the world he went, Schweitzer was never short of offers of hospitality and help.

This was the busy summer in which one evening in Strasbourg Professor Davison heard Schweitzer play on the organ of St. Thomas' Church; that night when, despite the clatter of the aging mechanism, Davison felt "the realisation of that so oft-dreamed ideal, the artist at one with the composer"; and sat, he and his students, talking to Schweitzer long after the concert at an open air café in the warm summer night.

Meantime Schweitzer was arranging an ambitious tour, and by autumn it was organized. It was to last well into the following year, and indeed he was seriously thinking of extending it as far as the United States, where he was in touch with Emmanuel Church, Boston. A Mr. Elwood Worcester was trying through friends at Harvard and Columbia universities to arrange for a series of lectures there, but the chief drawback, outwardly at least, was that "Americans as a rule are not very good linguists and the number of persons who would be able to follow your thought in either the French or German language would be limited."[12] This disadvantage, however, had not proved insuperable in other countries, given a good interpreter. Perhaps the additional cost and even a persisting mistrust of German-sounding names might have been the real reasons. It is interesting, however, in view of the number of occasions in later years when Schweitzer was implored to visit America and had to refuse for lack of time, to find him at this stage the proposer of the trip. The connection with Boston, too, is noteworthy. The Unitarians there were to prove an immense source of assistance during and after the Second World War, but this early correspondence has hitherto lain undiscovered in the files.

The tour, on which it seems Hélène accompanied him at least for some of the time, began in the wealthy countries, neutral in the war, which had already given him a welcome—Switzerland and Sweden. From there Schweitzer went in January to England, less war-torn than any other combatant country, where he had been invited to lecture at Oxford, at Cambridge, in London, and at the new Selly Oak College in Birmingham.

Anyone who followed him around England would have gained a good panoramic view of his intellectual preoccupations; Oxford had a preview of the coming book *The Decay and Restoration of Civilisation*; Cambridge was treated to "The Significance of Eschatology"; in London the Society for the Study of the Science of Religion heard about "The Pauline Problem"; and at Selly Oak he gave a series of lectures on his most recent study, "Christianity and the Religions of the World."

These last lectures were later published in book form—somewhat to Schweitzer's embarrassment. He felt he had failed, in so brief a compass, to do justice to a subject which he regarded as of great importance; and he was taken to task from time to time by people of other faiths for misrepresenting them. The book is of great interest, however, if only as a defense of Christianity against the fashion then beginning in Europe (and still with us) for upholding the religions of the East as far richer and more profitable.

Schweitzer had the greatest respect for Eastern religions, and considered that Christianity could learn something from all of them—a view which brought him into frequent conflict with more orthodox Christians. But he still believed that Christianity possessed some insights deeper than any of theirs.

Brahmanism and Buddhism, says Schweitzer, are logical, consistent religions, whose spirituality consists of a withdrawal from the world. They can have no ethical content; to do good is for them pointless, for it happens in a world in which good does not exist, in which the only good is to get out of it. Christianity too rejects worldly values but for quite a different purpose. "The Brahmans and Buddha say to men: 'As one who has died, and to whom nothing in the natural world is of interest any longer, you should live in the world of pure spirituality.' The gospel of Jesus tells him, 'You must become free from the world and from yourself, in order to work in the world as an instrument of God.' "[13] Hinduism, he believes, is tarred with the same brush as Buddhism. Though it has adopted an ethical element (perhaps from Christianity), and tries to be more closely in touch with the real world, the lure of world abandonment and pure spirituality is really still there at the bottom. "Hinduism tries in vain to hide the chain fastened to its foot."[14]

The Chinese philosophers, on the other hand, have mostly tried to find morality in learning to imitate the virtues of nature, to reflect in man's behavior the quiet but irresistible forces of the natural world. Where the Indians find salvation in totally rejecting nature, the Chinese totally accept it and try to conform with it.

But for Schweitzer, as we know, nature was far from benign. He could not accept that the cruelties of nature were a necessary part of some higher process. So the Chinese thinkers too, though noble in their pleas to mankind to stop fighting and struggling and to "live in accordance with the meaning of existence,"[15] lacked the positive compassionate will that informed Christianity.

Again and again he comes back to his central point—logical consistency is not enough. The strength of Christianity is that within a world whose
values it rejects, it yet finds another value which is as real if not more
so—compassionate love. Inconsistent it may be, illogical perhaps, but
true. Schweitzer proclaims the need for a special kind of naïveté—the
kind which has examined all the clever and consistent philosophies and is
prepared to say that they are irrelevant, because the facts tell a different
story.

With his usual thoroughness he had prepared for his lectures by studying how best to make himself understood through an interpreter. He had
first practiced the technique to some extent in his services at Lambarene,
where his addresses had been translated into the Fang and Galoa languages as he went along. But George Seaver in his excellent biography
records that the seed was sown earlier still.

In 1934 Schweitzer prefaced his Hibbert Lectures at Oxford by saying,
"I first learned that it was possible to talk to others whose language I
could not speak when, many years ago, I heard your Gerard Booth speak
through an interpreter at Strasbourg—the gift I had from him I now return
to the country that gave it."[16] And this is how, in his autobiography, he
describes the technique:

> What is most important is to speak in short, simple and clearly con-
> structed sentences, to go through the address with the interpreter with
> the greatest possible care beforehand, and to deliver it in the shape
> which he expects. With this preparation the interpreter has to make no
> effort to understand the meaning of the sentence to be translated; he
> catches it like a ball which he throws on at once to the listeners. By fol-
> lowing this plan one makes it possible to deliver through an interpreter
> even scientific addresses, and it is a much better way than for the
> speaker to inflict torture on himself and his hearers by speaking in a
> language of which he is not fully master."[17]

Reports from his audiences indicate that the method was highly successful; hearers often found that soon they quite forgot that they were listening to an interpreter. But all the same Schweitzer did want to learn
English. When Noel Gillespie went to Lambarene with him in 1924 one
of his functions was as English tutor.

From this tour for the first time we get an account of the impact of the
fully formed Schweitzer personality—that personality which was the outward sign of the character he had been molding for himself since, as a
boy, he had decided to break out of his reserve and seek for warmth and
spontaneity. When he was a young man people remembered him for his
energy and intensity, his masculinity, his acts of kindness; but no one
spoke or wrote of him quite as Dr. Micklem of Selly Oak College wrote
in his introduction to the published lectures. "It is not easy to explain in

words that will not appear extravagant how greatly we were drawn to the man himself. We know he was strong, but we found him gentle; we have not often seen such intellectual freedom coupled with so evangelical a zeal."[18]

Again and again, from now on, we have the same kind of reaction—"his personality was indescribable." People who met him speak of his complete concentration, a total, delighted, childlike interest in what was happening. He had learned to be permanently in touch with his own depths, his response coming always from the heart, unshadowed by self-consciousness or guile. Like Blake, he was a man without a mask. Whether chatting with a child about earwigs, rehearsing alone in Westminster Abbey for a recital, or talking to a church group about Lambarene, he withheld nothing. The art he had learned from Marie Jaëll of freeing the muscles of the arm so that the musical will went directly to the fingertips had also been used to free the personality from inhibition, and the result was overwhelming.

A good conversationalist is often less effective as a public speaker, and vice versa. Schweitzer had no such limitations. In private he would always give his companions his fullest attention. On a platform he knew how to hold huge audiences breathless, with a power that came from a marrying of deep emotional conviction with hard-won technique.

This new flowering of his personality, after the winter of sickness and depression, owed something to a special happiness—that all that he had sacrificed when he went to Africa had been restored to him—indeed had now become an essential part of the enterprise. He had renounced his joy in teaching; it was replaced by the joy of lecturing on his own favorite subjects. He had renounced playing the organ at concerts; now he played all over Europe, in the cause of his hospital. He had renounced financial independence when he resigned his salaried posts; now his own efforts were bringing in more than ever before, and he was no longer dependent on charity.

How was Hélène able to keep up with the surging energy of this new elation? A young journalist, Hubert le Peet, who later became editor of *The Friend* and also of the British edition of Schweitzer's hospital bulletins, went to Oxford to interview Schweitzer and found himself appropriated as his guide in London. He wrote of those days as "a strenuous time, conveying the burly black-cloaked figure from theologian to theologian, from organ to organ. . . . He sometimes forgets that other people are not quite so tireless as himself, and I've sometimes been quite sorry for dear Madame Schweitzer!"[19]

He returned home from England the way he had come, giving fresh lectures in Sweden and Switzerland en route—and only reached

Günsbach in March. The correspondence with the Paris Mission Society was dragging on all this while, and at the end of April he received a letter from Mr. Bianquis to which, by some chance, a copy of his answer has been preserved. At this distance we can see the archetypal comedy of the conflict between the committee mind and the creative mind, but at the time the raw edges of frustration must have been very sore. The letters deserve lengthy quotation:

MY DEAR FRIEND,
    I do not know where you are at the moment but I am sending this letter to Mr. Dieterlen who will certainly know how to get it to you. Our committee at its April meeting, has taken note of the discussion we had with you on March 10th. I was asked to produce a resumé, which I did from memory four weeks after our meeting, but I think it is sufficiently accurate. I enclose a copy.
    After hearing this . . . the Committee has instructed me to write to you again to clarify certain parts which were the subject of long discussion at this meeting.
    We are delighted to see you return to Lambarene to give your services, both to Africans and to the Europeans of the Ogowe, and in particular to our missionary personnel, and we are grateful for the great efforts you are making to collect the necessary funds. We are sorry, on the other hand, that you have not been able to accede more completely to the views of the Committee and take steps to hasten the building of your hospital and your dwelling at a certain distance from the mission station. However, we understand the reasons you give, and we are quite prepared to welcome you fraternally for a second spell on the following conditions:
    1. The committee requests you to choose, as soon as possible after your arrival at Lambarene, the plot of land on which you wish to establish yourself, and to communicate this to us within a maximum of three months.
    2. This plot should be at least 1 kilometre from the buildings of the mission station, either outside our concession, or on the concession's territory.
    3. In this latter case our society will not agree to sell you the land upon which you build, but it is willing to lend it to you free of charge for so long as you yourself remain in the Gabon. On your departure the buildings which you have raised on this land will remain our property, like the land itself.
    4. For the construction of these buildings we will put at your disposal one of our workmen, and even two if necessary, but all the expenses which arise will have to be your responsibility. Some of us even feel that we should require of you a certain indemnity for the time which our workmen spend in your service. In any case, the whole work will have to be effected during the dry season of 1923, and must therefore be finished towards the end of September 1923.

5. As to the hut which hitherto has served you at Lambarene as a consultation room and store for instruments and medicines, our society is prepared to grant you the title free of charge, but asks you to see to its removal to the hospital area as soon as possible, at your cost.

6. Finally, certain members have expressed the desire that our workmen should be asked as from now to prepare on the station itself a small hut, divided into two compartments, which can serve as your lodging from the time of your arrival and during the period of the building of your final domicile. This hut will subsequently be used by our missionaries for the benefit of their work.

We are afraid, in point of fact, that there is no room we can offer you in the actual Mission buildings if we add, as we wish, a second school-mistress in addition to Mlle Arnoux, and if the Hermann family is required by the Conference to settle at this station at the same time as the Lortsch family, M. Pelot and M. Tanner.

I should have sent you this letter a fortnight ago, for the committee would have wished to have your reply for its meeting of 1 May. I'm afraid now that it may be too late, particularly if you are in Sweden. But would you please reply as soon as possible, and forgive the delay, which results from my excessive work in these last weeks.

I hope that you have no objection to agreeing to the committee's wishes. I know that you do not much like written contracts, and that you would prefer to have carte blanche to reach verbal agreement with our missionaries. But it is very natural that our committee wishes to formulate clearly the conditions of a collaboration which, despite everything, is of a slightly delicate nature. We continue, you and we, to maintain the independence of our two kinds of work, vis a vis each other; but on the other hand there is between us an obvious solidarity.

I hope, my dear friend, that you are not tiring yourself too much before leaving! And I send, as you know, the most affectionate good wishes for your next trip.

Yours devoted,
Jean Bianquis[20]

The letter found Schweitzer at Günsbach, and on April 30 he wrote back. Here and there the letter—handwritten like all his letters—is illegible with age, but the bulk of it is clear enough.

DEAR DIRECTOR AND DEAR FRIEND,

I have just received your communication through the good offices of M. Dieterlen and I am replying straight away. I am forced to be brief, since I have a touch of writer's cramp which troubles and impedes me.

First of all I must correct one mistake in the resumé of our discussion. I have never thought of asking that M. Pelot or any other missionary-workman should be put at my disposition for my building. That would be tactless on my part. Perhaps M. Pelot and his colleague will be busy on other work, or tired. I have only ever spoken of *consulting*

M. Pelot, for whose experience and knowledge I have great respect. . . .

2. *The question of the kilometre.* First of all I must point out that it is not so easy to measure a kilometre through the bush. Besides, the question of the distance has not the same importance if my hospital is separated from the mission station by a stretch of water. That would be the case, if I were to establish myself either up-stream or down-stream of the station.

Furthermore, you may find that there are missionaries at Lambarene who will express their views against the kilometre and who will ask me to do them a favour and settle closer to the station! My hospital should oblige them by giving its services to the workers and to the children in the mission school! This is very important for them, seeing that there are a good number of rainstorms every day. If the hospital is at any distance from the station, it can no longer fulfill these functions. . . .

Furthermore, the station benefits from my hospital as regards its provisions. In return for my medicines, I receive fresh fish, hens and sweet bananas, which I am accustomed to sharing straightaway with the missionary households. This is important. If I moved too far away, the missionary tables will no longer be provided from the overflow from the hospital, because the "boys" of the missionary's wife could not be summoned quickly enough. . . .

If M. Hermann is still in your service, it is because during his fever in February 1914 I was able to stay with him for four weeks at Talagouga, since my hospital was under the supervision of the Lambarene mission. With the distance which you wish to impose on me, I can never do anything of the kind. I could give a consultation to a missionary when summoned, and that would be all, for I would not be able to abandon my hospital to robbery. It might well be that if it were decided that I am to place my hospital outside the station, I would put it two or three kilometres away, with all the disadvantages which would then result as regards the services rendered to the Lambarene mission station in general! In demanding this kilometre you are acting against the interests of the missionaries themselves. Please consult them.

3. *Construction of the buildings*—You ask me to agree that if you permit me to build on your land—which you refuse to sell me—the buildings are to belong to you. It will be difficult for me to agree to this clause. My death might occur at a time when my work was in deficit. In that case my heirs, who are responsible for the debts of my hospital, must be able to sell the materials of my buildings to cover the deficit. The great advantage of building on land lent by the Mission consists in this—that I can begin to establish myself without wasting months in asking the Government for my own concession. (You know the African bureaucracy!) For you the stretch of ground which you would lend me has no value. So why not let me have it, particularly if it is at a distance from the station?

I am sure that we shall still have time to discuss this question when we know whether I am interested in asking you for a stretch of land, when we know its situation, and when the missionaries of the Gabon have considered the question as it appears to them out there.

4. As to the length of time which you would like to fix for relieving the station of my presence, it is useless for me to agree today to dates which neither you nor I can accurately assess. Your situation in this is extremely simple. If you judge that the thing is going on too long for your convenience, you send a message to Lambarene, giving me my notice. So far as I am concerned, you will be obeyed within twenty-four hours. I will go and fix myself up somewhere in a bamboo hut. I can only repeat what I told you in our discussion—it is I who have the greater interest, once the question of principle is agreed, in establishing myself as quickly as possible outside the station. Why go on whipping a galloping horse?

5. Thank you for continuing to offer a corrugated iron hut. All the same, I only accept it, as I have already told you, if the missionaries there have no objection. The cost of moving I accept as my charge.

6. To conclude, let me once more say to you that only questions of principle, (as I said to you in our discussion) can be decided in Europe. Agreement on practical questions must be reached out there. Have no fear that my poor dialectic will carry away your missionaries. For the rest, believe me, they will make no decisions without consulting you.

My feeling is that we should not treat these matters like diplomats working out a treaty, but like Christians working for Christ and trusting in one another. I do not think I have abused your confidence nor that of the missionaries of the Ogowe. So I see no reason why we should impose on each other the torment of elaborating clauses as the diplomats do, instead of being towards each other what we wish to be; Christians who act in the spirit and who have confidence in the spirit.

Please accept my best wishes and pass on what I have written to the members of the committee. Please say a thousand good things from me to M.——.

Your devoted,
Albert Schweitzer

P.S. In the heat of the argument I almost forgot to say how touched I was by your thoughtfulness in lending me M. Tanner and M. Pelot for my building. As to the hut which you propose constructing for my temporary lodging, do nothing about it! If M. Hermann is at Lambarene he'll find a little place for the doctor to stay, believe me! You do not take into account the difficulties of the smallest construction at Lambarene. Since the whole land is on a slope, it is necessary first to level an area and that is only done with great difficulty because of the rock which one encounters everywhere—Unfortunately I cannot get this reply to you by the 1st May. Forgive me. I did not receive your letter in time.[21]

This uncompromising blast was thrown together so hastily, clumsily, and sometimes ungrammatically that Schweitzer almost certainly decided to make a fair copy when he had cooled down a little—and kept the first draft as a reference, which is why we are lucky enough to have it.

Soon after the letter reached Paris, the missionaries themselves, aware of Schweitzer's difficulties, tried to lend a hand. On May 6 they passed a resolution at Talagouga that ran:

The Medical Problem and Dr. Schweitzer

Our Conference has been called upon to re-affirm the absolute necessity for our Mission of possessing an organised and continuing medical organisation. The conclusions of the report which M. Lortsch sent you on this subject in September 1921 grow more and more apparent to those who want a proper foundation for our work.

In response to our needs, the arrival of Dr. Schweitzer might appear providential. He tells us we may expect his return in the month of September. We shall greet him with great joy, asking God to smooth over the difficulties which might prevent his establishment in our midst, and to grant us a fruitful collaboration with him for the good of the Africans and also of the missionaries. May He also permit him to give our medical installation the development and the stability which we would like. On his arrival, the most urgent questions concerning his position here will be examined by the board of the Conference in the spirit which you have indicated, and the others will be submitted to you.

We allow ourselves finally to point out that if a doctor seems indispensable to us for our work below, so much the more will he be for our work above.[22]

But before this could reach Paris, Schweitzer's broadside had achieved its purpose; for on May 11, M. Bianquis was able to write again to say that, without waiting for the committee's next meeting, he had contacted the executive members, who had taken counsel and agreed that since his return was "desired by all our missionaries out there," they were "confident that you and they can arrange the practical questions of your installation on the spot, each granting the other the maximum independence, but allowing for the mutual service each is called upon to render the other.

"I should like to believe," continues M. Bianquis, "that the Committee itself will recognise the force of your observations and will no longer insist on the somewhat trifling conditions that it felt it should impose."[23]

Together with this more or less official reply, M. Bianquis sent a very friendly personal note. He was evidently delighted at the outcome. The battle was won.

The following he was gaining through his tours now added a great deal to Schweitzer's correspondence. Small quantities of money came in a steady stream to the Günsbach house, and when he was not there himself his father would acknowledge these contributions and make a list for Albert. But for Schweitzer the important thing was to keep the cash flowing, and wherever his travels had taken him he began organizing the translation and distribution of newsletters and bulletins which he intended writing from the hospital to maintain the interest of his supporters. In addition to these tedious but vital activities he was writing to various experts about new drugs for gonorrhea, about the best sort of motorboat to order, about a hundred and one matters that needed dealing with before he went back to Africa. Small wonder his mother's writer's cramp was catching up with him.

Hélène's health had not kept pace with her husband's, and that summer they decided to build a house at Königsfeld, a village in the German part of the Black Forest. Hélène knew Königsfeld from earlier visits, and it had much to recommend it. In the first place the economic collapse of postwar Germany had made house building in that country very cheap; elsewhere Schweitzer might not have been able to afford it. And the air was excellent. In those days clear mountain air was believed to be essential for sufferers from tuberculosis, but on the other hand Hélène's heart would not permit her to live at too great an altitude. Königsfeld offered the perfect compromise. Though quiet and secluded it was easy to reach from the main road and railway line to Strasbourg. And finally it was the home of a branch of the Moravian Brethren, a strict sect of the Lutheran Church for whom Schweitzer had great respect, their hallmarks being simplicity of life, devotion to the Bible, and freedom from dogma. This was the sort of atmosphere in which Schweitzer would be happy to have his child grow up while he was away. So here they lived, mother and daughter, and Schweitzer was with them when he could be.

But in the autumn he was off again, in his worn suit and homespun overcoat, with his two big linen bags for correspondence (one for answered letters, the other for those still to be dealt with) and his selection of small linen bags carrying currency of the different countries he was to visit. After Switzerland he went this time to Denmark. And in November, Oskar Kraus wrote inviting him to come to Prague and lecture on the Philosophy of Civilization.

He went in January, and a great friendship with Kraus began, which three years later was to result in Kraus' writing a book about his friend. There is something touchingly comical about Kraus' attitude to Schweitzer, whom he regarded as totally wrongheaded, but at the same time unequaled "in originality, in manysidedness, and in the intensity of his intellectual, his artistic and above all his ethical qualities."[24] He himself was an unshakable disciple of a nineteenth-century speculative philosopher named Franz Brentano, and his book on Schweitzer is full of an infuriated perplexity that anybody could be as brilliant as Schweitzer and still not see that Brentano was right. Kraus is a glorious example of the kind of thinker, trained in the German schools of philosophy, of whom the half-German Roman Catholic philosopher and theologian Baron von Hügel says in *The German Soul* is much too inclined to think ideas important and meaningful just because they are efficiently and elaborately ordered. Such thinkers cannot rest content unless they can reduce the world to a verbal formula, to which end they are forever pulling apart phrases, comparing terminologies, referring every idea to another idea, and pouncing on paradoxes as though they were a proof of invalid thought.

With enormous triumph Kraus manages in his book to prove (what is partly true but quite irrelevant) that "Schweitzer's mysticism is nothing more nor less than a logically unjustifiable short cut to a desired aim which he is unable to attain in a logically justifiable way or which he prematurely despairs of ever attaining."[25] It never seems to occur to him that ideas need to be referred to life, and that inconsistencies can correspond to something inconsistent in reality. The fact that Schweitzer refused this kind of artificial consistency is just what marks him out from the German school and makes nonsense of those who claim that he had a typically German outlook.

Back in Königsfeld, while he was struggling to finish the two volumes of *The Philosophy of Civilisation*, preparations for Lambarene continued. One day samples arrived from the Rockefeller Foundation of a new sleeping sickness drug, Tryparsamide, with the request that he would test it under tropical conditions—an indication of how widely he was becoming known. In fact this proved to be one of the first of the great advances in tropical medicine which revolutionized Schweitzer's work during his lifetime.

Finally the books were finished—*The Decay and Restoration of Civilisation*, which is a fairly general statement of the problem and of Schweitzer's approach; and *Civilisation and Ethics*, in which he plunges, characteristically, into a historical survey of the course of civilization and the influence upon it of varying world views, before concluding with his own solution, the adoption of Reverence for Life as a basis for all future ethical and political systems. I have already tried to summarize the theme of the books; but they should be read in full, because they are so rich in insight and a sort of revolutionary commonsense. Every page of my copies is marked, often in half a dozen places. It is impossible to begin to quote. Let me hope that readers will seek out the books for themselves.

Schweitzer sent the books to Harper's in London, who before the war had expressed interest in a book on his philosophical ideas. But Harper's had changed their minds. When he told the story many years later to Norman Cousins, editor of *Saturday Review*, Schweitzer attributed the trouble once again to that German-sounding name of his. But his Berlin publisher was equally discouraging and in desperation he gave the manuscript to Mme Emmy Martin, a pastor's widow who since 1919 had been helping him with secretarial work, to take with her to Munich and dispose of as best she might.

Knowing nothing about publishers, Mme Martin offered it to a firm named Beck, which specialized in legal books. Herr Beck was not available but one of his associates, Herr Albers, after looking through a few pages took the manuscript home with him and before long the *Philosophy of Civilisation* had a publisher.

It was some time however before the books appeared, for this was the period of galloping inflation in the German economy and the government needed the printing press on which the books were to be printed to make paper money.

It so happened that thanks to Albers, Beck was already the publisher of Oswald Spengler's *Decline of the West*, which was enjoying great popularity at the time. One of Schweitzer's favorite stories was of the occasion when Albers, Spengler, and Schweitzer were all going to lunch together, Albers walking between his two authors. Schweitzer burst out laughing. "It reminds me," he said, "of a farmer with his two milk cows."

In May, Schweitzer was again in Switzerland. Some idea of the schedules he kept can be gained from the following list of engagements for this month—bearing in mind that excellent though the public transportation system was in Switzerland, the mountainous nature of the country added to the complications of traveling and that Schweitzer, as always, went third class—unless there was a fourth:

3 Mai	Frau Moser Kreuz Herzogenbuchsee	Cant. Bern
4 "	Prfr. Ziegler Burgdorf	" "
7 "	" Weiss Olten	" "
abends	" Schmid Balsthal	" Solothurn
8 Mai	" Gaun Liestal Baselland	
9 "	" Blumenstein Biberist	b/Solothurn
10 "	" Ludwig Biel	Cant. Bern
11 "	" Meier Baden	Cant. Aargau
12 "	" Nissen Schwarzenburg	Cant. Bern
14 "	" Friedli Ober—Diesbach	b/Thun
abends	" Dürrenmatt Kariolfingen–Stalden	Cant. Bern
15 Mai	" Buchmuller Huttwil	Cant. Bern
16 "	" W. Hopf Lutzelfluh	b/Burgdorf
17 "	" Matthys Worb	Cant. Bern
18 "	" Rohr Thun	" "
19 "	" Waber Munsinger	" "
20 "	" Roochuz Spiez	a/Thunersee

21	"	" P. Hopf Steffisburg	b/Thun
abends		" Ammann Trubschachen—Emmental	
22 Mai		" D. Müller Langnau	Cant. Bern
23	"	" Von Schulthess Männedorf	a/Zurichsee
25	"	" Weber Menziken	i/Seethal
abends		Lehrer Merz Rheinfelden Baselland	
27 Mai		Jac. Keller Winterthur	
28-29 Mai		Herrn Robert Kaufmann Belsitostrasse 17	Zürich
30 Mai		Günsbach Elsass	

As he crossed and recrossed Switzerland he found himself one afternoon with an hour or two to spare in Zürich, and called upon his friend Oscar Pfister—which is where, so to speak, we came in. Schweitzer lay and rested, Pfister persuaded him to speak of his early memories, and the result was *Memoirs of My Childhood and Youth*. This was the meeting which George Marshall, in his recent biography, quotes as additional evidence that Schweitzer after the war suffered ''a nervous breakdown.'' In fact by this time Schweitzer had been back on the top of his form for nearly three years—and there is a small epilogue to the story which clinches the matter. When, years later, Schweitzer damaged his hand and was taken by Erica Anderson to a Zürich doctor to have it attended to, the doctor's nurse turned out to be Oscar Pfister's daughter. She remembered the occasion well as a cheerful social visit and nothing more. The truth is that the worst thing Schweitzer suffered from at this period was an attack of *otitis media,* or inflammation of the middle ear.

Dr. Micklem, writing the preface to *Christianity and the Religions of the World* about this time, says that Hélène's illness postponed Schweitzer's return to Africa; but for that, he would already have been back in Lambarene. This certainly seems probable, but the delay was not to last much longer. By the autumn, when the proofs of the *Civilisation* books arrived for checking, he was busy in Strasbourg packing, as he had packed with Hélène eleven years before. He was due to sail in February.

The friendship with Oskar Kraus led to further expeditions to Prague before he left, and on one of these occasions he decided to break his return journey to visit Bayreuth again. This was not so simple, for a special visa was needed at that time to stop in Bavaria and Schweitzer had no such visa. At the frontier all passengers without visas were directed by the police to the express that went straight through Bavaria without stopping. Schweitzer, never an inconspicuous man, was made the more noticeable by the large bunch of white roses which he had been given after a concert in Prague and which he now wished to give to Cosima Wagner. But somehow, taking advantage of the inattention of the police, he crept onto the forbidden train.

As the reader already knows, it was all in vain. Sad enough that the great theater where Schweitzer had spent so many enraptured evenings was now unworkable, that there was no money to restore it to working order, and that no one knew whether or not there was still an audience for Wagner.

But the final blow was to discover that the great lady herself had grown very nervous and was often unable to see visitors. When she heard of Schweitzer's arrival she became so overexcited that her daughter grew anxious about her and Schweitzer, leaving the roses for her, went on with his mission unaccomplished. How he explained himself at the frontier is not recorded.

Kraus meantime had been badgering Schweitzer with questions designed to make him clarify his ideas. It was intolerable, felt Kraus, that a thinker should "vacillate" so. And on January 2, 1924, Schweitzer wrote him a letter, selections from which Kraus quoted in his book. The passage he quoted has become famous—Kraus' persistence had forced Schweitzer to set down, clearly and foursquare, the meaning he attached to the word "God" and the relationship he saw between philosophy, religion, and ethics. Looked at from Kraus' point of view, Schweitzer could see that what he had to say was not at all satisfactory. Yet he had to say it, because it seemed to him true.

Here is the passage:

Hitherto I have followed one principle; in philosophy I never express more than I have experienced as a result of absolutely logical thinking.

Because I express no more than I have experienced, I never speak in philosophy of "God" but only of "the universal will-to-live," which comes to consciousness in me in a two-fold way; first, as creative will perceived as manifestations in observable phenomena external to me; and secondly, as ethical will experienced within me.

Certainly there is a probability inference of which you speak that does suggest the existence of an external God, but it seems to me doubtful whether it is the province of philosophy to draw this inference.

Also it is doubtful that in making such a probability inference there is a gain thereby for the *Weltanschauung* or for the energy of such a total world view.

I prefer therefore to stop with a description of the experience of thinking, leaving pantheism and theism as an indecisive mystery within me. I am always thrown back to the reality of my experience.

When I must use the language of traditional religious idioms, however, then I employ the word "God" in its historical definiteness and indefiniteness.

Similarly I speak in ethics of "love" in place of "reverence for life."

When I use the language of religion, it is a matter of fidelity for me to convey the experience of elemental thinking in all of its affirmative vitality and in its relationship to our inherited religiosity.

In using the term "God" in this way, I distort neither my philosophy of nature nor the realities of traditional religion.

In the language of experience and the language of religion the content remains absolutely the same. In both idioms I renounce final knowledge of the world and I affirm the primacy of the universal will-to-live experienced in myself.

My lectures on religion contain much criticism of religious thought. But the views expressed in the lectures are put forth as universal experiences so natural that they do not hurt anyone. For ultimately the center of elemental religious concern is, in the traditional idiom, "the being grasped by the ethical will of God."

I am not able to get around the renunciation of all metaphysical knowledge of the world nor beyond the conflict: pantheism-theism. I say this in the philosophical as well as the traditional religious sense.

Ah, dear friend, how much would I rather follow together with you the unbroken lines which lead all the way to Brentano. But ever since my fifteenth year I have had to be content with discontinuity in my philosophy.

It is my fate and my destiny to think out while living how much ethical content and religiosity can be realized by reason in a *Weltanschauung* which dares to be incomplete.

But the point on which we are precisely and absolutely in agreement concerns the quality of active love as the ethical ordinance of the world view, which I call "the commanding power of the world view."

Our agreement on love and service makes clear our high task.[26]

On February 21, in pursuit of his high task, Schweitzer embarked at Bordeaux, accompanied by the young Englishman, Noel Gillespie. Hélène and Rhena stayed behind, in the Black Forest.

19

ADONINALONGO
The Second Hospital
1924-1927

SCHWEITZER loved the voyage. He always did love that voyage—the only holiday, he said, he ever had. This time he traveled on a cargo boat, to avoid interruptions by passengers; for this was a holiday rather in the sense of a change than a rest—the large sack of unanswered letters went with him, to be eroded en route. The customs men were incredulous and deeply suspicious, and spent some time searching for smuggled currency.

The steamer made more frequent calls at the ports of West Africa than did the passenger liners. Schweitzer was anxious to learn as much as possible about these other regions. He was even exploring the possibility of extending his activities by starting a second hospital at Nyasoso, in the British part of the Cameroons. Noel Gillespie and he left the ship at Douala, to spend a fortnight looking at the country and discussing possibilities with the British Resident. The plan came to nothing—probably because in the event Lambarene itself was more than enough to handle. But Schweitzer suffered, as we all do, from the persistent illusion that *next* year it will all be different, everything will be under control and we can relax, look around, and make fresh plans.

The journey continued in the mail liner *Europa*, and two days later they reached Cape Lopez, where Schweitzer and Hélène had spent the rainy season of 1916-17, seven years before, living on fish, and where the beaches are lined with the lost logs from the timber rafts of the Ogowe. Cape Lopez had been renamed since he was last there, and was now called Port-Gentil.

They went up the river on the *Alémbé*, the boat which had first carried Schweitzer that way in 1913—but which was a good deal older now and much the worse for wear. Schweitzer was comparing the country with the richer Cameroons and Gold Coast; richer because the very wealth of the Ogowe, its timber, took the labor off the land and left it quite uncultivated. The riverside tribes one and all followed the timber trade, and whenever the demand was high they moved to where the uncut trees stood and lived off imported food. Their lives had no continuity, no security against the whims of international trade. When trade was good they suffered from dysentery brought on by rice and canned meat. When it was bad they starved. At present, with postwar reconstruction still going on and two international exhibitions needing timber, trade was excellent, and nobody was left to prepare manioc or even to roof the village huts.

This nomadic, impermanent life of the Ogowe tribes was an important cause of their backwardness. In other areas clinics could be set up and local people trained to staff them. In a village forever on the move because its menfolk were periodically tempted by irresistibly high wages, this was a hopeless task.

Schweitzer and Noel reached Lambarene on April 19, 1924; Easter Eve. The war had torn six and a half years out of Schweitzer's life, since he last saw the scattered town on the long narrow island. The hot, rainy season was drawing to an end and the river was full. The mission station dugouts toiled the half mile up the river, hugging the bank to avoid the current, rounded the sharp nose of the island, and dropped more swiftly down the river's other branch, which sweeps the island's north side. From the moment they rounded the point they could see the Andende settlement, a mile and a half ahead, the river disappearing around a bend below it. This was unchanged.

But the hospital was changed. It barely existed. When men drop their guard the jungle moves in very fast. The buildings Schweitzer had worked on so hard were roofless and overgrown, the path up the steep little hill from hospital to house was invisible.

The work began again from the beginning.

This meant, first, putting a roof on the buildings which still stood. But even the makers of leaf-tiles (raffia leaves stitched over bamboo) had made none lately, so easy was it to earn more money from the timber merchants. Only by a hut-to-hut search, village by village, followed by bribery, cajolement, and the threat of refusing treatment to the sick (unenforceable and disbelieved), did Schweitzer and Noel manage even to get a roof over their heads.

Schweitzer missed Hélène sorely; everything reminded him of her absence. Joseph, like every ablebodied African, was busy on the timber trade. Noel Gillespie, young and enthusiastic but quite untrained, turned his hand to whatever needed doing—building, typing letters, and all kinds of unskilled medical assistance.

The patients came nevertheless—and many died, either because they came too late, their condition too extreme, or because to treat them properly in those circumstances was more than one man could do; or sometimes because lying in the roofless huts they caught fatal chills.

The hospital's mortality rate was boosted by another factor. "The praiseworthy habit of dumping sick persons at my hospital and then making themselves scarce has not been lost by the Ogowe people. . . . A woman from a village not far from Lambarene has been deposited here. She has no one at all belonging to her, so no one in the village troubles about her. A neighbour's wife, so I am told, asked another woman to lend her an axe that she might get a little firewood for the old woman to keep her warm during the damp nights. 'What?' was the answer. 'An axe for that old woman? Take her to the doctor, and leave here there till she dies.' And that was what happened."[1]

Sleeping sickness had increased. So had leprosy. For the latter the treatment was still at that time pitifully inadequate; the discovery of the sulfone drugs was years ahead yet. One sleeping sickness patient had fits of mental disturbance which made him violent, and a crude wooden cage had to be built for him. The enclosure was impossibly primitive, but better than the treatment his own people often gave to the mentally sick—to tie them up and pitch them in the river.

In June and July this desperate state of affairs began to ease. A Swiss missionary, M. Abrezol, arrived, bringing with him a powerful motorboat for the mission station. On the same day, all Schweitzer's packing cases finally reached Lambarene. Then the husband of a sleeping sickness patient turned out to have some experience of carpentry. ("The dread of being left without a carpenter at all made my lips so eloquent that under the mango tree at sunset I wrung the promise for him to stay. He cost me 300 francs a month besides his food (80 francs), and he cannot read measurements."[2]) Joseph returned to the hospital. And a nurse, Mathilde Kottmann, arrived from Strasbourg.

Here in a nutshell is the unpredictability of the struggle that was Schweitzer's lot from now on. For who could guess that within eight weeks M. Abrezol would be inexplicably drowned while bathing, though a strong swimmer; that the motorboat, which only he could master, would have gone aground; that Monenzali, the African carpenter, whom Schweitzer had persuaded to stay, would work faithfully on till his death years later; and that Mathilde Kottmann would live and work at Schweitzer's side till Schweitzer himself died in 1965.

Such were the swings and the roundabouts of Lambarene life. Noel Gillespie had to go home in August. In October a trained doctor arrived, an Alsatian named Victor Nessmann, who had been a fellow medical student of Schweitzer's. For the first time the immense burden of being the only doctor, as well as administrator, caterer, and builder, was lifted from Schweitzer's shoulders.

Now Schweitzer could, when necessary, leave the medical side of things to others, to concentrate on the expansion or consolidation of the hospital, on the correspondence with Europe which had to be kept alive, and on all the administrative details. From this time too stems the title the Africans gave him, *"le grand Docteur"*—a title which has been taken to imply some sort of self-aggrandizement, but which in fact only means "the old doctor," in contrast with the various younger assistants who joined him from time to time, who were *"les petits Docteurs."*

The migrant timber laborers from the even more primitive tribes in the interior, were a special problem. Unfamiliar even with the use of an ax, they were prone to every sort of accident and arrived in considerable numbers at the hospital, where they set new standards of blatancy in thieving and breaking things.

The rainy season was exhausting and depressing. Painful foot ulcers, brought on by constant injuries while building new wards, sometimes meant that Schweitzer had to be carried down to the hospital in order to work there at all. But after a wretched Christmas and a miserable fiftieth birthday, when all the white staff were feeling ill and despondent, the new year looked brighter. Another motorboat arrived, a present from Sweden. And when in March a third doctor, Mark Lauterburg, joined them from Switzerland, the team began to look really workable. Nessmann took the motorboat up and downriver, to deal with the cases that could not be brought in and to initiate some preventative measures, while Lauterburg dealt with major surgery, and Schweitzer, apart from his supervisory work, concentrated on experiments with the new treatments for leprosy and sleeping sickness.

At this stage the hopes of a second hospital at Nyasoso were still very much alive, and the British government had offered full support. A long fund-raising letter to *The Times* that August from Schweitzer's British Committee (including four bishops!) mentions it as "a feasible project."[3] But the very success of the hospital began soon to pose problems. The ever-increasing number of patients constantly threatened to overwhelm the facilities. New buildings were needed to house them, and the arrival of each new doctor or nurse meant additional building, all of which took away from time that could be spent on medicine.

Then, in the early summer, just after Schweitzer had received the long-expected but grievous news of his father's death, the number of dysentery cases began to increase alarmingly. The disease was reaching epidemic proportions.

This was a new type of dysentery, that did not respond to Schweitzer's drugs; and nothing would persuade the Africans of the vital importance of avoiding infection. Men would sooner catch the disease and die than be separated from their friends.

It was in the middle of this desperate time that Joseph made a remark that has gone into the Schweitzer legend. Some of the up-country tribesmen had once again been drawing infected water to drink, and Schweitzer, in despair, fell into a chair saying. "What a blockhead I was to come to Africa to doctor savages like these!" "Yes, doctor," said Joseph, "here on earth you are a great blockhead, but not in heaven."

The story is of course tailor-made for the more inspirational accounts of Schweitzer's life. But these all too often omit the comment with which Schweitzer ends the story, which is rather less edifying: "He likes giving utterance to sententious remarks like that. I wish he could support us better in our efforts to hinder the spread of dysentery!"[4]

In case readers find Schweitzer's word "savages" less edifying still, let me point out that the French "*sauvages*" from which it is translated is not quite so derogatory. As a description of wild, undisciplined, violent and primitive people it is accurate if not particularly tactful, and Schweitzer was always more interested in accuracy than tact.

The new rainy season approached, and the leaf-tile roofs were full of holes. Dreading what damp huts might do to his patients, Schweitzer ordered corrugated iron from Europe, though he had no idea how or whether he could pay for it.

And on top of everything came famine. The traders had miscalculated how much food would be needed for all the migrant labor, the weather had been worse than usual, and a supply ship had been wrecked. It added up to starvation. Schweitzer, having as usual scented trouble early, had laid in large quantities of rice, so his patients were better off than most. But an exclusive rice diet was conducive to dystentery. Among the hospital inmates were "dozens of walking skeletons."[5]

The realization was forced upon Schweitzer that in one major respect his foresight and his courage had failed. In bargaining with the Mission Society he had rejected the idea of starting afresh outside the station, largely because of the bureaucratic complications involved in getting a concession from the government for his own piece of land. But in staying within the mission grounds he had limited himself to an area which, as he wrote to his supporters in 1928, "was hemmed in on every side. On one side was the river, on another a steep hill, on another the graveyard of the Mission Station, on another a swamp."[6] He could never satisfactorily isolate infectious cases, never house noisy mental patients in any tolerable way or at a distance from the others, and never accommodate all the helpers he needed in any sort of comfort.

The only alternative to an ever more hopeless overcrowding was to write off all the work of the past eighteen months and begin absolutely afresh somewhere else. So much for the dream of getting all the building finally done and being able to concentrate on doctoring.

A possible site existed, very nearby. From the veranda of Schweitzer's house you could see it, less than two miles upriver, on a slight headland.

Today you can walk there in half an hour, along the riverside forest track, but in those days swamps made this impossible.

The site had once been the headquarters of the Sun-King of the Galoas, N'Kombe; and so the trees there were younger than elsewhere, the bush less dense, the soil at least a little less hard. Many of the trees were oil palms; the oil crushed from their nuts was a valuable addition to the local diet. On a wide front the ground sloped gently up from the river. In addition to the hospital there was room for a garden and a big fruit tree plantation, and Schweitzer was desperately aware of the need for the hospital to grow its own food, not to be dependent on supplies which could be interrupted by accident, by war, or by the varying fortunes of the outside world. The name of the place, which the world came to know as Lambarene, is actually Adoninalongo, which means "It looks out over the nations."

Schweitzer had long been tempted by Adoninalongo—even during his prewar spell here he had had an eye on it. Famine and epidemic now forced his hand. True to form he kept his thoughts to himself, until, his mind made up, he had been to see the district commissioner.

The commissioner was cordial. The formalities would be long-drawn-out, but in view of the urgency and the improbability of any opposition Schweitzer was given a provisional go-ahead. The concession he asked for was about 170 acres—which he would of course have to measure out for himself in the thick bush. The land remained the government's, but any building or development would be Schweitzer's property. A condition of granting the concession was that a quarter of the area must first be cultivated; but that was not hard to promise. The first thing Schweitzer intended to do was to provide the hospital with food.

When he announced the move to the assembled white staff, they were first stunned, then overwhelmed with delight. In Schweitzer's own case the delight was tempered not only by the thought of the immense task ahead but by the fact that now he would not be able to go back to Europe and his family, as planned, the following year. As before, his two-year spell was going to have to be stretched. No one else had the building experience or the ability to supervise the workers. Whatever the demands of his wife and his growing daughter, now six years old and much in need of a father, the hospital, for him, came first.

The work began. Workmen as such were nonexistent, so each morning all the more-or-less able-bodied men who could be mustered were herded into canoes and sent off upstream. The able-bodied were not many, for the dysentery epidemic raged on. In the hospital the medical work was as heavy as ever. Instead of the original forty or so, the patients now numbered well over a hundred—though additional nursing help had just arrived in the sturdy form of Emma Haussknecht, a former teacher from Alsace who was to be one of the hospital's greatest pillars of strength, sweetness, and good humor until her death in 1956.

The one ace in Schweitzer's hand, as he gathered his squad of hungry reluctant hobbledehoys, was that he had food—and in those famine-stricken days the offer of a little extra food for a day's work was a bribe few could resist. In the second of the bulletins which he now began to send, more or less regularly, to his supporters in Europe, he described his method of recruiting his laborers:

> I choose them from the fifteen to twenty persons among the 120 patients, women accompanying their husbands, children, slight cases, convalescents or ex-patients who are willing to give a few days' work out of gratitude. . . . They are told that friends in Europe are helping to support the hospital and have a right to expect each inmate to help the work in return. This truth does not easily make its way home to the hearts of my savages. They seem to believe in a "perfection of bounty" and that I should feed them, heal them, and leave them all day in the sociable circle telling stories, and even furnish them with tobacco to smoke! It is no easy task to embark them in the canoes for the plantation each morning. They prove, with every gesture of conviction, that their health requires that on this particular day they should rest at the hospital. . . . Naturally our convalescents work only in the degree their strength allows. Some on account of wounds cannot walk. They pull out weeds, seated on the ground.[7]

It was autumn, 1925. When the first tree fell at Adoninalongo, the site that was to become identified with Schweitzer, he was already nearly fifty-one.

So far as I can ascertain, the project for a second hospital in the Cameroons was never again seriously considered. As Schweitzer was known to say in his later years, when criticized for failing to do this or that: "One man can only do so much."

The measuring, pegging, clearing, felling, chopping up, snake killing, stone-breaking, leveling, pile driving, lifting, carrying, sawing, hammering, and tree planting went on for over a year. Schweitzer supervised it all—dovetailing it with the continuing needs of the old hospital and himself laboring harder than anyone. In *More from the Primeval Forest*, a fresh selection from the reports he sent to his supporters, he sets a typical day to music:

> A day with these people moves on like a symphony. Lento: They take very grumpily the axes and bush-knives that I distribute to them on landing. In snail-tempo the procession goes to the spot where bush

and tree are to be cut down. At last everyone is in his place. With great caution the first blows are struck.

Moderato: Axes and bush-knives move in extremely moderate time, which the conductor tries in vain to quicken. The midday break puts an end to the tedious movement.

Adagio: With much trouble I have brought the people back to the work place in the stifling forest. Not a breath of wind is stirring. One hears from time to time the stroke of an axe.

Scherzo: A few jokes, to which in my despair I tune myself up, are successful. The mental atmosphere gets livelier, merry words fly here and there, and a few begin to sing. It is now getting a little cooler too. A tiny gust of wind steals up from the river into the thick undergrowth.

Finale: All are jolly now. The wicked forest, on account of which they have to stand here instead of sitting comfortably in the hospital shall have a bad time of it. Wild imprecations are hurled at it. Howling and yelling they attack it, axes and bush-knives vie with each other in battering it. But—no bird must fly up, no squirrel show itself, no question must be asked, no command given. With the very slightest distraction the spell would be broken. Then the axes and knives would come to rest, everybody would begin talking about what had happened or what they had heard, and there would be no getting them again into train for work.

Happily, no distraction comes. The music gets louder and faster. If this finale lasts even a good half-hour the day has not been wasted. And it continues till I shout "Amani! Amani!" (Enough! Enough!), and put an end to the work for the day."[8]

The framework of the buildings was to be hardwood, the Ogowe's most plentiful product. This one commodity at least was much cheaper here than in Europe. True, it was extremely hard to work, blunting saws and bending nails; but softwoods would have swiftly been eaten by termites. "Any termite that tries to eat my hospital," Schweitzer told Erica Anderson, "will have to see a dentist."

For roofing the corrugated iron he had already ordered would be invaluable. Leaf tiles were far too much trouble. This hospital, however simple, must be weatherproof. Heat would be reduced by the insulating cavity between roof and ceiling.

All the buildings were raised on piles in order to let the storm waters pass beneath. The piles had to be brought from sixteen miles upriver where there was a plantation of especially hard wood, and then charred for extra preservation. Schweitzer had to supervise the charring, to make sure it was done enough and not too much; and had himself to move the heavy piles into their final position, for the Africans could not grasp the need for such precision. (Nor could they understand why, if a nest of ants were found where a pile was to sink, the doctor should carefully remove the ants rather than crush them. But so he did.)

The head carpenter, Monenzali, though industrious and reliable, could not read even a tape measure, so Schweitzer cut a series of sticks for him to the required lengths. In these circumstances the odds are high that a building will arise somewhat out of true. The price of a square and upright house was constant vigilance.

To create a garden, Schweitzer leveled a series of terraces near the water, protecting, with planks, each level from being washed away by the rains. Stones broken into gravel formed the base, through which excess water could drain off, and leaf mold was laid down to create soil. The goats and hens contributed their droppings, and the swift processes of decay in that hot steamy atmosphere soon rotted it all down to a fertile compost. Early in 1926 beans and cabbages were sown, and were eaten a few months later. In that dry season Schweitzer carried water every day for hundreds of fruit tree saplings. To stop the Africans from stealing fruit was impossible. The only solution was to have so much fruit that stealing would no longer be a crime.

In response to an appeal to Europe for a carpenter, a young Swiss, Hans Muggensturm, arrived in April and took over supervision of the building work. The first building completed was a store hut for the tools, to save carrying them to and fro each day; then a hut for the workmen, Monenzali and his assistants. After that there was no need to waste time each day in rounding the men up, transporting them by canoe, and getting them back home before the light failed. Things moved faster.

At Andende, Dr. Nessmann was replaced by Dr. Trensz, another Alsatian, who argued with Schweitzer about the design of the main hospital building and won the argument. "I often think that if I had not followed his advice," Schweitzer said later, "I might not have such a well-organized main building." [9] Frédéric Trensz also distinguished himself by improvising a simple laboratory and identifying in the river water a bacillus similar to that of cholera. It became clear that this was the bacillus responsible for many of the cases which had previously been diagnosed as bacillus dysentery—Schweitzer had in fact already had some success in experimentally treating dysentery patients as for cholera, but this had been a matter of lucky instinct, not scientific research.

Trensz was now able to prepare a vaccine, and as further precaution Schweitzer lost no time in having a well dug for drinking water. The discovery in fact revolutionized Trensz's career. He published a learned paper on the subject; and having gone out to Africa a surgeon, he returned well on the way to becoming a distinguished research bacteriologist. He now runs a highly successful laboratory in Strasbourg.

This was only one of many medical improvements. The new sleeping sickness drugs proved notably effective and new methods were discovered for treating the agonizing phagedenic ulcers of the feet, from which Schweitzer himself had suffered along with about a third of the hospital's patients.

Sometime in the dry season Joseph married a wife, and being unable with his hospital pay to support her in the manner to which she (and her relatives) felt she was entitled, left for a second time for the fleshpots of the timber trade.

And so the work went on until, on January 21, 1927, a fleet of canoes moved the patients to the new hospital:

> Night was falling as I made the last journey and, with Dr. Lauterburg, brought up the last of the patients, among them the mental cases. These, however, sat quite quiet, filled with great expectations. They had been told that in the new hospital they would have rooms with wooden floors; this was, to them, as if they were going to live in a palace. In the old hospital the floors of their rooms had been merely the damp earth.
>
> I shall never forget that first evening in the new hospital. From all the mosquito-curtains there looked out contented faces. "What a fine house you've built us, Doctor!" was the universal exclamation. The fact was that for the first time my sick were housed as elementary humanity requires the sick to be housed, and you may think how I thanked God for that. And how thankfully also I thought of the friends in Europe whose kindness has permitted me to face the cost of the removal![10]

The quarters for the staff were not yet built, so two doctors and a nurse moved into the house for European patients at the new hospital, and the rest stayed at Andende. Schweitzer set about demolishing all the buildings at Andende which belonged to him, to use every beam, plank, and nail for the interfittings of the new hospital—the bed frames, cupboards, and shelves. In March someone arrived from England who must be mentioned—though in the early bulletins she asks to remain anonymous. Mrs. C. E. B. Russell proved as much at home supervising the workers on the plantation as later she showed herself translating Schweitzer's lectures, and a lady of great talent and character.

> Early in July the chief buildings are finished, though there is still much to do in the matter of internal arrangements.
>
> The big pile-built village has quite a dignified look! And how much easier the work is now, for at last we have space enough, air enough, and light enough! How delightful we feel it, doctors and nurses all, to have our new rooms distinctly cooler than our old quarters were!

For the isolation of the dysentery cases wise precautions have been taken. Their rooms have no opening towards the hospital, and are approached on the side next to the river. But from the river they are separated by a fence, so that they cannot pollute the water.

For the mental patients eight cells and a general sitting-room are in prospect.[11]

Here in fact, is the nucleus of the hospital you may still see today. The ants have not eaten it, and though many of its original functions have been taken over by government schemes, and arguments go on about how and whether it should continue, it still provides a service for serious cases, especially on the surgical side, that is second to none among bush hospitals.

20

FAME
1927–1929

AT last he went home. Apart from anything else funds were running very low, and a new money-raising tour was imperative. The hospital was probably the cheapest ever built, with crippled labor and materials which either grew on the spot or were bought secondhand, but still the enterprise was more than had been budgeted for. Only Schweitzer could raise the necessary cash; so a real rest was out of the question.

Three nights only he spent at Königsfeld with the wife and child he had not seen for three and a half years, before he was off on his comfortless, third- or fourth-class travels across Europe, fulfilling engagements he had arranged before he left Lambarene.

In such circumstances little intimacy can have survived between husband and wife, but there remained a total and unquestioning loyalty and respect, which in itself is remarkable. Between father and daughter there appears to have been no particular tension such as one might have expected. About her feelings then Rhena writes, "I really don't know if I loved my father as a child or not. I certainly was happy when he was with us but I also adjusted when he left. I accepted his absences as a normal thing in my life."[1]

Children can and do accept almost anything as normal, but only if they are allowed to do so. Rhena's ability to adjust tells us a great deal about the atmosphere of equanimity that her mother must have created in the home and her acceptance that the demands of the hospital were supreme.

She still cannot have realized, however, that they would remain so for the rest of Schweitzer's life. Neither in Africa nor in Europe was there to be any escape. From now on his life was to be an alternation between physical work at Lambarene and fund-raising in Europe—with only one departure from the routine, when he went briefly to the United States after the Second World War.

Just beginning, and henceforward increasing to an almost monotonous flow, was the stream of honors which the world heaped upon him.

In the previous year he had been awarded the Universal Order of Human Merit at Geneva—"for the eminent services rendered by you to civilisation and humanity in the midst of the black peoples of Africa." This was his first award that had nothing to do with his academic achievements, but simply recognized his increasing fame as a humanitarian.

Another honor which had been offered him, but which he had had to refuse, was that of being the first recipient of an annual Goethe prize, also for Service to Humanity, which had just been inaugurated by Goethe's city—Frankfurt. The first presentation was made this year, 1927, on August 28, Goethe's birthday. Schweitzer had no hope of getting there, but he accepted the offer of the following year's prize.

Schweitzer was now fully in the world's eye. Wherever he went he was excitedly reported, not only for his hospital work but also—inevitably— for what he had been before and what he had given up to go to Africa. Whether or not he wished it, this was the story that brought money to the hospital; he had to make use of it or lose the income he so desperately needed to pay an increasing staff, to buy increasingly expensive drugs, and to feed and house an ever-increasing number of patients and their families.

Being in the world's eye he had another obligation—to be in himself the visible embodiment of Reverence for Life. He had set out to make his life his argument—he had mocked the Schopenhauers of this world for not living in accordance with their philosophy; now he was committed to making his argument unanswerable. The passion for what was true and serviceable, which had given him the strength for his merciless attacks on the flaws in philosophical and theological traditions, could hardly let him get away with any inconsistency in his own behavior.

Not that this was particularly difficult for him. Had there been any hypocrisy in him the strain would have been enormous, and doubtless the cracks would have shown. But he had been working on his own character since childhood, eliminating the bogus, finding his ideal in the depths of the natural man, and putting his truest impulses into action. "I am simply a man who does what is natural. The natural thing, however, is lovingkindness."[2] This was his true and tested belief.

The natural however is also other things—weariness, irritation, and in his case a continuing shyness, a fiery temper, and the need to be right. However vigorously he had molded himself, body and mind, to eliminate these accidental personal qualities and to let the basic loving-kindness through, he was, as he wrote in *Memoirs of Childhood and Youth,* "essentially as intolerable as ever."[3]

Before we go on then, let us look more closely at the self-portrait he gives us in that book, for it adds depth to the pictures we have from those who met him, on tour and at the hospital, in this last long stretch of his life. He is writing in his forty-ninth year, about his teens.

Between my fourteenth and sixteenth years I passed through an unpleasant phase of development, becoming an intolerable nuisance to everybody, especially to my father, through a passion for discussion. On everyone who met me in the street I wanted to inflict thoroughgoing and closely reasoned considerations on all the questions that were then being generally discussed, in order to expose the errors of the conventional views and get the correct view recognised and appreciated. The joy of seeking for what was true and serviceable had come upon me like a kind of intoxication, and every conversation in which I took part had to go back to fundamentals. . . .

The conviction that human progress is possible only if reasoned thought replaces mere opinion and absence of thought had seized hold of me, and its first manifestations made themselves felt in this stormy and disagreeable fashion.

However, this unpleasant fermentation worked itself off and left the wine clear, though I have remained essentially what I then became. I have always felt clearly that if I were to surrender my enthusiasm for the true and the serviceable, as recognized by means of thought, I should be surrendering my very self. I am, therefore, essentially as intolerable as ever, only I try as well as I can to reconcile that disposition with the claims of conventional manners, so as not to annoy other people. . . .

But how often do I inwardly rebel! How much I suffer from the way we spend so much of our time uselessly instead of talking in serious fashion about serious things, and getting to know each other well as hoping and believing, striving and suffering mortals! I often feel it to be absolutely wrong to sit like that with a mask on, so to say. Many a time I ask myself how far we can carry this good breeding without harm to our integrity.[4]

That was the picture from within. How did he appear to others? The acounts of people who met him in Europe show a quite extraordinary consistency. Even more unvarying are the letters he wrote, thousands of them; to friends, to the famous, to unknown contributors, to those who wrote for his advice. The biographer searching through this mass of material for the odd illuminating inconsistency, the flash of idiosyncrasy, is in for disappointment. The only striking thing is the contrast between the Schweitzer people met in the flesh, full of sparkling personality and resilient energy, and the Schweitzer of the letters, unrelaxed, a little formal, and generally complaining of weariness and a sense of mild desperation at the prospect of unending toil.

To record in detail the comings and goings of the next few years would be tedious in the extreme. Let us instead try to build up a picture of the man, his appearance, the sound of his voice, and the impression he made upon those who heard him, who escorted him, who went to visit him, who offered him hospitality. The exact dates are unimportant. He did not change from year to year; not at least until at last he began, much later than most, to grow old.

Even his clothes were always the same, and apparently everlasting. In Africa his outfit consisted of baggy trousers, white shirt, and a single clip-on bow tie which he took in his pocket on his way to formal occasions such as calling on government officials, to be donned at the last possible moment and removed directly the interview was over. In Europe he fetched out the black suit that the Günsbach tailor had made for him when he played in Barcelona before the King in 1905. His one and only hat went with him everywhere. At best, if someone suggested it was time he had a new one, he would examine it carefully and might concede that it needed a new band.

On one occasion Emmy Martin actually bought him a new hat, identical in style with the old, and left it on the hat stand in place of the old one. Schweitzer was going out to visit someone who had suffered a bereavement, and as he went to the door he had his mind fixed on understanding and sharing the loss, so that what he said might have some meaning. Absentmindedly he picked up the new hat, put it on, and went out. Mme Martin was triumphant. But when he came back he said, "This is not my hat. What have you done with my hat? I want it back." And he had it back.

All this, with his canvas bags and haversacks, seemed often to be a pose. People could not believe that there was not something perverse, an inverted flamboyance, about this ostentatious simplicity which was unaffected by time or circumstance. And certainly Schweitzer was not unaware of its effect. But the reasoning behind it was all of a piece. The money had been contributed for the hospital, not for him, and it was not his to spend. "Anything I spend on myself I can't spend on my Africans." His Lambarene trousers grew shorter and shorter as the bottoms frayed and he stitched them to a new level. And his shirts reached a condition in which observers could hardly tell which was darning and which was original material. He remained the canny peasant, whose grandmother had taught him to put the stalk of the apple in the fuel box and give the core to the pigs, who wrote his lists and letters on the backs of old envelopes, undid and preserved every piece of string, flattened every piece of used wrapping paper, straightened every used nail, and only for birthdays and similar celebrations allowed such luxuries as wine and butter on the menu at the hospital.

In a sense it was a demonstration. In Africa he was setting an example that was vital to the hospital, where waste was madness. In Europe he was flying a flag against the technological world of overconsumption, and when pressed could defend himself to some effect. He told a lady in America that his tie had been worn on ceremonial occasions by his father. She was astonished. "I know men," she said, "who have a hundred ties!" "Really?" asked Schweitzer. "For one neck?" The flag he flew was a true symbol of himself; to behave otherwise just because he was becoming notable would have been to be false to himself, to acknowledge that simplicity was not really important, that he was prepared to abandon it when it was no longer forced upon him. *"Je suis fidèle,"* he said.

And perhaps he needed his fidelity as a bulwark against the extraordinary tide of flattery which suddenly swept about him. He knew his strength came from his roots in the hills of Alsace, and his mind constantly returned there, even if his body could not, to draw fresh sap. His clothes and his habits were a statement that the traditions of his home were still strong within him. And though he often said he was a citizen of the world, he made it clear that he was also "a pine-tree of the Vosges,"[5] which would not change its characteristics, transplant it where you would.

As to the world's reactions to the way he looked, though he understood it, he was certainly not concerned about it. He was interested in his function, not in himself. Some part of the power of his personality and the effect he had on others must certainly be accounted for by the fact that he had had put himself at the disposal of something beyond himself. Such people present a paradoxical spectacle, in that their very self-abandonment enables them to be more themselves. They are not troubled, as others are, about their "images," so they inhibit themselves less and present themselves with greater force. In religious terms the experience of self-abandonment is expressed in a sermon which Schweitzer preached in 1905, the year of his decision to take up medicine, but which is appropriate to quote now, when we are trying to find clues to the mature personality which burst on the world at this time of 1927–28.

> To content oneself with becoming small; that is the only salvation and liberation. To work in the world as such asking nothing of it, or of men, not even recognition, that is true happiness. . . . There are things which one cannot do without Jesus. Without Him one cannot attain to that higher innocence—unless we look to Him in the disappointments of life, and seek in Him the strength to be childlike and small in that higher sense. . . .
> Whoever has gone through the world of smallness has left the empire of this world to enter into the Kingdom of God. He has gone over the border as one goes over the border in a dark forest—without taking

Marie Woytt-Secretan, Strasbourg

18. The chicken-house surgery.

20. View upriver from Andende.

Marie Woytt-Secretan, Strasbourg

19. The Andende settlement. The mission building and the Schweitzers' house on the top of the hill, the hospital at the foot.

Marie Woytt-Secretan, Strasbourg

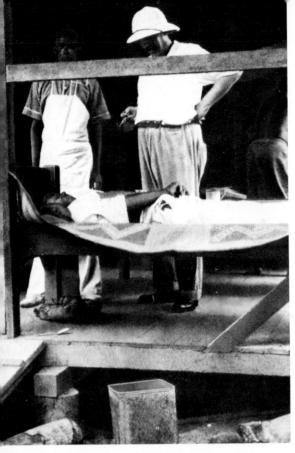

21. A ward in the new hospital.
Marie Woytt-Secretan, Strasbourg

22. Schweitzer treats an ulcer.
Marie Woytt-Secretan, Strasbourg

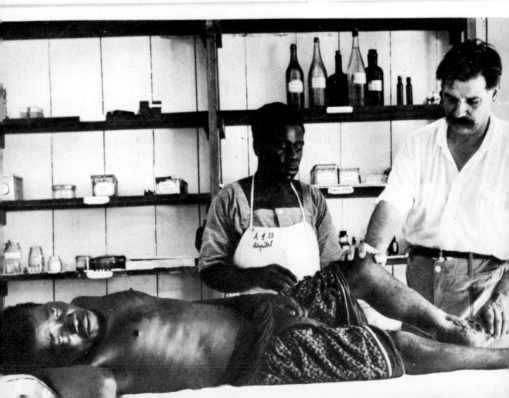

23. Schweitzer the foreman.

24. Patients live as they do in their own villages.

25. Left: Schweitzer in his fifties.
Marie Woytt-Secretan, Strasbourg

27. Right: Ground plan of the hospital in 1954.
Marie Woytt-Secretan, Strasbourg

26. Below: In the operating room.
Clara Urquhart

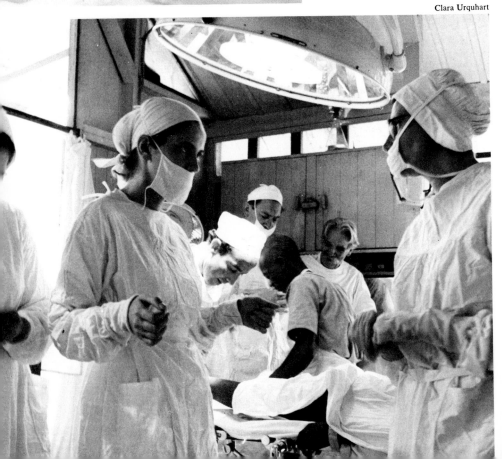

OF DR. ALBERT SCHWEITZER AT LAMBARÉNÉ

French Equatorial Africa

GABON

THE HOSPITAL, THE PLANTATION
AND THE LEPER VILLAGE

The Hospital has beds for 350 patients. The leper village has accomodations for 250 lepers. Two lepers occupy a room and a kitchen. The leper village was completed in June 1955.

The large trees are Kapocks which serve as lightning conductors.

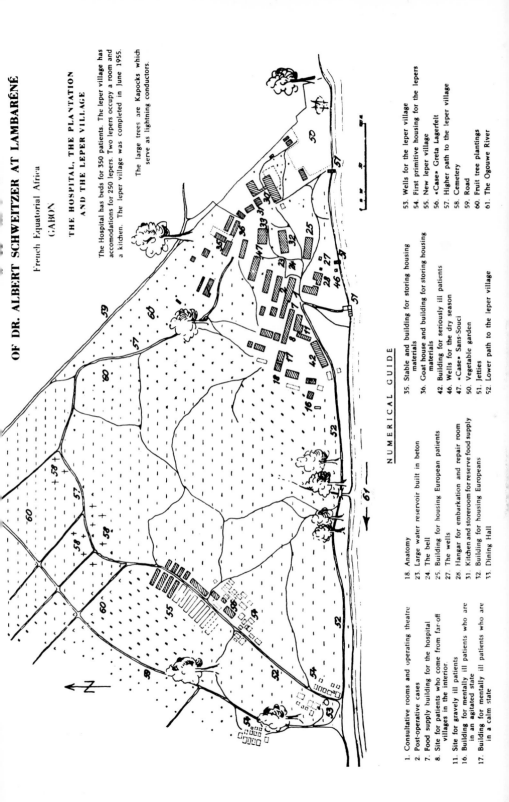

NUMERICAL GUIDE

1. Consultative rooms and operating theatre
2. Post-operative cases
7. Food supply building for the hospital
8. Site for patients who come from far-off villages in the interior.
11. Site for gravely ill patients
16. Building for mentally ill patients who are in an agitated state
17. Building for mentally ill patients who are in a calm state

18. Anatomy
23. Large water reservoir built in beton
24. The bell
25. Building for housing European patients
27. The wells
28. Hangar for embarkation and repair room
31. Kitchen and storeroom for reserve food supply
32. Building for housing Europeans
33. Dining Hall

35. Stable and building for storing housing materials
36. Goat house and building for storing housing materials
42. Building for seriously ill patients
46. Wells for the dry season
47. «Case» Sans-Souci
50. Vegetable garden
51. Jetties
52. Lower path to the leper village

53. Wells for the leper village
54. First primitive housing for the lepers
55. New leper village
56. «Case» Greta Lagerfelt
57. Higher path to the leper village
58. Cemetery
59. Road
60. Fruit tree plantings
61. The Ogouwe River

28. The working end of Schweitzer's room.

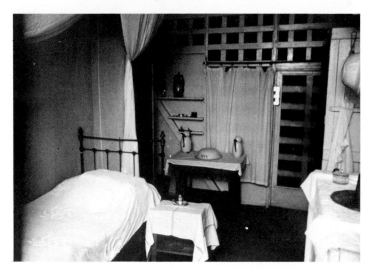

29. The sleeping end of Schweitzer's room.

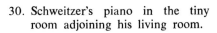

30. Schweitzer's piano in the tiny room adjoining his living room.

Clara Urquhart

31. One of his pet antelopes uses
Schweitzer's arm as a saltlick.

32. A family walk with his daughter Rhena, her
husband, and their four children.

Marie Woytt-Secretan, Strasbourg

33. Schweitzer besieged by autograph hunters.

34. The graves of Schweitzer and Hélène, Lambarene.

note of it. The way remains the same, the surrounding things the same, and only gradually does he realise that whilst everything is familiar it is different, that life is the same and yet not the same because of the clarity which lights up in him, and because of the peace and the strength which have taken possession of him because he is small and has finished with himself.[6]

This is not the false humility of the man who pretends he is unimportant. It is the ability to see oneself in perspective, judging oneself by the importance of the work one has to do, and be thrown neither to one side nor the other by the waves of popular hysteria. It amused him very much to find himself "as famous as a prize-fighter"; or perhaps not quite as famous, for he also loved to tell the story of the autograph hunter who said to him, "Now I've got three Albert Schweitzers I can swap them for one Max Schmeling." Wherever he went he might have been entertained, had he so wished, by the rich and the famous, by distinguished citizens and personality hunters who would have made much of him. In fact he often left his arrangements to the last moment, and trusted to luck to find a bed.

After he had spent two hard days in London, with rehearsals and recitals at St. Margaret's, Westminster, and St. Paul's, not to mention an impromptu talk to the Choir School, the wife of his organ assistant, Mr. Ashby, discovered that he had no plans for food or lodging that night. The Ashbys gave him supper and a bed, and their Putney home became his *pied à terre* in London for years thereafter.

In Amsterdam a widow, Mrs. Obermann, heard about Schweitzer in 1927, and with the help of friends made a great effort, collected a thousand guilders in a week, and sent them to Basel to a Mr. Baur, who acted as Schweitzer's collecting agent. Schweitzer wrote his thanks, and in his letter said that he would seek out Mrs. Obermann next time he was in Rotterdam and shake her hand personally. He came in 1928, to lecture in a church, and Mrs. Obermann managed to get a seat, though the church was packed to overflowing and mounted police were on hand to control the hundreds who were turned away. But she heard nothing from Schweitzer. She had not really expected to do so.

Throughout the introductions, while he waited to speak, she watched him sitting quietly "like a heap of tiredness." His turn came and he rose. His burly form had filled out now, and he was positively portly; though his face was extraordinarily young for a man of fifty-three, and his hair sprang dark and uncontrollable as ever. His arms hung loosely by his side, totally relaxed, in his characteristic pose, heavy and without grace, a peasant stance. He began quietly, in a voice which was unexpectedly high-pitched for such a big man—a pitch which he may have learned in order to overcome the abominable acoustics of churches and church halls.

"People often ask me, why did you go to Africa?" There was a long pause. He seemed to be brooding. The silence held through the packed church. Into the silence, slowly: *"Weil mein Meister es mir gesagt hat"*—"Because my master told me to." With its timing, its simplicity, its sincerity, the statement was one of those that makes an audience's skin prickle. Then, as he often did, he spoke of Africa as Lazarus, the beggar at the table of the rich man that was Europe. Whatever else the speech was, this was great oratory, a control of the audience coming from the personality but also learned in the schoolroom and the pulpit. American journalists in Lambarene in later years reported that Schweitzer's simple Bible readings after the evening meal outdid Billy Graham in their ability to grip an audience. A professional in all things, he had mastered his technique until it could be forgotten and the man himself was revealed.

The evening ended and Mrs. Obermann went home. There was a telephone call: "Did you receive my letter?" No, she hadn't. "I would like to take a meal with you tomorrow." So began a long friendship, of a kind which was repeated in numberless cities and towns of Europe.

On one occasion when he arrived, Mrs. Obermann's house was already full of relatives and friends, and she suggested a nearby hotel. "Haven't you a seamen's home here?" he asked. She happened to be on the committee of the seamen's home, and he picked up the haversack in which he carried his belongings and walked there to find a bed. Next morning he reported that he had enjoyed it very much because of the view.

Another time he had traveled all night and had rehearsed in the morning for an organ concert in the evening. These rehearsals were exhaustive and exhausting. Schweitzer would find an organ-playing friend to play the piece in question while he stumped about the church checking the effect of the different stops in different parts of the church. Having decided upon the ideal registration to use for the concert, he then began his own rehearsal. After he rehearsed he went back to Mrs. Obermann's house and lay down to rest. His hostess told her children to be particularly quiet when they came back from school for their lunch. When he got up Schweitzer asked where the children were—had they stayed at school? When he heard that they had been in the house but had kept quiet on his behalf: "If you ever again tell your children to be quiet just for me, I'll buy each one of them a trumpet."

His consideration had its limitations. When he really needed something he had no hesitation in asking for it—and one thing he always needed was a companion. A part of his shyness that he never lost was a real reluctance to go into a room alone. Whenever he visited Paris, for example, he would ring the Herrenschmidt household and demand that Adèle's younger sister (for Adèle had died in 1923) should drop everything and steer him around the city for two or three days. Did she ever refuse? "He was not a man one said no to," says her daughter. But did she not resent it?

"No, she loved it." He had a way of dominating women that many of them adored. It was done with charm and warmth; his manner of giving all his attention to his companion of the moment made it seem a compliment and a privilege. And even when he was ordering people about it was with a sort of attractive gruffness, like a terrier.

For the occasions when his displeasure was provoked (and such occasions were not infrequent in a man so sure of his own rightness and with so much of the teacher in him) he had learned a way of expressing it which took away much of the sting. His threat to Mrs. Obermann to buy all the children trumpets was typical. Another instance: he hated to see men wear shorts—he thought them undignified. So he would say to someone who failed or refused to do what he thought best: "If you don't do what I say I'll come out wearing shorts tomorrow."[7]

His biographer, George Seaver, whose book was published in 1948, gives many descriptions of encounters with Schweitzer, often from firsthand sources. After writing of the effect of the lectures he gave in England in 1928, Seaver goes on:

> Even more striking was the "terrific impact" of his presence within doors—a veritable tornado—with a riot of people surging round him; secretaries with their typewriters relegated to the bathroom and stairs; important and importunate callers, with whom he had light-heartedly made appointments and had forgotten all about, demanding interviews,—their indignation melting, when admitted eventually, "like wax in the sun." And when before his departure, itself an uproarious occasion, Miss Royden[8] tried to express in halting French their gratitude for his visit and the "honour" that she and her household felt in entertaining him as their guest, the Doctor, gravely shocked, drew her aside and besought her never to use such a word as that, *"parce que ce n'est pas convenable parmi les chrétiens."*[9]

Another encounter:

> So moved was Mr. Hudson Shaw by an address on Lambarene given by the doctor to a meeting of which he was chairman that, without a thought, he cast his gold watch into the collection. Remembering later that the watch, precious though it was to him, was of old-fashioned make and probably worth not more than the value of its gold, he offered to "ransom" it for a much larger sum. Somewhat to his surprise, Dr. Schweitzer asked if he might keep the watch for a few days longer. It was soon returned, but this time with an inscription: "Rev. Hudson Shaw et Dr Albert Schweitzer—fratres. 21/5/28." The considerate thoughtfulness of this gesture was noted by Miss Royden as characteristic of the "quality of perfection—and I should add, of exquisite care—that gives a grace and fitness to all he says and does—

trifles in themselves perhaps—but not trifles to those to whom beauty is as precious as strength."[10]

A singer, Clara Faisst, who had asked Schweitzer to hear her sing, wrote, "I have never been listened to as by you. . . . I felt your reviving force."

Yet during these outpourings of energy, physical and psychic (for to listen as he evidently listened to Clara Faisst demands the energy of great concentration), it seems that hardly anybody actually saw him tired; generally he easily outlasted his companions, snatching his rest as and when he could, curled up in a wooden-seated third-class compartment or stretched across a couple of hard chairs.* "He was the easiest of visitors to entertain," wrote Mrs. Ashby, "but a tyrant to work with; indefatigable himself, he would work others to exhaustion; and I remember his good-tempered but dismayed surprise when I told him so!"

Only the letters, with their constant and increasing complaint of weariness, provided the curious counterpoint. One wonders whether this became a more or less automatic ploy to excuse himself for the fact that he was so often late in replying; for the mountain of mail was now swelled by dozens of letters a week, from all over the world, asking Schweitzer to solve the writers' personal problems. He had become, as well as everything else, a guru.

It was a sad fate for one to whom, as he admitted in *Memories of Childhood and Youth*, letter-writing never came easy. Perhaps his epistolary style had been frozen forever by those dreadful post-Christmas sessions in his father's study as a boy, when he sat and envied his big sister's facile flow. Like thank-you letters, all his correspondence tended to fall into an unvarying mold: first the apology for lateness in writing, and the statement that he must be brief because his writer's cramp was troubling him; then a somewhat formal message, which, if on a philosophical or theological subject (and this would include life in general), would summarize the views set out in his books, sticking always to principles rather than individual cases: often a short rundown on the latest tasks awaiting him at the hospital, with a complaint about his weariness and the difficulty of getting things done; and a warm but formal conclusion. Even the signature was unrelaxed—amazing in a man who so studied to be natural in his relationships. Face to face he would ask people to address him by the intimate "*tu.*" But in letters, even to close friends, even to his daughter, he signed himself, not Bery, not Albert, not Papa, but the full and formal "Albert Schweitzer."

---

*The ability to relax, instantly and completely, in any circumstances is probably the secret of his stamina; and even when Mrs. Obermann saw him as a "heap of tiredness" he was more probably in a state of deeply concentrated relaxation.

Why was this? Was it that the written word was too permanent, and he too aware of the position he had taken up, to be able to unbend on paper? He did once say of Goethe, "If the poor man had known they would write down everything he said, he'd never have opened his mouth." Was he aware that he was moving into the same danger?

Or did he find it impossible to relate in a personal fashion unless the person were physically present? He certainly hated the telephone on the grounds that it was impossible to talk properly to someone whom one could not see.

Or were those Christmas letters so traumatic that the very thought of "letter writing" subconsciously and uncontrollably stiffened his mind, as it stiffened his fingers around the pen? Did the father image hang over him, saying, "You haven't written enough. Your aunt won't be satisfied with that." For he certainly often wrote much more than was strictly necessary; but it was wasted effort, for it said nothing new. Perhaps he was aware of this, for he did himself say that the colorful Gabonese stamps on the envelopes were the most interesting parts of his letters.

Königsfeld and Günsbach provided brief interludes from this Flying Dutchman existence. Here for short spells he could be with his daughter, and she with him. Hélène saw more of him, for she sometimes traveled with him and even did a little lecturing of her own.

During these breaks, Schweitzer worked on *The Mysticism of Paul the Apostle,* the book that had been so nearly ready when he first went to Africa fifteen years earlier. His retirement from the academic world had evidently not blunted his theological skill, for this is regarded by theologians as his finest achievement, though the subject is much less pertinent to the ordinary reader and never likely to attract the same attention as the books about Jesus.

But even Günsbach, even Königsfeld no longer provided complete sanctuary, for friends, acquaintances, correspondents, and now sightseers as well pursued him to every resting place; and a combination of his inherited hospitality and his own deliberate openness to all comers meant that nobody was ever turned away.

So when, in August, 1928, he went to Frankfurt to receive his Goethe prize, he had already decided what he would do with the money. He would build a house in Günsbach which could be his European headquarters and also serve as a guest house for his visitors. During the following year or two it was under construction, to his design. By his wish it was not set back, but opened directly onto the road, without even a pavement between; so that working at the window of the front room he could be close to the comings and goings of the villagers and chat with them as they passed by. It is this kind of touch (and there are many like it) that makes one ask oneself to what extent he as a person, shy as he was, *really* wanted things this way, and to what extent it was a demonstration of a conviction. The only way I find I can answer this is by saying that the conviction was as much a part of him as his shyness; by his own reckoning a more important part, because it was the product, as he always insisted, of thought, whereas shyness was an accident of inheritance. This is what he meant when he wrote to Professor John Regester in 1931: "I only understand myself from the philosophical point of view." He had dug his philosophy out of the depths of himself: now he molded everything about him to his philosophy.

The speech he made at the presentation of the Goethe prize is inevitably concerned with this interlocking of thought and life, for it was with Goethe's help that he first weaned himself away from the elaborate fairy-tales of speculative philosophy and on to the "simple, homely nature philosophy," which "leaves the world and nature as they are and compels man to find his place in them."[11] The speech, with its characteristic title "My Debt to Goethe," is Schweitzer's first public acknowledgment of the man whom he used to call "my father in thought." It describes how his admiration had developed into something like a personal relationship; how Goethe's example had strengthened him whenever practical tasks had seemed likely to overwhelm intellectual ones, as a curate, as a medical student, and recently as a building laborer. For Goethe too had lived by "the union of practical work with intellectual activity."[12] And when in Africa Schweitzer had been compelled to leave his medical work to others while he superintended the clearing of the jungle for the new hospital, "I thought, whenever I got reduced to despair, how Goethe had devised for the final activities of his Faust the task of winning from the sea land on which men could live and feed themselves. And thus Goethe stood by my side in the swampy forest as my smiling comforter, and the man who really understood."[13]

On the surface there were enormous differences between Goethe, the temperamental, many-sided creative genius, and Schweitzer, the single-minded ethical teacher. Werner Picht, who knew Schweitzer well, makes the most of these differences in his book *The Life and Thought of Albert Schweitzer.*

> The expansiveness of Goethe's nature stands against the homogeneity of Schweitzer's. Into a ripe old age Goethe still remained open to all possibilities of human activity, whereas from his earliest youth Schweitzer's way of life was already determined. Goethe added ring after ring to his personality like a growing tree, Schweitzer's nature is more that of the solid monolith. . . . For Goethe the all-important thing was to give permanency to the moment . . . for Schweitzer the meaning of life lies in ceaseless ethical activity. . . . The sensuality which combines Goethe rhapsodically with nature "in all her glory" is

not for him. For Schweitzer thought is the legitimate path to knowledge. Goethe attaches great importance to intuition. Schweitzer abstracts where Goethe keeps to the concrete.[14]

Rash though it may be to disagree with so fine a thinker as Picht, and one who actually knew Schweitzer, I feel certain that he undervalues the intuitive in Schweitzer. Schweitzer did, I am convinced, experience that rhapsodical sensuality, combining him with nature: only he did not find it enough. He had seen also nature's absurd cruelty in Africa, and that made a great deal of difference. "Nobody really knows me," he said, "who has not seen me in Africa." He was speaking of himself as a man of action rather than intellect, but also as a man in the midst of nature rather than in the midst of civilization. Africa's harsh indifference and man's insanity in the war had convinced him that the rhapsody needed directing. Indeed I believe it was precisely this tension, between the rhapsody and the despair, that forced him to think his way to his conclusions and that provided the motive force for his life.

So there was a genuine community of souls between Goethe and Schweitzer, though Schweitzer's style is the more formal and controlled. And the crucial link lies in what Schweitzer said, in 1932, speaking at Manchester University on "The Philosophical Development of Goethe": "With him thought and conduct were one, and that is the best thing one can say of any thinker."

Although he spent the Goethe prize on his Günsbach house, he felt badly about taking money out of Germany at a time when Germany needed every mark she could get for reconstruction and for the help of the crippled and widowed. So all the money he earned at this time from his concerts and lectures in Germany went not into the Lambarene fund but instead to German charities, until the full value of the prize had been equaled. And indeed throughout his life Schweitzer would often divert his takings to some other cause that he felt was especially needy, rather than to his hospital. His sense of justice was troubled by the feeling that the hospital enjoyed an unfair advantage in the ease with which he could fill churches and halls, and with them the hospital coffers. This was one of the reasons, not often understood, why the hospital remained simple when one might have expected it to be able to grow wealthy and elaborate. Schweitzer wished it so, certainly, on principle. But there was no vast fund lying idle, as has been alleged. The surplus was quietly distributed elsewhere.

In 1929, Schweitzer was fifty-four. A Leipzig publisher by the name of Felix Meiner decided that this was an appropriate age for him to embark on his autobiography. Schweitzer did not agree. A letter from Schweitzer to Meiner, on the latter's seventieth birthday in 1953, lets us into the genesis of the book:

> If you had not forced me to write *Aus meinem Leben und Denken* [Out of My Life and Thought] I never would have thought of it. . . .
> If you dear friend, had not enjoyed Oskar Kraus's co-operation, I doubt whether you would have succeeded. I did not like the whole thing, because at the age of 54 years I believed I was still too young to write a report of my life. An old clergyman in Strasbourg had stopped me in the street: "What have I been told, Albert, that you are writing your life already? That is a symptom of vanity. A man should do that only after his 70th birthday. I want you to hear this from me. Don't be offended." He spoke these words and left me. I did not think he was wrong, but it so happened that Mr. Felix Meiner thought differently.[15]

The book was commissioned, and Schweitzer wrote it the following year at Lambarene. But though he thought fifty-four was too young for an autobiography, he evidently felt it was time to think about who was to succeed him when he retired. Knowing as we do that he went on for another thirty-six years and that the succession was unclear to the very end, it seems odd to discover that he appointed a successor as far back as this—but in fact he did.

He was a young Swiss doctor, the son of a pastor, and his name was Erich Dölken. "Years before," wrote Schweitzer in one of his bulletins, "he had resolved to devote himself to my Hospital, not for a time only, but permanently."[16] But Dölken died before even reaching Lambarene. On the ship going to Africa, he was found dead in his cabin one morning—presumably from a heart attack—and was buried at Grand Bassam. It was the first of several abortive attempts to find the right successor.

One wonders what would have happened had Dölken lived. Would Schweitzer in fact have retired? Or would Dölken have been content to work as his assistant all those thirty-six years till his death before taking over? Or would the long haul finally have proved too much for Dölken? Would he have lasted just so long (as many others did), and then, through sickness or clash of temperament, the need to be his own master or the need to further his career, have moved on—back to Europe, or away to found a hospital of his own in some other unhealthy part of the world?

Dölken had been due in Lambarene in the autumn. Schweitzer was booked to return there on the next sailing of the same ship, arriving at Christmas, and for months ahead was superintending the fresh supplies he would take with him. We have a photograph which shows the room in the Rue des Greniers in Strasbourg, where the preparations went on. Here volunteers packed the cases, made by other volunteers, with drugs, rubber gloves, operating gowns, mosquito netting, sheets, blankets, etc., etc.,

etc., which had been bought, transported, stitched, hemmed, or otherwise contributed by hosts of yet other volunteers. It reminds us of something easily forgotten about this particular hospital—that the whole back-up organization, which in other cases would be provided by some mission society or some government department, had to be created and supported by Schweitzer alone. A multitude of friends and friends of friends gave up time to help; and among these a few key figures, honorary secretaries, honorary treasurers, honorary odd-job men of all sorts, unsung but beyond value for their industry and reliability, worked for years on end to keep the supplies flowing. But finally it was Schweitzer's responsibility and no one else's that everything needed on the Ogowe was thought of, obtained, and dispatched. Doctors, nurses, and patients must all have what they needed . . . and even the patients' families must be housed and fed, which is not a usual hospital facility.

This time when Schweitzer sailed, Hélène came with him, leaving Rhena behind with friends. The decision had not been easily reached, for Hélène's health was still far from perfect and they both knew all too well how merciless that climate could be to the weak. But simply to see the new hospital, to have that share at least in the work she had helped to start, that was her desire and her right.

With them on the ship went a Dr. Ann Schmitz and a trained nurse-cum-bacteriologist, Marie Secretan, the latter charged particularly with the care of Hélène on the voyage and at Lambarene. Marie Secretan's account of that journey makes intriguing reading:

> I had been told that this journey was dreadfully tedious, but we very soon discovered that no one who travels with Dr. Schweitzer can be bored. A bundle of proofs of his book, *The Mysticism of St. Paul,* which were awaiting correction, made the 22 hours seem quite short. . . . Then came the voyage—my first! . . . People had talked about the tedium of a three-weeks' voyage, but here too Dr. Schweitzer provided a way to make the time pass. He wrote while on board the final chapter of *The Mysticism of St. Paul,* and Frl. Schmitz and I provided him with two copies of it, in case the one sent to the printer should get lost. That also made the time pass very quickly.[17]

What kind of man is it who can prevail upon two healthy young women to check proofs and make copies of chapters of deep theology, amid the booming racket of an express train and the heaving and lurching of a coastal steamer, and make them feel he has done them a good turn?

Hélène too wrote about the return to Africa and her joy at seeing Lambarene again and the new hospital. What she does not mention is that on the voyage her tubercular condition flared up again, with a high fever. After so many years of waiting to come back and work at her husband's side this was a devastating blow—a sad indication that her full health was never likely to return. Long discussions took place on the ship as to whether she should continue the journey or whether she and Marie Secretan should transfer to a liner returning to Europe. Such a capitulation to weakness, however, was not in Hélène's nature, and she went on. They reached Port-Gentil on Christmas Eve, 1929. Quite unexpectedly, Mathilde Kottmann appeared with the motorboat in which she had come down river from the hospital to smooth over the customs formalities and organize the transfer of the 128 packing cases to the special tug she had hired. So Schweitzer was able to come upriver with the rest of them, instead of having to stay on the coast to deal with the paperwork and wait for the riverboat's next sailing. He spent Christmas Day chugging up the Ogowe and writing the preface to the St. Paul book. His last major book was finished.

At Lambarene there was further evidence of smooth and efficient planning. A timber merchant had lent a motor lighter to take the cases to the hospital. Another had offered the services of twenty of his African employees for the loadings. The barely completed cluster of huts which Schweitzer left behind had in the past two and a half years been completed to his specifications and had become a well-oiled medical machine, housing and treating between 250 and 300 patients. The staff now, including the African orderlies, the cooks, the washing and mending women, and the people who crushed the palm nuts for their oil, numbered about thirty-five. Among them, once more, was Joseph: the timber trade had let him down again. When Hélène had worked there, thirteen years previously, she, Joseph, and Schweitzer were more or less the entire personnel.

21

LIFE AT THE HOSPITAL
1929–1932

FROM his comment soon after arrival that the management and discipline were better than when he left,[1] it is evident that so far as the medical side was concerned his staff was perfectly capable of running the hospital without him, and that they could also organize the building and the garden maintenance that he had left in their care.

What they could not do was give the place the particular stamp that he gave it. Nor did they have to raise money for it, nor organize supplies, nor take responsibility for additional building. And this, it was instantly apparent, was already necessary.

The particular need was for a new mental ward, for the original one had had to be used for dysentery patients. Such a ward must be strong enough to restrain the mental patients during their violent disturbances, yet not too uncomfortably restrictive at other times. Pencil and hammer in hand, blue notebook with its string-threaded leaves in one hip pocket and folding rule sticking out of the other, Schweitzer set about it—and about any repairs and renovations that were required.

Though he still did a certain amount of doctoring, the hospital was now so complex that general supervision and administration, added to his building work and the writing of his autobiography, amounted to a full-time task. As time went on there were always improvements to be made—a big new building with partitions so that each family could have privacy from the others—a cement reservoir to collect rainwater from the roofs—all of them built with the same kind of laborious effort that had raised the main part of the hospital.

But the more he built, the more the patients came. Demand for treatment always exceeded supply. The spirit of mercy became indistinguishable from the struggle to keep abreast of the situation. Any romance that might be left was liable to disappear beneath the weight of what he called "the prose of Africa." It was vital that he preserve those moments when,

331

in philosophical work, in music, and in memory, his mind returned to the rich soil of the country and culture that had bred him and drew from it the fresh sap he needed.

At the same time the peasant in him also needed the manual labor, the challenge of physical mastery, without which he found the intellectual world meaningless. Though he constantly sought sympathy—and received it—for the way in which practical details kept him from his desk until deep into the night, he once confessed, in a quiet moment many years later, that he was unable to settle down to writing unless he had first done a hard day's work; that whether or not the work was needed, he needed the work. Since his university days work had always been a necessity—almost a drug. To wake each morning with the knowledge that the day held too much was the only way he knew how to live. Grumble though he might, his complaints were like those of a dedicated mother about her children; the tasks which were his burden were also his fulfillment.

At this time the fulfillment was great. The hospital was in that happy stage when a young, expanding project is full of life and growth. When Dr. Nessmann left in 1926 he had said it was like leaving paradise—not because the humidity was 90 percent and the place full of crippled, half-starved, desperately sick people—but because of the spirit of hope, cooperation, and achievement in face of odds. However great the contributions of others, this kind of atmosphere is always the creation of the leader of the enterprise; and perhaps it is the most satisfying creation of all.

For Hélène however it was too much, and at Easter she had to go home. She had been able to do no work, and for much of the time her weakness had forced her to remain sitting on the balcony of her room watching the activity go on around her. Finally, to her bitter regret, she had to acknowledge defeat. She said good-bye to the hospital, her husband, and the brisk women who could work with him in that climate and set off on the long voyage to Europe, health, and loneliness.

But at least she had seen and lived in the new hospital, and now when news came she could visualize and understand it. She knew the effort each task represented, she knew the feel of the dawn and the dusk, the routine of the day.

From that time till Schweitzer's death the routine scarcely varied. With days always the same length there was no change even from season to season. Doctors and nurses came and went, the hospital grew, medicines improved, but the long and detailed description Schweitzer sent to his supporters in 1936 of "A Day at the Hospital" can stand as a pattern for all the days from 1931 onward. This historic document is reproduced as Appendix A, and is the most complete and authentic account of the hospital's activities that we possess, and one which incidentally answers a great many questions, misapprehensions, and criticisms about the way it was run.

Schweitzer's own day began with a little Bach on the battered piano in the smaller room next to his own small room and a shave in cold water on the veranda, with a small mirror hung on a nail in one of the beams. After the day's work and the evening meal, when the oil lamps had gone their separate ways from the dining room through the rustling darkness to the various rooms, Schweitzer's own lamp sat in his window while he played again, and then wrote late into the night—letters, lists, and fresh pages of the projected third volume of *The Philosophy of Civilisation*. To prevent their being nibbled by ants or goats they were threaded on a piece of string and hung on nails above the windows, "like pheasants."

The work of healing was often complicated by the witchcraft, taboos, and superstition which still ruled the lives of the Gabonese. A patient's relatives, encouraged by a witch doctor, would attribute his sickness to poisoning by some enemy; and if the patient died it could trigger off a retaliatory murder. So the cause of every death had to be explained very carefully and convincingly to the relatives—though even then it was impossible to tell what random retribution might be exacted when the party got back to its village.

Within the confines of the hospital Schweitzer also had to act as headman and administrator of justice when one of the Africans' interminable legal arguments arose. Here is his account of one such occasion:

> In the night a patient had taken another man's canoe and gone out fishing by moonlight. The owner of the boat surprised him as he returned at dawn and demanded for the use of the canoe a large monetary compensation as well as all the fish he had caught. By the laws current among the natives, this was his actual right.
>
> The case was brought before me and, as often before, I had to act as judge. First I made known that on my land not native law, but the law of reason of the white man is in force and is proclaimed by my lips. Then I proceeded to examine the legal position. I established the fact that both men were at the same time right and wrong. "You are right," I said to the owner of the canoe, "because the other man ought to have asked for permission to use your boat. But you are wrong because you are careless and lazy. You were careless because you merely twisted the chain of your canoe round a palm-tree instead of fastening it with a padlock as you ought to dŏ here. By your carelessness you led this man into temptation to make use of your canoe. Of laziness you are guilty because you were asleep in your hut on this moonlit night instead of making use of the good opportunity for fishing."
>
> "But you," I said, turning to the other, "were in the wrong when

you took the boat without asking the owner's permission. You were in the right because you were not so lazy as he was and you did not want to let the moonlight night go by without making some use of it."

In view of the established legal usage, I then gave sentence that the man who went fishing must give a third of the fish to the owner as compensation, and might keep one-third for himself because he had taken the trouble to catch the fish. The remaining third I claimed for the Hospital, because the affair took place here and I had to waste my time adjusting the palaver.[2]

On Sunday only essential work was done. In the morning Schweitzer held a service, for the business of transporting everybody by canoe to the Andende mission would have been much too complicated; and besides, it satisfied a need in him.

At nine o'clock an orderly went around the hospital with a bell, summoning people to prayers. For the next half-hour Schweitzer sat playing on "the little harmonium," in the lane between the two main wards, under the shade of the wide roofs, while the people slowly came together; or else someone would play something appropriately religious on the gramophone. When eventually everyone had arrived Schweitzer began—not with a hymn, because nobody knew the hymns, and not with a prayer, because newcomers would not understand, but with a sermon. An interpreter on his left translated it sentence by sentence into Bendjabi, for the benefit of the tribes of the interior; another on his right translated into the Fang dialects; most patients knew one or the other, more or less.

> I cannot [he wrote] pretend that my hearers are as quiet as the faithful of a church in Europe. If anyone is in the habit of cooking their dinner on the spot where we are gathered, I let them get on with it. Mothers wash their children and comb their hair; men mend their nets, slung beneath the roofs; a native shamelessly lays his head in a companion's lap for a delousing. It is much better to let them go on than to interrupt the proceedings with remarks about discipline, which would have to be repeated each week, with this everchanging audience. Sheep and goats run bleating about the gathering. The weaverbirds that nest in the nearby trees make a deafening din. Even Mrs. Russell's two monkeys, let loose on Sundays, go through their tricks in the palm-trees and on the corrugated iron roofs, and finally snuggle up on their mistress's shoulders.[3]

In later years the Bendjabi language was replaced by Galoa, when less of the patients came from the wild interior tribes. And as literacy grew among the Africans Schweitzer provided hymn books and hymns were sung beautifully and with great enjoyment.

The sermons were rather different from those he had preached at St. Nicholas', Strasbourg, simple though even those were.

I restrict myself to the simplest experiences. Whatever my point of departure, I always come back to the central idea; letting oneself be seized by Christ. So even if someone only hears me once he has at least a hint of what it means to be a Christian.

I try to be as concrete as possible. No vague generalisations to explain, for example, Peter's question to Jesus: "How many times should I forgive my brother? Should it be seven times?" (Matthew 18/21). I talk to my people with complete realism, and I use everyday incidents to illustrate the meaning of forgiving seven times in a single day. This is how I recently tackled it:

"One morning, you have just got up, and you leave your hut. Coming towards you you see a man whom everybody thinks is a scoundrel. He does you an injury. You remember that Jesus has said that one should forgive; you keep quiet instead of starting an argument.

"Next your neighbour's goat eats the bananas you were keeping for your dinner. Instead of seeking a quarrel with him, you merely tell him what his goat has done and that it would be fair if he replaced your bananas. But if he contests this and pretends that it wasn't his goat, you go on your way peacefully and you reflect that the Almighty has provided so many bananas on your plantation that it's not worth the trouble of starting a fight over the odd bunch. . . ."

After another four misadventures evening comes and, "You want to go fishing but you discover that your canoe has disappeared. Someone has gone off in it to do his own fishing. Angrily you hide yourself behind a tree to await him, and you promise yourself that when he gets back you'll seize his fish, you'll make a complaint against him and make him pay a fair compensation. But while you lie in wait, your heart starts to speak. It keeps repeating to you the words of Jesus: 'God cannot forgive us our sins if we do not forgive each others'.' You have to wait so long that the Lord Jesus once more wins the victory. When the other fellow comes back at the crack of dawn, and stands all confused when he sees you step out from behind your tree, you don't start punching him, but tell him that the Lord Jesus forces you to forgive him; and you let him go. You do not even claim the fish which he has caught, unless he offers them of his own accord. But I think that he will give them to you, from sheer amazement that you haven't made a fuss.

"Then you go home, happy and proud that you have succeeded in forgiving seven times. But suppose that very day the Lord Jesus comes into your village; you introduce yourself to him, imagining that he will praise you before all the world for your good deeds. Not at all. He will tell you, as he told Peter, that seven times is still not enough—that one must forgive yet another seven times, and yet again, and a fourth time's seven times and plenty more times, if you also want God always to forgive you."[4]

Schweitzer, again and again confronted with the same indifference, the same negligence, the same thievish predilections, had ample opportunity to practice the limitless forgiveness he preached.

To complete the picture, the laughter must not be forgotten. Ali Silver, who spent nearly twenty years at the hospital, misses the fun more than anything else. Schweitzer's warm humor infected the whole place, and there was often plenty to laugh about in the absurdities of human or animal behavior. Almost anything could happen on the Ogowe, and Schweitzer treasured the comedies of life. From a collection of such incidents in the Günsbach Archives:

> My Uncle Charles was a great man, you know. He was a teacher at the Janson-de-Saylly College and much feared by his pupils. One day an African ran in to fetch me, because a white man had travelled up the river to visit me. That means a journey of three days! Flattered, I put on my Sunday jacket and went down to the landing stage, where the white man was waiting for me, surrounded by a crowd of gaping blacks. When he saw me in the distance he shouted, "Are you Albert Schweitzer?" I bowed. "Listen; your uncle is a rotten dung-heap. He failed me in my exam. So. . . ! I have only come here to tell you that." He turned round, clambered back on the motor-boat and left me standing there in my Sunday glory—and I laughed and laughed. . . ."[5]

Such a visit was a rare event. Mostly the comedy came from the hospital's own inhabitants, human and animal—the parrot that shouted "Get out of here!" to departing visitors; the lady who said, when Schweitzer mentioned a passage in one of St. Paul's Epistles, "In our village we don't read other people's mail"; and the local post office clerk who regularly ordered goods from Paris for people in his village, and when they arrived sent an official letter saying "Purchaser Deceased" so that nobody had to pay the bill. "That man," said Joseph, "is not stupid at all."

Such was a week at the Schweitzer hospital. Fifty-two such weeks in every year were what Schweitzer created on the banks of the Ogowe. The routine is something between that of a village, a hospital, and a farm; for it was really all three of these things, though for convenience's sake we must continue to call it a hospital.

One of the things that gave it its paradisical quality (though not everyone would have agreed) was the population of goats, antelope, cats, pelicans, monkeys, sheep, chickens, and dogs which shared Adoninalongo with the human beings. They added a touch of the Garden of Eden, for in that atmosphere of security the most diverse creatures played together.

The reason for the animals' presence were often practical enough. Some had been found wounded, nursed to health, and kept as pets. The chickens were there for eggs and for meat. And the goats for their manure, for their meat, and also because Schweitzer, anxious as much as anything to teach the local tribes how to feed themselves better, hoped to get milk from them. Milk was unknown on the Ogowe, because the tsetse fly killed the cows. Schweitzer unfortunately found that without a great deal of attention the goats suffered, often fatally, from mange. But he kept trying.

Alongside the practical reasons for keeping the animals however was of course the spirit of Reverence for Life. Even before he had hit upon the phrase he had felt that life without animals was only half life; in Alsace he had always had a dog, in Africa a selection of antelopes, and so forth. Now his natural feeling of the community of all life had become the central tenet of his philosophy, and the whole hospital was permeated by it. The animals were not merely used as a farmer uses his stock, though they were used. They were not merely loved as a lapdog is loved, though they were loved. They were respected. They had their inalienable place in the scheme of life. That was what made the difference. Attempts to pen them in always collapsed because patients, on their way to steal fruit or to steal the animals themselves, made short work of wire-netting enclosures. Besides, the patients' own animals, which came with the families, were quite uncontrollable, so the effort was scarcely worth it. When, later on, European visitors came to Lambarene and found the creatures roaming more or less unchecked through the hospital, their reservations were understandable. A goat in the wards of a European or American hospital might well seem out of place. We will look at the criticisms that then arose when we reach that part of the story. For the moment we are only concerned to see how the hospital developed and why it developed as it did.

Schweitzer's in fact was not the only hospital that looked more like a village. Dr. Clement Chesterman, for example, who was setting up a hospital in the Congo at about the same time, had also to face the fact that Africans could only be persuaded to come in for treatment if they were able to live there as they lived at home. They would not (and still often will not) be separated from their families. They would not (and still often will not) eat food cooked by anyone outside the family—for fear of poisoning. And the cooking had to be done outside the hut, in the traditional way. As recently as 1970, when African staff at the Schweitzer hospital were given new concrete homes with built-in kitchens, they refused to cook in them.

Late in life Schweitzer recalled that when he was planning his hospital two men from the Catholic Mission had said to him, "You must build a hospital here—but not up into the heavens, keep it close to the earth." He should not be credited with any exceptional foresight or insight. He built his hospital in the only way that supplies allowed or patients would accept. It cannot be emphasized too much that he never envisaged the size it would grow to, tiny though it still is compared with a big hospital in America or Europe. "I only meant to build a *small* hospital," he would say. And once—"It often seems to me as though I did it all half in a dream."[6] He simply wanted to be a doctor in the bush. He was forced to build a village because the Africans came in such numbers, families and all, and because their own villages were too impermanent for the setting up of clinics.

He was forced to grow vegetables, plant fruit trees, and keep livestock because otherwise his patients and their families starved. He was forced to organize a supply of doctors and nurses from Europe because the backwardness of the Gabonese made it impossible to find black staff who could even read. Lambarene, which even today is no larger than a sizable English village, is the Gabon's third largest town.

From the start—from the day when Joseph began to help in 1913— Schweitzer used all the local staff he could. He did not, it is true, set up a training course for Africans—"One man can only do so much"—and Schweitzer was primarily interested in teaching the Africans the elements of agriculture, handicrafts, and mutual help so they might become independent of the pressures of Western trade. Many thinking Africans today are coming around to a belief in the same priorities.

The only qualifications he could hope for in a population that had virtually no book learning were honesty and reliability. Africans who wanted to stay and help were given undemanding tasks at first, until it was clear whether or not they really had some firmness of intention. If this sounds patronizing, one can only point out that people's lives were at stake and Schweitzer did not feel like putting them in the hands of people who might decide to go fishing when an operation was due.

A number of black orderlies were already at work when Schweitzer returned in 1929, and through the following years they increased in number and responsibility. But he never had a black doctor there. Why? Because Schweitzer depended on volunteers—and no black doctor ever volunteered. The few who qualified in the Gabon stayed—understandably enough—in Libreville or headed for Paris. They felt no debt toward the ravaged tribes in the interior. Let the whites see to that.

Think then of Schweitzer as a headman in his village, a peasant on his farm, a superintendent in his hospital—all at the same time. He dispensed justice like a headman. He mended fences, dug drains, improvised outhouses, and tended the livestock like a farmer. He administered the hospital, saw to the welfare of the staff, planned for the future, authorized expenditure, took responsibility for treatment, like a superintendent. At important operations he was always present, day or night.

Indeed, he insisted that the whole staff should be ready for work at any hour, if work was needed. Suffering did not keep strict hours—nor could its alleviation. His own ear was the sharpest to hear the approach of a canoe in the night. His experience and instinct were often the quickest to diagnose trouble. Dr. Frank Catchpool, who worked with him in the 1950's said:

> He had a real understanding of when a man was sick, these critical moments in a doctor's career when he must decide to hold off treatment sometimes. When he was just causing the man more misery he would instinctively feel it. He could tell when a man was near death and he could tell—I can remember him ordering me to incise a big abscess sometimes when I thought I'd just wait another day. He'd say: "No, now, today, this minute, you must incise it today, no more delay." And he was right, every time. There would be a pint or two of pus in this man's leg—these big tropical abscesses.[7]

Whatever went on in the hospital, Schweitzer knew. As the number of doctors and nurses increased, the chances of emotional entanglement grew. The doctors were mostly young and vigorous, the nurses often young and pretty. The sun set at six P.M., and then little work could be done, there was nowhere to go, nothing to do to while away the time after dinner but to visit other people's rooms, talk, maybe play a gramophone. The place was as enclosed as a monastery, but for both sexes. The moon rose mistily above the palms, and love affairs, jealousies, gossip, and enmities were inevitable. The rooms might be mosquitoproof but they were far from soundproof; and though the sound of a gramophone can do a good deal to cover a whispered conversation, having to wind it up every few minutes makes for a somewhat piecemeal romance, and the love affairs (and hatreds) were mostly common knowledge.

Surprisingly, though, for a man so emotionally disciplined as Schweitzer, he was never censorious of other people's sexual indiscretions. Their lives were allowed privacy such as he wished for his own—so much so that when the irate father of one of the doctors demanded from Schweitzer confirmation and details of his son's liaison with a visitor to the hospital, he simply said, "You may tear me in pieces but I will tell you nothing."[8]

He did however dislike immodesty—he found it indecorous and possibly prejudicial to hospital discipline. Nurses were required to wear long dresses with high necks; and when a white woman patient received

Schweitzer in a nightgown of dramatic décolletage he instructed the nurses to find her something more Christian to wear.

This was a matter of taste however, not of moral condemnation. He never set himself up as any man's or woman's judge in matters of behavior. Only when passion interfered with the running of the hospital did he take action. And if the situation became so serious that those involved had to leave the hospital he would make all possible arrangements for them to start afresh elsewhere.

Otherwise, no judgments were made. Anyone who came for sanctuary was welcome and no questions were asked. A man who had been expelled from a mission for sexual misconduct stayed for years at the hospital, working in the garden. The only thing Schweitzer did require of anyone who stayed was that they undertook a share of the work, whatever their capacity—which was often not very great. But all could stay as long as they wished, and would be housed and fed.

As a result of this acceptance of all comers, Schweitzer was sometimes accused of being a hopeless judge of character. He was too naïve, it was said, to know whether people who came to him for sanctuary were genuinely desperate cases or confidence men looking for free board and lodging. The truth is that he did not care which they were. If that was naïve, he had always said he was not ashamed to be naïve.

In fact he knew something that the knowledgeable folk of this world do not know—that nobody can really tell the genuine from the bogus. The very need to abuse someone's confidence can often hide real desperation. A beggar whose only comfort is alcohol will never dare ask money for a drink—he will tell you he wants it to visit his sick mother. If you give him money and he spends it on liquor you have only yourself to blame for assuming you have the right to judge what he needs and whether that need is reprehensible or laudable. Nothing is more paternalistic than the view which is only slightly satirized in the cartoon of the well-dressed lady who says, "I never give food to tramps—they only eat it." Schweitzer would have nothing to do with such an attitude. He knew that the main reason for not judging others is that one can never be sure of being right. And he believed that people became trustworthy by being trusted. (Only persistent bitter experience and his responsibility for the hospital's survival forced him to become mistrustful toward the Africans, and even so he was constantly on the lookout for those whom he could trust, and to them he gave responsibility.) Combined with his lifelong refusal to pry into private lives, these considerations led him to make what many regarded as mistakes about the people he helped.

But he was careful enough about those accepted as his helpers. Applications came thick and fast from doctors and nurses, and their motives were by no means unmixed. Some wanted the cachet of Schweitzer's name to help them, after a few months at Lambarene, in their careers. Some were running away from failure or unhappiness at home—the thing Schweitzer had been accused of. Some simply wanted a romantic interlude in a humdrum life. Knowing the stresses not only of the work but of the confined life and the irritating climate, he could not give responsibility to anyone of an unstable temperament. "Idealists," as he said, "must be sober."[9] This, as much as considerations of language, accounts for the high proportion of Alsatian, Swiss, and Dutch names on the hospital records. These are races of low volatility. An equable temperament was as important as medical qualifications for his work, and his investigations before accepting new medical staff were suitably thorough.

Once accepted, such a person would receive the most meticulous instructions as to his requirements and his journey; his ticket would be arranged, and Schweitzer would write personally (and by hand—he never used a typewriter because the sound disturbed him and the mechanism came between him and his correspondent) to all the authorities whose approval was needed, to ease his passage. One of the recommendations to young doctors on the voyage out was that at ship's dances they should dance with the wallflowers—as Schweitzer had in his younger days.

Apart from the one or two faithful nurses—Mathilde Kottmann, Emma Haussknecht, Maria Lagendijk, who first went in 1938 and still works there, and later Ali Silver—the staff turnover was fairly rapid. Few people wanted to devote a lifetime to Lambarene. Few, for that matter, had the stamina to do so. Schweitzer, by nature a teacher, with autocracy bred into him from the Schillinger side, had autocracy thrust upon him in Africa, because nobody could match his experience of local conditions. He had, after all, gone there because he wanted to do things his own way. He had trained, studied, and observed, with all the formidable application of which he was capable, to become the complete bush doctor. He had designed the hospital himself and was personally responsible for its financial upkeep. So he had some excuse for claiming that he knew what he was doing, and little time for any arguing or explaining. The charge that he was an autocrat is true. The question is whether he was a good autocrat.

Dr. Mark Lauterburg, one of the few still living who worked with him in the early days, says (as do most people who worked there) that it took him a long time, a matter of months, before he fully realized why Schweitzer did things the way he did. One had to learn by experience that certain obvious "improvements" were in fact impractical; because of the climate, the behavior of the patients, or the distance from the source of supplies. To take the simplest thing—to maintain a supply of running water would have required a mechanical pump, and a pump meant fuel, spare parts, and a certain elementary understanding of and respect for machinery. Fuel was expensive—it had to be transported from Europe—and supplies were not guaranteed; a ship stranded, a world shortage, a war somewhere, and the flow would dry up, leaving the whole system useless. Spare parts were even less easily available. And every section of the system would be vulnerable to the ignorance and curiosity of tribesmen, who had never seen such a thing before and had no conception of its frailties. Better therefore an old-fashioned well and a hand pump one could rely on (though even that went wrong) than a complicated system that only worked some of the time.

Because running water was impractical, toilets had to be primitive—a hut for women, a hut for men; a hole in a piece of wood and a smell that pervaded the hospital when the wind was easterly. That was for the Europeans. The Africans simply used the bush, as they did in their villages. Visitors sometimes found this alarming, if not appalling, but the place was not designed for visitors; and what was the alternative? Such a system had served peasant communities for many centuries, and was entirely appropriate to this village. The huts were set on the outskirts of the clearing and were known as *"Hinter Indien"*—"Beyond India," a traditional German phrase for the end of the world. *Hinter Indien* became part of the legend of Lambarene. It was noted with some envy that Schweitzer, acute though all his other senses were, seemed quite oblivious to smell, but in fact this was not the case. He could smell flowers well enough, and perfume (which he disliked). He was simply able to ignore what he could not alter. Such conditions obviously necessitated careful attention to hygiene—but plenty of visitors to coastal resorts on the Mediterranean will confirm that few things are less hygienic than a flush toilet that has ceased to flush. The open hole is greatly to be preferred. And this was the principle on which many of Schweitzer's decisions were made. An electrocardiograph machine would be very nice but quite useless unless fully tropicalized against dust, humidity, and creeping things and accompanied by a technician who could service it. Better to perfect one's skills in diagnosing with the aid of a stethoscope, which would never go wrong.

Dr. Lauterburg remembers questioning Schweitzer's judgment on one point only—should he not have had an X-ray machine? Since Lauterburg was in Lambarene in the twenties, during the move from the old hospital to the new, the chances are that so complex a machine would have been beyond Schweitzer's pocket at the time, even if it had been technically feasible. When in fact Schweitzer was offered an X-ray machine in 1938, it was reluctantly and with very good reason that he refused it. As will be seen, he had a much more urgent use for the money. Apart from the X-ray machine, however, Dr. Lauterburg in the twenties like Dr. Catchpool in the fifties finally concluded that Schweitzer knew what he was doing. Here is Dr. Catchpool again:

I asked to introduce a new drug into the hospital for treatment of hookworm disease. I wasn't familiar with the drugs that he was using. I had been taught that these drugs were sort of out of date. Dr. Schweitzer asked me very sharply, he said: "What is this drug you want to use? Why do you want to use it? What advantages does it have over what I have been using with good effect over all these years? I know my drugs are toxic, but I have laid down exactly how they should be given, and we don't have toxic effects, because I have covered all of this with my patients, we don't allow this to happen." He said: "You know, I had a doctor who wanted to use a new drug for treatment of hookworm disease. I foolishly allowed him to do it, and we had three deaths. I have never forgiven myself for this." He said: "What proof do you have that this drug you want to use is efficient?" So I brought in the evidence. He said "Good, we shall do it." Then, later on, as he had a little bit more confidence in me, he made it quite clear that the medicine in the hospital should be practised in his hospital according to the way the doctors who were practicing medicine in the hospital at that time deemed they were able to best practice medicine. In other words, he said: "Whatever you want, tell me what you need, I'll get it for you. Whatever drugs you want, tell me what you want, we'll get them. You shall not want for any drug or any materials, or any instruments. You shall have everything you need." This he made quite plain to me. In this hospital we had all the facilities that we needed for doing even the most extraordinary work.[10]

The crucial thing was winning his confidence. The same point is made by Dr. Anna Wildikann, who worked at Lambarene before and during the Second World War:

Anyone who won his confidence had a free hand and could work independently. When new medicines were ordered, Dr. Schweitzer asked each of us if we had any special requirement. In the first week after my arrival in 1935, Dr. Schweitzer asked me if I needed any special medication. "Yes," I said, "I would very much like to have a new remedy for malformed bones which I have already used in Europe, but it is very expensive." His answer was: "I did not ask you about the cost, but about your wish. If the remedy is good, you shall have it."[11]

Schweitzer needed convincing that the new treatment, whatever it was, was not only new but better than the old, and would work not only in Europe but in Lambarene. Once convinced of that, he would move heaven and earth to get it. There is a story that he refused to use antibiotics. It is totally untrue. So familiar did antibiotics become at Lambarene that animals were named after them. But Schweitzer did refuse to allow young doctors, intoxicated with the success of the new wonder-drugs, to use them indiscriminately when there was not due cause. Sensational though they were, he saw no reason why they should be exempt from the law that, if overused, a drug will in the end produce an immunity to its action. "The old idiot is still living in the nineteenth century," some said. But the old idiot saw farther into the twentieth century than they did.

An illustration of the way in which Schweitzer gained a reputation for rejecting medical advance was the story of a visitor to the hospital (this was in the later years when visitors grew common) that he was seen pitching a load of drugs unopened into the river. The story gained wide circulation and Schweitzer, as was his custom, did not trouble to explain. The truth was however that on this occasion, as on several others, a consignment of drugs had been sent inadequately packed for the tropics and the contents had become useless. It is unlikely that these were drugs ordered by Schweitzer for he would have ensured that these were properly packed. But chemical companies would sometimes send quantities of surplus drugs to Schweitzer for tax deduction purposes and no special care was taken over their dispatch.

How keen he really was to find new solutions to medical problems emerges from an anecdote told by Dr. Ernest Bueding, who was working at the Pasteur Institute in Paris in 1934.[12] A new yellow fever vaccine had been discovered there but not fully tested for side-effects, when "a doctor from Colmar" telephoned for information about the new drug. On hearing of the possibility of side-effects he came to Paris the next day and insisted on being injected with the vaccine himself, despite strong warnings that this was unwise at the age of fifty-nine. Schweitzer, who of course had been recognized by this time, was very impatient when the institute hospitalized him for two days as a precaution. But he suffered no serious reactions and immediately put in an order for the vaccine.

Schweitzer, it is true, never liked technology for its own sake, and in this he was consistent from his youth onward. Claims that science could explain nature, when in fact all it did was to break it up into smaller pieces and give it new names, never impressed him. In this, too, he was ahead of the field. Physicists today recognize that every time they draw aside one veil they are faced by new mysteries; and Arthur Koestler recently described the education that young people receive today as "a package of information wrapped around a vacuum. . . . At the moment," he is quoted as saying, "we are before a splendid avenue of ignorance."[13]

As he grew older, Schweitzer liked the twentieth century less and less. He used his motorboats as little as possible, preferring a canoe paddled by lepers. It was good for the lepers to feel useful, and it was much more peaceful. He welcomed DDT at its first appearance and it was regularly employed in the operating theater, though he discouraged too widespread a use of it throughout the hospital, even when it might have simplified the nurses' work. It killed indiscriminately and did not, like antibiotics, specifically attack the carriers of disease. He would not have been at all happy, for example, about the wholesale destruction of ants. He was fond of ants, which he regarded as useful scavengers about the hospital; and he used to leave small pieces of food on his desk while he worked so that he could watch them crawl up the leg in a column and return beneath the floorboards with their booty; when the cat began to join in by sitting in wait for them and killing them with its paw, he protected them with a basket. He truly did love creatures simply for being alive, and refused to endanger anything, ants, mosquitoes, rats included, which did him and his hospital no obvious harm.

Inevitably such behavior seemed to some of his colleagues to be eccentric to the point of idiocy, so alien was it to everything they had been taught at medical school. There were battles which could only be ended by Schweitzer finally saying, "This is my hospital. While you are here you do as I say." Some doctors did not stay long enough to be convinced that Schweitzer's way worked. Others in the end decided that, against all their preconceptions, it did work. And they were prepared to let a few idiosyncracies go for the sake of the atmosphere of dedication and the obvious high success rate of the hospital.

One such idiosyncrasy was on the question of sun helmets. The warnings about sunstroke which Schweitzer had been given by old-timers on his first voyage out had been reinforced by cases within his own experience, and he was absolutely rigid about the need for his staff to wear something on their heads at all times. When people disputed this, on the grounds that they had survived in other parts of the tropics without hats and the pressure of a hat simply added to their discomfort in the humid heat, Schweitzer was adamant. He had known of cases, he said, where a few moments in the sun or a stray shaft through a hole in the roof had made people very ill. He was not going to let that happen in his hospital where he was responsible. And in the end his orders were nearly always obeyed.

It is true that the sun helmet is now almost obsolete, because it has been found that sunstroke does not automatically follow exposure. Except when in the open for long periods without shade, a covered head is now the exception rather than the rule on the Ogowe and no harm follows. Perhaps, as some believe, the climate has altered in the last fifty years. More probably it is a question of diet, for sunstroke affects the undernourished and we are better fed today. Or it is possible that Schweitzer was simply wrong, misled by incorrectly diagnosing the cases he came across; but this is most unlikely for he was rarely mistaken in his diagnosis.

When journalists began to visit him after 1950, men well experienced in the tropics, the sun helmet issue became an immediate cause of misunderstanding, for the first thing he did was to try to force headwear on them as well, thus branding himself a relic from nineteenth-century colonialism. This snap judgment was confirmed by his dislike of technology and his peasant ways and so the report grew that here was somebody who had retreated from progress into the jungle and had no understanding of the twentieth century—a well-meaning but irrelevant anachronism.

What, finally, was his real relationship with the Africans in his hospital? He had gone to Africa full of idealism. He had found himself in a region of greater poverty, disease, and backwardness than he had ever envisaged. He had suffered from the ingratitude and unreliability of those he came to help. He had seen other men lose patience with the blacks and take to cursing at them, and despite his own clear and compassionate analysis of the reasons why a tribesman could not and would not understand the Europeans' attitude to work, he too had often been driven to despair.

Now he had reached a kind of tolerant hopelessness toward them. Writing of them he used phrases that could be taken as very patronizing—*"Mes sauvages," "Mes primitifs."* Day after day the struggle was renewed to persuade them to take their treatment at the right time, in the right dosage; to discourage them from taking off their dressings to show their friends where the pain came out; to dissuade them from cooling their open sores in the infected river; to find help for the building work and the garden, and to keep them from drifting quietly away behind the bushes and disappearing. And day after day, at least some of the Africans defeated him. They failed to turn up for their medicine, they went for a swim, they consulted the witch doctor, they cut down a fruit tree for firewood; a lady being treated for gonorrhea spent a night entertaining a canoeful of gentlemen callers, themselves infected; and so on and so forth. In the end he was constantly shouting at them, he was calling them monkeys, and very occasionally he was hitting them.

A nurse who worked in Lambarene for two spells of over a year each, Trudi Bochsler, says that no one can judge Schweitzer who did not work at Lambarene for at least six months. The confinement, the climate, the endless frustrations and setbacks, the depredations of man and beast sooner or later take their toll and you are a different person from the one you thought you were. "If anyone who worked there for any length of time tells you that they never struck a native, they're lying," she says. She herself, a twenty-year-old idealist, finally struck a large African who was telling Schweitzer lies about her work. Schweitzer was horrified. "I never thought *you* would do that," he said.

Schweitzer himself horrified the great British journalist James Cameron, who visited Lambarene in 1953, by his violence of word and deed toward the Africans—though Cameron admits that a group of Africans he saw, who were supposed to be working, "moved with a deliberation I should scarcely have thought possible. It was like watching a slow-motion film! Sometimes work slowed down to a point where movement, if it existed, was imperceptible; it was like studying the hour-hand of a watch."[14]

Cameron was not the only visitor to be dismayed at finding this hero of so many uplifting articles and books shouting like a slave driver at his black crew and even sometimes laying a hand on them. The question is not, however, what James Cameron or any other brief visitor thought about it, but how the Africans themselves reacted. Few of the observers whose indignation was aroused on behalf of the humiliated blacks seem to have asked the victims for their views. Had they done so, the answers might not have been very reliable, for underprivileged people are not noted for confiding in rich inquisitive strangers. But if they had reached the truth it might have been very different from what they expected.

Schweitzer was a man for touching; he was not afraid of physical contact. And he could be impatient. He hit his young nephew for a mistake in Latin. He hit one of his nurses a considerable whack with a pick handle when she would not do things the way he told her to do them. The passion which in childhood made him strike his sister for not paying sufficient attention to their game was still there, however carefully held in check. His temper and his hand would flash out. A moment later, all would be over, and the swift reconciliation followed.

The Africans too were physical creatures, accustomed to physical expression of feelings. They understood the reasons for Schweitzer's impatience and they understood his way of expressing it. They knew that the shouting and the playful slap on the backside meant no ill will, and they knew something that educated Westerners, as prim about violence as their grandparents were about sex, have forgotten: that the ability to give or take blows without rancor is a mark of comradeship. A blow can only confidently be struck if no harm is intended. It is only when tension is high that it must be withheld, for then it would really matter.

The Africans knew too that the way he treated them had nothing to do with their blackness. His impatience, like his authoritarianism, was the same for everyone and it was only the visitors' own color consciousness that made them so uncomfortable. Clara Urquhart has an excellent story that when she was watching him supervise some Africans he grew so impatient with one that he said to her, "I should like to slap that fellow. I don't suppose I will, but if I should, just close your eyes and pretend I'm slapping a white man, and then you'll feel all right."

The understanding between Schweitzer and the Africans lay much too deep for penetration by those who came briefly to Lambarene. It was to help the blacks that he came to Africa, and kept coming—and the blacks knew it. They knew that they were secure in his heart, and he in theirs. Between such people, as between a long-married couple, small rows can flame and blow over and the underlying relationship is untouched. It is only with those we know less well that we must always be polite.

Schweitzer had no time for politeness. "I hate good manners," he said to Frederick Franck—though Franck qualified this by saying, "He has the most exquisite manners one could expect of a gentleman of the Old World. . . . What he really hates are the ape-like automatic tricks we indulge in."[15] At table everybody was told to reach for the food he wanted—there were better things to concentrate on than passing each other the potatoes. Nor did he care for any "After you" hesitations in a doorway; it was first come, first through. Hélène would have liked to refine him a little, but never succeeded.

Nor was he polite to Africans. If they were idle he shouted at them. If they still would not move, he abused them. For the most part they would shout back. But they would, even if briefly, move. And grin as they did so. "We do not become angry," a leper said to Norman Cousins. "How could we? Could a man become angry at his own father for telling him what to do?"[16]

But when Schweitzer shouted and nagged he knew what he was asking of them, undernourished as they were. Norman Cousins tells how, one day when he was at the hospital, Schweitzer suggested that he and three other whites should try taking over the jungle—clearing work the blacks had been doing. "After about ten minutes we looked as though we had been working ten hours. Our white shirts and khaki pants were drenched. All the while the Africans stood by, looking on us with boundless compassion and appearing desperately eager to spare us further effort." Schweitzer had "just wanted us to have some respect for the requirements of physical labour in Lambarene."[17]

When he first came back to Africa in 1924, Schweitzer evidently hoped for and looked forward to a less dominant relationship. He has been criticized for never having learned an African dialect, for having always played the part of an overlord, never that of a collaborator with the Gabonese of the Ogowe. A passage from *More from the Primeval Forest* shows that he was aware of this, and knew it to be a shortcoming:

> I daresay we should have fewer difficulties with our savages if we could occasionally sit round the fire with them and show ourselves to them as men, and not merely as medicine-men and custodians of law and order in the hospital. But there is no time for that. All three of us, we two doctors and Nurse Kottmann, are really so overwhelmed with

work that the humanity within us cannot come out properly. But we cannot help it. For the present we are condemned to the trying task of carrying on the struggle with sickness and pain, and to that everything else has to give way.[18]

If he had truly wanted to know the Africans as man to man, though, would he not have found time, or made time? Perhaps. And perhaps he would, as he suspected, have got more from them if he had. But though he respected their views on life and understood the origins of their super-stitions, he never joined in their celebrations or tried in any way to share their lives. The fashionable modern fascination with primitive cultures which takes film cameras into the intimate lives of lost tribes wherever they may be found he would have regarded as voyeuristic curiosity and an unpardonable invasion of privacy. He did not go to Africa to make clever discoveries about cultures which led people to eat one another, poison one another, and behave with total indifference to the suffering of anyone from the next tribe. He was there to improve their lot and he did it the way he found he could do it best. Possibly if he had learned a couple of Gabo-nese languages and lived closer to them, he might have accomplished more. On the other hand he could already talk with most of them in French. And perhaps by working side by side with them, ten times as hard as they, and bawling at them when things grew too much for him, he really grew as close to them as anybody could.

What news of these brusque encounters reached the supporters in Eu-rope? None at all, before 1950. Schweitzer's lectures and the bulletins that from time to time emerged from Lambarene were purged of such de-tail. They were sober, factual accounts, designed to give a brief picture of achievements and difficulties and to stimulate interest and the flow of cash. They were not dishonest, but they were far removed from the warts-and-all, now-it-can-be-told candid journalism that became fashionable later.

As a result, legions of good Christian people in Europe grew acquaint-ed with an imaginary Lambarene, where the warts were somehow ideal-ized and where sweat, pus, bad temper, and bad smells had no place. It was not surprising that when these people began to arrive to see for them-selves the sanctified jungle clearing, they often experienced fierce symp-toms of reaction—or that hardened journalists, whose experiences had given them a deep mistrust of heroes and dislike of halos, should begin to scent another clay-footed idol and to itch to bring him down.

"No one knows me who has not seen me in Africa." It was true. And almost no one ever had seen him in Africa. He was as remote, as mysteri-ous, as legendary as the gorilla or the pygmy, and romance built up around him in Europe; while in Africa the sweat fell off him in rivers as he wrestled with disease and mud, concrete and evil spirits, storms, snakes, other people's stupidity, and his own unquenchable temper.

And yet to Michael Scott, the priest who worked in South Africa from 1943 on, who truly tried to identify with the Africans and truly made their cause his own, Schweitzer said, in a moment of heartbreaking humility, "I helped Africa the easy way. You did it the hard way."

22

ANOTHER WAR
1932-1945

SO Schweitzer shuttled between his two lives, the myth thickening around him.

1932 was spent in Europe, where the new guest house in Günsbach was finished and Mme Martin, a pastor's widow, was installed as secretary. This is the house where the archives of Schweitzer's life are now held, superintended by his longtime senior nurse, Ali Silver. Here Schweitzer spent much of his time when he was not actually traveling, and here all sorts of visitors came to see him, invited and uninvited. Here all were welcomed and fed, and the cry often went upstairs to the first-floor kitchen: "Four more for lunch. Put some more water in the soup."

Plenty of these visitors have left a record of their impressions and of the homely everyday life into which they were absorbed. However distinguished, they were never allowed to disrupt the routine, for Schweitzer the theological rebel had never seriously questioned the simple traditions of Alsatian life, and now they were an essential part of his stability.

Time after time in these accounts we find the same elements—a sense of simple delight, a touch of hero worship, and the same incidents noted and treasured—Schweitzer's insistence on carrying the bags from the station; the family meals at which not only the family sits down but visitors, old friends, and staff from Lambarene; the strolls in the village and into the neighboring hills; the recruitment of visitors to do a little helping in the office or the kitchen; the constant interruptions of telephone calls or fresh arrivals; the evening sessions at the organ. Schweitzer preaches in his father's cassock and Geneva bands. Schweitzer chats with the villagers about their school days together. Schweitzer sits at his window, writing, writing, while neighbors leave little gifts on his windowsill—eggs, fresh vegetables, fruit from their gardens or picked wild on the hill.

Sometimes Schweitzer would decide to sit at the piano and launch into selections from *Der Rosenkavalier,* or even an interlude of "*Yotz,*" which is the Alsatian way of pronouncing "jazz." For his own private moments he preferred the place on the hill above the house where he had always sat since boyhood, the Rocks of Kantzenrain.

Hélène was often with him at Günsbach, but not always. Even here she felt out of things, as the activity buzzed about her. When Schweitzer was at Strasbourg, organizing matters in the Rue des Greniers and often sleeping there, she would stay in the Rue St. Aurélie with their mutual friends Christian Brandt and his wife.

As Schweitzer's star rose hers declined, and it is easy to feel the pathos of the picture—Schweitzer the center of attention, vital, brilliant, and admired, while Hélène sits half noticed in an unlit corner, talking of the old days. So easy indeed is the pathos that it is essential to remember that this was *not* a case of a beautiful marriage wrecked on the harsh shores of ambition. It was a case of a working partnership that almost by accident became a marriage and then through nobody's fault became unworkable. Tragic—and the tragedy spared neither of them—Schweitzer and Hélène had always understood and accepted the conditions of the partnership. Hélène's ill-health and the arrival of Rhena had meant that only one of the partners could go on with the work that both believed in, but neither would seriously have considered that the work be abandoned altogether to preserve the form of a conventional marriage.

Schweitzer himself, with his uncomfortable logic, saw the family tie as resembling the tribal tie of his Africans, which limited goodwill to the tribe alone at the expense of the rest of the human race. He criticized the same restricted vision in French family life. And steeped as he was in the Gospels he must have considered the relevance of the last verses of Matthew, Chapter 12: "While he was still speaking to the people, behold, his mother and his brothers stood outside, asking to speak to him. But he replied to the man who told him, 'Who is my mother, and who are my brothers?' And stretching out his hand towards his disciples, he said 'Here are my mother and my brothers! For whoever does the will of my father in heaven is my brother, and sister, and mother.'"

Hélène's tubercular condition, which had recurred on the way to Lambarene in 1928, had since been checked by a Dr. Gerson, an advocate of natural foods and a salt-free diet. According to Erica Anderson, Gerson actually saved Hélène's life at that time—though of course he could not restore the affected lung-tissue to its original elasticity. But Schweitzer was so impressed by Gerson's methods that he adhered to many of his principles—including avoidance of salt—to the end of his life.

Rhena saw almost nothing of her father. She could leave Königsfeld very little because of her schooling, and when Hélène was in Alsace she stayed with friends. Hers was not an easy life, though she made the best of it and enjoyed her father's brief visits while they lasted. He made great efforts, she remembers, to compensate for his absences, and she was grateful. Nor did she pine when the visits came to an end, for she says, "I always was objective with my father. I recognised his greatness and the importance of his work, even as a child, and I accepted my life as it was."[1] But she did find the Moravian Brothers uncomfortably strict. And when she was twelve something happened that caused her great distress—she caught her mother's tuberculosis.

Schweitzer had warned Hélène to take great care against infecting the child, but throughout the critical years of puberty, till she was eighteen, Rhena suffered from tuberculosis of the skin. Her face was affected, the skin pocked with holes full of matter, so that other children would not sit next to her. While Schweitzer found it impossible not to blame Hélène, there must also have been some feeling the other way—that had father been at home this might never have happened.

Before Schweitzer set off on the usual circuit of fund-raising engagements, a special occasion had to be fitted in. On March 22, the centenary of Goethe's death, he was to deliver a memorial oration in the Opera House in Frankfurt.

The gathering was notable, the audience distinguished, the Opera House packed. One hundred years after Goethe's death, to the exact hour, Schweitzer began to speak.

What he had to say was full of foreboding. With Germany still in a state of economic and political chaos after the war, thinking Germans were finding themselves forced into one extreme camp or another—Nazism or Communism. Schweitzer saw in Goethe the man who had stood supremely for the individual and for spiritual independence from any sort of mass will. He himself had been watching the approach of the mass will and warning against it ever since he had first seen the dangers in Nietzsche's philosophy in the 1890's. Now it was everywhere, overwhelming. Everyone sought, or had found

the magic formulas of some economic or social system . . . and the terrible significance of these magic formulas, to whatever school of economic and social witchcraft they may belong, is always that the individual has to surrender his material and spiritual personal existence, and may continue to live only as belonging body and soul to a plurality which controls him absolutely. . . .

The material and spiritual independence of the individual, in so far as they are not already crushed, are on all sides threatened most seriously. We are commemorating the death of Goethe in the most stupendous hour of fate that has ever sounded for humanity. And in this hour of fate it is his mission, beyond that of every other writer or thinker, to speak to us. As the most untimely of all men, he gazes into our era, because he has absolutely nothing in common with the spirit in which it lives. But as the most timely he tenders his advice, because what it needs to hear he has to say.

What is it he says to our era?

He tells it, that the frightful drama which is now being played through can only come to an end, if it removes from its path the economic and social magic to which it has surrendered itself, unlearns the incantations with which it has been befooled, and is determined, whatever the cost, to get back to a natural relationship with reality.

To individuals he says: "Do not abandon the ideal of personal, individual manhood, even if it run contrary to circumstances such as have developed. Do not believe this ideal is lost, even when it no longer seems tenable along with the opportunistic theories which endeavour simply to adjust the spiritual to the materials. Remain human with your own souls! Do not become mere human things which allow to have stuffed into them souls which are adjusted to the mass-will and pulse in measure with it!"[2]

So Goethe spoke through Schweitzer and Schweitzer through Goethe. For this speech is deeply revealing of Schweitzer himself, and not only on the political level.

Hundreds of people listened in dead silence that day to prophetic words whose truth they were to prove in their own minds and bodies in the next twelve years. They were breaking away from nature, he told them, and surrendering themselves to "a monstrous unnaturalness." Looking back from nearly half a century later we can see how exactly Nazism fulfilled his prediction. But it would be wrong to suppose that he was speaking only of Nazism, or that the end of Hitler has left Europe with a clean bill of health. All the time and everywhere the individual will is still threatened and submerged by the mass will. If Schweitzer was right, the evil of Nazism was not simply that the dogma it forced on individuals was false and cruel; the imposition of any dogma by force must in itself be evil.

The argument against him is that nothing can be achieved by individuals, that only united masses can be effective, and that if necessary unity must be created by coercion. In this speech in 1932 he did not evade that issue:

> There arises a question which even half a lifetime ago we should have regarded as impossible: Is there any longer any sense in holding on to the ideal of personal human individuality, when circumstances are developing in just the opposite direction, or is it not on the contrary our duty to adjust ourselves to a new ideal of human existence, in accordance with which man is destined to attain a differently constituted perfection of his being in unreserved absorption into organised society?[3]

Schweitzer had no doubt about the answer: this was precisely that "monstrous unnaturalness" he spoke of.

After that he went on with his tour, visiting Holland, Britain, Sweden, and Switzerland as well as Germany, the pace as furious as ever. "You can't burn the candle at both ends," someone said. "You can if it's long enough," said Schweitzer. "What do you think of the architecture of the city?" someone said. "I'll begin sightseeing when I'm seventy-five," said Schweitzer. (Though even that proved a pious hope.)

In the summer Oxford gave him an honorary degree in divinity. He went to Scotland, the country to which he had wanted to take his mother, for the first time in his life. Edinburgh University gave him degrees in divinity and music; St. Andrews in laws. He loved the long light midsummer evenings in Scotland, especially after the six o'clock sunsets of Lambarene. The students of St. Andrews were evidently impressed, for two years later they nominated him for rectorship of the university. A cable from the Students' Union dated November 1, 1934, says, "Nomination already well supported only difficulty speech in English essential." Despite desultory attempts to learn English, and ever-increasing ability to understand it when spoken, he was unable to oblige.

He stayed in Europe for the winter of 1933, and set off again for Lambarene in March. Hélène stayed behind, but not in Königsfeld. Hélène was Jewish by birth and Hitler was in power. She and Rhena moved to Switzerland and settled in Lausanne—much to Rhena's delight, for the move freed her from the rigidities of the Moravian Brothers.

The hospital was doing well. No special crises or disasters arose, the new building that was necessary was manageable, the surgeons completed more than 500 operations in the year; and a special fund raised in Alsace purchased the hospital's first refrigerator. Leftover food could now be kept fresh; and for the first time the parched workers had cool water to drink.

To ensure the continuity of the hospital a legal arrangement came into effect on October 13 whereby on Schweitzer's death the ownership passed automatically into the association that looked after his interests in Strasbourg.

So 1933 passed, and in 1934, Schweitzer was in Europe again. The notable events of this year were two major lecture series, the Hibbert Lectures on Religion in Modern Civilisation, first given at Manchester College, Oxford, and repeated at London University; and in Edinburgh the Gifford Lectures, a series of ten lectures on "The Problem of Natural Philosophy and Natural Ethics."

The two sets of lectures covered much the same ground, though the latter had a much greater range. Both were elaborations and variations on the themes of the first two books of *The Philosophy of Civilisation*, and both led up, inevitably, to Reverence for Life. "Everything that happens in world history rests on something spiritual. If the spiritual is strong, it creates world history. If it is weak, it suffers history."[4] Schweitzer was troubled that contemporary theologians were denying this powerful bond between the spiritual and the social, between religion and history. Karl Barth especially, he felt, was quite disastrously in tune with the spirit of the age when he taught that man's relationship with God was something quite apart from his everyday life.

> The terrible thing is that he dares to preach that religion is turned aside from the world, and in so doing expresses what the spirit of the age is feeling. The spirit of the age dislikes what is simple. It no longer believes the simple can be profound. It loves the complicated, and regards it as profound. It loves the violent. That is why the spirit of the age can love Karl Barth and Nietszche at the same time. The spirit of the age loves dissonance, in tones, in lines, and in thought. That shows how far from thinking it is, for thinking is a harmony with us.[5]

True and harmonious thinking, Schweitzer claimed, saw the progress of civilization as the expansion of Jesus' ethic of love into ever wider spheres—from tribe to nation, from nation to all mankind, and finally, with Reverence for Life, from mankind to all living creatures. The Gifford Lectures, leading to the same conclusions, began with a long section on Eastern philosophy. The subject had increasingly attracted Schweitzer, and his book *Indian Thought and Its Development* was nearing publication.

Two memorable meetings occurred in Edinburgh—the first with Sir Wilfred Grenfell, who was as it were a Schweitzer of the snow; what Schweitzer was doing in the hot swamps of Africa, Grenfell was doing in the frozen waters of Labrador, where he had founded a hospital for fishermen. A mutual friend invited them both and they met on the doorstep. George Seaver tells the story: "We began at once," says Schweitzer, "to question each other about the problems connected with the management of our hospitals. His chief trouble was the disappearance of reindeer for their periodic migrations; mine the loss of goats, from theft and snakebites. Then we burst out laughing: we were talking not as doctors concerned with patients, but as farmers concerned with livestock!"[6]

When they signed the visitors' book—the dark burly doctor from the African river and the white-haired doctor from the snows—Schweitzer was impelled to add under his signature: "The Hippopotamus is delighted to meet the Polar Bear."

And the great cellist, Pablo Casals, who was there for the first performance of a new cello concerto by Sir Donald Francis Tovey, wrote in his
autobiography, *Joys and Sorrows*:

> I had looked forward eagerly to meeting Schweitzer. Not only was I
> familiar with his writings on Bach, but I had of course an intense ad-
> miration for him as a man. On that occasion in Edinburgh there were a
> number of public and private concerts, and Schweitzer became very
> excited over my playing of Bach. He urged me to stay on—he wanted
> to hear more Bach—But I couldn't stay, because of other engage-
> ments. I had to catch a train after my last performance, and I had gotten
> my things together and was hurrying down a corridor when I heard the
> sound of running footsteps behind me. I looked around. It was
> Schweitzer. He was all out of breath. He looked at me with that won-
> derful expression of his which mirrored the great compassion of the
> man. "If you must leave," he said, "then let us at least say goodbye
> with intimacy." He was speaking in French. "Let us tutoyer one
> another before we separate." We embraced and parted.[7]

The rest of the tour took Schweitzer the length and breadth of England—Harrogate, Leeds, Peterborough, Sheffield, Manchester, Birmingham, London; and so back to the Continent. For his sixtieth birthday, in January, 1935, Strasbourg named a park after him. All over the
world, in fact, people took an interest in his birthday—even, surprisingly,
in Nazi Germany.

Schweitzer had made a vow never to set foot on German soil so long as
Hitler was in power. The distaste was mutual. The Nazi Party had been
going out of its way to find fault with Schweitzer's notions, which were
clearly not complimentary to them. But on his sixtieth birthday it seems
to have occurred to their propaganda ministry that he might be useful to
their image; and accordingly they tried to get in touch with him through
an old friend of his, Emil Lind, and to offer him various tempting musical
posts in Germany. Lind realized that they were using him to set Schweitzer up as an example of "National Socialist Bach worship" and warned
Schweitzer what to expect. When Goebbels, the Minister of Propaganda,
wrote shortly afterward to Schweitzer, he concluded his letter, "*Mit
Deutschem Gruss*"—"With German greetings." Schweitzer, declining
to have anything to do with the plan, signed off "With Central African
Greetings, Albert Schweitzer."[8] And three weeks after his birthday, back
to central Africa he went.

This time he was in Lambarene for only seven months. Expansion was
again necessary, for the hospital was full to overflowing, with thirty patients awaiting operations.

I could no longer close my ears to the frequent complaints of doctors
and nurses that our consulting room had become too small. On the days
when three or four doctors are all questioning patients, medicines are
being dealt out and many injections of Salvarsan, Tryparsamide and
Antileprol are being given, it is thronged as if there were a fair going
on. And often through all the din are heard the groans of a native ma-
ternity case lying behind a curtain. For the consulting room has also to
serve for accouchements![9]

Slowly the spread of technology was making itself felt, for better or
worse. The hospital was given a petrol lamp, which made it possible in
emergency to operate at night. And airplanes began to fly over Lambarene
on an air route which had opened between Europe and the Congo. One
witch doctor explained that this portended a month's darkness, and his
village cut all their plantains in readiness for the long night that never
came.

In October Schweitzer was back in Europe again—a Europe perturbed
by Mussolini's invasion of Abyssinia, which threatened the stability of
the whole of Africa. The chickens of dictatorship were beginning to fly
wide, before coming home to roost. Schweitzer's ear was cocked. He
knew the sound of the wings of war.

Honors were falling thick around him now. All over the world, from
Seville to New South Wales, organizations and cities were competing in
offering him honorary citizenships, honorary memberships, honorary
whatever they could think of. The previous spring a number of organizations in Austria, Switzerland, Sweden, Czechoslovakia, and England had
made a determined effort to get him the Nobel Peace Prize, but without
success.

In London he was asked if he would go to China with the Dean of Canterbury and Dr. Wilfred Grenfell to help with reconstruction work after
the flood disaster of the previous year. He would gladly have gone, he
told them, but he was an old carthorse who could still do some useful
work in the old shafts but might not do so well in new ones.

The months passed much as usual, but one meeting is particularly interesting. Jawaharlal Nehru was due to be released after one of his regular
spells in a British jail, and Mahatma Gandhi wrote to ask if Schweitzer
would look after him for a few days while he accustomed himself to freedom. So Nehru was briefly the guest of the Schweitzers in Lausanne. The
book on Indian thought had been published a short while before. In it
Schweitzer had written at some length and with enormous sympathy and
respect about Gandhi, though he had one or two minor criticisms to make
as well. Had Gandhi read this? And did Schweitzer discuss it with Nehru? How far did either of the great Indians agree with Schweitzer's interpretation of Indian philosophy? And what did they think of Reverence for

Life? It would be fascinating to know. But at least it is pleasant to think that Gandhi and Schweitzer, who from such totally different backgrounds had reached such similar conclusions, had at least this one very human and practical contact.

One mystery remains to be solved in the Schweitzer story—the mystery of the third and fourth volumes of *The Philosophy of Civilisation*. He was constantly reported to be working hard on these, and indeed he himself said so. Sheaves of notes were hanging on a nail in Lambarene, out of reach of the goats. This summer of 1936, for example, is one of the periods when he apparently put in a great deal of work on volume three. Yet volume three never appeared. For a man who could produce long and complicated books in six months or less, this seems extremely odd. The notes, which are reported to be extremely disorganized, are jealously guarded by the trustees of his intellectual work, but I am told that the edited version of some of them at least is shortly to be published.

When I inquired what was in them I was asked, "Do we need a forty-second symphony to understand Mozart? Surely forty-one is enough!" So far as I am concerned forty-one is not enough. I would be glad to have four hundred and one. But then Mozart did not repeat himself. Is the implication here that Schweitzer was repeating himself, that nothing new was emerging from all that work? Or was he grappling with something that even he was unable to master? It is important to know. For his subject was the application of Reverence for Life to society and to politics, and this is precisely where for many people the philosophy fails to convince. As a personal creed, yes. But how, for example, can politicians apply it to international affairs? Was Schweitzer's answer among those notes he worked on for so many years?

In the autumn another project loomed, which meant forgetting everything else for a few weeks. The Columbia Gramophone Company had already recorded Schweitzer's playing of a number of Bach works in London for the Bach Organ Music Society. The organ he had played on was that of All Hallows in the Tower. These first six works, advertised as "played by Dr. Albert Schweitzer, the greatest interpreter of Bach," had proved so successful that the company now wished to make fifty-two more records.

Though he liked the organ at All Hallows Schweitzer had not been entirely happy about the arrangements there. The rector had not been very enthusiastic about the enterprise, and Schweitzer had been able to work there only at nights. Moreover, much of the time he had spent on stepladders stuffing the windows with cotton wool to prevent vibration. He proposed instead the organ of St. Aurelia in Strasbourg—an organ built by his favorite organ builder, Silbermann, and restored by his friend Frederic Härpfer. The secretary of the Bach Organ Music Society went especially to Strasbourg to hear it and was so impressed by the organ's tone that Columbia agreed to spend a great deal of money sending their recording equipment from London to Strasbourg for what was at that time the "largest plan of consecutive gramophone record making ever undertaken by an artist."[10] The recordings were made in October, and took two weeks. They are now of course virtually unobtainable. But they sold extremely well, and Schweitzer must have earned a very large fee.

He stayed in Europe for his birthday, and on January 29, 1937, embarked again from Bordeaux. He arrived to find the hospital overcrowded as usual, with the additional complication that the rainy season had been less rainy than usual and many patients and their families could not go home because the river was too low. His determination not to get involved in any more building lasted a month or two, but in the end he had once more to give in to the pleas of the staff for more space, so the situation was back to normal. In addition it was found that some of the charred posts that formed the foundations of the huts had rotted more quickly than had been expected and were now dangerous. They had to be renewed.

Another task was the digging of a new well. The concrete cistern and the single well both dried up in a long dry season, leaving the patients with no choice but to drink the river water, which carried the risk of infection. In this predicament "I had the great good luck," Schweitzer wrote, "to come upon a spring of water which never runs dry."[11] And here he dug a well, lined it with concrete, and provided it with a good pump.

Now came the moment when Schweitzer had to turn down the offer of an X-ray machine. The grateful Europeans of the Ogowe had decided to show Schweitzer their appreciation. Many of them owed their lives, or those of wives or husbands, to the hospital; for often they would delay coming in until the last moment because of the difficulty of travel and the amount of money they stood to lose by abandoning their work at a crucial moment, and it required all the resources of the hospital to save them. Ninety thousand francs they collected, and an X-ray machine was the present they had in mind.

But Schweitzer had scented war, and much though he desired an X-ray machine, he had a feeling that his first need was going to be a large and varied stock of drugs. Ninety thousand francs' worth would go a long way to insure the hospital against a breakdown of supplies, and he persuaded the donors of the money to let him spend it his way.

1938 rolled onward. Schweitzer was still building, and in addition was extending the garden. As ever, each extension was undertaken with great reluctance, and each was to be the very last. Meanwhile, Lambarene town achieved the hallmark of civilization—a radio station.

In November and December of this year Hélène and Rhena went on a lecture tour of their own, to the United States. Schweitzer himself had never been able to find time to go, and though *My Life and Thought* had sold out there in 1932 (the name was slightly changed to *Out of My Life and Thought* and the first impression of 3,000 copies sold out in three weeks), he was inevitably less well known in America than in the European countries. This tour of Hélène's sowed seeds which were to bear fruit at a critical moment for the hospital when it might well have collapsed without American help.

On January 12, 1939, almost two full years after his last sight of Europe, Schweitzer set sail for a change of climate. But he was already too late. At every port where they put in warships lay at anchor. On the ship's radio he heard the saber-rattling speeches of politicians. Hitler had already occupied Czechoslovakia, calling the bluff of the rest of Europe, and now, as the ship crossed the Bay of Biscay, was busy announcing that he had no further territorial ambitions. Schweitzer, who was supposed to be naïve, was not so gullible as some politicians at that time; he did not believe a word of it. Before they reached Bordeaux he had booked his berth on the return voyage; he wanted to prepare his hospital for the war, and to be with the Africans who needed and trusted him when it came.

This gave him just ten days in Alsace before he had to head back for Bordeaux and the Gabon. He spent them ordering all the drugs and equipment he could afford—and seeing his family from whom he had been separated for two years. Rhena was now just twenty and engaged to be married to Jean Eckert, an organ builder working for Caraillé-Col in Paris. Though she had toured the United States with her mother on behalf of the hospital she had never actually been to Lambarene, and during Schweitzer's brief visit it was decided that she must now see the place that had kept her father away from her for most of her childhood. He left them making preparations, and on May 16 Rhena and Hélène sailed from Bordeaux in his wake.

They stayed only a few weeks. Rhena was anxious to return to her fiancé and the last thing anyone wanted was to have these two trapped in Lambarene throughout a long war. Schweitzer expected hostilities to break out at any moment, though few people showed his pessimism. The general belief was that either there would be no war, or it would be very short, or anyway it would not seriously interrupt shipping and supplies. As a result, Schweitzer, on the lookout for food to hoard, found that several traders were anxious to sell him quantities of rice at bargain prices because it was of inferior quality; it had weevils in it, and they were sure they could replace it. Schweitzer warned them that they might regret the sale, but was ignored. The hospital lived on this rice for three years.

In September the war began. Two nurses and two doctors had gone back to Europe in the spring and the summer. That left four nurses, including the perennial Emma Haussknecht, and one other doctor besides

Schweitzer, Dr. Ladislas Goldschmid, who had been attached to the hospital since 1933 and had recently returned from leave in Europe.

One other doctor, Dr. Anna Wildikann, reached Lambarene in January, 1940, before the war really began to blaze. But the optimists had to reconsider their outlook when the liner *Brazza,* which had several times carried Schweitzer between Bordeaux and Port-Gentil, was torpedoed near Cape Finistère and sank with almost all aboard. Nobody from the hospital was among the passengers but the last consignment of drugs and equipment was lost.

Schweitzer was not at all sure that the war would be short, and as soon as it began he started to send home all but the most serious cases. He had not the food, the medicines, or the staff to keep the hospital running for any length of time at its current rate:

> What sad days we spent sending these people home! Again and again we had to refuse the urgent entreaties of those who, in spite of all, wished to stay with us, again and again we had to try to explain what to them was inexplicable—the fact that they must leave the hospital. Many of the homeward bound were able to travel on steamers and motor-boats whose owners were kind enough to take them. Others were obliged to make their way to distant villages by long and difficult jungle trails. At last they had all gone and the heart-rending scenes were at an end. How dead the Hospital seemed with such a diminished number of inmates![12]

A few of those inmates were replaced by white women—wives of Europeans who had settled in lonely houses in the bush and were now called up. Unlike the Africans, these had no means of reaching their homes and rather than face the jungle alone they sought sanctuary at the hospital.

When France fell to Hitler in June, 1940, all her colonies followed suit in surrendering, except one—the bleak plateau country of Chad in central Africa. Félix Eboué, the remarkable and universally respected African governor of Chad, hated the Nazis and instantly responded to the call of Charles de Gaulle, exiled in England and rallying the forces of French resistance. A touch of persuasion and a little intrigue, and three other French colonies—the French Congo, the Cameroons, and Ubangi-Shari—followed Chad in declaring for Free France. Only the Gabon was left; and though for a while it looked as though the Gabon too would declare for de Gaulle, a pro-German submarine and various troopships which appeared off Libreville made the governor think again. This did not suit de Gaulle at all, for the Gabon was of enormous strategic importance. If he controlled the Ogowe he had a direct route to Chad and the heart of Africa, and from Chad the allies could harass the Italians in Abyssinia from the south and prevent them from moving any farther into Africa.

Moreover, he could offer the British a route to the Middle East and India—invaluable now that the Mediterranean was controlled by the dictatorships. With the Gabon, de Gaulle would have something of real importance to contribute to the Allied cause. Without it his position was intolerably weak for so proud a man. In September the Gaullist troops advanced from three sides into the jungle of the Gabon, making for the coast and Libreville, the capital.

It was at Lambarene that the defending troops made their one and only stand. Tiny as it is, Lambarene stands at the junction of river and jungle track and commands both. From October 13 to November 5 the battle for Lambarene continued. The hospital, a mile or two from the town, was declared neutral territory, and both sides forbade their aircraft to bomb it. All the same Schweitzer and the inmates hastily barricaded the windows against stray shots, and in fact a few accidental bullets did whistle across the water from the island.

On November 5 the occupying forces surrendered, the Free French moved on downriver to the coast, and before long the Gabon had fallen to de Gaulle and the whole of French Equatorial Africa was his. Félix Eboué was installed at Brazzaville in the Congo as governor-general of the whole vast area.

Every channel of communication with Germany or occupied France was now closed. Schweitzer's lifeline was definitely cut. But as one door closed another opened, and his friends in Britain and the United States could now contact him. Before the year was out he had received two offers of help from America. Dr. Edward Hume, secretary of the Christian Medical Council for Overseas Work, who had visited Schweitzer at Günsbach, offered to send drugs. And Professor Everett Skillings of Middlebury College, Vermont, wrote that he was collecting money. Schweitzer put the two in touch with each other. To Dr. Hume he sent a list of the most urgently needed drugs and equipment—the quantity to be determined by the size of Professor Skillings' collection.

Another year however was to pass before the consignment arrived. Sending across the Atlantic anything that was not connected with war was not the simplest of tasks. Meanwhile the gaps on shelves where the drugs were stored grew wider each week.

Those yawning shelves pointed up, as nothing else could have done, the vulnerability of Schweitzer's position, and his responsibility. It had been his decision to run his hospital without support of an organization; his decision too to hand over considerable quantities of his collections to other charities. Now he was reaping the results, pinned as he was in Africa and unable to go around with the collecting bowl.

Those who criticize him for being publicity-hungry doubtless forget that it was his name, and that alone, that stood between the hospital and bankruptcy; often indeed it stood between several hundred people and starvation. Publicity for Schweitzer was survival for the hospital. Such critics also forget—or perhaps do not realize—that until he was over seventy the publicity he received was not of the inflated kind, blown up by journalists in search of a good story. He had won it honestly, the hard way, and had done everything he could to ensure that the people who contributed to the hospital funds had the chance of actually seeing the man they supported. He had lectured to them, had played the organ for them, and multitudes of them knew him personally. For person to person was the only sort of communication he thought valuable. Without that communication he was crippled.

While the hospital was waiting for the drugs from across the Atlantic, help arrived in a totally unexpected form. On August 2, 1941, Hélène stepped onto the landing place, having managed to find her way from occupied France. She must have known what she faced, and that there was little hope of her going back till the war ended. She was sixty-two and not strong. Yet she had made that hard and dangerous journey alone and on her own initiative—a feat which in itself shows that, despite all the difficulties of the marriage, here was a woman who was still a match for Schweitzer in determination.

Early in the war she joined Rhena and her husband in Paris, but when the Germans came they made for Bordeaux—a nightmare journey that took about a month. They slept mostly in the car and ate when they could find something to eat.

To George Seaver, who wanted to know how she had contrived to get from there to Lambarene, she later wrote:

> I am glad to answer your enquiry, especially since it gives me the opportunity of paying a tribute of gratitude to your country, from which such efficient help came to my undertaking; and next to it, the most kind and active assistance from the Red Cross Society in Geneva. Knowing that a British visa was necessary, I asked the Red Cross to supply me with the address of the office in London to which to apply, stating as my reason the fact that I was the oldest of the nurses at Lambarene, and might be of some use since no young nurses were available. They replied that their delegate was on the point of leaving for London and would present my application, but that the reply might take a long time. It took a very long time. But then I had a wonderful surprise: a telegram, followed by a letter, informed me—not of the address I had asked for, but—that I was at liberty to proceed at once! Moreover, the competent authorities in London had given instructions that my journey should be facilitated as much as possible!
>
> The next step was to ask for permission to leave France. When this question had been discussed before, I had been told that if only I could

obtain the authority to prove admission to the colony, there would be little or no difficulty in procuring a permit. But when—contrary to all expectation—I had received this authority it took seven weeks to collect the necessary papers and permits to proceed from Bordeaux; and later on, four weeks longer, to continue my journey from Lisbon; in fact, I received my last permit just half an hour before the ship was due to leave that port!

My journey on the neutral [Portuguese] steamer was without accident, in broad daylight and brilliantly lit by night, and my reception in Angola quite in accord with the kind suggestions made by the competent authorities in London. I was relieved also of another trouble. I had prepared myself, with some apprehension, for a long and lonely journey of 3 months through the bush in unfamiliar territory, but found to my great relief that this was reduced to a week's drive by car on new roads, and finally to a cruise along the well-known river to the Hospital which I reached on August 2, 1941.

On my arrival I found that I was the first person—and so far as I know the only one hitherto—who has succeeded legally in coming here from France since 1940. Once again and with deep gratitude I would acknowledge my debt to that miraculous help which I have so often received in my life, and to so much undeserved kindness, to a large extent from strangers, which has made it easier to stand what would otherwise have been sad and difficult.[13]

Hélène stayed until the end of the war, deputizing in turn for each of the nurses, so as to give each one a break, and helping Schweitzer with his correspondence and administration.

Her health stood up unexpectedly well, though she did at one point have to have an operation on her foot. For fifty-six months she did not even go to the coast for the rainy season.

Schweitzer was of course having to do more doctoring than he had done for some time. Several times a week he was assisting Goldschmid at operations. Besides this he was taking advantage of the collapse of the timber trade and the consequent cheap labor to extend the fruit tree plantation and to renew deteriorating garden walls, drains, paths, and buildings. "I run from right to left, what with pumps to repair, missing keys to find, tools to mend, the refrigerators to set going, wood to fetch for the kitchen and laundry: bananas, cassava, and maize to buy from the natives who bring it in—et que sais-je encore. . . ."[14]

Funds kept trickling in—not enormous, but enough to keep the hospital working at reduced speed—from Britain, the United States, and the Swedish Red Cross. And in May, 1942, only just in time, the first consignment arrived from America—twenty-eight cases of drugs, instruments, extra-large rubber gloves for Schweitzer, who had been operating in a size too small, kitchen utensils, and every kind of useful article. In

1943, further shipments came from both America and Britain, and money with them, so that it again became possible to start taking in more patients. Numbers of these patients were whites, who were succumbing to the strain of their long enforced stay in the tropics and the inadequate diet. At the same time Dr. Goldschmid took a holiday in the Belgian Congo, and Schweitzer was himself operating three mornings a week. "Not to fall ill—to keep fit for work—is our constant care,"[15] he wrote.

Though things remained much the same at the hospital, the world outside was altering rapidly and constantly coming closer. Roads were driven through the jungle from west to east, from north to south, for military transport. The main highway, such as it was, that ran the full length of Africa from Algiers to Capetown, passed through Lambarene, crossing the two branches of the Ogowe on motor ferries. They were only red dirt tracks, these roads, but they brought the mail from the coast by truck in hours, instead of by boat in days. And the seeds for the garden now came from Capetown.

Politically, too, an immense change was brewing. Early in 1944 de Gaulle attended a conference at Félix Eboué's headquarters at Brazzaville and took the first step toward granting full French citizenship, with voting rights, to the black populations of the French colonies. The move was, of course, political—an act of acknowledgment for the help they had given him and an encouragement to further cooperation, rather than a farsighted piece of statesmanship. But by such gestures of expediency history is often pushed along, and two years later, when the war was won, the agreement was to be ratified—to the fury of most of the white colonists. The tragedy was that Eboué was not there to see the new era in, having died soon after the Brazzaville Conference.

As one might expect, Schweitzer viewed the whole thing with the darkest suspicion. He understood very well the political motives behind it and was not impressed; nor did he think it particularly sane to give the vote to people who could not read or write and who knew nothing of the issues they were voting about. For years he had been trying to teach them the basic principles of agriculture and carpentry so that they could feed and house themselves properly and cease to be the slaves of the seasons. He had hammered them about theft, foresight, honesty, and application, believing these to be the first essentials for the creation of any kind of stable community free from fear. His efforts had rolled off them like water off a duck's back.

He was convinced that in offering them any sort of self-government at this stage Europe was simply adding to its crimes by refusing responsibility for the mess it had got them into. European officials must remain, he believed, to protect them against exploitation by European trade.

He was thinking of course only of the Gabon, the only part of Africa he knew. And the Gabon was less able to become a political entity than almost any other area because of the lack of education and communications, and because of the large number of different tribes which did not like each other, did not understand each other's language, and did not wish to do so. After hundreds of years during which these tribes had been torn from their traditional ways of living, physically decimated and morally confused by the slave trade, the timber trade and the liquor trade, to leave them now to their own devices was something like criminal negligence. So Schweitzer believed. When he said, as he often did, that an authoritarian system was the only one that would work in Africa these were his reasons.

Other developments pleased him more. Those who claim that he ignored and mistrusted advances in medical techniques should read the notes he made during these years—"If only we had penicillin!" Of sulphonamides—"How much the existence of this valuable drug means to us!"[16] For heart disease—"Now we have from Switzerland a preparation of squills (Scilla Maritima) which is far less dangerous than digitalis. . . . Recently there has been hope of important progress in the treatment of leprosy. French doctors in Madagascar have since 1937 been making promising experiments with a drug obtained from a plant found on the island (*Hydrocotylus asiatica*). With this treatment they are achieving rapid cures of leprous ulcers. In America a drug called promin, related to the sulphonamides, is also being tried with success."[17] As to DDT, here he is writing in 1944 of termites—"these wicked insects" which crawl into everywhere and eat everything—"nothing so far had been of any use against them, but lately we have been trying DDT."[18]

For the first time, too, the government was lending a hand with medical problems.

> We have been less troubled with sleeping sickness than in earlier years because a Government doctor has been concerned with fighting it in our district. There is a large camp for sleeping sickness patients a little down the river from Lambarene. To carry on the fight against the disease in the right way it is necessary that at regular intervals the doctor or a white assistant should visit every village in a given district and examine all the inhabitants to discover by microscopic tests whether the germ of the disease is to be found in their blood or spinal fluid. Our concern is now limited to passing on to the Government doctor any patients in whom we suspect sleeping sickness.[19]

Unfortunately, though, even this relief boomeranged; the government doctor was called up, and Dr. Goldschmid had to take his place, so that he was able to work only part-time at the hospital. And everyone grew more and more tired. Schweitzer's letters kept coming back to it:

I dare hope that the greatest part of the work in regard to the maintenance of the buildings is about to be completed. I am glad about it, as I
could never tell how much I suffered in these years when I had to sacrifice so much of my time to such work, besides my other
activities. . . .[20] My wife is again well enough to help in the
household which is precious. I am always on my feet, though I need
rest. . . .[21] If I started going on holiday I would soon find out how
tired I am. I prefer to work from day to day. . . .[22] I surprise myself
by the way I am able to carry on with my work, week in, week
out. . . .[23] My capacity for sound sleep enables me to carry on like
this and keep going without a day's rest. But oh! for one free day when
I could at last sleep enough to get rid of the fatigue which more and
more invades me; to concentrate entirely on finishing my book, to
study my music and play the organ at leisure; to walk, to dream, to
read for pure refreshment's sake. When will that day come? Will it
ever come?[24]

In October, 1944—

We continue to go on well, although tired. I have more work than
ever. I begin in the morning at 6:45 and go on until 12:45. At 2 o'clock
I start again and continue until 7 pm. All this time I am on my feet in
the hospital and doing secondary things. I belong to myself only after
supper—but at 11 o'clock at night I am going on my last round in the
hospital.

My wife is also at work all day long. Mlle Emma looks after the garden, besides her other occupations. Mlle Koch does the household and
has charge of the kitchen. What luck that she returned safely!

How intensely I have been thinking of my friends in London when I
learned that you have been bombed again! But I do hope that is going
to be finished now, once and for all.[25]

It was, at last, nearly finished. One more wartime Christmas, one more
wartime birthday. He was seventy years old. For eight continuous years
he had been laboring in the sweaty confines of the hospital and the hope of
finding a successor was farther away than when he had first given the matter thought fifteen years before.

When in the evenings he sat down to write his thank-you letters, as his
debt to his benefactors compelled him to do, he was so weary that he
could find little but his weariness to write about; though often one can
see, reading these letters, how the enjoyment of communicating with his
friends lifted his spirits and restored his strength as he wrote, and a letter
which begins with apologies for lateness and brevity, using the standard
excuses of overwork and writer's cramp, ends by enlarging on the problems of the hospital for three or four pages. But for all the industry and
good intentions he put into his letters they were far from achieving the

fluency and grace he aspired to as a boy, and his harping on his tiredness, however justified, sometimes came dangerously close to self-pity; a sentiment which was far from his true feelings, for in fact he regarded himself as lucky to have escaped involvement in the war.

The seventieth birthday did not go unnoticed by the world. France and Germany were deep in the last few desperate months of fighting, and Alsace, after a war which had left it comparatively undisturbed by military action, was now the scene of rearguard battles as the Germans were driven back over their borders by the Allies. But in Britain, stretched to its utmost but now sighing with relief as the bombing eased and Hitler was clearly on the run, Schweitzer was richly remembered. London newspapers offered congratulations, if not canonization. One paper wrote:"If sainthood consists in making the good life attractive, Albert Schweitzer is a saint of our century. Yet his example does not belittle our own lives. He ennobles us, who are made of the same human clay. His story is a living sermon on the brotherhood of man. It gives perspective to the sufferings of our time." And the BBC broadcast a talk by Schweitzer's old friend, Nathaniel Micklem (somewhat patronizing about Schweitzer's theology, it must be said, though complimentary about everything else), and one of Schweitzer's organ recordings. Schweitzer actually heard it himself on the radio of a white patient—for this was another manifestation of the Brave New World, that occasionally the hospital could hear news of Europe direct by radio. Otherwise they relied on summaries fetched every few days from the radio station in Lambarene town.

While in Europe the war moved toward a ceasefire, Schweitzer was preoccupied by a new threat—one which mercifully had not loomed during the earlier war years, when it would have been totally disastrous—famine. The dry season of 1944 had not been dry enough, and the villagers had been unable to burn the bush and make their plantations of plantain and manioc. When this happened, as it occasionally did, the Africans, sooner than make the effort of digging up the trees and shrubs which would not burn, simply starved. Foreseeing the shortage, Schweitzer sent his empty rice sacks by truck to a region farther in the interior called Tschibanga, where a farsighted district commissioner had been growing rice since 1942, and bought as much as possible for the hospital.

And then—

The news of the end of the war in Europe we received on Monday, May 7th, 1945, at midday. While I was sitting at my writing table after dinner finishing urgent letters which had to reach the river steamer by 2 o'clock there appeared at my window a white patient who had brought his radio set with him to the Hospital. He shouted to me that, according to a German report relayed from the radio station at Léopoldville in the Belgian Congo, an Armistice had been concluded in Europe on land

and sea. But I had to go on sitting at my table in order to finish the letters which must be sent off immediately. Then I had to go down to the Hospital where the heart cases and other patients have appointments for treatment at 2 o'clock. In the course of the afternoon the big bell was rung and when the people at the Hospital had gathered, they were told that the war in Europe was over. After that, in spite of my great fatigue, I had to drag myself into the plantation to see how the work was getting on there.

Only when evening came, could I begin to think and try to imagine the meaning of the end of the hostilities and what the innumerable people must be feeling who were experiencing the first night for years without the threat of bombardment. Whilst outside in the darkness the palms were gently rustling, I fetched from its shelf the little book with the sayings of Laotse, the great Chinese thinker of the 6th century B.C., and read his impressive words on war and victory: "Weapons are disastrous implements, no tools for a noble being. Only when he can do no otherwise, does he make use of them. . . . Quiet and peace are for him the highest. He conquers, but he knows no joy in this. He who would rejoice in victory, would be rejoicing in murder. . . . At the victory celebration, the general should take his place as is the custom at funeral ceremonies. The slaughter of human beings in great numbers should be lamented with tears of compassion. Therefore should he who had conquered in battle bear himself as if he were at a festival of mourning.[26]

While Schweitzer quietly rejoiced that the disastrous weapons of war had been laid aside at last, the most disastrous of all was being primed for its first public performance. On August 6 the first atom bomb was dropped on Hiroshima—three days later, the second, on Nagasaki.

Man had discovered the opposite to Reverence for Life.

23

AMERICA
"The Greatest Man in the World"
1945–1950

THE first to arrive from Europe was the resourceful Mathilde Kottmann, who had been pining to get back to Lambarene and who managed
by dint of some string-pulling to get a much-sought-after seat on a flight
from Paris to Libreville. From there she traveled by car to Lambarene—
the first to reach the hospital from Europe in days rather than weeks. Soon
after she arrived, Hélène, who had endured those four and a half years in
Africa remarkably well, went home, along with numbers of whites who
had been living, more or less bedridden, at the hospital.

But if Schweitzer himself had hoped to be relieved as soon as the war
was over, he was disappointed. Permissions and papers were almost as
hard to get as ever, and though two doctors were ready to come they were
unlikely to reach Lambarene before the New Year.

And in the New Year they came. So did fresh nurses. So also did the
New Gabonese Constitution. "Now we are all Frenchmen," said the
Africans, "we don't have to work anymore." To Schweitzer one said,
"You can stay. The rest, we'll slit their throats." Allowing that these
stories may come from biased observers, there can be no doubt that the
niceties of democratic government were, and still are, far from clear to
the tribesmen of the Ogowe. A good many, when they were first required
to vote, wanted to know where they should put their cross for Dr.
Schweitzer.

For the hospital itself the change meant a steady increase in paperwork.
Nobody had hitherto troubled Schweitzer with that kind of thing; once
through customs he was his own man, and the hospital records, though
meticulous, were written on pieces of brown wrapping paper, luggage labels, and the like. They were for the use of the staff alone.

Now Schweitzer was answerable to a new government; what was
more, a black government, which inevitably had a strong antiwhite element and a vested interest in rejecting the works of all Europeans.

Schweitzer was forced to take his paperwork seriously, to justify his hospital not only to his patients on the spot but to the officials in Libreville. In fact the officials were mostly on his side; to anyone but a totally fanatical antiwhite his record spoke for itself. But still he was an alien, even if a friendly one, and to some extent on sufferance in the Gabon.

Despite the efforts of supporters in Britain and the United States, the hospital was beginning to run into debt. But for the bounty that had been flowing in from America it would have foundered long before; and when Schweitzer wrote of the work of the Albert Schweitzer Fellowship of America, "it seems to me in the nature of a miracle,"[1] he was hardly overstating the case. The fellowship had spread from the East Coast to the West, collecting thousands of dollars in California, and had even stirred inquiries in New Zealand. The Congregational and Episcopalian churches had added their blessings and their collections. The organist of the New York Philharmonic Orchestra, an Alsatian named Edward Nies-Berger, had organized benefit concerts among the American Guild of Organists, and other musicians too had contributed. All this in a land where Schweitzer was as yet barely known to the general public, and where even the moving spirit of the fellowship, a one-time missionary named Emory Ross, had never met him personally.

Ross made up for this as soon as the war was over. He and his wife, flying the Atlantic to visit Lambarene in 1946, were probably the first two people in the history of the hospital to come from a far land simply to have a look at what was going on. They were certainly not the last. They were in fact the first swallow of an Indian summer which along with great benefits and new friendships brought all kinds of fresh complications.

But despite all the efforts of all the committees money was still an urgent problem. Prices were soaring. Food, wages, drugs, fares—the cost of running the hospital had quadrupled since before the war and at the same time benefactors in Europe had grown poorer. Schweitzer was not sure that it would be possible to go on at all. "Something has to happen in someone's heart before anything happens in Lambarene,"[2] he said—but when the pockets of well-wishers were empty, the heart was less effective.

"My great and continued concern is how to feed them all," Schweitzer wrote in 1946. And as fresh doctors and nurses arrived from Europe, as the success of the new American sulfone drugs against leprosy brought greatly increased numbers of lepers into the hospital in search of treatment, the food problem grew more and more acute; by the summer of 1947, the hospital account was thousands of francs overdrawn. Schweitzer, struggling to get things back into peacetime running order before returning to Europe to raise fresh funds, was in an acute dilemma.

At this juncture—according to one version at the very moment when he

was on his way to the bank to discuss the possibility of closing the hospital—two Americans, Dr. Charles R. Joy and Mr. Melvin Arnold, arrived
at Lambarene. With them they brought a check for over $4,000—more
than enough to cover the debts and put the account into good shape for the
future.

Joy and Arnold had been sent by *The Christian Register,* a Unitarian
magazine published in Boston, Massachusetts. Dr. Joy was an administrator of relief programs, Arnold editor in chief of the Beacon Press, a
Unitarian publishing house.

The Unitarians had a special interest in Schweitzer, for they found his
theology very much to their liking, with its refusal to worry too much
about the doctrines of the Trinity or definitions of the divinity of Jesus.
The Unitarian Service Committee, with *The Christian Register* as its
mouthpiece, had already been active in collecting money for the hospital
during the war. And now Melvin Arnold, on taking up his post with the
Beacon Press, had decided on "a long term publishing program seeking
to make America as familiar with the work of Albert Schweitzer as is
Europe."[3]

Charles Joy in fact had already collected an anthology of Schweitzer's
writings, which the Beacon Press was in the process of publishing, and
this had occasioned considerable correspondence with Schweitzer, so
perhaps the doctor was not totally taken by surprise when Arnold and Joy
and the check arrived at Lambarene. But they were nonetheless welcome;
and the visit was the beginning of a long friendship which was of value
not only to the hospital (and presumably to the Unitarians) but also to the
present-day biographer of Schweitzer, for Joy's enthusiastic researches
brought to light and preserved a good deal of material which but for him
would have vanished completely. With Joy and Arnold the Indian summer began in good earnest.

They returned to Boston, and their contribution to a special Albert
Schweitzer number of *The Christian Register* in September, 1947, put
the Schweitzer bandwagon firmly on the road in the United States.

Not that their articles were the first to salute him with superlatives.
Reader's Digest had already, a year before, published an article about
him by a Fr. John O'Brien entitled "God's Eager Fool—The Story of a
Great Protestant, told by a Catholic Priest." An eminent divine had de-
scribed him as "the greatest soul in Christendom"; and a poll taken in
Europe and quoted in *The Christian Register* had classed him alongside
Goethe and Leonardo da Vinci as one of the three all-around geniuses of
Western Europe.

These plaudits however had not yet become part of a full-scale campaign. *Reader's Digest,* it is true, has a tremendous circulation; but this
periodical discovers a new genius or saint every other month—a new one

from central Africa was nothing to stir the pulse especially. America had been softened up a little, that was all, for the barrage of publicity which now began. *Life* magazine, one of the biggest guns of all, ran a major article on October 6, 1947 (almost simultaneous with *The Christian Register*'s special number), headed "The Greatest Man in the World— that is what some people call Albert Schweitzer, jungle philosopher."

After that nothing could stop the runaway myth.

Arnold had described how on leaving Lambarene he had written in Schweitzer's visitors' book "a few lines, telling what it meant to have the privilege of knowing 'the greatest soul in Christendom.' "[4] Schweitzer instantly crossed it out; thereby of course confirming his greatness. The tale itself became part of the myth.

For the America of that time, a label such as "the greatest man in the world" was irresistible. Schweitzer grew furious when he heard of it, but what could he do? His story had moved uncontrollably beyond the level of personal encounter at which he had tried to keep it in Europe and into the realm of the mass soul, which he dreaded and disliked. And what was more, those unrelieved, overstrained war years at Lambarene had turned the big, bull-like figure into something highly suitable for canonization by popular demand. The springy hair, though just as vigorous and unruly, was going gray. The face was growing lined, the eyes were a little gentler, the frame a little stooped. Schweitzer was ideal for the sort of presentation America loved, as the craggy old he-man saint, the peasant philosopher who had seen it all, the frontiersman with the homespun wit and unquenchable kindliness.

So much popularity was, of course, very good for the hospital's finances; the money that now flowed in made its reestablishment merely a matter of time. But before Schweitzer left for Europe two things happened which were to have a long-term effect on the hospital. Ali Silver arrived, the bright, energetic and totally devoted young nurse from Holland who, with Mathilde Kottmann, was to support and serve Schweitzer to the end, still nearly twenty years ahead. And over in Lambarene town a new hospital came into existence, founded by the Gabonese government. It began almost as modestly as Schweitzer's had—a few mud huts, very little equipment, a young doctor and his wife as the entire staff.

Dr. Weissberg's first encounter with Schweitzer was not auspicious. When, stammering and nervous, he came face to face with the great man, he began by explaining that he had read some of his books, then failed to remember which, then asked if Schweitzer enjoyed hunting. The story is a fair illustration of the sort of awe-inspiring figure which Schweitzer, the prophet of simplicity, had by now become in the world's eyes.

But after this unpromising start the friendship eventually ripened— Weissberg stayed only a few months on this occasion but returned a few years later—into a mutually valued collaboration, a very different relationship from the one described or implied by many of the reporters from postwar Lambarene, who wanted to use the government hospital as a stick with which to beat Schweitzer's.

Enough for the moment to say that what Schweitzer had gone through in 1913 and 1923, Weissberg in some degree repeated in 1947 and in the 1950's. It was Weissberg who said that out there you were always Charlie Chaplin when the bomb dropped—you looked around for somebody to hand it to, and there was no one. Schweitzer's hospital at that time seemed to Weissberg a place of dazzling equipment and gleaming efficiency.

In 1948 approaches began to reach Schweitzer from the American universities. First Dubuque offered rectorship. Then Yale proposed an honorary degree in divinity, which had to be refused because acceptance involved appearing in person to receive it. (Some universities were prepared in Schweitzer's case to waive this rule and grant an honorary degree "in absentia," but not Yale.) And Princeton invited Schweitzer to come and finish his philosophical work in peace and quiet at the Institute of Advanced Studies, run by Robert Oppenheimer, the physicist who had been so closely involved in the development of the atom bomb. The reasons for Schweitzer's refusal to go to the States are obvious enough, but they are spelled out in a letter he wrote in April, 1948, to Albert Einstein, who lived and worked at Princeton.

DEAR FRIEND,
Many a time have I written you in thought, because from afar I follow your life and your work and your attitude towards the happenings of our time. But my writer's cramp, an inheritance from my mother, hinders me, so that many letters planned in thought remain unwritten. But now that circumstances make it impossible for me to meet you in Princeton I really must tell you in writing how sorry I am about it. And now in an issue of *Life* magazine which came into my hands I see pictures of the Institute which further increase my regrets about the renunciation. The picture of Dr. Oppenheimer with you is touching. When I see a picture of you there always comes back the memory of the beautiful hours I spent with you in Berlin. . . .
Through Dr. Oppenheimer you will have heard about the reasons for my renunciation. I am no longer a free man; in everything I have to consider my hospital and have always to be alert and ready for any action required for its running. Every enterprise is nowadays so burdened by all possible regulations, records and the like that it needs firm guidance all the time. So my absences from Lambarene are limited by this need for constant alertness. At present I have no doctors who are thoroughly acquainted with the hospital's management. The two who are with me now will this week have finished their two years and will be

replaced by two new ones whom I will have to introduce to the work. And for the management as a whole I have nobody who could take over the necessary decisions and responsibilities.

For instance—at one time it began to "smell" like inflation of the franc (in spite of official reassurances that this would not happen), and in order to convert the shrinking paper currency into merchandise before it was too late I had to risk putting all available money into rice, petroleum and other materials which could be had in the factories and stores. In this way I risked having insufficient funds later on to pay outstanding bills and the wages of the numerous black personnel of the hospital. Nobody else could have taken the risk of getting the hospital into great financial difficulties by emptying the money chest, which was already in a precarious situation. I took the risk and saved thousands through hurried buying which was above our means. It saved the hospital from the financial crisis in which it would have been involved if we had had to pay the prices which soared high on the day of inflation. This is just one of many examples. How could I, a good theologian, ever have thought that I would become a speculator and a gambler to keep the hospital above water? However, though I have become a slave to the hospital, it is worth it.

Nonetheless, I am not giving up the hope of being able to continue with my other work. One thing to which I still rigidly adhere is practising the piano with the organ pedal, even if it is only for three-quarters of an hour, to keep in form and also to improve.

The Philosophy I carry with me constantly. Many chapters of the third volume of the Philosophy of Civilisation are finished and others are so far completed in thought that they can be put on paper right away. Only I must first get much extra work behind me (some of it masonry work), in order to be able to keep at it with some degree of quietness and regularity.

At the moment I am trying to eat my way through a mountain of thick gruel to reach the "Lubberland," the land of the lazy. It will be a very modest "Lubberland" but it will suffice my desires. These consist in having the morning and night hours to myself and to use the afternoon for work at the hospital. And if I can achieve that, even in a modest way, I could still give "The Philosophy of Reverence for Life" its definitive form. The whole question is: will I have around me efficient people who are capable of relieving me of as much work as possible, especially the stupid secondary work? The third volume is conceived as a symphony of thoughts—a symphonic performance of themes. Never before in my life have I thought and felt so musically as in these last years. In the third volume I have worked in chapters about mysticism and religion, as revolving around ethics.

We are at present three doctors and seven white nurses, among them an American. Without the material help of the U.S.A. the hospital could not be kept above water despite the economies we practise. My special field is Urology. At the same time I am the Top Apothecary, working out all the orders and keeping the large Pharmacy in order. At the moment I am especially occupied with the treatment of Leprosy. We are using the new American remedies Promin and Diasone, which actually achieve what the former remedies could not. At present we have about fifty lepers under treatment. Leprosy is widespread here.

I am enclosing a map of the hospital. A Swiss engineer who passed through here made it and gave me several copies. Most of these buildings I erected with our black carpenter; in particular I did the masonry work. Among the new generation of natives there are none of the good workmen we used to find among the old ones. The old ones went through the regular apprenticeship and fellowship at the Catholic and Protestant labour missions. Those of the new generation get their knowledge at the so-called Industrial Schools. They consider themselves too good to become workmen. On the whole, *what* will become of the native population in all the colonial territories now that the tendency of the present generation is directed towards emancipating itself from the tilling of the soil and from trade! Nearby and seen from within, rather than from outside and from a distance, colonial problems look quite different.

Now I have let myself go and imposed upon you many pages of my scribble. But it was a pleasure for me to be with you in thought at my desk in these night hours. When will it be granted to us really to be together? Will it even happen?

I read in the "Aufbau,"[5] which I receive regularly, that you received a prize which imposes on you a flight around the world. I hope you will be able to play hooky, to use a good old college expression. . . .

Please remember me to Dr. Oppenheimer. I would have liked to make his acquaintance. How is your violin?

With best thoughts, your devoted
Albert Schweitzer

The writer's cramp hand has stood up well this evening. My wife is at present in Europe, staying in the Black Forest in Switzerland. She is relatively well. My daughter lives in Switzerland with her husband and four children.[6]

Einstein's reply was brief but warm:

I regret of course that you cannot visit the Institute, as you had intended. I am convinced, however, that the work you have pursued for so long is much more important. You are one of the few who combine extraordinary energy and many-sidedness with the desire to serve man and to lighten his lot. If there were more persons such as you are, we would never have slid into so dangerous an international situation as

now prevails. Against the blindness of human beings there unfortunately does not yet exist any remedy.
With warmest regards and wishes,

Yours
Albert Einstein[7]

Schweitzer's long letter is interesting for several reasons. It is a good example of the stiffness of his letter-writing style, even when writing to old friends, and of the repeated themes of all his correspondence. (Ten years later he wrote another letter to Princeton, to the president of the university, most of which might have been written on the same day.) But the fact that he was already in correspondence with Oppenheimer is also interesting, in view of Oppenheimer's subsequent stand against the development of the hydrogen bomb and Schweitzer's deep involvement, along with Einstein, in banning atomic testing.

The brief mention of Hélène in the postscript concealed the fact that she was in fact not at all well, and very unhappy. No sooner had she returned to Europe than she was hankering to get back. "I was pretty miserable in Europe, more than I could tell you," she wrote on June 25 to Hermann Hagedorn.[8] And that dry season she did fly out for a brief and happy interlude. Then she had had to return to extract their Königsfeld house from the military authorities who had requisitioned it and to put it straight again—all of which had proved very tiring.

A tantalizing feature of Schweitzer's letter is the reference to the "symphony of thought" in the long-awaited third volume of *The Philosophy of Civilisation.*

The previous year either Joy or Arnold had actually touched the famous Third Volume. Their account in *The Christian Register* relates with awe:

> The last night that one of the American visitors was to be at the hospital, the doctor called him in and told him to hold out his arms. Then the doctor reached up to a shelf and began piling into the visitor's arms stacks of sheets of paper, yellowed and brown with age. He continued until the paper stood a foot high, and then he exclaimed: "Third Volume!"
>
> So this was it: the distilled wisdom of this scholar, for which the learned world had long been waiting.
>
> "How soon?" the visitor asked. The doctor chuckled, and spread his hands. There are more chapters to write, and rewrite. Some of the chapters already have been done six times.
>
> Looking at the oil lamp on the desk and thinking of the inflammability of this single copy of the precious manuscript, the visitor suggested microfilming. The doctor laughed: Microfilming? Too modern! His manuscript was durable. "Look—see how these chapters have survived the teeth of the antelopes!"[9]

In September, 1948, at long last, Schweitzer set sail from Port-Gentil. Air travel had arrived since he was last there, but nothing would induce him to fly. He enjoyed the sea voyage too much.

Apart from the one hurried round trip to Günsbach and straight back in 1939, he had scarcely moved outside that tiny, hemmed-in cluster of huts on the riverbank for eleven years and seven months.

The homecoming was triumphant. Jacques Feschotte, an old friend of Schweitzer's and a regular visitor at the Günsbach house, wrote:

> I cannot describe with what joy he was welcomed by those who had waited so long. The road to Günsbach was soon crowded with pilgrims. They found the Doctor at seventy-three as strong and as upright as ever. His hair had silvered over and his face was thinner, but his eyes—if such a thing were possible—seemed even keener than before. The whole of Alsace was bent on fêting him. His native town, Kaysersberg, Colmar, Strasbourg, his University, and representative bodies of every kind vied with one another in their touching expressions of regard for this great son of Alsace.[10]

There were, of course, those four grandchildren to visit in Switzerland, none of whom he had ever seen. But for the most part the next few months were extremely peaceful and static by Schweitzer's standards, as he fell back into the rhythm of Günsbach life, writing, talking, strolling in the evenings, playing the organ, and entertaining visitors by the score. Thanks to the stir going on in America, there was no pressing need to go on tour for the moment. Wealthy, enthusiastic, generous, and very very large, the United States represented a newly discovered fairy godmother to the hospital.

Nor had Americans given up hope of inducing Schweitzer to cross the Atlantic. Yale and Princeton had failed. Harvard had invited him to deliver the Lowell lectures, but he had not risen to that bait either. But a more seductive attempt came in the form of an invitation to speak at Aspen, Colorado, on the occasion of the Bicentenary of Goethe's birth.

Aspen was originally a silver-mining town. A wealthy enthusiast named Walter Paepcke had founded an organization known as the Aspen Institute for Humanistic Studies, which held its meetings in a huge specially designed tent in Aspen, though much of the planning was done in Chicago.

About the beginning of January, 1949, Paepcke sent a cable to Schweitzer asking him to come and speak at Aspen the following July, and offering a fee of $5,000. Before long came the reply: Dr. Schweitzer regrets. . . . After a little consideration a new cable went to Günsbach, offering the same sum, only this time in francs, and payable to the hospital. It arrived soon after Schweitzer's seventy-fourth birthday, and was accepted. Goethe, the money, the chance of visiting the pharmaceutical companies that produced the sulfone drugs, and, most important, the chance of saying thank you in person to the people who had kept the hospital alive—all added up to an irresistible proposal.

In accepting, Schweitzer was apparently unaware that Aspen was half a continent away from Chicago, the origin of the cable. He was under the impression that it might be a suburb of the city or a nearby town. "Schweitzer would never have come to America in the first place," said Mrs. Paepcke later, "had the great doctor not laboured under an illusion."[11] A confirmatory letter arrived toward the end of February, clarifying matters but by now Schweitzer was committed, and during the following months he worked on his speech, as well as on the legendary third volume and also on an important epilogue to a projected book on his theology by the Englishman, Colonel E. N. Mozley.

In England meanwhile the first serious criticism of Reverence for Life had appeared, in the form of Middleton Murry's book, already mentioned, *The Challenge of Schweitzer*. Though Murry's whole exasperated argument is destroyed by his failure to understand what Schweitzer meant by "thought," the book is important as giving the intellectuals in England their first respectable lead in questioning the perfection of Schweitzer's ideas.

America was troubled by no such doubts, and prepared excitedly for the arrival of the World's Greatest Man. The University of Chicago had seized the occasion to offer him an honorary degree in laws, which he accepted. The date for its presentation was three days after the Aspen speech, which was to be given twice, once in French, once in German, early in July.

Schweitzer had never aimed to be great, only to be human. And when the liner SS *Nieuw Amsterdam* docked at New York on June 28 and sixty-eight reporters and photographers thronged around him and Hélène, he appeared to enjoy himself greatly, posing for the photographers in his Günsbach suit, his high wing collar, and his father's bow tie, and backchatting the reporters. "What do you think of the New World?" they asked him. "You live here," he replied, "you tell me. . . . I was afraid I'd find you all so materialistic," he said, "but here you are treating a philosopher like the King of England or a prizefighter."

Dr. Emory Ross went with him to Colorado, marveling at his childlike enthusiasm, his swift absorption of what he saw and heard, the extraordinary range and accuracy of his knowledge, the "quality of understanding, solidarity, oneness with others quite different from himself"; and in particular that special vision which gave him the constant flow of images of everyday life with which he made his points. For example, here is Ross' account of an interview with Fulton Oursler for *Reader's Digest*. They are talking about the practical application of Reverence for Life.

> Man should forgive wrongs against himself, yes. Before the wrong-doer asked forgiveness? Certainly, replied Schweitzer, and cheerfully, freely without grudging or reservations—just sweep it out clean, and again and again if required. That's the only way a man can live at peace within himself, and have a room free within for enjoyment and growth. He remembered a fortnight before, in New York's Pennsylvania Station. He was waiting with Mrs. Schweitzer and their small party of friends to board the train for Aspen, Colorado. The usual crowds were milling before the gates. It was the first American railway station he had ever encountered. There must have been a thousand things to see. But Schweitzer saw a sweeper with broom and pan. He was steadily sweeping up paper, cigarette stubs, refuse, moving among the people. He swept a space clean and moved on. When he looked back, there was more paper and refuse already thrown by people. Did he fume and fuss and hate? Not at all. He went on steadily, serenely sweeping. That was his part. He did it. In the business of forgiveness, we must always be using our broom and pan.[12]

During the 2,000-mile journey an incident occurred which no book about Schweitzer can omit. The story has many versions; the most authentic is probably that from the 1951 bulletin to British supporters, vouched for by Mr. and Mrs. T. D. Williams, the treasurer of the Schweitzer Hospital Fund in Britain and his wife. Both had traveled with Schweitzer from Europe.

"As they were travelling over the plains of the Midwest two ladies stopped diffidently at the door of Schweitzer's compartment and asked, 'Have we the honour of speaking to Professor Einstein?' 'No, unfortunately not,' he replied, 'though I can quite understand your mistake for he has the same kind of hair as I have (rumpling his up), but inside my head is altogether different. However, he is a very old friend of mine—would you like me to give you his autograph?' And he wrote, 'Albert Einstein, by way of his friend Albert Schweitzer.' "[13] (Schweitzer and Einstein, incidentally, were to figure as first and second respectively in a nationwide poll conducted in December, 1950, by *The Saturday Review of Literature* to select the world's greatest living nonpolitical persons.)

Aspen turned out to be 8,000 feet high—a great deal higher than anything in the Vosges—and the altitude did not suit Schweitzer. "Aspen," he said, "is built too close to heaven." All the same, despite a late arrival caused by a rockfall on the rail track, he was up bright and early on his first morning there, to the embarrassment of his hostess, Mrs. Elizabeth Paepcke.

The Schweitzers had been told that breakfast was at 8:00 sharp. But at 7:45 the bathroom flooded while Walter Paepcke was showering and Mrs. Paepcke related how she was still endeavoring with mop, bucket, and sponge to control the situation when "our Victoria clock chimed 8:00. The front door opened. There stood the great man himself, amused brown eyes, immense drooping mustache, thin black folded tie, old fashioned long coat . . . and on his arm an elderly lady in gray and garnets who looked like a pale moth. '*Dénoument.*' I stared at the doctor.

" 'Oh,' I cried, 'our plumbing has backed up, there is water all over the floor, and I have to rescue my husband from the bathroom.'

" 'I see,' said Dr. Schweitzer slowly, as he looked me over from tousled hair to bare feet and mop. 'I see,' he repeated, 'Mrs. Schweitzer and I are just in time to witness the second flood.' "[14]

The first lecture, in French, was translated by Emory Ross. When Schweitzer repeated it in German, two days later, the translator was the novelist and playwright Thornton Wilder. "Schweitzer stood," Mrs. Paepcke remembered, "with folded hands, hardly moving, speaking in a surprisingly high and childlike voice. He wore his usual long, black coat, and high, stiff winged collar, but instead of looking pontifical in these he gave the illusion of frailty and extreme vulnerability. It was hard to believe that this man was he who had hewn a hospital with his bare hands out of a disease-infested jungle."[15]

The audience included all kinds of distinguished people. José Ortega y Gasset was there, Artur Rubinstein, Gregor Piatigorsky, Martin Buber, and Ernst-Robert Curtius, son of the Frederick Curtius who had helped Schweitzer in his student days, had come all the way from Strasbourg for the occasion. *Life* magazine managed to take a photograph in which Schweitzer was surrounded by philosophers, theologians, and historians from Spain, France, Holland, and Norway, as well as from Harvard and Washington.

The content of the lecture would not have been unfamiliar to anyone who already knew Schweitzer's other lectures on Goethe. He went into the different sides of Goethe's personality in greater detail than on previous occasions; and there was none of the lowering sense of coming disaster that had marked the last one, in Frankfurt in 1932. But the main theme is the same—Goethe's attachment to nature, to simplicity, to resignation in the face of mystery, to commonsense and observation and action, as opposed to speculative and sterile intellectual exercises. Schweitzer is, as usual, singling out the elements in Goethe which he himself valued—and is puzzled here and there by elements that he cannot sympathize with.

We do not understand for instance, his behaviour toward Christiane Vulpius. They live as man and wife for eighteen months before he legally marries her and gives her, in the eyes of the world, the status to which she is actually entitled. How is it possible for him to prolong a situation which must bring him, and especially her, so many difficulties and so much humiliation? How shall we understand, in general, the spirit of indecision which he displays on more than one occasion?

And this lack of naturalness which he also exhibits! When his prince and friend, Karl August, dies, he does not render to him the last honors, which he should have done in any case as the prince's prime minister. Instead he asks Karl August's son and successor to excuse him from taking part in the funeral ceremonies, so that he may retire to the country to master his grief. He does not even take part in writing the necrology.[16]

Schweitzer the traditionalist breaks through here, the man who, for all his other revolutionary notions, valued the stabilizing force of the rules and rituals of society. A later generation than his came to feel that these rules and rituals were themselves often the forces that destroyed individuality. Rejecting these rules, they could perhaps understand that side of Goethe better than Schweitzer did. But the society that bred Schweitzer had given him his individuality, not taken it from him, and he was faithful to it.

For the most part, however, the lecture is one of gentle and understanding admiration. "This is Goethe—the poet, the sage, the thinker and the man. There are persons who think of him with gratitude for the ethical and religious wisdom he has given them, so simple and yet so profound.

"Joyfully I acknowledge myself to be one of them."[17]

* * *

Schweitzer did not stay long on the heights of Aspen, but while he did the reporters were around him in droves, wanting a good quote or two. One, who had been keeping him from his dinner, said to him, "You're a great man, but what is this business of Reverence for Life?"

"Do you want to practice it," asked Schweitzer, "or do you want me to explain it to you?"

"You explain it first," said the reporter, "and I'll decide if I want to practice it."

Schweitzer liked that.

"If you let me go and eat my soup while it's warm," he said, "you've already practiced Reverence for Life."

It proved a successful and lasting quote.

After leaving Aspen he rested for a day at Denver, then went on to Chicago, where he received his honorary degree, and after it attended a luncheon reception in the Grand Ball Room of the Stevens Hotel. Among those who paid him tribute at that luncheon was Governor Adlai Stevenson, and the Grand Ball Room (as Schweitzer noted on his copy of the program) held over 1,700 people. The invitation with which the lady who organized it drew them all there deserves reprinting in full, for surely it must be one of the high points of the legend, the ecstatic call of a Maenad to the worship of her deity:

CONFERENCE OF CLUB PRESIDENTS AND PROGRAM CHAIRMEN

A WONDERFUL DREAM COME TRUE!
You are to have the high honor of presenting the award
FOR DISTINGUISHED SERVICE TO HUMANITY
TO
DR. ALBERT SCHWEITZER
Philosopher - Musician - Doctor - Theologian - Writer, "Man of God"
"The Thought of him was always a Beatitude, a Great Light, a Wind of Courage."
JULY 11—12:15 NOON, STEVENS HOTEL, GRAND BALL ROOM—CHICAGO

MRS. FREDERICK TICE	MRS. JAMES R. BRYANT
Chairman Luncheon Tickets	Assistant Chairman
440 Linden Avenue, Oak Park	6316 Louise Ave., ROdney 3-1624

Reservations made in order of checks received. Tickets $4.00 including tip and tax. Tables seat ten. **DR. ERNEST CADMAN COLWELL**, President, University of Chicago, will give a tribute, as will **DR. RUDOLPH GANZ**, President of Chicago Musical College.

This invitation includes ministers, **FRIENDS OF CHICAGO PUBLIC LIBRARY** and those who deeply appreciate Dr. Schweitzer as a glowing exemplar of what religion can be in the Life of Man.

NOTE—This is the only place in U. S. outside of the GOETHE Festival at Aspen, Colorado, where this great scholar will appear, nor will he come again.

MRS. CHARLES S. CLARK, President

Schweitzer would not have been human had this kind of adulation left him completely untouched. For one thing it must have affected those around him, making it less and less possible for anyone to treat him as an ordinary human being. And now *Time* magazine gave him a front cover, as well as an article, and another article appeared in *Life. Reader's Digest* added their piece. He was on every bookstall and in every cinema, blown higher than any human creature could survive. If not the greatest, he was certainly the world's most admired man, with several popularity polls to prove it. From now on there was nowhere he could go in the world's estimation but down, and who could wonder that among journalists there was a feeling that the bubble should be pricked sooner or later and speculation as to who would be the first to prick it.

But whatever dismay, amusement, satisfaction, embarrassment, or sheer amazement Schweitzer may have felt at finding himself the world's favorite, shrewd amusement and a childlike delight in all that was happening were his most apparent reactions, and his lifelong sense of proportion ensured that in essentials he was unchanged. He continued to play any organ he could lay his hands on until he was dragged away (organ playing, he used to say, is the best exercise in the world). He went to see friends in Cleveland, Ohio, he visited pharmaceutical works in New York, and on July 22 set sail again for Europe.

It was at this high point of his fortunes that many of the books about Schweitzer appeared, publishers naturally being keen to ride the wave. George Seaver's book had come out in 1947, and others by Hermann Hagedorn, Colonel E. N. Mozley, Joseph Gollomb, and Jacques Feschotte followed in 1948, 1950, 1951, and 1954 respectively.

Most of these books, as one might expect, were to a greater or lesser extent hagiographies. They made little attempt to comprehend Schweitzer, but simply accepted that he was some kind of force of nature, to be wondered at and if possible emulated rather than understood.

The correspondence between Schweitzer and Hermann Hagedorn in 1944 and 1945 shows how little Schweitzer did to encourage this adulation. Hagedorn, whose *Prophet in the Wilderness* is one of the most imaginative and appealing of the books about him, was anxious to fill in some of the gaps, factual and emotional, in the autobiography *My Life and Thought,* and many of the questions he asked were very pertinent. They dealt mainly with the early years, the Strasbourg years; and the striking thing about them, and about Schweitzer's answers, is the light they shed on the insidious way in which the hindsight of admirers colors the past of a famous man, so that an aura of significance rises around what was at the time very matter-of-fact.

In question after question Schweitzer cuts away the ground from beneath the biographer's feet. Hagedorn, for example, writes about the temptations Schweitzer must have felt to abandon the resolution he made at twenty-one and go after the honors that were beckoning at thirty— about "the spiritual struggles that you must have known. The inward story remains untold." What does Schweitzer reply? "I did not know the temptations of which you speak. . . . I was so absorbed in work during those years that I didn't have time to think of myself. I am no superman. Far from it. There is no 'inward story' of those years. I was very happy, very busy, very tired, and I lived in the shadow of St. Thomas' Church; when I wanted to relax I often went there at ten o'clock at night to play the organ—it was a fine instrument—in the dusky church. . . ." And again and again: "Don't forget one thing: people thought very little about me. . . . I don't believe that Catholic Scholars attached any particular importance to my book. I was a quite unknown young man. . . . I was no prodigy, one way or another. I got somewhere thanks to good teachers, and thanks to my industry. . .   There is nothing 'unique' about me whatsoever. . . .[18]

But nobody was interested in Schweitzer's own valuation of himself, even though it was borne out by Elly Knapp (that friend of Hélène's whom Schweitzer married to Theodor Heuss in 1908) in her book *Ausblick vom Münsterturm*. At that time, she remembered, nobody paid any special attention to him. But now the glory of the present shed a transforming light on the past.

Only Colonel Mozley's book ignored the saintly figure with the shaggy head and twinkling eyes, brooding with patient wisdom over the world, and went with enthusiasm for the theology, which had long been neglected or at best regarded as just another alpha plus for the prize boy.

With indignation Mozley discovered that the Church had failed either to answer Schweitzer or to take him seriously, and his book summarized, in seventy-five good clear pages, all Schweitzer's conclusions. This was important and timely. More so still was the epilogue which it drew from Schweitzer himself, in which he followed up his theories about the early Church and traced the course of Christianity thereafter. We have already glanced at this in Chapter Eight but it is worth reminding ourselves, that now, fifty years later, Schweitzer still retained these thoughts not only as an intellectual conviction but as the very foundation of his daily activity.

As Schweitzer saw it, the vivid expectation that Jesus originally had of the coming of God's kingdom had inevitably been whittled away over the centuries after his death. Gradually, as the kingdom receded into the future, the hope of a new age for all mankind had become transmuted into something quite different—the self-centered attempt of isolated individuals to ensure their ticket into bliss after death. The Church's function had changed from that of fostering communal life in the Spirit of Jesus to that of forgiving sinners so that they could die "in the sure hope of glorious resurrection."

In Schweitzer's view this aberration must now be reversed:

> We are no longer content like the generations before us, to believe in the Kingdom that comes of itself at the end of time. Mankind today must either realise the Kingdom of God or perish. The very tragedy of our present situation compels us to devote ourselves in faith to its realisation,
>
> We are at the beginning of the end of the human race. The question before it is whether it will use for beneficial purposes or for purposes of destruction the power which modern science has placed in its hands. So long as its capacity for destruction was limited, it was possible to hope that reason would set a limit to disaster. Such an illusion is impossible today, when its power is illimitable. Our only hope is that the Spirit of God will strive with the spirit of the world and will prevail.
>
> The last petition of the Lord's Prayer has again its original meaning for us as a prayer for deliverance from the dominion of the evil powers of the world. These are no less real to us as working in men's minds, instead of being embodied in angelic beings opposed to God. The first

believers set their hope solely upon the Kingdom of God in expectation of the end of the world; we do it in expectation of the end of the human race. . . .

But there can be no Kingdom of God in the world without the Kingdom of God in our hearts. The starting-point is our determined effort to bring every thought and action under the sway of the Kingdom of God. Nothing can be achieved without inwardness. The Spirit of God will only strive against the spirit of the world when it has won its victory over that spirit in our hearts.[19]

The apocalyptic end of the world that Jesus saw coming had made a new appearance in the world, in the shape of the threat of atomic destruction. But if the end came, there was no promise this time that God would send a new ruler and a new world order after it. Only man could do that, through the spirit of Jesus which now had a new name, Reverence for Life; and it must be done before the disaster, not after it. The confrontation between Life and limitless Death was imminent.

This epilogue was a brief sketch for a longer book which Schweitzer contemplated and on whose manuscript he did in fact work in 1950 and 1951, but which he never published in his lifetime. It was found among his effects after his death and published under the title *The Kingdom of God and Primitive Christianity*—his last statement about God, about the Church, and about life.

A couple of months in Europe for packing and preparation, and Schweitzer was en route once more for Africa, with Hélène still with him.

From there, soon after he had completed three-quarters of a century's living, he wrote: "I am still standing. That is really something. . . . I am in the process of giving to the hospital the impulsion so that it may go on one day when I am no longer in this world, in my tradition and in my spirit."[20] He had not only made his life his argument, he had made his hospital his argument, for his hospital was now his life.

How long had Schweitzer been aware of the hospital as something embodying his spirit and his tradition? For most of its life it had simply "grown half in a dream," reflecting his personality to some extent certainly but mostly reflecting the sheer forces of necessity.

But now, with the world's eye on him, with all the Albert Schweitzer councils and committees all over Europe and the United States thriving and multiplying, he could take the hospital's survival for granted and think more about preserving its style.

For with the publicity came also the pressures. It would have suited many of the big international companies well to sponsor the hospital to the tune of thousands of dollars and garner the glory. Schweitzer had several such offers. He might have raised, if he had so wished, air-conditioned palaces with spotless antiseptic wards and long echoing concrete corridors, full of all kinds of equipment which humidity made useless in his wooden village. In return, he would only have had to allow the use of his name—and lose control of his hospital. For whatever promises he might have been given, he must have known that the image-makers of any respectable American concern would never have allowed life to go on at Lambarene as it now did. He had enough experience already of the shock registered by hygiene-conscious Europeans when they saw his open drains and found chicken dung in the wards to know that his Africans' needs would have to take second place to the demands of the benefactor's publicity men. An army of white technicians would have arrived to install and maintain the new-style hospital. The Africans would have been separated from their families, forced to eat unfamiliar food cooked by strangers, and imprisoned in impersonal wards functionally designed not for living in but only for being ill in.

No amount of superior equipment, Schweitzer felt, could make up for the psychological harm that would follow. In his hospital the whole cycle of life and death was integrated. Health and enjoyment were there, as well as pain and disease. The place asserted life, in a way no American or European hospital could do. And probably most important of all, it was a teaching hospital.

The constant criticisms that Schweitzer did not teach the Africans medicine and did not contribute to medical knowledge miss the point that all the time he was trying to teach them something else, something much more basic and essential: how not to get ill in the first place; how to grow food; how to plan for the future; how to avoid infection; how to defeat suicidal superstitions and hatreds—in short how to live.

Schweitzer had originally come to Africa to be independent, in his service of mankind, of a civilization he thought was on the wrong road. He was not going to sell out to that civilization now, however great the inducements it offered him. His creation was not just a hospital, which could be improved by spending money, but a way of life. That was what he meant by his spirit and his tradition, and that was not for sale. It could be passed on only by personal example and personal influence. All the millions of the drug companies and the film companies (for Hollywood was vainly offering huge sums to make a film about him) were powerless to do that simple thing.

More and more, as the outside world increased the pressure in the ensuing years, Schweitzer was forced into autocracy. It seemed self-evident to a great many people that his hospital was as it was only because he could not afford to make it any better. Now that money was available for the asking, why did he pigheadedly cling to its primitive inadequacies? His reasons, though they were quite capable of rational explanation, lay deep in his instincts—as had his reasons for going to Africa in the first place. And just as then he had grown tired of the hopeless task of convincing his friends by argument and had simply said, "I'm going," so now he laid down the law and let everybody think what they pleased. *"Fais ton devoir sans discuter,"* he used to shout at the Africans—"Get on with your work and don't argue about it." And so he did himself.

He had always been a hard man to say no to. As with age and pressure he grew more dogmatic and less inclined to discuss his decisions, the chances of his sometimes being wrong increased. The marvel is how rarely it happened. The only person with the courage to tell him when it did happen was Hélène. She had always been irritated by some of his characteristics, and now the unquestioning deference he received really exasperated her. So of course did her impotence, as the young and vigorous nurses took over and she found herself again without a function at Lambarene. The tension between husband and wife was inevitable and not always well concealed. For example, Hélène had much less love for animal life than he had, and would keep a stick handy against any creature that presumed too much on her reverence for its life.

All the same, Schweitzer may have needed that touch of acid in his life, and may have known it. For though he very humanly liked to be admired, he hated to be separated from other people by too much respect; and one thing he missed very much at Lambarene was the company of his intellectual equals and the chance of exercising his wits with them. At least Hélène's skepticism offered him something to push against, even though it was complicated by personal emotion.

But in July, 1950, Hélène had to go back to Europe. The hurly-burly of the American tour and the hurried preparation in Alsace had told heavily on her remaining energies. Schweitzer accompanied her to Port-Gentil and put her on the ship. "The farewells at Lambarene," he wrote to America, "were moving for it is scarcely probable that my wife will return . . . together we looked at the hospital until at the bend of the river it disappeared from our horizon. I still cannot get myself away from the emotion of that farewell."

In the hospital, though, all was well. "The doctors and nurses are doing their work well . . . the spirit is excellent . . . my dream is accomplished."[21]

It seems to have been during this happy period, when the hospital was running smoothly, there were no financial worries, and the Schweitzer spirit ruled unquestioned in Lambarene, that he wrote a tiny, odd little book of immense charm, which, like *Memoirs of Childhood and Youth,* tells us more about the man himself than all his philosophies do.

Three young pelicans had been brought in by Africans, and were named Parsifal, Lohengrin, and Tristan. Parsifal became Schweitzer's own favorite and lived in the hospital until his death from the pellets of a hunter's shotgun, already described in Dr. Catchpool's story.

For Schweitzer's birthday Dr. Anna Wildikann presented him with a collection of photographs of Parsifal, with which he was delighted. Dr. Wildikann was shortly leaving the hospital to work in Israel, and Schweitzer knew that she needed a car for her new work. So he sat down and in one night wrote the biography of Parsifal to go with the photographs so that she could buy her car with the royalties.

The book is called *The Story of My Pelican,* and it is told in the first person by the pelican himself—"I am the pelican, the hero of this book." The story begins with the pelican's "confused recollections" of his infancy, with his brothers, in a high nest above the river and the forest:

> My exact memories start from the moment when some black men, shouting and waving branches, drove my parents off and carried us away, all three of us, with our feet bound together. In the village we were placed in a basket in which we could not move. . . . [They are then taken by canoe on a three-day journey, till they reach a place where] among the palms and the mangoes are many red roofs.
> . . . Dogs flung themselves yelping in our way and I promise you we were very frightened. Then a powerful voice broke in, restoring silence, and there appeared a man of burly stature accompanied by a person in white. It was, I discovered from what followed, Dr. Schweitzer and the nurse Emma Haussknecht.
> For a moment or two the doctor looked at our kidnappers and our basket. Then he said, "Three pelicans to feed, that's all we needed!"
> After that there was another silence, at the end of which the doctor spoke to the two blacks: "Didn't you know it's a sin to take little ones away from their parents? How could you do that? Just wait and see; the good Lord will surely find a way of punishing you! Didn't the missionary tell you that at school?"
> The doctor's expression was fearsome, and the blacks were uneasy. But they quickly pulled themselves together and said: "We thought that you liked pelicans and that's why we've brought them. If you pay us for them you can have them. If not, we'll take them to another white man."
> The doctor went all red: "Out of the question! Do you think I'm going to let you drag these poor creatures around half dead with hunger? They'll stay here. Here you are, here's a couple of coins for the cost of the journey and the fish you had to buy for them. And now, clear off!"
> So the pelicans stayed, and were fed, and "the doctoresse" [Anna Wildikann] came and looked at them, and said: "They have a remarkably stupid look about them! But aren't they nice, with their little round behinds all covered with down." They would have liked to pick us up and stroke us, but we dealt out a few sharp nips all round.

[After that the doctor set about building a hutch to keep them warm at night.]
He busied himself all afternoon under the house, crawling about and making no attempt to hide the bad temper these extraordinary activities put him in. I never had any experience of man and I found it very strange that such a good man could grumble such a lot. . . .
[The story continues, the pelican grows up, and the doctor teaches him to fly.]
At the end of the dry season, when the other pelicans returned to the region of the lakes and swamps, my brothers went with them. "Good riddance" said the doctor to Miss Emma; "let's hope the little one will follow suit."
But the little one—me—I'd no intention of doing them such a favour. At the hospital I was at home. . . . I swore that the doctor wouldn't get rid of me so easily. I know better than he does what's good for me. . . .
From time to time lady pelicans have made suggestions to me about leaving the hospital and making a home with them, somewhere a long way away, in a tree. But I've always stuck to the hospital grounds and I intend to go on sticking to them. . . . .[22]

It is impossible to convey at secondhand the warmth and the humor and the loving enjoyment of people and creatures that glow from this book. Sentimentality and whimsy are somehow effortlessly avoided, and in their place, in a frivolous vein, is that same entering into another's world that marked Schweitzer's understanding of Jesus and of Bach. Perhaps his word "solidarity" is as good as any to describe the process.

Everyone who knew Schweitzer speaks of his eyes. They were alert, they were direct, they fixed you, they were amused, they twinkled. Reading *The Story of My Pelican* I find I can see those eyes as clearly as in any photograph.

24

SCHWEITZER ON FILM
1950-1954

THE hospital now housed 400 patients, of whom half were lepers, attracted by the efficacy of the new sulfone drugs. The staff numbered twenty-four, of whom about two-thirds were white.

Apart from one or two who had made Lambarene their life's work (Emma Haussknecht, Mathilde Kottmann, Ali Silver), these white doctors and nurses came for spells of two years at the most—frequently less. Some returned for a second period, but most moved on elsewhere.

In a sense therefore the larger the hospital grew the less continuity it had, for the proportion of people who were untried and new to the work was always increasing.

These doctors and nurses comprise a roll of honor which is and always will be unsung in Schweitzer's story, but we must not forget the sum of adventure, enterprise, and often self-sacrifice represented by this ceaseless flow of trained medical personnel to the Ogowe; nor the constant efforts of Schweitzer's allies in Europe and now in America to find and persuade the right people to go out there; nor from Schweitzer's point of view the ever-increasing paperwork—negotiations, instructions, tickets, permits, passports—which he insisted on seeing to personally.

For the biographer, who has been troubled by the underdocumentation of the early years, the problem now is rather that of an excess of information. For though the outlines of the story are clear enough, different accounts often contradict each other in detail; and meanwhile the inward Schweitzer, whom we have been trying to follow and comprehend, is in danger of becoming swamped under a torrent of facts.

Because Schweitzer's autobiography came to an end twenty years earlier we no longer have his own vision of his life to go by. He published no more books. And the bulletins he wrote and the vast bulk of his letters concerned only the practical needs and problems of the hospital.

More and more people could claim to have met Schweitzer, but very few of those could claim to know him; and even of those few none could know his every side—human communiation does not allow such total identification. So one of his closest friends could say to me, "Schweitzer could never have written such a thing," when in fact he did write precisely that. Another could claim that he occasionally struck Africans in momentary anger, while a third will hotly deny that he could ever have administered more than a friendly slap on the backside. One nurse will say that he was remote and authoritative, another that he was warmly human toward everyone. And on a simple point of fact, someone who was a long while at the hospital will say that Schweitzer was never concerned about fire because everything there was always so damp, while his own remarks in his bulletins show that possibility did worry him and that for that reason he replaced wooden walls with corrugated iron and also abandoned wooden floors in wards and went back to earthen ones.

But what is clear from every account is that for all the increasing complexity of the hospital Schweitzer never did lose the "inwardness" he valued so much, nor his sense of wonder and delight. "The prose of Africa" might overwhelm his days so that there was rarely time to give himself, as man to man, to those who worked with him or those for whom he worked, but the impulse never died. Nor did the need to withdraw and commune with nature. Clara Urquhart remembers how he would say to her, "Come and sit with me"—and they would go to a bench overlooking the hospital and sit together hand in hand for half or three quarters of an hour without speaking, as once he used to go, alone or with his goddaughter, Suzi, to the Rocks of Kantzenrain above his village in Alsace. Times like these were his only holidays.

The great influx of lepers into the hospital posed very special problems, the most obvious of which was that there was simply not enough accommodation for them—especially in view of the long period during which they needed to be kept under observation before the disease could be considered checked. They were inclined to vanish back to their villages as soon as the pain ceased, only to return, much worse, when it recurred.

Into this situation came an enthusiastic young nurse, Trudi Bochsler, who immediately made the lepers her special concern. Soon indeed she began to argue with Schweitzer and fight hospital regulations in her determination to see that "her" lepers got a fair share, or if possible more than their fair share, of the available facilities. She noted that the effectiveness of the new drugs was often reduced because the patients were suffering from other diseases or from malnutrition and their systems were unable to benefit as they should. The other complaints therefore had to be diagnosed and treated before the leprosy treatment could begin, and this made fresh demands on the hospital in general.

It is probably from this time that the popular imagination began to identify the Schweitzer hospital exclusively with leprosy, and it is worth reiterating that until the end of the Second World War leprosy treatments were so laborious and ineffective that lepers made a very small proportion of the patients. Ten or fifteen years later the hospital's usefulness in the leprosy campaign was ending as the government took it over, and once again lepers were in a minority there. But at this particular juncture Schweitzer's hospital was the only place for hundreds of miles offering the newest treatment.

The place where the lepers were treated was not even a building, simply a leaf canopy to keep off sun and rain, and their accommodation was the isolation building at the top of the hill, a few minutes' walk from the main hospital.

Here before long Trudi Bochsler was taking upon herself the building of a number of huts for the lepers. Here she coaxed and bullied and cajoled the lepers, who now loved and trusted her like a mother, to do for themselves, so far as their maimed limbs allowed them, what no one else had time to do—build themselves a village. Defying Schweitzer when she disagreed with him, oblivious to the problems she caused in the rest of the hospital, she yet wrung from him such respect that he granted her an autonomy within the organization that no one else had achieved.

Another arrival at the hospital at this time was the filmmaker, Mrs. Erica Anderson, who has already been quoted but now met Schweitzer for the first time.

With her she brought her camera equipment and an assistant—in defiance of Schweitzer's wishes, for when she had first broached the idea of making a film about him he had refused permission, as he had done to numbers of other applicants before her. To Clara Urquhart, through whose good offices Erica had first managed to contact Schweitzer, he had written, "I would rather burn in hell than have a film made of my life."

However he had invited Erica to come, if she wished, to the hospital, but *not* to film. She had only brought her equipment because a collector of African art had asked her to shoot some film for him in the Congo—though she also had a secret hope that once at Lambarene she might overcome Schweitzer's objections.

And so it proved. After a while she had regretfully reached the conclusion that Schweitzer was right—anyone making a film would only interrupt hospital routine and be an extra and unproductive mouth to feed—when Schweitzer sent for her. Having come to know her he had changed his mind—with two stipulations. There must be no publicity for the film, and it must not be released until after his death.

So began a friendship which Erica was to record in her book *Albert Schweitzer's Gift of Friendship*—by far the most vivid, and I suspect the most accurate, portrait of Schweitzer ever put into print, lovingly written and full of the kind of significant day-to-day detail that so many books about him lack.

With her independence from hospital routine and her different background from the nurses Erica was able to see Schweitzer in a different light from the medical staff. She saw him as someone whose gaiety and spontaneity was inhibited by his responsibilities at the hospital, and she felt that to some extent at least his authoritarian pose was forced on him by the need of some of the medical staff for a father figure. He told her, for example, that he much disliked being called *"le grand Docteur,"* the title which some of the staff insisted on using. To Erica he would refer to himself humorously as "Grandfather," or "the old idiot."

The staff in turn tended to mistrust Erica as an alien force in the atmosphere of Lambarene. But nobody could fail to admit that her film, when it was finally shown several years later, was a loving and unique record of the hospital as well as of Schweitzer himself and his home in Alsace.

* * *

He returned to Alsace in May, 1951—this time only for six months. He was growing older, and Europe was growing more exhausting. Though he undertook no further tours and went only briefly to Holland, Scandinavia, and England on more or less private visits, he was inundated by visitors of all sorts—among them the Queen of the Belgians, who came quietly and privately to see him.

Erica Anderson had already returned to America to develop the film she had shot and to report progress to her producer, the railroad millionaire James Jerome Hill. He sent an album of her photographs to Günsbach and shortly received an ecstatic letter from Emmy Martin, thanking her for such "an abundance of beauty" and inviting her to Alsace. "On the 28th July, the anniversary of Bach's death, Dr. Schweitzer will play a concert in St. Thomas's Church in Strasbourg. You should be present! It would also be good if you could be here in Günsbach between the 7th and 14th of August, because there will be much music in our house."[1]

Such an invitation was exactly what Erica had hoped for, and Jerome Hill decided to come with her. They arranged to be in Strasbourg in time for the concert, but not to disturb Schweitzer by calling on him before it. Erica's account of what followed provides a good example of Schweitzer's captivating charm.

> The night of the concert we arrive at St. Thomas Church at six o'clock. Hundreds of people are already gathered there, standing outside the church, though the concert does not start until seven-thirty. We've inched our way forward to about the fourth row of standees,

when Schweitzer arrives. His European clothes strike me as very strange: a black Loden coat, a large black hat, an old-fashioned collar and black tie. He looks very much the proverbial German professor, quite different from the worker of Lambarene with his sun helmet, sand-colored trousers, and the white, open-collared shirt.

He walks briskly, waves at the crowd, but does not stop to talk with anyone before entering the church. A few minutes later the church door opens and Mme Martin beckons to someone in the crowd. I turn instinctively to look for that someone behind, not believing she could mean me. But I feel myself pushed forward.

"Yes, I mean you," Mme Martin says. "The Docteur told me that he made you a promise. Follow me."

Schweitzer is already in the organ loft when we reach him. "An elephant does not forget," he says taking my hand. "Didn't I promise you that someday you would be with me when I played on a beautiful church organ, instead of an out-of-tune piano with pedal attachments?"[2]

After the concert Schweitzer spent hours signing autographs (having refused to let the police "protect" him from the crowd) and at last went to the restaurant where he had arranged to meet with, among a number of others, Jerome Hill.

Hill remembered how that evening Schweitzer went methodically from table to table, concentrating unhurriedly on each group of people who wanted to meet him; and how when he came to Hill's table and spoke to him, Hill immediately felt entirely at ease, as though he had known him all his life. "Schweitzer's power was to bring out the person you really were," writes Erica. " 'So you are the generous soul who let this creature come to Lambarene despite all my objections' are the words with which Schweitzer takes Jerome's hand. 'The girl's stubborn as a dog,' he continues. 'Like a flea which digs in where the dog can't scratch. That's the way she is. I just could not refuse her.' "[3]

Before long, as filming progressed at Günsbach, Jerome Hill began planning to bring tape recording equipment there, to record a concert for the film on Schweitzer's own village organ.

The two Americans entered closely into Günsbach life, and both grew close to Schweitzer's heart.They saw how "he is asked to aid all kinds of human suffering. A father comes to him, in deep despair about placing his Mongoloid child in a mental home; a young bride terribly disillusioned by her marriage; a lonely widow. Schweitzer offers far more than general advice. There is something deeply and distinctly personal in his dealings with people. When the widow is leaving him, for instance, Schweitzer follows her a few steps away from the house. 'This is the spot where your husband said good-bye to me for the last time,' Schweitzer tells her gently. For some astonishing, inexplicable reason, he remembers the day, the

month, and the year of the event, though it happened thirteen years
ago!''[4]

Hélène was there most of the time, her bowed figure contrasting with
the uprightness of her husband. Though the flesh was sinking on his broad
figure and the face falling into the lines of old age, he was still a formidable physical presence. The secret of life was, he believed, to live "as a
man who never gets used up.''[5] But Hélène was used up. Her body gave
her no choice.

Rhena too was a frequent visitor, bringing one or more of her children,
as her aunts had brought their families up the valley before her to visit the
old manse. She was all too aware of the tensions between her parents, and
of her mother's jealousy of Mme Martin, on whom Schweitzer relied
completely.

The old jangling doorbell rang unceasingly with visitors or with mail
arriving. Honors were still pouring in—offers of honorary degrees, invitations to become a freeman of the city, or president or vice-president of
charity committees and musical organizations. Schweitzer can never have
known that so many organizations even existed. He would generally accept, so long as all they wanted was his name on the letterhead and no
work or responsibility was required.

The happiest occasion was when a prize of 10,000 marks was awarded
him by the West German Association of Book Publishers and Book Sel-
lers for his contribution to world peace. It happened at Frankfurt. His last
visit there for a public occasion had been for the centenary of Goethe's
death in 1932, with the Nazi threat looming. Things were different now.
The President of West Germany, who presented him with his prize, was
one of his oldest friends—Theodor Heuss, whom Schweitzer, reeking of
anesthetic, had married to Elly Knapp in 1908. We have already heard the
story of the famous frock coat, which Schweitzer wore to that wedding
and wore again today—and Heuss congratulated him on the excellence of
his Günsbach tailor.

The prize money Schweitzer gave to German refugees and destitute
writers. He could afford to do so now—so long as he kept his hospital
simple and made the Africans work for what they got. The council which
organized collections for him in Britain had a balance of £10,000 or so, of
which he only asked them to send about a tenth to Africa. The rest he
wanted to set aside as a pension fund for his workers; for this purpose he
trusted sterling more than the other European currencies.

A visit to Stockholm to receive the Grand Medal of the Red Cross of
Sweden and membership of the Swedish Royal Academy of Music gave
him a good story to add to his repertoire. At a dinner at which the King of
Sweden was present a fish was placed before him which he was not famil-

iar with—a complete fish, head, tail, bones, and all. Not knowing what to do with this fish or whether he liked it, he waited till nobody was looking and slipped it into his pocket. A newspaper report the next day noted that the famous doctor had learned some interesting habits in central Africa, for he could swallow an entire fish and leave no trace behind.

Unfortunately Schweitzer forgot about the fish, and a day or two later Hélène grew seriously worried about the drains before the decomposing corpse was traced.

On October 6 Jerome Hill's recording van arrived in Günsbach, and work began on that section of the film. Schweitzer was naturally delighted with the fidelity of the recording and the instant playback, making it possible to check and rerecord unsatisfactory passages. He began to ask about the possibility of recording a whole series of works the following autumn—Bach, Widor, César Franck, and Mendelssohn. Jerome Hill immediately put the wheels in motion.

While Schweitzer's days were filled with vigorous enthusiasm, his letters, as usual, told a different story. He wrote at this time to friends in America: "Since I have been in Europe I have not had one day, one afternoon to rest. There are visitors, journalists, friends.

"I cross one crisis of fatigue after another. On shipboard I have given definite form to two important chapters of *The Kingdom of God,* but in Europe not a single hour on it. I am in despair because of this. I am trying to work on the chorales of Bach which I promised to Schirmer before the first world war. Nies-Berger is helping me with this."[6] (Edouard Nies-Berger's own recollections of the time are somewhat different—a humbling amazement at finding himself quite unable to keep pace with a man, almost twice his age, who worked with unflagging delight and passion and seemed to need neither rest nor sleep.)

Schweitzer, it may be remembered, had been working with Widor on this edition of the complete Bach organ works for Schirmer's of New York before the First World War, but had not been able to finish it before going to Lambarene in 1913. After the war, Schweitzer's German-sounding name and the general chaos of the economy had discouraged the publishers from going ahead with the project. But now that that same name represented such glowing publicity value, the scheme was resurrected and urged to a conclusion.

Though Schweitzer did not in the end manage to complete the edition himself, Nies-Berger went on to finish it alone, and this monumental work, the fruit of all the detailed research Schweitzer had put into fingering, registration, and ornamentation, as well as the original score, finally saw print in its entirety.

While this was going on, Erica Anderson had been happily making herself useful by acting as chauffeur. When the filming and recording were finished she went on to Germany to visit friends, leaving word that she was at Schweitzer's disposal if he needed her, and it was not long before she was summoned back into service.

The summons was courteous but peremptory:

> DEAR ERICA,
> Now I have to call on you, if it is possible for you to be at my disposal. I arrive in Heidelberg from Hamburg on Thursday, November 1 at 5:05 P.M. I have to visit friends in Württemberg. The train connections are very bad, and I would lose a day that way. Now my request: Wait for me on the Heidelberg train station on November 1 at 5:05 P.M. Drive me to the place where I have to be, and the next day on to Strasbourg. Should I not arrive at 5:05 P.M. wait in the station restaurant until ten in the evening. Then take a room in a hotel as near to the station as possible. Then wait for me on November 2 from eight in the morning on, again in the station restaurant, until I show up. You help me out greatly. I thank you from my heart and I am happy to see you again. In haste with kind greetings,
>
> Yours,
Albert Schweitzer[7]

When Schweitzer took such journeys by train he went alone, so we have no way of knowing what happened. Thanks to the fact that he never learned to drive a car and relied on a chauffeur we have Erica's account of this trip, and it adds valuably to our knowledge of him. A few extracts will have to suffice here:

> On the way to Heilbronn, Schweitzer tells me about his recent trips through Sweden, England, and Germany, about the enthusiastic response of new friends and old to his philosophical ideas. His talk is so animated, his voice so youthful, that in the dark of the autumn evening I feel as though I have a very young man next to me who has just returned from his first trip into the world.
> I am not sure of the road, and in the darkness it is difficult to read the signs. But it is always Schweitzer who jumps out of the car to seek directions, grabbing the hand of whomever we encounter, and always displaying such a rare combination of politeness, directness and warmth.

When in the dark they lost their way and the car became stuck in a muddy ditch, Schweitzer, though he had been two days and two nights in a third-class train compartment, insisted on walking off across muddy plowed fields in search of help.

Fortunately Erica managed to extricate the car by herself, and when he was back in it again, " 'The adventures we experience!' he says. 'One must allow life to come up with such accidental situations. It is always they which turn out to have been the most memorable' . . ."

Erica left Schweitzer with his friends for the night and herself went to the local inn, picking him up again in the morning.

> In daylight the road is much easier to follow . . . Dr. Schweitzer talks in a constant flow about the poet Mörike, who grew up in this part of the world, about art, politics, philosophy, and he grows more exuberant as the sun rises higher and the day brightens. Every well-cared-for field we pass gives him joy, every little cart, every dungheap. Especially dungheaps! He explains to me their importance: "Once when a journalist asked me about civilisation, I answered, 'It all begins with the dungheap. If a dungheap is looked after well and built as it should be, you can be sure that the people who built it are civilised.' I'm afraid that journalist did not understand what I meant, but ever since then I say, 'Civilisation starts with the dungheap, the *Misthaufen*.' "
> While he talks on, the sun shines in his eyes, and like a boy who has taken a day off from school, he says: "Think of it. No one in the world knows exactly where we are!"
> A little girl, braids flying in the wind, is running down the road ahead of us.
> "Pull over," he says. "Maybe we can give her a lift." Then to the child: "Hey, you little frog, where are you off to in such a hurry?"
> "To the pharmacy,' the little one pipes up. "My mother is sick, and I have to get her some medicine."
> "To the pharmacy then," replies Schweitzer. "Get in, and we'll take you there. Tell me, does the druggist give you some licorice when you buy something?"
> "No. Never," replies the little girl.
> "Then tell him that the old fellow who gave you a lift is a doctor," says Schweitzer. "And that when he was a child, he always got some free candy in a pharmacy. It's a good old custom and should not be abandoned. What do you want to be when you grow up?"
> After a slight pause, the small high voice rings out: "A fashion designer!"
> "Fashion designer," Schweitzer says, imitating her high voice. "Tell me," he continues in his own, "do you know how to sew?"
> "No. But I can draw beautifully," the child replies.
> "That is good," says Schweitzer. "But you must also learn how to sew. That way you will be a better fashion designer later on. And don't make skirts that are too short, do you hear? And the same applies to your hair—leave it long, whatever fashion dictates."

Later they gave a lift to a young man who, despairing of the purpose of life, was on his way to enter a monastery.

For seven miles Dr. Schweitzer tries to touch something in the young man which still has a glimmer of faith, a spark of hope. I can feel that the young man, although by no means easily convinced, is listening intently. At last he speaks too, slowly, but with less bitterness and self-pity than before.

"Maybe you have something," he says. "Maybe it is not a coincidence that you picked me up. I did not even bother to raise my hand for a lift any more. I was sure that people didn't care, that people are no good. I have no friend—"

Here the Doctor interrupts him.

"You must not expect anything—from others," Dr. Schweitzer says. "It's you yourself of whom you must ask a lot. Only from oneself has one the right to ask for everything or anything. This way it's up to yourself—your own choice. What you get from others remains a present, a gift!"

"Thank you," says the young man when he steps out of the car. "I'll think about what you said. I will take time before I make a decision."[8]

Finally, after visiting another friend of Schweitzer's in the mountains of the Black Forest—a professor of geology who had been exiled by the Nazis and never reinstated by the French, and whom Schweitzer had not seen for twenty years, they drove home.

Though Schweitzer grew accustomed to cars and appreciated the time they saved, he never quite accustomed himself to the guilt involved in traveling in the softly sprung American limousine—"It's like a pram," he said—and he tried to assuage it by insisting on offering lifts to all and sundry. As with his passion for helping people with their baggage, the impulse occasionally got a little out of hand and led to situations that were humorous rather than helpful. But that was a small price to pay for adherence to his principle of giving himself to all humanity, and for the constant contacts he made with all kinds of people on his travels.

25

A CRACK IN THE MYTH
1951–1954

WHEN he returned to Lambarene in December, 1951, Schweitzer found everything in very good running order, except the leper situation. The number of lepers was still increasing, and the huts they had built under the driving encouragement of Trudi Bochsler were of the very vulnerable bamboo and leaf-tile construction that needed constant repair. There was nothing for it but to build a complete new section of the hospital, a permanent village, for the lepers alone—somewhere for them to live out their lives even after the disease was arrested, for their villages often refused to have them back.

Monenzali, the carpenter who had helped Schweitzer build the beginnings of the hospital, had retired to his village. He was too old, he said, to work any more. Schweitzer sent a message that if he came back and built again he would grow younger every day; and Monenzali came.

His relationship with Trudi, fighting for her lepers with a single-mindedness which took no account whatever of the interests of the hospital as a whole, remained unsettled, and his famous Schillinger temper was often on display—as was his technique of swift reconciliation. At the end of one row he shouted : "Don't you know you're talking to Albert Schweitzer? Get out of the room and don't come back!" Before she had reached the door—which could not have been more than three paces, he said "Do you like books?" She stopped and said she did. "Take any book you like from my shelves," he said. She took her time and chose a book by Kierkegaard, a philosopher she thought she should know more about. She thought Schweitzer showed signs of regretting his offer, but he said nothing, and she carried the book off to her room. The moment was typical. Schweitzer never actually apologized; he simply did something to show that the incident was canceled.

The Kierkegaard book turned out to be underlined and annotated so heavily that there was barely any white space left on the pages. Schweitzer's Bible too was black with annotations, but that one might have expected. It is more interesting in the book of a philosopher whom he mentioned little, and then often dismissively, but who shared with him the conviction that religion is a matter of the individual soul's deep response to God, beyond reason and beyond dogma.

Kierkegaard is often quoted as the father of Christian Existentialism, the apostle of the personal, immediate encounter with God in the circumstances of daily life. Allowing for tremendous differences of temperament, one could easily make the same claim for Schweitzer. When I first started researching this book I was struck by this similarity and asked Dr. Hermann Baur, who has made a deep study of Schweitzer's thoughts, whether Schweitzer had ever mentioned Kierkegaard. Dr. Baur had never read nor heard of any serious comment by Schweitzer on the subject, and I was surprised and disappointed by the implication that Schweitzer had failed to take note of so important and relevant a philosopher. But the incident with Trudi shows once more the comprehensiveness of Schweitzer's interests and the concentration he gave them. One can never assume that he has ignored or dismissed anything of importance simply because there is no recorded utterance on the subject.

Erica Anderson was in Lambarene again in March, continuing to shoot her film. Six more years were to pass before it was finished. And the correspondence with Jerome Hill about the new recordings at Günsbach was touched with an intimacy very rare in Schweitzer's letters. He is overwhelmed, he says, by the money that Hill is spending on him, in putting that marvelous recording apparatus at his disposal again. "I'm afraid one day an article will appear in 'The New York Times': 'Doctor Schweitzer has ruined Jerome Hill.' " And meanwhile he hears from Erica that Hill is sending him an incomparable new record player as a belated birthday present. "Don't trouble to send an electrician—we have plenty of people who can install it, given clear instructions. But send the most essential spare parts."[1] He leaned too on Hill's advice about the contracts for the sale of the recordings. Hill planned to do this through the American Columbia Company, and the contract excluded the British section of Columbia, to whom Schweitzer felt he owed gratitude for recording him when he was less well known. "Gratitude has been one of my guiding stars. Now I look like having to renounce it."[2]

As to the film he reiterated that it must not be shown before his death. "How can I allow such personal scenes to be shown while I am still alive? How could I possibly bear it? This is impossible. I could not do it because I have given myself to you both with all my heart. I have unlimited confidence in you both that you will not only make a good film but also do it with great tact. To no-one else but you would I show such trust."[3] It ran quite counter to his reserve, and particularly to his dislike of personal adulation, to think of himself as the subject of a film. His work, yes. Himself, no. In fact he had grown so involved in the film that he decided to write the commentary himself—but not in a hurry. "I can't hurry. It must be a good and beautiful job." There was plenty of time, since the film was not to be shown in his lifetime, and "I have more imagination than is usually believed of me." [4]

On the leper village front things were less smooth. In the end Trudi Bochsler crossed him once too often and in May she went home after a final confrontation. She went to various centers in Switzerland to study the latest treatments of leprosy, and Schweitzer continued the leper village without her.

July saw him on the boat for Bordeaux again, for a brief five months in Europe during which the new recordings were made. Nies-Berger came from New York for further work on the Bach edition, and Schweitzer was installed as a member of the French Academy of Moral and Political Sciences. In his address to the Academy on October 20, entitled "The Problem of Ethics in the Evolution of Human Thought," he covered much familiar ground; but one thought is perhaps given clearer articulation than before:

> The term "Reverence for Life" is broader and, for that reason, less vital than that of love, but it bears within it the same energies. This essentially philosophical notion of good has also the advantage of being more complete than that of love. Love only includes our obligations towards other beings. It does not include our obligations towards ourselves. One cannot, for instance, deduce from it the necessity of telling the truth; yet this, together with compassion, is the prime characteristic of the ethical personality. Reverence for one's own life should compel one, whatever the circumstances may be, to avoid all dissimulation and, in general, to become ONESELF in the deepest and noblest sense.[5]

In November he completed the recordings in Günsbach church. Rhena's husband, the organ builder Jean Eckert, who himself took a keen and informed interest in the problems of recording music, had always tried to dissuade Schweitzer from using the Günsbach organ for recording purposes—not because the organ was unsatisfactory but because the acoustics of the small church muffled the effect. But Schweitzer, it seems, was not interested in making perfect recordings, only in preserving the sound of his beloved instrument. He was well satisfied with the result, but the recordings certainly appear to lack the clarity and definition of which this beautiful little organ is capable and on which he himself laid such emphasis.

The recordings over, he went back to Lambarene, this time for eighteen months. More and more now Lambarene, not Günsbach, was home. In Lambarene he was his own man, he could organize his life, he could give himself time to think.

For extraordinary though it may seem, no major journalist had yet actually penetrated to the hospital or seen what actually went on there. And though visitors were growing more frequent, they were still for the most part people who already had some personal interest in Schweitzer and his work. The tourist trade had not yet discovered Lambarene.

For a year things went more or less smoothly in the hospital. The building of the leper village took up the greater part of Schweitzer's time, for the clearing and the leveling of the site meant moving quantities of hard rocky soil by hand—

> Why did we not hand the work over to a building contractor, instead of doing it ourselves? If we had engaged a white contractor, who would have had to employ native workers and earn something for himself, the cost would have been prohibitive. Nor could I, to reduce his wage bill, let him use the able-bodied lepers, because I would have had no guarantee that he would look after them properly, while they on their part would not have wanted to work under him or obey him. Now, as before in the Hospital, the village has had to be built with the labour of the inmates who are able to work, and those lepers whose general state of health is more or less satisfactory. And since I am the only one with the authority to keep them at the job I have to be my own contractor again.
>
> Moreover, I regard it as a matter of principle that those who find shelter and care in this Hospital maintained by gifts should serve it with the labour of which they are capable, and so acknowledge what they are receiving. They owe it to those who make donations to the Hospital to do their part in keeping the costs of its maintenance and operation as low as possible.
>
> At the end of the week, of course, those working on the building site get some money, and two or three times during the week they are given some good confectionery; they also like gifts of sugar. They have a right to all their clothes, and on Sunday the women who during the week have been carrying earth can be recognized by their pretty dresses and headscarves.[6]

A timber merchant helped by lending Schweitzer a length of light rail and some trucks in which the earth could be carried more easily; but it was still a formidable task.

From the outside world, pressures were now being exerted on Schweitzer from various sources to involve himself in politics, especially in the efforts to get international agreement on the control of atomic bombs, for many people thought his moral influence would be invaluable.

But he always refused. His method had always been the slow, personal one, not the high-level political approach; and besides he was not sure that he knew enough about the subject.

In November, 1953, however, something happened that had been in the cards for a long time. He was awarded the Nobel Peace Prize. And this had several results, the first being that he could afford to buy and import corrugated iron for the roofs of the village, for the prize was worth $36,000. Without that money the huts, though built on concrete and of hardwood, would apparently have had raffia roofs.

The question immediately arises why Schweitzer did not plan to use his reserves in Britain for this purpose; and there is no way of knowing the answer, for he kept these decisions very much to himself. At a guess, however, he was determined not to find himself without a sizable contingency fund if war came again—which in those uneasy years, when the threat of atomic war was always at the back of everyone's mind, seemed not all unlikely.

The prize had to be awarded in absentia, and was accepted on Schweitzer's behalf by the French ambassador to Norway, for Schweitzer was much too involved in the building of the leper village to get away. But it was of course widely publicized. And this was the moment when at last a British journalist decided to make the great expedition and confront the doctor in his mythical habitat. James Cameron took some pride in having been the first actually to penetrate to the lair of the legend, but his achievement was not so tremendous when one considers that inexperienced young nurses now made the trip regularly and it was possible to fly all the way to Lambarene's own airstrip. Schweitzer had been doing it the hard way for forty years.

Cameron wrote a series of three articles for the *News Chronicle* about Schweitzer and the hospital, which he adapted fourteen years later into a chapter for his semiautobiographical book *Point of Departure*. He also broadcast a talk on BBC radio. Some of what he wrote has already been quoted. But now it is time to go into it more thoroughly, for Cameron was in fact the first man to open a few cracks in the surface of the myth—the reaction the world was ready for.

The effect of Cameron's articles was due to a combination of factors. He was the first man to have visited Lambarene and reported it with an eye unprejudiced in Schweitzer's favor—he had no ax to grind. He wrote much more vividly and entertainingly than most of Schweitzer's adulatory biographers had done. And he was known as a paragon among journalists for sensitivity and integrity. He was a man to be trusted.

Much of his report ran along fairly familiar lines. He found that he liked Schweitzer ("the only man in this century," as he described him in his radio talk, "who has become famous by being good")[7] more than he had expected. He had come prepared to find him smug, ready to be preached at. This did not happen. "It may be hard to communicate that a man may be good, and testy; of legendary resolution, but frail; capable of universal tolerance and sudden superb impatiences; full of Christ and fun. . . . I often forgot in the mornings that Albert Schweitzer was The World's Finest Man: I felt him merely to be one of the friendliest." (In the heat of the afternoon nobody was quite so good-tempered.) He liked his "famous and intensely expressive moustache—a massive affair of no especial shape, or rather of a multitude of shapes, since it appears to pay great attention to the doctor's mood; now a battery of questioning antennae, now an unpromising curtain." He enjoyed the way "he roared at the dog chasing hens: 'Stop that! Don't you know this is a Peace Prize house? Be a Nobel dog, and quick.' " And he admired Schweitzer's "prodigious wink."[8]

Cameron's broadcast used mostly the same material as the articles, and we can hear from his tone of voice how much he liked the fact that in Schweitzer's ethic there was no fanaticism, only reasonableness, and that the sole rule was kindness. He liked the way Schweitzer's conversation ranged between the state of the world, the best way to eat a mango, and the will of God. He respected the fact that most thefts were merely irritating, but that it was a desperately sad day when somebody stole some penicillin. And in a voice of great warmth he told how Schweitzer, asked when he would go for his Peace Prize, said, "I can't go yet. If I do these lazy brutes will never get their houses built. And they need them so badly!"[9]

Though he found himself somewhat disconcerted when Schweitzer talked "like a Kenya settler" about the idleness of the Africans, he conceded in the articles that "In this context he could of course say what he liked. . . . You do not negate 40 years of selfless devotion to the African by reacting to his more maddening aspects. I liked it. He made people work, and did most of it himself."[10]

But however much he liked Schweitzer personally, evidently bearing no ill-will over the inevitable tussle about wearing a hat in the sun ("'If you are determined to become ill, become ill elsewhere, near some other doctor,'"[11] said Schweitzer), the things that disconcerted him were bound to disconcert his readers over the breakfast tables in December, 1953, even more. Fair though he tried to be, Cameron's understanding of Schweitzer was far from complete, and the majority of his readers were much less well informed than he was about the reasons why things at Lambarene were done as they were.

Early in the first article, for example, comes the description of "the primitive dugout canoe that fulfils the doctor's insistence on remoteness, self-containment, his resistance to progress." For those who skimmed over the page and did not even read the text there was a picture of the hospital with the caption LIFE IN THE GIMCRACK COLONY OF HOPE. And of the hospital itself ("a place of surpassing ugliness"), Cameron writes, "I would say that the hospital today exists for him rather than he for it. Here it is: deliberately archaic and primitive, deliberately part of the jungle around it, a background of his own creation which probably means a good deal more philosophically than it does medically."[12]

That was very damaging, and irresponsible in its inaccuracy. And what must the good Liberal readers of the *News Chronicle* have thought when they read that Schweitzer shouted at his native workmen, " 'Run, you! Work like a white man, can't you?' "[13] Nor can they have liked Schweitzer's reported views on the subject of African self-government: " 'They have citizens' rights now—but no citizens' responsibilities. They destroy most things they touch. . . . You ask whether the *indigène* can ever develop to responsibility without us, and the answer is No, they cannot. Others disagree. The United Nations Trusteeship Commissions and so on—they think in terms of *politics*. Do they ask who plants the trees that the African can eat, who bores the wells that he can drink? No, they say, How are they progressing to self-government? Self-government without resource, without thrift? Democracy is meaningless to children!' "[14]

Out of the context of the upper Ogowe these too were damaging, however accurate; and it is clear that Cameron did not ask the right questions of Schweitzer to get a complete picture—or else that Schweitzer did not take Cameron seriously enough to give him the full answers.

In a rather perfunctory attempt to explain the hospital Cameron wrote, "There was the theory, or heresy, that somewhere in this monument to sacrifice rests a trace of spiritual pride—the mystique that maintains the hospital as a slum, because it is thus that Schweitzer has always seen it; that denies to his patients and staff the minimum of amenity, and indeed human contact with le grand Docteur himself, because his mind is elsewhere.

"The doctor's answer is very nearly clear: this is a mission before it is a hospital: it is maintained in African squalor because it is indeed part of Africa: in any case were it otherwise no African would come. One asks why, with tuberculosis patients the hospital should refuse offers of essential radio-therapy, and the answer again is simple: Dr. Schweitzer does not like it. That answers everything: it may be right."[15]

The consistent philosophy that lay behind everything that Schweitzer did had evidently escaped him, leaving him with the belief (headlined by the subeditors of the *News Chronicle*) that "here was not one man but two"—[16] the moral impulse and symbolism of being good, its practical expression worthless.

Reading the later version in *Point of Departure* one finds that time has hardened Cameron's negative feelings about Schweitzer. Perhaps as the warmth of Schweitzer's personality faded from the memory he was left with only his indignation at the doctor's views. He was probably affected too by the growth of the antimyth which he himself fostered and which had become firmly entrenched by the time of Schweitzer's death—for reasons that we shall come to.

But though these feelings may have grown through the years, they were certainly there in embryo from the start. And Cameron was sensitive enough to record and remember a small stab which Schweitzer made at his profession. Cameron had raised the question of "the many shadows of despair that haunt this continent and seemed somehow this week to obsess me," but Schweitzer would not be drawn. " 'I am a man of limited experience,' " he said. " 'A man must occupy himself with what he knows and lives among. I would suggest there are too many people hurrying around having everybody's troubles at once. Yours must be a distressing occupation: rather useless.' " "It was," says Cameron, "the only acid remark he allowed himself."[17]

What also emerges from *Point of Departure* is that even in 1954 a heavy undertow of reaction already existed against the Schweitzer image. Cameron ends his section on Schweitzer thus:

> When I returned to England there was much pressure to write a book on the visit, which had, it seemed, been the first. I did not; I am uncertain why. Among the wistful fancies that had haunted the reveries of biographers and journalists for years with a guilty and unreasonable itch was the definitive exposure of Dr. Schweitzer. There, it had been felt, would be the really outstanding essay in tastelessness, the truly resounding iconoclasm. The endurance of the Schweitzer legend was a permanent challenge to explode it, or at least to question it: to examine with some sort of objectivity the man who through half a century conned the world into an adoration in which the mere investigation of his pretensions was a sort of heresy.
>
> It was not hard to know what had for years been argued only by a few; that while the original achievements of Schweitzer were considerable and his sacrifices notable, yet his accomplishments were negligible: his mission an illusion; his hospital in the Equatorial forest medically valueless, or even dangerous, existing solely as a frame for his immeasurable ego; his own philosophical contribution to the advancement of Africa rather worse than negative.
>
> Everything lay in the decision of timing, and this I mistrusted. When I stayed with the patriarch in Lambarene it was long ago, before the Doctor began to discover and enjoy the reverent pilgrimages of journalists and TV teams. Then did the theme become popular; that the Schweitzer hospital was no place of light and healing but a squalid

slum, from which the Doctor excluded all the advantages he was forever being offered simply because he did not personally understand them; that his immense personal vanity insulated him from anything less than sanctimonious worship; that his celebrated "Reverence for Life" contrasted bitterly with the cruel loneliness imposed on his own wife and daughter, just as his arrogant contempt for those around him contrasted with his cultivation of the rich dilettante women who affected to nurse at his shrine. To that could be added that it was the Doctor who proposed to me his opinion that the most salutary influence on the African race question had been the late Dr. Malan; that he had never in forty years taken an African to table, and that indeed in no circumstances could he contemplate even the possibility of an *indigène* being seated in his presence. There was at the time the baffling suspicion that he was pulling my leg; only later I knew he was not.

I reflected much on these things, and came to the decision that while the life of Dr. Schweitzer was indeed a paradox with very unwholesome undertones, to argue so would almost certainly be defined as unreasonable sensationalism and probably rightly. Numbers of people were presumably deriving some sort of value from the inspiration of the Schweitzer mystique, and if the price of that were to let this strange old man perpetuate his peculiarities, then it might be dishonest, but was not particularly harmful.

It was possible that in redressing the balance of unreasonable devotion one could be ungenerous to those aspects of Schweitzer's life that must command admiration—the almost inhuman industry of the young Alsatian who *did* become a distinguished scholar, theologian, musicologist and all the rest; to surrender such a rare virtuosity for the sake of a dream was not a small thing, albeit the end was so little.[18]

When I spoke to Cameron recently about this he reiterated his belief that in some way and to some people the myth was of value, so must not be destroyed—in its way a less ruthless attitude than Schweitzer's own about Jesus. But in fact his articles had damaged the myth considerably. And though in the *News Chronicle* he had written nothing as damning as the reference to Dr. Malan or those phrases about Schweitzer's accomplishments being negligible, his mission an illusion, and his hospital valueless or even dangerous, he must have let these views be known to his colleagues in Fleet Street and elsewhere, all of them eager to hear about Schweitzer at firsthand. Dr. Malan in particular was political dynamite, for as leader of the South African Nationalist Party and Prime Minister of South Africa at that time he was setting in motion the policy of separate development of black and white known as apartheid—though in a less vicious form than it later assumed.

Perhaps as regards Schweitzer's accomplishments and his mission readers of this book should be left to make up their own minds. They have the information with which to do so. The statement that the hospital was medically valueless (which was echoed by various doctors then and later and almost certainly came from medical sources) begs the question—to whom?

It was indeed valueless to medical research. It was not equipped for that nor designed for it. But to the patients? The question answers itself; and in doing so reveals the horrifying self-centeredness of some of the medical profession, to whom sickness is a matter of professional interest rather than compassion, and a place which merely makes people suffer less is valueless.

With regard to the criticism about Schweitzer's behavior toward his family, Cameron admitted that he knew neither Hélène nor Rhena. "It would seem," he said, "from what one hears, that he behaved very badly towards them"—a piece of hearsay reporting that inclines one to take the rest of his criticism with a pinch of salt.

The Malan issue, however, must be faced, and here Cameron's comments were interesting. After admitting that the Ogowe Africans were much the most primitive of the continent, he went on: "Schweitzer argued, and I think with some reason, that Malan was a patriarchal tyrant, rather than a fascist tyrant, the way his successors became. And I think there's something to be said for that." And he said, "Although Schweitzer was totally undemocratic, and refused to discuss anything, that may have been exactly what these chaps [the Gabonese] liked about him."

This however would by no means fully explain Schweitzer's apparent defenses of Dr. Malan. Malan for example was a Nationalist of the most extreme kind—Schweitzer detested Nationalism. Malan admired Nazi Germany—Schweitzer had abominated it. Malan's policy was that South Africa should become an all-white territory and that the blacks should be moved from their homes to new areas of separate development— Schweitzer was on record that such enforced movement was a crime by the white man against the black. If Cameron assumed that Schweitzer approved of everything about Malan, he misunderstood him completely.

The key to the misunderstanding lies in Schweitzer's "no discussion" attitude. He had grown tired of theoretical arguments before he was thirty. More recently he had grown accustomed to doing without the company of his intellectual equals. Nor was there time for going over and over the same ground with new people. We know already that he had spent immense care studying Kierkegaard, whom he once in a letter dismissed as "that psychopath." And he much distressed Cameron by apparently speaking contemptuously of Gandhi as someone with a great gift for education who had been misled into politics. This was conversational shorthand tinged with a certain amount of sheer naughtiness, as Cameron would have realized had he read the thirteen pages on Gandhi in Chapter 15 of Schweitzer's *Indian Thought and Its Development*.

"The philosophy of Mahatma Gandhi," Schweitzer there begins, "is a world in itself." And after exploring that world with the greatest sympathy and admiration he ends: "By a magnificent paradox Gandhi brings the idea of activity and the idea of world and life negation into relationship in such a way that he can regard activity in the world as the highest form of renunciation of the world. In a letter to the Brahmin ascetic, he says, 'My service to my people is part of the discipline to which I subject myself in order to free my soul from the bonds of the flesh. . . . For me the path to salvation leads through unceasing tribulation in the service of my fellow-countrymen and humanity.' So in Gandhi's spirit modern Indian ethical world-and-life-affirmation and a world-and-life-negation which goes back to the Buddha dwell side by side."[19]

Such was Schweitzer's true assessment of Gandhi, as opposed to his curt remark to Cameron. And what increasingly emerges from the whole of Cameron's article is that Schweitzer was not taking Cameron very seriously. The exchange about the gorilla, Schweitzer's comments on Cameron's profession, the remark about Gandhi—all suggest that Schweitzer was teasing Cameron a little and deliberately trying to shock what he regarded as Cameron's somewhat overdelicate and theoretical sensibilities.

There are many other accounts of Schweitzer's liking to tease overearnest visitors. Frederick Franck, the dentist who worked at Lambarene in 1958, relates the reply he made to a visitor who at lunch embarked on a solemn speech asking the Lord to preserve Schweitzer in health for many years to come. All Schweitzer said in reply was, "Let us hope the Lord is listening."

"On such occasions," writes Franck, "he has a twinkle in his eye which no professional snake charmer could improve on, and usually the twinkle is followed by a special wink which will disappear from this earth with Schweitzer."[20] I suspect that the twinkle and the wink were in evidence when he talked with Cameron, whether Cameron realized it or not, for nothing could have been more calculated to arouse the reactions of someone whom Schweitzer suspected of sentimentality toward the blacks than praise of Dr. Malan.

Similarly the remark about never taking an African to his table and never contemplating the possibility of an African being seated in his presence gives an impression so totally at variance with the facts that some grave misunderstanding must have occurred, whether deliberately induced or otherwise. Africans sat, lay, and sprawled in Schweitzer's presence all the time—even while he was taking the Sunday morning service. It is true that no African took a meal in the staff dining room, for two reasons—reasons which might well have led Schweitzer to say that he could not imagine it ever happening. The first, as we have seen, was a matter of discipline. As head of the hospital he believed, from sufficient experience, that his authority would be diminished to the detriment of the patients if he allowed the Africans to feel that he and they were socially identical. Some separation was necessary for the efficiency of the hospital. The second was the Africans' own refusal to eat from any pot but their own—a refusal that had its origin in fear of poisoning but had become an unbreakable social custom. But naturally when in the course of time Africans—mostly officials—came to the hospital as visitors they ate in the staff dining room like any other guests. Schweitzer was the man who in Alsace had insisted on traveling fourth class in order to be among the real people. Whatever he may have said to Cameron, the implications of the way Cameron reported it are totally foreign to Schweitzer's nature.

Though Schweitzer may not have taken Cameron very seriously, Cameron unfortunately took Schweitzer very seriously indeed. Schweitzer knew what he was talking about when he said of Goethe, "If he had known they would write down everything he said he would never have opened his mouth." And perhaps he was unlucky that the first writer to take a critical line about him was the well respected and widely read James Cameron.

Not long after Cameron came the equally popular and distinguished American writer, John Gunther, who was working on his book *Inside Africa*. Unlike Cameron, Gunther came by personal invitation. Friends had recommended him to visit Schweitzer after a family tragedy and Schweitzer had no idea that he intended to write a chapter in his book about the hospital.

Gunther's piece was much better informed than Cameron's and showed more understanding of the local conditions. His description of Schweitzer as "august and good . . . but cranky on occasion, dictatorial, prejudiced, pedantic in a peculiarly teutonic manner, irascible, and somewhat vain"[21] was as reasonable a thumbnail sketch as one could expect. And though he got a few facts wrong, his research was remarkably thorough and accurate. The things that upset Cameron about the hospital Gunther took in his stride: "The hospital startles some visitors because almost everybody thinks beforehand that it will be like an Indian ashram, an aseptic harbor of tranquillity, spirituality and out-of-worldness." What distressed Gunther was being told never to leave anything unlocked. "It was sharply disillusioning, in this community dedicated to good works, to find that there should be so much overt distrust."[22] Perhaps when Gunther was there nobody stole any penicillin.

He did appreciate the reasons for many things however—that the smoke from the Africans' outdoor fires, blowing through the buildings, kept down the mosquitoes; that the animals were not only loved but made use of—"as we walked into lunch one day Schweitzer encountered Thekla, the red pig, and calmly wiped his shoes on her. Obviously the pig enjoyed this process, and her stiff bristles gave the Doctor's shoes a formidable shine."[23]

Medical standards were high, said Gunther, nor did he see any harm in shouting at workmen who "were not too ill to work, but just plain lazy."[24]

Gunther's piece, though written second, actually appeared before Cameron's; and despite its well-informed and moderate approach aroused Schweitzer's indignation. Schweitzer very rarely protested about what people wrote about him—he made it a principle not to do so. So his letter to Gunther on this occasion is surprising, and is probably to be explained by the fact that he felt he had been caught unfairly off guard. "I spoke with you naturally and openly," he wrote.[25] Cameron had come unashamedly as a journalist, and as such had suffered Schweitzer's irony and watchfulness. Gunther had outraged Schweitzer's feeling that personal and public statements must be kept separate, and that nothing of his must be published which had not been carefully drafted and redrafted into a formal statement.

Paradoxically, though, his very guardedness with Cameron had produced much worse results than his openness with Gunther. As for his protest to Gunther and his request that certain passages be omitted when the article appeared in Gunther's book, that produced no result at all. He never attempted such a thing again.

After these two articles, Cameron's especially, the antimyth began to gather momentum on both sides of the Atlantic. To most people Schweitzer remained a selfless saint, a dedicated healer. But to a small but growing group, a modish minority, he was suddenly a self-centered bully, a publicity-seeking tyrant who knew nothing of medicine and sought only to grope his way to a questionable heaven. Both views were absurdly wide of the mark. And perhaps at that time it was really not possible for any writer to see things properly in perspective—especially if at the same time he was trying to hold the interest of a public to whom illusion and disillusion seem equally desirable, but who often find the truth more than a little tedious.

A note from the hospital bulletin about this time discusses the Africans' wearing—or not wearing—of sandals. Some time later a distinguished visiting South African physician, Dr. Jack Penn, seeing a number of Africans walking barefoot, noted that more good might be done by providing all the patients with sandals than by the equivalent value in drugs. The suggestion was sensible and well-meant but like many such suggestions was made in ignorance of the practical problems—and of course implied that Schweitzer had not thought of such a simple piece of preventive medicine. Here however is Schweitzer:

> Our native inmates have decided to wear sandals. From the very beginning I tried to persuade them to make themselves sandals of thin

wood or hide as a protection against thorns and stones and the splinters
of glass that lie around their dwellings. But I was preaching to the deaf.
Not even when I told them that Homer makes the god Hermes tie sandals on his feet before every journey, even a journey through the air,
could I arouse any interest in this kind of footwear. The pictures which
they saw in the illustrated newspapers and magazines that fell into their
hands showed that whites, men and women alike, wore shoes and not
sandals. And for them that settled the matter. Since the cost of shoes
was prohibitive, they preferred to go around barefoot, and took no notice of me. When I tried to persuade them to wear sandals it was also
because the patients who wore foot bandages would no longer get them
dirty, wet and muddy.

Just as I had about resigned myself to failure, the illustrated papers
began publishing photographs of elegant ladies wearing sandals, and
so now for about ten years our natives have been wearing them too. All
the hospital inmates wear them, not only those with bandaged feet. We
can't afford to get them in Europe, but a native who sits on a cobbler's
stool on the veranda by my room puts together sandals out of old tyre
tubes which we are given locally. The soles are made of cloth and the
rubber is used for the straps. We have to thank the ladies of fashion that
the bandages on the feet of our lepers remain clean.[26]

The Africans whom Penn saw were backsliders, immune for some reason to the influence of fashion.

Another great medical advance was the installation, at long last, of X-
ray equipment. It was specially designed for tropical use, and Dr. Emeric
Percy, who for a long while had been one of Schweitzer's chief assistants, went to the Philips factory in Holland where it was built to study its
operation and maintenance before bringing it back.

Schweitzer himself was doing less and less actual medical work. The
leper village occupied most of his active hours—though he still made sure
of being present at all major operations, so that he could take responsibility. Correspondence took up more time than ever, though he delegated
much of it to various assistants and nurses. One extraordinary fact is that
the handwriting of all the three chief nurses who helped him, Mathilde
Kottmann, Emma Haussknecht, and Ali Silver, came to look almost identical with his own. Mathilde Kottman's in particular was said to have
been seen by handwriting experts and pronounced indistinguishable from
Schweitzer's.

(Friends of Schweitzer's once sent a sample of his handwriting to an
expert for analysis—without of course saying whose it was—and then reported the result to Schweitzer. The expert, so Schweitzer related later,
"said some very nice things about it, but added that there was a tendency
to despotism.")

One letter which he wrote at this time links the old days, when the hospital was cut off from the world, with the new period of Schweitzer's emergence into international affairs. The subject was Dr. Goldschmid, who had stood by Schweitzer through the war years. The addressee was Dag Hammarskjöld, Secretary-General of the United Nations.

DEAR MR. HAMMARSKJOLD,

When you were elected Secretary-General of the United Nations I learned through an English review that you had sympathy for my ideas and that your device was to Serve. I intended to write you at that time, not to congratulate you on your election—for you should not be congratulated on having to fill one of the most difficult of posts—but to send you my good wishes. But as I am overwhelmed by work and fatigue, this letter to you was never written—as has been the fate of a good many others. But I did send you my best wishes through my thoughts.

Now I am writing to ask you for information and perhaps a favor.

The doctor who had served my hospital from 1932 to 1944, and who was subsequently, from 1945 to 1953, in the service of the Government of French Equatorial Africa, has now reached the age limit of 54. It would still be possible for him, with his vast medical knowledge and great experience as a physician and surgeon, to make a place for himself in France, but he would much prefer to have a position where he would continue to serve in colonial lands and use his experience relating to these regions. . . .

Dr. Goldschmidt's qualifications followed, and Schweitzer concluded:

Perhaps I shall some day have an opportunity to see you in Sweden. I go there during each of my European sojourns, especially to see my friends the Lagerfelds at Gammalhil. Baronne Lagerfeld, my Swedish translator, has been seriously ill for many months and has become nearly blind.—I am also to go to America, but I do not know when my work and my fatigue will allow it. In any case I should be very happy to make your acquaintance,

With my good wishes,
Your devoted
Albert Schweitzer

I apologize for making you decipher my handwriting. I do not use a typewriter because of the noise it makes.

Hammarskjöld's reply was swift:

13 January 1954

DEAR DR. SCHWEITZER,

I have received your kind letter of December 19, 1953, and wish to tell you how touched I am by your good wishes and what encouragement I found in it. I know no better way to reply to what you have so kindly said about me than to send you herewith the text of a brief talk I am to give on television in the near future, and which will show what a source of inspiration your own life and thought has been to me.

From the information you have given me, it would indeed seem that Dr. Goldschmid is fitted to render great services in an international organization concerned with the welfare of the peoples of Africa. I naturally think first of all of the World Health Organization. This Organization, as you are no doubt aware, has a regional office at Brazzaville which serves the territories to the south of the Sahara and which concerns itself with public health and the fight against certain tropical diseases. . . .

Hammarskjöld promised to consult not only the Director General of WHO, but also the Director of UNICEF and the Director General of UNESCO, and the letter continued:

I am delighted at the prospect of meeting you. Please do not fail to keep me informed of your plans for travel to Sweden and the United States. There are so many things I would like to talk with you about, in the realm of pure thought, as well as about the services which the United Nations can render those indigent peoples who have so long been the object of your preoccupations.

I must not end this letter without mentioning the Nobel Peace Prize which has recently been awarded to you. The Nobel Institute has acted with great discernment; no man of the present day has contributed more than you have to the development of the spiritual conditions required for world brotherhood and a lasting peace.

Please accept, dear Doctor Schweitzer, my cordial and devoted good wishes

Dag Hammarskjöld
Secretary-General

So there were compensations for the overburdened, ill-paid, and ill-equipped workers at the Lambarene hospital; a note of recommendation from *le grand Docteur* was a passport to work and recognition anywhere in the world.

26

THE NOBEL PEACE PRICE
1954-1957

IF ever a prophet earned the right to say "I told you so," it was Schweitzer. Before 1914 he was already warning the world against rampant nationalism, the dehumanizing effects of technology, and the growth of vast, soul-demanding organizations, whether commercial or political.

In the Second World War irreverence for life had reached new levels, in the torture and slaughter of the Jews and in the mass killings of the atom bomb. Things that human beings would never, except under extreme pressure, dream of doing on their own behalf, they did cold-bloodedly in the name of some national or political mystique. And as their humanity dwindled, their power grew.

Schweitzer's moral stature was enhanced by his very rejection of size and power. And after the announcement of his Nobel Peace Prize people who knew about the diabolical effects of atomic radiation began increasingly to see him as a valuable champion of their cause against the ambition of politicians and the apathy of the public.

Schweitzer had for long been in touch with people close to atomic development, as we know from his letters to Einstein and Oppenheimer at Princeton. And he had concerned himself with finding out the results of research on the survivors of Hiroshima and Nagasaki. But he had resolutely refused to be drawn into any public discussion, and had asked that anything he wrote in letters remain confidential and not be passed on to journalists. He wanted to be able to say freely what he thought.

Early in 1954 however he was approached by the London *Daily Herald* for his comments on a proposal by Professor Alexander Haddow that the United Nations should set up a conference of scientists on the subject of the hydrogen bomb. On April 14 the *Herald* gave half a page to his reply, complete with photographs of himself and his signature and a potted biography ("the scholar-genius who renounced the world to become a medical missionary").

Schweitzer's contribution was characteristic. The first three paragraphs explain how tired he is and that therefore an article of 800 words is out of the question—and one wonders anew at the obstinacy which makes him write these laborious longhand letters, writer's cramp and all, sooner than risk becoming glib by learning to dictate to a secretary or to use a type-writer. The letter continues:

> I am, however, most anxious to give my views to you personally. The problem of the effects of H-bomb explosions is terribly disturbing, but I do not think that a conference of scientists is what is needed to deal with it. There are too many conferences in the world today and too many decisions taken by them. What the world should do is to listen to the warnings of individual scientists who understand this terrible prob-lem. That is what would impress people and give them understanding and make them realise the danger in which we find ourselves. Just look at the influence Einstein has, because of the anguish he shows in face of the atomic bomb. It must be the scientists who comprehend thor-oughly all the issues and the dangers involved who speak to the world, as many as possible of them all telling humanity the truth in speeches and articles. If they all raised their voices, each one feeling himself im-pelled to tell the terrible truth, they would be listened to, for then hu-manity would understand that the issues were grave. If you and Alex-ander Haddow can manage to persuade them to put before mankind the thoughts by which they themselves are obsessed, then there will be some hope of stopping these horrible explosions, and of bringing pres-sure to bear on the men who govern. But the scientists must speak up. Only they have the authority to state that we can no longer take on our-selves the responsibility for these experiments, only they can say it. There you have my opinion. I give it to you with anguish in my heart, anguish which holds me from day to day. With my best wishes and in the hope that those who must advise us will make themselves heard.

Schweitzer wanted to bring out into the open the personal, individual fears and obsessed thoughts which scientists had expressed in letters to him. These personal nightmares of the scientists never found their way into the prepared statements and public attitudes that they brought to con-ferences, so conferences were useless. Conferences had agendas and nightmares were out of order. In the hope of publicizing their anguish, Schweitzer revealed his own. And the *Herald* made the most of it with its huge headline—THE H-BOMB: THERE IS ANGUISH IN MY HEART, SAYS DR. ALBERT SCHWEITZER.

The most important effect of this letter was to make known to the pub-lic, anguished itself but kept totally in the dark, that their anguish was shared by those who knew the facts. But Schweitzer's hope that the scien-tists might now speak out for themselves was for the most part doomed to disappointment, for the scientists were in trouble. Governments were touchy about the bomb, being involved in the desperate race to build bigger and better ones in order not to be at a disadvantage when the next one fell. Scientists therefore who condemned the bomb were as good as committing treason. Robert Oppenheimer himself, after rising to dizzy heights in the American scientific and political world, fell under suspicion of Communist leanings that year because he gave voice to his doubts about the ethics of proceeding with the atomic arms race, and suddenly found himself stripped of office and barred from any access to the work of the U.S. atomic energy program.

Schweitzer went back to Europe in May. In the autumn he was due to collect his Peace Prize in Oslo and make an acceptance speech. The hopes of those who thought he might take the opportunity to preach a really passionate sermon on the evils of atomic testing were unfulfilled, for he was still waiting for others to speak, more qualified than he. The speech he worked on throughout that summer was in his other style—a historical survey of war, its causes, its results, its justification or otherwise—very coolly argued and to tell the truth, considering the potential of the subject, rather dry and dull. It was to sober reason, not to emotion, that Schweitzer was appealing.

The occasion itself was anything but dull however. To begin with, the domestic tension at Günsbach suddenly flared high when Hélène flatly refused to go to Oslo with Schweitzer if Mme Martin went. Schweitzer was not used to being blackmailed in that way, and besides he needed Mme Martin, he said, to guide him through the throng of notables he was to meet. And he set off for Oslo without his wife.

The progress was triumphal, the stations the train stopped at jammed with people. Everybody wanted to shake his hand, and he had to exercise. a long-learned discipline to drink very little because it was so hard to get away to the toilet. An article appeared in a Norwegian newspaper suggesting that everyone who wanted a handshake should instead give a krone to the hospital; and that one article gave Schweitzer as much again as the prize.

The style of it all troubled Schweitzer. He had to travel first class, at the Prize Committee's insistence. He found running water in his hotel at Oslo and wanted to know, "What do I need running water for? Am I a trout?" Bouquets of flowers were banished from his room, because he hated to see flowers wither. He tried to see everyone who came, but refused to speak into an impersonal microphone.

Erica Anderson was there, as well as Emmy Martin. So was Clara Urquhart. Charles Joy, who with Melvin Arnold had brought succor to Lambarene from the Unitarians after the war, had arrived from Boston to report on the presentation. And then came a message from Rhena that her mother was now on the way, in a very bad humor and quite prepared to destroy the whole thing by publicly threatening divorce. On his side Schweitzer was equally at the end of his emotional tether. "Let her," he said.

It never came to that. Hélène arrived and sat by her husband's side through the ceremony, but they did not speak to each other. Whether anybody outside the Schweitzers' immediate circle knew of the private stress of the speaker is hard to say. But Charles Joy noted that "Dr. Schweitzer was not an effective speaker with his manuscript. He seldom looked up from it; his voice was not strong and had little resonance; his inflections were regular and monotonous. The occasion was too important for extemporaneous utterance, but Dr. Schweitzer would have made a much more dynamic impression if he had spoken directly from his heart."[1]

It was not like Schweitzer, however important the occasion, to read from his written speech. Normally he would write and rewrite, thereby making sure he knew what he had to say and how to say it—and then he would speak without reference to the written word at all.

In this case he was suffering from the fact that on arrival at Oslo he had had to cut the talk from eighty minutes or so to thirty-five—a butchery he was not at all happy about, since he felt he could not properly develop his points in the time. "For a moment," he told Norman Cousins later, "just before I got up to speak, I was tempted to reach for the full message even at the risk of being stopped half way through my speech. But I downed the temptation out of courtesy to my hosts."[2]

So everything combined to make it hard at this moment to speak directly from the heart—the importance of the occasion, the truncation of his speech, and the tensions of his private life.

His theme was simply that organizations could never, by themselves, bring about peace:

> I am well aware that there is nothing essentially new in what I have been saying about the problem of peace. I am profoundly convinced that the solution is this: we should reject war for ethical reasons— because, that is to say, it makes us guilty of the crime of inhumanity. Erasmus of Rotterdam, and several others since his day, have proclaimed this as the truth to which all should rally. The only originality which I claim for myself is that not only do I affirm this as true, but I am convinced, intellectually convinced, that the human spirit in our time is capable of creating a new attitude of mind: an attitude based upon ethics. This conviction persuades me to affirm that truth anew, in the hope that my testimony may perhaps prevent its being set aside as a well-meaning form of words. People may say that it is "inapplicable to

reality"; but more than one truth has long remained dormant and ineffective for no other reason than that nobody had imagined that it could
ever have any application to reality.[3]

The speech was simply an affirmation of faith. Now, Schweitzer believed, it was for the specialists, the scientists, to say their say; and for
the politicians then to do their job of peacemaking.

* * *

As soon as might be he returned to Africa and to work, reaching Lambarene in December—though for a while he found himself among the patients there, having slipped and hurt his leg at Port-Gentil. The role did
not suit him. His impotence exasperated him and he vowed to be rid of his
crutches by January—which he was.

The Peace Prize address, though it gave heart and strength to individuals and organizations all over the world who were fighting to get a hearing
for the voice of humanity, produced little immediate result. The letter to
the *Daily Herald* on the other hand had the effect of stimulating a young
French atomic physicist, Noel Martin, to publish some of his conclusions
about the effects of radiation in a communication to the Paris Academy of
Sciences. His calculations had shown that, quite apart from the fact that
hydrogen bombs were "terrible and inadmissible death-dealing machines," their explosions also resulted in "numerous irreversible and cu-
mulative phenomena, which will irremediably affect the existence of
life."[4]

In December he wrote to Schweitzer to say that as a result of this communication to the Academy, the press of the whole world had publicized
his conclusions and he was now sought after by radio, newspapers, and
television. He was the man of the moment. And he would like Schweitzer, whose letter had been the starting point of the whole chain of events,
to contribute a preface to the book he was writing on the subject.

Schweitzer wrote very warmly in reply, but declined to provide the
preface—on the usual grounds of not wishing to become involved in specific issues on which he was not qualified to speak. And he had good reason to be cautious at this particular moment, because a small cloud of hor-
nets was buzzing around his head as a result of his having agreed to become honorary patron of a German Communist Youth organization.

Such honorary appointments he often accepted, whatever their political
background, if their aims seemed humane, and this organization claimed
to be interested in peace and cooperation and humanity. Schweitzer was
somewhat dismayed therefore when letters from friends suddenly began
pouring in warning him gravely of the way in which this Communist

group was certain to exploit his name for ends very different from the ones he approved of. Schweitzer took alarm and swiftly withdrew his patronage. It was the first of several occasions in his last ten years when he found himself in political trouble, as often as not simply through an undiscriminating politeness and goodwill. But his goodwill was now, quite against his wishes, valid political currency, and he had to learn painfully that in the world of 1955 it could not with impunity be distributed to all and sundry.

Age, seclusion, and the rapidly changing world were at last robbing him of some of the sureness of his political instinct. For he had reached eighty.

Among the plaudits that came thick and fast to the little red-roofed settlement was a statement by Einstein:

> I have hardly ever met a person in whom kindliness and the desire for beauty are so completely fused as in Albert Schweitzer. This is a particularly fortunate blessing in someone who enjoys robust health; he is fond of using his arms and hands in order to create what his nature urges him to achieve. This robust health, which makes him very active, as well as his moral sensitivity have kept him from being a pessimist. In this way he has been able to preserve his joyfully affirmative nature, in spite of all the disappointments which our time inflicts upon every sensitive person.
>
> He loves beauty, not only in the arts proper but also in purely intellectual efforts, without being impressed by sophistry. An unerring instinct helps him to preserve his closeness to life and his spontaneity in everything.
>
> In all his activities he has avoided rigid tradition, and he fights against it whenever the outcome is promising. This can be clearly felt in his classical work on Bach where he exposes the dross and the mannerisms through which the creations of the beloved master have been obscured and were impaired in their simple effectiveness.
>
> It seems to me that the work in Lambarene has been to a considerable extent an escape from the morally petrified and soulless tradition of our own culture—an evil against which the individual is virtually powerless.
>
> He has not preached and he has not warned, and he never expected that his dream would become a comfort and a solace to innumerable others. He simply acted out of inner necessity.
>
> There must be apparently an indestructible good core in many people, or else they would never have recognized his simple greatness.[5]

The statement reached Schweitzer in a special Birthday Volume from his admirers, and he replied swiftly and delightedly:

"Even without writing we are united in thought, because we experience our terrible times together and in the same way, and we worry together about the future of mankind. When we met in Berlin we could never have imagined that we should be united by such a bond. It is strange how often our names are linked in public. It delights me that we have the same first name.''

The progress of events had evidently caused him to change his mind about conferences, for he went on: ''About the new tests with the latest atomic bomb, it amazes me that the United Nations Organisation cannot make up its mind to set up a conference about it. I get letters asking that you and I should speak up and demand that UNO should do something of the kind. But we have spoken up enough. We cannot dictate to UNO. It is an autonomous body and must discover for itself the incentive and the responsibility for trying to halt the disaster that threatens. From this distance I cannot make out what it is that prevents them from rising to the occasion. If they failed at least the attempt would have been made, and the opposition would have been forced to show its hand. . . .''[6]

He was indeed a long way from the involved personal, national, and international politics that were plaguing the United Nations. The individual protesters were in a weak position. The dynamic Oppenheimer was discredited and powerless. The gentle Einstein was old and sick and in despair. And Noel Martin, the man whom Schweitzer had encouraged to speak out, was learning the cost of his honesty; in a letter to Schweitzer he described how as a result of publicizing his findings he had been discreetly but swiftly dismissed from the National Centre of Scientific Research, where he had been on the point of getting his doctorate; and how even his colleagues now looked askance at him.

In April came the news of Einstein's death. ''Why won't they listen? Why won't they listen?'' he had repeated hopelessly before he died. Schweitzer was haunted by his despair.

Britain, the first country to recognize Schweitzer's theology and one of the first to offer him honorary degrees, had one last great honor to bestow. Only one other non-Briton had ever received the Order of Merit, and he was a general who as Allied Supreme Commander had led the British Armed Forces to victory over Hitler's Germany—Dwight Eisenhower.

Schweitzer was in Europe in May, his friends gathering around as ever. His younger brother Paul, now a retired businessman, lived opposite the Günsbach guest house, where his widow Emma, née Münch, still lives.

When he went to England in October to receive his Order of Merit from the Queen, his private audience with Her Majesty delighted him and he decided that other European countries had made a great mistake in abolishing royalty. He wrote a thank-you letter to the Privy Secretary: ''Please convey to Her Majesty my great and respectful gratitude for the friendly way she deigned to receive me on October 19th. It touched me deeply. Would you please also ask if she would be kind enough to accept these two copies of my "Memoirs of Childhood and Youth" which I have signed for Prince Charles and Princess Anne. I wrote them for children, and to be read to children. I would be very happy if Her Majesty would kindly pass them on to her children one day when they are old enough to read."

Three days after his visit to Buckingham Palace he went to Cambridge, where he was presented with an honorary doctorate of laws. ("Laws is for general excellence," wrote the master of Magdalene College. "A degree in Medicine, Letters or Music would be too specific.") And while at Cambridge he insisted on visiting Grantchester to see the grave of Professor F. C. Burkitt, who had been responsible for getting his youthful theological work translated into English. Schweitzer always had a liking for visiting graves of friends when the friends were no longer to be visited alive. It was a part of his "inwardness" to be able to summon up the past in an awareness of how it had nourished the present, in much the same way that he summoned up the mountains and woods of Alsace to nourish him in Lambarene.

During the few days he spent in London Schweitzer himself was treated something like royalty, holding court in a back room of his friend Emil Mettler's restaurant in Petty France, by St. James's Park. A "closed" notice was hung on the door, and the famous lined up to meet him. A nurse from Alsace who worked then in a London hospital was invited by Mettler to attend the reception, and she watched, awed, as the great men arrived. The composer Vaughan Williams, also an OM and three years older than Schweitzer, was led to the head of the line. Bertrand Russell followed and Dr. Leslie Weatherhead; and George Seaver, Schweitzer's biographer, met him for the first time, to be overwhelmed by his personality. Augustus John, yet another OM, had persuaded a friend to stay all night with him to make sure he remained sober and woke up in time for the interview; and he sat sketching Schweitzer for nearly an hour. In between the celebrities came the dozens of ordinary people who simply wanted an autograph or a word with the great man. An Indian wanted to kiss his feet but Schweitzer gently forbade him. "We should love each other," he said, "but one should never stand in awe of another human being."

So he left England for the last time. In November his old friend Theodor Heuss presented him with the German Order of Merit, to the accompaniment of the usual throngs, and in December he went back to Africa. A little while later Hélène joined him. She found the long pointless months without him even worse than the humid climate and the prickly relationships at Lambarene. She was truly a sick woman now, walking with difficulty, drawing breath with difficulty. Some of those who knew her had little sympathy for her, finding her snobbish and catty. Others admired her courage, her proud intelligence, and her refinement. But she was certainly a tragic figure. However weary he became, it is doubtful whether Schweitzer can ever have experienced the exhaustion of body and spirit that a chronic weakness imposes—except perhaps in those few far-off years after the First World War, just after Rhena was born and before he "straightened himself like a pine-tree shaking off the snow" and obtained Hélène's agreement that he should go his own way alone.

In Lambarene town Dr. Weissberg had arrived back at the government hospital, and a friendly partnership began. On the whole it was the government hospital that benefited the more, since Schweitzer had a trained and dedicated staff whom Weissberg could borrow, as well as equipment and drugs. Weissberg himself had no white staff, and he swears that so far as his experience went the difference between white and black was that the blacks had no conception of dedication. The midwife would turn up for duty when it pleased her, not when she was needed; nurses would have no interest in healing patients from a rival tribe. He envied Schweitzer a great deal.

On his side he could, as time went on, offer to keep drugs for Schweitzer in his large refrigerators; and he would help Schweitzer with his paperwork—"his weak point," says Weissberg. "He would send a message to me saying, 'Come as quick as possible. I need you.' When I got there he would show me all these papers. 'What am I supposed to do with these forms?' he'd say; 'you'll have to help me. Do you think Beethoven could ever have composed his symphonies if he'd had to fill up so many forms?' He was never really organized," says Dr. Weissberg.

The hospital was now well and truly on the tourist circuit, and the day of the rubberneck had come. Travel agents arranged visits for parties, without knowing anything of the conditions there. One day Weissberg was summoned by Schweitzer (there was no telephone—nor is there still) who waved a letter in his face and said "Seventy Norwegians are arriving tomorrow and they all want a room with a bath. What are we going to do?" When the laughter had died down beds of a sort were found for twelve at Schweitzer's hospital, for twenty at Weissberg's. After their first night Dr. Weissberg saw his twenty marching off with their luggage and an indignant expression on their faces—looking for something better. Some hours later they crawled back, very tired, very apologetic, and very glad to have somewhere to lie down. What happened to the remaining thirty-eight is not recorded.

Naturally all visitors, after they had been shown around the hospital, felt entitled to see and speak to the real object of their pilgrimage, Dr. Schweitzer. "Why, it's a zoo!" cried one disenchanted tripper. "Yes," he said, "and I'm the chief gorilla."[7] A tourist association invited him to become their honorary president, an honor which he felt was not really suitable; "as the new type of elephant which the tourists come here to shoot—not with guns but with cameras—I feel it would hardly be fitting for me to be president of your association."[8]

To deal with the hordes Schweitzer had inevitably to develop something of an act—a performance which could be switched on and would keep an awestruck group entertained for half an hour or so. He gave good value; he could amuse, instruct, and charm, and the visitors went away happy. But what they went away with was not the real Schweitzer. "Anyone who only met Schweitzer once," said Clara Urquhart, "met only the myth."

Erica Anderson was finishing off her film, and Schweitzer wrote to Jerome Hill: "As I write to you it seems to me very strange that there was ever a time when I did not know you and say 'tu' to you. For a long while you were simply the mysterious boss of Mrs. Erica; I thought of you as an elderly stiff gentleman who had succeeded in doing a very strange thing— persuading this strange creature, me, to have a film made about me; without even being sure whether it would ever come to anything."

Trudi Bochsler, the nurse who had left after disagreements with Schweitzer about the lepers, had returned. After extensive study of new leprosy treatments, she had been to other leper colonies elsewhere and found them too much influenced by politics for her taste. Schweitzer or no, Lambarene had much to be said for it. Schweitzer for his part knew how the leper village missed her, and the hatchet was buried. When she came Schweitzer gave her responsibility over the new leper village which had been laboriously growing while she was away. There she became, in Norman Cousins' phrase, "general manager, nurse, interne, teacher, confidante, minister and family head."[9] Medically and psychologically her effect on the lepers was excellent. Even so, some of the nurses found it hard to forgive Schweitzer for forgiving Trudi. She had committed high treason, and even Schweitzer was not allowed to condone that. Truth to tell, Schweitzer was not finding it easy to imbue all the staff all the time with the authentic Schweitzer spirit. There was no difficulty now in recruiting staff—the problem was to select the right ones from the huge numbers of young doctors and nurses who were anxious to begin their careers here, many of whom wanted mainly to borrow a little glory to help them on their way. So the very success of the hospital began to militate against the maintenance of its unique qualities. And though Schweitzer himself was able to withstand the demands for change, he knew they existed; not only in the world outside but within the hospital itself. "They can turn it upside down when I'm gone," he said once or twice, "but while I'm here it stays the way it is."

All of course hung upon finding the right successor, and Schweitzer was not satisfied that he had done so. A regular theme in his letters now and for many years is that "I have a permanent staff of very good and devoted doctors, but no-one is really capable of taking over the entire management of the hospital. In the backwoods everything is more complicated than in Europe or the U.S.A."[10]

In fact the search for a successor was complicated by another problem—that nobody knew what the government would do with the hospital once Schweitzer was gone; and in any case it would be a bold man who would take over from a myth, with the eyes of the world's press on him.

In April, 1956, Emma Haussknecht died. If anyone could be described as having been Schweitzer's right hand, it was she. Thirty years earlier, when Schweitzer decided to move out of the old, small hospital and build a new one, she was there—and but for her spells of leave had stayed ever since. Of the three women who, like Schweitzer, gave their whole lives to Lambarene, she was the most like him in temperament, sturdy and cheerful and compassionate. The penalty of living too long is that your friends die around you—but Emma's death was quite unexpected. A sudden illness, a return to Europe, a quick operation, and death.

Her ashes were returned to Lambarene, and over them, in a service attended by the whole hospital, Schweitzer made a short speech of recollection and thanks—"She did not live to herself. She lived for her duties, and to be kind to others. She had indeed a good heart. All those who had anything to do with her knew this. . . ."[11] And then came a little ceremony: "He asked that each one present should throw a little earth into the grave, himself the first, followed by his staff, and then all who were there. It took half an hour for all the men, women and children to file past. The old people were helped, the blind were led; there were lepers with bandaged feet, and last of all came Joseph, Dr. Schweitzer's old orderly at the Hospital.

"Dr. Schweitzer himself stood with bowed head by the open grave, watching how it gradually filled, now and then himself drawing a little Alsatian soil [brought specially from Alsace with the urn] from the small bag in his hand until it was empty. Then he received from Mlle Kottmann two small wreaths from Emma Haussknecht's homeland, and tied them on to the wooden cross underneath the date palm."[12]

Erica Anderson had at last finished her film. More than that, she and Jerome Hill had succeeded in making Schweitzer change his mind about not showing it until after his death. One reason was no doubt that he had come to trust them as he had never expected to do, and had got closely involved in the making of the film, himself writing the commentary. But the immediate reason for its release was the fact that screens the world over were changing shape. The panoramic screen was taking over from the old "academy" shape in which every film had hitherto been shown, and Hill was afraid that his film might seem too old-fashioned in a few year's time to get a showing.

Hill's idea was that the proceeds should go to the hospital, but Schweitzer was anxious that he should first recover the costs of making it and if money were left over that other charities should benefit. "It's a question of tact. My hospital gains a great deal of sympathy in the world because I myself am well known. This gives it a tremendous advantage over other works of benevolence; so I am vulnerable to the world's criticism simply for accepting this privilege . . . and also one has to take into acount the possibility that one day my hospital may cease to exist. . . . Finally I would like to ask you if one can't allow my four grandchildren to benefit—in Switzerland—to some small degree. With the difficulties of transferring money from France to Switzerland I haven't been able to help these children as I would have liked to." In fact, for whatever reason, the children never did benefit from the film.

In January, 1957, Erica wrote an article for *American Weekly* which told the story of her making of the film, and announced that it was shortly to be shown in New York, with Fredric March speaking Schweitzer's words and Burgess Meredith doing the narration. The film was a great success, and rightly. The fact that it was about Schweitzer would in itself have ensured its popularity, but this was a very good film. It attracted huge audiences, earned a lot of money, and the following year won an Academy Award. Schweitzer was delighted—though he himself did not see it till 1959.

For the last three years Schweitzer's determination to avoid being involved in the politics of atomic radiation had been coming under increasing pressure. Dag Hammarskjöld himself had written to him in 1955 in terms that must have been hard to refuse:

> You know, as I do, that the whole world absolutely needs an ideology which can confer a valid meaning to the efforts of all nations and give fresh and solid bases to the principle of "co-existence." Thus, I am persuaded that it behoves you, even within the strictly political field that concerns the United Nations, to send forth an essential message to the world. I have already had an opportunity to tell you that in my opinion it would be possible to animate international life with a new spirit by making better known the very attitude that you have tried to explain to the men of our generation. It is precisely for this reason that

we at the United Nations have contracted a debt of gratitude to you for
what you have done and what you symbolize; but this is also why we
make bold to hope that you will perhaps choose to add your powerful
voice to the appeals made in favor of mutual respect among nations, in
the very sense that we understand this term at the United Nations.[13]

Schweitzer had held firm at that time. But as the months passed it became evident that the politicians would never of their own accord adopt
the humanitarian line. Indeed they were continuing to hush up the scientists' fears. At the same time his sense of debt was coming into play
again: "They gave me the Peace Prize—I don't know why. Now I feel I
should do something to earn it." And at the same time a plot was being
hatched among friends of his, which was to swing the balance.

Emory Ross, still head of the Schweitzer Fellowship of the United
States, first approached the editor of *Saturday Review,* Norman Cousins.
Cousins, who had made a name for himself as a champion of cultural
freedom and public morality, and had written and lectured a great deal on
the problems of the atomic age, had already published an editorial entitled
"The Point about Schweitzer," taking issue with the critics of Lambarene's "primitiveness"; he was also involved in discussions with Mr.
J. D. Newth of A. & C. Black, Schweitzer's London publishers, as to
how to persuade Schweitzer to finish and deliver the famous Third Volume of *The Philosophy of Civilisation.*

Thirty-three years had passed since the first two volumes appeared, and
all that existed of the third was those yellowing, curled, goat-chewed
pages now lying haphazard in a trunk in Schweitzer's room at Lambarene. No carbons, no photocopies, no security at all.

The two projects—to rescue the third volume and to persuade
Schweitzer to speak out about the atomic horror—came together. Clara
Urquhart lent her influence, and early in 1957 she and Cousins arrived in
Lambarene. With them they brought a letter from President Eisenhower
and the good wishes of Nehru, now India's Prime Minister.

In the few days he stayed there Cousins achieved a great deal. First he
persuaded Schweitzer to look in the trunk where he kept his manuscripts,
to extract *The Kingdom of God and Primitive Christianity,* and to spend
several hours sorting it out before handing it over to be photocopied.

> I opened the bundle [Cousins wrote]. Here, for all I knew, was one
> of the most important books of our time. The sheets had been perforat-
> ed at the top and were tied together by a string. But I gasped when I
> saw the kind of paper that had been used for the manuscript. There
> were sheets of every size and description. Dr. Schweitzer had written
> his book in longhand on the reverse side of miscellaneous papers.
> Some of them were outdated tax forms that had been donated to Lam-

barene by the French colonial administration. Some were lumber re-
quisition forms used by a lumber mill not far away on the Ogowe River. Some came from old calendars. I couldn't even begin to count the
number of manuscript pages which were written on the reverse sides of
letters sent to him many years earlier.[14]

Cousins had less luck with the bigger manuscript, the Third Volume. It
already amounted, it seemed, to something like 400,000 words, and to
put it into order would take days of uninterrupted work. Schweitzer admitted he had done very little work on it for several years, though his
mind had been ticking away "like an old clock a long time after the key
has been lost."[15]

What had certainly happened was that the life had gone out of the
book. Any writer knows that an idea must be given birth within its proper
time, or it dies in the womb; and Schweitzer once told Erica Anderson
that the hardest thing in his life was to keep his thoughts warm and vital
until he had time to get them onto paper. He may well have found his
ideas going cold and had worked and reworked on them, trying to breathe
fresh life into them, until he himself scarcely knew where they began or
ended.

On the atomic question however his response was swift and positive.
Cousins spoke to him of the hazards of the arms race, of the immorality of
the tests which were spreading radioactive dust across the world, of the
rapid increase in radioactivity in certain foods as a result of the fallout test
explosions, of the genetic hazards for future generations; but Schweitzer
needed no telling. The questions in his mind were practical ones: first,
should he make a statement at all, and what good would it do? Second: if
he did make a statement, should it be about peace and disarmament in
general, or about the more limited subject of nuclear testing. And third:
what form should it take?

After a night or two of consideration Schweitzer had answered his three
questions. To the first the answer was:

"This crisis intimately concerns the individual. The individual must
therefore establish a connection with it. . . . The leaders will act only
as they become aware of a higher responsibility that has behind it a wall
of insistence from the people themselves. I have no way of knowing
whether I can help in this. Perhaps I may be justified in trying."

In answer to the second question he felt it was better to aim first for the
limited objective, the banning of nuclear tests. The issues here were
clearer, the involvement of peoples worldwide, the chances of success
were greater. "If a ban on nuclear testing can be put into effect, then perhaps the stage can be set for other and broader measures related to the
peace."

As to the form of the pronouncement, Cousins felt that "a direct statement, released to all the news agencies, might be effective." Schweitzer disagreed. He had serious doubts about the news release type of story. What it gains in immediate attention it tends to lose in long-term impact. "Besides one runs the risk of competing with all the other news that may be breaking on a certain day."

"I am worried about present-day journalism," he told Cousins. "The emphasis on negative happenings is much too strong. Not infrequently, news about events marking great progress is overlooked or minimized. It tends to make for a negative and discouraging atmosphere. There is a danger that people may lose faith in the forward direction of humanity if they feel that very little happens to support that faith. And real progress is related to the belief by people that it is possible."[16]

When Cousins departed he took with him the photocopied manuscript and a letter to President Eisenhower:

DEAR MR. PRESIDENT:

I send you my heartfelt thanks for your friendly letter in which you send me your good wishes and those of Mrs. Eisenhower on the occasion of my eighty-second birthday. This expression of your good wishes was the first birthday greeting I received. Your generous and kind thoughts touch me deeply. In my heart I carry the hope I may somehow be able to contribute to the peace of the world. This I know has always been your own deepest wish. We both share the conviction that humanity must find a way to control the weapons which now menace the very existence of life on earth. May it be given to us both to see the day when the world's peoples will realize that the fate of all humanity is now at stake, and that it is urgently necessary to make the bold decisions that can deal adequately with the agonizing situation in which the world now finds itself. I was very happy to have Mr. Cousins, who will take this letter to you, here with me in Lambarene. It was rewarding to spend time together and to see how many ideas and opinions we shared.

With assurance of my highest esteem, I am,

Yours devotedly,
Albert Schweitzer[17]

Schweitzer was left to work out the details of his statement. And within a week or two we find him writing to Gunnar Jahn, President of the Nobel Peace Prize Committee in Oslo. He has been pressed, he says, because of his views on Reverence for Life, to express publicly his concern about the increase in radioactivity from nuclear tests. And he has decided he would like to do so by radio from the Peace Prize city, Oslo. Would Gunnar Jahn please talk to the Director of Radio Oslo about this?

The arrangements were quickly made. After his experience at the

Peace Prize presentation, Schweitzer wanted unlimited time "to develop the facts very fully. I don't want to be criticised for leaving large gaps in the argument." But he would compress it as tightly as possible, making it simple and universally comprehensible. But—"don't ask me to come to the microphone myself," he wrote. He did not like speaking to large faceless audiences, and the difficulties of recording the statement at Lambarene were too great—there were no glass windows to keep out the noises of the hospital and the jungle. Someone else had better do it.[18]

If other national radios wished to broadcast the statement they might do so simultaneously with Radio Oslo or later, but in no case before: and then only with Radio Oslo's permission.

On April 24, Schweitzer's "Declaration of Conscience" was issued by Radio Oslo, and simultaneously by several other national radio stations. As he had intended, it was carefully documented as to the history of atomic tests, the quantities of fallout, and the effects of radiation, short-term and long-term.

All these things were known to the statesmen of the atomic powers, he said, "and we must also assume that they are alive to their responsibility.

> At any rate, America and Soviet Russia and Britain are telling one another again and again that they want nothing more than to reach an agreement to end the testing of atomic weapons. At the same time, however, they declare that they cannot stop the tests so long as there is no such agreement.
>
> Why do they not come to an agreement? The real reason is that in their own countries there is no public opinion asking for it. Nor is there any such public opinion in other countries, with the exception of Japan. This opinion has been forced upon the Japanese people because, little by little, they will be hit in a most terrible way by the evil consequences of all the tests.
>
> An agreement of this kind presupposes reliability and trust. There must be guarantees preventing the agreement from being signed by anyone intending to win important tactical advantages foreseen only by him. Public opinion in all nations concerned must inspire and accept the agreement.
>
> When public opinion has been created in the countries concerned and among all nations, an opinion informed of the dangers involved in going on with the tests and led by the reason which this information imposes, then the statesmen may reach an agreement to stop the experiments.
>
> A public opinion of this kind stands in no need of plebiscites or committees to express itself. It works through just being there.[19]

That was the message. "The broadcast," wrote Dr. Kaare Fostervoll of Radio Oslo, was "incredibly successful." Among other things it stimulated an American scientist on the General Advisory Committee, Dr. Willard Frank Libby, to write Schweitzer an open letter claiming that the radiation involved was insignificant compared with normal quantities from other sources. Did Schweitzer wish to reply? asked Dr. Fostervoll.[20]

Schweitzer had already dealt with this argument by pointing out how even insignificant amounts of radioactive material in river water became stored in ever increasing quantities in the river plankton and in the creatures that lived on the plankton—and particularly in their reproductive systems; so that the radioactivity in the egg yolks of river birds on such a river was a million times higher than that in the water itself. Libby's letter was precisely the kind of "reassurance propaganda" from the Establishment that he was fighting. But he had no intention of involving himself in disputes. He preferred to make his statement and leave it to make its effect. "Do not reply to the Libby letter," he cabled.

For all the success of the broadcast in terms of public response, the effect on politicians was negligible. Perhaps Schweitzer underestimated the time it takes for a grassroots movement to make itself felt at a political level. But one major political figure did react—Adlai Stevenson, with whom Schweitzer had been in touch for some time.

This correspondence was another result of Clara Urquhart's benevolent diplomacy. The previous year, when Stevenson was for a second time running for the Presidency against General Eisenhower, Schweitzer had written to him:

> I take advantage of the letter Madame Clara is writing to you, to say Hello. I read with great interest everything that concerns you, and I admire your courage in throwing yourself again into the electoral struggle. What emotions and fatigues you have in prospect!
>
> I too have a difficult life, but less difficult than yours. I do my work far from this world, in the forest, at the end of a river. I enjoy a certain solitude which gives me the strength to do my work. I have no vacation, no free day, no Sunday. But nevertheless I have the privilege of belonging in a way to myself. This year I cannot go to Europe. I am enjoying Madame Clara's visit, and having news of you through her.[21]

In his reply Stevenson had written with deep envy: "I think your felicitous phrase 'belonging in a way to myself' comes close to identifying what I long for most in this exposed and relentless life."[22]

In June, 1957, after the "Declaration of Conscience," Stevenson finally came to Lambarene, combining the trip with an inspection of the mines and dams of the Gabon. Afterward he issued a statement:

> Dr. Schweitzer is gratified by the world's reception of his declaration in April on the dangers of testing atomic devices. Heretofore man

has had to obey nature. But now he has learned how to subjugate nature and Dr. Schweitzer considers this the most dangerous period in history. He commented that his views were not as widely reported in the United States, Britain and France as elsewhere. But he feels that his declaration may have encouraged scientists to express their views more freely, and he was much pleased by the recent petition signed by two thousand American scientists calling for an end of nuclear bomb tests.

His information agrees with the reports I brought him, and he feels that public opinion, led by scientists who know the facts, is now moving rapidly in the right direction and will soon influence governments.[23]

We have no means of knowing how much effect Schweitzer's Declaration in fact had. But those 2,000 scientists did sign their petition shortly afterward; and the following February the Campaign for Nuclear Disarmament was launched in Britain by Bertrand Russell and Canon Collins. Both events represented precisely what Schweitzer had urged: the raising of the voices of the people against the apparent blindness of their rulers. At the very least, he gave great impetus and courage to a movement that needed all the support it could muster—and did so at exactly the right moment.

27

THE LAST OF EUROPE
1957–1959

For eighteen painful months Hélène Schweitzer had not left Lambarene. She had stayed by her own choice through the rainy season, her health failing more and more. In January Norman Cousins had noted that "the blue veins stood out against her forehead and seemed stark against the pure whiteness of her skin. She had lovely grey-brown eyes but they seemed to look at you through a mist. When she spoke it was with considerable effort. Her breathing was labored. Despite her difficulties she would not allow anyone to treat her as an invalid. She insisted on coming to the dining room for lunch and frequently for dinner. It was easy to see how much of a struggle it was for her, even with the aid of a cane, to negotiate the two dozen or so steps across the compound and climb the short stairs to the dining room."[1] In fact, as the autopsy was to show, she must have had several slight heart attacks during these years: and the lung tissue, though completely cured by Dr. Gerson's treatment in the twenties and thirties, was so extensively scarred that much of it was useless. In an atmosphere that took away the breath of the healthiest, she was breathing on severely limited capacity.

But the decision to stay was hers. When her husband urged her to go back to Europe she would complain to friends that he was trying to get rid of her. She must have known all too well that her presence was a worry to him, and he must have resented the fact that she knew it; a sore relationship, perhaps mitigated, perhaps aggravated, by the long years of companionship and mutual trust that led up to it.

In May, 1957, a few weeks before Adlai Stevenson's visit, she could hold out no longer. A Dutch nurse, Toni van Leer, was flying back to Europe to her sick father, and Hélène, who certainly could not have made the journey alone, said a final good-bye to Lambarene and set off with her to Paris. There Rhena met her and took her to a clinic in Zürich. Ten days after she left Lambarene she was dead. Had she gone sooner she might have lived longer, but probably not much, for the doctor who performed the autopsy told Rhena that the organism was completely used up.

Some staff members were surprised how silent and sad the Africans were, not for their own loss, but for him. "But the doctor and Mrs. Schweitzer weren't happy together," one nurse said. "Perhaps," said the Africans, "but she was his wife."

As for Schweitzer, his feelings had never in his life been on display—nor were they now. Nobody knew what he felt, and it would have been a rash person who claimed to do so.

In August, as soon as he could get away, he went to Europe to clear up Hélène's affairs. The house at Königsfeld was handed over to the Moravian Brothers, and all Schweitzer's belongings were moved from there to Günsbach. Meticulous as ever, he made out an inventory, like the ones he and Hélène had made out together the first time they went to Africa.

> Objects which Dr. Albert Schweitzer is moving from his house on the Rue de Schramberg in Königsfeld, where he will not be living any more, to his house in Günsbach, Upper Rhine, on the road to Münster:—

Used Books (1300)	value: 30,000 francs
Used Music notebooks (400)	value: 25,000 francs
Packets of notebooks with choir notes (12)	no value
Manuscripts of Dr. Schweitzer (12 packets)	no value
Notebooks with notes (15 packets)	no value
Old white paper (2 packets)	no value
Concert programmes (1 packet)	no value
Little boxes of old writing materials (2)	no value
Old letters (2 sacks)	no value
1 70 year old piano, out of tune	no value
A plain wooden bed, used	6,000 francs[2]

Erica Anderson was in attendance with her car, and we find Schweitzer writing to Jerome Hill.

> I was very happy to see Madame Erica at my return here, for I have had to make a journey of four days from Günsbach to Switzerland, from Switzerland to Frankfurt and then to Stuttgart—partly to assist at the anniversary of Goethe's birth, and afterwards for other reasons. During this period I shall have to travel a good deal from Alsace to Switzerland and Königsfeld to put my wife's affairs in order. I don't know about Madame Erica's plans but if she still finds a little time to help me in my journeys I shall be extremely grateful. I hope that the film will be as great a success in Switzerland as it has been in the States, France and Germany. I hope also to see you in Alsace.[3]

Jerome Hill had had a new electric heating system put into the Günsbach church, and "this afternoon I went with Madame Erica, Mlle Mathilde and my brother to the church. What a joy it was for me to see it in this state!—despite the fact that I was so attached to those horrible furnaces. The electric heating which has replaced them is very well installed."[4]

Among the friends Schweitzer visited was Nikos Kazantzakis, one of the great Greek novelists and poets of this century, best known as the author of *Zorba the Greek* and *The Greek Passion* (in Britain entitled *Christ Recrucified*). Two years earlier he had visited Schweitzer and had afterward written him a lyrical note: "I am still under the charm of your presence. That blessed day of 11th August was an astonishment to me. It seemed for the first time that our ideal can be realised on our hard earth without being compromised. You have renewed my confidence in man and in his high possibilities. . . ."[5]

Now, on a sudden impulse, as they drove through Freiburg Schweitzer went to see Kazantzakis, only to find that he had just had a relapse after recovering from an infection which he had contracted when vaccinated in China against his will. Now he was mortally sick, and three days later he died.

Equally important to Schweitzer was the old woman in a remote Swiss village who for years had sent Schweitzer the money from the eggs in her small farmyard. It was because of her, and such as her, that the hospital had existed at all in the first place; and because of her and such as her that Schweitzer refused to allow any unnecessary expenditure, even when he might have done so.

By November Jerome Hill was beginning to inquire what kept Erica in Europe, and Schweitzer was writing:

> I'm afraid I've kept her here in Europe against her will, because I fractured my little right finger. I have lost a lot of time and I needed her very badly; particularly for following the news about the danger of radioactivity in the newspapers, and the journals in German, French and in particular English and American. I have to stay up to date on this question. My time and my eyes don't let me do this work and so I asked her to do it and she's done a tremendous service in cutting out interesting articles and making me a packet every day. The result is that I'm now up to date with the results or non-results of all the congresses and the discussions exchanged between the east and the west bloc and I can judge what point the situation has reached."[6]

This broken finger was the result of an accident climbing up to his favorite old sitting place—the Rocks of Kantzenrain. Admirers had installed a bench on the spot and Schweitzer insisted on going up the steep path in the rain to look at it properly before thanking the donors. The eighty-two-year-old gentleman was not as sure of foot as the boy who had first found the place and slipped on the wet soil.

Immediately after the accident his travels took him through Zürich and Erica took him to a doctor there for treatment. The nurse turned out to be the daughter of that same Oscar Pfister, the psychiatrist, who had persuaded Schweitzer to recollect his childhood and youth in 1923.

On Christmas Day Schweitzer arrived back in Lambarene, bringing with him Hélène's ashes. They were interred near those of Emma Haussknecht, close below Schweitzer's window, and Schweitzer carved the cross.

For his birthday that January there was a guest at the table who was also celebrating a birthday—his daughter Rhena. It was years, she had written to him, since they celebrated their joint birthday together. All right, he had replied; come to Lambarene for this one. And she had come.

Despite the difficulties of her childhood, Rhena had loved her mother dearly and still wanted the love of the father she hardly knew. Once, in Lausanne, when she was about sixteen, he had waltzed with her at a party, and waltzed very well. Once he had borrowed a book of hers about Red Indian trappers and retired with it to his room. "You'd better come and fetch it back in half an hour," he said, "because once I'm into it I shan't be able to put it down." Such domestic memories were few. She had married young, and friends thought it might have been because she needed love and a home of her own. She had borne and raised three daughters and a son, and when Clara Urquhart first visited her the impression she had left with Clara was of a highly domesticated woman smothered in children and chows.

Now the children were in their teens, and her marriage was beginning to go wrong. She had a feeling that the course her life had taken had been without her full understanding and consent, and she wanted to do something of her own before it was too late. As a child she had wanted to be a doctor, and her father had discouraged her. The life was too hard, he said. Now it was too late for that, but the Lambarene which she had only once in her life visited still exercised a great fascination. She might yet do something there, she thought; or failing that, she might try publishing.

On this trip to the hospital, for her thirty-ninth birthday and her father's eighty-third, it struck her that what the hospital really lacked was a good pathology laboratory. Perhaps she should train as a pathologist. On her return home she wrote to her father with this proposal. His reply was crushing. "You won't even let me die in peace," he wrote, explaining later that he did not like the idea of his daughter working under him alongside the doctors; the relationship might be uneasy. But she was not his daughter for nothing; and she was stronger now than in her teens. She went ahead with the training. It was a two-year course, and before it was even finished, while she was in Lambarene again during her vacation, Schweitzer gave her sole charge of the laboratory.

Apart from his daughter, Schweitzer's concerns at the hospital were all too familiar—more patients than ever, more nurses, and more doctors: five doctors by now, fourteen nurses, and room for 360 African patients, besides the 200 lepers. The problem of feeding them all was complicated by the shortage of rice, so a switch had to be made to bananas and manioc for a staple diet. How were they to collect enough? In a talk in Switzerland the following year Schweitzer told a group of helpers on their way to Lambarene about the coming of "modern times" to the hospital. This talk, so eloquent of Schweitzer's charm, his humor, and his whole approach to life, is printed as Appendix B. It tells of the great moment when the automobile came at last to the hospital, in the form of a Mercedes-Benz truck that Schweitzer had to buy to collect the bananas. It tells of the road that had to be built by hand for the truck to run on. And it defines once and for all Schweitzer's attitude to machinery.

But although he gave in with a good grace when the internal combustion engine proved itself really necessary, there is no denying the glee with which sometime earlier he had announced one lunchtime at the hospital: "The twentieth century has finally arrived here. There are only two motor vehicles in the district, and today the inevitable happened. They collided. We have patched up the drivers. Anyone who feels reverence for machinery is welcome to look after the vehicles." Nor did he ever use a motorboat when a canoe could serve the purpose. But could anyone, reading that talk, suppose this was a man blinded by a Canute-like prejudice against progress?

The progress of the world toward nuclear self-destruction can have given him little cause to reconsider his mistrust of technology. Negotiations in London had collapsed in the summer, and Russia had walked out of a United Nations Conference in the autumn.

In December a request came from Linus Pauling for Schweitzer's signature to add to a new appeal against the proliferation of nuclear weapons. Schweitzer signed—along with over 9,000 scientists, thirty-six of whom were Nobel Prize winners. But Schweitzer felt that still more was needed. By chance he had met Kaare Fostervoll of Oslo Radio in Basel while shopping for medicines in the autumn, and he was wondering about another broadcast. In February, 1958, he wrote to Fostervoll and to Gunnar Jahn about it. "Since October I have spent the greater part of my time in keeping myself informed about the progress of atomic weapons, and I am in touch with experts on the subject." He had in mind two talks on the radio, one of about thirty minutes on "Peace or Atomic War," another of forty or forty-five minutes on the renunciation of atomic weapons. "Address letters and cables,'' he added, ''to Mlle Mathilde Kottmann. Journalists are getting at my letters, I don't know how.''[7]

In fact, journalists were frequently to be found ensconced, rather uncomfortably, in Lambarene town, making interesting offers to postal officials for a sight of Schweitzer's correspondence. Several things drew them there; the hope of an interview—the possibility of Schweitzer's death—and according to several people I have spoken to, the desire to discredit him and his campaign against nuclear testing. There is no proof of this last allegation, but a good many interested parties would have preferred so influential a voice to keep quiet on the atomic issue.

The broadcasts were finally made on April 28, 29, and 30. A summit meeting between the political heads of Britain, the USA, and the USSR was impending, and Schweitzer spoke out much more directly than before. Now he was really entering into the political world, naming the villains:

> The Soviet Union has recently made a disarmament proposal
> . . . the proposal is difficult for the United States and Britain to accept. They spoke against it when the matter was discussed in the spring of 1957. Since then ceaseless propaganda had been directed against the view that the radiation following nuclear tests is so dangerous that it is necessary to stop them. The American and European Press is constantly receiving abundant propaganda material supplied by government atomic commissions and scientists, who feel called upon to support this view.[8]

After going in some detail into this ''reassurance propaganda'' put out by the physicist Edward Teller and others, he went on:

> It is not for the physicist, choosing to take into account only the radiation from the air, to say the decisive word on the dangers of nuclear tests. That right belongs to the biologists and physicians who have studied internal as well as external radiation, and those physicists who pay attention to the facts established by the biologists and physicians.
> The declaration signed by 9,235 scientists of all nations, handed to the Secretary General of the United Nations by the well-known American scientist, Dr. Linus Pauling, on 13th January 1958, gave the reassurance propaganda its death-blow. The scientists declared that the radioactivity gradually created by nuclear tests represents a greater danger for all parts of the world, particularly serious because its consequence will be an increasing number of deformed children in the future.[9]

He spoke of the new Intercontinental Ballistic Missiles, with a range of 5,000 miles, and quoted the statement of an American general to some Congressmen: ''If at intervals of ten minutes 110 H-bombs are dropped over the U.S.A. there would be a casualty list of about 70 million people, besides some thousands of square miles made useless for a whole generation. Countries like England, West Germany, and France would be finished off with 15 to 20 H-bombs."[10]

He warned against "the extreme danger of an error in interpreting what appears on a radar screen, when immediate action is imperative, resulting in the outbreak of an atomic war."[11] And he begged that the nuclear powers separate the disarmament issue, on which there was little chance of agreement, from the banning of further tests, which concerned the whole world and was a feasible first step.

With Linus Pauling and his 9,000 dissenting scientists in the United States and with the Campaign for Nuclear Disarmament making itself felt in Britain, the people were beginning to speak, as Schweitzer had hoped, and the world's politicians found it worth their while to be seen crossing and recrossing the oceans in pursuit of agreement on the nuclear issue. This in fact was the year when the Nuclear Powers voluntarily suspended testing and the talks began which were to end in the Test Ban Treaty five years later.

All this increased Schweitzer's incoming correspondence even more. He continued to keep in touch with the international situation, so far as he could from Africa, by corresponding with people in high places and low. He wrote worried letters to Adlai Stevenson about the way the Heads of State were beginning to fly to and fro uttering banalities without making any practical moves toward peace, receiving warm and anxious replies from a man who thought very much as he did, but had to deal with the sluggishness of popular reaction. "I am afraid that most Americans think of peace as peace on our terms and unconditional surrender by the Soviet. Nor do our politicians or press do much to erase this naïveté."[12]

Pauling had written a book entitled *No More War,* in which he wanted to include Schweitzer's "Declaration of Conscience" as an appendix. For the dust jacket he asked Schweitzer to contribute a statement such as "By his efforts to prevent nuclear war and to bring the powerful forces of nuclear energy under international control Professor Linus Pauling is rendering a great service to humanity." With the omission of the word "international," Schweitzer signed it as suggested.

But the mass of the letters was still from the common people, terrified of nuclear war for themselves and their children. For all the help he had from Mathilde, Ali, and anyone else who could be pressed into service (even typewriters were welcome so long as they were kept out of earshot), there was no hope of keeping up with it all—especially since the hospital paperwork was growing all the time. A plebiscite was held in the Gabon in 1958, as a result of which the country became fully self-governing; and the documentation required of Schweitzer changed again and still increased.

Among the incoming mail were invitations from Princeton and Yale. Yale offered the Howland Memorial Prize, worth $3,000, but with the qualification that it must be received in person. Princeton offered an honorary degree, with appeals both from Robert Oppenheimer and Adlai Stevenson that Schweitzer should come. But nothing could tempt him across the Atlantic again.

One more trip to Europe was arranged, however, during which he received the Sonning Prize (the bequest of a Danish journalist) in Copenhagen, and the Joseph Lemaire Prize in Brussels; he received the freedom of the City of Frankfurt; and visited Switzerland, Holland, Sweden, and France as well. In Paris he spoke at a meeting of the French Association, of which his old friend Jacques Feschotte was vice-president.

His speeches here and at the Lemaire Prize presentation have been preserved, probably transcribed from tape recordings. They are condensations of all he believed, pithily expressed, the opposite of verbose German philosophy:

"No philosophy can have the assurance or the simplicity of those which existed before Einstein gave the world his insights.

"The mystery of being, the mystery of life, dominate our age.

"The distinctions between the learned man and the man without learning is leveled down by this mystery of being.

"All beings are together in the foundations of the essence of life.

"If you have the same feelings as I have, try to speak to others about spiritual things. I guarantee you one thing. You will find that without your realising it the spirit in these other men will understand you."[13]

In Günsbach this last time Schweitzer was helping to organize the restoration of the organ. It had been rebuilt in 1932, but the parish then had not been able to afford new material throughout and many of the parts used had been salvaged from the original seventeenth-century instrument. These had now deteriorated seriously.

Moreover, the rebuilding had been done at a time when organ builders had abandoned tracker action for pneumatic linkage. Since then Schweitzer's disquisition on organ building had brought tracker action back into favor, and organ builders had relearned how to install it. With financial help from the American Guild of Organists, from Jerome Hill and elsewhere, a complete new restoration was embarked upon.

And in Münster Schweitzer finally saw the film he had helped to make about his life and work. A cinema had recently opened in the town, seating about 500 people. By word of mouth alone the cinema was packed to overflowing that Saturday night, and the film had to be run twice. No lights showed in the houses as Schweitzer's party drove in Erica Anderson's car the two miles from Günsbach. "You've started something, Erica," Schweitzer said. "Movies now on Saturday night! Where will it end?"[14]

He refused a special seat, and pushed his way among the people, perching with two children on his knees. Erica watched his reactions and noted that "he seems particularly moved when he sees photographs of his father and mother and hears his own confession: 'They educated us for freedom. My father was my dearest friend.' "[15]

Let the commentary which he wrote for this film, full of the unashamed emotions he had always felt for the place of his upbringing, round off his life in Europe:

> I long once more to have the freedom to live in memories, to be allowed to wander among them. I recognise how wonderful it is that in my old age I can be at home where I was in my youth, that the themes of the beginning of the symphony of my life resound again in the finale.
>
> This privilege is to be twice valued in a time when so many men, as a result of the terrible events of two wars, are denied the right to enjoy the home of their youth. This loss has brought homesickness to their hearts.
>
> Yet to me it has been given in my old age to be at home in the village in which I grew up, in the surroundings where I received my first impressions. Because of the demands of the work of my student days I had to deny myself much that I longed for. But I do not want to give up now the heartfelt wish which I have cherished so long of enjoying the splendor of being at home once more and searching out those places that remind me of my youth. So let me, after these long years of work, be lighthearted again in the most beautiful sense of that word. The autumn sun calls to me; there is no autumn sun in Africa, only here.
>
> I remember four or five periods of my life when nature spoke to me here when I was small, before I went to school. In the vineyards which my father had newly planted and which bore their first harvest, my father called me to hunt for grapes. When I found none, he showed me finally where some were hidden in the leaves. And here along the line of the brook, in the small valley behind the hills, we walked to the interior of the Günsbach valleys. Here at these rocks I used to sit so often during my later student days, reflecting on my plan to go to Africa to help. Here in the meadow covered with flowers we rested. And then we went further up on a winding mountain trail. And suddenly the valley stopped, shut off from the world outside. Here the mountains drew together and I could no longer see the way to the valley leading to the plain.
>
> I came here many times before leaving for Africa, to experience the mystery of remoteness from the world. Here on the path along the woods one can look beyond the valley onto the plain and the world. My mother loved this path and this view. Always in the first days of vacation we came here with her and rested in the grass. I would suggest that the ruins at the end of the valley lifting high above the plain be the

boundary for our excursion. Lying on the wall, I looked down on the castle and considered what would rule my life. How I have loved the castles of Alsace! In the shadow of the proud castle of Kaysersberg, I was born. Often I have returned to it, to the wonderful church at the foot of the hilltop castle. I always imagine that men such as I who are rooted in the past have a special relationship to it for their entire lives.

Now I come down into the valley to a small mountain lake. How often we walked here with my mother after the four-hour journey from Günsbach, to sit here with her. When she came down from the high mountains around the end of the valley she would say, "Here, children, I am completely at home. Here among the rocks, among the woods. I came here as a child. Let me breathe the fragrance of the fir trees and enjoy the quiet of this refuge from the world. Do not speak. After I am no longer on the earth, come here and think of me." I do think of you, Mother. I love as you did this refuge from the world, this niche.

Now I have left the mountains and the castles and the woods. I stand before the church and see the swallows once more. The swallows are gathering for the journey south. We will set out together. But a time will come when I will not see you when you gather for this journey, and you will set out for the south without me, for I will have gone on a longer journey from one world to another. Hurry with your going, so that cold and death from starvation do not surprise you here! Farewell, until we meet in Africa under the southern sky.[16]

28

THE FINAL YEARS
1959-1965

IN November, 1959, Schweitzer was offered an honor that could well be regarded as the most extraordinary of all. The new government of the Gabon, under León M'Ba, asked him to represent the African states on the French delegation to the United Nations Commission on the Rights of Man. So much for the contention that all the Africans mistrusted him and his paternalism. If any Africans might have cause to resent him, it was the government of the Gabon. They might well have felt that his hospital was some sort of reproach to their own medical services, staffed as it was by whites and run by a man who was known not to believe in African independence. The invitation does credit to them as well as to Schweitzer. But the reply was predictable; scribbled across the invitation is "Impossible. My hospital needs me."

On the ship going back to Africa, Clara Urquhart had a message that a very old friend of Schweitzer's was dead—Emil Mettler, the Swiss at whose restaurant Schweitzer had set up headquarters when in London. When Clara told Schweitzer he showed no sign of emotion at all. His grief was certainly deep—he later wrote a memoir of Mettler which shows how deeply attached the two had been. But he had seen much death. And whatever other spontaneities he had learned, personal grief was still something for himself alone. The story is a warning not to suppose, as many did, that they could divine Schweitzer's feelings, or lack of them, by what he did or did not do. Feelings as powerful as these he took deep into himself, to the place where death and life were all part of life's significance.

He reached Lambarene on December 31, a fortnight before his eighty-fifth birthday, never to leave again. And still the hospital grew.

Still Schweitzer built, still he did not rest, still there was more to do than he could ever find the time for. In the midst of all the normal activities, a stream changed course, cutting across the road taken by the banana truck, and they had to build a new concrete bridge. And there were the everlasting letters. "Long after I'm dead I feel I'll still be answering letters."[1]

The pathology laboratory was finished and in operation, and Rhena was working there full time. Among those who had helped her to set it up was Joseph Bissengai, "young Joseph," who had been at the hospital only twenty-five years, in contrast to "old Joseph," Joseph Azowani, who was Schweitzer's first assistant at Andende forty-six years before. Old Joseph did little work now, preferring to yarn with visitors about his early days with the doctor, and maybe pick up a tip or two. But he was still there.

Like everyone else Rhena had her fights with Schweitzer. She was disobedient about sun helmets and would hide when she was hatless and saw him coming. And there was a battle over the use of electricity for the laboratory. But like everyone else she found she had only to prove that her proposals were necessary, practical, and economical, and she would get her way.

The world outside was seething. In the United States the hawks were after the blood of Linus Pauling; he was summoned before the Internal Security Subcommittee of the Senate Judiciary and questioned about the petition he had organized against nuclear testing. His action, it seemed, had been somewhat un-American. He appealed to Schweitzer for help. Although the McCarthy era was over, Pauling was for a while in some danger, and the committee seems to have allowed the case to drop only because they did not wish to be in the position of prosecuting a Nobel Prizewinner.

Trouble was also brewing in the Belgian Congo, which gained full independence in August, 1960, about the same time as the Gabon. But where the Gabon had been reasonably well prepared, the Congo was hurled into independence hastily and without forethought. Chaos ensued, and soon civil war. Dag Hammarskjöld flew over the hospital on his way to Brazzaville to seek a solution and cabled his good wishes to Schweitzer.

And Adlai Stevenson was appointed ambassador to the United Nations at the end of the year by the newly elected President John F. Kennedy.

Tucked away in his wooden hut on the Ogowe Schweitzer maintained his contact with the protagonists of these great events; but all his correspondence constantly reiterated that his letters were personal, not for publication. And before long he had good cause to regret it when someone did not honor his request.

Walter Ulbricht, the head of East Germany, had written to Schweitzer earlier to congratulate him on an honorary degree conferred on him by the East Berlin Humboldt University, where he had studied in 1900.

Schweitzer had in fact as much sympathy with Russia and East Germany as he had with America and the West. He was constantly pointing out to Adlai Stevenson that America's insistence on encircling East Germany with nuclear missiles was bound to make Russia nervous and invite reactions. And despite the fact that he had no more sympathy with Communism than with any other dogmatic political creed and in letters referred to Ulbricht as a tyrant, he replied as politely as he would have done to anyone else, adding a few lines about the importance of peace and Reverence for Life and concluding with his good wishes.

Unfortunately for him he was late, as so often, in replying; and in the meantime the situation between East and West Germany had reached a point of high tension, for this was the time of the Berlin crisis and the building of the Berlin Wall. When Ulbricht received Schweitzer's letter he published it—and the reaction in Europe, especially in West Germany, was violent. It was alleged that at this critical moment he had declared himself in favor of the East German Democratic Republic. Schweitzer was hurt and indignant. They were calling it, he said, the end of the Schweitzer myth of political impartiality. Why? All he had done was to offer Ulbricht the same courtesy as he did to anyone else.

The result was that when Bertrand Russell wrote in September of that year, 1961, to ask for his support in making protests about Berlin and about the nuclear threat, Schweitzer replied that, though he fully agreed with Russell and would sign whatever Russell wished, he felt too out of touch, as well as too busy and too tired, to write the text.

Indeed he was so busy and so tired that he did something he had never considered at any previous time—he gave up playing Bach. It was a real sign of capitulation when he crated up the famous piano with organ pedal attachment, which the Paris Bach Society had given him in 1913 and which had been his daily solace for almost fifty years, and sent it back to Günsbach.

For all his caution the year was not to end without another misunderstanding, another indiscretion, and another row. George Marshall, minister of the Church of the Larger Fellowship, Unitarian Universalist, in Boston and an associate of Charles Joy and Melvin Arnold, had written to Schweitzer in April, suggesting he might like to become an honorary member of the Unitarian Church. In reply Schweitzer, seeing no harm, wrote back (in November!):

> I thank you cordially for your offer to make me an honoured member of the Unitarian Church. I accept with pleasure. Even as a student I worked on the problem and history of the Unitarian Church and developed sympathy for your affirmation of Christian freedom at a time when it resulted in persecution. Gradually I established closer contact

with Unitarian communities and became familiar with their faith-in-action. Therefore I thank you that through you I have been made an honoured member of this church.[2]

George Marshall published Schweitzer's letter in its entirety on the front cover of his church's *News Bulletin for Religious Liberals*; and very naturally a great many people, Unitarians and others alike, took it to mean that Schweitzer, whose orthodoxy in the Lutheran Church had long been highly dubious, had now finally thrown in his lot with the Unitarians.

The religious rumpus was as noisy as the political one had been over the Ulbricht letter, and for once Schweitzer was persuaded to break his habit of not replying to criticism. In an interview in *Time* magazine, which had followed up the story, he stated: "For a long time now I have had connections with the Unitarian Church. But there is no question of my breaking with the Lutheran Church. I am a Protestant, but above all I am a scientist, and as such I can be on good terms with all Protestant Churches."[3]

The Belgian Congo situation was growing worse. Within weeks of the declaration of independence, the wealthy Katanga area had seceded from the rest of the Congo and set up its own government. The Belgians had prepared the country so badly for independence and granted it in such haste that the central government in Léopoldville (now Kinshasa) had no chance of imposing order on the situation.

Katanga, with its huge deposits of copper, possessed all the wealth of the country, and the great international mining companies which operated there had brought with them organizing ability and technical skills which the rest of the country totally lacked. Katanga, in fact, was the industrial center of the whole of the Belgian Congo, without which the rest of the country was bankrupt. The secession, headed by Moise Tshombe, was backed by Belgian money and Belgian mercenary soldiers; for part of the stated policy of the new Léopoldville government was to rid the country of whites and in Katanga at least the whites intended to stay.

Dag Hammarskjöld had persuaded the Security Council of the United Nations to send troops to the area, in the hope of forcing Tshombe to allow the large earnings of Katanga to be spread over the rest of the Congo and thus make it possible for the new government to control and develop the whole country. And in August, 1961, after a series of atrocities, murders, plots, counterplots, alliances, and betrayals, UN forces were ordered into action against Katanga.

World opinion was bitterly divided. A month later Hammarskjöld was on his way to negotiate with Katanga when his plane crashed and he was killed—the victim, many believed, of another murder.

Sporadic fighting went on for another year and more. And in December, 1962, Schweitzer broke his rule of political silence and made a statement.

His thesis was simple: Before the Belgians colonized that part of the world, Katanga and the rest of the Congo had nothing to do with each other. Colonization welded the two together quite arbitrarily, simply because Belgium happened to occupy both. Therefore, when independence was granted and colonization was reversed, the two territories reverted to their old separation. There was no legal or historical reason whatever why Katanga should feel any responsibility toward the new Congolese Republic or vice-versa.

Moreover, since Katanga was well organized, wealthy, and well-disposed to cooperation with the whites, it deserved its prosperity. To hand over large amounts of that prosperity to the totally disorganized, feckless, and malevolent Congolese would simply be to throw away good money—which itself was a feckless and irresponsible act.

There is of course a certain cold logic about this argument. What it ignores, astonishingly, is precisely the thing that sent Schweitzer to Africa in the first place—the debt owed by the white man to the black. For the bulk of the money from the mines was not going to Katanga at all—it was going back to Belgium. Tshombe's support came from Belgian interests of an entirely selfish nature. Belgium had exploited the whole of the Congo—and the only reason Katanga had done better was because that was where the mines were and that was therefore where the money had been invested. The rest of the country was impoverished and inefficient for precisely the same reasons as the Ogowe was impoverished and inefficient—the capitalist countries had put money in only where they hoped to get more money out. Hammarskjöld and thousands with him agreed with the new government that it was now time to restore the balance and use the Congo's assets to feed the whole country.

Schweitzer was quite sincere. It clearly hurt him to find himself opposing the views of a man he admired as much as Dag Hammarskjöld. And when Bertrand Russell wrote to say that European interests were bribing Tshombe and milking Katanga and that they should be forced to help the Congo to industrialize, he replied that the only trouble with the Congo was that its government was corrupt and inefficient, whereas Katanga's was efficient, hardworking, and peaceful. "Please forgive me for not being able to agree with you," he wrote, "because I know the facts."[4]

The facts which Schweitzer referred to were local, not international. The white traders and engineers he personally met were none of them rascally exploiters; they were mostly humane men struggling to earn a living in very hard conditions. These were not the men who bribed governments and organized private armies of ruthless mercenaries to protect their investments. They were themselves cannon fodder for the financial field marshals who sat in the capitals of Europe and disposed of millions of francs. Things, as Schweitzer often said, looked very different from out there.

But it does appear that for once his respect for thrift, order, and legality, combined with his oft-stated mistrust of black self-government, had overwhelmed his sense of natural justice and the rights of man as man.

Across the Atlantic the nuclear threat reached a climax with the Cuba crisis of October, 1962. Both Kennedy and Defense Secretary McNamara said that they were prepared to use nuclear weapons if necessary to keep Russian missiles out of Cuba. Full-scale nuclear war seemed very possible and Schweitzer wrote in great perturbation to Bertrand Russell: "We must act!!"[5]

No action Schweitzer took could in fact have had any significant effect at that critical moment. His great strength lay in his ability to speak to the ordinary people of the world and to remind them that their futures were at stake. This he had already done, and that worldwide call and the tide of popular feeling to which it had given impetus certainly had their effect on the peaceful outcome of the Cuba crisis. More he could not do.

In the long-term issue, too, that of nuclear testing, the humanity to which he had appealed was gradually winning. The talks that began in 1958 resulted in a formal Test Ban Treaty in August, 1963, and Schweitzer began to see President Kennedy in a new light. When Kennedy was assassinated in November of that year, Schweitzer wrote to his mother, Mrs. Joseph P. Kennedy: "I do not know who else has his clear-sightedness, his tenacity and his authority and could continue his great humanitarian and political work.

"At present we walk in the dark again. Where are we going? Your son was one of the great personalities of the world's history. Millions of us mourn with you."[6]

But at least the treaty was signed. And not the least of Schweitzer's rewards must have been the many letters he received from the ordinary defenseless folk who stood in most danger from atomic radiation—and from some who already knew what it was. Here is one, from Sueo Muta, Hospital for Atom Victims, Nagasaki, Japan:

DEAR DOCTOR SCHAITZER [sic] AND MRS. ECKERT!
I wish you a Merry Christmas and a happy new year.
Looking at the photograph taken on the occasion of your visit to our hospital, I am thinking of you at far distant land in Africa. I wish that doctor Schweitzer is in good spirits. My health comes to a state of lull. It is difficult to me to get good health. Thanks to endeavour of doctor Schwaitzer and other peace-makers a partial atombomb test ban was realized in the last sommer. It is big joy for us. From now we need not

fear rain and air contaminated by radioactivity which causes atomdiseases to many persons.

But production, storage and use of nuclear arms are not yet prohibited and minace [sic] humanity. I hope that the coming year 1964 will be the year of annihilation of nuclear arms and of establishment of eternal peace.[7]

Einstein had died in despair at what science had let loose on the world. Schweitzer was luckier—he saw at least a milestone on the road he had pointed out back to sanity.

Earlier in 1963 he had passed another landmark—one he could never have expected—the fiftieth anniversary of his arrival at Lambarene. He had come in April, 1913, his achievements all put aside for the sake of one ambition—to give something back to the Africans whom the West had used and abandoned; fifty years later that gift to the Africans had itself become his greatest achievement. He had come with his wife to a single bungalow; fifty years later his daughter was able to write:

> Lambarene hospital is in great degree an African village, which now comprises 72 buildings grouped around the central core: operating theatre, X-ray room, laboratory, dental clinic, delivery room, doctor's offices, and a dispensary where drugs are issued and injections given, and where, in cases of accidents, first aid is administered. About a thousand operations a year are performed, mostly hernias, but including urological, gynecological, abdominal, orthopedic and some eye surgery.
>
> About 350 babies are born each year at the hospital. Besides the 450 to 500 hospitalized patients, we also treat a large number in our outpatient clinics.[8]

All he had wanted was a small hospital, but it had grown and grown. Since 1927 he had been trying to get it finished, to get the building over and done with and to concentrate on his medical work, his writing, his philosophy. But the hospital had defeated him—Rhena writes, "His most important task now, however, is the construction work, especially during the dry season. The roofs of the new houses must be on before the rains start at the beginning of October."[9]

In fact, the hospital was growing faster than ever. Between 1961 and 1964 the number of patients rose from 450 to 600. It was so big that Schweitzer no longer knew everybody by name. His was in his late eighties, still working a longer, harder day than his daughter could, but here and there the hospital was beginning to slip out of his control. He had not a single day off for many years. And when suddenly he felt very tired and for two days was not seen around the hospital, it was as though the sun had failed to rise. After those two days he was back at work, but for a while he himself had thought that he might die.

In a letter to Wernher von Braun, the rocket physicist, who wrote to him that year about immortality, he had said, "At eighty-eight a man is rather like an over-ripe plum hanging on a tree—it only needs a little gust of wind to shake it off." But he was not tempted, as the old so often are, to console himself with thoughts of everlasting life. "I do not believe that life after death is a field for deep religion. Deep religion is a matter of a spiritual way of life, in which man enters into the life of the spirit with which Jesus came into the world. Deep religion does not make demands as to the continuation of life after death. Religion leaves all this to God. In religion the point is to follow the saying of Jesus: 'Go up into the heights.' "[10]

It was the same answer that he would have given at thirty. Nothing had changed. His fidelity still held.

In the administration of the hospital he was helped by his two "archangels," Mathile Kottmann and Ali Silver. As it grew bigger and he grew more tired, more and more responsibility devolved upon them. They had been there so long—Ali for sixteen years, Mathilde for nearly forty, that they had reason to feel they knew his mind. They worshiped him, and he relied on them. To look after him and the hospital was their joy and privilege, and to Ali, writing in the bulletin for 1963, all was for the best in the best of all possible hospitals.

> There is something of a small paradise about Lambarene. We live and work in mutual trust and confidence, each trying in the best way he can to alleviate suffering. Whenever necessary doctors and nurses work without regard for hours or time, day and night. The patients have freedom throughout the hospital: they fish in the river, they take their firewood from the forest, they eat all they wish of the fruits of the plantation, and they have no cares concerning payment, for everything is free for them. Children are playing everywhere, the little ones often completely naked, enjoying the sun or the waters of the Ogowe river. The animals know that they can live in security here, they are not killed for food and when they die they die a natural death.[11]

Ali was not the only one to feel this. It was the raison d'être of the hospital, and the feeling to a greater or lesser degree affected everyone who worked there for any length of time. In Erica Anderson's film something of the enchantment comes across, and the viewer is captivated by the atmosphere of a life that is busy and purposeful yet unflurried, serious but gay, and in which the companionship of all creatures is taken for granted.

Schweitzer's own personality had become, as he had wished, the spirit of Lambarene, and those who allowed themselves to respond to it were warmed and enriched—men as well as women, though men were the more inclined to resist the spell.

But the sunshine of that paradise was not always unclouded. Ali herself had grown so furious on one occasion that she almost left, and Schweitzer had implored her to stay "at least until I die." Mathilde had grown stiff-lipped with disapproval when Schweitzer forgave a man who stole drugs and allowed him back into the hospital for treatment; also when he took back the heretic Trudi Bochsler and gave her charge of the leper village.

Some of the other doctors and nurses resented the power of the archangels—particularly when, in those last few years, Schweitzer grew too tired to dominate them. Almost by definition anyone who came to work at Lambarene was a person of exceptional personality, someone who had made a break from the accepted pattern. Such people held strong and far from identical views. To hold these people together, in those cramped and wearying conditions, needed a personality as big as Schweitzer's. For him they would do what they would do for no one else. As his dominance began to wane, clashes of interest and temperament became more apparent.

Part of Schweitzer's great strength as a leader was that the fierce authoritarianism that he wielded in hospital matters gave place to a total generosity in everything else. People's religious beliefs, their sexual inclinations, their taste in music and the way they spent their spare time—these were their own affair. Schweitzer might tease them—and some sensitive souls might find the teasing a little heavy-handed—but he would never judge and never interfere. Indeed he would greatly enjoy the kaleidoscope of character. And when he wanted something, he knew how to handle people with kid gloves. "Please don't make me sad," he would say when deviations occurred from the Schweitzerian way.

Nor did it escape him, as was commonly supposed, that some of his helpers were less dedicated than others. "Some come to help," he said once; "and others come to help themselves."[12] To both kinds he indiscriminately offered a place in the hospital. And here we must mention the well-publicized tale that Schweitzer encouraged wealthy socialites to cluster around him, feeding on their money and their flattery.

The two who are specifically cited are Marion Preminger (subsequently Mrs. Marion Mayer) and Olga Deterding, daughter of an oil millionaire. They must be mentioned only because they have figured so largely in other books and articles (one book contrived to devote almost a whole chapter to the two of them) that they are now, willy-nilly, part of the story.

The idea of poor little rich girls working among the tumors and the leprosy was much too good to escape the journalists, and they made the most of it. In England, if you ask almost anybody what name they associate with Albert Schweitzer, they will say Olga Deterding—a fine example of both the power and the perspective of the press. In Lambarene she was no more important than any other guest, though it was tiresome that from time to time she had to be hidden from reporters and photographers who had come a long way to get at her.

Marion Preminger's function in the hospital was to collect money for it and to arrive every year for Schweitzer's birthday to hand out expensive and incongruous gifts to all and sundry. On the strength of this she called it "my hospital."

To both Schweitzer offered precisely what he offered hundreds of others—if they wanted to come they were welcome. If they wanted to stay, a place would be found for them. If they wanted to help, with work or with money, so much the better. "I'm a past master at putting people to work," he said; and money was always welcome. But no one was going to force them. And if a rich woman wished to spend some of her money on exotic gifts, though the staff might feel the money could have been better spent, Schweitzer would not judge. He would, as Erica Anderson said, like you for what you were—whatever you were—even if you were rich; and he would try to give you what you needed, even if what you needed was a sense of your own bounty or an escape from your own uselessness.

The archangels could not be expected to have the same breadth of vision. For years they had tried to protect Schweitzer from his own generous refusal to discriminate, his giving of himself to activities and people they thought unworthy of his time. He had had to fight for the right to make his own decisions as to what was important. At last he began to give in and allow himself to be organized. He allowed the archangels to take decisions he would once have taken and to come between him and the people of the hospital.

Minor inefficiencies increased. We have Dr. Weissberg's word for it that Schweitzer was never really organized, and his sisters were always astonished that their dreaming brother had gained such a reputation for efficiency; it never seemed evident at home. He had run the hospital on the basis of intimate personal knowledge of its every aspect. As the details slipped out of his grasp, gaps appeared in the smooth running of things which, while they had little effect if any on the actual medical excellence of the hospital, loomed large in the minds and the gossip of the workers there. One nurse for example, badly needing fresh linen, was denied the key to the store and broke in, only to find it infested with rats. It had always been next to impossible to keep rats and termites out of the stores (much of the trouble with the famous out-of-tune piano in the dining room was diagnosed as caused by rat urine), but the nurse felt that this piece of neglect would not have happened had Schweitzer been fully in charge.

The small beginnings of the hospital became an ever more obvious liability. Schweitzer might build houses and import staff and buy trucks and jeeps, but the drainage, such as it was, was never designed for such numbers. An outside toilet that is adequate for half a dozen people is a very different matter for a staff of twenty plus a dozen or more visitors. The open drain down the middle of the village, which was intended to serve at most forty or fifty patients with their families, now carried the litter of ten times that number; and some of that litter consisted of pus-and-blood-soaked dressings torn off by patients or by animals and dropped by the wayside. To keep this Augean stable in order was a Herculean task, and its Hercules was growing old.

Rhena too had her difficulties. Suspecting the well water, of which her father was so proud, she analyzed it and found it to be more infected than the river water. When she told Schweitzer he was furious and ignored her suggestion that a pipe should be run out into midstream where pollution was minimal, and water pumped into the hospital from there. But when, next dry season, all the wells fortunately ran dry, Schweitzer did exactly that, and she noticed that he did not go back to the wells. Before long he was showing off his water supply to visitors as if it were his own idea.

But still the patients came—and were cured. The opinions of doctors about the hospital's efficiency varied tremendously, and one has only to consider the wrangles that divide and subdivide the medical profession on every possible subject to know that no such thing as an objective medical opinion exists.

Dr. Stanley Browne, an expert on leprosy and now in charge of the British Leprosy Research Association, visited the hospital after Schweitzer's death and pronounced it a disgrace—chiefly on the grounds that it was not occupied in preventive medicine but concentrated on what he regarded as the more showy side of doctoring—surgery.

At least one television program has been based on this view, which ignores the fact that at this time the Schweitzer hospital was handing over the early treatment of leprosy to a government campaign in the villages. The leper village itself remained for one reason only—the cured lepers refused to go home. "This is now our village," they said, "and if you turn us out we will build ourselves a new village nearby." And indeed several who did return to their original villages found themselves rejected and driven back to the leper village. Schweitzer promised that they might stay there as long as they lived.

Stanley Browne's life is dedicated to the fight against leprosy. The fact that the Schweitzer hospital was not concentrated on that one thing was enough to damn it in his eyes.

On the other hand Dr. Jack Penn, a South African plastic surgeon who began by calling the hospital "a magnificent failure," later revised his opinion after working and operating there. He told Clara Urquhart, "This show is a Rolls-Royce; maybe a fairly ancient model, but still a Rolls-Royce. To my mind nothing could be gained by changing anything so as to make a streamlined Ford—even the very latest model—out of this tried and tested Rolls-Royce."[13]

But even he, as has already been quoted, is said to have remarked that a consignment of sandals would do more good than a lot of surgery—as though Schweitzer had not been trying to get the Africans to wear sandals since he first came.

Finding fault with Schweitzer in fact had become something of a fashion. And the more one studies the evidence the more one is forced to the conclusion that the opinions of anyone who did not actually stay and work with him are virtually worthless. Time and again a criticism that looks intelligent and valid proves to be so ill-informed as to be quite irrelevant. So, although figures too can lie, let me refer to some that were collected by a Swiss doctor, Rolf Müller, who did work for some while at Lambarene and who published these figures in leading medical journals in Geneva and Munich.

These show that the number of patients treated rose from 3,800 in 1958 to about 6,500 in 1963. The number of operations performed in 1962 was 802—in 1963, 950, an average of over three in every working day. The operation mortality rate was lower than 1.17 percent—less than the European average.

The equipment in the operating theater, which now had two operating tables, each with powerful modern electric lamps, was better according to one visitor than that in the average large Swiss hospital; and the same was true of the supplies in the dispensary.

Schweitzer himself had of course long ceased to do any surgery personally, though he sat daily in the dispensary, keeping himself informed of all that went on and ready to give any advice required. And he still insisted on authorizing serious surgery, for he was responsible to the families of the patients.

The only relief he found from the pressure of his overgrown creation was in his visitors. While he complained regularly about yet another day wasted on tourists, in fact he welcomed them gladly and sometimes appeared restless if several days passed without any arrivals. He would show them proudly around and talk to them about his philosophy. Perhaps the performance which, as we have seen, he was compelled to put on for their entertainment (and from Appendix B we have some idea of the quality of that performance) also gave some satisfaction to him. In age the bones of character, like the bones of the body, begin to show through, and Schweitzer, by his own account a schoolmaster, was by now the headmaster of a school for living. A few inmates had access to the real man. For the rest it was: "No discussion." The myth spoke and was not to be questioned.

Among the visitors came a writer called Gerald McKnight. After a few days' stay and a couple of conversations with the doctor, he felt equipped to write his *Verdict on Schweitzer,* a book which deserves to be passed by in silence but for one thing—that in many libraries, in Britain at least, it is the only work to be had on the subject and it is therefore the source book and compendium of practically the whole range of misinformation about Schweitzer. The book needs some attention so that people with a vague feeling that Schweitzer was a fraud should be quite clear about the origin of that feeling.

To itemize the inaccuracies, false insinuations, and out-of-context quotations in McKnight's book would take a chapter in itself. A few samples will have to suffice, though they cannot hope to indicate the range and frequency of his distortions. The difficulty is to select from such a rich crop.

The Preface immediately establishes McKnight's view that Schweitzer's hospital appears to some people to be "in reality, a jungle sore suppurating into the fresh body of emergent Africa, hampering the advance of clean, clear-minded and progressive Africans who are now building modern and fully equipped hospitals in the vicinity . . . in a word Schweitzer's hospital is redundant . . . an old man's private dreamworld overtaken by realities he refuses to accept."[14] What it appears to others to be McKnight does not trouble to state.

In fact the only "modern and fully equipped hospital in the vicinity" (Dr. Weissberg's) was described by one of the few reporters who actually went there, a Swiss named Roman Brodmann, who went to Lambarene in 1962 armed with all the standard prejudices against Schweitzer. Here are his words:

> I found at the hospital a young French doctor who was responsible for the running of the place. He showed me round the building, which was of stone and disgustingly dirty (*Time* Magazine: "A modern antiseptic hospital") and shrugged his shoulders in resignation. "I'm a doctor, not a charwoman." The beds are of iron. The mattresses have a dosshouse look about them—a real paradise for germs. The operating theatre is inadequately equipped, which is relatively unimportant since there is a complete lack of a second doctor to assist at any operation that presents any difficulty. So the doctor sends cases that are at all complicated across the river to Schweitzer's hospital. I found nearly half the beds unoccupied at the government hospital; Schweitzer's hospital is full to overflowing, and being expanded all the time.[15]

And Frederick Franck, in his delightful and perceptive *Days with Albert Schweitzer,* writes:

> I saw many much better equipped hospitals in Equatorial Africa [than Schweitzer's]. I was shown modern government hospitals after having been told that they put the Schweitzer Hospital to shame. And, indeed, they had better buildings, cleaner wards, mosaic floors, and sometimes better equipment. The quality of the medicine practiced, however, was often incomparably poorer. In some of these hospitals the staff consisted of a single overworked doctor who, having to waste most of his time on useless paper work and statistics, was forced to leave treatment to incompetent orderlies. Often there was no doctor at all and a lonely, overburdened nurse had to try to diagnose and treat everything from toothache to leprosy. Intricate instruments, no longer in working order, were standing around; gleaming electrocardiographs or anesthesia machines had become corroded and irreparable after a short time in the equatorial humidity.[16]

Having discussed the hospital, McKnight goes on, in a chapter entitled "How Good a Doctor?" to assess Schweitzer himself. He makes the point that Schweitzer was not a brilliant surgeon and that for many years he had practiced very little medicine or surgery himself, and continues, "We must accept the fact that Schweitzer did not have any great stomach for healing men's bodies, while his time could better be used in trying to patch up their doomed souls"[17]—a statement diametrically opposite to the truth that Schweitzer went to Africa precisely to get away from word spinning and devote himself to physical healing.

It was McKnight, too, who if he did not invent them, gave a great boost to the titillating tales of desperate women with an unhealthy longing for self-sacrifice, offering their lives to Schweitzer in a sick and hopeless devotion and loving him for the ruthlessness with which he sucked them dry. It was McKnight who devoted a chapter to Olga Deterding and Marion Preminger. The chapter is called "Beauty in the Jungle." Out of twenty chapters, four others are devoted to this exciting theme—"Women and the Lure," "Eccentrics' Goal," "The Novice," and "Unsung Heroines."

The chapters on "The Bach Book," "Is Schweitzer a Christian?" and "Philosopher of Doom" also have their special highlights. Conor Cruise O'Brien remarked in *The New York Review of Books* that "Mr. McKnight's writing has the worst features of the kind of British journalism which formed it; cockiness, ignorance, carelessness, prurience, innuendo, and lip-service to the highest moral standards."[18]

Finally we come to the "Verdict." Here McKnight poses the wholly fatuous question, "Is Schweitzer a saint or a fraud?"[19] and then brings evidence that he is not a saint. So he had to be the other thing. Schweitzer was unlucky to live just long enough to see the fashionable tide swing against him; and now in magazine after magazine the new cry was taken up, "Schweitzer is a fraud." Schweitzer refused to reply, or to let anyone do so for him. He never believed in justifying himself. "The philosophy of stoicism has its advantages," he said. McKnight's book came out in the middle of 1964. That summer Schweitzer had his coffin made. And to look after the medical side of the hospital after his death he sent for Dr. Walter Munz, who had worked with him already for some years, to return as physician-in-charge. But still he had apparently not nominated an administrator to succeed him. To inquiries—and there were many—as to what would happen when he died, he was evasive.

For his ninetieth birthday BBC television sent out a team to do a program for the Panorama series, and the interviewer, Michael Barratt, asked him, "What arrangements have you made for the future of Lambarene after you're no longer able to run it?" Schweitzer replied: "The one who will take over as leader of the Hospital when I am dead—but [laughingly] I am not going to die too soon—he's already been nominated and is already on the staff. That's all been taken care of."[20] But still nobody knew who the successor was. Schweitzer had not told even the two archangels. The mystery thickened. He could not have been referring to Munz, for the interview took place before January 11, and Walter Munz had not yet come back to Lambarene to take up his position. In any case, the post of physician-in-charge was not the same as Schweitzer's successor.

The conflicts that were bound to break out at his death were already casting a shadow before them. Should the hospital survive? And if so in what form? As an indication of how far it had changed already, it now boasted six refrigerators, two deep-freezes, two jeeps, an American convertible donated by Erica Anderson, traffic signs requesting a speed limit of ten kilometers per hour, and a parking area. ("If they park anywhere else I'll put down tin tacks," said Schweitzer.)[21]

There was air conditioning in the windowless X-ray room. One nurse had made a start on preventive medicine by taking a traveling inoculation clinic to nearby villages. The number of patients had risen to 600, with six doctors and thirty-five nurses to look after them. Sometimes they had to rent beds in nearby villages to accommodate the walking patients.

But the aged motorboat was never used. Schweitzer felt no need of it. The toilet facilities were unchanged, and when a nurse, Joan Klent, was discovered building a lavatory for her patients Schweitzer was furious— though in the end, as usual if anyone stood up to him, he growled, "You'll never change," and gave in.

Rhena found that she could never predict exactly how her father would react. Though she was his daughter, she was only now beginning to know him properly and her feelings toward him were a curious mixture of love, irritation, admiration, and detachment. For all his unshakable consistency at the elemental level—perhaps because of it—he could be whimsical, he could change his mind, he could give in to impulse. And if she began: "But yesterday you said—" he had a standard answer: "I'm not a book with a well-constructed plot. I'm a man, with all a man's contradictions."

A man who lays down rules is allowed to break them—and knows when they should be broken. It was harder for Mathilde and Ali, indoctrinated with his belief that what was good enough for the Africans was good enough for those who tended them and in love with a way of life they felt was threatened. They resented the force of the change they could feel coming, and their rigidity was resented in turn.

Among those who wanted change was Rhena—not a great deal of change, but some. She wanted, for example, running water, and electric light throughout the hospital. Schweitzer would not budge. It was not necessary, so it need not be. He had doctors, nurses, patients, and a good medical record. Why change? His view was entirely reasonable. Rhena, however, thought that the people who came to work there deserved better than a bucket to sluice over themselves for a shower and oil lamps to read and write by.

During those last years Rhena not only worked in the laboratory, she also traveled all over the world on her father's behalf, speaking, showing slides, and collecting money. She went to Scandinavia, to South America, and most successfully of all, to Japan. Japan took to Schweitzer's thought more enthusiastically than any other country, and in many Japanese schools his books became required reading. (From these visits comes the reference in Sueo Muta's letter to "your visit to our hospital." Schweitzer himself never went—only Rhena).

Schweitzer's writer's cramp was now getting serious. But he still wrote letters, as many as ever. Bertrand Russell was trying to persuade him to join the campaign to look into the assassination of President Kennedy, but he declined, on the grounds that he knew too little about it. "People have to often criticised me for concerning myself with the world's affairs, though I live in the virgin forest. You would not wish to expose me to this criticism again."[22]

The atomic issue was different. Schweitzer felt that they should campaign against Barry Goldwater's election to the Presidency, and Russell agreed. Schweitzer signed a manifesto.

Thousands of letters still went unanswered. A sad Indian who had written once and had no reply writes desperately: "I expected your kind word of comfort and appreciation from your own hand would arrive to console and encourage the heart of this poor despairing boy. But God did not will it so far. But, truly, my dear Grandfather, I am left by Him as a miserable ship with its destination of a high goal but struggling in the midst of great agitating waters of impediments both of body and of circumstances. Really my position is thus. I find no other go but to run to you crying for help and a lift by your own strengthening arm."[23] What a burden of responsibility, the knowledge that so many hung so on his words! No wonder he confessed to Trudi Bochsler that he was sometimes afraid of not being able to live up to his professions.

As he grew weaker and had to be driven in the jeep on his visits to the leper village, everyone around him was constantly concerned for his health. They worried about the effect on him of the sudden spate of malice directed toward him in the world press. He was often said to be untouched by criticism, but it was not true. "He strides through his self-created world," said the commentary of the Panorama film, "impervious to criticism from outside and deaf to it from the people around him." But to Dr. Weissberg he said, "Always ask yourself how much of the criticism is justified." And on his ninetieth birthday he said to the assembled Africans, "Do you want me to leave you? If you say so, I will." They howled him down, because they loved him deeply. But he had never needed to ask such a question before.

Another blow awaited him. *Les Mots,* the autobiography of Jean-Paul Sartre, came out with its dismissive references to the family in general and especially Sartre's grandfather, Schweitzer's Uncle Charles. Schweitzer had always visited Sartre's mother when he was in Paris and they got on well together. He visited Sartre too, when he could, and had read all his books and plays. He admired them if he did not like them. But Sartre seems to have neither liked nor admired Schweitzer in return. "I am sad," wrote Schweitzer in a letter to a friend, "that he writes so derogatorily about his grandfather, who had a good knowledge of German literature and had a great love for his only grandchild."

And he went on, with one of the few personal asides in his correspondence:

> I met Sartre very early, when he was still in his baby clothes. I lived near my uncle, close to the Bois de Boulogne and so my cousin often asked me to push the pram to the park for her. I was supposed to lift him out of the pram to do a wee-wee; but he never did it when he was lifted out, only in the pram. One could see that he was already himself in that pram.
>
> Sometimes he spent his holidays with his mother at the vicarage in Günsbach. He is supposed to have written his first pieces in the vicarage garden, when he was still a pupil. We are correct and friendly with one another, but we have no deep relationship. His philosophy is witty and clever but not profound. He is a follower of Husserl and Heideg-

ger. His plays are better than his philosophy. In them he deals with ethics, which have no place in his philosophy. . . .[24]

That year Ali Silver began to sleep in a hammock in Schweitzer's room
to be near him at all times. But he kept going. If any whisper of illness
escaped, the deluge of inquiries about his health doubled the normal flow
of letters. So he still took care always to be seen around the hospital. And
indeed he seemed to be as fit as ever—only a little less active.

But in June there was concern about his blood sugar, which was 265.
Sweet things were cut from his diet, but he was not a good patient. He resented even being asked how he felt and was as difficult as a spoiled child
about his food. He would try to snatch a piece of cake if it was within
reach and nobody seemed willing or able to stop him. His color was not
so good as usual, especially the color of his hands; and his memory was
growing erratic.

Rhena's situation as laboratory nurse was made more difficult by the
fact that the patient was not only a crusty authoritarian but also her father.
Nevertheless, she sent particulars to her husband's doctor in Zürich, a
specialist in diabetes, who prescribed Orinase. This brought the blood
sugar down to 165, and Schweitzer seemed better.

For a number of years now he had not eaten meat (he could no longer
bear, he explained, to eat anything that had been alive) and now he lived
largely on soup—often lentil soup—of which he never tired.

Erica Anderson had been at the hospital during the spring and early
summer, and when she left in the middle of July there was no immediate
cause for concern.

On August 10 Schweitzer wrote to Jerome Hill, and his handwriting,
usually so consistent and firm, was spidery and wandering, the final sentence almost illegible. The letter is of no great interest in itself—he wants
Jerome Hill to help a friend while he is in Europe. And, "If you are able
in one of your journeys to pass by Lambarene, which has an airport now,
I would be very glad to see you again."

It was one of the last letters he penned himself. Two days later a small
group of friends arrived, including Charles Michel, who for so many
years had supervised the purchases and deliveries of supplies to the hospital from Strasbourg, and Fritz Dinner, the vigorous leader of the Swiss
Committee. "He looked very well for his age," they wrote, "though he
was a little more stooped and his movements were slower than in previous
years. His voice was softer but extremely clear."[25]

He worked every day, as usual, in the pharmacy, in his room, or on the
building site and still took most of his meals with the staff and read the
Bible after the evening meal.

On Monday, August 23, instead of the Bible reading, he announced in
a clear, firm voice, his instructions in case of his death. That same day he

dictated and signed a letter to the Strasbourg Association of the Hospital, who would become responsible for the hospital on his death:

> To the Association of the hospital of Dr. Albert Schweitzer, Lambarene, Gabon, Strasbourg.
> To the Members of the Association,
> GENTLEMEN,
> I the undersigned, Albert Schweitzer, doctor of medicine in Lambarene, Gabon, declare that my daughter, Mme. Rhena Eckert-Schweitzer, Uetikon a See, shall take over the direction of my hospital at Lambarene after my death. Given at Lambarene, the 23rd August, 1965.

It was the first Rhena had known of it.

From that moment he began to fail. He was not always present at meals, he was not always out at work. On Thursday and Friday he had himself driven through the hospital grounds, and on the Friday he walked through his orchard. Walter Munz said, "His last walk was wonderful. Once more he passed through the orchard supported by his cane. He identified every tree he had planted, praised them for their sturdy growth and for their beauty. From the top of the hill he looked over the hospital and was very happy about it."[26]

Once when the criticism had been high, he had sat and looked at his hospital and said quietly. "All the same, it is a charming hospital." Walking through the orchard he said good-bye to his charming hospital.

On Saturday the twenty-eighth he had breakfast in the dining room, and the staff could see that a change had taken place. Then he went back to his room and talked to Rhena. He said he was very, very tired.

He tried to walk a little way, but got no farther than the porch outside his room. He returned to his bed.

Dr. David Miller wrote the medical report:

> The terminal illness of Albert Schweitzer was caused primarily by cerebral vascular insufficiency which manifested itself quite abruptly on August 28, 1965, with impairment of consciousness and of cerebral regulation of cardiac and respiratory function. During the preceding week he had seemed more fatigued than usual, with some unsteadiness on his feet.
> On the evening of August 29, because in his semi-comatose condition he was unable to take sufficient fluid by mouth, he was given an intravenous infusion of physiologically-balanced electrolyte solution, slowly through the night.
> For the most part thereafter he remained semi-comatose and bed-rid-

den, with transient periods of increased reactivity. Until September 3, he was able to take clear fluids, including beer (which he had asked for) in small amounts by mouth. His blood pressure was well maintained until nearly the end, and an electrocardiogram on September 2 revealed no evidence of myocardial infarction.

On 3 September, his fluid intake and urinary output diminished, his temperature rose gradually, his respirations became more rapid with evidence of diminished aeration of the right lung, and his coma deepened.

Because of the evident irreversibility of his condition—deepening cerebral coma, increasing uremia and developing pneumonitis—no further diagnostic measures or specific therapeutic measures were carried out. He continued to receive constant and excellent nursing care but he did not require any analgesic medications, for at no time was there any evidence of suffering. Over the last few hours of his life his pulse grew weaker and his coma deepened further. At 11:30 p.m. September 4, 1965, he passed away quietly in peace and dignity in his bed at the hospital he had built and loved.

Fritz Dinner and Charles Michel's account of the funeral was published in the hospital bulletin, the American Schweitzer Fellowship's *Courier,* and elsewhere:

His mortal body was laid in the coffin which had been made during the summer of 1964 according to his instructions, and with him the little sack filled with rice which he used to carry with him constantly, and leaves of the wild vine climbing his Günsbach house; his old felt hat from which he never parted was placed there too and his loden coat was spread over him.

On the eve of his impending death the natives of the hospital had gathered and all of them, irrespective of creed, had held a moving service for their "Papa pour nous" with singing and Bible reading, expressing their love and devotion.

On Sunday 5th September at 5:30 in the morning the big hospital bell tolled and was joined by the bell from the leper village to signal the death of the "Grand Docteur." The tom-toms of the natives began to mingle with the bells to spread the sad news.

From six o'clock in the morning onwards, without interruption until the funeral in the early afternoon, the inmates of the hospital, the people of the leper village and those who had come from the surrounding countryside filed past the coffin in the room in which he had lived and died, to take leave in reverent dignity of their beloved dead.

The grief of these African men and women as they expressed it in their songs was deeply touching—an audible witness of their gratitude, their devotion, and most of all their love for their "Grand Docteur" who had helped them and had understood their actions, their joys and their sorrows.

The funeral took place on 5th September at three in the afternoon. The coffin was placed on a small platform under the palm trees in front of Doctor Schweitzer's room. The only tributes on the red shining coffin, made from native wood, where a small wooden cross and a sprig of red blossoms from the African jungle, placed there by one of the doctor's workmen who has served him for many years, Obiange.

In spite of the short time between the announcement of Doctor Schweitzer's death and burial, a great grieving multitude had gathered. There were members of the Government, the Minister of the Interior, the Minister of Defence, and the Minister of Public Health; the Director of the Cabinet of the President of the Republic of Gabon, the Prefect of the Moyen Ogowe, the Under-Secretary of Lambarene, representatives of the Gabonese and French Administrations, Deputies of citizens of Libreville and Lambarene, as well as many from surrounding villages. Representatives of Catholic and Protestant Missions and presidents of many different organisations had come, and Ambassadors or those representing them from France, Germany, England, America and Israel. A guard of honour of the State Police appeared and paid their respects to the bearer of the highest decorations of the French and Gabonese Governments. Uncountable people from near and far filled the big compound of the hospital.

Dr. Walter Munz officiated at the service, during which hymns were sung by the European nurses of the staff, by the Protestant evangelists, and by the people of the leper village. The choirs of the natives, singing with emotion, expressed their immeasurable sorrow at the loss of their "Grand Docteur" in a deeply touching way.

Following the religious service the official representatives of the Gabonese Republic honoured the great personality of Dr. Schweitzer in speeches in the warmest terms. Finally, Monsieur Michel, as representative of the Strasbourg Association of the Hospital, and speaking for the diverse other supporting organisations in different countries, as well as in the name of the entire staff of the hospital and of those from Dr. Schweitzer's distant homeland, Alsace, addressed the last words of gratitude and the last farewell to the beloved dead, in these simple words:

"I thank you, dear Docteur, in the name of all—for all you did."

In the name of Mrs. Rhena Eckert-Schweitzer he thanked all those who had come that day for the sympathy they showed and the grief they shared.

After this, the mourning visitors gathered round the grave. Four African and four European helpers carried the coffin and lowered it into the African earth under the palm trees beside the Ogowe river. After the blessing of the grave, the final prayer, and the Lord's Prayer spoken in unison, there followed a chorale sung by the hospital community. Then innumerable hands let African earth fall on the coffin as their last greeting and thanks to their "Grand Docteur" so deeply beloved.[27]

EPILOGUE

THE man was dead. The myth lived on—and the antimyth. So, against many expectations, did the hospital. This book is not about the hospital but about Albert Schweitzer, but perhaps it should be reported here how it has fared since he died.

Disagreements arose, as was inevitable, about whether and how far it should be changed. But today it is still there and still working. Running water has been added; there are shower and toilet blocks. Electric light is available throughout the hospital until the generator is switched off at ten each night. But the room the visitor sleeps in is identical with the room James Cameron and hundreds of others have slept in; the wards, the surgery, and the operating theater are still the simple, tough, hardwood buildings Schweitzer put up for his patients in the years before the hospital grew famous and the money easier. Survivors still live in the leper village. The staff still gathers for meals in the dining room, though the old long table has gone and been replaced by several small ones. On Sunday a service is still held by one of the staff, a Fang interpreter on one side, a Galoa on the other—though now it is held in the new recreation hut, not in the open space between the wards.

Schweitzer's room remains as he left it—a memorial and a museum for the many visitors who still come by and wish to see where he lived and worked. But reports of a morbid Schweitzer mystique—of meals set in his empty place—are certainly not true now and I am assured never were. The rest of the hospital stays as it is because it is still efficient and it serves a purpose which the government values. It now specializes in difficult cases, and particularly in surgery.

The hospital is dependent on government goodwill, for without Schweitzer's presence the flow of donations from the world outside has dwindled to a fraction of what it was. The government's stipulation is that new facilities should be added; and on the neighboring site, recently purchased, new wards and clinics are rising.

The work of healing goes on, but has the Schweitzer spirit survived? Well, the goats are gone. The hospital no longer grows all its own vegetables, for labor is no longer obtainable on the old barter system. There are minimum wage rates to be considered and it is now sometimes cheaper to buy the vegetables. Pets are still common, but anywhere in the world people keep pets. The Garden of Eden touch has vanished. People there may believe in and to some extent practice Reverence for Life, but nobody any longer passionately embodies it. Things have become more ordinary. The myth is evaporating.

This would not have troubled Schweitzer too much. It was his Lambarene, but as he said to his granddaughter Christianne, when she wanted to go there to help: "You can have your Lambarene anywhere." The true heirs to Schweitzer's hospital are other hospitals, many of them directly inspired by his—Dr. Mellon's in Haiti, Dr. Binder's in Mexico, Dr. Rhee's in Korea, Dr. Humberto's in Brazil—and not only hospitals but many other ventures undertaken with the same concern and dedication. The criterion is not that others should try to preserve what Schweitzer made nor even to imitate it, but that they should try to find a true and valid expression, in action, of their own most humane and human impulses.

For the hospital, as Schweitzer said himself, was really only "an improvisation." He made it up as he went along. The theme on which he was improvising was a certain attitude which, once the name had come to him, was called Reverence for Life. Other people's improvisations on the theme could be, and should be, quite different. What mattered was the theme.

Unlike the hospital, the theme was anything but improvised. From his early childhood he had been aware of it and all his life he had worked at its perfecting. Rabbi Leo Beck said that Schweitzer's greatest achievement was his own personality. Jung said that he seemed to have no neurosis. However much or little this book can convey, it can never present the personality which, whether admired, loved, or resented, was always overwhelming.

In the autobiography we find the events and the thoughts that built up the man. In the books of philosophy the thoughts are expanded and enriched. In the sermons the soul's deeper feelings are revealed. But it is in the slighter, more casual works, that came from him almost by accident, *Memoirs of Childhood and Youth* and *The Story of My Pelican,* that we come nearest to the flavor of that personality—childlike without being in the least childish, undeceived without being critical, loving without being indulgent, and in every way appreciative. He drank life and savored it.

With the poet Terence he could say, "I am a man. No human thing is foreign to me." Further he could say, "I am life. No living thing is foreign to me." Because he entered so simply into the realm of living creatures, he seemed its king.

By another paradox, the thing that made him rich was his overwhelming sense of indebtedness. In fact, though he appears not to have noticed it, his sense of debt was very selective. He felt no urge to pay anyone back for harm done to him, only for good. He was aware of being privileged and of owing that privilege to various people in particular and also to life in general.

Guessing wildly, we might wonder whether his near-fatal illness in infancy left him with a profound subconscious gratitude for being alive at all. It is the only clue as to what might have made him different from his brother, or from many other children born in similar circumstances.

His theology will probably never satisfy the theologians. It ignores all the fascinating blind alleys they love to explore. His philosophy will never satisfy the philosophers. It fails to put the universe in its place, and it fails to pursue verbal distinctions down long dark burrows leading nowhere. It speaks to the whole man, not to the intellect alone.

Even his ethics will never satisfy the students of ethics. They fail to lay down clear and definitive regulations as to what to do in all circumstances. (Two years before his death, a Roman Catholic journal in Iowa, in a gesture toward the new goodwill between Churches, published a very friendly article about Schweitzer by Fr. Ernest Ranly, CPPS; but Fr. Ranly found it a great failing in Schweitzer's ethics that he could not tell us "how or to what degree we are to help others, pay our taxes, work for social justice and obey civil laws.")[1]

On the other hand, the ethics of ethicists, the philosophy of philosophers, and the theology of theologians will never satisfy ordinary people. Schweitzer's might.

The things that Schweitzer believed and fought for are believed by millions and millions of people already. Is there anything startlingly new in the proposition that life is to be preserved and encouraged, and death, disease, and human destructiveness to be fought against?

Did Schweitzer carry this to excess, with his plea that no life, animal or vegetable, large or small, shall be taken without due and careful thought for the consequences? It seemed so to a great many people. But within a few years of his death that thought of his has received grand new names—conservation, and ecology. The casual use of pesticides which he was mocked for banning has been found to have effects which reach out and threaten the whole world's balance of existence. As I write today, even his refusal to install electric light and so become dependent on diesel oil for the generator becomes almost laughably relevant, as great stores and offices are lit by candles and camping lamps.

Today the economists of the world have executed a hasty, ragged, and rather humiliating about-turn to fall into line with the ecologists—and with Schweitzer. We all know now that simplicity, thoughtfulness, and the cherishing of our world is the precondition for survival. We have not yet understood (and perhaps an even deeper crisis yet is necessary for this) that to cherish each other is also something more than morality. It is, as Schweitzer said, a necessity of thought. It is commonsense, practical politics, and the health of the human soul.

We may be thankful for Schweitzer's schoolmasterishness and passion for teaching, whatever authoritarian quirks they may have led him into. For they forced him to demonstrate with a grand QED something that the world badly needs to know—that goodness works; that to be effective it is not necessary to belong to a huge consortium or to indulge in political intrigue or the power game.

The vast majority of people, as he knew, are at heart peaceable and neighborly; and for that very reason they never reach the places of power where the world's fate is decided. The dilemma has always been that power and influence go to the ambitious and the aggressive—so that gentleness and humanity are less to be found in the corridors of power than anywhere else, and it comes to be accepted that the simple neighborly values in some way unfit a person for responsibility. Schweitzer put into the service of kindness a personality that could have dominated governments, thereby proving that goodness was not after all a disability.

I began this book by quoting Erica Anderson: "He was not so much righteous, as right." That does not mean that everything he said or did was correct, but that he was normal, he was human, he was balanced, he was sane, he was free. He was normal, in fact, to an abnormal degree. He was superhumanly human. He was excessively balanced. He took simple, everyday qualities, gave them intellectual respectability, and then pushed them to their limits and proved that they worked in practice.

Great men usually achieve greatness at the cost of some distortion of personality. They pay for their exceptional strength in one sphere by exceptional weakness in others. In Schweitzer two things only were truly exceptional. His conviction that his simple instincts were not to be despised but were desperately important. And his sheer physical stamina.

The passionate boy who would not wear an overcoat; the passionate youth who was forever arguing the truth; the passionate young man who had learned the uselessness of argument and instead kept his thoughts and intentions to himself till they were ready to be acted upon; the passionate explorer of music, the hero-worshiper of Jesus, of Wagner, of Goethe; the never-satisfied searcher for the root of all human impulse; the unwavering, uncompromising exemplar of his beliefs—at every stage of this consistent progression he was dependent on the ability of his body to stand up to the demands his passion imposed on it. In one of his last letters, with the pain of the writer's cramp very visible in the writing, he says, "The hand has stood up to it after all. My body generally sees reason in the end."

Once the passion and the strength are understood, many of the seeming paradoxes of Schweitzer's life fall into place. That a man so consistent and so basically simple could have so many divergent interests is not really surprising. Everything mattered to him; the only limitation on the things he could do was the number of waking hours in a day—and his waking hours were more than most. That he should be both musician and philosopher, pastor and physician, is only surprising to those who believe that specialization is in the nature of things. Most people are interested in all kinds of things, but few have the energy and determination to do more than dabble outside their own professions.

Schweitzer never allowed the false distinctions of convention to trouble him. Conventional thinking opposes reason to instinct, art to science, theory to practice, tradition to revolution. Schweitzer was not interested in such labels. Both reason and instinct are aspects of mental concentration; art and science are forms of creative discovery; practice is useless without theory and theory without practice; revolution loses itself without knowledge of tradition, and tradition stiffens without revolution. Most people are temperamentally disposed to one or the other of each pair, and the balance of society depends on the interaction of opposing and complementary types. With Schweitzer all the elements came together in a single man. His imagination and intelligence took him into the deep places of the mind, where all these things begin. His ecstasy before the manifestations of nature led him into the origins of thought and will and impulse, where nothing human—indeed nothing conscious—could be denied, where the mind is aware of its solidarity with all consciousness.

Reverence for Life is the acknowledgment that deeper than all division is the mystery of solidarity. Solidarity is not unity; nor is it identity; nor is it love. It respects the separateness of individual lives as the very condition of their mutual concern and interdependence. In finding that mystery and deliberately giving himself to it, Schweitzer released a force in himself which encompassed the whole range of existence. "With consciousness and with volition I devote myself to Being. I become imaginative force, like that which works mysteriously in nature, and thus I gave my existence a meaning from within outwards."[2]

So Schweitzer described what he was trying to do. The result was described by his close friend Werner Picht:

* * *

During the years the goodness inherent in his nature . . . has permeated his being into its uttermost recesses like yeast. It manifests itself in the least significant word and in the most casual action. His self-renunciation is complete. His life is spent absolutely and exclusively in the service of love, caritas. But this, as the ethic of reverence for life clearly shows, is exclusively based on the consciousness of solidarity with everything living and the responsibility which flows from it. It is humanitarian. It is compelling not by its theoretical justification, but by its perfection. [3]

Schweitzer was a practical mystic, whose mysticism led him into the ordinary lives of men and women and of all creatures—into a normality filled with significance.

He was a genius, one might say, in the art of living—using the word genius in his own sense of one who constructs a new unity out of what appeared before to be divided. He was certainly a religious genius, breaking down old structures and taking from them the pieces he needed to build a new unity. But the religious genius was inseparable from his genius in living, in which he welded an unprecedented new unity out of elements which normally divide men within themselves—intuition, reason, and will.

To do this he had to learn to use himself to the limit. Once he had discovered where the center of his life lay, and learned not to be ashamed of it but to express it, the joy of that liberation lasted a lifetime. In his teens it made him insufferable. In old age people would say of him, ''He is the most self-centered man I have ever met.'' That self-centeredness was the visible sign of the concentration he gave to being true to himself. It was the price he paid, and made others pay, for his fidelity to his vision.

And the vision? He himself would have said that everything that mattered was in his books, that he understood himself philosophically, that as a fallible individual he was unimportant.

The books, it is true, are vital. They explain and complement the life. But all the same, the image of a living man is more potent and more effective than any sermon or symbol or set of exhortations. Schweitzer was not the ultimate or only illustration of his vision; he was formed by Alsace, by liberal Protestantism, and by the nineteenth-century German academic tradition, and he carried the marks of that place, that time, and that mental discipline. But through that particular individual the vision shone with a power that is the greater because it is more personal. The theory, in short, worked.

The life was the argument, and a very strenuous argument it was. After ninety years, eight months, and some days the body that had carried it grew very tired and lay down for the last time.

With it, his case rests.

APPENDIX A

A DAY AT THE HOSPITAL
by Albert Schweitzer

"DR. SCHWEITZER'S HOSPITAL FUND"
Reprinted from the British Bulletin No. 12 (Spring, 1936)

When the first gong sounds at 6:45 a.m. the doctor who for a week is taking the duty of making the first round of the wards, the nurse whose turn it is for early service and the nurse who has charge of the workmen descend to the Hospital. The latter calls the roll of the paid labourers, the companions male and female of the patients who are eligible for work and the convalescents who are in like case, deals out to them axes, saws, spades, rakes and bush-knives and sends or leads them to where they are to work, whether it be in the forest, in the plantation, in the garden, on a building-site or in the laundry. At the same time the nurse in the consulting room is calling over the names of the native orderlies and visiting the people who are seriously ill.

At 7:30 the gong summons us to breakfast. It is only after breakfast, at 8 a.m., that the real Hospital work is supposed to begin. But in spite of all exhortations I cannot prevent nurses and doctors, even when it is not their turn for early work, from being down in the Hospital at 7. The nurse who has to do the bandaging in the operated patients' ward generally begins soon after 6. But nevertheless I hold fast to the principle that the main work in the Hospital shall only begin at 8, for in this equatorial climate one must economise one's strength. One can only get through three-fifths of the work of which one is capable in Europe. The newcomers and the overzealous often pay dearly for their contempt of this truth.

It must also be remembered that doctors and nurses do not always enjoy undisturbed rest, but are often fetched down to the Hospital two or three times in the course of one night. It is often the greatest savages who have the least consideration for their need of sleep and have them called without any urgent reason.

When we come down at 8 a.m. the six Hospital washerwomen have the boilers on four big fires under a roof which protects them from sun and rain. They get the water from a pump near. These women who work down by the Hospital have to wash the bandages and operation linen. Their place is just in front of the consultation room, so that the nurses can overlook them from its windows and stop their gossiping and idleness by calling to them. Up near our dwelling houses six other women are busy with our household washing. We need far more clean linen in the Tropics than in more temperate zones. In the hot season we may each of us need a change three times a day.

At least six men are occupied every day with the felling, cutting-up and transport of the necessary firewood. In the course of the years the plantation has pushed in between the

473

Hospital and the forest, so that the forest is now a good half hour's walk from the Hospital. Carts are no use in such hilly country so all the wood must be carried by hand. It is not only the washerwomen and the women who are making palm oil who use up the firewood, but there are fires burning nearly all day long for disinfecting the surgical instruments, and for cooking the food prepared for the very sick and the mental patients under the supervision of the nurses, and there are fires in the dysentery ward (to which relations are not allowed access) kept burning day and night. And in addition there is the firewood required for our own kitchen, for the bread oven and for our laundry.

Often we get whole rafts of splendid okoume wood as presents from timber merchants who for one reason or another cannot sell their logs. A nurse takes a crew and goes to fetch them, but the sawing of these huge logs is a laborious business.

As the washerwomen and the palm oil women are recruited from those who have come with patients and are constantly changing, it is impossible to think of training them to economy in the use of fuel, or to reasonable methods of work. This causes the nurses much trouble.

The patients and their friends fetch their own firewood from the forest for the fires over which they cook their meals, fires which they keep burning from early morning till far into the night. As unfortunately we have not enough sheds which can be locked up they often manage to help themselves from our stores, and even the beams and planks ready for use in building are not always secure from their depredations.

At 8 o'clock the patients and out-patients begin to congregate on the landward side of the consulting room. Plank beds are arranged under the big ward for the operated patients which lies opposite and stands on piles, and on these they sit or lie protected from sun and rain.

Three times a week, on the days when injections are given, the Hospital orderly Dominique goes through the wards at 8 a.m. with a big cow-bell, and summons the sleeping-sickness and elephantiasis patients, the lepers, the tuberculous and the patients who need injections of Neo-Salvarsan. An hour passes before he has collected at all events the majority. So that they may not promptly melt away again, they are shut up in a big wire-enclosed room alongside the consulting room and fetched out one by one when their turn arrives. But when a doctor calls the roll of those on his list for injections, at least a third are missing. Then Dominique, who is the shrewdest of the orderlies and has most authority over the patients, starts out again. He looks for the dawdlers among the patients who sit gossiping on the steps by the landing stage, among those who are bathing, those who are fishing, those who are fetching firewood, those who are gathering palm nuts, and drives them in front of him to the Hospital like a flock of sheep. He does not attempt to get the "Incorrigibles." These go off into the forest or the plantation for the whole morning and then appear in the consulting room in the course of the afternoon or towards evening reproachfully to establish the fact that they have not yet been "pricked." It is nothing to them that the necessary solution must be prepared afresh, and it is in vain that we try to make clear to them how they render our work difficult by their heedlessness about days and hours. They cannot even be trained to punctuality by the loss of their rations for a day or two if they repeatedly fail to attend at the right time for their injections. They always find helpful friends who let them share the contents of their cooking-pots, and thus they need not be unfaithful to the principle that freedom is the highest good.

The injections are given by Hospital Orderly N'Yama. He has held this office for years and is a master of the art of finding veins which defy both eyes and fingers when sought. He prepares the solutions under the supervision of a doctor who tells him the exact quantity required for each patient. When it is a question of Tryparsamide, which is used for sleeping sickness, or of various other drugs, the doses are calculated by the weight of the patients. At the request of Mr. Holm, the Swedish doctor, who had the care of the sleeping sickness cases, a Swedish lady gave us a weighing machine, and this enables us to weigh these patients every week.

The work is generally distributed among the three doctors as follows: one has the white patients, the mental patients and the urological cases, undertakes the main part of the work in the operating room and looks after the dispensary. The second is mainly concerned with leprosy, sleeping-sickness, tuberculosis, tropical ulcers and native confinement cases, and supervises all patients who regularly receive injections. The third undertakes some of the operations, is responsible for the bandaging of all who have undergone operations and all accident cases and has the care of the dysentery patients.

Of the eight nurses three are occupied with the housekeeping, garden, kitchen and livestock. One of the three looks after the little motherless babies who are brought up on bottles. These infants—of whom there are usually ten or twelve—pass the day in an airy room protected from mosquitoes, in charge of a native woman. They spend the night with the relatives who have brought them. We make these relatives stay with us to wash the babies' clothes and, if they are capable, to work for the Hospital in return for the milk given to the children. Usually it is the father, or an old aunt or a grandmother who is with the baby. I have built a house with eight rooms near the crèche for these people so that the infants can always be under the nurse's supervision.

A fourth nurse has charge of the workpeople. Her chief responsibility is the upkeep of the plantation, the supervision of the harvesting of the bananas and palm nuts, and the care of the young fruit trees, which are greatly endangered by fungi and grasshoppers. She also directs the clearing of the forest and has to provide the Hospital with the necessary amount of firewood.

The four nurses who serve in the Hospital divide their work as follows: The first serves in the operating room, sterilizes the linen and bandages and supervises the washerwomen who wash these things. The second bandages the operated patients and those wounded by accidents, has charge of the white patients and assists the operation sister. The third serves in the consulting room, dispenses the medicines as the doctor directs, looks after the native confinement cases and the new-born infants and supervises the people who are seriously ill in the various wards. The fourth bandages the tropical ulcers (this work claims many hours of the day), looks after the mental cases, supervises the women who make palm oil, buys the plantains and manioc (cassava) needed to feed the patients, gives the ration, and sees to it that the wards and surroundings of the Hospital are kept clean.

At 11:30 this nurse has a horn blown to announce that the distribution of the ration is about to begin. This is done from a room on a level with the ground with a large window with a counter inside it. The patients file past the window and each takes his ration from the counter. But before receiving it he has to hand in his card with his name and number so that the nurse can mark his name on her list as having received his day's ration. Otherwise the same person might fetch a ration four times over.

The ordinary patients and those who accompany them are not given cooked food, but materials to form two meals, which they prepare as they please over their own little fires.

When we have enough plantains and manioc the ration consists entirely of these, with the addition of a little salt and a large spoonful of palm oil. Two or three times a week we also give a piece of dried fish.

If there are no plantains and manioc to be had, we give rice. Plantains are far more nourishing than bananas, but when we are obliged to give rations of rice we add bananas. In our plantation we only grow bananas, not plantains, as the former require far less labour. If we were to cultivate plantains they would cost us more than those we buy from the villagers.

All the inmates of the Hospital have permission to fetch from the plantation all the palm nuts, bananas, paw-paws, lemons and mangoes they need. In this way we know that if we are compelled to feed them on rice they will nevertheless get enough vitamins.

The nurse who distributes the rations has a difficulty in the fact that those who file before her also fetch the food for the lying-down cases. She knows the ration is given but cannot be sure that it reaches its destination. A thorough savage will think nothing of gobbling up the share of a lying-down patient who has been committed to his care.

Both the nurses who have to look after the patients lying in the wards have great difficulties with those who are unaccompanied by relatives. There are plenty of people who are only suffering from slight illness and can be detailed to act as attendants. But it is quite another matter to get these to fulfil their duties properly, namely cook the patients' food and give it to them, fetch their drinking water, and be constantly about ready to render any necessary service instead of passing their time as best they please.

We hesitate to ask anybody to be a patient's attendant unless he belongs to the same tribe, for we know in advance that he will regard the request as outrageous. In many cases it is impossible to get a man to render neighbourly service to a "stranger" either by kindly exhortation, presents, threats or punishment. But even people of the same tribe do not readily consent to undertake such duties and, when they do, need very strict supervision. The nurses are often quite in despair about the difficulty of the problems concerned with the patients who cannot leave their beds.

Our eight native orderlies are so busy that they cannot devote as much time as is necessary to individual patients in the wards. We cannot think of facing the expense of having more paid attendants when the people with slight illnesses can perfectly well perform these duties. So we still take the trouble to try and teach savages that the patients assigned to their care are their neighbours. When we succeed in making them understand, we are happy indeed.

Three mornings a week are devoted to consultations for out-patients and the reception of new patients, and three to operations. But we cannot observe this routine very strictly. Sometimes for weeks at a time it is necessary to perform operations every morning as otherwise we could not get through the surgical work. On the other hand we cannot prevent out-patients and new patients from arriving on the operation days. For we cannot restrict those who come long distances by canoe to landing on certain days, nor even if it is an operation day can we refuse to receive sick people brought by some canoe which is going to Lambarene on business when its occupants have given them a passage out of compassion. Many patients, especially the old and the lonely, can only reach the Hospital if they can find such an opportunity.

A card like a luggage label is filled up for each patient. On it is inscribed the date of the consultation or reception as an in-patient, his name, his Hospital number, his age, where he comes from and the diagnosis. If it is an in-patient, a note is also made to show whether he is to receive the ration or not. People who come from a short distance—up to about twenty-five miles around—are not provided with food, as their relatives ought to bring them plantains and manioc. And similarly patients who are not altogether poor are expected to provide their own meals. It is not always easy to decide who ought to have the ration. The new doctors generally refer the question to one of riper experience. I have laid down as a principle that it is better to give food to a patient who might perhaps provide it for himself than to let him go hungry when he ought to be having the ration.

It also happens that people who are able to provide their own food for a time have to be supplied by us later on when they have spent all their money or their relatives are weary of spending whole days bringing them plantains or manioc. A few weeks ago I had to give orders that a well-to-do chief from the interior who had come to us for an operation should along with his two wives receive the ration. On a journey far from his own village he had been forced suddenly to resolve to get freed from the hernia which was troubling him badly. So the rich chief was with us like any poor stranger and his wives had to condescend to laundry work in order to earn their food. He promised to give the Hospital a fine present in return for his operation and board, but it has not yet arrived.

Those who accompany a patient are also given cards. On each of these is the name and number of the patient, the name of the companion and a note as to whether he is entirely occupied with his duties as attendant or whether he can also work for the Hospital. So by a glance at the card each of us can quickly know all about every native he meets at the Hospital.

For every patient a second, larger card is filled up on which is entered the history of his illness, the diagnosis and the treatment. This card is kept in the consulting room and the results of later examinations and an account of the course of the disease are added from time to time.

When a patient is discharged, he keeps his little card to show if he ever returns for treatment. But one corner, the corner in which it is marked that he is to receive the ration, is snipped off, otherwise he would leave it to a friend who would thus be enabled with two names to fetch a double ration, if the nurse were not very observant. It has actually happened that patients about to leave have pretended their cards were lost so as to be able to give them to others with the instruction to give the ration still intact.

As a rule we have not finished with the consultations when the gong summons us to dinner at 12:30.

From 1 to 2 p.m. the doctors and nurses are supposed to rest in order to be fresh for their afternoon work. On the Equator a siesta is almost a necessity.

After 2 p.m. the doctors are busy with the out-patients who have come for consultations or with the reception of new patients for whom there was no time left in the morning. But our principal work in the afternoon is with the serious cases lying in the wards. It is at this time that we undertake the often lengthy examinations necessary to pronounce or confirm a diagnosis. How glad we are to be several doctors and able to consult each other! It is a principle among us that any doctor who has a serious case under his treatment shall introduce it to his colleagues. And each of us is entitled to talk to his colleagues about all his cases, to communicate his opinion about the diagnosis and get advice about the treatment. In very difficult cases the doctor who has been longest at the Hospital decides on the treatment to be employed and assumes the responsibility.

In so far as their work permits all the doctors make the evening round of visits together.

As I have mentioned in previous reports, we have great difficulty in repatriating the patients who have come from far distant districts. We have to rely on passing steamers or motor boats taking them with them. So that no opportunity may be missed, the two nurses who are busy in the consulting room with a view thence of the landing stage have the duty of inquiring of the owner or native skipper of each boat that calls whether there is any possibility of taking some of the patients who have been restored to health. The owners and skippers are naturally not very enthusiastic about giving our natives a free passage and thus adding to the weight of their generally overloaded boats. So if we do not take the initiative by inquiring as to the goal of their voyage and begging them to take some patients, they simply go on. There are but few so far advanced in virtue that they come and offer to take some people with them.

When it becomes clear that a boat is available, Dominique is hastily sent through all the wards with a bell such as railway porters use, and as he goes he shouts, "An opportunity of sailing in the direction of——! Anyone who wants to go is to come to the consulting room at once!" And in the consulting room all other work comes to a standstill while a doctor decides whether the aspirants can really be discharged. Whilst he writes for the successful a recommendation to the officials through whose districts they must pass on their journey, and the nurse puts up a stock of provisions for several days and finds presents for those who have been workers, the patients who may leave fetch their belongings from the wards. But they cannot be left to do this by themselves. A native orderly must go with each to make him hasten and prevent him from going all round the Hospital to take a long farewell from all his acquaintances. The captains of the boats are in a hurry to go on, but for our savages time is nothing. Often the people who ought to be going have to be fetched out of the plantation. So in spite of all the trouble we take, frequently more than an hour goes by before all are on board the boat. Doctors and nurses are left quite exhausted by the running up and down and the shouting of directions. And then we are always afraid that the affair did not go well enough, so that that owner or skipper will not touch at the Hospital again for a long time lest he run the risk of having to take people with him and so losing time.

It is but seldom we know in advance when a boat will be passing so that we can quietly assemble the travellers and equip them for their journey.

On the afternoon of the last day of the month the monthly roll-call is held. As our natives often depart without announcing the fact, we have to make sure from time to time who is still on the list as a Hospital inmate and who is missing. And in addition the roll-call gives us an opportunity of questioning the patients and their companions when we can all discuss them together. At 2 p.m. the doctors and Hospital nurses with the orderlies around them sit down at a table in the consulting room. To begin with the nurses display the cards of the bed-patients for which each is responsible, whilst Dominique assembles the people outside. First come the labourers sent to us from the big timber camps or from other employers or missions, and then come the rest. It takes about four hours before the three hundred patients and their companions have filed past the doctors and nurses, for all haste while calling the roll is prohibited, and all the questions which arise in connection with any inmate are quietly discussed. The diagnosis and treatment of the patient's malady, his right to receive a ration, the length of his residence and other details are all passed in review. Every inmate can make complaints or express his wishes; but he must also be prepared for nurses and orderlies bringing up against him any acts of insubordination of which he has been guilty.

The roll-call is also the hour of judgment, especially feared as such by the companions and wives of the patients and by the convalescents. For doctors, nurses and orderlies now discuss whether this woman or that attendant is still needed entirely for nursing the patient, or whether they cannot also work for the Hospital, and which of the convalescents is far enough advanced towards health to be able to render some service until such time as he can be sent home.

The nurse who supervises the workpeople sits, notebook in hand, watching for her victims. Now a washerwoman or a palm-oil woman is assigned to her, now a man for cracking palm nuts, now a woman for weeding the garden, now a woman for carrying water, or a man to fetch water for the garden, now people who are fit for any kind of work, even for felling trees. Each of these has a note entered on his or her card to the effect that he shall now no longer fetch his rations from the nurse who distributes food to the patients, but from her who supervises the workpeople so that he becomes dependent upon her.

It avails nothing to be an absentee from the roll-call, for fate is decided even in absence. When such people come to fetch their rations next day they are referred to the nurse in charge of the workmen. They cannot even escape work by always remaining invisible when the doctors make their morning and evening rounds and by renouncing their claims to a ration by begging a miserable living from other people's cooking-pots or finding what they can in the plantation. Attention has been directed to them by the study of their cards at the roll-call and they may be sure that on one of the following days an orderly, a nurse or a doctor will stop them and hand them over to the nurse in charge of the workers. And if they have once been seen by her, she will not let them disappear from view again.

It is one of our principles that all people capable of work who are not needed in attendance on the sick, whether they receive the ration or provide their own food, shall in some way or other work for the common good in payment for the treatment and drugs provided for themselves or their relatives. There is always any amount of work to be done.

Of course those who take trouble to remain un-noticed sometimes succeeded in escaping work for a time, especially if we are very busy with the sick people or there are new nurses at the Hospital who are not sufficiently familiar with their dodges. "The savages are cleverer than I am," said one of the new nurses at a recent roll-call when it came out that a Hospital inmate owed several days of delightful idleness to her inexperience.

We keep such strict watch over the inmates and are so careful that each carries a card-label, because without these precautions our wards would become lodging houses and places of refuge for all the riff-raff of the neighbourhood.

When there is room, we gladly receive as lodgers genuine unemployed until they can find work. They draw the ration and a little payment according to what they do.

When they leave we also give convalescents and companions of patients money or a present in return for the services they have rendered. Good washerwomen or palm-oil women can go home wearing fine head-cloths or loin-cloths.

We see that evening is approaching when the poultry and duck-herd and the sheep and goat-herd come down to the Hospital and drive the livestock up the hill to their quarters near our dwelling houses. When the birds and animals are fetched it is a sign to doctors and nurses that it is time to begin the evening round of the wards.

A little before 6 p.m. the gong is sounded to announce that work is at an end. The workers are already back from the forest and from the planation, having known the time by an alarm clock carried by one of them on a cord. Now there is a great throng round the room where the tools are kept. Axes, saws, bush-knives, spades, pickaxes and rakes are given back, and the nurse in charge has to be careful that this does not happen too quickly so that she has time to see that all she gave out has been brought back. If the tools were not counted, many men would put the best axes and saws aside for their own use or leave them in the forest to save the trouble of carrying them home. The last of the tools may be put away by lantern-light. For we are close to the Equator. At six o'clock—the difference between winter and summer is only about a quarter of an hour—night suddenly descends.

We all find it unpleasant that darkness comes so quickly. One has to break off work instead of finishing it at leisure. For with the darkness there immediately come the mosquitoes which spread malaria. We are specially in danger from them because the Hospital contains so many malaria patients. As the consulting room, like the rooms in our dwelling houses, is protected by wire mosquito netting, people who are urgently requiring attention can be brought to it on stretchers or on their light wooden beds. The two operation rooms, the room for confinements, the bandage room and the large and small dispensaries are similarly protected.

At 6:30 p.m. a second gong reminds the over-zealous to cease work so as to change and rest before supper, which is announced at 7 o'clock by a third gong. The meal is followed by prayers. Then we often remain together for another half-hour. At 8:30 the evening bell—which except at this time is only rung for the Sunday Services—sounds, and after that there must be no more noise. Even the white patients' gramophone must be silent. The nurses visit each other's rooms with their needlework. The doctors read medical journals with an ear on the river in case a motor boat is approaching with fresh patients.

By 10 p.m. most of the lights are out, but this does not mean that all are sleeping. To begin with there are the cicadas and toads which make a tremendous noise from 9 p.m. till 2 a.m. And often the white patients' house contains mothers with new-born infants which sleep by day and cry by night. Or the two hippopotami that live in front of the Hospital engage in a bellowing competition. Or one, if not several, of the lunatics drums for hours at a time on the wooden walls of his cell. Or in one of the villages across the river there is dancing all night to the sound of the *tam-tam*. When Dr. Goldschmid complained to the chief of a village in which the *tam-tam* did not cease during the whole of a night illuminated by the full moon, he replied, "But Doctor, what will become of a people that does not get any amusement?"

But we are compensated for all these disturbing noises by the mild, fragrant night air and the mysterious rustling of the palms.

I am very glad that during my last stay I was able to enlarge the rooms for the examination and treatment of the patients. It makes the work quite different. Each of us now has enough room for his work, whereas up to now we kept getting in each other's way.

The airy new ward for the T.B. patients has places for about twenty and will soon be in use.

I should like friends all over Europe to know how grateful we are to them that their kindness enabled us to make these building improvements in such hard times and so allow us to fight the misery of disease more efficently than before.

ALBERT SCHWEITZER

APPENDIX B

Part of a talk given by Albert Schweitzer to Swiss and Alsatian helpers of his hospital before they went to Lambarene—summer, 1959. Reprinted from *Albert Schweitzer's Life of Friendship,* by Erica Anderson, pages 144–48.

In history, every school-boy can tell when modern times started; in regard to the hospital I, too, can determine this pretty accurately.

Modern times at the hospital started in the year 1958. I will tell you how. The year before I had made a vow that no one would ever persuade me to build again. We had enough space and did not need any new buildings. I really thought that I was old enough to say sincerely: "I will not build any more. I have no one to help me with such things anyway. Therefore, all that's finished." This was a nice thought for me, but it worked out differently, because very strange things happened.

I first had to face the fact that we needed some space to store petroleum for our generators, and it had to be stored a good distance from living quarters in case it should be struck by lightning and start a fire. So I decided to build near the garden, away from our houses, a room where we would store oil and petrol.

But I said to myself: "This is only a little diversion. My vow of not building still holds." So I was getting set to start that when something else happened. An engineer from Zürich offered to build me a house, a prefabricated house made of aluminium.

First I thought, what would we do with aluminium? But the fellow finally convinced me that the house would be good for us and that it would be good for everybody to find out what experience one can have with aluminium in the tropics. So I told him: "Yes, and thanks."

Then they said: "You know, of course, you only have to make the foundation, but that is a trifle." Then they gave me the blue-prints. Just to read them was a nightmare for me. I am so used to building without plans. But then they told me that the foundation did not have to fit to the exact millimeter. Same story that was! If I'd not had a doctor who was knowledgeable about construction, I would have had to give up the thing at the start. But I had to work at that foundation for weeks and weeks. I who swore never to build again!

So this became building project number two, and I have to admit that the building was important because I did not really have enough space for all my patients. We have about

481

three hundred and fifty couchettes, or mats covered with straw and a blanket. On these they sleep well enough, but there aren't enough of them. Because we have so many patients, I decided to agree to that aluminium building. This is the one that has worried me most and completing it has taken months. But when I left Africa, all was going well, and a fortnight ago I got the message that it is finished. How well an aluminium building fares in the tropics we shall soon see.

Now to building number three. I could ask you to guess what I might be referring to, and no one would. Could you imagine what else we would need in Lambarene? No one knows? Well, I did not know it either. A building for an automobile, a Mercedes-Benz truck weighing five and a half tons, imagine that! How did such a thing come about, and why?

You might think that we got high-hatted, that the hospital became big and that we got proud and modern, but those who know me know that the danger of my becoming too modern is not great. But necessity stepped in, namely, the problem of feeding the hospital patients and of being sure that we always had enough to eat; we have to have twenty-seven tons of rice on hand in advance, because there may be months when no shipment comes from Saigon. At least that was always my working principle, to have that much rice on hand.

But suddenly in the year 1958, no rice is forthcoming. I asked in Lambarene: "What is this? No rice has come. Are there no ships bringing rice from Saigon?" They answered me: "Oh, be calm, Monsieur. It will come. This is Africa. Don't worry. It will come. You must have patience. It does not come just when you wish, but it will come." So I kept my patience, as they had advised. Oh, yes. But one sack of rice was eaten up and then another and another and another. Finally I said, "What is this? We have only enough left for another week. What will happen?" So I went again to the officials in Lambarene, and again they answered: "Don't worry. It will come. It will come."

But I'd heard enough of that. No, I thought, this is a time when more exact information is needed, and I found out that through political circumstances the rice traffic had been interrupted. Saigon had left the business pact with France, and did not accept payments in French money any more. It wanted dollars. You can imagine that we did not have too many dollars around. Anyway, we could not count any more on a regular supply from Saigon. The day had come when I had to admit that I had not enough food for my people. What could I do?

I went to the local administrator and said: "Listen. I have no more food for my people. I want to give up my hospital. Half of my patients I will send away and the other half I will bring to you, and you must feed them and care for them." This did it. The man finally understood what it all meant and he answered: "What can we do, cher Docteur?" Then I replied that the only alternative was for him to put a car at my disposal so that I could get to villages and buy bananas for my people. He said: "But certainly, of course, absolutely, Docteur." And he finally sent a car. So we had to change our staple from rice to bananas, a very serious thing.

How does the banana market operate in the tropics? In the old times, while the hospital was small, we had almost enough bananas. They were delivered to us by riverway. But not from down the river, only from up the river. This is because one cannot expect the men to paddle upstream with a heavy load of bananas. They can paddle back upstream after unloading the bananas. But with this system we were not getting enough bananas.

Then the Government built a road linking Libreville and Lambarene because they also need bananas from the villages, where there are lots of plantations. One cannot expect the *indigènes* to carry bananas on the paths through the jungle to the Lambarene hospital, because bananas are very heavy. Another disadvantage is that they spoil quickly and so cannot be stored for long. In fact, after four days in the tropics they start to rot. So I stood facing the problem, "How can I get hold of enough bananas quickly and steadily?"

After a week my great friend, the administrator, decided that I had used his car long enough. He said that he needed it for other projects. My luck had run out. But there was an *indigène* who did have a car and I told him I would make an agreement with him. I said: "On Thursday you drive from the hospital about twenty miles to those villages which sell bananas. I will send a nurse along with you. She will take along a scale to weigh the bananas, and help you load and unload!" That was fine, he told me, and so we made a contract. But one thing I forgot—to examine the car.

European people from Lambarene came to me and said, "Docteur—how can you send your nurses off in a car which may burst into flames at any moment? It is a dangerous thing, and how its brakes ever work not even the Good Lord knows." I also realized that no such car would ever solve the problem permanently since we now required eight tons of bananas a week. What we obviously needed was a truck. But the road was not strong enough for a truck so we also needed a new road. And a road that would even hold after heavy rains. At that point the connecting link to the government road was only a narrow path: moreover, it mounted to a steep hill.

So I had to build a road, and that turned out to be one of my biggest adventures. I even confessed to myself: "This you can't do." And in truth it was most unlikely that I could ever finish it because the road had to be widened about two and a half meters, and the foundation had to be filled in to about one meter, and the earth had to be carried by my good workmen.

But they are not favorably inclined to shovel tons of earth. Not very enthusiastic, at first they had to carry heavy earth for about half a kilometer, and the soil was wet besides. So you can see the beginning was one of the most difficult performances I started in Lambarene. At first the *indigènes* really did not want to co-operate. We also had to hew the stones out of the ground, carry them to the road, and stones that were too big we had to crush with a hammer. I told myself: "Now, I, myself, will have to stand for at least four months to supervise this job." I who promised myself never to build again! I who had vowed to do only the hospital work from now on!

But at this point a miracle happened, a genuine miracle. A Volkswagen appeared on the horizon. Now a Volkswagen has a good reputation. Half of the cars that travel through the Sahara are Volkswagens. It's one of the few cars that can travel through sand. Anyway, from this Volkswagen four youths from Hamburg emerged, one of them slightly injured from an accident in a ditch. We took good care of him, and his companions walked through the hospital, looking very interested. They watched us work, and it was not long before they said to me: "Docteur, we have seen how hard you work, and we've decided to stay a while and help you build that road."

They took the tools and started to hew the big stones from morning till night, and the ambition of these German fellows had a most infectious effect on the *indigènes*. They became different people and started to work, as though it were fun. The spark took, and in three months we finished that road. It is a great road, sweeping behind the hospital in a big turn, and it rises to a hill of about thirty meters, and it serves well. Now the big question was, What kind of automobile would be must useful? I held a meeting of mechanics and asked them. Unanimously, they replied: "A Mercedes-Benz, five-and-a-half-ton diesel."

"Perhaps that is right," I thought. I had just read a report that the President of the French Republic and the German Chancellor had embraced each other at a political meeting so I figured the time was ripe to buy a German car even if living in a French territory. You see how wonderful it is when two people suddenly start up a friendship which no one would have expected! Anyway, I was lucky again. I contacted the Mercedes firm, and they delivered me the truck for a truly Christian price, I must say.

And so all is in order. The truck travels well on the new road; once a week it brings us about eight tons of bananas. Thus we've become independent of the arrival of rice. I need rice only for the summer months when bananas are more scarce. So fifteen tons of rice suffice. And that is how my hospital has entered into the modern age. But one thing I will guarantee you, modern times will not alter the old spirit of modesty and economy, the spirit of small beginnings. In this spirit the hospital developed, and in this spirit it shall live on.

Bibliography

American Scholar (Winter, 1949–50).

ANDERSON, ERICA, *Albert Schweitzer's Gift of Friendship*. New York: Harper & Row, 1964.

————, *The Schweitzer Album*. New York: Harper & Row, 1965. London: A. & C. Black, 1965.

Anecdoten um Albert Schweitzer, ed. by Roland Schütz. Munich: Bechtel Verlag.

BAILLIE, D. M., *God was in Christ*. London: Faber & Faber, 1948.

Begegnung mit Schweitzer. Festschrift edited by Hans Walter Bahr and Robert Minder.

BENTHAM, JEREMY, *The Principles of Morals and Legislation*. London: Basil Blackman, 1948.

BREMI, WILLI, *Der Weg des Protestantischen Menschens*. Zürich: Artemis Verlag, 1953.

BRODMANN, ROMAN, *"La Vérité sur Lambarene."* Article in *Saisons D'Alsace*, No. 14.

CAMERON, JAMES, *Point of Departure*. London: Arthur Barker, 1967.

CASALS, PABLO, *Joys and Sorrows*. London: Macdonald, 1970.

The Christian Register and *The Register Leader*.

CHURCHILL, WINSTON, *My African Journey*. London: Holland Press and Neville Spearman, 1962. Reprinted from the original edition of 1908.

CLARK, HENRY, *The Ethical Mysticism of Albert Schweitzer*. Boston: Beacon Press, 1962.

The Convocation Record of the Albert Schweitzer International Convocation at Aspen, Colorado, May, 1966.

COUSINS, NORMAN, *Doctor Schweitzer of Lambarene*. New York: Harper and Brothers, 1960. London: A. & C. Black.

The Courier (Magazine of the American Albert Schweitzer Fellowship).

DAVISON, ARCHIBALD T., "The Transcendentalism of Albert Schweitzer." In Jubilee Book of 1954, A. A. Roback, ed. Cambridge, Massachusetts: Sci-Art Publishers, 1954.

FESCHOTTE, JACQUES, *Albert Schweitzer—an Introduction*, tr. by John Russell. London: A. & C. Black, 1954. Boston: Beacon Press, 1955.

FORKEL, JOHANN NICOLAUS, *Uber Johann Sebastian Bachs Leben, Kunst und Kunstwerke*. Leipzig: Hoffmeister und Kuhnel, Bureau de Musique, 1802.

FRANCK, FREDERICK, *Days with Albert Schweitzer—The Story of His Life*. London: Peter Davies, 1959. New York: Holt, Rinehart and Winston, 1959.

GOLLOMB, JOSEPH, *Albert Schweitzer—Genius in the Jungle*. London and New York: Peter Nevill Ltd., 1951.

GUNTHER, JOHN, *Inside Africa*. London: Hamish Hamilton, 1954. New York: Harper & Brothers, 1955.

A Handbook of Christian Theology. Cleveland: World Publishing, 1958.

HEUSS-KNAPP, ELLY, *Ausblick vom Münsterturm*. Tübingen: Rainer Wunderlich Verlag Hermann Liens, 1952.

HOLTZMANN, HEINRICH JULIUS, *Das messianische Bewusstsein Jesu*. Tübingen: Verlag von J. C. B. Mohr (Paul Siebeck), 1907.

HUNTER, A. M., *The Work and Words of Jesus*. London: S. C. M. Press, 1950.

JACK, HOMER A., ed., *To Dr. Albert Schweitzer: A Festchrift Commemorating His Eightieth Birthday*. New York: Profile Press, 1955.

JOY, CHARLES R., tr. and ed., *Music in the Life of Albert Schweitzer*. New York: Harper, 1951. London: A. & C. Black, 1953. Beacon Paperback, 1959 (from which quotations here are taken).

KINGSLEY, MARY, *Travels in West Africa*. London: Charles Knight, 1972.

KRAUS, OSKAR, *Albert Schweitzer—His Work and His Philosophy*, tr. by E. G. McCalman. London: A. & C. Black, 1944.

LANGFELD, GABRIEL, *Albert Schweitzer—A Study of His Philosophy of Life*, tr. by Maurice Michael. London: George Allen and Unwin, 1960.

MARSHALL, GEORGE, *An Understanding of Albert Schweitzer*. New York: Philosophical Library, 1966.

———, and David Poling, *Schweitzer*. New York: Doubleday & Co., Inc., 1971. London: Geoffrey Bles, 1971.

McKNIGHT, GERALD, *Verdict on Schweitzer*. London: Frederick Muller, 1964. New York: John Day & Co., 1966.

MOSS, NORMAN, "Koestler in Wonderland." From *The Sunday Times Magazine*. (October 14, 1973).

MOZLEY, E. N., *The Theology of Albert Schweitzer for Christian Enquirers*. London: A. & C. Black, 1950. New York: Macmillan, 1951.

MURRY, MIDDLETON, *Love, Freedom and Society*. London: Jonathan Cape, 1957.

OSWALD, SUZANNE, *Mein Onkel Bery*. Zürich: Rotapfel Verlag, 1971.

PICHT, WERNER, *The Life and Thought of Albert Schweitzer*, tr. by Edward Fitzgerald. London, George Allen and Unwin, 1964.

PIERHAL, JEAN, *Albert Schweitzer—The Story of His Life*. New York: Philosophical Library, 1957.

ROSS, EMORY, "Portrait: Albert Schweitzer." Article in *The American Scholar*, Vol. 19, No. 1 (Winter 1949–50).

SARTRE, JEAN-PAUL, *Les Mots*, tr. by Irene Clephane. London: Hamish Hamilton, 1964. Paris: Gallimard & Cie. New York: George Braziller, Inc.

SCHWEITZER, ALBERT, "Albert Schweitzer Speaks Out." Article published in *The World Book Year Book* of 1964. Reprinted in *The Courier* (May, 1964).

———, "Childhood Recollections of Old Colmar." Part of a speech given at a reception in Colmar on February 23, 1949. Printed as an Appendix to Jacques Feschotte, *Albert Schweitzer*.

————, *Le Choeur de St. Guillaume de Strasbourg—Un Chapitre de L'Histoire de la Musique en Alsace.* Compiled by Erik Jung. Strasbourg: P. H. Heitz, 1947. Reprinted in Joy, *Music in the Life of Albert Schweitzer.*

————, *Christianity and the Religions of the World,* tr. by Johann Powers. London: George Allen and Unwin, 1923. New York: Henry Holt and Co., 1939.

————, *Civilisation and Ethics,* tr. by C. T. Campion and Mrs. C. E. B. Russell. London: A. & C. Black, 1923. New York: Macmillan, 1929, 1950.

————, "The Conception of the Kingdom of God in the Transformation of Eschatology." Appendix to E. N. Mozley, *The Theology of Albert Schweitzer for Christian Enquirers.*

————, *The Decay and Restoration of Civilisation,* tr. by C. T. Campion. London: A. & C. Black, 1923. New York: Macmillan, 1932, 1950.

————, "A Declaration of Conscience," radio broadcast on April 24, 1957. Printed as an appendix to Norman Cousins, *Dr. Schweitzer of Lambarene.*

————, *Deutsche und Französische Orgelbau-kunst und Orgelkunst.* Leipzig: Breitkopf und Härtel, 1906. Reprinted in Joy, *Music in the Life of Albert Schweitzer.*

————, *Histoire de mon Pélican.* Paris: Albin Michel, 1963.
1936).

————, *From my African Notebook,* tr. by Mrs. C. E. B. Russell. London: George Allen and Unwin, 1938. New York: Henry Holt and Co., 1939.

————, *Goethe. Three Studies,* tr. by C. T. Campion and Mrs. C. E. B. Russell. London: A. & C. Black, 1949.

————, *Goethe. Five Studies,* tr. by Charles R. Joy. Boston: Beacon Press, 1961.

————, *Un Grand Musicien Français: Marie Joseph Erb.* Strasbourg-Paris: Editions Le Roux & Cie. Reprinted in Joy, *Music in the Life of Albert Schweitzer.*

————, *Histoire de mon Pélican.* Paris: Albin Michel, 1963.

————, *Indian Thought and its Development,* tr. by Mrs. C. E. B. Russell. London: Hodder and Stoughton, 1936. Reissued by A. & C. Black, 1951. Boston: Beacon Press, 1936.

————, *J. S. Bach,* tr. by Ernest Newman, with alterations and additions at Schweitzer's request, from the German version of 1908. London: Breitkopf und Härtel, 1911. Reissued by A. & C. Black, 1923. New York: Macmillan.

————, *J. S. Bach, Le Musicien-Poète* (French version) Paris: Costallat, 1905. Leipzig: Breitkopf und Härtel, 1908. Tr. in part by Charles R. Joy and reprinted in *Music in the Life of Albert Schweitzer.*

————, *Memoirs of Childhood and Youth,* tr. by C. T. Campion. London: George Allen and Unwin, 1924. New York: Macmillan, 1931.

————, "Mes Souvenirs sur Cosima Wagner." Article in *L'Alsace Française,* Vol. XXV., No. 7 (February 12, 1933). Reprinted in Joy, *Music in the Life of Albert Schweitzer.*

————, *More from the Primeval Forest,* tr. by C. T. Campion. London: A. & C. Black, 1931. New York: Macmillan, 1948.

————, *My Life and Thought,* tr. by C. T. Campion. London: George Allen and Unwin, 1933. Quotations taken from the paperback edition, 1966. New York: Henry Holt and Co., 1948.

————, *The Mystery of the Kingdom of God,* tr. by Walter Lowrie. London: A. & C. Black, 1914. New York: Dodd, Mead & Co., 1914. Macmillan, 1950.

————, *The Mysticism of Paul the Apostle,* tr. by William Montgomery, B. D. London: A. & C. Black, 1931. New York: Henry Holt and Co., 1931. Macmillan, 1955.

————, *On the Edge of the Primeval Forest (Zwischen Wasser und Urwald),* tr. by C. T. Campion. London: A. & C. Black, 1922. New York : Macmillan, 1948.

————, *Paul and His Interpreters,* tr. by William Montgomery, B. D. London: A. & C. Black, 1912. New York: Macmillan, 1912.

————, "Peace or Atomic War." Three broadcast talks transmitted on April 28, 29, and 30, 1958. London: A. & C. Black, 1958. New York: Holt Rinehart and Winston, 1958.

————, *A Psychiatric Study of Jesus,* tr. by Charles R. Joy. Boston: Beacon Press, 1948.

————, "The Problem of Ethics in the Evolution of Human Thought." Address given before l'Académie des Sciences Morales et Politiques on the occasion of Schweitzer's installation as a member of the Academy at the Institut de France on October 20, 1952. Printed as an appendix to Jacques Feschotte, *Albert Schweitzer—An Introduction,* tr. by John Russell. London: A. & C. Black, 1954. Boston: Beacon Press, 1955.

————, "The Problem of Peace in the World of Today." Nobel Peace Prize Address. London: A. & C. Black, 1954. New York: Harper & Brothers, 1954.

————, *The Quest of the Historical Jesus,* tr. by W. Montgomery. London: A. & C. Black, 1910. New York: Macmillan, 1945.

————, "Un Culte du Dimanche en Forêt Vierge." Article in *Cahiers Protestants,* No. 2 (March, 1931).

————, "Religion in Modern Civilization." Two articles summarizing his Hibbert Lectures given in the autumn of 1934. Printed in *The Christian Century* (November 21 and 28, 1934).

————, "Warum es so schwer ist einen guten Chor in Paris Zusammenzubringen." Article in *Die Musik,* Vol. 9, No. 19. Berlin: Bernard Schuster. Reprinted in *Music in the Life of Albert Schweitzer,* Charles R. Joy, tr. and ed.

————, "Zur Reform des Orgelbaues." Reprinted in Joy, *Music in the Life of Albert Schweitzer.*

SEAVER, GEORGE, *Albert Schweitzer—The Man and His Mind.* London: A. & C. Black, 1948. New York: Harper & Brothers, 1947.

————, *Albert Schweitzer: Christian Revolutionary.* London: James Clarke & Co., 1944.

————, *Albert Schweitzer, A Vindication.* London: James Clarke & Co., 1950. Boston: Beacon Press, 1951.

URQUHART, ˙CLARA, *With Dr. Schweitzer in Lambarene.* London: George G. Harrap, 1957.

WEST, RICHARD, *Brazza of the Congo.* London: Jonathan Cape, 1972. New York: Holt, Rinehart and Winston.

NOTES

Unless otherwise indicated, all works are by Schweitzer. Shortened titles and last names of authors are used after the first reference.

CHAPTER 1

1. *Memoirs of Childhood and Youth*, p. 10.
2. *Ibid.*, p. 13.
3. Commentary written for Erica Anderson's film, but not used.
4. Letter dated December 16, 1944, now in the Hermann Hagedorn Collection in the George Arents Research Library at Syracuse University, New York.
5. Jean-Paul Sartre, *Les Mots*, p. 60.
6. *Ibid.*, p. 7.
7. *Ibid.*, p. 36
8. *Memoirs*, p. 17.
9. *Ibid.*, p. 19.
10. *Ibid.*, p. 16.
11. *Ibid.*, p. 39.
12. *Ibid.*, p. 42.
13. *Ibid.*, p. 49.
14. From "Childhood Recollections of Old Colmar," speech made at a municipal reception in Colmar on February 23, 1949, in Jacques Feschotte, *Albert Schweitzer—An Introduction*, p. 110.
15. *Ibid.*, pp. 111–13.
16. *Memoirs*, p. 81.
17. *Ibid.*, pp. 40–41.
18. *Ibid.*, p. 34.
19. *Ibid.*
20. *Ibid.*
21. *Ibid.*, p. 65.
22. *Ibid.*, p. 33.

CHAPTER 2

1. *Memoirs*, p. 51.
2. *My Life and Thought*, p. 195.
3. *Memoirs*, p. 52.
4. *Ibid.*
5. From "Un Grand Musicien Français: Marie-Joseph Erb," in Charles R. Joy, *Music in the Life of Albert Schweitzer*, p. 6
6. Letter dated February 12, 1945, in the Hagedorn Collection.
7. *Memoirs*, p. 55.
8. *Ibid.*, p. 60.
9. *Ibid.*, p. 72.
10. *Ibid.*

CHAPTER 3

1. *Memoirs*, p. 75.
2. "Warum es so schwer ist einen guten Chor in Paris zusammenzubringen," in Joy, *Music*, p. 56.
3. *My Life and Thought*, p. 86.
4. "Deutsche und Französiche Orgelbaukunst und Orgelkunst," in Joy, *Music*, p. 168.
5. Preface by Charles Widor to *J. S. Bach* (German edition).
6. Letter dated December 16, 1944.
7. *My Life and Thought*, p. 10.
8. St. Matthew, Ch. 10, verses 1, 5–18, 22–23.
9. St. Mark, Ch. 6, verses 7–13.
10. St. Matthew, Ch. 11, verses 2–6.
11. Letter dated February 12, 1945.
12. "Le Choeur de St. Guillaume de Strasbourg—un Chapitre de l'Histoire de la Musique en Alsace," in Joy, *Music*, p. 37.
13. *Ibid.*
14. *My Life and Thought*, p. 76.
15. Sermon preached at St. Nicholas', Strasbourg, January 6, 1905.
16. *My Life and Thought*, pp. 74–75.

CHAPTER 4

1. *My Life and Thought*, p. 15.
2. "Mes Souvenirs sur Cosima Wagner," in Joy, *Music*, p. 58.
3. *My Life and Thought*, p. 63.
4. St. Matthew, Ch. 26, verses 26–28; St. Mark, Ch. 14, verses 22–24.
5. St. Mark, Ch. 14, verse 25.
6. "Philosophy of Religion," in Thomas Kiernan, ed, *A Treasury of Albert Schweitzer*, p. 235.
7. *Ibid.*, p. 336.
8. *Ibid.*, p. 312.
9. *Ibid.*, pp. 325–26.
10. *Ibid.*, p. 329.
11. *Ibid.*

12. *Ibid.*, p. 330.
13. Preface by Widor to *J. S. Bach* (French edition).
14. *Ibid.*
15. *My Life and Thought*, p. 20
16. *Ibid.*
17. Suzanne Oswald, *Mein Onkel Bery*, pp. 77–80.
18. *Memoirs,* p. 41.
19. *Ibid.*, pp. 95–96.
20. *My Life and Thought*, p. 122.
21. *Ibid.*
22. *Ibid.*, p. 123.

CHAPTER 5

1. Oswald, *Mein Onkel Bery*, pp. 80–83.
2. *My Life and Thought*, p. 122.

CHAPTER 6

1. *My Life and Thought*, p. 25.
2. *Ibid.*
3. Sermon preached at the afternoon service at St. Nicholas', May 14, 1900.

CHAPTER 7

1. *My Life and Thought*, p. 27.
2. *Ibid.*
3. Letter to Felix Raugel.
4. Joy, *Music*, p. 144.
5. *Ibid.*, p. 152–53.
6. *Ibid.*, p. 152.
7. "Zur Reform des Orgelbaues," in Joy, *Music*, p. 224.
8. "Orgelbaukunst," in Joy, *Music*, p. 156.
9. Werner Picht, *The Life and Thought of Albert Schweitzer*, p. 198.
10. *My Life and Thought*, p. 28.
11. *Ibid.*

CHAPTER 8

1. *The Mystery of the Kingdom of God*, p. 6.
2. *Ibid.*, pp. 5–6.
3. St. Luke, Ch. 17, verse 20.
4. Isaiah, Ch. 53, verses 4–5.
5. St. Mark, Ch. 14, verses 61–62.
6. Werner Picht, *Life and Thought*, p. 46.
7. St. Mark, Ch. 9, verse 1.

8. H. J. Holtzmann, *Das messianische Bewusstsein Jesu*, pp. 8–9.
9. *Mystery*, pp. 18–19.
10. *My Life and Thought*, p. 48.
11. *Ibid.*, p. 54.
12. *Mystery*, pp. 18–19.
13. Adolf Harnack, *The Sayings of Jesus*, p. 232.
14. *Hibbert Journal*, No. 32 (July, 1910).
15. *The Quest of the Historical Jesus*, 3rd edition, p. xviii.
16. Glasgow *Herald* (May 20, 1910).
17. Manchester *Guardian* (May 20, 1910).
18. *The Nation* (June 11, 1910).
19. *Encyclopaedia of Religion and Ethics*, Vol. 5, p. 382.
20. *Quest*, 3rd edition, p. xii.
21. *Ibid.*, p. xiii.
22. E. N. Mozley, *The Theology of Albert Schweitzer*, p. 77.
23. *The Pelican Guide to Modern Theology*, Vol. 3., "Biblical Criticism," p. 256.
24. A. M. Hunter, *The Work and Words of Jesus*, p. 13.
25. W. J. Wolf, *A Handbook of Christian Theology*, p. 57.
26. D. M. Baillie, *God Was in Christ*, p. 24.
27. *My Life and Thought*, p. 51.
28. C. H. Dodd, *The Authority of the Bible*, p. 233.
29. *My Life and Thought*, p. 48.
30. *Quest*, 3rd edition, p. xiv.
31. *Ibid.*, p. 25.
32. *Mystery*, p. 248.
33. *Quest*, pp. 368–69.
34. *Mystery*, pp. 251–52.
35. *The Mysticism of Paul the Apostle*, p. 2
36. *My Life and Thought*, p. 51.
37. *Mystery*, p. 274.
38. *Quest*, p. 401.
39. *Ibid.*
40. *My Life and Thought*, p. 50.
41. *Ibid.*
42. *Ibid.*
43. *Ibid.*, p. 51.
44. Picht, *Life and Thought*, p. 88.

CHAPTER 9

1. *Mystery*, pp. 274–75.
2. Sermon preached at the afternoon service at St. Nicholas', February 23, 1902.
3. *Ibid.*
4. St. Luke, Ch. 10, verse 21.
5. Sermon preached at the afternoon service at St. Nicholas', May 11, 1902.
6. *Ibid.*
7. *Ibid.*
8. *Ibid.*
9. *My Life and Thought*, p. 55.
10. *Ibid.*, p. 56.

11. *Ibid.*, p. 56–57.
12. *Ibid.*, p. 75.
13. Sermon preached at St. Nicholas', July 27, 1919.
14. *My Life and Thought*, p. 75.
15. *Ibid.*, pp. 76–77.

CHAPTER 10

1. Letter dated December 16, 1944.
2. *My Life and Thought*, p. 77.
3. Letter dated December 16, 1944.
4. Picht, *Life and Thought*, p. 16.
5. *My Life and Thought*, p. 77.
6. Sermon preached at the afternoon service at St. Nicholas', January 6, 1905.
7. *My Life and Thought*, p. 88.
8. *Ibid.*, p. 77.
9. *Ibid.*, p. 83.
10. Widor in Preface to *J. S. Bach* (French version), tr. by Charles R. Joy.
11. *My Life and Thought*, p. 58.
12. *J. S. Bach*, Vol. II, pp. 253–54 (English version).
13. *Ibid.*, p. 2.
14. Johann Nicolaus Forkel, *Life of Bach* (French version), p. 69.
15. *J. S. Bach* (French version), from Joy, *Music*, p. 74.
16. *J. S. Bach* (English version), Vol. I, p. 20.
17. *Ibid.*, Vol. I, p. 183.
18. *Ibid.*, Vol. II, p. 131.
19. *Ibid.*, Vol. I, pp. 188-89.
20. *Ibid.*, Vol. I, p. 137.
21. *Ibid.*, Vol. I, p. 158.
22. *Ibid.*, Vol. I, p. 114.
23. *My Life and Thought*, p. 40.
24. *Ibid.*, p. 74.

CHAPTER 11

1. *My Life and Thought*, p. 78.
2. *Ibid.*
3. Elly Heuss-Knapp, *Ausblick vom Münsterturm*, p. 64.
4. *My Life and Thought*, p. 78.
5. *Ibid.*
6. Picht, *Life and Thought*, p. 162.
7. *My Life and Thought*, p. 78.
8. *Ibid.*, p. 79.
9. Sermon preached at the afternoon service at St. Nicholas', November 19, 1905.
10. Letter to music critic Gustav von Lüpke, quoted in Jean Pierhal, *Albert Schweitzer—The Story of His Life*, p. 59.
11. *My Life and Thought*, p. 80.
12. *Ibid.*
13. *Ibid.*

14. *Ibid.*, p. 78.
15. *Ibid.*, p. 88.
16. Frederick Franck, *Days with Albert Schweitzer*, p. 166.
17. Joy, *Music*, p. 180.
18. *My Life and Thought*, pp. 82–83.
19. *Ibid.*, p. 84.
20. *Ibid.*
21. *Ibid.*
22. *Ibid.*, p. 80.
23. *Ibid.*, p. 81.
24. George Seaver, *Albert Schweitzer—The Man and His Mind*, p. 160.
25. Letter to Gustave Bret in the Princeton University Library collection.
26. From an article in *Die Musik*, "Why Is It So Difficult to Organize a Good Choir in Paris?" Reprinted in Joy, *Music*, pp. 48–49.
27. *Ibid.*, p. 53.
28. *Ibid.*, p. 55.
29. Archibald T. Davison, "The Transcendentalism of Albert Schweitzer," published in *The Albert Schweitzer Jubilee Book of 1954*, pp. 200–1.
30. Preface by Widor to *J. S. Bach* (German version).
31. Davison, "Transcendentalism," in *Jubilee Book*, p. 201.

CHAPTER 12

1. Davison, "Transcendentalism," pp. 202–5.
2. Joy, *Music*, p. 254.
3. *Ibid.*, p. 202.
4. *Ibid.*, p. 206.
5. *My Life and Thought*, p. 113.
6. *Ibid.*, p. 112.
7. Joy, *Music*, p. 181.
8. *My Life and Thought*, p. 92.
9. *The Psychiatric Study of Jesus*, p. 27.
10. *Ibid.*, p. 14.
11. *Ibid.*, p. 33.
12. *Ibid.*, p. 28.
13. Sermon preached at St. Nicholas', January 21, 1912.
14. *My Life and Thought*, p. 194.
15. Sermon preached at St. Nicholas', February 25, 1912.
16. *Ibid.*
17. *My Life and Thought*, pp. 97–98.
18. From the Günsbach archives. The stranger is not identified.
19. Sermon preached at St. Nicholas', March 9, 1913.

CHAPTER 13

1. *On the Edge of the Primeval Forest*, p. 14.
2. *Ibid.*
3. *Ibid.*, pp. 14–15.
4. *My Life and Thought*, p. 89.
5. *Primeval Forest*, p. 17.

6. *Ibid.*, p. 21.
7. *Ibid.*, p. 19.
8. *Ibid.*, p. 21.
9. *Ibid.*, pp. 21–22.
10. Mary Kingsley, *Travels in West Africa*, pp. 129–30.
11. Winston S. Churchill, *My African Journey*, pp. 101–2.
12. *Primeval Forest*, pp. 22–23.
13. *Ibid.*, p. 23.

CHAPTER 14

1. *Primeval Forest*, p. 25.
2. Kingsley, *Travels*, pp. 214–15.
3. *Primeval Forest*, pp. 30–31.
4. *Ibid.*, p. 32.
5. *Ibid.*, p. 28.
6. *Ibid.*
7. *Ibid.*, pp. 28–29.
8. Letter in the Günsbach Archives.
9. *My Life and Thought*, p. 119.
10. *Primeval Forest*, p. 36.
11. *Ibid.*, p. 37.
12. *My Life and Thought*, p. 118.
13. *Primeval Forest*, p. 65.
14. *Ibid.*, p. 69–70.
15. *Ibid.*, p. 85.
16. *Ibid.*, pp. 85–86.
17. *Ibid.*, p. 90.
18. *Ibid.*
19. *Ibid.*, p. 95.
20. *Ibid.*
21. *Ibid.*, pp. 95–96.
22. *Ibid.*, pp. 96–97.
23. *Ibid.*, pp. 97–98.
24. *Ibid.*, p. 96.
25. *Ibid.*, p. 51.
26. *Ibid.*, p. 98.
27. *My Life and Thought*, p. 120.

CHAPTER 15

1. *The Decay and Restoration of Civilization*, p. 1.
2. *My Life and Thought*, p. 124.
3. *Ibid.*, pp. 129–30.

CHAPTER 16

1. Middleton Murry, *Love, Freedom, and Society*, p. 187.
2. *Decay and Restoration*, p. 88.

3.   *Religion in Modern Civilisation.* Summary of Hibbert Lectures in *The Christian Century* (November 28, 1934), p. 1520.
4.   Interview on Radio Brazzaville, 1953, quoted in Anderson, *The Schweitzer Album,* p. 153.
5.   *Civilisation and Ethics,* pp. 12–13.
6.   *Ibid.,* p. 13.
7.   *Ibid.,* p. 197.
8.   *The Mysticism of Paul the Apostle,* p. 12.
9.   *My Life and Thought,* p. 130.
10. *Ibid.*
11. *Ibid.*
12. *Ibid.,* pp. 130–31.
13. *Ibid.,* p. 131.
14. *Ibid.,* p. 132.
15. *Ibid.*
16. *Civilisation and Ethics,* p. 9.
17. Jeremy Bentham, *The Principles of Morals and Legislation,* Chapter 17, Section 1.
18. James Cameron, *Point of Departure,* pp. 169–70.
19. Talk by Dr. Frank Catchpool, printed in *The Convocation Record* of the Albert Schweitzer International Convocation at Aspen, Colorado (May, 1966), Section VI, pp. 27–28.
20. *Civilisation and Ethics,* p. 221.
21. *Ibid.*
22. "Albert Schweitzer Speaks Out." Article in *The World Book Year Book* for 1964, p. 148.
23. *Civilisation and Ethics,* pp. 218–19.
24. *My Life and Thought,* p. 179.
25. *Civilisation and Ethics,* pp. 198–99.

CHAPTER 17

1.   *Primeval Forest,* p. 115.
2.   *Ibid.,* p. 103.
3.   *Ibid.,* p. 108.
4.   *Ibid.,* p. 109.
5.   *Ibid.,* p. 108.
6.   *My Life and Thought,* p. 7.
7.   Letter dated August 15, 1916.
8.   *Primeval Forest,* p. 109.
9.   *My Life and Thought,* p. 141.
10. *Ibid.,* p. 142.
11. *Ibid.,* p. 143.
12. *Ibid.,* p. 144.
13. *Ibid.*
14. *Ibid.,* pp. 145–46.
15. *Ibid.,* p. 146.
16. *Ibid.*
17. *Ibid.*
18. *Ibid.,* p. 147.
19. Oswald, *Mein Onkel Bery,* p. 97.
20. *Primeval Forest,* pp. 124–25.

CHAPTER 18

1.   Sermon preached at St. Nicholas', October 18, 1918.
2.   *Ibid.*, December 1, 1918.
3.   *Ibid.*, February 16, 1919.
4.   *Ibid.*, February 23, 1919.
5.   *Ibid.*, August 17, 1919.
6.   *My Life and Thought*, p. 151.
7.   *Ibid.*
8.   Memorial Article to Archbishop Nathan Söderblom, May, 1933, now in the Hagedorn Collection.
9.   *Ibid.*
10. *Ibid.*
11. *My Life and Thought*, p. 168.
12. Letter from Elwood Worcester dated September 27, 1921.
13. *Christianity and the Religions of the World*, p. 46.
14. *Ibid.*, p. 68.
15. *Ibid.*, p. 54.
16. Introduction to the Hibbert Lectures, quoted in Seaver, *Albert Schweitzer*, footnote to p. 80.
18. Foreword by Nathaniel Micklem to *Christianity*, p. 8.
19. Seaver, *Albert Schweitzer*, p. 86.
20. Letter dated April 25, 1922, quoted by permission of Le Service Protestant de Mission et de Relations Internationales, Paris.
21. Letter dated April 30, 1922.
22. Resolution passed by the missionaries of Talagouga, May 6, 1922. Permission by above.
23. Letter dated May 11, 1922. Permission by above.
24. Oskar Kraus, *Albert Schweitzer—His Work and His Philosophy*, p. 1.
25. *Ibid.*, p. 50.
26. Letter dated January 2, 1924.

CHAPTER 19

1.   *More from the Primeval Forest*, p. 24.
2.   "Dr. Schweitzer's Hospital Fund," British Bulletin No. 2, (Summer, 1926), pp. 3–4.
3.   Letter to the London *Times* (August 22, 1925).
4.   *More from the Primeval Forest*, pp. 80–81.
5.   *Ibid.*, p. 84.
6.   Bulletin No. 3 (Spring, 1928), pp. 3–4.
7.   Bulletin No. 2 (Summer, 1926), pp. 2–3.
8.   *More from the Primeval Forest*, pp. 91–92.
9.   Anderson, *Albert Schweitzer's Gift of Friendship*, p. 143.
10. Bulletin No. 3 (Spring, 1928), p. 6.
11. *More from the Primeval Forest*, p. 126.

CHAPTER 20

1.   Letter to the author dated May 24, 1974.
2.   Picht, *Life and Thought*, p. 199.

3. *Memoirs*, p. 75.
4. *Ibid.*, pp. 75–76.
5. Letter dated December 16, 1944.
6. Sermon preached at the afternoon service at St. Nicholas', June 6, 1905.
7. Related by Anderson.
8. Maude Royden, DD, CH, pioneer of the women's movement.
9. Seaver, *Albert Schweitzer*, p. 109.
10. *Ibid.*, p. 108.
11. Goethe Prize Address, August 28, 1928.
12. *Ibid.*
13. *Ibid.*
14. Picht, *Life and Thought*, p. 169.
15. Letter to Meiner, quoted in Anderson, *The Schweitzer Album*, p. 138.
16. Bulletin No. 4 (Spring, 1930), p. 4.
17. *Ibid.*, pp. 14–15.

CHAPTER 21

1. Bulletin No. 4 (Spring, 1930, p. 10.
2. *From My African Notebook*, pp. 101–2.
3. "Un Culte du Dimanche en Forêt Vierge," article in *Cahiers Protestants*.
4. *Ibid.*
5. From the Günsbach Archives.
6. Picht, *Life and Thought*, p. 166.
7. *The Convocation Record* (May, 1966), Section VI, p. 26.
8. Related by Anderson.
9. *My Life and Thought*, p. 78.
10. *The Convocation Record*, Section VI, pp. 26–27.
11. *Ibid.* Section VI, p. 38.
12. Postscript by Skillings to *My Life and Thought*, p. 204.
13. Interview with Arthur Koestler by Norman Moss in *The Sunday Times Magazine* (October 14, 1973).
14. James Cameron, *Point of Departure*, p. 166.
15. Franck, *Days with Albert Schweitzer*, p. 32.
16. Norman Cousins, *Doctor Schweitzer of Lambarene*, p. 94.
17. *Ibid.*, p. 95.
18. *More from the Primeval Forest*, p. 53.

CHAPTER 22

1. Letter to the author dated May 24, 1974.
2. "Goethe's Message for Our Time." Address on the Centenary of Goethe's death, March 22, 1932, in *Goethe*.
3. *Ibid.*, pp. 49–50.
4. From a summary of the Hibbert Lectures printed in *The Christian Century*, November 28, 1934, p. 1484.
5. *Ibid.*
6. Seaver, *Albert Schweitzer*, p. 148.
7. Pablo Casals and Albert E. Kahn, *Joys and Sorrows*, p. 215.
8. Roland Schütz, *Anecdotes of Albert Schweitzer*, p. 56.

9. Bulletin No. 11 (**Autumn**, 1935), p. 8.
10. Bulletin No. 13 (Autumn, 1936), p. 6.
11. Letter to Dr. Maude Royden. Quoted by Seaver in *Albert Schweitzer*, p. 155.
12. Bulletin No. 18 (Spring, 1946), p. 3.
13. Seaver, *Albert Schweitzer*, pp. 159–60.
14. *Ibid.*, p. 161.
15. Bulletin No. 18 (Spring, 1946), p. 11.
16. *Ibid.*, p. 12.
17. *Ibid.*, p. 15.
18. *Ibid.*, p. 16.
19. *Ibid.*, pp. 14–15.
20. Bulletin No. 17 (January, 1945), p. 4. Letter dated May 24, 1944.
21. *Ibid.* Letter dated April 30, 1944.
22. *Ibid.* Letter dated May 24, 1944.
23. *Ibid.* Letter dated September 21, 1944.
24. Seaver, *Albert Schweitzer*, p. 162.
25. Bulletin No. 17 (January, 1945), p. 5. Letter dated October 25, 1944.
26. Bulletin No. 18 (Spring, 1946), pp. 17–18.

CHAPTER 23

1. Postscript by Skillings to *My Life and Thought*, p. 217.
2. Anderson, *Schweitzer Album*, p. 60.
3. *The Christian Register*, Vol. 126, No. 8 (September, 1947), p. 324.
4. *Ibid.*
5. The German-language paper published in New York.
6. Letter dated April 30, 1948.
7. Letter dated September 25, 1938.
8. Letter in the Collection of American Literature, Beinecke Rare Book and Manuscript Library, Yale University.
9. *The Christian Register*, Vol. 126, No. 8 (September, 1947), p. 327.
10. Feschotte, *Albert Schweitzer*, pp. 62–63.
11. *The Convocation Record*, Section I, p. 12.
12. Reprinted from *The American Scholar*, Vol. 19, No. 1 (Winter, 1945–50), page 85.
13. Bulletin No. 19 (June, 1951), p. 6.
14. *The Convocation Record*, Section I, pp. 13–14.
15. *Ibid.*, p. 14.
16. "Goethe—His Personality and His Work." Address at the Goethe Bicentennial Convocation, Aspen, Colorado, July 6 and 8, 1949. In *Goethe—Five Studies*, pp. 58–59.
17. *Ibid.*, p. 65.
18. Letter dated December 16, 1944.
19. "The Conception of the Kingdom of God in the Transformation of Eschatology." Epilogue by Schweitzer to Mozley, *The Theology of Albert Schweitzer for Christian Enquirers*, pp. 107–8.
20. Letter dated February 7, 1950, quoted in *The Courier*, (Autumn, 1968), p. 11.
21. Letter dated July 7, 1950, quoted in *The Courier* (Autumn, 1968), p. 11.
22. *Histoire de mon Pélican*, pp. 10–40.

CHAPTER 24

1. Anderson, *Schweitzer's Gift*, p. 89.
2. *Ibid.*, pp. 89–90.

3. *Ibid.*, p. 90.
4. *Ibid.*, pp. 91–92.
5. *Memoirs*, p. 101.
6. Letter dated October 23, 1951. Quoted in *The Courier* (Autumn, 1968), p. 12.
7. Anderson, *Schweitzer's Gift*, p. 95.
8. *Ibid.*, selections from pp. 96–103.

CHAPTER 25

1. Letter dated February 3, 1952.
2. Letter dated March 31, 1952.
3. Letter dated May 9, 1952.
4. Letter dated April 14, 1953.
5. "The Problem of Ethics in the Evolution of Human Thought." Printed as an appendix to Feschotte, *Albert Schweitzer—An Introduction*, pp. 129–30.
6. Bulletin No. 22 (January, 1955), p. 10.
7. Radio broadcast, January 14, 1955.
8. Articles in the *News Chronicle* (December 7, 8, 9, 1953).
9. Radio broadcast, January 14, 1955.
10. Articles in the *News Chronicle* (December 7, 8, 9, 1953).
11. *Ibid.*
12. *Ibid.*
13. *Ibid.*
14. *Ibid.*
15. *Ibid.*
16. *Ibid.*
17. *Ibid.*
18. Cameron, *Point of Departure*, pp. 173–74.
19. *Indian Thought and Its Development*, pp. 237–38.
20. Franck, *Days with Albert Schweitzer*, pp. 158–59.
21. John Gunther, *Inside Africa*, p. 698.
22. *Ibid.*, pp. 706–7.
23. *Ibid.*, p. 710.
24. *Ibid.*, p. 709.
25. Letter dated July 28, 1954.
26. Bulletin No. 22 (January, 1955), p. 16.

CHAPTER 26

1. *The Christian Register* (December, 1954), p. 17.
2. Cousins, *Doctor Schweitzer of Lambarene*, p. 186.
3. "The Problem of Peace in the World Today," Nobel Peace Prize Address delivered November 4, 1954, pp. 18–19.
4. Letter dated December 5, 1954.
5. From *To Albert Schweitzer. A Festschrift Commemorating His Eightieth Birthday*, privately printed by Homer A. Jack.
6. Letter dated February 20, 1955.
7. From Anderson's film, *Albert Schweitzer*.
8. Clara Urquhart, *With Dr. Schweitzer in Lambarene*, p. 39.

9. Cousins, *Doctor Schweitzer,* p. 147.
10. Letter to Robert F. Goheen, president of Princeton University, dated March 27, 1959.
11. Bulletin No. 23 (July, 1957), p. 7.
12. *Ibid.*
13. Letter dated July 21, 1955.
14. Cousins, *Doctor Schweitzer,* p. 171.
15. *Ibid.,* p. 122.
16. *Ibid.,* pp. 173–76.
17. *Ibid.,* pp. 189–90.
18. Letter dated February 20, 1957.
19. "A Declaration of Conscience," radio address broadcast on April 24, 1957. Printed as an Appendix to Cousins, *Doctor Schweitzer,* pp. 235–36.
20. Letter dated May 3, 1957.
21. Letter dated August 14, 1956.
22. Letter dated September 18, 1956.
23. Statement dated June 24, 1957.

CHAPTER 27

1. Cousins, *Doctor Schweitzer,* pp. 108–9.
2. Anderson, *Schweitzer Album,* p. 112.
3. Letter dated August 30, 1957.
4. *Ibid.*
5. Letter dated August, 1955.
6. Letter dated November 24, 1957.
7. Letter dated February 25, 1958.
8. *Peace or Atomic War,* pp. 5–7.
9. *Ibid.,* p. 9.
10. *Ibid.,* p. 15.
11. *Ibid.,* p. 17.
12. Letter dated February 8, 1960.
13. Address by Schweitzer to the French Albert Schweitzer Association, November 6, 1959.
14. Anderson, *Schweitzer's Gift,* p. 150.
15. *Ibid.,* p. 152.
16. Anderson, *Schweitzer Album,* pp. 19–20.

CHAPTER 28

1. Anderson, *Schweitzer's Gift,* p. 69.
2. News Bulletin of the Church of the Larger Fellowship, Unitarian Universalist, Boston (November 24, 1961).
3. *Time* (December 8, 1961).
4. Letter dated February 7, 1963.
5. Letter dated October 24, 1962.
6. Letter dated December 19, 1963.
7. Letter dated November 29, 1963.
8. *The Courier* (May, 1964), p. 150.
9. *Ibid.*
10. Letter dated February 10, 1963.

11. Bulletin No. 26 (April, 1963), p. 4
12. Anderson, *Schweitzer's Gift*, p. 53.
13. Urquhart, *With Dr. Schweitzer in Lambarene*, p. 24.
14. Gerald McKnight, *Verdict on Schweitzer*, pp. 13–14.
15. Roman Brodmann, "La vérité sur Lambarene." Reprinted in "Albert Schweitzer dans la vérité: hommage pour ses quatre-vingt-dix ans." From *Saisons d'Alsace*, No. 14, p. 136.
16. Franck, *Days with Albert Schweitzer*, pp. 80–81.
17. McKnight, *Verdict*, p. 217.
18. *New York Review of Books* (August 20, 1964).
19. McKnight, *Verdict*, p. 16.
20. BBC "Panorama" program, transmitted January 19, 1965.
21. Related by Anderson.
22. Letter dated October 9, 1964.
23. Letter in the Archives dated August 25, 1963. From D. Packiarajan.
24. Letter to Herbert Speigelberg dated April 4, 1965.
25. Bulletin No. 28 (November, 1965), p. 3.
26. Quoted by Joy in *The Register-Leader* (December, 1966), p. 3.
27. Bulletin No. 38 (November, 1965), pp. 4–6.

EPILOGUE

1. *The Catholic Messenger* (August 29, 1963).
2. *Civilisation and Ethics*, p. 190.
3. Picht, *Life and Thought*, p. 198.

INDEX

(Continued from front flap)

Perhaps the reason for the subsequent controversy surrounding him was that he became a myth in his own lifetime. More than twenty years before his death in his ninety-first year, he reached the worldly beatification of a front cover of *Time* magazine, with the caption "The Greatest Man in the World?" Inevitably, he became both the victim and the perpetrator of his own reputation. As times and attitudes changed, his once-hailed humanitarianism was transmuted into charges of racism and patronization.

Now James Brabazon describes Schweitzer's life in what is by far the most comprehensive biography ever written about this amazing man. In so doing, he has interviewed countless people, analyzed Schweitzer's own writings and been given access to papers not previously available. What emerges is a fully rounded portrait of the public man and his accomplishments, but what also comes through is an original picture of Schweitzer as father, husband, fund raiser and friend.

As the book makes clear, the celebrated hospital at Lambarene was not the beginning and the end of Schweitzer's significance. Rather Schweitzer's life in itself became the embodiment of his beliefs and the fulfillment of his writings. He translated the intuitions of all religions into language that is startlingly valid today, and in making his life his argument he provided a message that will endure even longer than will his amazing accomplishments.